LIFE AND *Love*

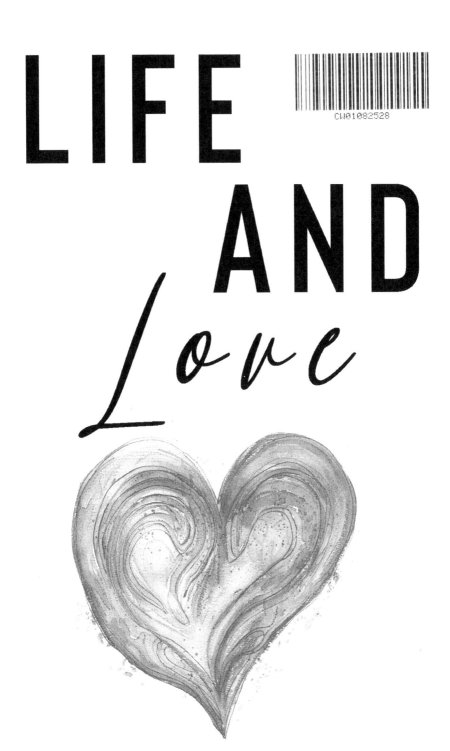

MT CASSEN

CONTENTS

TOO LITTLE TOO LATE?
LIFE AND LOVE (BOOK ONE)

AT WHAT COST?
LIFE AND LOVE (BOOK TWO)

PASSION WITHOUT TENSION?
LIFE AND LOVE (BOOK SIX)

A dedication from Morgan Cassen to medical workers in all corners of our world:

Morgan is in awe of the work done by the frontline workers of the noblest profession. The recent events have only increased my appreciation of the difficulty and danger associated with your line of work. I would like to thank you from the bottom of my heart.

Too Little, Too Late?

LIFE AND LOVE:
A Lesbian Medical
Romance Series

M.T. CASSEN

CHAPTER ONE

RACING HEART

Pounding, pounding, pounding. The echo of Maddie's heartbeat continued to pound loudly in her ears. She was almost there. She could make it. Her breath came in quick bursts as she tried to relish each inhale. Even in the Spring, the bitter Chicago wind stung her face. Her legs ached as she listened to the wind whistle and the steady pounding of her heartbeat. *You've got this. Don't give up now.* She'd raised over $2,000 via sponsorships for this race, surpassing her initial goal by almost $500. Now all she had to do was finish the damn thing. Tears stung the back of her eyes as she stared forward and tried to drown out the sound of her breathing. *You've got this!*

Maddie Anderson knew she had no choice. Despite all the pain and agony, she had this. If she could trust those voices in her head, she could crumble. *Don't think that way. You've got this!*

Pounding, pounding, pounding.

With every race Maddie ran, she refused to listen to the doubt inside her. Yes, she was sore. She was on the verge of collapse. Yet, she had one person she had to do this for. He counted on her, and most importantly, he believed in her.

"Just a little while longer, Maddie. Don't stop now." From her peripheral vision, she saw the people standing on the sidelines. Many of them were friends who she had met through various charity races. They bonded over their love of runner's highs and their shared commitment to the American Heart Foundation. Many of her friends ran to raise money in memory of the loved ones that they had lost to heart disease. Maddie knew she could count on her friends at the foundation to counsel her through the highs and the lows. They weren't just friends; they were practically family. Some of them even drove out from the suburbs to watch her today. *That* was worth fighting for. The aching in her body wouldn't even allow her to stop that fight. She couldn't give up on the American Heart Foundation. She wasn't about to give up on herself. She could see the edge of the banner flapping in the wind signaling the finish line. She took in a deep breath and grinned. *Just a few more steps, and I'll be there. Her whole body buzzed with the thrill of success as she crashed through the banner noting the finish line.*

Her head came forward. She was panting. Her hands dropped to her knees. Eventually, she smiled. Just like the voices encouraged Maddie to continue, she didn't allow anything to get in the way. She did this, and she was proud that she succeeded.

Maddie fished her phone out of her pocket, sweat dripping from her face. She needed to mark this occasion. She pulled up Instagram and took a selfie. Her green eyes squinted in the sun, and her long, blonde ponytail was slick with sweat. She wore a pink nylon running top with her race number pinned squarely on the center of her chest, black running shorts, and her trusted Nike running shoes. She zoomed out and angled her camera so she could fit most of her outfit in the frame. Thankfully, Maddie never had to worry about the perils of running with large boobs. She was 5'3, and surprisingly muscular. In the photo, Maddie looked exhausted but happy. Satisfied with her selfie, she got to work perfecting the caption. She typed: Another *½ Marathon for American Heart Foundation. Mission Accomplished.* "And send," she mumbled.

"Young'uns, nowadays, they're so self-absorbed. Why don't you look up from your phone for once and live a little?"

She looked up to see an older man shaking his head. He glared at her, and Maddie fought hard not to frown. He spun on his heel and started walking away, grabbing hold of the hand of a young boy.

"Sir, I don't see you running a half marathon!" Maddie yelled out.

The man never once stopped to acknowledge her remark as the boy beside him scrambled to keep up. Based on the age gap, she deduced it to be his grandson. The man moved faster, never once turning around to acknowledge her words.

Some people didn't understand the power of fighting for a cause with a tangible goal. She turned from the man and toddler, nearly bumping into a woman who approached her, towel in hand.

The woman held it up with a smile. "Thank you!" Maddie dabbed off the beads of sweat and wrapped the towel around her neck.

"Good race," the woman said. She smiled, but she left before Maddie could thank her.

Maddie headed off towards the cooling tent. The minute she entered it, she released a sigh. Now that's what was truly needed. She took a sip of her water and scanned the crowd. Her eyes landed on her father—the man behind her mission.

Her junior year of high school came rushing back to her. The memory was as vivid today as it was back then. A call that nearly changed the trajectory of her whole life. *Your father had a heart attack and is in ICU.* To Maddie, he seemed the spitting image of health. Little did she know that just because one doesn't get sick often doesn't mean they're the picture of health. He was always the strong one in the family, but a fried food and beer diet wasn't going to cut it. Knowing that she could lose him practically killed her. Luckily, he survived, and two weeks later, he was home.

She opened her eyes and stared back at him. He knew then that he had to live a healthier lifestyle, and Maddie ensured he never forgot that. Now in his mid-'60s, Dave Anderson's once thick, curly hair had thinned, and his beer gut had slimmed to a fatherly paunch. But, even though his round face had a couple more wrinkles, he had the same bright blue eyes that sparked whenever he heard anything interesting or caught a World War II documentary on T.V. He was Maddie's best friend. Maddie was with him every step of the way. Together they worked to incorporate healthy foods into his diet, and much to his chagrin, he even accompanied Maddie on the occasional run.

If she lost him, her world would never be the same. Her father was her one true rock, and doing what she could to ensure she was always there by his side was necessary.

When she drew closer, he looked up from his phone and grinned, slipping his phone into the pocket of his navy vest, which he wore over a white T-shirt emblazoned with the American Heart Foundation logo. "You did great out there, sweetheart."

He kissed her cheek.

"Thanks, Dad. Hope I made you proud."

"Always and forever." He held up his phone, and your fans seemed to agree. A twinge settled in her stomach, and Maddie clenched her gut. "Everything all right?" He arched an eyebrow and instinctively wrapped his arm around her shoulder.

Maddie quickly straightened up. "Of course."

Maddie forced a smile, despite the earlier tug that startled her. "I'm starving. I only had a couple of eggs and a smoothie before this." She got through the race thanks to a double shot of espresso and willpower. She released a slow breath, and her stomach lurched. She told herself that she was just hungry. It'd been a long morning. Her dad's smile returned, relieving Maddie.

"Let's go get something to eat," he said, keeping his arm around her.

Maddie grinned. That was what she needed— quality time with her dad and a good hot meal.

CHAPTER TWO

FRESH REVELATIONS

Maddie stifled a yawn. How could she be so tired when the day was barely beginning? She shook her head, "Focus, Maddie. Focus." She blinked a few times, shook her head, and then returned to the chart. The half-marathon over the weekend was still catching up to her. Why wouldn't she be exhausted? Her body was begging for rest.

"Not now. You have seven hours left in your shift," Maddie reprimanded herself.

Maddie glanced over the chart. Her next patient, Mike Bishop, was a regular. It wouldn't take her long to finish his session, and she could be onto her next patient. She heard a slight murmur and turned to see Lourdes Russo. Her cheeks flushed when she saw Lourdes staring at her. Lourdes was a cardiac nurse practitioner. She was higher up on the chain of command, compared to Maddie, who was just a nurse. Lourdes arched an eyebrow, then snickered.

"Talking to yourself?" Lourdes glanced around the empty nurse's station and winked, and Maddie felt a blush creeping up her cheeks. Why could she always get caught in the most awkward of situations?

"Are you sure you didn't see them? You just missed 'em," Lourdes grinned. Her face lit up most beautifully. Lourdes Russo was downright gorgeous. She had luminous brown eyes framed by ink-dark lashes and an olive-toned heart-shaped face; Maddie could barely force herself to look her in the eye. Lourdes wore her curly, dark hair in effortless waves that cascaded down her back. She was the only person Maddie knew who made scrubs look sexy. Maddie could see the outline of her curves beneath the cotton fabric of her scrubs. She couldn't help herself as she noted Lourdes' ample breasts straining beneath her top. Lourdes was a Mediterranean goddess. She looked like she should be sunning in Mykonos, not fielding patient concerns. She made Maddie look like a middle-school boy in comparison. While Lourdes was all soft lines and curves, moving through the hospital with ease and leaving behind a jasmine-scented cloud of her perfume, Maddie was flat as a board and practically tripped over her feet.

Maddie's heart clenched as she forced herself to look away and focus on Mike's chart. Besides, she consoled herself it had been years since she had been in a relationship or even gone on a date. Her last serious relationship ended after she graduated nursing school three years ago. Even though it was painful, Maddie and her ex Allison kept in touch, liking each other's Instagram posts now and again. Sure, it got lonely sometimes, but once work took over, she didn't even have time to focus on her broken heart. Nor did she have the time to plan elaborate dates for gorgeous Mediterranean women. Not that she ever thought about going out with Lourdes.

If she didn't look up, Lourdes was bound to leave. She heard a couple of pops and looked up to find Lourdes cracking her neck. Maddie's mouth was agape, and she stared. Lourdes' olive skin glowed, and her high-rise cheekbones shone below her light ruby blush. Lourdes shifted her neck, and a couple more pops sounded.

"Rough day?" Maddie asked.

"You could say that," Lourdes mumbled. She put on a bright smile.

"But hey, I didn't stop by to discuss my day. I wanted to talk to you."

Maddie tried not to frown," Oh yeah?"

What could Lourdes possibly have to discuss with her? Lourdes probably wanted to remind her of how green and inexperienced she was, unlike Lourdes.

"Patient concern?"

"Russo to room 124. Russo to room 124."

Lourdes turned from Maddie. Lourdes groaned and darted her gaze over to the room. "Hold that thought. We'll catch up later." She tossed a wave over her shoulder and rushed off. Lourdes disappeared into a room. Still, Maddie tried to hold her gaze.

Now she'd have to wait for however long to see what Lourdes needed to discuss with her. Surely, it had to do with work. What else could it be? Lourdes had only been with the department for three months. Before that, she worked in the ER for less than a year. They couldn't exactly be considered friends. Yet, acquaintances seemed harsh. She liked Lourdes, even though she didn't know much about her. But everything she did know seemed to point to the fact that Lourdes and her could get along outside the walls of CAPMED. Assuming Maddie's introverted nature wouldn't turn Lourdes away.

Someone cleared their throat behind her. She jerked and turned to see her best friend, Eric, a fellow nurse. Eric was stocky and jovial, with dirty blonde hair and brown eyes. Round dimples appeared on his cheeks whenever he smiled, which was often. He was only 5'9 but made up for it with his larger-than-life personality.

Eric chuckled, "What's with the thousand-yard stare?"

Maddie rolled her eyes. "I don't. Just thinking. Why do you always read too much into a situation?" She looked back down at the chart and then checked her watch. She still had some time before she had to grab her patient. "Has it been a long morning? Or is it just me?"

"I don't think it's been too bad. I'd say it's moving along rather nicely," Eric shrugged, and Maddie arched an eyebrow. It would have been nice if Eric had just nodded and agreed, but Eric was grinning, which caused Maddie to snicker.

"Then I guess it's just me."

The grin continued on Eric's face. "But seriously, though. Were you staring at Lourdes?" He wiggled his eyebrows when Maddie looked up to meet his gaze.

"What?" Maddie hissed. "You weren't just reading too much into a situation. You're downright foolish. Besides, why does it matter even if I was looking at Lourdes? Am I not allowed to look at a co-worker? Perhaps I should be forbidden to look at or even talk to another person besides you. Is that what you're saying? People can look at other people!"

Eric tilted his head. "Too much caffeine?"

"You started it," Maddie mumbled. She cringed. Why the sudden urge to go off on Eric? She grimaced and looked down at her patient's chart.

"You had a busy weekend. I saw your post on the 'gram. Your dad must be very proud. I know I was."

"Thanks, Eric." She forced a smile after rambling a few minutes earlier.

"I like to think I made him proud," she replied. "I raised another $500 once I posted the selfie at the finish line." Sometimes hiding behind the phone helped ease Maddie's nerves. While the thought of public speaking made her want to barf, social media allowed her to share her story without the added pressure of face-to-face interaction.

"I saw that pic, too."

Maddie looked up when another voice joined the conversation. Shannon, a fellow nurse, came into the station. She picked up a bottle of water hidden by the phone and took a swig. "I was there, too," she added.

"I thought I saw you before the race started," Maddie replied. "Great job to you, as well."

Shannon nodded. "You were ahead of me, but it was still exhilarating to be able to run."

"Exactly," Maddie said. "Not about who's ahead, just who participates. No one gets ahead by sitting on the bench."

Eric arched an eyebrow. "You're making me feel like a complete dud," Eric replied. He offered a teasing grin.

Maddie laughed. "You had an excuse. Someone had to work."

"Best get back to work. See ya around." Shannon waved and left the station.

"Weird," Eric mumbled. "That's the most she's ever really talked." While it was true, Maddie didn't think much about it. "But as you can see...everyone thought you did great."

Maddie smiled, brimming with pride. She released a yawn and covered her mouth. "Now, if this day would just speed up a little, I can go home, have a long bath, and get some rest. But, enough about me. How's James?"

Eric's grin grew wider. "As gorgeous as ever."

Maddie giggled, grabbing Mike's chart. "I swear, the two of you make the cutest couple."

Eric sighed. "Don't stop. Tell me more. Tell me more."

Maddie playfully slapped his shoulder with the chart. "Give James a kiss for me," Maddie said, winking.

"My patient awaits." She held up the chart.

"Talk to you soon." Maddie barely survived Eric's teasing. Her heart hadn't stopped racing since Lourdes disappeared into the patient's room.

"Looking forward to it," Eric called out, sitting behind the computer. Maddie's thoughts shifted to the other woman, and she couldn't help but smile. Suddenly, Maddie wasn't so tired after all. Still, she wondered what Lourdes could ever want from her.

CHAPTER THREE

A FLUTTERING HEART

"Hey, Mike! How are you doing today?" Maddie called as she entered his room. The rapport she developed with patients was one of her favorite parts of her job. She got to know the patients almost as well as her family and friends.

Mike smirked and gave a slight grunt. "Same ol' same ol', you could say." Maddie helped guide him through the triage area, nodding at other familiar faces as they trudged down the hall. He didn't walk as quickly as Maddie would have liked to report. His breathing seemed a bit raspy after just a few words. He shrugged, "I've had worse days, I suppose."

Maddie smiled, letting Mike lead them into the room where the rest of the session would occur. "Before you know it, you'll have some of your best days." She winked, and he grinned in response.

"I'll hold you to that."

Maddie motioned for the chair, but Mike had already started to take his seat. Most of these therapy sessions consisted of a routine built over time. Maddie was confident that many of her patients would rather be anywhere but here. Some would choose a root canal over the pain therapy brought them. Yet, it was Maddie's job to maintain the comfort they received. It was how she wished her father had been treated when he was in the same position. Sadly, she was aware that when he was in the hospital under emergent care, most times, he was a number. The staff appeared overworked and rushed, sometimes coming across as bothered. From that moment on, she vowed that once she became a nurse, she would always do her best to make her patients valued and welcomed. But nursing didn't come as naturally to her as she had hoped during her days at school. Some days, she felt a panicked ache in her chest the moment she walked through the doors of CapMed. Even so, every day she walked into work, she made good on that promise to herself, her father, and her patients.

"So, it's been a week since you were last here. Have you noticed an increase in stamina and endurance?" She tossed his file down on the counter and moved over to him. She grabbed the blood pressure cart and wheeled it over to him. As she put on the cuff, he shrugged.

"Not particularly." He quickly looked away from her, glancing at the corny painting of Lake Michigan that hung on the back wall beside the clock. Maddie heard his labored breathing.

She documented his pulse and grabbed his blood pressure as the machine beeped. "It's a little high today. Are you sure you're not exerting yourself more than usual?"

He shook his head, but his face fell. "Guess I forgot to take my meds the past couple of days."

Maddie groaned. "Just a couple?"

Again, he shrugged. "Maybe a few."

"That's not a good sign. The meds are needed to make sure your BP stays regulated. Long periods of hypertension increase the risk of heart attacks. That's not good for you or your loved ones," Maddie admonished.

"Geez, doctor. I'll do better." He added a teasing smile, but Maddie wanted him to take it more seriously. When things got intense, Mike tended to overcompensate with the jokes, and Maddie feared he didn't truly realize how important his health was. She felt her palms start to sweat. A tinge of pain tugged at her heart, and she released a shaky breath.

"At least try, Mike. You owe it to yourself and that son of yours."

"I know. You're right." The earnest look on his face relieved Maddie slightly. "But I guess I'm just getting frustrated. I keep telling myself that we haven't been doing this for that long and that I have to be patient and have faith that things will be back to normal one day."

Maddie removed the cuff from him, pushed the machine to the side, then sat on the stool and continued watching him. His lips curved downward, and he shifted his eyes to the floor.

"It hasn't been that long. But I have to ask...." Maddie smirked slightly. "After all, it's in my contract and how I get paid." Mike snickered but never spoke out of turn.

"Besides the not taking your medicine part, are you going by the doctor's orders? Have you been doing your breathing exercises? Have you been gradually working on your cardio?"

"Of course," he quickly responded. His eyes dropped the minute he met Maddie's gaze. "Mostly."

Maddie groaned. She was so close. "I see." She jotted down a note. He wasn't the most responsible patient, but being a single father, she knew he took pride in being there for his son. "How's Myles doing? He's getting ready to try out for the little league, right?"

He nodded. " He wants to be a pitcher." Mike proudly sat up in his chair, a huge grin crossing his lips.

"If memory serves me, you were a pitcher in college, right?" Maddie inquired.

"Until a shoulder injury took me out. I don't want Myles to have to deal with the same suffering I had to. Once that happened, I felt like I had lost my way. I'll be damned...." He snapped his mouth shut. "Pardon the language."

Maddie smiled. "No need to apologize."

"I just want to ensure he's ready and prepared for what life is about to throw him."

"So, have you been helping him? Probably doing some conditioning on the field?" Maddie arched an eyebrow.

He smirked. "Hey, you said cardio, right?"

"Well, there is such a thing as too *much* cardio. Whatever you do, don't overdo it." He opened his mouth to argue, but Maddie held up her hand. "Myles is everything to you. You want the best for him. I get it. Just don't overdo it."

"Aw shucks, Maddie. Keep that up, and people will start to believe you care." He gave her a wink.

Maddie shook her head. "And you, kind sir, are just trying to change the subject."

"Did it work?" he teased.

Maddie laughed and nodded. "You know the drill. Follow me."

Maddie led him out of the room and down the long corridor to the physical therapy room. "Noelle will be right with you." She put her hand on his right shoulder and squeezed slightly. "Take care of yourself. I'll be seeing you next week."

"See ya, Maddie."

She closed the door behind him and returned to the nurse's station. She wouldn't be doing this job, living the stress that came with it, if she didn't care. She hoped all patients realized how much she truly cared for each of them.

When she got back to the station, she glanced at her watch. "You still here?" she teased. "Don't you have patients to take care of?"

Eric glanced up from the screen. "I've been gone and back. What took you so long?"

Maddie shrugged. "Guess I provide a little more TLC than the next person." Maddie glanced over her shoulder, and he scowled. It was all good fun, as Eric could dish it out as much as the next person. Turning back to her computer screen, she spotted Lourdes and gave her a slight nod before returning to her documentation.

"It's been one hectic morning," Lourdes said, sighing as she entered the work area. " I've been trying to eat this freaking apple since 9:00 A.M. That's how bad it's been. No downtime. Nothing. Guess the good part is that the day is zooming by." Lourdes snuck over to the nurse's station and fished an apple from her canvas tote bag, which she had stashed under the desk.

The apple crunched loudly. Lourdes chewed and swallowed before glancing up at Maddie and giving her a friendly smile. Maddie returned the smile, then tried to look back at her computer. "Definitely a busy one. I don't know where the day's gone."

Eric shot a confused glance in her direction, "Well, you know what they say, time flies when you're having fun. And with gorgeous co-workers such as yours truly, not to mention L—."

Maddie kicked his shin, and he shot her a look, then grinned and looked away from her. "You were saying?" Lourdes asked.

Eric shrugged, "Never mind."

"It certainly has been a crazy day," Maddie said, staring at her computer. She could see Eric smirking out of the corner of her eye.

"Not always a bad thing, I suppose. But sometimes, these patients are enough to drive anyone up the wall," Lourdes exclaimed.

Maddie looked up, suddenly intrigued by the conversation.

Lourdes continued, "Take room 124. I'm getting called every thirty seconds because her oxygen is slipping." She rolled her eyes. "It's not. She's just a hypochondriac, and everything goes wrong in her eyes." Lourdes heaved a sigh. "But I don't have to tell you about troublesome patients. You both experience that, in many ways, more than I do." Lourdes took another bite of her apple.

Maddie looked back to her computer and quickly finished the notes, ensuring that Mike's physical therapist, Noelle, had everything she needed in Mike's chart. Another crunch of the apple and Maddie turned to Lourdes.

"Yeah, sure, we all have those patients."

Lourdes smiled and tossed her half-eaten apple into the trash can. "Enough about that, though. Seeing I have about five minutes, I was going to talk to you, Maddie."

"Oh yeah. That's right." Maddie was glad Lourdes had brought it up again. She didn't want to appear eager to hear what she had to tell her.

"I saw your Instagram post after the race. Kudos to you for raising so much money. I heard that you raised over two grand. That's amazing! Good job."

"Yeah, I raised over my goal, so that was pretty cool," Maddie said.

Maddie's cheeks burned once again. How exactly did she hear this? To her knowledge, Lourdes didn't follow her. Right? Perhaps she heard others talking and just happened to glance at the post. Either way, Lourdes acknowledged it. Maddie didn't do charity runs for recognition or to give people an excuse to pat her on the back. But sometimes, running these races felt thankless, even isolating as she dipped out on plans with Eric to train. While it was the last thing Maddie expected, it felt great that someone like Lourdes acknowledged her hard work.

"Wow, thank you. That's nice of you to say. I was just happy to do my part."

Lourdes glanced at her watch. "Keep up the great work. Back to work, I go." She waved, then rushed away from the station. Maddie's gaze followed after her. Lourdes' ponytail swung behind her, exposing her elegant neck. Lourdes moved through the world with a dancer's grace. Her back muscles rippled in her scrubs as she walked. For a moment, Maddie wondered how holding her close and kissing her would feel. She thought about how it would feel to have those strong arms hold her and finally muster up the courage to press her lips to hers. Maddie bit down on her lower lip and couldn't tear her eyes away.

Eric laughed. "So, apparently, James and I will have to duke it out with you and Lourdes to see who's the cutest couple in this hospital."

Maddie twirled around. "Huh? What? Excuse me?'

Eric grinned. He cupped his hands together and swayed back and forth, cooing like a love-sick teenager. Maddie's jaw dropped as Eric continued to smile.

"You ladies would be on fire." He shook his hand. "Sizzling hot. Like, grab the hose and water you down, hot."

Maddie rolled her eyes. "In your dreams."

He laughed. "I mean it. I saw the way you looked at her. You looked like you were in heat or something."

"Are you serious?"

She cupped her hand against his mouth. "Shut up! You're making me sound like an absolute horn dog. Besides, I don't even sound like that. I was strictly having a simple conversation with another employee. Or am I not allowed to converse with other co-workers either?" He laughed, and she slowly pulled her hand away. She playfully slapped his wrist.

"And what do you think you were doing? You were out here trying to make me sound like a whiny fool. Some friend!"

His jaw dropped, "Why do you even care? I mean, if she's just a co-worker and all."

Maddie rolled her eyes. "Just because I don't want my co-worker to think I'm lazy doesn't mean I have a crush on them. I just don't want to look like a slacker. Besides, Lourdes is a mature woman. Even if I were the least bit intrigued, it wouldn't happen."

Eric scoffed. "Maddie, give yourself some credit! You're smart, you're funny, and you're an absolute catch! Perhaps if Lourdes knew you were interested, things would move right along." He winked as Maddie looked away from him. Her eyes landed on Lourdes, who was now talking to another woman, someone Maddie didn't recognize.

"You're relentless," Maddie mumbled. She could see her silhouette as she laughed and spoke with the stranger. Her smile was gorgeous. Her eyes seemed to dance with every movement she made. Anyone would have to be blind not to notice how beautiful it was inside and out. "We're so different." Maddie turned back to him. He was smiling so big that the skin around his eyes was crinkled.

"You heard the way she talked about her patient. It's like she doesn't even care or have empathy."

"Maddie, girl, stop making excuses! Lourdes has plenty of empathy. She's just a little more cynical than you. You might be the woman that can break through that rough exterior." Without another word, he left her, and she glanced at Lourdes. At that exact moment, Lourdes turned and caught her staring. Lourdes smiled slightly, catching Maddie off guard. Lourdes turned back to the other woman. She didn't misread that, did she? Lourdes genuinely smiled, almost like she could read Maddie's mind. Maddie spun on her heel, swallowing the lump in her throat. Her cheeks were on fire again. It was ridiculous even to consider. Even if, at that moment, her knees were about to buckle and her heart was aflutter.

CHAPTER FOUR

GROWING INFATUATION

An intercom screeched to life as Maddie walked towards the break room.

"Just five minutes," she whispered, practically willing the loudspeaker to call another name. She waited, then waited a few more seconds. How long has it been? She glanced at her watch like she wanted to count the minutes. All she heard was the sound of fuzziness and soft chatter. Perhaps a mistake. Then the intercom went dead. She sighed, and a smile crept to her lips. She might get those five minutes after all.

She pushed into the break room and grabbed the seat furthest from the door, feeling her body sigh with relief. Today was a mad-house. Three patients came in on an incorrect day and had to be worked into the schedule. Two other patients were nearly twenty minutes late for their appointment. It seemed as if the minute she felt caught up, another bevy of problems appeared, vying for her attention. Maddie yawned just as a notification vibrated on her phone.

She slid the phone out of her pocket and pulled up Instagram, smiling when she spotted her dad's name. He liked her latest post on eating healthy when you're addicted to carbs. *Everything is necessary for a heart-healthy lifestyle.*

"Thank you, Dad," she mumbled.

He had come a long way when it came to social media. Maddie never thought she'd see the day when her dad liked her posts and followed everything she had to say. But sometimes, people have a way of changing, even when kicking and screaming.

She scrolled through her posts; each one garnered more and more likes. It was all about getting noticed, which would ensure people were talking. That's when you get awareness out there, and that's when you make a difference. She smiled. It worked.

The door to the break room swung open, and Maddie looked up to catch Lourdes' gaze as she entered. Lourdes smiled widely. "Hey there!"

"Hey!" Maddie warbled. She swallowed. Why was she suddenly so nervous?

"Mind if I sit down?" Lourdes motioned to the seat across from her.

"Of course not." Maddie quickly slid her phone back into her pocket.

Lourdes took a long swig of her water, and Maddie couldn't look away. Her skin glistened with beads of sweat as if she had just been outside in the blazing sun. As Lourdes smiled at Maddie as she put down her water. Maddie looked away quickly. She had been gawking long enough. She needed to control herself. In the space of one week, her crush on Lourdes became an infatuation. Whenever she thought of Lourdes, her heart quickened and her breath grew ragged.

"It's a hot one on the floor. I sometimes think administration thinks when it's colder outside, they need to bump the heat up to 100." Lourdes laughed. It was like the sound of music moving through the air. Maddie could listen to Lourdes laugh for hours. Unfortunately, it died way too soon.

"Don't ya think?" Maddie met her gaze, realizing she probably had been gawking at Lourdes. "Yeah, absolutely. They can never seem to regulate the temperature correctly."

"Another busy day. At least I can grab a few minutes to sit down."

"Agreed." Lourdes' foot briefly brushed over hers. Maddie jerked but tried not to dwell on the simple movement. Lourdes didn't seem to notice as she took a long drink of her water.

"But hey, I was gonna talk to you more about the half-marathon."

Maddie quickly jolted back to attention, moving her gaze to Lourdes'. "Oh yeah?" Maddie assumed they had all the conversation they needed to regarding the race. It'd been five days since they first discussed it. She hadn't anticipated a replay of that conversation. Yet, at that moment, she would have talked to Lourdes about the break room's new carpet if it meant getting a few more minutes with her. "What's that?"

"The truth is," Lourdes started, taking another sip of her water. "I was supposed to be there, too."

"Really?"

Lourdes shrugged. "Got called into work early. Not much you can do when they're down a practitioner. But, as for you, I see you're continuing to gain the pledges. Even a week after the race is over. Truth be known, I pledged under your campaign. Don't tell the other staff members." She winked, and Maddie got lost in those eyes of hers. When Lourdes quirked up her lips into a smile, Maddie blushed.

She wished she had her bottle of water to hide behind. She didn't even have a chance to grab her phone.

"Thank you, Lourdes. Won't say a word." She crossed her ankles and accidentally kicked Lourdes. "Oh, sorry," Maddie mumbled.

"No worries." Lourdes took another sip, and Maddie stood up from the table. As she walked over to the vending machine, she was mindful of the sound of her feet tapping against the linoleum. "Well, now that you mentioned, I'm surprised you're into social media and all that stuff." *I'm especially surprised that you follow me.* Maddie bit her tongue so that she wouldn't word-vomit all over Lourdes. She got herself a bottle of water and turned to face the table. Lourdes had her eyes fixated on Maddie.

"Are you kidding me? The hospital is abuzz with the star athlete. I have no choice but to check it out." She winked again. Maddie's toes curled. She looked down, so Lourdes wouldn't notice how one moment had turned Maddie into mush. Maddie opened the water and chugged it before returning to the table. "It's impressive, Maddie. You should be very proud of yourself." Lourdes grinned. "I'm embarrassing you."

"No, you're not," Maddie quickly blurted, staring Lourdes square in the eye. Lourdes nodded, giving a knowing smile.

"You should be used to people gushing. After all, the way you get likes and comments on your Instagram, you're very popular."

"I wouldn't go that far," Maddie softly stated. "Besides, I did this for my Dad."

Lourdes arched an eyebrow, and the table was silent. Maddie didn't know how much she wanted to dive into more information. She had already said way more than she expected. Lourdes didn't waver from the staring match that had ensued.

"It's a long story," Maddie continued.

"I see." Lourdes took a long swig of water, finishing off the bottle. "Perhaps you'll tell me about it sometime. Maybe even over coffee?"

"Maybe," Maddie whispered.

Lourdes stood up from the table and tossed the bottle into the trash can, making a perfect score, then glancing back at Maddie momentarily. Maddie swallowed another lump that was lodged deep in her throat.

"How about tomorrow?" Lourdes asked.

Maddie's jaw dropped slightly. Was she asking her out on a date? Or was this strictly platonic? *Breathe, Maddie. Breathe.*

"I've made you uncomfortable," Lourdes replied. "It's just an idea. Forget I ever said anything." She turned around. "I'll be seeing ya."

"Yes," she blurted out before Lourdes could reach the door. "I'd love to grab a coffee with you. That sounds nice. Have you ever been to Jolt?" Jolt was a trendy coffee shop located a couple of blocks from CapMed that served artisanal lattes made with house-made syrups that were small-batch, healthy alternatives to the store-bought syrups that Starbucks shilled. Maddie liked to buy their beans in bulk. Whenever she felt down, one sip of their cardamom rose latte never failed to brighten her day. She suspected Lourdes would enjoy it if she weren't already a regular. Lourdes looked over her shoulder, grinning in a way that made Maddie's stomach drop. "I love Jolt! It's one of my favorite spots in the city. Let's plan on it! I'll see you tomorrow, yeah?"

Lourdes left the break room, and Maddie sank back into her chair. She couldn't wait. The next day could be one of the best days of her life as long as she didn't get in her own way. She tried to tamp down the burgeoning hope that was bubbling in her stomach, but she couldn't stop smiling.

CHAPTER FIVE

COFFEE FOR TWO

Maddie spotted Lourdes as soon as she walked into Jolt. She wore a ribbed forest green crop top paired with dark-wash high-waisted jeans and beat-up Converse sneakers. Lourdes gathered her long, dark hair into a ponytail at the nape of her neck. She looked gorgeous, as always, sun-kissed and undeniably alive. Maddie yanked at the hem of her favorite flannel, wondering if she'd dressed too casually. After an hour-long pep talk from Eric last night where he urged her to "just be yourself," she'd picked her favorite flannel and perfectly worn Wrangler jeans. It was early Spring, and the sun was starting to shine more, but it was still chilly during the day. She paired the flannel with a black short-sleeved T-shirt. She'd had this flannel since she was twenty. The red and black buffalo check pattern had faded, and the fabric was soft. It felt like a hug. It made her feel confident, and she figured she could use all the extra confidence she could get. She'd stuffed her wallet and phone into a beat-up tote bag and practically shoved herself out the door before she could devise an excuse. Except now, standing next to Lourdes in a hip coffee shop decorated with hanging Edison bulbs and a mural made out of dried flowers, she felt like a lumberjack who stumbled into the wrong place.

Lourdes smiled when she saw her, "Hey! I was just looking at their new Spring specials. Do you have a favorite?" she asked.

Maddie walked over to her, and to her surprise, Lourdes enveloped her in a hug. Her shampoo smelled like lavender and thyme, earthy yet feminine.

"I, uh, the, uh, rose cardamom latte is really good," she stuttered.

Lourdes beamed, "That's what I was looking at!" She turned to the barista, an artfully tattooed hipster in their mid-twenties, "Two rose cardamom lattes, and," she glanced at Maddie, "Do you want any snacks?"

"Their vegan breakfast bars are great," Maddie said. Her stomach growled. She had been too nervous to eat before she met up with Lourdes.

"And two vegan breakfast bars," Lourdes added. Maddie dug around her tote for her wallet, but Lourdes grabbed her wrist and stopped her.

"I've got it," she grinned, handing over her card before Maddie could protest.

After a couple of cursory laps around the shop, Maddie and Lourdes found an open table. Lourdes grabbed their drinks from the bar and passed Maddie a steaming mug and a breakfast bar. Maddie nibbled the edge, trying to find comfort in the familiar sweetness of carob chips and maple syrup and the crunch of oats and pepitas.

Maddie glanced at Lourdes over her coffee cup; her breath caught again. Why was it she was suddenly feeling like a princess in a fairy tale, and Lourdes was the woman there to whisk her away? She cleared her throat and took a quick drink. Lourdes' eyes latched onto her, and a hint of a smile sparked on her lips.

"I have to tell you something, Maddie." Lourdes put her cup down, her eyes steady.

"I didn't think you would say yes."

Maddie smirked, staring down at her coffee, then looked up, hoping her eyes were filled with flirtatious curiosity even though she felt so timid.

"I'll admit I wasn't sure I should." *Or whether this was even classified as a date.* The flirtatious smirks and lust-filled glances Lourdes tossed her way slowly reassured Maddie that nothing about this was platonic.

Maddie situated herself in her seat, hoping to straighten her posture and project an aura of maturity and confidence. Lourdes didn't need to know that she was a total introvert just yet; that was a third-date problem. Maddie slid a finger around a strand of her dirty blonde hair and pushed it behind her ear. She was glad she had let her hair down from her usual ponytail at work. It helped to make her into the strong woman she hoped she could be.

"I'm glad you did." Lourdes took a sip of her coffee, then grinned wider. "I don't know a ton of people in the department. Since I've been there for a few months, it's hard to know who I can trust and count on. It's lonely when you don't feel like you have a confidante."

"For sure," Maddie shifted again in her seat.

"So, I need to know what's up with the staff. Who can I trust? Who should I avoid? I need a tour guide. I need someone who can give me the lay of the land." That's what this was. Maybe all the flirtation was so that Lourdes could use Maddie. Was that all?

Disheartened, Maddie continued, "Well, I can tell you that everyone in our department is great. You can pretty much count on them to do anything for you."

She reached for her cup of coffee. "But, I imagine it's probably similar to the ER." She drank from her mug, forgetting it was fresh and piping hot. She gasped, choking, nearly dropping the mug on the table.

"Are you alright?" Lourdes jumped up and hurried over to Maddie's side, quickly patting her on the back as Maddie attempted to catch her breath.

"I'm fine. Good." She coughed loudly and shook her head. She wasn't fine. She practically choked to death in front of the woman she was romantically interested in. What had gotten into her? This wasn't like her. She didn't go outside of her comfort zone. Where did it leave her? Choking and red-faced, looking like a complete dweeb.

"Hang on a second," Lourdes' returned a few seconds later. She forced a glass of water to Maddie's lips.

Maddie grabbed the glass. "Thank you!" she muttered, taking a sip of ice water, desperate to soothe her burnt throat. "All better." She choked, forcing a smile, but Lourdes knelt before her. Lourdes' brows furrowed. "I mean it; I'm fine. It just went down the wrong pipe. No need to be concerned."

Lourdes tilted her head but then backed up to her chair and sat down. "I know CPR and the Heimlich maneuver if you would have needed either one." She winked, which caused Maddie to drop her gaze to her water. Why was Lourdes flirting with her if Maddie was just a work friend? Why the mixed signals at all? She took a drink of her water.

"So, as I was saying...." She tried to calm her breathing with a couple of short breaths.

"Our department probably isn't much different than the ER. I'm sure you made friends and such there. You were there for a year, right?"

"Ten months," Lourdes replied.

"And I suppose, but there really wasn't anyone I hit it off with. I mostly came to work, did my job, went home, and that was it. Sure, I know people, but what does it really matter when you have no true outside connections? You know what I mean?"

Maddie nodded slowly, quite surprised by Lourdes' response. Lourdes seemed talkative. She was personable and always in good spirits. Maddie couldn't fathom that Lourdes didn't make friends everywhere she went. She sipped on her water, her throat slowly getting its sensation back.

"Plus, I've never really vibed with anyone to the point where I wanted to really get to know them."

"Well, I can assure you that if you need anything, you can come to any of us."

"That's always great to hear," Lourdes replied. "But since you're here, I want to know more about you."

"I'm not going anywhere," Maddie laughed, taking another sip of water, then pushing it out of the way to get back to her coffee. Slowly her embarrassment dissipated. They were there. She would sit back and see what Lourdes' agenda was.

"You're pretty athletic, aren't you? You did the half-marathon. You've got those runner thighs of steel. ."

Maddie's cheeks burned from the compliment. "I do my best. I enjoy jogging whenever I get the chance. Eating a healthy diet is also very important to me."

"Same here," Lourdes replied.

"I choose to stay mostly vegetarian. Once I went that route, I felt much better. I used to be constantly exhausted. Ever since I started eating organic, I've felt like I could run a marathon. I'm not a star athlete like you, of course."

Maddie felt herself blushing again.

"That's amazing." Maddie leaned into the conversation, putting her choking fiasco behind her.

"I had a friend in high school who had chronic fatigue. She had to see all these specialists, but maybe she should have gone that route."

Lourdes smiled, "It isn't for everyone, but I can't imagine my life any other way." Maddie watched as Lourdes sipped her coffee. Her olive complexion continued to glow behind the coffee cup. Maddie's heart did a flip-flop. When Lourdes met her gaze, Maddie diverted her gaze and reached for her coffee cup. This wasn't a date, not in Lourdes' eyes. Now that she knew that, she had to force herself not to get lost in every word Lourdes spoke.

"What do you want out of life, Maddie?" The question surprised Maddie; she feared she would start choking again. Maddie tried to avoid ever pondering those sorts of questions her whole life. She always believed that nothing else mattered as long as she was with her father, a belief that only intensified after his health scare. Why dream? Why have goals? Why not just live in the moment, and whatever happens, happens?"

"I guess I never really considered it," Maddie admitted.

Lourdes sat back. Her mouth hung open.

"You never drew out a road map to your life? You've never wondered where you would be in five years or ten? You never desired something so intensely that if you didn't have that one thing in your life, you would break?"

Maddie giggled. Yet, Lourdes didn't shake her attention." I..." She closed her mouth, then shrugged.

"Tell me about your dad."

Maddie frowned. "Huh?"

"Well, you said that you did the half-marathon because of him. Right?" Maddie nodded.

"Tell me about him because I'll tell you that you were glowing in that picture from the race. I saw passion there and a desire to help others. So, share that with me. Please?"

Did she see all that from a single picture? Maddie began to tell her everything, from how she nearly lost him to the moment she realized she had to be the one to change his lifestyle. If she didn't, who would? Maddie shared how she hated seeing the nursing staff treat her dad and how that inspired her to become a nurse. She told her more than she had ever confided in another human, and Lourdes followed every word.

Maddie blushed. "You ask, and you shall receive. I tend to overshare.."

"That's why you do what you do. That's who you are, and if that isn't passion, then I don't know what is," Lourdes said. She reached across the table and placed her palm on Maddie's hand. Maddie didn't move away.

Instead, Maddie met her gaze again, "So, now that you know my life story, what about you? What makes Lourdes, well, Lourdes?"

Lourdes leaned back into her chair, "I knew from a young age," Lourdes began, "that I wanted to see the world. I have traveled close and far, helping others, volunteering where needed."

She smiled and grabbed her phone. Maddie watched as she swiped through several images before showing Maddie the picture, "Here I am at the Pyramids in Egypt."

"Wow!" Maddie exclaimed.

"That's amazing."

"I can't imagine not traveling. And I can't imagine not helping others." She grabbed her phone back and slipped it back into her pocket.

"You and I are alike in so many ways. We go all in for things that are important to us. We both like to exercise. We try our best to eat healthily," Lourdes continued to tick off things. Maddie nodded after each one. Maddie was exhilarated by what they did have in common. It made their differences seem so trivial.

"We do have a lot in common. More than I even realized. It's just ..." Her words trailed off, and she sipped her coffee. She couldn't stop the burning question that played in her mind.

"I guess I'm a little confused about what this is. You know, us together in this coffee shop," Maddie confessed.

Lourdes tilted her head, a sparkle in her eye. "What do you think it is?"

"I'm not sure," Maddie cautiously admitted, laughing.

"That's why I ask."

When Lourdes didn't attempt to move, Maddie proceeded. "I mean, I guess there was a part of me that thought maybe it was a date." She choked out the last word, leaving a bad taste in her mouth.

"But after we talked, I thought maybe it was just that you wanted a friend. But then I opened up about my dad, and you talked about your trips. I'm just as confused as ever."

"I see." Lourdes sipped her coffee as she pondered Maddie's confusion. "Let me rephrase the question. What would you like this to be?"

Maddie shook her head, "Nope, I'm not falling for that one."

"It's just a question." Lourdes laughed, and her eyes twinkled. "I can tell you're a thinker. Come on, go for it."

"It's not that easy," Maddie argued. "Not for me."

"Well, perhaps you'll change. It's possible. But the question remains. Do you want this to be a date? It's as simple as that." *Simple?* Nothing was simple about this. However, Maddie knew she wouldn't be the one caught in expressing her thoughts and feelings. That wasn't her. Not now. Not ever. She remained quiet. After a brief moment of hesitation, Lourdes proceeded. "I've done some research at the hospital. It's a mutual love-fest."

Maddie frowned. "What do you mean?"

"I just meant that when I asked around the other day. Everyone said I wouldn't find a better person than you." She snickered, "Especially Eric. He gushes about you. I can see why."

"Eric is a good guy. I've known him awhile."

"That's what I hear. The whole staff loves you."

"Is that so?" Maddie asked quietly.

Lourdes nodded enthusiastically, "I just knew that you were someone I needed to get to know better. I suppose you could say that I was hoping this was a date. I mean, you seemed pretty pumped to grab a coffee with me."

"I did not!" Maddie argued, just as Lourdes winked. Maddie snapped her mouth shut. "You're teasing me."

Lourdes shrugged. "It's so much fun."

Again, a bright red blush crept up her cheeks as Lourdes leaned into her, her eyes fixated. While Maddie knew the temptation was there. The chemistry was on fire, and everything aligned just right. There was still something throwing her off.

"When doing your research, did you happen to find out my age?" Maddie inquired, staring into her coffee.

"Maybe," Lourdes replied. Maddie looked up to catch Lourdes smirking. "Do you know how old I am?"

Maddie snickered and looked away from her. "Not exactly, but I imagine mid-thirties. While I'm—"

"Twenty-five." Lourdes winked. "Age is just a number. So what if there's a ten-year age difference? It doesn't bother me. I hardly notice."

Maddie smiled, sitting back in her seat. Perhaps it wasn't enough to warrant concern. Then why should Maddie make it such a big deal?

The date continued with no break in the conversation, leaving Maddie enthralled about the future. They exited Jolt, walking down a side street to get to Maddie's car. Maddie unlocked her car and awkwardly shifted her weight from one foot to the other.

"So, I had a great time. I must confess I'm happy that we determined date vs. no date," Maddie admitted.

"Me too." Lourdes laughed. "It was nice." Lourdes' laugh and smile were so sexy that Maddie was confident she wanted Lourdes to lean in for a kiss. The feeling was mutual; she could see the desire written all over Lourdes' face.

"Well, Maddie..." Lourdes began.

Maddie snickered. "Well, Lourdes," she replied with a teasing smirk.

Lourdes slowly leaned in. Maddie could smell the scent of Lourdes' perfume and feel her soft breath on her upper lip. But the moment vanished before she could make a move. Instead of closing the distance between them, Lourdes jerked away like a frightened animal.

"I have to get back to work. I'll be seeing you." Lourdes grumbled, affectless.

Maddie's jaw dropped as Lourdes hurried towards her bike. She watched as she got on, rode off, and left Maddie clueless. What just happened, and was the last hour only a dream?

CHAPTER SIX

JOGGING ENCOUNTER

"**A**re you heading out for the night ?" Eric asked as Maddie approached the nurse's station.

"Yep. I'm going for a quick run before heading home. Wanna join me?"

"Thanks for the offer, but James and I have a hot date planned tonight, and I need to shower. Can't be having my man disgusted."

Maddie smirked. "No, you can't. You guys have fun. Don't do anything I wouldn't do." She winked at him and then turned to see Lourdes headed their way. When Lourdes caught her eye, she diverted her direction and walked away from them. Lourdes hadn't said one word to Maddie since their date. Maddie sighed.

"That was awkward," Eric noted.

"Even I felt the chill over here. You guys haven't talked, have you?"

"Nope." Maddie groaned. Lourdes had been avoiding her like the plague for the past week and a half. They had a great time. They both agreed that it was a date. Lourdes paid for it, and all was well until that awkward moment at the car, where their spark fizzled just as quickly as it occurred.

Maddie shrugged, "I don't get it, but I probably never will. And this, my dear friend, is why I'm probably still single."

Eric rolled his eyes. "You just never know what will happen along the way. Maybe you'll meet your Ms. Right. And who knows, maybe that person will still be Lourdes. You guys would be so great together."

"Well, you thinking that and me thinking that does not mean that she's thinking that." Maddie shrugged.

"It is what it is. I best be going. I want to get that run in, and I hear there may be a storm brewing. Catch you later." She waved and hurried out the back way to get to the trail. Once outside, Maddie popped in her earbuds, pulled up her playlist, and started to run. It was already clouding up, so she closed her eyes and ran. The piercing wind invigorated her. She took a deep breath of fresh air. This was exactly what she needed.

A Black Eyed Peas song played in her headphones as she raced around the track adjacent to the hospital's East entrance. With the approaching rain, there weren't many people on the track. It allowed for some clear thinking. Unfortunately, her mind was mush when it came to having an idea of her thoughts.

The song switched to a slow ballad, and Maddie stopped running to change the song. As she skimmed through her playlist, she didn't notice anyone watching her until she heard Lourdes' voice,

"You come here often?"

She jumped and looked up, then laughed. "Oh, you startled me."

She dropped her phone into her pocket and looked around to see if anyone else was around.

"I go for a run here when I want to clear my head. You? I've never seen you running out here before." She regarded Lourdes coolly, tamping down her bubbling irritation. How dare she show up as if nothing happened in Maddie's secret spot of all places?

Lourdes shrugged. "Same situation. I needed to clear my head."

Lourdes looked up at the sky. "And the sky's about to break, so I don't think we have much longer. Care if I join you?"

After almost two weeks of radio silence from Lourdes, Maddie didn't anticipate this moment. Just to get back at her, she left her hanging for a few minutes as Lourdes matched her stride.

"Sure, go ahead," Maddie acquiesced.

They turned and continued to jog together in silence. Maddie could feel the shift in the weather. The sky would let loose at any moment, and they would be running in the rain. Yet, neither one seemed to care, especially Maddie. The thought of getting drenched in the rain brought a hidden desire from within her that she never knew existed. How many romantic movies caught the main couple together in the rain, dancing and kissing? Too many to count. It had been three years since she'd kissed anyone, and she couldn't help but contemplate how good it would feel to kiss Lourdes. "Busy week?" Lourdes asked.

"Yeah, work and life have been hectic. You?" *Seeing that we haven't exchanged a single word in 10 days.* Maddie bit down on her tongue. She would give Lourdes a chance to talk if she had anything to say.

"Same."

That wasn't much of a conversation. A few sprinkles landed on Maddie's nose, and Maddie looked up. "Well, we should head back, or we'll get drenched."

"Yeah, you're right. Let's go."

Once they reached Maddie's car, the rain started to come down even more. "Where are you parked? "Maddie asked.

"My bike is up there." Lourdes pointed to the rack of bikes, where her bike was the last one remaining. Maddie tilted her head and shook it. "I'll be fine."

"Let me take you home and bring you back tomorrow for your bike. You'll never make it before the hurricane hits."

Lourdes snickered. "Aren't you being a bit dramatic?"

Dramatic or not, there wasn't any way she could leave Lourdes there to fend for herself, even if she were irritated with her. She wasn't that petty "Get in the car," she ordered.

With no more convincing than that, Lourdes got into the car, and Maddie headed toward the direction Lourdes mapped for her. She only lived five minutes from the hospital, so it was obvious why she chose to take her bike.

"Best on gas, too," Lourdes reasoned.

"If I lived so close, I'd do the same. Makes sense." Maddie turned into the driveway and stopped her car. The rain started to pelt the windows harder. "See, you would have never made it."

"My hero," Lourdes smiled as she looked over at Maddie. That same flirtation instantly returned, along with the heated gaze they shared. Maddie quickly shifted from it and reached into the backseat for her umbrella.

"I'll walk you up to the door so you don't get drenched ."

"You don't have to do that," Lourdes argued, but Maddie was already out the door and around to help her out of the passenger side. The wind started to pick up, moving her umbrella, but she held it steady as Lourdes exited the car.

"Thank you!" Lourdes turned to her once they reached her porch. "Maddie," Lourdes started. Hearing her name come out of Lourdes' mouth made her melt. It was getting harder to stay mad at her. *Remember what she did.* Maddie coached herself. Lourdes led her on. Now she had the gall to stand here with her gorgeous brown eyes, the color of melting chocolate, and soft, luscious lips.

The rain fell harder, crashing to the pavement. "What's that?" Maddie leaned in closer, their faces inches from one another's. Her eyes locked on Lourdes, and Lourdes smiled.

"I was just going to say I'm sorry I have been avoiding you this week."

At least the truth was out there, and it wasn't all in Maddie's mind. She felt vindicated at that moment. She wasn't crazy.

"The truth is," Lourdes went on. "The other day, I wanted to kiss you."

As Lourdes spoke the words, Maddie listened. She nervously bit down on her lip. In one moment, she has this overly-hyped anticipation of what it'd feel like to be kissed by this beautiful woman.

"Why didn't you?" Maddie asked. "I wouldn't have objected."

"I know you wouldn't have. I saw it in your eyes, but I was scared. I was scared that it would have been too forward and would have pushed you away. I didn't want it to look like I was taking advantage of you. I guess because you mentioned the age difference, it worried me that it would appear like I felt I could overpower you or something." She snickered as Maddie opened her mouth, appalled by the statement.

"I freaked. I'm not too old to admit that. I swear, I wanted to kiss you. Then, the moment I told myself to buck up and do it, I swear, I saw my ex. She just moved back to Chicago from Denver about a month ago, and I didn't think we'd run into each other so soon. It freaked me out, so I bolted." Maddie shook her head, feeling a pang of sympathy settle in her stomach. Lourdes was so confident. It was hard to imagine her being nervous enough to flee a date like it was a crime scene.

"That bad, huh?" Maddie asked.

"It was terrible. I nearly mowed her over on my bike. I biffed it," She showed Maddie her elbow, sporting a nasty multi-colored bruise.

"And then, I was too embarrassed to say anything," Lourdes explained.

"I thought you were pushing me away because as we had gotten close, you realized it wasn't what you wanted. Then when you avoided me, I convinced myself that the date meant nothing."

"The date meant everything." Lourdes brushed her hand against Maddie's cheek as she moved closer.

"I want to see where things can go, Maddie. As long as you feel the same way," Lourdes whispered.

Maddie nodded. Finally, Lourdes leaned in, caressing her lips so softly against Maddie's. The kiss deepened, and Maddie went all in. She drew her arm around Lourdes. Her whole body sparked with the warring forces of pleasure and excitement. This was the romance she longed for, where the two lovers stood in the rain as it showered down over them.

"I'd invite you in," Lourdes teased.

"But then we both know where that would lead."

Maddie pulled back from the kiss. Her eyes lingered passionately on Lourdes'. Lourdes smiled and grabbed Maddie's hand, pulling her back towards her, and their lips reconnected. Lourdes pushed Maddie up against her front door, not breaking from the hold. The rain enveloped them. Nothing was more right than being locked in Lourdes' arms as the rain poured around them.

CHAPTER SEVEN

HIDDEN AFFAIRS

A couple of weeks after their fateful meeting in the rain, a notification sounded on Maddie's phone. Maddie smiled as she read the message.

Lourdes: Hey, Gorgeous. I hope your day is fantastic. Can't wait to see you tonight.

Maddie: Lovely, you are a breath of fresh air. Until tonight ...

"I guess I don't have to ask what you're grinning about," Eric said, approaching the nurse's station. Maddie blushed and quickly put her phone in her pocket.

"I don't know what you're referring to." She looked over to where Shannon was leaning against the wall, resting her eyes until her next patient.

"She can't hear a thing. She's in Zen mode." Eric rolled his eyes. "You know exactly what I'm talking about. You've been grinning like a school-girl with a crush since Lourdes, and you decided to make this thing work."

Maddie playfully pushed him backward, and he pretended to stumble. She snickered. "Things aren't bad between us."

"Aren't bad." He scoffed.

"That's like someone saying it's not bad that they won the lottery. Please don't kid yourself or me. You are one happy lady, and you love every minute of it. You have been a busy little beaver since things started to heat up between you two. Have you done the deed? Gone downtown? Spent an evening of Sapphic seduction on the 'ol Isle of Lesbos?"

Maddie arched an eyebrow, "Eric, seriously! Get your mind out of the gutter. We are taking things at our own pace, and it's good."

Her grin deepened. "Really good. But I'm beginning to think you know way too much about my love life."

"Come on. You wouldn't want it any other way." Eric teased, bumping his hip against her.

"You like that someone is privy to your secret desires," Eric pretended to swoon.

Maddie sighed and continued. "We went running this morning. I never thought I'd meet someone that could outrace me, but to my surprise, she holds her own." Maddie smiled. She loved the challenge when it came to running with Lourdes. Lourdes could keep her on her toes, and she admired that.

"And you went to dinner the night before last."

"We gotta eat, right?" Maddie looked down at the file in her hand. "And she's making me dinner tonight."

"Oohhh...how cozy. But can she cook?" He arched an eyebrow.

"That would be the question. Guess I'll find out tonight." She laughed.

"Although, I haven't found something she hasn't been amazing at."

"Keep searching. Keep searching." He winked at her, and Maddie shook her head, unable to stifle her giggle.

"Didn't you go wine tasting over the weekend?"

Maddie nodded, "Right after a picnic in the park. Then a cycling event the weekend before."

"What haven't you done?" Eric replied.

"Oh yes...the deed. Don't you think it's about time? It's been just about a month! That's like ten years in lesbian! You have far exceeded the three-date limit."

Maddie rolled her eyes. "When you're playing by your own rules, there are no rules."

She looked behind him as Shannon, a fellow nurse, inched closer to them, most likely interested in their conversation. "Anyway, as I was saying, this pediatric fundraiser will be a huge event. I'm excited to be part of the raffle. How many tickets can I put down for you and James?"

"Depends. What's the winner getting?"

Maddie opened her mouth, shocked that he would inquire about that. "The joy and satisfaction of knowing you are helping make a difference. Isn't that enough?"

He chuckled. "Of course. Put me down for ten."

"That's better," Maddie giggled.

"I'll take five," Shannon piped up. "Sounds like a terrific cause. Good for you."

"Thanks, Shannon."

Shannon spun on her heel and walked away, and Maddie snickered. "That was a close one. The last thing Lourdes and I need or want is to be ground through the hospital rumor mill.'

"As if people don't already know," Eric teased. "But in all seriousness, Shannon is right. Good for you, but you get involved in so much. I don't know how you do it."

"And I don't know how you do so little," Maddie teased, playfully punching him in the shoulder.

"So little? I'm buying ten raffle tickets, and James and I will come to eat the food. It's all about giving." He winked, and Maddie could hear his laughter ringing as he walked away from her. Still, she couldn't tear the smile from her face. She was a woman intrigued with her new relationship, which was something to celebrate. Her past relationships tended to die down after the initial honeymoon phase of week-long dates, but with Lourdes, it seemed like they would never run out of things to talk about. With Lourdes by her side, Maddie felt she could conquer the world. Still, part of her worried that the other shoe would drop, that Lourdes, just like her previous partners, would find her combination of ambition and anxiety too much to bear.

CHAPTER EIGHT

INTIMATE DINNER

Maddie smelled the earthy scent of Spring rain as she stood on Lourdes' front porch. She smiled, images of their first make-out session coming back to her. That was one night she wouldn't forget, even if it were over three weeks ago. Standing there, drenched, the scent of Lourdes mingling with the smell of heavy rain, it was the closest she had ever been to a perfect moment.

Lourdes opened the door and greeted her with a huge smile. "I thought this night would never get here," she teased, pulling Maddie into the foyer and embracing her. They kissed, and the busy day faded away. Maddie's heart quickened, and she slid her hand up Lourdes' back, feeling her toned back muscles, desperate for the moment to last just a few seconds longer. Her breath escaped loosely through her lips as Lourdes slowly broke away. "You look nice," Lourdes added.

Maddie blushed, ashamed to admit that she had dug through her entire closet in preparation for tonight. She settled on a black turtleneck and jeans, hoping to convey her stylishness. She even started wearing a new flavor of tinted chapstick: cinnamon flush.

The taste of Lourdes' lips lingered on her own. Maddie looked Lourdes over longingly. "You look extra lovely," Maddie said, giving an equal-sized grin. Lourdes stood wearing a black pair of pants and a red blouse that dipped down, revealing her cleavage. It was an outfit that matched her curves splendidly, leaving very little to the imagination.

"Thank you, Gorgeous!" Lourdes winked. "Make yourself at home. Dinner's almost ready."

Maddie dropped her gaze to Lourdes' ass as she walked away. The outfit hugged her curves in all the right places. When Lourdes disappeared around a corner, Maddie glanced around the foyer. There were running shoes by the door and a yoga mat propped in the corner. It was as if she was ready to escape to the realm of physical fitness whenever possible. From the conversations they had, it didn't surprise Maddie one bit. She peeked in a room right off the foyer and saw more exercise equipment, with dumbbells and a treadmill. Perhaps this would be another activity they could do together.

"There you are," Lourdes said.

Maddie jumped and whirled around. "I'm sorry if I was being nosy. You said to be at home and...."

"Calm down ... I just missed you! I was wondering where you ran off." She kissed Maddie, calming her racing heart. Lourdes grabbed Maddie's hand, and they left the room and went back through the foyer and to the kitchen.

Maddie took in a big whiff and nodded with approval. "It smells amazing."

Lourdes looked over her shoulder from where she resumed her place at the stove. "Thanks! I just got a new perfume," she winked before returning to her preparations.

Maddie couldn't believe they had gotten to this point. In just three short weeks, she was already feeling like maybe Lourdes was the one she had been waiting to connect with emotionally and physically. Yet, the mere thought of taking their physical relationship to the next level caused her heart palpitations to increase. Why was she so nervous? When they kissed, it was like the world melted away. Any worries and stress just dissolved. But the minute she contemplated moving forward, she always wanted to take a step back. It had nothing to do with their chemistry and everything to do with her fears and failures. She couldn't shake the feeling that she would be the one to mess this up.

"Uh oh."

Maddie turned back to Lourdes as Lourdes' voice echoed in the kitchen. "Huh? You look worried. Want to share?" Lourdes moved in closer to Maddie.

"I was just thinking about a plethora of stuff. It's nothing you need to worry about." *Plethora of stuff? Why the sudden need to break out a thesaurus in front of Lourdes?*

Lourdes frowned but never pried.

"I'm good. Is dinner ready?" She brushed past Lourdes but felt Lourdes' eyes following her.

"Uh, yeah. It is. Let me grab your seat for you." Maddie waited as Lourdes pulled out a seat and waited for Maddie to sit down.

"Thank you!" Maddie sank back in her seat and waited for Lourdes to sit across from her.

"How was work today, Gorgeous?" Lourdes asked as she moved in and took the first bite. Maddie sighed, grateful to have any awkwardness behind them.

Maddie was centered and anxious to enjoy the meal and the company. "Busy, but the thought of meeting up with you made the day go smoothly." Maddie took a bite of her spinach salad and sighed. She could now tell Eric that Lourdes was a fantastic chef.

"This salad is amazing. So delicious," Maddie exclaimed.

Along with the salad were tofu and noodles. The tofu was spicy and perfectly crisp. Whenever Maddie tried to make tofu, it tasted like wet cardboard. She made a mental note to get the recipe from Lourdes. She always wanted different healthy ideas.

Lourdes laughed. "I appreciate the satisfied look on your face. I don't recall anyone looking so pleased with a salad," Lourdes took a bite, and Maddie laughed.

"It's not just the salad. This tofu is divine — compliments to the chef. Please remind me to get the recipe to share with my dad. He'll love it." Maddie winked and went back to savoring the meal. She was less nervous than when she arrived, but earlier thoughts and fears circled her mind.

"Thank you! It's a secret family recipe. But I suppose my ancestors wouldn't mind." Lourdes gave a teasing wink.

Maddie took a sip of her water, but her gaze never dropped. "Tell me about your family." Maddie had spent time discussing her dad. It was only fitting that Lourdes discussed hers. "I want to learn about your parents. Do you have any siblings? Tell me everything." While Maddie and Lourdes had been on several dates, they were mostly activity-based. This dinner was the first time since the coffee shop they had the chance to talk.

"There's not much to tell. My mom died when I was young. She immigrated to the United States from Italy in her twenties. Then, she met my dad. I was only a couple of years old when she died. My dad took great care of me. I'm an only child, but I was close with my cousins. A couple of them live in Italy, where my mom grew up. My dad owns an oil company in Texas."

"Wow, he must be rich." Maddie bit down her tongue. "Sorry, I didn't mean to butt in."

Lourdes shook her head. "No worries. He's well-off, indeed. He provided well. He remarried a few years ago, and she's a nice enough woman. I'm glad he's happy, but I don't see any of my family as often as I should. I guess we just drifted apart."

"You travel, so maybe you should make a point to visit Texas and visit them. You could even go to Italy!" Maddie took a bite of her salad.

"Yeah, maybe you're right," Lourdes quietly replied. "But tell me about your mom."

Maddie moved her salad around with her fork. "I don't like to talk about her. She abandoned my father and me when I was six. So, in one aspect, we have that in common, too. I don't have too many vivid memories of her. Until two years ago, I didn't even know my dad knew her whereabouts. It turns out she died of breast cancer. My dad saw the obituary. She lived just about twenty-five miles from here. It's a shame she never wanted to reach out or anything."

"I'm so sorry. Do you know why she left?"

Maddie shrugged. "Possibly depression. Who knows? My dad just said that they grew apart. In one way, I get that. You'd think she'd want to stay in touch with her child. But, it was her loss. She didn't want to be around us, so it is what it is. And no siblings. No cousins." Maddie snickered, "Just me and my dad."

"Depression can put people in a world of hurt that not everyone understands. I'm sorry she chose to leave you and didn't want to get help."

"It's alright. My dad never left me wanting for anything, so I didn't feel deprived."

Lourdes was very easy to talk to; she was a thoughtful and attentive listener. Maddie hadn't shared that information with anyone: even her first love, Raven. After Raven, she dated a couple of other people casually.

But Maddie was starting to suspect that this thing with Lourdes was anything but casual. They continued to eat, making idle chit-chat. Maddie never once checked the time. She didn't want the night to end.

"How about I get us some wine and take this conversation to the living room?" Lourdes grinned, standing up and grabbing both of their plates from the kitchen table.

Maddie nodded. She would need the wine if the evening went as far as she thought it could go. After all, three weeks and several dates later, she was ravenous for Lourdes.

"Here you go, Gorgeous."

Maddie jumped when she heard Lourdes' voice. "Oh. Thank you! That was fast."

Lourdes grinned. I didn't want to be away from you longer than necessary." She winked, and Maddie felt the heat building between them, but her nerves didn't lessen. Lourdes moved in closer to her. "Everything is going to be fine," Lourdes whispered. "Trust me." She grabbed Maddie's hand and led her to the couch. They sat just inches from one another and sipped on the wine. A fire softly glowed in the background.

"Everything was great," Maddie choked out through her sip of wine. "The food was wonderful."

"Glad you enjoyed it." Lourdes brushed a strand of hair away from Maddie's eyes and slowly moved in, kissing Maddie with a hunger that Maddie felt tenfold. Maddie released a moan as Lourdes' tongue slipped between her open lips. She tasted the wine on Lourdes' tongue, sending shivers down her spine.

As they kissed, Lourdes slipped her hand up Maddie's shirt, gently caressing her breast. Maddie groaned. She wanted to take things further, but she couldn't relax. It had been over a year since Maddie had slept with someone. What if Lourdes thought she was terrible in bed? Lourdes was experienced. If she knew what good sex was, then surely she'd been able to tell if someone was inexperienced. Maddie quickly pulled back. "We can't."

Lourdes' mouth hung open, and she distanced herself from Maddie as if Maddie had slapped her across the face. "I'm sorry if I moved too fast. I just thought it was going in that direction. I guess I was wrong."

"It's not that. We were going in that direction. But at the same time, I don't want to rush things. Can you understand that?"

Lourdes gave a weak smile. "Honestly, I can respect that. Before we went down this path, I thought maybe we should talk. I had no intention of taking it to that level right here. Right now. But then, as we were kissing...." She smirked.

"I guess I read too much into it and didn't want to do what I've accused you of doing."

"Overthinking?" Maddie asked.

Lourdes sighed. "Exactly. The moment just felt right."

Maddie grimaced. Lourdes wasn't wrong. The moment felt perfect, right up until she pushed her away. Lourdes' suspicions were spot on. Maddie was a thinker, and that was her demise at times.

"Lovely, I would love to go there. But it's been a while...." She quickly stopped herself, dropping her gaze.

"How long?" Lourdes asked, arched eyebrow.

Maddie looked up, then shook her head. "Around a year, but it doesn't matter. I'm not as experienced as you are. I can leave if you want me to."

"What?" Lourdes caressed Maddie's cheek. "I would never do that," Lourdes moved her hand down to cup Maddie's chin in her palm.

"I would never kick you out for that reason. I would never kick you out for any reason. You're not like any other woman I've met, Gorgeous. You are truly someone special."

"You mean that?" Maddie softly asked. Maddie was preparing for a walk of shame to her car. But she could see the sincerity in Lourdes' eyes. Lourdes was being honest.

"Maddie, what kind of woman would I be if I didn't respect you? You think we should wait; then we'll wait." Lourdes stood up from the couch and went over to the overstuffed chair. Maddie watched her, where she now sat halfway across the room. Maddie looked at the fireplace, the soft romantic glow encapsulating the space. She swallowed. She wanted Lourdes to return to her, but she couldn't get the words out. It'd been a long, lonely year. Maddie could feel herself longing for Lourdes. Her heart fluttered in her chest. No one had ever encapsulated her thoughts and desires like Lourdes Russo. She took a deep breath to psych herself up and told herself to be brave.

"Maybe we shouldn't wait," Maddie suggested.

"What?" Lourdes asked.

Maddie got up from the sofa and walked over to the chair. Lourdes stood up. Her eyes narrowed in on Maddie's. "Maybe we are right," Maddie said.

Lourdes paused for a moment, arching her eyebrows. "Maddie, are you sure? Again, I don't want to pressure you."

Maddie took a deep breath, pushing past her anxiety once and for all.

"Yes, I'm sure. Lourdes, I want this. I want you," Maddie said.

Lourdes smiled. Finally, Maddie closed the distance between them, kissing her fiercely. Maddie groaned. She reached up and threaded her fingers through Lourdes' thick hair attempting to demolish any molecule of space between them. At that moment, Maddie had never wanted anything more in her life.

Lourdes wrapped her arms around Maddie, enveloping her in her warmth. Her hands tugged at Maddie's shirt until it was over her breasts. Lourdes kissed her chest, licking the underside of her breasts.

"Yes," Maddie groaned. Lourdes pushed Maddie down to the couch and slid her mouth around her left nipple, hungrily tugging at it before swirling her tongue around it and releasing it with a loud groan. "Lourdes!" Maddie growled just as Lourdes engulfed her other nipple between her teeth. Maddie released a breath, digging her nails into Lourdes' shirt.

"Let's get this off of you," Maddie said. For the first time, she felt confident, sexy even.

She unbuttoned Lourdes' blouse as fast as her fingers let her, revealing Lourdes' ample breasts, pouring out of the top of a black lace bra. Maddie was practically drooling. She kissed Lourdes again, reaching behind her to unhook her bra. She tossed Lourdes' bra behind her and began to lick, trailing her tongue along Lourdes' large, dark nipples, which soon pebbled with desire. Maddie took one of her nipples in her mouth and sucked. She left a trail of kisses along her chest until she finally made her way to Lourdes' lips, slipping her tongue into Lourdes' mouth. Maddie rolled her hips toward her instinctually. She felt her underwear grow slick with desire as she ground her crotch into Lourdes.'

Lourdes pulled away, grinning as she unbuttoned Maddie's jeans.

"Lie back for me, baby," she instructed. Maddie did as she was told and laid back on the couch. Lourdes slid off the couch and knelt in front of Maddie, a devilish grin spread across her face as she yanked Maddie's jeans off her legs, peeling her slick underwear off. She got up onto her knees and started to kiss the muscular plane of Maddie's stomach. Desire formed a molten pool behind her belly button as Lourdes' lips got closer and closer to her center. Maddie's hips bucked, and the back of her thighs ached with anticipation. Her heart hammered inside her chest, but she wasn't nervous ... she was enthralled, that same mixture of fear and awe that occurs when you reach the crest of a roller coaster.

Even though it seemed Maddie was about to burst, Lourdes paused, "Is this okay?"

"Yes," Maddie said breathily.

With that, Lourdes slung Maddie's legs over her shoulders, adjusting her position. She parted the lips of Maddie's sex. She began to lick, slowly exploring the contours of her molten, wet center. Lourdes traced her tongue along the arch of Maddie's clitoral hood. Lourdes took Maddie's clitoris in her mouth and sucked, savoring it as if it was a world-class delicacy. Maddie's hips bucked, pleasure fissured along the backs of her thighs. Encouraged, Lourdes began to increase the speed of her licks, adding more pressure with her tongue. A guttural groan escaped from the back of Maddie's throat. Lourdes licked even faster, swishing her tongue upward around Maddie's clitoris. Maddie could feel her orgasm starting to build. Her legs were beginning to shake, and Lourdes licked even faster. Maddie gasped, her hips rocked upward, and Lourdes grabbed onto her hipbones, meeting the rhythm of her body. Lourdes' sucked at her clit, and Maddie came hard. It was as if every nerve ending in her body had transformed into a firework. There was no such thing as pain, only wave after wave of pleasure. Maddie soared along the crest of her orgasm, crying out, "Lourdes!" in a ragged yell. This was bliss. This was heaven. This was everything. How was she supposed to go to work tomorrow when she knew this existed? Lourdes lapped along her sex, slower now, savoring the taste of Maddie as the last fissures of her orgasm fizzled out. Lourdes looked up at her, grinning, a ring of Maddie's juices shining slick around her mouth.

Maddie was breathless, "What ... how did you ... when?"

Lourdes shrugged, "What can I say? I've got a couple of years on you," she teased. She got up and sat beside Maddie, who rested her head in her lap. Lourdes stroked her hair, "You're an angel," she whispered.

"No, you," Maddie insisted. She leaned up on her elbows and captured Lourdes' lips in hers.

"Is it your turn now?" She teased.

She got up and straddled Lourdes, leaning forward to kiss her again. But then, Lourdes' phone rang, vibrating against the coffee table.

Lourdes grabbed it, "Shit, it's work. I have to take this," she said.

"Of course," Maddie replied.

She tried not to listen as Lourdes pressed her phone between her cheek and the crook of her shoulder, "Yes, this is Russo. How often? Ugh, that's not good. Okay, I'll be right there." She hung up quickly and turned to Maddie.

"Marilyn is complaining of chest pains and is ordering them to get me. But you know her; it's probably nothing."

"Right...124." Maddie shrugged. "If you need to go, then you need to go."

"But I want to stay here with you," Lourdes whined, pressing her face against Maddie's bare chest. It was cute how indignant she was.

"You have to work. It's okay, I understand," Maddie reassured her.

Lourdes groaned again and bent down, retrieving her bra and top from the floor. Maddie grabbed her clothes that were flung about the living room. Once she was decent, Maddie gave her a quick peck. "Call me later," she instructed Lourdes. They grabbed their coats, and Maddie drove Lourdes to the hospital, silently furious at Marilyn Evans for interrupting her chance to go down on the inimitable Lourdes Russo.

CHAPTER NINE

CRASHING DOWN

Maddie anxiously tapped her fingers alongside her keyboard. "Don't fail me now." Technology was great, most of the time. However, on this particular day, Maddie could scream at the computer. While it was bad enough that the day was busy, with a full schedule of patients coming in, Shannon called in sick. The hospital had a strict policy on tardiness and sick days, and Shannon had used up her quantity and then some. But what could you do if you weren't feeling well? She said she had a fever, so it was all they could do but believe her. The last thing the patients needed was a nurse to give them their germs. And with Covid still going around, nobody needed to take that chance.

"Hey, Gorgeous. Wanna stop and get some lunch?"

Maddie smiled back at Lourdes' eager grin. They hadn't talked since the previous night's rudely interrupted love-fest. Maddie would have loved to have a few minutes to catch up and find out how Marilyn was doing. "I'd love to, but I'm swamped. I'm not sure I'll get lunch today." Maddie got up from her computer. "The computer's lagging. Plus, Shannon's out sick. I have three new patients in a matter of 2 hours. I'm overwhelmed." Maddie turned, but Lourdes grabbed her arm.

"Calm down, Gorgeous," she whispered. "If you work yourself in a frenzy, it won't be good for anyone." Lourdes rested her head against

Maddie's. "You're going to pass out from all this stress. Just take a deep breath and breathe."

Maddie closed her eyes. Feeling Lourdes' hands on her did ground her at that moment, but she quickly came to her senses. If someone saw them, they would think Lourdes was picking favorites, and she couldn't have the staff believing she had the edge over everyone.

"You're right. I'll try my best. How's Marilyn doing? Was everything alright?"

She nodded. "A bit hypertensive, and her EKG was abnormal, but I think it was just a case of anxiety. Two hours later, she improved, and I went back home. I'm sorry that it interfered with our night."

"That's alright. The patient has to come first. Speaking of, I really should get to my next one."

"Understood." She felt Lourdes' eyes on her as she darted away from her. While she was getting more comfortable being around Lourdes, she still struggled with how the other employees would handle seeing them together. It's not that she wasn't proud to be a lesbian. Most of her friends at the hospital knew that she was gay. But it was another thing for strangers to know so much about her personal life. She didn't want her sexuality to be the first thing that popped into people's minds when they thought of her. The only thing that worked quicker than triage at CAPMED was the hospital's rumor mill, and she didn't want her and Lourdes to be subject to the relentless scrutiny of the entire hospital, at least not yet.

Maddie focused back on the task and stepped into the packed waiting room, "Jennifer," she called. There weren't any open seats left in the waiting room. When she escorted Jennifer to the room, she saw Lourdes still watching her. She released a breath and looked away. She led Jennifer to the scale and noted her height and weight in her chart. "Please take a seat. My name is Maddie, and I'll be your nurse for the day." She grabbed the blood pressure cart and wrapped the vinyl cuff around Jennifer's arm.

"Now, are you on any medications we should know about?" Maddie prompted.

Jennifer paused, thinking hard, before she responded, "I'm on 15 milligrams of Corgard, and I take 20 milligrams of Lexapro. Plus, I have an albuterol inhaler for seasonal allergies that I use as needed."

Maddie noted the medications on her chart.

"And what brings you here to see us today?" Maddie asked.

"My primary doctor said that my last echo showed an arrhythmia. He wanted a specialist to take a look. However, I heard great things about CAPMED's Cardio therapy department and decided to come to check it out. I'm sure I need some help with breathing exercises, or maybe some meds would help. I'm exploring this first, and if a specialist is necessary, I will pursue that as a last resort."

"Alright, today you'll get to see one of our finest physical therapists." Maddie escorted her to the physical therapy room, "Tami will be right with you."

"Thank you!" Jennifer replied as Maddie left the room and returned to the nurse's station. To her relief, Lourdes wasn't there anymore. However, Eric was at the computer as she approached.

"Trouble in Sapphic paradise?"

"You saw that?" Maddie mumbled. If anyone saw it, she was glad it was him, though. At least he knew about their relationship. It was the nurse practitioners and doctors that Maddie wanted to steer clear of.

"I tried to look away," he replied. Maddie chuckled. She knew he was lying.

"What's going on?" Eric prompted.

"I'm way too busy to talk. Lourdes wanted to grab lunch, and I didn't have the time. Did you see the waiting room out there?"

"Believe me, I saw it. But you have to eat. You can't run yourself ragged. It sucks that Shannon isn't here, but you and I can only do so much." He touched her arm. "Don't stress yourself out."

"You're sounding like her," Maddie snapped, pulling her hand away.

"I literally write about managing stress and healthy living. You and Lourdes don't have to tell me how to handle my stress levels. Got that?"

Eric frowned. "Got it." He stood up from his chair. "We're just trying to help because we both care. Don't push us away just because you don't like what we have to say." He headed to the waiting room as Maddie sank into a chair. Maddie clutched her stomach as a pain tugged at her insides. She was hungry, starving. Maddie appreciated their concern, but she had it all under control. She hurriedly put in Jennifer's vitals and the information she gathered at the appointment, then reached for another chart.

Her phone vibrated in her pocket. She grabbed it and looked to find a text from her dad.

Dad: So, I don't want you to worry, but if I didn't tell you, I know you would be upset. I was in a minor car accident today. I'm fine, but the car didn't have it so lucky. Don't worry about me, though. I'm fine.

Maddie swallowed a scream just when it felt like the day couldn't get any more stressful. She called her dad, and he picked up on the first ring.

"Maddie, I already told you I'm fine! It was just a little fender bender," he insisted.

Adding after a beat, "Wait, aren't you at work?"

"Yeah, I'm at work, but leave it to you to downplay a car accident," Maddie snapped. She felt terrible as soon as she said it, but the stress of the day was getting to her.

"Maddie, it's okay. I'm already back home! My car will be in the shop for a few weeks, but I got a rental."

"Dad, this isn't about the rental!"

"Maddie, listen to me. It is okay. I am okay. I feel fine now, but the moment I notice any issues, I'll go ahead and get them checked out. I promise."

"You promise?"

"Yes, now get back to work. Don't you have lives to save?" Her dad teased.

"More like charts to update. It's been a crazy day."

"Well, you better get back to it then. I'll call you later. I love you."

"I love you too, Dad," she hung up the phone and tried to steady her breathing.

Maddie's heart started to pound, and her breathing turned ragged. She slipped her phone back into her pocket. Her stomach clenched, and her chest tightened. A slow breath escaped her lips. "You've got this." She made her way to the waiting room, her legs trying desperately not to shake. She paused at the wall and grabbed onto it to steady herself.

"Robert?" A man that looked about the same age as her dad and a younger woman came walking toward her. "Hello, my name is Maddie, and I'll be the nurse assisting you. Follow me."

They walked to the triage room, and the younger woman put her arm around the older man's waist. "I have you, Dad," she said.

Flashbacks came rushing back to her. Suddenly, it seemed like she was back in high school again, terrified and clutching onto her dad as they sat in an unknown hospital waiting room, frightened about what the future would hold. When the woman looked up, Maddie smiled, then motioned to the chairs against the wall. An image of her dad continued to play in her mind, playing tricks on her. When Maddie turned to the girl, she saw her own face staring back at her. Maddie wondered if it would always be like this if part of her were still stuck in that waiting room today. She thought again about her dad's accident. He was always one to downplay his health. What if he had internal injuries that no one would catch until it was too late? What if the accident made him forgetful? What if he forgot to take his medication? What if he had a concussion and fell asleep, only to not wake up the following day? The myriad ailments and injuries that could occur to the person she loved most flooded her mind. Her brain was a continuous loop of gore and flat-lining vitals. There was no escape. She would never escape. No matter how fast she ran.

Maddie felt a tear stinging the corner of her eyes. "Alright, so what are we seeing you today for?"

"I recently had a heart attack, and now my daughter is forcing me to have therapy." The guy's voice was rough, but his daughter clutched his hand. He gave her a loving look, then offered Maddie a smile. "I think it scared her a bit, and I would do anything for my daughter. So, that's why I'm here."

A tear seeped from Maddie's eye, and she quickly flicked it away. "Um, can you please excuse me?" She hurriedly escaped the room before they would see her tears. Eric sat behind the desk; by this time, she was bawling.

"Eric, please ... I have Robert in the triage room. Will you please do his vitals? I just can't. I just can't."

"Maddie? What's wrong?"

Maddie swallowed, but she couldn't speak. She couldn't breathe. Maddie felt her airway beginning to close. She thrust the folder into Eric's hands and rushed away from the desk before someone else could spot her and ask questions.

MADDIE COLLAPSED INTO A CHAIR. THE WEIGHT ON HER shoulders had pushed her down entirely. Her sobs echoed in the break room. She heard the door swing open and sighed. So much for alone time.

"Maddie? There you are." Maddie looked up, tears streaming down her cheeks. "What happened?" Lourdes rushed to her side, taking the seat beside her and throwing her arm around her shoulders.

"How'd you find me?" Maddie sobbed. "Or even knew I needed someone to find me?"

"Eric, but that's not important. What's going on?" Lourdes pulled Maddie closer, and Maddie rested her cheek against hers. "Everything is going to be alright. I promise you." The loving words she whispered to Maddie were well-received. Lourdes had no idea how much Maddie needed to hear them at that moment.

"It's my dad," Maddie whispered.

"Your dad? Another health scare?" Lourdes' eyes widened, and Maddie quickly shook her head.

"Well, not exactly." She sniffed and then sat back up, grabbing her phone from her pocket to show the texts to Lourdes. Lourdes read them to herself, then handed the phone back to Maddie.

"At least he's okay."

"Well, that's what he says. He's not planning on getting checked out unless something happens. You know as well as I do that sometimes something happens when it's too late to do anything about it. You work at a hospital; you should get that." Lourdes' eyes darkened, and Maddie winced. "I'm sorry. I shouldn't have snapped."

"No, it's fine. And you're right. Sometimes it can be too late, but you also have to have faith that everything will turn out all right. You can't go around believing that something will automatically go wrong. That's no way to live."

"But..."

Lourdes brushed her finger to Maddie's lips. "I know you're concerned. He's your father."

"He's all I have," Maddie added.

Lourdes looked away from her. Her eyes dimmed. When she turned back, she had a tear in the corner of her eye. She was the strong one, so where did those tears come from?

"There are times when you have to let people in, Maddie. Even if it's difficult."

"I rushed out on a patient earlier. That's not like me." Maddie looked down at her knotted hands.

"Wanna talk about it?" Lourdes asked. Her hand ran along Maddie's fingers as Maddie considered whether she did. But there was one thing for sure. Maddie needed to open up more if she wanted to explore this relationship.

"A man, my father's age. The same situation my father was in several years ago. A loving daughter who looks like her world would come crashing down if something happened to him."

"That piled on top of everything was sure to break you. I get it, but you can lean on me." Maddie moved in closer and put her head on Lourdes' shoulder. Those words were the signal she needed. "What do you say tonight we go for part two? You come to the house, and I'll cook you dinner again. We'll have wine, and we can talk. I think we deserve that much."

"I don't know," Maddie scrunched up her face. Before this nightmare of a day had started, she woke up dreaming of Lourdes. Now the thought of being away from her father, unavailable with her phone shoved in a bag, racked her with guilt. "I should be with my dad. At least check up on the fact of how he's doing. He tends to play things off when they're more serious."

"I get that. So, here's my offer. If tonight doesn't work, you choose the night. I want you to feel comfortable that he's doing alright. Once you know that's the case, I'll wine and dine you. But it's your choice when it happens."

"I love that you're around," Maddie whispered.

Lourdes pulled Maddie to her. "That's always good to hear." Lourdes kissed Maddie and held her for a few moments until Maddie felt ready to return to the floor. After work, she would call her dad to ensure he wasn't just blowing her off. And then, she would gladly take that do-over.

CHAPTER TEN

BURNING HEAT

"Y ou're sure you're doing alright?" Maddie asked for the twentieth time.

"For the eightieth time, I'm doing great. Enjoy yourself tonight, and don't think about your dear old Dad," Dave insisted.

Maddie smiled, the knot in her stomach finally going down in size. "Twentieth," she mumbled.

"What was that?"

"Nothing, Dad. You call me if you need anything. You know how to reach me."

"Honey, if anything changes in my health, you'll be the first to know. Have a good time tonight with your friend." He enunciated friend as Maddie turned to look at Lourdes' house.

She hadn't told her father anything other than Lourdes was a co-worker she was getting to know. She didn't even mention her name. It was more of a need-to-know basis, and she would surely tell him if there was anything he needed to know in the future.

"Love you, Dad."

"Love you, Kiddo. Talk soon."

She finally relaxed her shoulders. He was good. There wasn't anything to worry about. Now, all she had to do was focus on Lourdes.

The door swung open before Maddie could even finish knocking. Lourdes had a bright grin that lit up the whole night. She wore a classy suit, jet black to match her long eyelashes. She looked elegant. Yet, Maddie wasn't kidding anyone. She also looked ravishing. Maddie stood there, gobsmacked, as her breath caught in her throat. Lourdes had this dimple on her cheek that only appeared when she was excited. Tonight, it was one of the first things Maddie saw.

"Are you going just to stand there looking gorgeous, or are you going to come in?"

Maddie blushed but didn't tear her eyes away from Lourdes' breathtaking gaze. "I'm not nearly as gorgeous as you," she retorted. Lourdes pulled Maddie into her house, barely touching her arm as she tenderly greeted her with a kiss.

"You're wrong about that," Lourdes whispered. "And tonight, you're absolutely radiant." She returned to the kiss, Maddie's lips opening slightly to welcome Lourdes' tongue. Maddie trailed her fingers around Lourdes' neck and held her in place. If she didn't ever have to stop, it would be too soon.

"If we don't stop now, dinner will burn," Lourdes whispered, slowly parting from the kiss.

Maddie inwardly groaned. And? She'd let dinner scorch for a couple more seconds in Lourdes' arms.

Already, Lourdes made Maddie's life infinitely better. Maddie intertwined her fingers with Lourdes'. Lourdes escorted Maddie back to the kitchen. "Have a seat, Gorgeous, and I'll grab the food off the stove. I hope you like salmon?"

"Yum...love it. But I thought you were a vegetarian?"

"Mostly vegetarian," Lourdes corrected. "Sometimes, on special occasions, I make exceptions."

And just like that, they were back to sitting in that kitchen, talking, laughing, and enjoying conversation as if they had known each other for years. Maddie's worries evaporated. Her dad was fine. He wanted her there, and more importantly, she wanted to be there.

As the dinner ended and they lingered in the kitchen sipping on wine, Lourdes turned the conversation to Dave. "Have you spoken with your dad? How's he doing?"

"We've talked, and he's doing alright. He told me to go out and have a good time tonight." Maddie took a sip of her wine as Lourdes arched an eyebrow.

"What?" Maddie asked, giggling.

"Does he know about me? Come on, spill the juicy details."

Maddie laughed. Her face was on fire, and she could only imagine how red she had gotten. She looked down at her hands nestled in her lap. "Let's say he knows you're someone I want to get to know better. And speaking of, tell me more about your travels. It's all so fascinating." She leaned forward. Lourdes laughed and nodded, then started speaking.

Maddie enjoyed that Lourdes could easily carry on a conversation, and this night didn't disappoint. "I would have to say my most recent excursion was one of the most exciting. I went to Iceland."

"Iceland? Wasn't it cold?" Maddie squealed.

Lourdes snickered. "Precisely why I enjoyed the hot springs most of all." She gave Maddie a wink. "Soothing and relaxing. Simply perfect. Iceland, though, was more of a personal trip. Maybe we can go sometime and slip into those hot springs. You wouldn't want to be anywhere else." Lourdes winked, and Maddie imagined them enjoying the hot springs together. Lourdes' foot brushed against Maddie's, and Maddie kept her lower lip clenched between her teeth. If Lourdes continued to flirt like that, she wouldn't be able to pass up any trip with her. She took a sip of her wine, and Lourdes' gaze dropped to Maddie's lips. Maddie opened her mouth slightly, feeling Lourdes' gaze shift up to her eyes.

Lourdes cleared her throat. "Anyway...that wine?" she began, her gaze still locked on Maddie's. Maddie nodded. "It's from France. I volunteered over there and kept it for a special occasion. I can't think of anything more special than this."

"Special?" Maddie softly inquired.

Lourdes nodded. "Special. You've had a rough day. You deserve it." Lourdes took a sip.

Maddie moved in her seat, eager to finish what they had started the other night.

"So, you've talked to your dad and know he's doing alright. And yet, you still seem so stressed."

Maddie looked up into Lourdes' dark eyes. "I'm not," Maddie argued. "I've never felt so relaxed in my life."

Lourdes scrunched up her nose, as in thought, then stood up from the table and reached for Maddie's hand, a soft smirk on her lips. Maddie didn't budge. Lourdes tilted her head. "Even if you're not stressed, I have some great techniques that can help a person ease some tension." She grabbed Lourdes' hand and pushed herself up on her feet. "You and I are similar in so many ways. And yet, there are moments when we're just so different."

"Shhh..." Lourdes cooed. "Relax. You won't even know what tension is once I'm through with you." She winked and pulled Maddie behind her. Those words left a tingling sensation in Maddie's core. As they reached the living room, Lourdes pointed. "Sit on the floor."

"Is that an order?" Maddie asked, curving her lips into a smile. Lourdes snickered but kept pointing. Maddie took a seat on the floor, with Lourdes quickly joining her. Lourdes pulled Maddie back, placing her in between her legs. She promptly found the knot in Maddie's shoulder and began to work at it with her nimble hands.

"Just relax," Lourdes whispered.

"I'm telling you, I'm, oh God."

Lourdes snickered just outside her ear. "You were saying?" Lourdes kneaded Maddie's shoulders, her hands moving deep into her surface. Maddie's head fell to her chest, and she groaned with Lourdes' strong hands kneading her shoulders. She wasn't expecting this once they reached the living room, but she wasn't arguing. Lourdes had magic hands. The knot in Maddie's shoulder melted.

"On some of my adventures, one of the best things I could give myself were these massages. You get out there and do work to help people but catch yourself not taking care of yourself. These massages would always keep me moving. I felt centered and in control."

"I can see why," Maddie moaned, feeling the warmth and strength of Lourdes' hands. Lourdes reached down and touched Maddie's inner thighs. "Oh God," Maddie moaned again.

Lourdes snickered. "Yes, it can be very sensual. But we'll get to that later. Right now, I want you to relax." Lourdes gently massaged her thighs as Maddie felt the pressure building inside her. "Unfortunately, I never had the benefit of being attracted to whoever was massaging me. So, I imagine you're getting a better experience." Maddie looked over her shoulder as Lourdes grinned. "At least, I would hope so."

Maddie twisted around and kissed Lourdes, "It's not so bad," she said. She leaned forward to kiss her again, but Lourdes raised her hand. "Face me." Another order Maddie jumped to follow. Maddie turned around and sat before Lourdes as Lourdes raised one arm and started doing stretches. "As you do this, breathe in and out so your diaphragm slowly rises and falls."

"Like this?" Maddie asked.

Lourdes smiled. "Almost. Just move your arm forward a little." She moved in, touched Maddie's arm, and slowly pulled it forward. "Like this." Their eyes locked, and Lourdes trailed her hand down Maddie's arms, tenderly caressing her, with Maddie closing her eyes, enjoying the sweet and simplest of touches. As Lourdes' hand grazed over the side of Maddie's left breast, Maddie's eyes flung open.

Finally, they kissed. Their tongues darted around one another like a dueling battle until Maddie could barely breathe. She broke away and grabbed her shirt, quickly pulling it up and over her head. She grabbed Lourdes' shirt and pulled it over her head, shooting it in a different direction.

Lourdes continued to grin while Maddie kept possession of the heat in the living room. She pushed herself up and wrapped her legs around Lourdes' waist, then grabbed onto the hook of her bra and released it, sliding it off to press her bare breasts against Lourdes' chest. There was no need for words or questions. She kissed Lourdes again, sucking on her bottom lip.

Slowly, Lourdes massaged Maddie's breasts. Lourdes took Maddie's breasts in her palm and rolled them upward, releasing the tension in her chest. Maddie's nipples pebbled with desire at Lourdes' touch. She leaned in and undid the clasp of Lourdes' bra, allowing it to fall away. She pulled away from the kiss and shifted her attention to Lourdes' breast, grabbing her right nipple into her mouth as Lourdes hungrily kneaded Maddie's breasts through her fingers. Maddie captured Lourdes' lips in a kiss once more. She shifted her hips upward. Lourdes reached down and unzipped her jeans. Deftly, she slipped her middle and ring fingers into the entrance of Maddie's sex, arching her fingers upward in a motion that unleashed a torrent of pleasure within Maddie. Her hips bucked. Maddie felt the back of her neck grow hot as her orgasm fizzled up her spine; emboldened, Lourdes increased her pace. Maddie whimpered, leaning into Lourdes' touch. Finally, she cried out, enveloped in ecstasy and Lourdes' strong arms. When she emerged from the haze of her orgasm, she saw Lourdes smiling.

Lourdes pressed her lips to Maddie's sweaty forehead.

"Feeling Better?" Lourdes asked.

Maddie grinned sheepishly, "Much better."

"See, I told you so. Stress is no match for me," Lourdes quipped.

CHAPTER ELEVEN

MORNING AFTER TEMPTATION

Lourdes' snores echoed in the living room as Maddie quietly pulled her pants on. She turned to look for her shirt and caught it resting against the lamp. Images of Lourdes and her in the wild heat of passion flashed back through her mind. Lourdes' olive skin shone beneath the slither of the crescent moon, barely coming through the front window. She shuddered; that image brought her rushing back into that moment. Maddie looked over as Lourdes continued to sleep on the sofa. Falling asleep in her arms was heavenly.

She reached for her shirt and tugged against the lamp, bringing it crashing to the floor. "No, no, no...." Maddie moaned, rushing around the table and picking it up, sighing when she saw the lamp was still in one piece.

"Gorgeous? What are you doing?"

Maddie groaned. The lamp wasn't broken, but the noise still caused Lourdes to wake up. She situated the lamp and turned to where Lourdes leaned on her elbows, the blanket shielding her naked body.

"I didn't mean to wake you."

"I'm glad you did. What's going on? It's two o'clock in the morning." Lourdes pulled the blanket up, and her nakedness vanished. Maddie made an inward growl, then shook her head, trying to clear away that sexy image.

"It's three thirty. Much later than I should have slept." Maddie pulled on her shirt. "I tried to get out of here before you woke up."

"Early shift?" Lourdes asked. She sat up, the blanket slipping down to reveal her upper half. She leaned over and grabbed her shirt, pulling it over her head and not even making eye contact.

Maddie nodded, "I have to be at work at six this morning. Or rather, I should be at work at six. I left a mess with documentation. Yesterday was a nightmare, and I don't want to start the day off already behind. So, that means getting a shower and dressed, and I think it's best if I get out of here. The earlier, the better. That's all."

Lourdes was now fully dressed and standing in front of her. "Shit, that's too bad! I was hoping we could spend the morning together, possibly take a shower together." She quirked up a smile. "Then have some breakfast before we both go into the hospital. I wanted to spend our first morning together, actually, together. If you know what I mean." She reached for Maddie's hand, and her fingers traced slowly over Maddie's digits. "But that's just how work goes, isn't it? When you think you're caught up, they throw something else at you. I wish you could stay," Lourdes said.

" I know." Maddie sighed

She sighed, not daring to close her eyes for more images to come racing back into her mind. Last night was perfect. Spending the night together strengthened their bond, and Maddie undoubtedly knew she wanted all her nights spent with Lourdes.

"But it's more than just a work thing. I can see it in your eyes."

Maddie sighed. "I don't know, Lovely." She plopped down on the couch, where moments ago she had been cuddled up against this vibrant woman, and she looked over to where the blanket was a chaotic mess. "I guess I worried that you'd think we rushed into things."

"How could I possibly?" Lourdes reached for Maddie's hand and held it as they sat on the couch, staring longingly into one another's eyes.

"Last night, in the heat of the moment, I thought there was silent agreement. We both wanted this week to happen. Maddie, when I'm with you, everything is perfect. There's no doubt in my mind about it."

Lourdes dropped her gaze. "If anything, I feared that you would regret it. If we're going to be together, I don't want either of us to be on the fence about it. I'll admit, I've questioned our age difference, but mostly I questioned how someone like you would want to be with me."

"Get that thought out of your mind right now. I'm here with you because it's the only place I want to be. Got that?"

Maddie nodded, and Lourdes brushed her thumb along Maddie's lower lip. Maddie shifted in the seat next to her and moved in, bringing her lips to Lourdes' as they gently kissed one another. All of Maddie's fears melted away.

"When we're together, our connection feels so real." Maddie leaned her head against Lourdes'.

"I don't want this to come across as some fling." Her heart raced as Lourdes' gaze met hers.

"I could never see this as a fling, Maddie. The connection you feel, I feel it, as well. You may see differences, but I focus on just the similarities. We go about things differently, but our similarities are our spark." She winked, and they were making out on the couch before Maddie could stop it; Maddie's hands roamed the soft cotton material of Lourdes' PJs. Just five more minutes, she'd rush out of there and get home and get ready for work. Lourdes slipped her hand up Maddie's shirt and touched the back of her bra, tugging it to try to unclasp it. Lourdes groaned when Maddie's bra wouldn't budge.

Maddie laughed, pushing herself away. "Keep doing that, and I'll never leave."

"Promise?" Lourdes asked, giving a flirtatious smirk.

Maddie stood up from the couch. "I better go. We'll see each other at work."

Lourdes jumped up, snaked her hand through Maddie's, and walked her to the door."So, does this mean that I get to call you my girlfriend at work?" Lourdes asked.

Maddie blushed, "Let's see how things go. I don't want to make everyone jealous right away. See you soon, Lovely."

Lourdes stood at the door, and Maddie felt her eyes on her as she drove away. Maddie was a bit more private than Lourdes. But she would accept whatever happened. She'd never smiled so big.

CHAPTER TWELVE

CALM BEFORE THE STORM

Maddie whistled as she exited the break room, bumping into the person headed the other way. "Oh, sorry, Eric." She laughed and continued to whistle.

Eric tilted his head. "You're in a chipper mood. After your day yesterday, I expected a permanent scowl."

He took a look at his watch and then arched his brow. "And you're here at least two hours early. What gives?"

"Well, I have a boatload of work and thought I would get an early start. As for the scowl, it's supposed to be a beautiful day outside. What's there to scowl about?" She reached up and pinched his cheek, and his jaw dropped.

"Oh, my goodness. Oh, my goodness."

"Oh, my goodness? What are you, an eighty-year-old woman?" Maddie laughed. She started to push past him, but he reached out and grabbed her arm, knocking her back to him. "You and Lourdes had sex, didn't you? Didn't you?" His eyes narrowed, and there was a devious grin on his face. His smirk deepened. "I'm right, aren't I? You and Lourdes finally banged, and now everything is rainbows and puppy dogs."

Maddie's cheeks were on fire. "Will you be quiet? Rainbows and puppy dogs? Really?" She laughed, unable to hide her grin. "What

74

happened between Lourdes and me is for me to know and you to contemplate."

She whirled on her heel and smirked as Eric's eyes widened. "Have a good day, Maddie. Just remember, your silence speaks volumes."

Maddie rolled her eyes and continued to the elevator. He could inquire all he wanted, but she wouldn't budge. Let him imagine what happened. Once she reached the nurse's station, she saw a pile of charts. Her smile couldn't last much longer.

"Ugh!" she groaned. "And why did I leave these charts until today?" It was a question she didn't need anyone answering. She didn't want to get to Lourdes' house any later than she had to. She reviewed the charts individually to clarify the documentation and get everything into the computer. Over thirty charts were waiting there; this was going to take forever. When eight o'clock rolled around, she still had five charts to do.

"Maddie?"

Maddie looked up and smiled. "Hey, Louisa. Is the first patient here?"

"Actually," Louisa grimaced. "Mike Bishop is here for an add-on."

"Did you see the schedule? There's no way. You can try working with him next week, but we're swamped."

"I told him all that. But the thing is, he had a mild heart attack at the end of last week, and the doc said he needed to work him in right away. But if you insist, I'll let him know. I just thought I should tell you."

Maddie's heart lurched as she stared at the computer, looking at the schedule, hoping that she had miraculously overlooked a cancellation. It was going to be a nightmare, and she immediately put them back behind schedule, but she couldn't be the one to tell him that he'd have to wait.

"Sign him in."

"Thank you." Louisa hurriedly left the nurse's station and returned to the lobby. Maddie glanced at the lobby as Gretchen, one of the nurse practitioners, headed towards her. "First patient here yet?"

"Not quite checked in, but there's been a minor delay in scheduling. We're working with Mike Bishop. He had a heart attack last week, and his PCP told him to get an appointment asap."

Gretchen rolled her eyes. "Everyone's a priority. There's only so much we can do, Maddie. We can't work all the patients in just because they have a story. Everyone has a story." She stared at Maddie, but Maddie couldn't back down. This was Mike; if she wanted to work anyone in, it was him. She didn't like to pull the favoritism card, but she had to take her stand in this case. "Get him roomed, but this will have to be it. We can hardly keep up with the patients we have. I don't mean to be harsh, but it's the truth. Got it?"

Maddie nodded, her cheeks flushing. "Got it." She turned from Gretchen. Only a few minutes into her actual shift, she was already getting reprimanded over her attempt to help the most patients. "I'll get him checked in." She quickly walked to the waiting room without even bothering to grab his chart. "Mike?" she called.

He walked even slower than usual as he made his way to her. He gave a weak smile. "Hey, Maddie. I appreciate you getting me in."

"That's all right, Mike." On the way to the room, she made conversation to gather some information. "When did you have the heart attack?"

"Last Thursday. Before you freak out, I know I need to be more careful. But I was exerting myself, and it was mild. Nothing much to worry about. I was only in the hospital for a couple of days."

Maddie frowned; why no one was informed of his stay was beyond her. It was just another classic inter-hospital miscommunication.

"Have you been doing the exercises and monitoring your BP? And most importantly, have you remembered to take it easy when you play ball with Myles?"

"Of course," he argued. "But..." His face fell, and Maddie waited for him to continue. "My brother was moving, and I offered to help. I might have overdone that because I wasn't feeling well that night. I thought it was indigestion. It didn't feel anything like the last one...." He gave a short shrug. "Sometimes it's hard to say no."

Maddie knew that phrase all too well. It was hard to say no, especially when the people you loved most asked for help. She saw some of her stubbornness reflected in Mike, making her feel even more sympathy for him. Mike refused to make eye contact with her as she took his blood pressure and pulse, then made a mental note of the numbers. "Gretchen will see you, so follow me."

"Gretchen? I usually see Noelle."

Maddie nodded. "This is a little more serious, as you just had a heart attack, even if only mild. You need to see one of the nurse practitioners, and Gretchen is waiting for you." When she reached the exam room, she turned to him. "I don't want you being here again unless it's for regular therapy. Got that?"

"I'll do my best." He winked, then chuckled as he leaned back in his chair. Her duty for the moment was through, but walking back to the nurse's station, she didn't feel any better about that. If Mike wouldn't listen, what good was it to keep talking? Feeling helpless, she dug through her pocket and retrieved her phone from the pocket of her scrubs. Maddie opened Instagram and scrolled until she found the draft of her latest post about the benefits of stretching. She added a couple more tips about using yoga as a stress management technique and pressed "post." Sometimes posting online felt as useless as chastising repeat patients, like she was talking to a brick wall, but she didn't know what else to do. So much of her life felt uncontrollable. From her work-load to her father's health, Instagram was something she could control. She could decide what she wanted to talk about and when. She could encourage strangers to make healthy choices, which had to count for something.

The fax beeped to life as she approached the desk, and she pulled the paper off the machine. Maddie shook her head. "Just a week too late," she murmured. She tossed down the pages to the desk and grabbed a seat.

Shannon came hurrying by as she did, rushing off to the waiting room. Her eyes appeared red, she was frowning, and she looked as pale as the hospital bed sheets. Maddie frowned. It was crazy how staff needed to be there even when they weren't feeling well, and from the look of Shannon, she looked like she wanted to hurl. Sure, Shannon called off way more than hospital rules allowed, but if you're sick, you're sick. Maddie hated that everyone felt obligated to be there because of rules and regu-lations.

Maddie turned back to the computer and quickly put in Mike's stats, then reached for the first chart of the scheduled patient. She took a glance at her watch and then over to the hallway. Maddie hadn't seen Lourdes yet and hated to admit it, but she missed her. This morning was already turning into a stress fest, and she would have loved to have been able to wake up next to Lourdes and spend the morning together. Instead, she was stuck drowning in paperwork. *Get it together, Maddie. Quit complain-*

ing. You'll see her tonight — no need to U-haul. Maddie grinned as she dug for her phone and pulled up Lourdes' name.

Maddie: Just checking on your morning. Another busy one. Maybe we can grab lunch together?

Maddie stared at her phone, hoping that Lourdes would send her a quick reply, but the response never came. She groaned and tucked her phone back in her pocket. Hopefully, after her next patient, she would return to a text.

Maddie went out to the lobby and grabbed her next patient. As the morning went on, she tried to give each patient the same courtesy she always offered, but she slowly began to get further behind. This only left her more stressed and scrambling through the assessment process. She always smiled but felt depleted with each patient she rushed through. When lunch arrived, she grabbed her phone, disappointed that Lourdes never replied. Besides that, she had yet to see her in the department. This wasn't unusual, especially since the morning had been one big blur of activity. She didn't have much time to take note of anyone. Most of the staff appeared too stressed to focus on anything but work.

Shannon sighed as she sunk into the chair next to Maddie. "Is this day over yet?" she groaned.

"I wish. It's been busy for us all." Maddie side glanced over to Shannon. Shannon's cheeks were peaked, and Maddie felt a pang of regret for her co-worker. "You know, Shannon. Maybe you should go on home. You don't look so great."

"Gee, thanks a lot," Shannon mumbled. "If I went home, then you would be all alone. I'm feeling better. Besides, I don't have any more sick days." She looked up and shrugged. "It's all good. No fever. No contagion. Do you want to go to lunch? Or I can go first, whichever."

Maddie opened her mouth when she spotted Lourdes for the first time. Lourdes grinned and gave a slight wave, then walked over to the desk. "Ready for lunch?" she asked.

"You read my mind ...." Maddie's words fell off as she turned to Shannon. "Are you going to be alright here?"

"I'll be just dandy. Enjoy." Shannon turned back to her computer as Maddie and Lourdes left the desk. Once they were alone in a hallway, Lourdes reached for Maddie's hand.

"I missed you," Lourdes whispered. She lifted Maddie's hand to her lips, then frowned.

"Are you okay? You're frowning."

"I'm fine. I haven't seen you at all this morning. And I texted you...."

"And you missed me...." Lourdes replied, grinning, squeezing Maddie's hand.

"Are you being smug?" Maddie teased, quirking up her lips.

They entered the elevator and waited for the doors to close before Lourdes pushed Maddie against the wall. "Never." She hungrily kissed Maddie, and there was a thirty-second gap in time, where Maddie forgot how stressed she was throughout the morning. She slipped her tongue into Lourdes' welcoming mouth, and they kissed until the bell dinged in the elevator. Lourdes pulled away and gave Maddie a wink, and the doors opened. "Sorry, babe. It's been a crazy morning. But I saw you running around like a gorgeous blur."

Maddie blushed. "I know what it's like to be busy, that's for sure. I'm glad we can grab lunch, though." They entered the cafeteria and went in separate directions as Lourdes went to get a salad, and Maddie grabbed a chicken wrap from the deli. Maddie paid and then looked around the cafeteria, locating Lourdes in a secluded corner.

She sunk in the chair, and Lourdes gave a teasing grin. "I wish I could kiss your stress away every day."

"That elevator wasn't a bad start," Maddie replied, smirking. They started eating their lunch, and Maddie picked at her wrap, unsure she had the energy to eat.

"Wanna talk about your day?" Lourdes asked, nibbling on her salad.

"Well, it starts with the last-minute patient. He was seen in the ER last week and then admitted to the hospital for two nights of observation. We never received this information until today. That's a week after they admitted him! The doctor wanted an immediate follow-up. The truth is, he should have been here at minimum four days ago. But how would we know this without getting the information? It's the lack of staff, and it sucks. Patients aren't getting the care they deserve."

"And I feel it's only going to get worse," Lourdes mumbled.

Maddie shook her head. "Why would you say that? Why would you think that?"

Lourdes circled her fork in her salad before glancing up to meet Maddie's gaze. "This morning, I forgot I had a board meeting. The truth is, they're talking about budget cuts. They're asking older nurses to retire early. Other staff members might be laid off. The nursing staff is in danger. That's all across the hospital. I worry about—" Her face fell, and Maddie leaned back in her chair. "Even if you keep your job, there will be many more days like what you're experiencing today. Things are liable to get worse, not better."

"As it stands, we're talking about one nurse to every fifteen patients. How exactly can it get worse than that?"

"It can always get worse."

Lourdes was looking at a worst-case scenario, right? The struggle was already so real, and Maddie feared they hadn't seen anything yet.

CHAPTER THIRTEEN

HEATED CONFRONTATION

An hour after her shift ended, Maddie walked out of the front door of CAPMED and headed to her car. She hadn't stopped thinking once about Lourdes' mention of budget cuts. She knew that it impacted her interactions with the rest of her patients.

"Maddie? Maddie, wait up?" She turned around and saw Lourdes running to her. "Geesh," Lourdes said, stopping short of Maddie's car. "I didn't think you were ever going to stop. I've been hollering for you ever since you clocked out."

Maddie smiled. "Sorry. I've got a lot on my mind. I didn't hear you." She stared at Lourdes' perfect complexion. Her hair was pulled back into a neat ponytail, whereas Maddie felt like a dingy mess. Half her ponytail was undone, and her face smudged with dirt. She could feel a volcanic zit forming under the skin on her chin. Deep purple bags were forming under her eyes from stress and lack of sleep. It was most likely all in her mind, but Maddie felt gross. "You look worried. I didn't mean to freak you out earlier. Let me take you out for dinner. It's the least I could do."

"That's nice of you, but I'm a mess. I should get home. I need to shower, put on some sweatpants and have a frozen dinner. It wouldn't hurt to get to bed earlier tonight, either."

Lourdes frowned. "First off, you look beautiful. You're not a mess.

Secondly, don't go home and sulk. It puts on some unnecessary worry lines on your gorgeous face." Lourdes reached up and drew her finger along Maddie's cheekbone. Go out to dinner with me. Nothing fancy. Please. My treat."

"Lourdes, you've done so much for me. I should repay you by picking up the tab."

"If I agree, will you go?" It didn't take much convincing for Maddie to say yes.

Lourdes led the way to a corner diner that was a favorite amongst hospital staff. It would be good to spend another evening just talking with Lourdes. At least she had that to look forward to.

Lourdes held the door open for Maddie as she stepped into the diner. Inside the restaurant, it was downright cozy. A Sam Cooke song warbled through the tinny speakers. The lighting was warm, a perfect contrast to the unforgiving fluorescents of CAPMED. Customers sat in worn vinyl booths. Teens nibbled on French fries as they puzzled over their homework. Couples shared milkshakes, and old men sat at the counter eating pie and drinking steaming mugs of coffee. It was a warm and friendly atmosphere, a welcome change from the dismal mood that hung over the halls of CAPMED like a storm cloud, ready to burst.

They found an open booth near the window and took their seats. A waitress was there to grab their drink orders and food. Once she was gone, Lourdes reached out and held Maddie's hand. "I have a confession," Lourdes began. "I can't stop thinking about these past couple of nights.."

Maddie giggled, "Honestly, same. Work's been hell lately, but the past few nights have been actual dreams come true," Maddie confessed.

"Agreed." Lourdes pulled Maddie's hand to her lips and placed a kiss between her knuckles. "I saw your latest Instagram post. Now that I follow you. Ah, the benefits of stretching. I believe I inspired you there, at least partly."

"Well, my dear, you were the biggest inspiration." Maddie skimmed her fingers over Lourdes'.

"I feel you might inspire me more and more as time goes on."

"I'll certainly do my best," Lourdes wiggled her eyebrows flirtatiously. The food came, a veggie burger for Lourdes and a harvest salad for Maddie. It was a spinach-based salad with gorgonzola cheese, dried cranberries, and walnuts. Maddie poured a small cup of balsamic dressing onto her salad and mixed it up. They ate silently, with Maddie and Lourdes staring at one another between bites and drinking water. "How are the raffle baskets going?" Lourdes asked, causing Maddie to raise an eyebrow.

"What?" Lourdes inquired. "I remember you mentioning them when we were out jogging once."

Maddie grinned. Lourdes wasn't only a great conversationalist. She was also a great listener. Maddie practically glowed from the attention.

"They're coming along great. We've met periodically to go over plans. There's going to be a dance, too. You're more than welcome if you want to come to a meeting."

Lourdes grinned. "Perhaps, but I might leave the talent to you and show up with some money."

"That's always needed, too," Maddie joked.

"The charity is going to be a huge success, though. I can feel it in my bones." Her smile slowly faded. That was if she would still be there once the fundraiser got underway. Maddie knew that she wasn't the best nurse from a technical standpoint. Maddie had to double-check the equations for converting med dosages that her coworkers could do in their heads. Her desire to connect with patients meant that her patient turnaround time was slower than others on staff.

To top it all off, Maddie was significantly behind in planning this fundraiser. She hadn't even started making a list of previous donors to reach out to. Her promotional Instagram post was currently a one-line note on her phone about putting the 'fun' in 'fundraiser.' She was supposed to draft an E-vite to send to the hospital staff, and she hadn't even picked a template.

Maddie felt her chest twinge. Her throat tightened. Was her airway closing up? Did she have a walnut allergy that no one told her about as a child?

"You're eyes instantly darkened," Lourdes commented. "I feel like you're thinking way too much." Lourdes reached across the table to grab her hand, but Maddie shied away from her touch.

Maddie huffed. "Lourdes, did it ever occur to you that I'm not thinking enough? The fundraiser is a month away, and I haven't even started reaching out to donors! I need to cut down on my patient turnaround time. I still have a huge pile of charts left to update. And now, you come through talking about budget cuts! I'm scared that people are going to start losing their jobs. Maybe I'll lose my job, and then what? So, I'm freaking out a bit? Can you blame me?"

". Maddie, I understand where you're coming from and that you're feeling overwhelmed."

"Don't tell me how I'm feeling," Maddie snapped.

Lourdes continued, "But I don't think worrying about it will help change the situation's outcome. If anything, all it's going to do is stress you out more, and you've already got a lot on your plate," Lourdes' tone was dripping with sympathy, pity even. Suddenly, Maddie was irritated. Did Lourdes think that she was in over her head? Who was she to judge? Maddie didn't see Lourdes taking on extra tasks at the hospital. Her solution during a crisis was to grab a slice of pie and not worry about it!

"Are you trying to suggest that I can't do my job, that I'm incompetent?" Maddie asked.

Lourdes straightened up her spine, adopting a stern demeanor. She took a deep breath, trying to calm herself before continuing, "Maddie, that's not what I'm saying at all. You're a wonderful nurse. But I've been through staffing cuts aplenty. It's all a part of the business world. Nothing much anyone can do about it. Senior nurses never really like to retire early because they don't want to lose their retirement benefits. So, that means they have to find other people to cut. Sometimes they lower a person's hours or give them less desirable shifts. They move them to other departments or fire them on the spot."

"And that's just okay?"

"It is what it is. Such is life." Lourdes shrugged, and Maddie stared at her. Lourdes' nonchalant attitude was appalling. Maddie was genuinely angry now. How dare Lourdes be so blasé, not only about their livelihoods, but the quality of patient care that was sure to plummet as staffing cuts swept the hospital?

"Such is life? No biggie? That's how you feel? So, if I lost my job, it would suck to be me? Politics have no place in healthcare, Lourdes. Money shouldn't take priority over patient care. And I can't believe that you think that's alright. You don't even care about the patients that get lost in the shuffle." Maddie couldn't take it anymore. She couldn't breathe. Maddie had to get out of there. She could feel sweat pooling under her armpits. Maddie slapped her hands on the table, and Lourdes dropped her gaze to Maddie's hands. Maddie's eyes kept locked on Lourdes.

Slowly Lourdes raised her gaze, and her eyes were dim. "It's hard to care about patients when you don't have a job. You have to cut your losses somewhere, Maddie."

"Cut your losses? It's not that simple."

Maddie reached into her pocket for money and tossed it on the table. She stood up, but Lourdes reached out and grabbed her arm.

"Maddie, I know that came across as harsh, and I'm sorry. Do not rush out like this. I don't like this any more than you do, but it's the harsh reality. Now, I'm not saying this will happen to you, but when you lose a job, it's hard to think about the patients suffering. You're out a paycheck and having to put food on the table. You're scrambling to get by. It will be awful if you, or anyone else, loses their job. Yes, I will care about that. It will be a mess for the patients having to deal with even fewer bodies on the floor. But, dammit, my heart can't go out to them when I have to see coworkers getting cut. Or if I lose my job. No one is safe, and that's the harsh reality."

Maddie sighed, shaking her head. "There has to be a balance," Maddie argued.

"Care about yourself, but empathize with the patients. It's not always black and white."

Lourdes slowly pulled her hand away, and Maddie looked towards the door; Lourdes' eyes softened. "Stay. If you leave, it won't solve anything. I don't mean to be callous, but sometimes you can't do everything. It's not always in our hands."

MADDIE SUNK BACK DOWN IN HER CHAIR AND STARED straight ahead. Yet, there had to be some way to make a change. There had to be some way to help everyone.

CHAPTER FOURTEEN

TOUGH TIMES WON'T BREAK YOU

Maddie skimmed through the schedule for the day. It wasn't as intense as the last couple of days, and she'd be lying if she said she wasn't looking for a little reprieve. Even ten minutes she could get back in her day would be well worth her time. She leaned back in her chair and pulled out her phone. It was still on the last text she received.

Lourdes: We're good, right? I didn't mean to freak you out last night or insinuate that you might lose your job. I know it's scary. I'm scared, too. I'm off today, so perhaps we could meet up later for a jog?

Maddie slipped the phone back into her pocket, still contemplating a response. While they ended dinner with a friendly wave, the romance had evaporated. How could Lourdes be so cynical about a profession dedicated to helping others? How could their beliefs be so different, and how could they overcome that?

Eric popped around the corner, and his brown eyes diverted from Maddie's. Plus, there wasn't even a hint of a smile. "Hey there?" Maddie began. He barely acknowledged her with a nod. Did Lourdes get to him first? Was he seriously on her side after having known Maddie for years? Maddie opened her mouth, then snapped it shut. She really didn't want to know if that was the case.

"Let's hope the day flies by," Eric mumbled.

Maddie tilted her head. That wasn't like her jovial friend. "Are you doing alright? You seem, um, a bit out of sorts. We haven't worked the same shift recently, but is everything okay?"

"Not even a little bit," he gruffly replied. He looked up, eventually meeting Maddie's gaze. "Did you hear about Shannon?"

"Ugh. Is Shannon still sick? Poor thing. She didn't look so great the last time I saw her."

"Apparently, you didn't hear." Maddie looked up as Eric turned away from his computer. "She was let go of the department. They said they had to get rid of someone. Frankly, I suspect it has to do because of her absences. They're trying to save face."

"Wow. I hadn't heard that." Maddie sunk back in her chair, recalling Lourdes' concerns about budget cuts. It had already started before she could figure out how to fix things.

"How'd she take it? Was she fired, fired? Or sent to another unit?"

"They offered her geriatrics, but she gave an excuse that she lost her grandma last year and didn't think she could see the patients suffering. Apparently, that was a lie. So, she's gone. How would any of us take it, though? I imagine she was blindsided and didn't know how to deal."

He shook his head. "I'm sorry, Maddie. I'm not taking it out on you. It's just I'm frustrated. With the workload the way it is, we will look at longer hours, and before you know it, we'll be drowning." He stood up from the computer and grabbed a chart. "Speaking of, I have to get to the first patient."

Maddie considered those words all morning as she called her patients and did everything she could to keep that look attentive. With fewer patients, the morning dragged on. She crossed paths with Eric a few times, but they were mostly in separate areas, like two ships passing at sea.

"Mind if I take a break?" Maddie asked when she finally caught up with him just after eleven o'clock.

"Nah! I'll go when you're back." Maddie made sure she had her cell phone tucked in her pocket, then left the nurse's station and headed to the elevator. Her phone vibrated once she had gotten through the elevator doors.

Lourdes: Thinking of you, Maddie. Please give me a call.

Maddie fell back against the elevator and stared straight ahead. On the ride to the break room, the elevator stopped off at another floor, and another pediatric nurse, who Maddie only knew in passing, stepped onto the elevator. She gave Maddie a curt nod, then turned to face the front. Maddie appreciated the silence, and as the doors opened, she waited for her to get off and followed her.

She sighed in relief when the nurse darted to the exit, and Maddie entered the break room. She was the only one there and could use the moment of solitude. Maddie retrieved her phone again and pulled up her dad's number. Lourdes' messages stared her in the face.

"Hello?" A woman's voice answered.

"Oh. I'm sorry. I think I have the wrong number." She glanced at her phone. Dad flashed across the screen. She frowned and turned her attention back to the phone. "Is this Dave Anderson's phone?"

"Yes, honey. Give me just a minute. David?"

David? Maddie hung onto the phone, trying desperately to hear anything else, but there was silence.

"Maddie? What a nice surprise."

"Hey, Dad. Who was that?"

"Oh, that? Just a friend. I was away from my phone, and she grabbed it." Maddie arched an eyebrow. *Friend?* She couldn't remember the last time he had a woman over to the house. It was probably something like eighteen years ago. Let alone someone comfortable enough to pick up a phone call on his cell.

"How are you doing?"

"Um, I'm fine. I just wanted to check up on you. How are you feeling?" She'd visited him briefly after the accident, stopping by to drop off some salmon filets she'd made with Lourdes' recipe. While he seemed perfectly fine, save for a cut on his forehead, Maddie still wanted to check up on him.

"Oh honey, I'm still fine. Nothing's changed in the past three days! No worries." He hesitated. "But are you sure you're fine? Remember, I'm your father. I can tell if something isn't right."

Maddie huffed. "Well, if you want the truth." Maddie collapsed into the nearest chair. "I'm not doing so great. I just found out that one of my co-workers, a fellow nurse, was let go from the department. She's had some health problems and had to miss some work, but that's not every-thing. There's talk about more budget cuts; if I'm being honest, I'm nervous. I'm nervous I'll be the next to go."

"Honey," Maddie's dad's soothing voice came through the receiver. "You are a hard worker, and they know that about you. They would be foolish to let you leave. However, even if they did, you could find another job. There are plenty out there. I have faith in you. Just remember, the world is a better place when you're in it, and you are meant to do great things."

Maddie exhaled. "Thanks, Dad, but I can't imagine having to start all over again. What if I'm not prepared for that? What if I take losing my job as my biggest downfall, and then I spiral, and I can never get another job?"

There was a long hesitation on the other end of the line. Maddie checked her phone twice to ensure the call hadn't been dropped. "I know it's difficult when your mind and heart are struggling. But you have to remember that you and I faced many hard times when you were growing up. Do you remember when I got laid off? You were only eight, and it was Christmas. You feared we would lose the house, but I assured you that as long as we were together, nothing bad could ever happen."

"You got a new job on New Year's Eve, and it was like none of that had ever happened." Maddie tried to smile, though it couldn't even reach her eyes. "I remember"

"And how about college? You swore that you were failing all your classes and would never be able to pass and get your degree. But look at you now. Bad times are inevitable, but you'll get through them. We always do."

Maddie always felt good after talking to her dad. However, in this instance, she was still depleted and too anxious to hold onto hope that all would be well. Her stomach tightened, and she winced.

"Are you there?"

"Yeah, Dad. I'm here. I know you're right. It's just...." Her words trailed off. "I better get back to work. Glad you're still feeling alright. Love you, Dad."

"Love you, too. And please try not to worry. Nothing good will come of that." As soon as he said that, her mind returned to her heated conver-sation with Lourdes.

"I'll do my best." She hung up the call and looked at Lourdes' two messages. *Just breathe, Maddie.* As Maddie sat there, she did a few breathing exercises, hoping they would lessen the stress that had quickly built inside her. Alongside the breathing, she worked on her stretches, keeping her eyes closed and practically feeling Lourdes right beside her. After ten minutes, she felt a tad better, but still a slight twinge of pain in her gut. "Everything is going to be alright."

Maddie grabbed her phone and pulled up her Instagram. She took a selfie, forcing through a smile, then added her message. *Reminder, don't get caught up in daily stress. You'll only burn yourself out. Do those stretches, and you'll be feeling better in no time. Keep stretching. Keep smiling.*

"And post." She stood up, and her phone vibrated as she headed to the door. Lourdes had left her a like, and Maddie frowned. It would look suspicious if she didn't respond to her texts. She pulled up Lourdes' messages.

Maddie: Hey, babe. We're absolutely swamped over here, so I haven't had time to check my messages. Talk soon?

That should suffice at the moment. Things would be alright with them. She just needed to get out of this funk. Eventually, she'd get there.

CHAPTER FIFTEEN

UNEXPECTED VISITOR

The rain started to fall the minute Maddie exited the hospital. She looked up into the sky, and a splash hit her face. "Go figure!" She ran towards her car but was soaked when she slipped into the front seat. Maddie backed out of her parking spot and drove to her apartment building. Her phone started ringing, and Lourdes' number came over Bluetooth.

"Answer," she mumbled. "Hello?"

"Oh, good. Glad I caught you! Are you going home right after work?"

"Um yeah, but it's been a long day, and I want to rest. So, I'll be home, but I'm not really into...." Her words trailed off as her building came into view. Lourdes parked her car in the first parking spot behind Maddie's building. Maddie lived on the second floor of a two-flat on the outskirts of Little Village. Lourdes stood outside near the back door, umbrella in one hand, roses in another. "And you're here."

"I hope you don't mind. I was just in the neighborhood. I thought I'd surprise you. Surprise."

Maddie smiled. All of the tension that she had been holding in her body evaporated. Maddie worried that her last conversation with Lourdes had left them on bad terms. Even with the rain pouring down and Lourdes struggling to keep her umbrella up, she looked elegant and beautiful. "Glad to see you." Maddie hung up the call and got out of her car. Lourdes held the flowers up, a wide-toothed grin on her lips.

"Okay, hear me out. I know it's cliche, but I had no idea what your favorite flower was. I hope you like roses!"

"They're beautiful. Thank you. But let's get out of the rain." She grabbed the flowers from Lourdes and fished her keys out of her pocket.

"Just one moment." Maddie hurried past Lourdes and to the front door, unaware of what Lourdes was doing, until she reached the stairs to her apartment with a pizza box in her hands. "I brought dinner. I hope you're hungry."

"Famished." They went up the stairs, and Maddie motioned to her door. Maddie opened the door for her, and they were both dripping wet, standing in the narrow front hallway. Once the door was closed, she turned to Lourdes. "Hi," she said again. Lourdes beamed.

"I hope you don't mind an unexpected visitor," Lourdes smirked, and Maddie was in awe of how beautiful someone could appear with wet hair matted around her face. Still, Lourdes took her breath away.

Maddie opened her mouth and looked around her small foyer. This was the first time Lourdes stepped foot in her home, and that realization quickly hit her. She wondered what Lourdes would think of her apartment. While Lourdes lived in an elegantly furnished apartment with framed reproductions of famous paintings and a cloud-soft velvet loveseat, Maddie still used her futon from her college apartment as her couch. She found her kitchen table on Craigslist and the accompanying plastic chairs in the alley behind her apartment. After work, she barely had time to think, let alone decorate. The walls were bare except for a *Love and Basketball* poster that Eric got her for her birthday last year. That movie had been her gay awakening in high school. Lourdes was staring at it now.

She looked back and met Lourdes' inquisitive gaze, then shrugged. "I'm happy to see you. The living room is in there. I'll grab some plates and wine and be there in just a moment."

"Do you have any beer?" Lourdes inquired.

Maddie looked over at her. Once again, she was awe-struck. "You're so elegant. You drink beer?"

Lourdes laughed. "There's still so much you need to learn about me, Maddie." She winked and then disappeared into the living room

Maddie went towards the kitchen and took in a whiff of the roses. And there was so much Maddie wanted to know. The roses smelled just as lovely as Lourdes. Maddie smiled, and suddenly her worries about their relationship vanished. She could compromise. Maddie grabbed a vase, filled it with water, and dropped the roses in it. She grabbed a stack of napkins and two beers and was ready to get the evening going.

Once back in the living room, she stopped short of the couch. Lourdes had lit all three of the candles that Maddie owned, allowing the living room and Lourdes herself to take on a soft, atmospheric glow. Maddie stared at Lourdes from a short distance, where Lourdes was oblivious. She attempted to lean closer and heard Lourdes humming a gentle melody. Maddie couldn't make out the tune, but Lourdes was engrossed.

After several minutes of gawking and listening to the song, Maddie cleared her throat. Lourdes twirled around; her cheeks flushed. "How long were you standing there?"

"Long enough." Maddie quirked up her lips. "Beautiful song."

"Thank you. My mother wrote it."

"Are you ready to eat? Again, I had to guess your pizza preferences. Do you like veggies with black olives?"

" Perfect," she replied, turning back to her guest.

They sat down and began eating and drinking their beers, neither rushing to make any small talk. Maddie wiped her mouth halfway through her slice and smiled. The silence didn't bother her. Even if there was any leftover awkwardness from the previous night, Maddie was already over it. Her mind returned to the song Lourdes had hummed as they sat there. Her mother wrote it. Those words played in a loop in Maddie's mind. Her reverie was interrupted by a soft meow. She turned to her cat, Cheddar, as he entered the living room.

"You have a cat?" Lourdes asked, eyes wide.

"Um yeah, I do. You're not allergic or anything, are you?"

Lourdes laughed. "No, I love cats." She reached out and immediately scratched behind Cheddar's ear. Cheddar started to purr.

"Better watch out," Maddie warned. "He'll think you're here only to see him, and he'll hang all over you."

Lourdes grinned. "What's his name?"

"Cheddar."

"Like the cheese?" Lourdes asked.

"It is my favorite," Maddie confessed.

Lourdes smiled, leaned in, and began baby-talking to Cheddar as he purred and crawled up into her lap. She laughed, snuggling her nose into his fur. Maddie shook her head in disbelief. He was a friendly cat, but sometimes it took days for him to warm up to a stranger. In this instance, it seemed like he knew Lourdes even better than she did. Maddie ate her pizza, with Lourdes seemingly forgetting she was even there. Lourdes continued to talk to Cheddar, leaving Maddie shocked.

After a moment, Maddie caught herself a bit jealous. She would laugh at it later, jealous of a cat, somehow watching Lourdes interact with Cheddar only endeared her to her more. Maddie cleared her throat, patting her mouth with the napkin.

"So, anyway, that song from earlier," Maddie began. "You mentioned your mother, but I thought she died when you were only two."

Lourdes nodded, finally looking up, but still scratching behind Cheddar's ears, then moving to under his chin. "She did, but a few years ago, I started to have flashbacks, memories I never held onto before then. Those memories included thoughts of that song. Then I started to think vividly about her and how she would hum that song to me to get me to fall asleep. I have journals from her younger years discussing singing and writing music. Those journals made me realize that I didn't just have random memories. I remember the days when my mom was alive. I strongly believe that children latch onto early childhood memories."

"Wow! That must be so exciting for you."

Cheddar moved away from them and hopped into his bed, closing his eyes and settling down to snooze. Maddie turned her attention back to Lourdes.

"Memories are sometimes all you have, so you should hold onto those. And I hum the song, so I never forget." She gave a gracious smile.

Maddie smiled. She loved how Lourdes' brain worked. Lourdes' vulnerability inspired her to be more open.

"What about you, Maddie? Do you have memories of when you were a child?"

Maddie considered the question. Outside of what she and her father had discussed earlier, she couldn't recall many memories before she was eight. Maddie had one picture of her mom, but looking at it made her question why her mom had left her. She couldn't remember her face on command.

"I don't know. I guess not. I blocked out most of my childhood. I had a few memories of experiences with my dad when I was eight, then maybe ten. But most of my memory comes from my teenage years." Maddie sipped on her beer.

"Well, I firmly believe that memories have a strange way of working themselves in, so don't ignore them if they happen to pop into your mind one day."

"I won't." Maddie dropped her gaze to her pizza and grabbed an olive, tossing it into her mouth.

After another few minutes, the silence was thick, and Lourdes looked at Maddie. "So," Lourdes began. "The truth is, I didn't just come here for pizza and flowers. Although, I like to believe it cheered you up a bit ."

"Absolutely! I didn't know how much I needed it until you arrived."

Lourdes glanced over to Cheddar, a pensive look overtaking her expression. "But when we left each other at the diner, I got the feeling that things were so awkward with us. Then, I texted you, and you seemed to be avoiding me. I was hoping it wasn't intentional. But then you posted the Instagram picture, and I thought, okay, she's got her phone, so she must be upset. Perhaps even angry."

"I wasn't angry," Maddie argued. "I guess you could say I was upset." Maddie finished off her beer, then shrugged. "I don't want to discuss it. Everything is fine now. Do you want another beer?" She stood up and reached for Lourdes' napkin and beer bottle.

"Nah, I'm good," Lourdes quietly replied. "Every relationship has conflicts, Maddie. It's how we deal with them that matters." Maddie put the bottles and napkins on her coffee table and sat back down. "If you were upset with me, I would prefer we work it out sooner."

Maddie paused. In past relationships, she tended to stuff conflict down and avoid it at all costs, but she could tell that what she had with Lourdes was different.

Maddie took a deep breath, "There are moments when I worry that maybe we're living in a fantasy world."

Lourdes frowned. "How so?" Lourdes' bright eyes had lost their glow.

"You and I are so different. I question how we could keep a connection going when sometimes I wonder if you are too abrupt about your patients. I feel like you sometimes have a business-like sense regarding patient care. Whereas I like to believe that we can save all patients and do what we need to, for the better of the patients, regardless of money matters."

"You are optimistic, and that's a great quality, Maddie. I envy you for that. But I'm not sarcastic, and I'm not pessimistic by nature. And regardless of what you think, I care about the patients just as much as you do." Lourdes sighed.

"Maybe I've become more cynical than I used to be. The fact is, I used to be a lot more like you when it came to patients. I suppose you can say I was a hopeless optimist."

Her eyes softened. "I use a lot of trips as my getaway, so I can truly relax, center myself, and then work even harder when I get back. A couple of years ago, I booked a trip to the Caribbean. I was excited about it. There would be volunteering, but I would also have time for myself." She shook her head, and Maddie saw a tear on her cheek. Lourdes flicked it away like she didn't want Maddie to see.

Maddie touched Lourdes' hand, causing Lourdes to look up and smile briefly. "What happened on the trip?"

"Actually, it happened before the trip," Lourdes quietly recounted.

"I had a patient that I was super close with. You could say she was my favorite patient, even though you're not supposed to have those." She laughed, and Maddie knew the feeling. She didn't interrupt, just listened, waiting for Lourdes to continue.

"The night before I was supposed to leave, I left the hospital I was working at early. She seemed fine. There wasn't any reason to think that something horrible was about to happen. I got the call at eleven o'clock that night that she had a massive heart attack and died instantly. I nearly didn't go on the trip, but her voice played through my mind. You'll regret this, Lourdes. Don't stay on my account. She was young, just a few years older than me. And I questioned life, my Faith, and whether I even wanted to continue this career. Despite missing her funeral, I opted to go on the trip. But you could say her passing changed my life, made me change. Her passing showed me that you couldn't get too involved because if something happens, it can practically kill you. At least kill your spirit."

A tear peeked out of the corner of Lourdes' eye, and Maddie reached up and brushed it away. "Losing a patient is never easy," Maddie quietly replied.

"Some are just harder than others. I don't want you ever to have to feel this way because it ate me up inside. I started to realize that you can't get overly invested. I know it seems callous. But it's not that I don't care. Sometimes I care too much, and I see that inside of you. There's only so much a body can handle." Lourdes' eyes widened, and she stared directly into Maddie's soul. You and I have a lot in common, eating healthy, exercising, and loving life. That's why I feel it far outweighs our differences."

Maddie snaked her hand around Lourdes' neck and pulled her to her. Her forehead rested against Lourdes,' and they stayed in that position for what seemed like an eternity. Lourdes' breath brushed against Maddie's lips, but she didn't move to end their intimate connection.

Cheddar meowed, breaking that moment and causing them both to laugh. Maddie pulled away, and Cheddar scooted onto Lourdes' lap. Maddie reached out and petted her cat, then looked up at Lourdes. At that moment, she realized that Lourdes and her dad were right. Moments of conflict were a part of life; it wasn't something you had to avoid. If you were lucky, you got to work through it together.

CHAPTER SIXTEEN

READY TO BREAK

Lourdes grabbed Maddie's hand and pulled her into an empty exam room. She pressed Maddie up against the wall and gave her a passionate kiss, her tongue sweeping across Maddie's, causing a deep moan to release through her mouth.

"We have patients," Maddie protested, letting Lourdes' body hover over hers, keeping her warm and safe. Lourdes ignored her, pressing a trail of kisses along her neck. "We should get back," Maddie argued, letting the kiss deepen as Lourdes didn't utter one word.

"Just five minutes," Maddie whispered, snaking her hand up Lourdes' shirt and clamping onto Lourdes' bra. If only five minutes was enough.

"Maddie? Maddie?" A bell sounded, and Maddie jerked awake from her daydream. Sierra Hinshaw, the head nurse of her department, stared at her, squinting her blue eyes, radiating scrutiny. She'd fallen asleep at the nurses' station! Maddie could have sworn she was resting her eyes. She hadn't slept in days. Every night she went to bed, she tossed and turned as an endless loop of worries and disasters circled her mind. A hot clod of dread settled in her stomach. Maddie wanted to throw up. "Do you have the time to sit around? Did I see your eyes closed?"

"No, Sierra. I was thinking," Maddie insisted.

"About the waiting room full of patients, I hope." Sierra's eyes widened as she gawked at Maddie.

"Something like that," Maddie mumbled. "I'm going." She turned and hurried to the waiting room. The waiting room was packed, and the encounter with Sierra left her reeling.

"Mike?" she called.

Mike came walking up, a grin on his lips. "Hey, Maddie. I've been feeling pretty good now. That should get me at least a sucker. Or, I could go for a cup of Joe."

"We'll see about that," Maddie muttered. "Take a seat, and I'll grab your vitals." Without looking in his direction, she grabbed the blood pressure cuff and pulse oximeter and worked on getting his vitals. "Looks good," Maddie said, quickly jotting some information down. "How are you feeling?"

He frowned. "Uh, pretty good; no complaints this week. I might miss my son's baseball game, but I am trying to get some hours in at work. Overall, just awesome."

"Good!" It'd been nearly two weeks since his latest mild heart attack, and his improvement was a relief. She looked down at his chart and stood up from the stool. "Follow me."

He reached out for her arm before she could get away. "What about you? How are things?"

Maddie's cheeks flushed. "Um yeah, it's great." She couldn't even lie her way through that one. She forced a smile.

"Really good. You said your son has a game coming up. So, he made the team?"

"Was there any doubt," Mike teased. "He'll be a star just like his father. Let's hope a bum shoulder doesn't take him out like his good ol' Dad."

"Hopefully, he'll be fine, but I'm sure he has plenty of years for you to worry about that." Maddie winked, and Mike's grin returned. "Follow me." On the walk to the exam room, she looked over at him, ensuring she kept her steps in line with his. "Anything else new? Diet? Exercise?"

"I'm feeling great, Maddie. I swear. I feel better than I've felt in years. I'm looking forward to living life to the fullest and loving every minute of it." She was glad that at least someone was feeling good. Maddie, on the other hand, was exhausted. She felt like a shell of a human being. She was still behind on her plans for the charity auction. Only one donor had gotten back to her, and it seemed the entire hospital ignored her e-vite, except for Lourdes.

She was too stressed to eat or sleep. Maddie's normally healthy diet had been reduced to protein bars and Red Bull, which she hated, but needed to stay awake. The Red Bull made her jittery, so even though her limbs felt like they were made of lead, her heart pounded a mile a minute. She couldn't keep down any real food. It was impossible to focus on one patient, and her caseload had increased since Shannon's untimely departure.

She forced a smile, "That makes me super happy to hear. Hang out in here, and Noelle will be with you shortly."

"Thanks, Maddie. Good to see you."

"Good seeing you, too, Mike. Take care."

Maddie smiled, feeling relieved that she could return to her old ways. If Mike knew something was off, it could hinder his continued improvement. She needed him to stay as calm as he possibly could.

As she left the room, Lourdes met her outside. "Hey," Maddie replied. She wanted to pull her into an exam room and reenact the fantasy from this morning, but with Sierra watching, nothing of the sort could happen. Even after five weeks, the sparks continued to fly between Maddie and Lourdes.

"I don't want to make you stressed," Lourdes whispered. "But the waiting room is packed, and people are complaining about waiting longer than necessary for their appointment. I'm not sure if you noticed, but Sierra has her eyes on the department."

"I noticed," Maddie mumbled. "I'll pick up the pace." If she wasn't pleased, then no one was pleased.

Lourdes gave Maddie a weak smile, dismissed herself, and rushed in the opposite direction. Maddie turned to see Sierra staring right at her; just another thing to worry about. She quickly walked to the nurse's station and grabbed another chart.

"Maddie?"

Maddie whirled around. "Yes, Sierra?"

"When your shift is over, can I please see you in my office?" Without another word, she turned and walked away.

Maddie looked down at the chart, tears threatening to fall. *Don't cry, Maddie. It's all going to work out.* But Maddie wasn't really sure about that. She had to pick up her pace and get through the rest of her shift, but it would likely be the longest six hours of her life.

———

MADDIE'S HEART BEAT FASTER AND FASTER AS SHE NEARED Sierra's office. She hesitated right outside the door. What could she possibly need to see her about? *It's obvious. Isn't it? You will be just another rung on the ladder that will be cut.* Maddie released a breath and knocked on the door. She heard a slight murmur but couldn't make out the words, so she opened the door and peeked her head in.

"Is now okay?"

Sierra looked up and motioned for her to enter, then Maddie closed the door behind her. If she was going to be fired, she wanted it when no one could hear it all happening. Maddie sat in the chair directly before her, and her leg started to tap nervously. She touched her knee, willing it to stop moving.

Sierra looked up, zero expression on her face. "I've been going through the documentation in charts and on the computer, and I must admit that I'm disappointed, Maddie."

A punch to the gut wouldn't have hurt anymore. "Excuse me?"

"There are missing holes. The timelines are hard to follow." Sierra shook her head. "It's lackluster work, to say the least."

"I apologize. I'll do better."

Sierra sighed. "It's not even just the documentation. You continuously run behind. I observed most of your day; you took the longest with all your patients. We have a waiting room full of nervous patients waiting to be seen, but you weren't anywhere to be found."

"Sierra, I was in with the patients. I might take more time, but that's because I want to take extra care and show them compassion." Sierra arched an eyebrow, and Maddie bit on her lower lip. It wasn't the time to argue with Sierra, so why even try?

"I will speed up my turnaround time," Maddie mumbled. And right along with that, cut the empathy in half. What about that? She wanted to scream that out, see if Sierra cared, but she continued to bite her lip, holding back everything she longed to say.

"And there's more," Sierra continued. Maddie sunk back in her seat and nodded. "I have noticed that you have worked lots of overtime lately. Unapproved, I might add." Sierra looked down at some papers in front of her. "If you would have gotten the work done while doing overtime, then that'd be one thing, but the way I see it, you haven't. So, the OT needs to stop. Understood?"

"Yes!"

Sierra grimaced. "If I were allowed to not pay you for the extra time you worked, I'd gladly take back the payment. Maybe that would assist with some of the budget issues." The latter part was mainly built-in grumbles and not meant for Maddie to hear. She continued to stay quiet, not inquiring about it further.

"I don't want to let you go, Maddie. You're one of my more compassionate employees, but rules are rules, and we must keep the ship running, or else we'll sink. Got it?"

"Got it." Maddie stood up. "Am I free to go?"

Sierra nodded, and Maddie dismissed herself by quickly leaving the office, the door shutting behind her a little louder than she anticipated. She felt the tears threatening to fall as she hurried to the elevator to take it down to the lobby and out the front door. Before the elevator could close, Lourdes rushed to it and stopped it with her hand.

"Just the person I wanted to see!" Lourdes panted. Maddie quickly flicked away a couple of tears that escaped. "Are you hungry? I thought we could go to Ginkgo. It's been a long day, and we both deserve it. What do you say?"

"I don't know, Lourdes," Maddie whispered. "I don't think I'm great company tonight."

Lourdes tilted her head. "Are you crying?"

Maddie shook her head but then fell back against the elevator wall. "Sierra called me into the office and reprimanded me for taking too much time with patients and extra overtime. I'm just trying to be compassionate, not drain the hospital budget dry! I don't know how much more of this I can take. If I hurry through the patients, then they're upset. If I don't, then my boss is upset."

"Maddie!" Lourdes pulled her into her arms and gave her a warm embrace. "You need dinner tonight! Let me take you out and do whatever I can for you not to think about Sierra and this hospital."

Maddie nodded. That seemed like an enticing offer that Maddie couldn't refuse.

CHAPTER SEVENTEEN

WHAT DOESN'T KILL YOU

Maddie stared at her reflection in the bathroom mirror of Gingko. She had just about got the red out of her eyes, but the conversation with Sierra wouldn't leave her mind. Maddie splashed water on her cheeks and pulled her hair out of her ponytail holder. She fluffed her hair with her hands, hoping she looked more presentable than when she first entered the restaurant's bathroom.

Ginkgo was an upscale vegan restaurant that served homemade Vegan Asian fusion. She'd only been there a couple of times, but their spring rolls were to die for. The soft, sensual lighting and cozy booths made it date-night-ready. She looked down at her scrubs and snickered. Not many customers probably dressed so down, but Lourdes made her baby-blue scrubs look runway ready. She wore her hair in a loose ponytail, her gold hoop earrings peeking out beneath her curls. Unlike Maddie, Lourdes didn't seem bothered by the fact that they were stuck wearing medical-regulation scrubs. The waitress didn't seem to mind.

She gave herself a once over and turned from her reflection. She had to return to the table so Lourdes didn't think she had ditched her.

The waitress had arrived, poured them wine, and dropped off their food by the time Maddie returned. Lourdes ordered spring rolls for the table and lettuce wraps with gochujang-infused jack fruit.

"Thank you," Lourdes replied as the waitress left. "Feeling better?" she asked.

"Absolutely." Maddie grinned, hoping that smile did what she desired. Lourdes smiled, but it didn't even look all that convincing. "The food looks delicious. Thanks for the recommendation." She picked up her fork, but her stomach churned, and she feared she would throw up if she attempted to take a bite.

"You know, Maddie. A boss is there for one reason: to dictate how things should work. I know you feel that Sierra scolded you." She shrugged. "But that's their job." Maddie looked up as Lourdes continued. "With the budget cuts, sadly, the supervisors will have to monitor everyone's actions more closely. I'm not trying to scare you. I don't think you have anything to worry about. Everyone knows how great you are with the patients." Lourdes took a big bite of a spring roll and smiled.

Maddie smiled hesitantly and looked down at the lettuce wraps on her plate. She picked up her fork and deconstructed a lettuce wrap, scraping the filling. "I get what you're saying. I do." Maddie took a small bite but had to smile through it. "I was worried that the reason I was getting called into her office was my turn to turn in my name badge, no goodbye, nothing. I can't imagine not getting a chance to say goodbye to your friends."

"Well, Maddie, if you're truly friends, you'll see each other after you get fired. Just because you've been let go at the hospital doesn't mean your real friends will abandon you." Again, with that matter-of-fact attitude. It was truthful but still disheartening at the same time. She was always so cynical, yet spoke with grace. After seeing Lourdes' vulnerability, the remarks didn't come across as harsh.

Maddie fished her phone out of her pocket and pulled up her Instagram. She snapped a picture of her food with a thumbs up, then pocketed her phone. Looking up, she saw Lourdes staring at her.

"Why do you do that?"

"Do what?"

"When we're in the middle of a difficult conversation and talking about something serious, you pop out your phone and take a selfie or take a picture of your food, or write something motivational. It feels like you're focusing on your followers instead of me." Lourdes insisted.

"I don't do that," Maddie argued. Lourdes nodded, and Maddie looked down at her food, sensing another scolding about to take place.

"I guess because it's easy. I interact with them because I know they'll always be in my corner. Even when I might lose my job or get reprimanded because someone doesn't like my work, I'll still have my Instagram and all of the friends I've made through my account," Maddie explained.

Lourdes slowly nodded, then smirked. "Just your followers? You think they will be the only ones that stick by you?"

"That's not what I'm saying."

"Well, that's what it sounded like. Maddie, I'm in your corner. I am doing everything I can to help you, but getting a small reprimand from Sierra isn't anything like losing your job. At least she warned you. Now all you have to do is heed that warning. You know how to fix it. She says that you should take less time with each patient."

"And spend more time on documentation. All while making sure I don't go into overtime. That doesn't even seem feasible."

"It's doable. Anything is doable."

"You're always so confident. I don't know how you do it."

Lourdes snickered, "It hasn't always been that way. I've had my fair share of setbacks. I thought if I pushed and pushed, I could do it all. It turns out I was so focused on getting everything done that I was missing out on what life had to offer. Then I was hospitalized for exhaustion when I was in college. Striving to be the best nearly took me out of the running."

"I understand what you're saying." Maddie dropped her gaze to her food. She needed to eat, gather some energy, and relax. But it was all easier said than done. She grabbed her fork and took a small bite. The lettuce was crisp, and the jackfruit absorbed the spice of the gochujang sauce well. It would have been delicious on an average day. Yet, with her stomach lurching and jumping a thousand hurdles, it wouldn't be long before she would have to excuse herself to the restroom. She pushed her fork around her plate, hoping Lourdes didn't notice that her plate was still full.

"Well, I hope you don't worry too much about Sierra." Lourdes reached out and placed her palm over Maddie's hand. Maddie looked up, and Lourdes winked at her. "We all know that you are the hardest working nurse there. Just appease her for a few days, and she'll move on to someone else to harass. Trust me." She moved her hand against Maddie's, and that quick motion softened Maddie's heart. Lourdes was trying, and that was more than she could acknowledge about other people in her life. She was right, too. Sierra would move on as long as Maddie took a little less time with each patient and didn't log all the overtime. She would find a way to treat the patients with the courtesy they came to know from her, even if she didn't give them as much time. It was all about balance. Maddie would soon have to figure it out or lose everything she had worked for. She wouldn't go down without a fight, and with any luck, she would come out stronger in the end.

CHAPTER EIGHTEEN

BASKETS FOR CHARITY

Maddie stifled a yawn as she left the break room. Her phone buzzed, and she reached into her pocket and checked her texts.

Noelle: Are we still on for tonight in making the baskets?
Maddie: Just leaving the hospital. I'll meet you, ladies, there.

Even though she was exhausted after a long day, she looked forward to getting the raffle baskets made. She reached the elevator and was about to push the button when she felt an arm around her, dragging her towards another direction. She giggled when she recognized the lavender and thyme scent that washed over her.

"Lourdes? What are you doing?"

Lourdes pushed through an empty exam room, startling Maddie. She finally released her, and Maddie turned to see Lourdes locking the door. Maddie tapped her foot and stared at her captor. Lourdes whirled around and leaned back against the door.

"Hello," she said, smirking as she closed the gap. "We didn't get two minutes alone today, and that's a crying shame." She looped her arms around Maddie's neck and pulled her to her, the hunger dancing in her eyes. She kissed Maddie, sucking on Maddie's lower lip, sending a shiver up and down Maddie's spine.

"Lourdes," Maddie argued, attempting to pull back but to no avail. Granted, she didn't try all that hard. "I was just about to leave. I have plans."

"Break them," Lourdes replied, kissing her harder. She slipped her tongue into Maddie's mouth and weaved her fingers through her hair.

Maddie laughed and snaked her hands up the back of Lourdes' scrubs. She grabbed Lourdes' shirt and pulled it over her breasts. Briefly, Maddie broke from the kiss to unhook Lourdes' bra. She kissed Lourdes once more, surprising herself with the force of her desire. Maddie moved her lips down, tracing the soft skin of her throat with her tongue, peppering her collarbone with kisses. She paused, admiring Lourdes' supple breasts, before taking her nipple in her mouth and sucking. Maddie felt Lourdes' nipple pebble inside of her mouth. Satisfied, she moved onto the left breast; Lourdes groaned. Maddie knelt in front of Lourdes, running her tongue along the smooth plane of her tanned stomach. She toyed with the waistband of Lourdes' scrubs, grinning as she felt Lourdes begin to squirm. Lourdes stepped out of her shoes, and Maddie carefully peeled off her pants, revealing the lacy, dark red waistband of Lourdes' underwear. She tugged on the waistband of Lourdes' underwear with her teeth as Lourdes' leaned back against the bed. Once her panties were on the floor, Maddie could see that Lourdes was dripping wet. The soft flesh of her thighs glistened with desire. Maddie took Lourdes' wrists and shoved her back onto the bed, ready to take charge.

"What's gotten into you?" Lourdes asked as Maddie trailed kisses down her belly.

"I just missed you," Maddie replied. Quickly, Maddie shrugged off her scrubs.

Maddie dropped to her knees and moved in to greet Lourdes' femininity. She slid her tongue into Lourdes, slowly at first. Maddie licked upward, tracing the delicate skin of her clit, lapping up and down, feeling the warmth of Lourdes in her mouth. She licked upward, sucking on the mound of Lourdes' clitoris. Lourdes' breath hitched. She reached down and grabbed Maddie's hands, slinging her legs around Maddie's neck and settling her feet on Maddie's shoulders. Maddie felt Lourdes' thighs begin to shake as she licked, increasing her speed.

"More," Lourdes panted. Maddie was more than happy to oblige. It felt as if she was drowning in Lourdes. Her cheeks were pillowed between Lourdes' impossibly soft thighs. She felt Lourdes' thighs clench around her face; Lourdes was starting to whimper, emboldened. Maddie lapped even harder, sucking on her clit as Lourdes' hips bucked as she rode the waves of her orgasm. The sound of her name echoed as Lourdes came. Time stood still. What would ten minutes hurt?

Forty-five minutes later, they were getting dressed, with generous smiles playing on their lips. "What's the plan?" Lourdes asked.

Maddie laughed, standing at the door of their hospital room. "You were the one that thought up this plan."

Lourdes winked. "I guess our desires took over. But how about you leave first, and I'll wait about ten minutes and duck out of here. Will I see you later?"

"Are you kidding me? After this, you won't be able to get rid of me." Maddie wrapped her arms around Lourdes and kissed her. She could still taste sex on her lips. "I'll call you later."

"I'll be waiting for it."

Maddie opened the door and peeked out into the hallway. The coast was clear, or so she thought. As she stepped into the hallway, two nurses came around the corner. They nodded, but Maddie barely acknowledged them. She rushed to the elevator, all while putting her ponytail back together. Once in the elevator, Maddie fell back against the wall and stood there with a sappy grin. It wasn't until the elevator doors opened and she rushed towards the front door that she heard her phone buzz.

She fished the phone out of her pocket but didn't hesitate to hurry to her car.

Noelle: Hey, Maddie! Just checking in! You were supposed to be here an hour ago.

Maddie: Sorry. Wound up getting called back to the department. Emergency. Leaving now.

Granted, it was less of an emergency than a fulfillment of her wildest fantasies, but Noelle didn't need to know that.

Maddie jumped in her car and quickly backed out of her parking spot. It'd been three days since Sierra had spoken with her. She had tried to abide by all the rules and succeeded. And based on the last encounter with Lourdes, her relationship was thriving. Overall, Maddie was feeling much better. Truthfully, she didn't mind missing the overtime. She missed a few breaks here and there to ensure she got her documentation done, but she could do without her breaks if Sierra left her alone. To her relief, Sierra hadn't seemed to be paying too much attention to how Maddie coped with the reprimand. Maddie's most challenging task was taking less time with her patients, but as each day progressed, she got quicker at the tasks. So, maybe it was all doable, especially with Lourdes by her side.

Maddie turned into the parking lot of Cayman's Event Hall and saw that the parking lot was packed. She parked in the furthest spot away and headed to the front door. Once inside the banquet hall, she saw the other women sitting at tables, working on their creative basket designs. They had already worked hard to plan the event, but the fun part was this: putting the baskets together for the raffle.

"And there's our fearless leader," Noelle remarked. "An hour late, but who's counting?" She winked, and Maddie shrugged.

" I'm hardly the leader. Sorry for my delay. Duty called."

"What was the emergency?" Noelle asked. "I thought I left things relatively quiet."

Maddie opened her mouth, then snapped it shut. *Think, Maddie. Think.* "You know, Marilyn. Well, there's always an issue. She's getting ready to be discharged. She had a panic attack. We couldn't find Lourdes, but crisis averted."

Noelle rolled her eyes. "Yeah, she's sort of a hypochondriac, but glad she's able to get out of there and go to rehab."

Maddie gave a weak smile, but inside, she was beaming. She had gotten away with the small fib, and no one needed to know the real reason behind the delay. Before taking her seat, Maddie opened up the camera on her phone and took a selfie in front of the sign for the Pediatrics event. She quickly typed up a caption. *Tonight we're prepping for the big event. Show your support by purchasing a raffle ticket! Link in bio.* She put out the link and a smiley face, then slumped in her chair. "Those look great!" she exclaimed, glancing at the in-progress baskets.

"Thank you!" The women responded nearly in unison.

"And we have a whole slew of them over there that we've finished," Noelle motioned.

"Wow, you guys have made great progress." Maddie wasn't the least disappointed. She had her forty-five minutes of excitement before arriving at the hall. She wouldn't trade that for anything.

"Here's a basket, Maddie." Gina, a receptionist from the pediatric ICU wing, slid one in front of her.

"Thank you!"

They fell into a steady rhythm of decorating and gossiping. The conversation turned to the topic of the hospital's most eligible bachelor. Maddie always just listened, minding her business, as the other women remained engrossed in their little world.

"Did you see Micah?" Noelle asked. "He looked mighty fine today when I was in the break room."

Maddie laughed, unable to hold it in. "Um, aren't you married, Noelle? Isn't Micah married?" Maddie looked up, mid-bow tie, as she gawked in Noelle's direction.

Noelle smirked. "My hubby and I have an agreement. We can look, not touch." She winked. "And the fact that Micah is married, all the better. I mean, he's not an easy target to snag, so you might as well have a look. No strings attached."

Maddie snickered, looking down at her basket.

"Noelle has a point, though. He is mighty fine. It's good for me that he is married because I would be on the prowl for that one." Maddie didn't know Theresa as well as the others, but her face said it all. She was equally eager to dish about the radiology hottie.

"Speaking of studs," Gina began. "There's a new doctor in the pediatric wing. He's quite the looker. He's straight out of med school. And every sign points to him being single. I think he'd be great for you, Maddie."

"What?" Maddie squealed, looking up. Her jaw dropped.

Gina nodded. "He's a great guy. And did I mention he's a doctor? If I showed him your Insta, I imagine he'd be down to get to know you. Give me the word, and I'll make it my mission."

"Don't bother," Noelle replied, a smirk on her lips. Maddie frowned as Noelle met her eyes.

"Come on, Maddie, everyone in the department knows you and Lourdes are an item. You're not fooling anyone."

Maddie's cheeks flushed. "I don't know what you're talking about."

She looked away, but the red on her cheeks was every indication of the truth.

"There's no reason to deny it." Noelle continued to work on her basket. "It's cute the way you two look at each other. And if I were a lesbian and single, I'd go for her, too." Noelle reached across the table, her eyes finally rising to meet Maddie's. "Nothing to be ashamed of there. You love who you love."

"No one said anything about love," Maddie blurted. "We're just exploring things and getting to know one another. That's all," Maddie blushed.

"Love, infatuation, whatever you want to call it. No need to hide from it." Noelle shrugged. "Infatuation can always lead to more, as well. My hubby and I sure were infatuated with each other back in high school."

She laughed. "You should have seen us." She then frowned. "But, even then, I'm not sure that we looked at each other like that. I don't know what we do after ten years of marriage." She laughed loudly.

Maddie opened her mouth to respond, but a familiar sound stopped her.

"Is there room for one more?" Maddie turned and looked towards the sound of Lourdes' voice. She had changed out of her scrubs and into her street clothes, high-waisted jeans, and a red T-shirt. Lourdes slipped her hands in her pockets, giving a sheepish grin, " I thought I'd check this place out." Maddie stared at her. Lourdes was just as radiant, with no sign of how they had sex moments earlier. Maddie only hoped that she looked as well put together.

"Not at all. Plenty of room," Noelle said, a little too eagerly.

"Um yeah, let me get you a basket." Maddie jumped up and grabbed Lourdes' hand, pulling her behind her towards the table of baskets and more decorations. "How'd you know where I was?"

"Your Instagram," Lourdes nonchalantly replied. "After leaving the hospital, I couldn't stop thinking about you."

"So, you're stalking me?" Maddie teased, arching an eyebrow. She lowered it when Lourdes grinned. "I'm glad you're here. I can't stop thinking about you either."

"Good to hear." Maddie dipped her gaze down to Lourdes' lips, longing to kiss her again. "What were you guys talking about? I got the feeling I interrupted something."

Maddie looked past her to the table of women. Everyone was staring at them, but they quickly looked away when Maddie caught them staring. "If you'd believe it, we were talking about you." Lourdes raised her eyebrows. "And how lucky the department is that you came along."

Lourdes smirked. "And that's all?"

Maddie nodded, not wanting to divulge where their conversation went. But she was glad to see Lourdes and the other women were right. If they made each other happy, then maybe that's all that mattered. Noelle seemed to have her own ideas about their relationship, which made Maddie smile. Now, if she could calm her worries, things might be where she needed them, ready to progress.

CHAPTER NINETEEN

SEXUAL INTIMACY AT ITS HIGHEST

They worked on making baskets for two hours, all while laughing and enjoying one another's company. Every time Maddie looked at Lourdes, her breath caught. How could she be so lucky that someone as beautiful as Lourdes was there with her? And it was sweet that Lourdes had shown up at the event hall. After their time in the exam room, it was a new step in their relationship. She had invited her in the past, but Lourdes was adamant that it wasn't her thing. So, it was a pleasant surprise. Maddie was sure it all had to do with their rendezvous. Maddie was disappointed when the evening ended, sulking as she made the long trek back to her car.

"I had a good time," Lourdes replied as she stopped next to Maddie's car

"Granted, nothing beats exam room sex," She smirked. "But it was cool to see you in your element, Ms. Charitable Cause."

Maddie laughed and nodded, "I never thought I'd see the day when you lent a helping hand. I'd say some of your baskets were the best."

Lourdes laughed, "No way. You are the creative one." She gave Maddie a wink; it was undeniably tender.

Lourdes stood up straighter, "So, I thought maybe I could come back to your place. If you wouldn't mind?"

Mind? Maddie couldn't think of one thing she would want more than that.

"I miss Cheddar. I could use some kitty time."

Maddie's jaw dropped. "Oh, well yeah, if that's what you're wanting. I'm sure Cheddar feels the same." Maddie reached for the door handle. "Follow me." Lourdes touched Maddie's hand, then pulled her to her. Maddie's lips caressed Lourdes' before Lourdes returned with a genuine smile. "I guess I'm feeling a little selfish, and I think I'd prefer to give a quick hello to Cheddar and spend the rest of the night with you. If you know what I mean." She quirked up her lips.

Maddie wrapped her hand around Lourdes' neck and pulled her to her, crashing her lips against Lourdes' and dipping her tongue between Lourdes' lips. Lourdes growled, and Maddie smirked. Maddie went ten miles over the speed limit back to her apartment. She kept checking her rearview mirror to ensure Lourdes was still following her. She whipped into her parking spot, and Lourdes grabbed the spot beside her. They laughed all the way, sprinting up the stairs to her apartment, hand in hand. Already, Maddie could feel the palpable heat between her and Lourdes. They ran into Maddie's elderly downstairs neighbors, slowly creeping down the stairs. "Good evening, Mr. and Mrs. Jenkins," she said, her face flushed, her eyes shining. Her heart was pounding from excitement. Mrs. Jenkins looked perplexed. Maddie gave a quick smile and worked her key on the lock. Lourdes laughed behind her. "I don't think they're used to the noise."

Maddie grinned, looking over her shoulder, "If they think that's noisy, then it's a good thing they're going out." She winked as Lourdes rested her chin against Maddie's shoulder, nuzzling her lips against her ear.

Maddie pushed open the door and pulled Lourdes in after her, letting the door slam behind them as she pulled Lourdes into her arms. She kissed Lourdes with a voracious hunger, already feeling the desire pool deep in her belly. Maddie pressed Lourdes back against the door and wrapped her leg around Lourdes' waist. Two minutes into the kiss, she felt Cheddar's body brush against her leg, and Lourdes laughed.

"Mood. Killer." Maddie groaned, breaking from the kiss.

"Hey there, pretty kitty," Lourdes squealed, kneeling in front of him. "Aren't you such a good kitty? Yes, you are."

Maddie shot a look at Cheddar, who seemed oblivious to the fact that Maddie and Lourdes were in the middle of something

" Do you want a drink or anything? "She turned back to Lourdes

Are you trying to get me drunk?" Lourdes asked.

"I'm all good. All I want is you," Lourdes stood up and slinked toward Maddie. Maddie felt the heat slowly moving from the bottoms of her feet up her legs and radiating around her midsection. She swallowed, "I just thought you'd be thirsty."

"Hungry is more like it." Lourdes winked and headed towards the living room, Cheddar following closely behind. She looked over her shoulder. "Are you coming?"

Maddie nodded and moved into the living room. Lourdes pulled Cheddar onto her lap and continued to pet her. "You're hungry. I have plenty of choices. I could throw in a pizza or whip up some nachos. You name it, and it's yours."

Lourdes patted the spot next to her. Maddie smirked and plopped down into the seat, reaching over to pet Cheddar as he purred and nestled his nose against Lourdes. For the second time this week, she was jealous of a cat. Suddenly, Lourdes leaned in for a kiss, taking Maddie by surprise. Maddie savored the feeling of Lourdes' soft lips against hers, eagerly slipping her tongue into Lourdes' mouth. Cheddar purred, head-butting the bottom of Maddie's chin. Maddie reluctantly pulled back. She grabbed Cheddar and took him to the laundry room. "You are fine," Maddie snapped the minute Cheddar meowed. She closed the door and hurried back into the living room. Lourdes glanced toward the laundry room, where Cheddar emitted a muffled meow.

"He was killing the mood. Can you blame me?"

Lourdes laughed, "Never."

"Besides," Maddie whispered.

"You said we could be selfish. I want your attention. All of it." Maddie stood before Lourdes and raised her shirt up and over her head. Lourdes' eyes lit up as she saw Maddie's small, pert breasts resting in their light pink bra and her toned stomach.

"You have it, Maddie. You never lost it."

"Good." Maddie pulled off her pants and kicked them to the side. She moved closer to Lourdes. She wrapped her legs around her, straddling her with ease, before capturing her lips once more. As they kissed, Lourdes reached up and withdrew Maddie's hair tie from her hair. Her hair fell in waves around her shoulders. Lourdes splayed her fingers along Maddie's back, unhooking her bra with the flick of her wrist. Maddie grinned through the kiss, slipping out of her bra and letting it fall away. She pulled back, arching her back as Lourdes moved in to kiss her cleavage, running her tongue along the underside of Maddie's breasts, lapping upward to suck on her nipples. Lourdes took her nipple between her teeth, and Maddie groaned. Oh God, yes, she needed to be selfish more often.

Lourdes slipped her hand inside Maddie's panties and slowly parted Maddie's sex, slipping her middle and ring finger into Maddie's molten center. Maddie moaned. She tilted her head upward, and their lips collided with a cosmic force. It was the sort of collision that could create a brand-new galaxy. Instead, Lourdes and Maddie were in their own separate universe. Maddie's hips matched the rhythm of Lourdes' strong, capable hands. Every touch sent a shiver down her spine as her hips started to shake. Lourdes' other hand cupped her ass. She felt herself growing even wetter as Lourdes continued to coax her to explore the depths of her pleasure.

"Come for me, baby," Lourdes whispered, her voice low and soft as her fingers tenderly pressed against her clitoris. The sweetness in Lourdes' voice and the jasmine cloud of her scent mingling with the scent of raw desire sent Maddie over the edge as her lips crashed into Lourdes'. Her hips bucked as she came, and her whole body lit up from within as the fiery tendrils of her orgasm enveloped her. She cried out. Time stopped as she raked her nails down Lourdes' back, desperate to bring her even closer to her.

MADDIE SHIFTED IN BED AND OPENED HER EYES. SHE SMILED when she saw Lourdes sound asleep next to her. Yesterday was the first time she felt like she and Lourdes made sense. From the sexual tryst they shared at the hospital to choose to end the evening in Maddie's apartment, it all just fit. Maddie always longed for the day she would find someone to satisfy her mind, body, and soul. With Lourdes, there seemed to be a mutual and constant fascination that was only further fueled by the fact that they couldn't keep their hands off each other. She moved in and kissed the top of Lourdes' shoulder, the only part of her skin revealed from under the sheets.

Careful not to cause Lourdes to wake up, she slipped out of the covers and grabbed a robe from her dresser. She looked over her shoulder, and Lourdes hadn't moved a muscle. Maddie blew her a kiss, then left her bedroom.

She walked into the kitchen, and Cheddar immediately wound his way around her legs, eager for his breakfast. Maddie scooped some dry food into his bowl and added a bit of wet food on top as an apology. She felt guilty for ignoring him last night. Usually, Cheddar slept on her bed. She'd locked him out last night, so she and Lourdes could continue where they left off in the living room. Cheddar glowered at her as he ate a mouthful of food.

"I'm sorry! We can hang out tomorrow night," Maddie reassured him. Cheddar ignored her apology. Maddie snickered and went back to the living room. She grabbed her pants, still on the living room floor, and retrieved her phone from where it lay on the coffee table. It only had a little battery left, but it was enough. She hurried back to the room, so Lourdes wouldn't wake up and wonder where she went. Maddie pulled up her Instagram and typed. *Breakfast and an early morning jog are a surefire way to start the day off right! Shout out to antioxidants and endorphins.* She skimmed through a list of recipes until she found one for a spinach breakfast shake. She added it and a selfie from one of her morning jogs. She posted it and then read it back.

Lourdes reached out and touched her hand. "What are ya doing, Gorgeous?" she asked.

Maddie shrugged. "Just posting my early morning routine."

Lourdes tilted her head. "At four-thirty in the morning? Is anyone going to be up to see it?"

Maddie laughed. "Some people like to get an early start!" She leaned in and kissed Lourdes. "Speaking of, wanna wake up and go for a jog?"

Lourdes snickered. "Give me a couple of hours. I'm still wanting to be a little bit selfish." She winked and wrapped her arm around Maddie's back, pulling her to her.

"Don't deprive me of that." Maddie opened her mouth to a sensual kiss, grinning as Lourdes pulled back the covers to invite her in. Maddie slipped out of her robe and moved in on top of Lourdes. Lourdes tenderly held Maddie in her arms as they made out under the covers. It was early morning. The moon still lit up the sky, casting a shadow through the bedroom window, and Maddie broke from the kiss, pressing her hands down along Lourdes' side. She rested her head against Lourdes' chest, hearing the faint sound of her heartbeat as she closed her eyes. An early morning makeout sesh definitely beat an early morning run.

CHAPTER TWENTY

VOICE OF REASON

Maddie poured the shake into a glass and snapped a picture of it. She pulled up her message from earlier, editing it to add the photo she just took. *Now off to my jog.* She already had a hundred likes that went along with her post, including her dad and half of the hospital. She sipped on the shake until it was half gone, then dumped the rest into the trash. A little went a long way. Her espresso machine dinged, and she rushed over and grabbed two mugs, then poured them each a cup. She sighed as the espresso went down her throat. *Perfect.* That was enough to get through her day.

"What happened to the shake?" She twirled around and saw Lourdes leaning back against the wall, a smirk on her face.

Maddie looked over her attire, shorts, and a t-shirt that said CAPMED, courtesy of Maddie's wardrobe. "I see you found something to wear."

"Well, it beats running in my work clothes from yesterday. Seeing that I haven't been home to change." Maddie moved in and held up a mug. "You ignored my question, though. "Per your latest Instagram post, you prefer something a little greener."

"I already had it. But this," Maddie held up the espresso. "Will help me push myself a little further. If I'm going to keep up with you, I must have something that adds a little edge." She winked and turned from Lourdes. "Hope you slept well last night."

"I didn't get much sleep if I remember correctly."

Maddie laughed and looked over her shoulder, downing the rest of her espresso. "Touché," she replied, smirking. "Finish up your drink, and we'll go out and get our jog on." She turned back to the sink as a pang hit her gut. She grabbed onto the counter and leaned forward to try and catch her breath.

"I don't drink this stuff. Too much caffeine for me." Lourdes reached over Maddie's shoulder and poured the espresso down the drain. Maddie tried to smile, but the pain in her gut went a little deep this time. She turned around and leaned back against the counter.

"I envy you."

Lourdes smirked. "Why? Because I pass up on caffeine? It's not too hard to bypass when you have steered clear of it. I'll have a cup of coffee here and there, but tea is more my thing. I'm surprised you chose to drink that in the morning. You go on these health kicks and all. I pegged you for a matcha girl, at least.."

"Are you judging me?" Maddie teased.

"Not judging, just asking." Lourdes looked around the kitchen until her eyes landed back on Maddie's. "Everyone's got their own taste; if you enjoy it, then no argument here."

Maddie shrugged, taking another sip. "Maybe someday I'll give it up." She grabbed her phone and pulled up the group chat for her fellow basket makers.

Maddie: Today at 6 to finalize plans for tomorrow night?

Lourdes reached into the refrigerator and grabbed some water. "You spend a lot of time on your phone, don't you?"

"Social media is the wave of the future; it has been for years. Doesn't everyone?" Lourdes stood there, and Maddie turned away and started washing the two mugs. "I was checking with everyone to see if six o'clock was still a good time to meet at the event center and finalize details." Her phone dinged repeatedly, and she took a look. "Looks like it'll work. Since you were there last night, you're welcome to join us."

Lourdes sighed, "I have to work at noon and don't get off until eight."

"Bummer, I get off at five."

"We'll be there a little bit together. Also, we can still go for a jog before you head to work. Thanks for the offer."

Lourdes took a sip of her water. "Are you ready?"

Maddie nodded. "I'll drive us to the park and bring you back to your car."

"No need." She held up her keys. "I'll follow you."

"I mean, it just makes sense. That way, you don't have to rush home." Lourdes walked over and kissed Maddie. "By the way," she said, grinning. "Yesterday was amazing. And this morning wasn't so bad either." She winked and pushed past Maddie, heading to the front door.

They left the apartment and drove to the park. Maddie led the way and pulled into her familiar parking spot. She and Lourdes walked to the trail, and Maddie was the first to bust out into a jog. It wasn't a slow and easy jog, one where they could chat next to each other. It was a fast run that left Lourdes in her dust. For ten minutes, she ran as fast as she could. She was exhausted, but the espresso was taking over and allowing her to take off. She thought Lourdes was still at the starting line when she felt a hand on her shoulder.

"Maddie, hold up!" Lourdes yelled.

Maddie slowed and laughed when she saw Lourdes breathing heavily, hunched over with her hands on her knees. "What was that about? I thought this was a jog, not the Olympic trials," Lourdes panted.

Maddie grinned. "If you need me to slow down, say it. Perhaps it was because you didn't take advantage of the espresso." Lourdes frowned, and Maddie tried to smile. "Sorry, I guess I can get a little competitive. And you have outrun me in many other cases, so I was trying to show you I could keep up. I guess now's not the time.".

Lourdes shook her head and stood up, clutching her stomach as she grimaced. "I don't know. It just seems like you were running from something. I get being competitive and all. Healthy competition is great, but I didn't realize you could be so fast."

"Only when I want to be." Maddie slowly started to walk, with Lourdes keeping in step. "I sometimes get a little too competitive for my own good."

"A little? If I didn't know better, I would say you were running away from me. Or trying to prove something to yourself."

Maddie stayed silent. From the corner of her eye, she saw Lourdes glancing at her, looking away, opening her mouth to say something but stopping.

"Sometimes it feels like everything I say around you will lead to a misunderstanding. But Maddie, you can only do so much. And while I appreciate that you're ambitious and want to take advantage of every minute of every day, it is a lot to take in." Lourdes released a heavy sigh. "No one can be expected to do all that. I don't want you overextending yourself. You don't have to prove anything to yourself or me."

Maddie stopped walking and turned to Lourdes. "You say I think too much, but maybe I'm not the only one. I'm fine, and you don't have to worry. I only do what I want to do. Everything is great."

"You don't think you're pushing yourself too hard?" Lourdes raised an eyebrow.

Maddie shrugged. "I'm pushing myself because it makes me feel alive and refreshed. Other than that, everything is perfect. Trust me." She then grinned harder.

"Now, let's race." Before Lourdes could respond, Maddie sprinted back toward the cars. Lourdes ran behind her, but once Maddie reached the parking lot, she turned and saw Lourdes was still several yards away. Maddie withdrew her phone from her pocket, panting, sweat dripping down her face, and snapped a couple of selfies. *Perseverance is critical,* she posted, then looked to find Lourdes jogging toward her. "Did you get your next Instagram post?" Lourdes rolled her eyes as she walked past Maddie to get to her car. Maddie whirled around and stared at the back of Lourdes.

"Don't go away like this," Maddie argued.

"Go away like what?" Lourdes rested against her vehicle, locking eyes with Maddie. "Maddie, I'm not trying to chastise you or anything. All I'm saying is that it wouldn't hurt if you tried to relax just a bit. But it's only because I care."

Maddie moved in closer to her. Lourdes had beads of sweat trickling down her cheeks, yet she still looked radiant and beautiful. Maddie had yet to pull something like that off. "If you think I need to chill, I'll try."

Lourdes stood up straighter. "You mean it?"

Maddie smirked, "No one's ever looked out for me like that before. I mean, except for my dad. If anything, I'm always the person who's telling other people to take it easy. And with work and the auction, I guess I really have been spreading myself a little thin these days.

Lourdes grinned. "So, you promise me you'll try to relax?"

Despite both being sweaty, Maddie went in for a kiss. If it upset Lourdes, then she would try to hold back.

"If you're really concerned, I promise I will do what I can to stress less for the both of us.." Maddie kissed her slowly, once again aching to be as close to Lourdes as humanly possible. She caught Lourdes' smile between her lips, which was enough to motivate Maddie to try her best to keep this promise. However, it wouldn't be an easy task, especially when a million things were on her mind.

CHAPTER TWENTY-ONE

A PROMISE FALTERED

Noelle: *Headed to the event hall, running a few minutes behind.*

Maddie: *I'm still at work. Getting ready to leave now, so I'll meet ya there.*

Gina: *I can't be there until 6:30 now. I don't have a babysitter until then.*

Noelle: *Gina, we might be able to get through without you. I'm just putting some finishing touches on the hall and making sure everything is ready for tomorrow night.*

Gina: *I appreciate that. I've been neglecting my mini-me and feel that if I could have a few hours with her tonight, she won't forget what her momma looks like, lol.*

Maddie: *Absolutely. No worries at all. Noelle and I will be there, and so will Jamie. That should be plenty. You have done enough. Take the night off and enjoy your time with your daughter. Rumor has it they don't stay babies forever. ;)*

Gina: *lol. You girls are the best. I'll see you tomorrow night at the event. I'm excited.*

Maddie pushed out of the break room and tossed her bag over her shoulder. Another busy day in the books, but ever since she had gotten reprimanded, she had tried to steer clear of overtime. Today was unavoidable, and she hoped no one noticed since she worked off the clock.

The elevator doors opened, and she stepped on. Maddie heard someone shuffle onto the elevator behind her. "Hold the door!" she hollered. Maddie reached out just before the door closed, and it whipped back open in time for Lourdes to rush in.

"I thought I was going to miss you."

"Glad you didn't." Maddie wrapped her arm around Lourdes' shoulder and drew her into a kiss. Once they broke apart, she sighed, falling back against the door, "Another busy day."

"Too busy." Lourdes crashed back against the wall. "And I still have a couple of hours to go."

She laughed. "I feel like we hardly saw each other." Lourdes' gaze dropped to the numbered keypad as Maddie pressed the button for the main lobby. "I was hoping we would have been able to grab lunch or something. Hell, I would have settled for a five-minute chat or jog along the track. I was busy, but your day seemed to be ten times worse. I don't even know that you took two minutes to yourself." She smirked, her eyes darting back to Maddie's. Her one eyebrow arched up, and Maddie shrugged. "Besides, I thought you were only working until five."

Maddie groaned. "Pretend you didn't see me. Please."

Lourdes shook her head. "I won't say a word, but please tell me you were gentle with your hands" Her voice was syrupy sweet, and she shot Maddie a meek grin.

"I was the only nurse on the floor. They had Eric working admin, stuck in a file room somewhere. It was the only way to manage the day. But I'm good. I promise," Maddie reassured her.

Lourdes crossed her arms and gave Maddie a wary look. "You also promised me this morning that you would take it easy. I'm pretty sure that we have different definitions of easy."

"I will, at least once this event is behind me. Then I'll have one less thing to focus on. Things are bound to get easier from there. The stress will dissipate, and all will be well. You'll see." The elevator bell dinged, and Maddie smiled. "And that's my cue ."

She stepped off the elevator and turned to Lourdes. Lourdes dropped her gaze, which caused Maddie to step in closer, keeping the door from closing behind her. "I know you probably don't trust me."

"It's not you, Maddie. I trust you. I do. But I also know the situation and how difficult it can be when you're spreading yourself thin. It can be impossible not to overdo it, but I don't want you to forget that a human body can only take so much."

"After tomorrow night, things will improve. You'll see." She pulled Lourdes to her, kissing her, finally feeling Lourdes relax in her arms. I have to run."

"How about you coming by the house tonight when you're done with the committee? We can do Netflix and chill. Unless you think that you'll have to work all night."

"It shouldn't be more than an hour or two. I should finish up right when you get out of work."

"Perfect. I'll chill the wine, and you pick the movie. I probably should get back to work. See you tonight, Maddie." She gave a wave, and Maddie turned on her heel and hurried out of the hospital to get to Cayman's Event Hall. She was excited about what the whole night had in store.

As she drew closer to the event hall, she began humming. Why couldn't she have it all? She could slow down, be happy with Lourdes, and life would be great. When she pulled into the parking lot, her face fell, and her anxiety rushed back into her chest. The parking lot was filled with vehicles, from cars to construction trucks -- at least twenty-five more than usual.

She jumped out of the car and hurried towards the door when she saw Noelle and Gina pacing in front of the main entrance. "What's going on?" She looked at Gina. "I thought you weren't coming tonight."

Noelle threw up her hands. "Don't you reply to texts?" Maddie dug in her pocket and withdrew her phone. She had a dozen text messages waiting for her reply. The last one was from Noelle.

Noelle: A pipe burst, and the venue flooded! The whole place is ruined. We've lost the venue.

Maddie gawked at them. "I was a bit distracted. What do you mean we lost the venue? The event is tomorrow night?"

Gina thrust her phone towards Maddie. "We saved most of the baskets. A few were hopeless."

Maddie skimmed through picture after picture, her eyes growing as she saw each one. That panic feeling pumped through her chest as she shook her head. "What now?"

"Jamie is attempting to get a venue, so we can still have it tomorrow, but we're going to have to make calls, send out emails, text people, do whatever we can to let everyone know."

"I can't believe this. It's not salvageable?"

Gina snickered. "Did you see the pictures?" Her voice was thick with sarcasm.

From a distance, Maddie saw Jamie hurrying towards them. "I have an idea, but it will take some work. I hope no one has plans tonight because we'll need all hands on deck."

"We have to do what we have to do," Maddie replied.

"Let's get started." Her anxiety still felt heavy in her chest, but she knew she had to push through it to ensure that tomorrow night was unforgettable. The hospital and the children were counting on her.

Every inch of Maddie ached as she made her way to her car. She glanced at her watch and grimaced. How had it gotten so late? What started to be a quick trip ended five hours later. She yawned, but the tension in her shoulders remained.

Maddie slid into the front seat and started the car. Her eyes dipped down to the clock radio, where the time stared her straight in the face. *Lourdes!* Maddie pulled her phone out of her pocket and cringed at the messages on the screen. The last one ended with, *Maybe you just decided tonight wasn't a good night. After considering it, I don't know that tomorrow is a great night either.*

Maddie closed her eyes. It was clear that Lourdes was upset. Maddie felt terrible. Why was everything just so hard? *Maybe you are self-sabotaging the relationship. It wouldn't be the first time.* One voicemail popped up on her phone. Maddie swiped the notification and pressed the phone to her ear.

"Hey, Maddie. So, it's just after ten. I'm starting to worry. You aren't at the event hall, as I've checked. On the verge of checking the hospital. Please call me."

"Call Lourdes!" Maddie yelled into her Bluetooth. She backed out of her parking spot and hurried towards Lourdes' place. Her phone rang once, then; it went straight to voicemail. She disconnected the call and kept driving. Ten minutes later, she pulled up in front of Lourdes' house, barely wasting time to get out of the car. The rain had started to fall just as she reached the porch. Maddie pounded on the door, waiting for the moment Lourdes would open up, and she would talk to her, explain herself, and make sure that Lourdes realized that she didn't mean to bail. "Lourdes? Please open up!" Maddie hollered. She looked over her shoulder; Lourdes' car was still parked in the driveway. She just needed five minutes. "Lourdes!"

Finally, the door flew up as Lourdes stood before her, wearing her hair in a messy bun. She wore a robe hanging open to reveal her pajamas. "Do you know what time it is?" Lourdes asked. She tapped her foot, impatiently waiting for a response.

"I rushed over here as soon as I realized how much I screwed up. I'm sorry." Maddie stepped into the doorway. Lourdes arched an eyebrow. "Things didn't go as planned. We lost the venue. There was a flood, and I know it could have been much worse, but thankfully we could salvage some things. We found a new venue." Maddie rambled, all while Lourdes kept her eyes lowered. "I should have called. I'm sorry."

Lourdes sighed, holding back tears, "Maddie, I was genuinely worried about you!"

"And I can understand if you don't want to forgive me. I shouldn't have screwed up. The truth is...." Her words trailed off, tears threatened to fall, and Maddie clamped down on her lower lip. "I've never been good at relationships. Most likely never will be."

"I don't buy that," Lourdes whispered. "When you have too much on your plate, it's hard for you to focus on everything. You could have at least shot me a text so I didn't have to worry about whether or not you were dead in a ditch somewhere. I guess I felt sort of blindsided, especially after this morning. It felt like you stood me up, that's all." She shrugged. "But you couldn't help it. You lost the venue. Can we talk about it?"

More than anything, Maddie wanted to express her whole heart.

Lourdes would comfort her, and they would hold one another. The exhaustion settled in, and Maddie slowly nodded, with Lourdes reaching for her hand and pulling her into the house. They sat in the living room, and Maddie gushed about what had transpired five hours earlier.

"There wasn't any way to save anything! Literally, all of our hard work was wasted."

"Maddie, I'm so sorry. I know how hard you all worked to guarantee it was a perfect night." She reached up and caressed Maddie's tear that had slipped from her eye. "I'm sorry I immediately jumped to the worst conclusions."

Maddie shook her head. "I should have called you instead of letting you freak out. But we found a venue. We only had four hours to put everything together. It's not perfect, but we don't have to cancel the event."

"Is there anything I can do to help?" Lourdes asked. There she was, once again, trying to calm Maddie down even though she was upset.

"Just one thing," Maddie added.

Lourdes nodded.

"Still take me tomorrow," Maddie pleaded.

A smile crossed Lourdes' lips, and she moved in. "It would be my pleasure." Maddie sighed as the kiss deepened. Lourdes would always be by her side. If only she never doubted that.

CHAPTER TWENTY-TWO

LOVE IS IN THE AIR

I t had taken forever to get to this very moment. Maddie could hardly believe they had gotten there. She glanced around the new venue, a convention hall at Jamie's boyfriend's office. They'd decided to go with a pastel color scheme to celebrate Spring. An archway made of flowers, donated by one of Maddie's followers who worked events at the Garfield Park Conservatory, adorned the entrance transporting guests into a Spring wonderland. Centerpieces of paper flowers held down the egg-shell white tablecloths that decorated each table. Thanks to the dozens of paper lanterns that lit up the space, the room was filled with a soft glow. Maddie and the other volunteers had set up a photo booth in the back of the room where guests could pose with props and have the photos air-dropped to their phones. It was a perfect size, even offering an extra room where guests could chill and chat with their partners for the evening. Maddie looked over at Lourdes, and Lourdes offered her a gracious smile.

"You look radiant tonight," Lourdes said, a slight shimmer coming from her lip gloss. Maddie wore a fitted lavender suit. The suit jacket was low-cut, so she wore a sheer crop top beneath it. She gathered her hair in a sleek ponytail at the nape of her neck. A thin gold chain glimmered around her neck. Though she rarely wore heels, she found a comfortable pair of nude wedges online. Now she and Lourdes could look each other in the eye.

"Me?" Maddie asked, her eyes unable to stay away from Lourdes' slight cleavage. The diamonds sparkled just shy of her breasts. Lourdes looked equally dazzling in a slinky aubergine silk cocktail dress. Her hair flowed effortlessly down her back.

Maddie lifted her gaze to meet a beautiful grin. "You always look gorgeous, but tonight you defied all odds. I still can't believe we match."

Neither Maddie nor Lourdes had consulted the other about their outfit before showing up to the hall.

Lourdes laughed, "A classic case of lesbian telepathy."

Maddie laughed along with her and sipped her champagne just before Lourdes leaned in and pressed her lips against Maddie's. She tasted like champagne.

"I couldn't disappoint when you put so much love and effort into this evening."

Maddie braced herself, anticipating that Lourdes would say something about her stress levels. She let out a soft breath, relieved that for the night, at least, Lourdes would keep worrying to a minimum. Perhaps it was because of the night they had shared just eighteen hours earlier. Maybe Lourdes finally understood that what she saw as stress was merely Maddie giving it all and that Maddie could handle more than anyone gave her credit for.

Maddie opened her mouth when she spotted Eric and James closing in on their table. They wore pastel blue suits that looked straight out of the seventies. Eric had gelled his hair back. James stood by his side, gorgeous as ever, the blue in his eyes brought out by the powder blue fabric of the suit. His dark, curly hair brushed his shoulders. He was growing his hair out into a mullet. It would have made most people look like truck drivers, but James looked like a model.

"There's the lovely couple," Maddie said, winking.

"Not lovelier than you," he whispered, leaning in and kissing her cheek. Maddie blushed as he parted from her. "You both look great." He gave an approving nod."

"So do you, Eric." Lourdes nodded to James. "As do you. You both clean up quite nicely."

"Thanks! Can you believe these suits? We found them at a Vintage shop on Halstead," James gushed.

Maddie beamed as Eric and Lourdes held the conversation. It was as if they had all been friends this whole time. Eric laughed as Lourdes said something funny. Maddie was too caught up in her thoughts even to recognize the words. Maddie cleared her throat.

"So, Eric, I hope you spent all your money on the raffle tickets for the baskets. It's all for a good cause, you know."

Eric rolled his eyes. "As you have been telling me at least a hundred times." He tossed a look to James, who snaked his arm around Eric's waist.

"James wanted the season passes to the theater. All my tickets went into that. You better not let me down." He held up his finger, and Maddie laughed.

"I'm simply one of the organizers. Good luck, though!"

"Thanks, Maddie. You, ladies, have a great rest of your evening." Eric waved, and they disappeared, with Maddie turning to Lourdes.

"What about you?" Maddie arched an eyebrow, "Anything interests you?"

Lourdes looked over to the baskets and shrugged.

"I don't know. Everything looks pretty dull over there. I'm more enticed by what's in front of me." She leaned in and kissed Maddie again. This time Maddie let her guard down and wrapped her arm around her, unfazed at the prospect of her coworkers watching her and Lourdes make out. If Noelle was right, the whole hospital most likely knew they were a pair, anyway.

The night went better than Maddie could have dreamed. With the venue working its magic and everyone laughing and having a good time, Maddie reminded herself that sometimes stress isn't bad. Without pushing herself to accomplish things, they might not have had this unexpected miracle happen. And she might not have Lourdes in her arms right at that moment.

They had dinner, all catered. The food was divine; scallops, shrimp, roast, potatoes, and a vegan grain bowl with spicy tofu. There wasn't one person that seemed disappointed by the food options. Everyone was thrilled to be there. Even more interesting, Lourdes seemed to know every-one. Maddie didn't mind taking a step back and allowing Lourdes to do her socializing because, in the end, she knew they would have their alone time. Eventually, Lourdes and Maddie found a secluded table in a corner where disruptions were minimal, and they could enjoy each other's company.

Maddie lowered her hand over Lourdes' chest, barely grazing her cleavage, and Lourdes snickered between their sweet and tender kisses. "The night is still young. Do that again, and I'm liable to pull you into the restroom and make passionate love to you. Screw the party."

"Promise?" Maddie whispered, her breath lingering over Lourdes' smile.

"You naughty girl." Lourdes laughed and started to move in to kiss her again when she abruptly stopped. "You know, Maddie. I'm proud of all this extra work you've put into making this event successful."

Maddie frowned. What happened to going into the restroom and having a party of their own? Maddie was ready to rip Lourdes' dress off in the gender-neutral bathroom. She opened her mouth.

"I hear you have a lot to do with how this evening turned out."

Maddie turned to see Sierra, who was actually smiling for once.

Maddie quickly nodded. "It was a group effort, but I tried to do my part."

"It turned out great. I just wanted to let you know that." She nodded, then shot a look at Lourdes.

"You both have a good night."

Maddie turned and watched Sierra walking away. Her jaw dropped. "Well, it would've been a little awkward to make out with you in front of Sierra." Lourdes took a sip of her champagne and then laughed, covering her mouth. "I can only imagine the look on her face."

Maddie felt her cheeks burn. "Then I suppose I should thank you for pulling away. Even though I was slightly disappointed."

"Slightly?" Lourdes tilted her head.

"Maybe a smidge more," Maddie teased.

Lourdes looked around the room, and her eyes got a faraway distant look. "What you did to transform this place is quite impressive. You had less than twenty-four hours. Kudos to you."

Maddie's smile grew brighter. "You know, the truth is, I wanted to make tonight special for you" Lourdes frowned.

Maddie continued, "I wanted to share this night with you. Knowing that we'd be here together pushed me to make sure everything turned out magnificently. And I can't wait to do more of these types of events. As long as we're there together, I know they'll be special."

Lourdes' smile faded, and Maddie heard a faint sigh leave Lourdes' lips. "You know, Maddie...." Lourdes began. Her eyes dropped, and she shrugged. "Nevermind. Let's dance." She stood up, still frowning. Maddie didn't budge, despite Lourdes reaching out for her hand. Lourdes eventually took her seat while Maddie stayed seated. "When you do things, I want you to do them solely because it's what you want to do. Because it's what will make you happy; after all, that's the greatest gift you can give me."

"I think you misunderstood me. This event never felt like a burden. It didn't feel like I was doing too much. I loved seeing the smile on everyone's faces. That's what makes me the happiest."

Lourdes shook her head, "But all the hard work and stress isn't good for you."

"That's just it. I might be stressed, but this wasn't one of the reasons." Maddie reached out for Lourdes' hand.

"You're right. We need to dance." Her fingers grazed over Lourdes' hand until she grabbed on and pulled Lourdes to her feet.

"But if you try to do everything, you'll never want to plan another event. I'm only looking out for your best interest, Gorgeous."

Maddie smirked. "One of the many reasons I love you." Lourdes' eyes widened. "I mean, I love that about you." She cringed. "You know what I mean." She nervously laughed. "Now, let's dance." With those words still lingering, she pulled Lourdes onto the dance floor. When she turned to face her, Lourdes had a giddy grin, and she pulled Maddie into her arms just as a slow song played over the stereo. Maddie wanted to be here in Lourdes' arms; if the whole world saw, she wouldn't even care.

MADDIE LOOKED OVER TO LOURDES, WHO HAD GAZED AT HER the whole way back to her house. Maddie gave a smile and looked up to the front door. "I'll walk you home." She winked, and that caused Lourdes to laugh.

"All that way? Such a lady." Lourdes grabbed Maddie's hand and kissed her softly between the knuckles. "I'm a lucky woman."

Maddie giggled, and they exited her car. Before they reached the sidewalk, Lourdes reached for her hand, and they slowly made their way to the porch. Maddie didn't want the evening to end. The way Lourdes held back, she seemed to feel the same way.

Maddie stopped at the porch and turned to face Lourdes. "I had a wonderful evening."

"As did I." Lourdes continued to caress Maddie's fingers between hers, and her warmth lingered. Lourdes' eyes latched on hers; they were always magnificent. Every time she stared into them, it was like she had discovered a new shade of green. Their lovely hue transfixed Maddie.

"Maddie," Lourdes whispered, leaving Maddie no choice but drop her gaze to her lips as she nodded. "What do you want out of life?"

"You!" Maddie blurted. Lourdes smiled sincerely.

"What else?" Lourdes squeezed Maddie's hands.

"I want to help people," Maddie admitted, the seriousness in the question showing its face.

"You are a vibrant woman full of life, wonder, and a beautiful soul. Your kindness knows no bounds, which scares me. But that heart, that's what makes me love you."

Maddie grinned. "You love me?"

"I might have said that." Lourdes laughed.

Maddie relaxed as those words played gleefully in her mind. "I know you heard me earlier tonight, but I played it off. Call me scared or confused or just plain stupid...." Her words trailed off as Lourdes moved in closer to her. She kissed her passionately, taking Maddie's breath away. "I love you!" Maddie gasped, sliding her tongue into Lourdes' open mouth.

"I'd love to have you back in my bed," Lourdes replied between kisses.

Maddie wrapped her arm around Lourdes as Lourdes worked on the door, their lips still entangled on one another's. They stumbled their way into the foyer, and the darkness faded. It was a beautiful thing to be in love.

CHAPTER TWENTY-THREE

CRASH AND BURN

Maddie wiped the beads of sweat off her brow as she quickly typed out her notes. "Maddie!" Noelle hissed, approaching the counter.

"Yes?" Maddie asked, unable to look up, the words running together. How could the week start like a dream only to turn into a nightmare? Between understaffing and the constant rollover of patients coming in and out of the department, Maddie was ready to pull her hair out. Not to mention, it felt like everyone had a bigger problem than the patient before. Her stomach clenched, and she braced herself against an accompanying wave of nausea.

"Do you have Mr. Johnson roomed?"

Maddie looked up. "Johnson?" She returned to her list and saw that he had arrived an hour earlier, but she still had two patients she needed to room before him. "He got here early."

"But his appointment was forty-five minutes ago." Noelle arched an eyebrow.

"I'll grab him next," Maddie mumbled, standing up from the desk. "Sorry." She pushed past her before rushing back to the desk, realizing she'd forgotten his chart. She was so frazzled it was a miracle that her head was still attached to her shoulders. The recent staffing turnover left a mountain of work for the remaining nurses. For starters, they had to pull all their own charts. The only nurses left in the department were Eric and Maddie. They would fill in with staffing from around the hospital. None of this was a genius plan.

"Johnson!" she called.

A man and woman stood up, one on the left side of the waiting room and one on the right. Maddie mentally groaned. "David," she called.

"I've been waiting over thirty minutes," the woman complained. "If I don't get seen soon, I will reschedule; this is ridiculous." The woman crossed her arms and glared back at Maddie. Maddie looked at Rachel behind the front desk, who shrugged. What did she care? Her only responsibility was to check the patient in. As far as she was concerned, her job was done. Maddie tossed a look back to the woman.

"I apologize. I'll be calling you next. I swear." David rolled his eyes as he approached Maddie, and Maddie wanted to do the same, but she had to keep her composure. The day would be over soon enough, and she could forget this monstrosity even occurred. "Follow me."

Maddie heard the huffing behind her and felt her feet dragging behind her as she made her way to the triage room. As long as Sierra didn't come out of her office and offer her words of advice, she might be able to make it through the rest of the day.

"My name is Maddie," she began.

"Have a seat, and we'll get you through relatively quickly. What are you being seen today for?"

"Isn't that in my chart?" he asked. "I would think you would have some idea of why I am here. I was referred, after all. Isn't that part of your job?" His face was red, but not nearly as red as Maddie's probably was. Trying to be friendly to the patients was one thing, but when they insinuated that you were dumb, it made an already awkward situation even worse.

"I apologize, but we're given the bare minimum. If you could give me a brief synopsis, that would be most helpful."

"Fine," he muttered. "Just a little on edge. I was diagnosed with a heart murmur, and they said I needed to come to see someone. I don't even know what that means." His eyes narrowed in, and Maddie sat back in her seat.

"I understand you're concerned, but rest assured that many people live a long and happy life. I can guarantee that you are in the right place."

A small smile graced his lips, and he fell back into his chair. "I've always been healthy. My parents never had any health issues, and I fear I'll pass this down to my kids. Thought it's best not to take it lightly."

"And you are correct. The earlier we can get you a diagnosis, the better we can do to manage the symptoms. Let's take a look at your BP. Do you have hypertension?"

His eyes widened, and Maddie smiled, "High blood pressure," she explained.

"Oh. No. I never had any concerns. Sometimes it runs low, but it's usually normal. "

"That's a good thing. We'll have all your questions answered before the end of your appointment. I promise you that." He relaxed, and Maddie was able to get his vitals without fail. The assessment lasted ten minutes longer, but when Maddie walked him to meet up with Noelle, she felt a tad better.

"Here's your patient, Noelle." Maddie's voice was chipper, but Noelle shook her head and kept her eyes on the chart. Maddie glanced back at him. "It was nice to meet you, Mr. Johnson. I'm sure I'll be seeing you." She patted his shoulder, and he left her with a kind exit.

Maddie returned to the nurse's station, where Eric sat at the desk. "You're looking too happy for the number of patients in that waiting room." The tension in his voice didn't even upset her.

"I saw the charts and nearly went running." He smirked.

Maddie scowled at the charts as her heart started to pound again. "Ugh." She plopped down into the seat and logged into the computer.

"I'm glad you didn't because, as you mentioned, it's been a nightmare."

Eric laughed, "That's better."

He shook his head. "I don't know how much more we're going to be able to do to keep up running this office this way. We might have to utilize the hospital more. They said we can get someone here when the patients outweigh the employees."

"That's every minute of every day," Maddie grumbled. "Besides, if we show them we can't keep up, that will give them a reason to push us out the door and bring in someone that can do the job of ten nurses."

"I'd like to see them try," Eric scoffed.

When they couldn't find a reason to joke around, that's when Maddie knew things were getting worse.

Maddie continued to type in notes for David's appointment, her stomach churning. It was another day with nothing to eat. She hadn't even been able to stop to have a cup of coffee, and she could feel the exhaustion settling in her bones. "Remember" patient in, patient out, patient in, patient out, like it's a factory of sorts. Who cares if we don't give every patient the same amount of time?"

He shrugged. "It's all in how we manage our time. And if patients complain, we'll look at Sierra and the physicians and say, "You're the ones that wanted this."

Maddie turned from her documentation and stared at him. "How do you do it, Eric? How do you whip through your patients like it's nothing more than snapping your fingers? We have a stack of charts, and even though you grumble about it, you act like it's no big deal. Who cares if we don't give every patient the same amount of time? Is it like a factory? How do you do that? Just snap your fingers and shrug your shoulders like it's so easy."

"Well, it's like this...." He clenched his fists together. "I think I need to give you a lesson in being a cold-hearted bitch. It's not that hard, and it might do you wonders." He winked, and Maddie rolled her eyes.

"Not helping."

She stood up and reached for the next chart, "Ugh, do you want to do this, patient? Consider it a gift from me to you." Maddie held up Marisa Johnson's chart.

Eric grabbed the chart, looked at it, and then turned his attention to her. "If you're this eager, then I would say no thank you" He handed the chart back, then laughed.

"We had a moment earlier. She had some complaints, and I just stood there like a bumbling fool. Either way, I don't want to deal with the glares this woman will give me."

"Sorry, Maddie. I have to finish up this before I grab my first patient.

I'm sure you'll be fine, though. Just remember, you don't have to be nice to everyone." He winked and left the station.

Maddie was a nurse by nature. She wanted to fulfill the patient's needs, all while doing the best job she could. The idea of deliberately rushing with a patient made her skin crawl. Maddie looked at the walkway, where Lourdes ran from room to room. They hadn't even had ten minutes to talk, and now she was forced to be nice to a stranger who wanted to chop her head off. She pushed through with a smile and made her way to the waiting room. "Johnson!" she called out.

"It's about time," the woman mumbled. Her frown stayed on her face as she looked down at the floor and marched over to where Maddie stood.

"My name is Maddie, and I'll be assisting you before you get to the practitioner. Follow me."

Again, with a groan, the woman continued to mumble as they walked back to the room. Maddie tossed a look in her direction as they entered the room, and the woman marched over to the chair and sat down.

"So, let's see. Why are we seeing you today?"

The woman stared, just as she expected. "I have to do your job for you? Is that what you're saying?" She sighed. "I had a heart attack a year ago, and I'm starting to have an arrhythmia. My cardiologist told me to come here, and now I think it would be more pleasant to die at home." The woman dropped her gaze, and Maddie's heart went out to her.

"Ma'am. Surely you have loved ones at home that wouldn't want to hear you say that. I understand this is a stressful situation, but we're here to help you. I promise you that." Marisa looked up and cocked an eyebrow, and at that moment, they reached a silent agreement.

Maddie finished up with Marisa and got her back to where she needed to be, then tried her best to ensure the rest of the day went without a hitch. She could feel that it was a losing battle. Her co-workers kept glaring at her. Her anxiety and stomachache returned. Maybe this was all her fault. She clearly couldn't balance good patient care and rushing them through like they were only a number.

She clocked out late, which only added to her stress. Tears stung the backs of her eyes as she rushed to the elevator, fearful she would crumble in front of her co-workers, desperate to get behind those closed doors where she could fully crash and no one would be the wiser.

When the doors opened, Lourdes stood there, ready to enter the break room. "Maddie?" Maddie fell into Lourdes' waiting arms, and she couldn't hold back the tears that had her riddled with anguish.

"I'll never be able to do enough. I'll never be enough." She sobbed, her cheek resting against Lourdes' shoulder.

"It will be okay," Lourdes whispered. "Trust me." No words would calm Maddie's worries. Maddie's mind was set; she was a complete and total failure.

CHAPTER TWENTY-FOUR

TWO SIDES OF A RELATIONSHIP

Maddie inhaled a whiff of fresh air and slowly exhaled. Lourdes remained extra quiet next to her. As they slowly walked, Maddie reflected on the day: the rush, and the fury, how she fell into Lourdes' arms as Lourdes attempted to console her. Even so, Maddie was still reeling. She couldn't calm her pounding heart or her racing thoughts. "I needed to come here," Maddie began. She glanced over to Lourdes. "The fresh air has done me some good."

"I'm glad, Maddie." Lourdes smiled weakly.

"You had me worried back there," Lourdes admitted.

Maddie sighed and turned straight ahead. She was used to running in this park, but now the one coffee she had for sustenance wasn't giving her the strength to move. Perhaps a shot of espresso would have given her that push. But walking out in the fresh air wasn't so bad. At least it was a place she could clear her head.

"I feel like whatever I do. It's not enough at the hospital. As a nurse, I want, or rather, I should do more. But I don't want to rush patients through the triage process. It's just not right. We should want to do more for these patients. They deserve at least that much."

Lourdes remained quiet, her eyes set straight ahead. Maddie sighed, continuing the slow jaunt along the trail. Why didn't Lourdes understand that? Why was this so foreign to all other employees? Sure, Maddie had a leg up. She had experienced the world of lackluster patient care when her Dad went through it, but that was ten years ago! Maddie would have hoped that there would be growth in patient care. If anything, Maddie had hoped she would be the difference.

"We should probably head back to the cars," Maddie mumbled, turning to walk in the opposite direction. After several more minutes of silence, she stopped walking and turned to Lourdes.

"Am I alone here? Am I foolish in thinking that patient care should be our top priority?"

Lourdes huffed, "No, Maddie."

Lourdes hesitated and tilted her head, "Sweetheart, you're not the only one that cares about the patients. I care, too. But I couldn't spend as much time with the patients because your assessments took too long. Maybe you should consider this a group effort, not just an individual task."

Maddie's jaw dropped, more tears threatening to fall. She began to sprint. Her legs carried her only so far. But she couldn't dare let Lourdes see how the words stung. She considered herself a good nurse, but perhaps that was part of her foolish nature. What if Maddie was the annoying one? What if she was the reason why the senior staff was left hanging, wanting to know where their patients were?

It was one thing for all the other staff to question this, but Lourdes? She believed Lourdes was on her side. She stopped at her car, her head racing as fast as her heart. She turned and jogged back toward Lourdes, who was now in a solid sprint. Maddie looked away. She could get in the car and leave, never looking back. That was one idea. She swallowed the lump that had grown in her throat and looked over her shoulder. Lourdes stopped, her breathing heavy as she stared at Maddie. Maddie didn't want to run. Not away from Lourdes. Not away from anyone.

"I'm sorry if I sounded harsh." Lourdes shook her head. "But I'm trying to be realistic. When you're with the patients, they are in great hands, but since we are short-handed, we must move it along. Does it stink? Yes, of course, it does." Lourdes grabbed Maddie's hand, and Maddie instinctively pulled back.

"I don't know how to do that," Maddie spoke.

"That's where your heart comes into play. Maddie, I love your heart. I hate when you think I don't understand where you're coming from. When I watch you with the patients, my heart swells, and you know what I think?"

Maddie slowly shook her head.

"I think that's my girl! That's the woman that the patients need. That's your girlfriend talking. Heaven knows I wish with all my might that that's the only person in play here. Unfortunately, I also have a job to do. I don't particularly appreciate when Sierra, Noelle, or other doctors look down on and judge you. I want to protect your heart. But, on the other hand, I can see where they're coming from. When one person gets behind, we all get behind. That puts more stress on the department, as a whole."

"And that's all my fault."

Lourdes shook her head. "No, it's not all your fault. We all have to take responsibility. But there's a team effort. If one person falters, the whole team goes down. If we're not all doing our part, then a part of the team will crumble. That's where you come into the equation."

Hearing Lourdes' breakdown, it all made sense. "I just don't know if I'm cut out for nursing if that's how it's going to be," Maddie confessed.

"You have to think about what you're truly passionate about, Maddie. Things have changed. There's no doubt about that." Lourdes reached up and cupped Maddie's chin in her palm. "But everyone should take inventory of their lives and if they're pleased. Just remember that I am on your side, Maddie. Even if you don't always see it."

Maddie dropped her gaze. Suddenly, she had even more things to think about. "I should get going."

Lourdes scrunched up her nose, "Wanna go get a bite to eat or something? My treat!"

She gave a genuine smile, but Maddie just shook her head.

"I'm not hungry," she leaned in and kissed Lourdes, hoping the kiss didn't feel forced on Lourdes' side. "Goodbye!"

"Bye, Maddie." Maddie saw Lourdes staring after her from her rearview mirror, unmoving, but the tears couldn't be delayed. She flicked a tear away and kept on driving. She was so exhausted that she could barely keep her eyes open. When Maddie returned to her apartment, she tossed a frozen dinner into the microwave. She couldn't even bring herself to cook something healthy, but if she didn't eat, she was liable to pass out.

As she went through the evening, Lourdes' words were heavy on Maddie's heart. In many ways, Lourdes was right. Just as much as they were romantic partners, they were also co-workers. Maddie would have to decipher between the two, or it would never truly work out. A call came through from Lourdes at ten o'clock, and Maddie stared at the phone until she had no other option.

"Hello?"

"Hey, Maddie. I just wanted to check up on you. Do you want to talk?"

"Actually, I was just about to go to bed."

The phone went still, and Maddie leaned back against the couch, rubbing the back of Cheddar's ear. "But you've given me a lot to consider. I guess I never contemplated how we have two relationships. Maybe we just need some more distinct boundaries. That makes much more sense in my eyes."

"In a good way or bad?" Lourdes asked.

"Guess I haven't decided that yet. But I love you, Lourdes. I know that. "

"I love you, too, Maddie. Rest easy."

Lourdes hung up, and Maddie tossed her phone to the side. While rest was necessary, she wasn't sure it was possible. With everything running through her mind, sleep was rough. Maddie tossed and turned before finally settling back on the couch, pulling Cheddar into her lap. If she couldn't sleep, why force it?

CHAPTER TWENTY-FIVE

RECOIL

Maddie closed her eyes, if for just a second. She felt like a walking zombie driving to the hospital the following day. She could make it through the day on less than an hour of sleep, but she had no choice. The patients needed her as the staff shortage was already too overwhelming for those who were left. She pushed away from the wall, her coffee still in hand.

"You've got this, Maddie. Don't let the lack of sleep consume you." Maddie downed the last of her coffee and tossed the cup away. Her stomach tightened as she reached the break room door to go out onto her long shift. Maddie grabbed the wall for her support. She closed her eyes briefly, straightened herself, and exited the room. To her relief, the hallways were empty, and she could ride the elevator up to her floor without interruptions. When the doors opened, she was greeted by the familiar commotion. Maddie felt her chest tighten and took a deep breath, trying to center herself as she approached the nurses' station. Eric was already behind the desk, working and looking frazzled. He looked up and scrunched up his face.

"Sierra wants to see you."

"What now?" Maddie murmured. He shrugged, grabbed a chart, and went out to the lobby.

Maddie made her way to Sierra's office and knocked. Sierra looked up and, with no emotion. She pointed to the chair.

"Sierra, with all due respect, there's a madhouse out there. Eric is alone. Can this wait?"

"Not really." The tense words came out in one breath. Maddie entered the office, closing the door behind her, her stomach clenching again. She sank into the chair. She couldn't bring herself to look Sierra in the eye. "I won't take any longer than I need. Maddie, you are good with the patients, but you have had your warning. I noticed you worked overtime again over the past week, and I have been forced to put you on a seven-day probation."

"Seven days?" Maddie squealed. "Like if I don't shape up in seven days, you ship me out?" Tears stung her eyes as she finally looked up.

"It's not technically like that. But you have seven days to make a change." She pushed a paper in front of Maddie, and Maddie skimmed her eyes over it, her tears blurring her vision.

"And if I don't sign?"

Sierra sighed. "Maddie, don't make this more difficult than it already is. No one likes reprimanding someone, but I have given you ample time, and it doesn't look like it's gotten through to you. The biggest thing is you have to move your patients through more quickly. If you take more time, you are depriving the physician of their time. That's your first step. And you have got to monitor your time better. You can't have any overtime unless we approve it. Your documentation has gotten better, but not by much. If you don't sign this paper stating that we went over this, I'll have no choice but to let you go, effective immediately. I'm hoping you don't put me in that situation."

Maddie picked up the contract and stared at it, making out some more of the words. It was a lot of legal mumbo jumbo that Maddie didn't even quite understand. Essentially, if she didn't change her ways, she was out. If she didn't sign the papers, she was out. Either way, the same result was imminent. She shook her head and tossed the papers down on the desk.

"So, basically, I'm screwed. Unless I can find some way to change in seven days miraculously?"

"Eric isn't having any trouble following the department's rules."

He also doesn't care if he's deemed a cold-hearted bitch. "How long do I have to decide?"

"What's there to decide, Maddie? You need this job, don't you?" Maddie looked down at the contract as Sierra continued, "Sign the papers, Maddie. Go back to work and do your best. The way I see it, that's your only option here."

Maddie rolled her eyes and pulled the contract towards her. Sierra held a pen out to her, and Maddie reluctantly grabbed it. Her hand trembled as she signed the contract. She pushed it back towards Sierra and stood up from her chair. Her arm wrapped around her stomach as it tightened.

"Maddie, don't think about it. Just go out there and do your job."

Maddie looked over to Sierra as she pondered those words. That wasn't her. How could she not think about it? She turned and left the office, leaving the door ajar. Eric wasn't around when she returned to the nurse's station, just a stack of charts. She grabbed the chart off of the top and saw Mike's name. Maddie couldn't even smile as she recognized the patient's name. She would have to force her way through a smile, which was impossible.

She kept a smile as she made her way to the lobby. "Mike?" she called out.

He came up, a grin on his lips. "Hey, Maddie."

"Hi, Mike." She lost the smile and turned away from him. "Follow me." When they reached the triage room, he hitched up an eyebrow.

"Everything okay?" he asked.

Maddie smiled, quickly moving to the stethoscope and blood pressure cuff. "All good." When she started to pump up the cuff, he cocked his head.

"I'll be fine," she replied.

Her regular patients wouldn't believe her even if she was a great actress. She had to put the probation out of her mind until her shift was over and she could fully reflect on it. It wouldn't be easy, but she had to do it.

"Maddie, it's Lourdes. I heard about the probation, and I just wanted to check up on you. Please call me back."

Maddie dropped the phone on the counter and downed the rest of her coffee. She took a bite of her burger and dipped a French Fry in a small container of ranch dressing. Maddie had listened to Lourdes' message at least a dozen times but couldn't force herself to make that call. She took a bite of the fry but dropped it into the paper container, her appetite quickly fading.

She poured herself another coffee and sipped it, hoping it would take off the edge. The more she considered the probation and her job, the more she questioned if she wanted to be there. Why settle for a company that was willing to put its patients second? She grabbed her phone and pulled up Indeed once she got home. She wasn't sure what that would entail if she decided to find something else. She suspected that even if she switched hospitals, she would still run into the same problems. All places would likely have the same rules, and she wasn't thrilled about the prospect of dealing with another Sierra. "Who are you kidding?" She tossed her phone to the side. At that moment, the phone rang. She quickly grabbed it, realizing she hoped it would be Lourdes on the other end of the line. "Hey, Dad? How are you doing?"

"Doing well, Sweetheart. How are you?"

I've been better. I'm not doing great. What have you heard? "I'm doing great!" The words tasted stale, rolling off her tongue. "How are you doing?"

He laughed. "You already asked me that. I'm doing well. No complaints here." The phone went silent for an extra-long time. Maddie slowly nodded, waiting for him to continue. She glanced at her watch. It was only nine o'clock, but she wanted to urge him off the line and give a lame excuse that she needed to get to bed or some nonsense like that.

"I just thought I'd reach out. It's been a few days. You haven't even posted on Instagram," he noted.

She snapped her mouth shut, seconds from inquiring if anything was new.

"Are you sure you're okay?" he prodded.

"Oh yes. Of course. I didn't have anything new to post." She frowned, not even realizing time had passed since her last post.

"I was going to post something right before you called." Another lie. When did it become so easy to spew these fibs out of nowhere? She clenched her teeth together. "I didn't know you were that invested in my posts."

He snickered from the other end of the line. "I guess I am, more than I ever even imagined."

They laughed for a few seconds, the laughter aching as she sat there. " I love you, Dad."

"Love you too, baby girl."

He paused again. "So, I'd like us to catch up with dinner or something. I have a couple of things I want to run by you."

"Oh? What's up?" Maddie could use the break from worrying about her own life.

"Forget about it. We'll catch up later -- nothing major or anything. I just miss you."

He chuckled, "You take care of yourself until then."

"Alright. Be on the lookout for my new post."

"I'll be looking forward to it. Talk soon."

She disconnected the call before she opened up her Instagram and stared at the post from nearly a week ago. She began typing but then stalled, unable to find the words to motivate her followers. She quickly erased them, then started again.

"Life is..." Her words trailed off, and she closed her eyes and leaned back against the couch. *Think, Maddie, think.* The longer she sat there, the more those words faded from her mind. She had no desire to add to that post, which startled her. A task that once was ingrained in her brain was now a heavy weight she had to carry.

Her phone rang, and she looked at it and saw Lourdes' name.

"I was just thinking about you," Maddie replied, answering the call.

"You were? I wasn't sure if I should try you again or wait until you called me. How are you doing?"

"I'm okay now, but it was definitely a shock at first. I needed some time to take it all in. Ultimately, I know that it will push me and make me stronger. So, I don't want to take it as a negative."

"I'm glad to hear you say that, Maddie."

Maddie took a deep breath. She would make the best of the situation, even if it seemed difficult to fathom right now. Maddie appreciated the call from Lourdes. She promised herself that she would keep her head up and not let the probation get her down.

CHAPTER TWENTY-SIX

SHATTERED HEART

Eric approached the nurse's station, a sheepish grin on his face. "Hey, Girl!"

Maddie glanced up and nodded, "Long time since we've had thirty seconds to talk. How are you? How's James?" She checked the computer and looked up again. They could talk while she was waiting for the next patient, but that was about it. At least today, she could finally relax for a few minutes between being bombarded with more work. It helped that two patients did not show up, and the afternoon was just beginning.

"I'm doing well. James, even better." He winked, and that got a laugh from her. It'd been a while since she'd been able to laugh. If only there were more days like this.

"And how are you?" He leaned forward, checking both ways before smirking, "And Lourdes."

Maddie looked back down at the computer. Truthfully, she had no idea how Lourdes was doing. It'd been three days since their last serious conversation; they hadn't even worked the same shift for two of those days. They worked the same shift today, but the influx of patients and the lack of staff left virtually no downtime. There'd been no calls, no late-night rendezvous' and certainly no clandestine hook-ups in exam rooms.

It'd been disappointing, but with work being so crazy, there was only so much they could do.

On cue, Lourdes walked out of her room. They made eye contact. She glanced at Eric, turned the other way, and disappeared into another room. Maddie looked up at Eric, who had instantly taken note. "Does that answer your question?"

"Trouble in paradise?" He scrunched his nose.

"It all depends on your take. As far as I can tell, we're not angry with each other. We're just busy, and since the probation, it's hard to really get a chance to communicate. You know as well as anyone else. If you can't communicate, sustaining a relationship is hard."

"But you're talking, just not talking." He put his fingers up in quotations, and Maddie laughed.

"Let's just say we haven't had any ... sensual conversations lately," Maddie felt a blush creeping up her cheeks.

He groaned. "Sorry to hear." He reached out and touched her arm. "Give it time. Before you know it, you two will be back on better terms. Mark my words. You'll see. This probation will be behind you, and you'll be back on cloud nine with your lady."

The computer lit up, signaling her next patient, and Maddie shrugged. "At this point, I'm not going to worry too much about it." She turned, and her stomach tightened; so much for not worrying about it.

"Baker?" She called out.

The new patient got up and gave her a welcoming smile. Things at work were a bit better. She kept up, moving the patients along and slowly finding that balance. With only a few days left on her probation, the timing couldn't be better. Maddie coasted along the afternoon, feeling a smoother transition between patients. None of the providers seemed upset with her. Sierra didn't have reason to pull her into the office. She even had five more minutes on break than usual, which allowed her to chow down on a sandwich before returning to work.

Two hours before the end of her shift, she spotted Lourdes again. This time Lourdes tossed up a simple wave and started to turn away. However, she slowly turned and made her way to the nurses' station, where Maddie stood alone.

Lourdes' lips curved up slightly. "How are you?

"I'm doing pretty good." Maddie rocked back and forth in her chair. "You? I meant to call, but time has gotten away from me."

"I'm doing pretty good. But yeah, I've wanted to call, too."

"Lour..."

"Madd..."

They then laughed, and Maddie bit down on her tongue. "You go first."

"Well, I was hoping we could meet up after work. Perhaps grab some coffee or tea or whatever you desire. I think we need to talk."

Maddie nodded. "Agreed. We do."

"Okay. Meet you outside in two hours? Next to door 4?"

"I'll be there." Lourdes nodded, then turned away and seemed to hurry further away from Maddie. Maddie watched her, mixed emotions welling up inside. Maybe the meeting was a good thing, right? They could reconnect, have some good conversations, and possibly rekindle their spark. Yet, there was a heavy feeling in the pit of her stomach, and the longer she stared at Lourdes' disappearing frame, the bigger the pit grew.

MADDIE'S TIMER DINGED, SIGNALING THAT HER SHIFT WAS over. She quickly finished off the documentation and practically sprinted to the elevator. She didn't see Lourdes when she got onto the elevator, clocked out in the break room, and returned to the elevator to take it to the lobby. She was probably already outside the door, anxiously awaiting Maddie's arrival. Maddie hoped Lourdes was anxious, indicating that not all hope was lost. When she got outside, though, Lourdes wasn't waiting. Maddie checked her watch, sat on the bench, and did her best to look comfortable. She flipped her legs across, from one side to the other, posing in various ways, wanting the least nonchalant position. After several minutes, Maddie got up and began pacing, checking her watch a few times. "Where are you?" she muttered.

"I hope you weren't waiting too long?"

Maddie whirled around, and Lourdes had two cups in her hand. "Caramel Mocha, extra Caramel. I hope that sounds alright."

"Oh. Delicious. I thought we were going to go to the diner or something."

Lourdes shrugged. "It's a beautiful evening. We have an hour of daylight left. I thought I would grab some drinks from the cart. I hope you're not too disappointed."

Maddie shook her head, taking the coffee from her. "This is great. Thank you." She sipped on it and nodded. "Perfect."

"Let's walk, shall we?" Lourdes motioned in the direction of the trail. Maddie fell into step and casually drank her coffee as they walked silently. The birds chirped overhead, and the sun rested low in the sky. It was beautiful out, and the longer they walked, the more certain it was the best place for them to be, one with nature. "Thanks for agreeing to meet up with me."

"I was glad to meet. We're both so busy we haven't had the chance. I've missed our alone time— this is perfect."

"I'm glad to hear you say that. The truth is, I know you've had things on your mind. I've had things on mine. I sort of felt this coming.."

"Right. I've had things on my mind, but I should have made a better effort for us to communicate. With this probation, I've just been so focused on improving, so the probation ended victoriously. I should have sought you out more. I haven't been the girlfriend that you deserved."

"It goes both ways, Maddie. I could have made more of an effort, as well. It's just...." Her words died down, and Lourdes hesitated, sipping her tea. When she swallowed, she turned to face Maddie, pausing.

"The thing is, Maddie, I've taken the past few days and put a lot of thought into life and relationships. I've thought about everything happening in not only my life but yours. Seeing you get so stressed out all the time gets to me. I want to be there for you and support you in any way possible. And, if I'm being completely honest, you're all I ever think about. I'm consumed by how you are and what you're doing. I hope you feel me there with you in your soul, even when I'm far away. And Maddie, I love you. I love you so much that it kills me to see you in pain."

Lourdes took a long drink of her coffee and sighed. "Remember during the beginning of the pandemic when there were so many cases of nurses getting burned out? All these nurses felt stressed because of the environment around them. They didn't know how to deal with it, and Maddie, it worries me that the stress will get to you in ways that your body isn't going to know how to deal with it."

"I'm fine. Really I am. Today has been a good day, and things have been improving gradually."

Lourdes nodded. "I'm happy to hear that. Today you seemed to be smiling more. Your posture is relaxed. You're carrying less tension. Those are the moments I long for. Unfortunately, I fear those days are so slim that tomorrow you'll be right back to stress. You're an idealist, Maddie. That's one thing I love about you. But sometimes you're too idealistic, which can cause your demise."

Maddie swallowed hard. What could she say to that? She nodded, not wanting to face the criticism that the words seemed to dictate.

"The last thing I want to do is hurt you, Maddie."

Maddie frowned. "I would hope that's true." Lourdes shifted her gaze to the ground. "What are you trying to say?"

Lourdes looked back up at Maddie's wondering eyes. She looked like she was on the verge of tears for the first time. Her eyes were red, almost bloodshot. Maddie had never seen her this vulnerable before; she looked wounded.

"You have to take care of yourself, Maddie. So you can be resilient when times get tough." A rush of air left Lourdes' lungs, and Maddie heard it.

She continued, "I wish things were different. I do. This would never happen in a perfect world. But, Maddie, I'm only thinking of your best interest. A relationship between us won't work. Not now, anyway."

Maddie opened her mouth, then quickly shut it, dropping her gaze to the ground. "Before fully committing to a healthy relationship, you have to learn how to take care of yourself."

"Lourdes, I beg to differ." Maddie looked up, the tears threatening to fall, "Maddie, for three days, I've thought about this. I've considered all options. I went down several avenues in my mind. They all led me back to this one decision. Our relationship isn't going to work when there's so much uncertainty. You must take care of yourself before you can let anyone into your heart. We both know this. If things could work between us right now, you would have reached out to me. And, in turn, I would have reached out to you. I know that this decision is the right decision. I'm sorry, Maddie." She backed away from Maddie. "So very sorry." Lourdes turned and sprinted away from Maddie. Maddie stared after her. Her heart shattered into a hundred pieces, but she couldn't bring herself to beg Lourdes to stay.

CHAPTER TWENTY-SEVEN

LATE-NIGHT EMERGENCY

C heddar meowed as Maddie fell onto her bed. Her tears hadn't once subsided, and she sniffled as she looked down at her cat. She remembered how lovingly Lourdes interacted with Cheddar, and she was immediately hit with another tidal wave of sadness.

Maddie grabbed Cheddar and pulled him into the bed with her. "Lourdes and I are so different. This is just for the best. I could never be satisfied with a woman with no empathy for her patients and their treatment."

Cheddar snuggled up against her as the tears continued to flow. She knew that wasn't fair. Lourdes had empathy, but she was also practical. Maybe Maddie's heart was in the right place, but she didn't know how the business aspects worked. Cheddar purred and cuddled against her. Her tears dampened his fur. Lourdes failed her, giving up on her when the going got tough. That, alone, should tell her they weren't suitable for one another. Maddie was too disappointed to console herself.

Cheddar moved away from her and made a bed at her feet, snuggling into a comfortable spot as the tears stung Maddie's eyes. A notification popped up on her phone, and Maddie quickly grabbed it and pulled it up. *Lourdes?* Her face fell -- just an advertisement for shoes. Maddie pulled up her Instagram and sifted through her old posts. Each selfie looked more and more positive. Yet, none of those pictures conveyed how she truly felt nowadays. Her gaze dropped to the photo of her at the finish line, the crowd behind her cheering her on, the smile on her face. Briefly, she remembered how it felt to be happy and fulfilled. She scrolled through hours and hours of pictures, most filled with likes and comments, people thanking her for her help. Maddie felt the love behind each one of them. But that was over a week earlier. Lately, she had steered clear from Instagram and her followers. She had missed a lot, as each new post reminded her of how she had stepped away from social media.

"Just me and my daughter," she read aloud. Her father had posted a picture. It was the only time he had ever posted on Instagram, and it was a picture of them together. Was it from Christmas last year or the year before that? They were grinning, with wide eyes and mischievous smiles, enjoying the holiday as they always did. She hadn't gotten the notification of the picture. But he had made a valiant effort to take part in social media. Maddie never thought she'd see that day. She forced a smile, running her fingers over the outline of their photo. Her face fell. She didn't even look like the picture anymore. The stress had overtaken her body, leaving her a shell of the person she once was. The Maddie on the screen was unrecognizable. She never smiled like that anymore.

Her followers showered her with likes and positive comments, but it still wasn't enough. Maybe Lourdes was right; she had to focus on caring for herself. But how exactly should she do that? Maddie always felt positive; lately, her optimism faded. She pulled up her Instagram again and typed out a message.

Just remember that just because someone always smiles doesn't mean they're not struggling. Take care of each other, online and off. Sending y'all love and positive vibes. XOXO.

She stared at the message for what felt like hours and then ultimately deleted it. Maddie pulled up her dad's texts and sent him a message.

Maddie: Love you, Dad.

Dad: Love you, too, Sweetheart.

Maddie grabbed her pillow and sobbed into it as the tears suddenly took over her body, causing massive convulsions. She hadn't cried this hard for as long as she could remember.

THE PHONE RANG, THE SOUND DEAFENING THE DARK bedroom. Or was it just in her dream? The longer the ringing continued, the more convinced Maddie was that it wasn't just in her dream. Her eyes shot open, and the moon crept into the bedroom window.

Maddie grabbed her phone and squinted to see the name on the screen. "Dad?" she quickly answered. According to the alarm clock on her bedside table, it was 2:30 A.M. "What's wrong?" Maddie's heartbeat quickened.

"I don't want you to worry." Maddie sat up in bed. The phrase immediately caused her to panic. "My chest is a little tight. I'm sure it's fine, nothing more than indigestion."

Maddie tossed the covers back, glancing down at her outfit. She was still fully dressed. Suddenly better just in time to help her dad.

"Are you there?" he asked.

"You can't possibly tell me not to worry. I won't have you lessen the severity of the issue on my account. Stay on the phone with me. I'm on my way."

"Honey, you don't have to do that," he argued as Maddie grabbed her keys and purse and quickly left her apartment. She had to be there for him. If anything happened, she shuddered at the thought, another tear threatening to fall on her cheek. "Just be careful," he murmured. "Again, I'm sure it's fine. I had spicy chili for supper, and I'm sure that's all it is. Please be careful."

The words drowned in her ears as she nodded, concentrating on her drive to his house. She arrived at his house ten minutes later, with him still trying to console her. "I'm here." She disconnected the call and hurried to the front door, her heart never stopping its race. The door was unlocked, and she burst through the front door, spotting him at the kitchen table.

He looked up, sheepishly grinning. "See? I'm fine. You really shouldn't have rushed over here like this." He reached out for the table and closed his eyes.

"Dad!" She rushed over and grabbed his arm. "We're getting you to the hospital."

He mumbled some words that Maddie was still curious about, but she couldn't decipher what he was saying when she carefully walked him out the front door and got him to her car.

"You don't have to do this," he whined.

"Dad, if anything happens to you, I'd be lost. Don't ask me not to." She looked at him, and he slowly nodded and slipped into the passenger side. Maddie helped him with his seatbelt and then closed the door. Her mind was a mess as she rushed him to CAPMED. What would she want to say to him if this was the last time she saw him? She watched him as he closed his eyes and rested the whole way.

She pulled him up in front of the Emergency Room doors, where a man brought a wheelchair out as if he were waiting for that moment.

"Dad, they'll get you checked in, and I'll park and be right there."

He nodded. "Honey, don't worry. I'm sure it's just indigestion."

Maddie would feel better hearing the doctor say that over her father. She loved her dad, but he wasn't a physician. Maddie parked the car in the nearest spot, which was still too far. When she got inside, she looked around and couldn't see her father.

"Good morning. May I help you?" The woman behind the desk asked in greeting.

"My father just came in here. He's having shortness of breath, tightness...."

"Room E-3," the woman replied before Maddie could even continue. Maddie went through a set of double doors and made her way down the hallway until she reached the room. He was alone, sitting on the bed, his phone to his ear.

"I'll let you know once I hear what's going on. Talk soon." He disconnected the call, and Maddie frowned.

"Who was that? It's nearly three in the morning."

He gave a weak smile. "It's just a friend." He reached out and touched Maddie's hand, but his whole face lit up the way he said, friend. "The nurse said she would grab the EKG machine and get me checked out." Maddie's face clouded over. "Honey, I'm fine. My chest isn't nearly as tight as it was. I promise you."

Maddie nodded, but it wasn't doing much to convince her. Once she was given the green light from the doctor, she would feel better. She opened her mouth when there was a knock on the door.

"Come in," she said, snapping her mouth shut. She stepped back and out of the way when the nurse came in with the EKG machine. She nodded and then worked on it with her dad. Maddie sunk into the chair, watching the whole scene play out. It brought about a bit of déjà vu while she waited.

"The nurse practitioner is finishing and will be with you, but I'll get your EKG monitor on. How long has the pain been for?"

"About four hours. It happened after I had supper. I'm telling my daughter that I'm sure it's just indigestion."

"Even so, it's best to have it checked out," the nurse said. She looked over her shoulder and smiled. "My name is Tiffany."

"Maddie," she mumbled.

"My daughter works here," her father boasted. "Cardio area."

She smiled. "Is that right? It's a good place to work."

Maddie kept her mouth shut. Instead of being stuck in this rut, she wanted to feel that way. Maddie wanted to be proud of the place where she worked. Perhaps she needed to change departments if the other staff disagreed with Maddie's approach to patient care.

A knock on the door, and Maddie jerked out of her thoughts.

"Is this a good time?"

Maddie looked towards the door as Lourdes entered, smiling until she turned and spotted the woman staring back at her. Lourdes' face instantly dropped.

"We're ready for you, Lourdes," Tiffany remarked, upbeat and completely oblivious. Lourdes cleared her throat and turned to Maddie's father.

"My name is Lourdes, and I'll be the nurse practitioner on duty this morning. Why don't you start telling me how you're feeling now."

Maddie dropped her gaze to the floor. Instantly tears wanted to spring back to her eyes. What was Lourdes doing there, and how could she stop her heart from yearning for her?

CHAPTER TWENTY-EIGHT

PROPER ASSESSMENT

Indigestion. Maddie finally allowed herself to unclench her jaw once Lourdes confirmed her father's suspicion. Lourdes had deduced a full hour of panic using a single word.

"See, I told you." Her father smiled with pride. "I guess from years of being around my nurse daughter, I was able to pick up a few things. But she was worried."

Lourdes smiled. "The heart is something you shouldn't mess around with, so I can understand her fears. Just rest for a couple of days, and try not to eat anything spicy, and you should be good as new." Lourdes shook his hand, then glanced over at Maddie.

Maddie quickly looked away. She had spent the last hour ignoring Lourdes' attempts at eye contact. She didn't intend on reading too much into them now. After some awkward silence, Maddie glanced over and saw that Lourdes was still looking in her direction. Maddie gave a weak smile as Lourdes stood to her feet.

"Um, may I speak privately with you for a minute?" Lourdes asked.

Maddie's brows furrowed, and she looked over to her dad, who had his eyes on both of them. He nodded, which pushed Maddie to follow Lourdes into the hallway.

"What are you doing here?" Maddie asked.

Lourdes spun around and shrugged. "They were short-staffed and didn't have anyone to fill the department. They called me in a panic. I had no idea this was your father when I went in."

"I'm sure it was strange to see me."

"Something like that." Lourdes looked down at the floor. "But Maddie, I couldn't stop thinking about you and how things were left yesterday. I'm sorry if I hurt you. I would never want to cause you more pain. I'm only...."

"Putting my best interest at heart." Maddie finished for her. She shoved her hands in her pocket and looked at her father's room.

"The truth is, I have done some thinking since we parted ways, and I guess I am starting to understand where you're coming from. I was terrified when I got the call from my dad. My stress levels are through the roof."

"At least it was only indigestion," Lourdes replied, comforting. Her hand reached out, and she touched Maddie's arm, "In this case, I can understand why you would be worried. I mean, I know you don't want to lose your father. That could stress anyone out, but managing our stress matters."

"Lourdes," Maddie started before catching her eye. "I want you to know that I have never loved another woman the way I loved you."

Lourdes smiled. "The feeling is mutual."

"But you're right that I can't be with someone until I fully care for myself. This morning has made me see that."

"I'm glad you see that." To Maddie's surprise, Lourdes leaned in and hugged Maddie. Maddie rested her head on Lourdes' shoulder, wishing she could stay there forever. Eventually, she pulled back. Lourdes' eyes were dark, but she smiled, "See you around, Maddie." She moved past her, and Maddie tossed a look over her shoulder.

"See you around."

Maddie's breath hitched, and she returned to her dad's room. He was on his phone, texting someone in a frenzy. Maddie reached for the phone, but he pulled it away, causing Maddie to tilt her head.

"You heard her. You should be resting." He looked up and grinned, slipping his phone into his pocket.

"Believe me. Texting won't give me a heart attack. Are you ready? I've got the papers, and I'm raring to go."

Compared to how she found him at his house, he was good as new. They headed towards the front of the hospital, but she reached out for his arm to steady him.

"Should I get you a wheelchair?"

"I'm fine. Much better than when we arrived," he insisted.

She shrugged, and they kept on walking.

"Who was that woman? She said her name was Lourdes, right?"

Maddie smirked. "You heard her right. Just a co-worker in my department."

He snickered, "Looked more chummy than just that."

Maddie stopped at the car and turned to him. "You think?"

He shrugged, "Us fathers know these things. She looked at you like she was interested. I just thought maybe there was a story to tell. That's all."

Maddie grinned. She liked that her father noticed that, but she wasn't quite sure where she could take the story. "Let's not change the subject. Tell me about that phone call and the texts. Who are you talking to? Looks like maybe someone you're quite interested in."

He laughed, "Perhaps I have something I need to tell you. Only if you'll tell me about Lourdes first." He winked, and Maddie was grateful that he was in better spirits.

MADDIE DOWNED HER COFFEE AND GLANCED AT HER reflection in the mirror. Outside of the bags under her eyes, she didn't look half bad. No one could tell that she had been up most of the night.

"Are you sure you should be going to work?" She fumbled with her cup and laughed as she looked over her shoulder, gently placing the cup on the counter.

"You startled me."

Her dad smiled. "Well, I would say you haven't slept a wink because of me. I would feel much better if you stayed home. Surely the hospital can manage without you for one day."

Maddie shrugged. "I'm good, honestly." She left it at that. Giving the hospital another reason to get rid of her during this probation wouldn't be beneficial.

"But how are you doing?" She raised an eyebrow, and he grinned.

"Can't complain. I'm at least a nine on a scale of one to ten."

Maddie turned away from him. If only she could believe that. Maddie would stay home with him in the perfect world and not worry about rushing off to work. But, as she knew, this wasn't a perfect world. "Can I get you anything?"

"Coffee," her dad replied.

Maddie shook her head, "Not happening. I can't have you back in the hospital."

"Not fair," he whined, like a little kid, then laughed. "I'll just take water."

"As you wish." She poured him a glass from the filtered water jug and handed it over. "Please rest today. I don't want to find out that you overdid it. Understood?"

"Aye, aye, doctor." He teased, offering up a wink. "I promise. I will be a good patient."

"Good." She kissed his cheek. "I'll stop by after work. Love you!"

"Love you, too."

She hurried out of the kitchen and straight out the front door. As she drove to the hospital, she remembered their conversation at home. For the first time all week, Maddie smiled. She couldn't believe her father had a woman in his life after all these years. She also couldn't believe this was the first she had heard about it. She had answered the call the one time Maddie called, and Maddie suspected something was up between all those secret texts and calls. She was grateful to see him so happy.

The hospital employee parking lot was dead once she arrived at her usual spot. She waited a few minutes before getting out of the car, her eyes surveying the hospital momentarily. "Just get me through the day," she muttered.

She headed to the elevator without encountering one person. The hospital used to be so lively. Who would have ever thought they would get to this point? She exited the elevator and spotted Eric at the nurses' station. At least she wasn't alone for her whole shift. Eric looked up, though, instantly tilting his head.

"What are you doing here?"

"What do you mean? I work here." She snickered, attempting her hand at a joke, no matter how small.

"Is it a busy morning?"

"A tad. Nothing record-breaking. But I'm confused. I heard about your father and the early morning ER visit."

"Word travels fast," Maddie replied, skimming through the patient list. I'll grab Roma, and you grab Noah?" She jumped up from the desk, and he reached out and touched her arm.

"You should be home resting, Maddie. I can handle this. If we get backed up, I'll call down for help. You must be exhausted, and now you're rushing through like breaking the triage record is imperative. This isn't like you."

"Well, maybe it needs to be," Maddie argued. "I need this job, and if my probation depends on me rushing through like I don't care, then so be it. It's all about that cash, right?" She turned, but he still had his hand grasped around her arm. She closed her eyes and waited for him to release her.

"How many coffees?" he asked.

"Three, but what does that matter?"

"Maddie!" he argued.

She turned around and glanced at him. "I'm fine. And you should know Lourdes and I broke up. It's all good. Grab Noah, and I'll grab Roma." She spun on her heel and hurried out to the waiting room. Before calling out her name, she leaned against the wall. The walls wobbled in her field of vision. *You can't lose it now, Maddie.* She took a deep breath and counted to ten to steady herself.

"Roma?" she called. She had this, no matter what anyone else believed.

CHAPTER TWENTY-NINE

A NEW CHANGE

Maddie was extremely frazzled the rest of the week, but she had no choice but to continue to work. She would try hard to get the work done; otherwise, she'd lose her job. Was it ideal? Not particularly, but it got easier as the days slowly moved by. When Friday hit, she was confident she had done enough to keep her job and get off probation. She only encountered Lourdes a couple of times. They greeted each other with a friendly nod before continuing with their days. After seeing each other in the emergency department, Maddie knew it was for the best. At least for now, until they got their bearings. Her heart hurt every time she thought about the breakup, but until Maddie proved that she could take care of herself, there was no need to even wish for it. Part of her knew she was in no shape to be someone's partner right now. The stressors were piling up around her. Every time she took care of a problem, five new ones appeared. She had to figure out how to manage her workload without putting herself on the back burner, like that dumb cliche about loving yourself before you could love someone else. Maddie dragged herself into work on Friday morning. Her jaw ached, and she'd started grinding her teeth in her sleep. Maddie could barely keep her eyes open. Still, she had to be on her A-game. There was no saying when Sierra would want to have their meeting about the probation. She continued working throughout the morning, keeping the extra speed in her step, ensuring all documentation was done, and practically bending over backward to transform into Sierra's ideal employee. Sierra approached her right before lunchtime.

"Here it goes," Maddie mumbled.

"Good luck," Eric replied before skirting off to the next patient and leaving them alone.

"Hey, Sierra," Maddie wanted to portray the hopeful employee her voice attempted to portray. Sierra gave a quick nod, then motioned with her finger for Maddie to follow her.

"We can talk out here," Maddie argued.

"After all, I feel like things have greatly improved. The staff doesn't seem rushed, and I apologize for the part I played in bringing us to this point."

Sierra turned as they reached her office, and Maddie dropped her gaze and entered the office. She jumped when Sierra closed the door behind them, and Maddie could feel her frustration mounting. She had worked hard to get to this point. Just another situation for Maddie to see that hard work was never enough.

"I have decided to transfer you to post-op recovery."

Immediately, Maddie's heart sank. Post-op recovery was the sterile, unfeeling part of nursing care she had always disliked. Instead of interacting with patients, she'd monitor patients as they awoke from surgery. If she talked with patients at all, they would most likely be coming out of anesthesia. She'd barely get to interact with patients, which is what Maddie loved the most about her job. She loved caring for people and making them smile. Now she'd only be talking to doctors. Her patients probably wouldn't even know her name. And who would look after Mike, Noelle, or even Eric back in her department? She'd be on the opposite shift schedule of all her friends. . The apathetic nature of the work, combined with the loneliness of a new department, would crush her spirits in a matter of days.

"What? I don't understand. Sierra, I have done everything you have asked of me. Just ask Eric and the other nurses. Ask Lourdes or Noelle. Come on. You can't do this to me."

Sierra looked up with that same grimace that stopped everyone in their footsteps. Maddie looked down, her cheeks burning. It just wasn't enough.

"I have seen improvement, Maddie. I will give you that." Maddie looked up as Sierra's eyes softened. "This isn't about the probation or the fact that you haven't improved, but you still haven't improved enough, Maddie. I think you'll find this isn't a bad thing in time. You'll like post-op recovery. I think it'll be a bit more," Maddie could have sworn she saw her grimace, "Your pace."

Maddie gulped back tears, "What do you mean my pace?"

Sierra sighed, "Maddie, I know you've worked really hard to improve, but I can see that you're struggling to keep up."

"I'm not!" Maddie insisted.

Sierra continued, "Maddie, yes, you are. I know you think you have it all together, but anyone can see you're drowning. I'm not doing this as a punishment for you. I'm doing this as a favor. If you keep going at the pace that you're going, you'll burn yourself out and never want to touch a stethoscope again. I've seen it happen to far too many nurses in my day. And you're a good nurse. I don't want it to happen to you, too."

Maddie couldn't believe it. This was her worst-case scenario playing out before her. Well, second worst-case scenario. She swallowed the lump growing in her throat and nodded numbly.

"We all wish you the best, Maddie." Even Sierra's tone didn't convey that she was speaking the truth. She signed the papers in front of Maddie, then pushed them towards her, waiting for Maddie to do the same. Maddie stared at them.

"When does this go into effect?"

"They expect you in the department on Monday morning. You can leave for the day. We canceled your shift, and you'll have the weekend off. That should give you some much-needed rest. I heard about your father."

Maddie mentally groaned. Everyone said she needed to rest, everyone except her. Maddie signed the papers and stood up from her chair. Without a word, she turned and left Sierra's office. Maybe she should see Eric or call Lourdes? However, neither thought seemed to add much enthusiasm to her step. She clocked out and left the hospital. Her mind was a blur. What would she do in a department she knew nothing about? Tears sprung to her eyes as she drove the long way to her apartment. It wasn't until she got there that she could let the tears dry.

Maddie dialed her father's number, "Hey, Pop. How ya feeling?"

"Are you at work, worrying, again?"

He gave a light-hearted chuckle. "Sweetheart, I'm doing well. I promise you that. How's work?"

Again the tears stung. Maddie released a slow breath. "Actually, great. I just got some exciting news. I've been transferred to Post-op recovery. It's a great department to be a part of. I'm super excited."

"Really? That's great. You never even mentioned that you put in for a transfer. I look forward to hearing all about it."

Maddie sunk back in the seat of her car. She couldn't fool her dad. Now what? He would see right through her lies. She flicked a tear away. "Maybe we can grab some lunch this weekend, and I'll share the details. I have to go. Talk to you soon!"

Her phone dinged with a text message, and she looked to find a message from Eric.

Eric: I just heard the news. How are you doing? Can we talk? I get off in an hour. Text me.

Maddie didn't reply as she got out of the car and hurried to her apartment. What could she say? Her heart now had two reasons to shatter.

ERIC'S FACETIME CALL CAME THROUGH JUST OVER AN HOUR later. Maddie stared at the request, nearly missing out on taking the call, but in her heart, she knew that pushing Eric away wouldn't help. She needed someone in her corner who wasn't her dad.

"Hey!" Maddie answered. Her tone was hopeful and confident, unlike the onslaught of tears she had experienced over the past hour and a half.

"How's it going? How was work?"

"Maddie! Don't even get me started. How are you doing? Are you okay? I see your eyes are red. I'm so sorry. Tell me how things have been. We haven't been able to talk. Spill the tea. Do we hate Sierra now? I think I hate Sierra now. Whatever, screw her. I'm here to listen."

"You're driving. You need to focus."

"Don't even try that. I just reached my destination."

Maddie frowned when she recognized the trees and stairs and heard the knock on her door. "You're here?" She ran downstairs and unlocked the front door. He smiled at her.

" I thought you could use a hug." He disconnected the call, and she threw her arms around him. The tears quickly started to flow once more. He let her cry it out as he held her.

"It's going to be okay," Eric whispered.

Maddie sniffled and pulled back from the hug, pulling Eric into the apartment. "Is James upset that I'm keeping you away from him?" Maddie asked.

Eric smirked. "James knows he'll see me tonight, and I'll make it up to him. Just don't you worry about that."

Maddie pulled him into the living room, and they sat on the couch. "I have so much to tell you. My heart has been a cluttered and shattered mess. I don't even know where to start."

"Let's start with Lourdes," Eric dropped his gaze to Maddie's hands as he laced his fingers between them. Maddie watched Eric as he didn't give her a condescending look like so many people would if they were in the same situation. He was soothing, comforting, and gentle. Maddie could speak with him with no judgment.

"I don't know where to begin," Maddie huffed.

"Well, I'll tell you what I know. I know that Lourdes cares a great deal about you. And I know that anything that happened between you is because she only wants the best for you. So, please remember that."

Maddie arched her eyebrow. "What do you know? What have you heard?"

He shrugged. "I know what you told me. You guys broke up."

She arched an eyebrow. "That's all?"

He shrugged. "Also, maybe I heard that Lourdes is worried that the breakup only stressed you out more. Maddie groaned, "Well, you know more than I expected you to. You have the courtesy of hearing from her and me. Ain't that lovely." Maddie grabbed a pillow and wrapped her arms around it, releasing her fingers from Eric's.

"Don't be upset. Lourdes was worried about you. She came into work a couple of hours ago, heard the news, and knew you would need a friend.

I'm pretty sure Lourdes thought you'd already told me everything. She probably thinks we chat every night. It's not a big deal. When she started talking, she immediately changed the subject once she figured out that you hadn't told me everything. I'm the one that forced her to spill the tea. It doesn't matter. She was concerned and wanted you to know that she only has your best interest at heart. She even said that she fears changing departments could negatively impact your mental health, so she does care."

Maddie looked up at the ceiling, her eyes picking out various dots from the markings above her. "I wish I could be sure about that. Getting the news from Sierra today practically crushed me. Then I thought about Lourdes and how this would put the nail in our coffin. At least periodically, I would see her, and we would have reason to interact. But now, what would that reason be?"

"After speaking with her, I believe you two will end up back together. I really do."

Maddie looked over at him. For some reason, Eric was beaming, "You know, it's going to be tough not seeing you every day. But I know that you and I will remain friends."

Maddie groaned, "I can't imagine starting over in a new department. I won't know anyone up there."

"You'll know Jamie. Didn't the two of you work on the charity event together? That's her department."

Maddie hadn't considered that. She didn't know who worked on the floor, but it wouldn't be the same. She had made so many friends in her current department. And it took some time to make that happen.

"I don't know if my heart will be into this change. I mean, maybe now's the chance I have to break out and do something else?"

"Like what?" Eric inquired softly.

Maddie shrugged. That was one of the many questions she had running through her mind. *What?*

"I appreciate you coming here. I did need the company." Maddie reached out and grabbed Eric's hand, then stood to her feet.

"But James needs it more than I do." She leaned in and gave him a bear hug.

"Go on and make out and make up for the lost time. Tell James I said thanks for letting me steal you for a bit."

He smirked, leading the way to the front door. "I will! Let me know if you need anything." He turned and faced her, "And remember that just because you and Lourdes aren't currently together doesn't mean it won't eventually work out. Trust me on that. Take care of yourself."

"I will. Talk soon." Maddie watched until Eric disappeared, then looked down at her phone and pulled up Lourdes' number. If she called her, it could be the first step to rekindling their relationship. *Or it could be a sign of desperation.* Maddie longed to hear Lourdes' voice, though, telling her she wasn't saying goodbye.

CHAPTER THIRTY

DEPARTMENT CHALLENGES

Maddie's first week in Post-op was off to a rocky start. As Maddie decided to go forward, she wanted to make a good impression and make sure that no one thought she didn't deserve the transfer. The department placed her with Jamie for training, which was a relief, but even knowing the one person she worked closely with left some challenging moments.

"Maddie," Jamie began approaching her, her eyes looking down at the chart. "It says here you just put in a request for Hydrocodone after surgery for George Bartlett."

"Yeah? I thought that's what the notations said."

"George is allergic to Hydrocodone. Misty Bartlett is supposed to get the Hydrocodone, while George gets the Fentanyl. It's the little details that you have to be most concerned with. If it would have made it through to the pharmacy and he took it, there could have been dire consequences."

"Sorry," Maddie mumbled.

"Don't apologize. Just be more vigilant. Bed 6 is complaining about being cold. Will you get her a warming blanket and finish the documentation for these four charts?" She handed the charts over to Maddie, and Maddie nodded, barely able to make eye contact with Jamie. That was how the week seemed to be going. The only time anyone talked to her was to tell her about the mistakes she was making, which made her want to cry. And she couldn't stop thinking about her patients in the Cardio-Pulmonary department, especially the regulars, who she couldn't even say goodbye to.

How was Mike? Did he understand that she didn't just suddenly ditch him? She hoped Eric would be sure to let him know it wasn't her choice. She would give anything to be back there and do the job that she had become accustomed to doing.

Nathan Scott, one of the doctors, approached the nurses' station as Maddie's mind wandered to the floor a few floors down. "Is someone getting Bev her blanket? She's freezing."

"I'm on it." Maddie quickly left the station, grabbed the blanket, and rushed to deliver it. The day-to-day routines of each department were remarkably different. Her day was now an endless barrage of IVs that needed placing and medication orders. She felt like she was drowning in a sea of IV bags and charts. It took her longer than she anticipated to get into a rhythm when assessing post-op patients. Maddie longed to have the issues she had faced the previous week rather than being forced to learn a new structure altogether.

Maddie returned to the station and began the documentation Jamie had left for her. Another instance that Maddie didn't quite comprehend. Why was it the new person's job to ensure that everyone else looked good? She didn't even work with half the patients Jamie had left her. Although, she was sure that probably made sense to all of them. Let them deal with the more intense job tasks, especially when Maddie seemed to fall short in understanding various aspects of her training.

Apparently, she couldn't even transcribe one medication correctly. *They had the same last name, and it could happen to anyone.* Maddie wanted to prove it wouldn't happen to her. Not again.

When she took her lunch, she finally used the time to decompress. She grabbed her phone and pulled up the texts she missed from Eric as he flooded her phone with cat memes, bringing a smile to her face. One of the few times she had smiled —not including the fake smiles she tossed her patients. That thought left a scowl on her face. She scrolled through the memes, laughing at each cat she encountered. She then loaded them into her gallery in case she needed a reason to smile again.

She continued to scroll as she spotted several pictures she had practically forgotten. She and Lourdes smiled back at the phone as they snapped selfies. Each time their smiles grew more prominent and filled with more enthusiasm. Maddie closed out the photos and pushed her phone to the side. Being reminded of the relationship only brought another cloud over her. As she sat there, nibbling on her salad, she returned to her conversation with Eric. Apparently, Lourdes still cared about her if he wasn't messing with her. Even with the sudden flood of changes, Maddie had been trying her best to care for herself. She fought the constant need to work overtime to catch up on charts and silenced the anxious voice that told her she was just another burden for her overworked co-workers in Post-op.

She made good on her promise to relax after the charity auction. Now, she concentrated on relaxing every night after her shift. Her next race wasn't until May, and she had plenty of time to reach out to donors. Instead of pushing herself to the limit when she was already exhausted from trying to learn new things all day, she started taking advantage of the extra daylight and going for leisurely jogs around her neighborhood after her shifts. She couldn't remember the last time she ran or did anything for fun. Much to her chagrin, she invested in a puzzle to work on to entice her to relax and stay off her phone after work. Though it made her feel like an elderly woman, she had to admit that she was having fun, even though Cheddar accidentally ate one of the pieces.

When her dad suggested meditation, she laughed in his face at first, but eventually, she discovered that having a dedicated time to relax was actually relaxing. Slowly yet surely, she was learning how to sit with her feelings, realizing that what she told herself about herself might not be accurate.

Maddie grabbed her phone and pulled up Lourdes' number.

Maddie: I just want you to know I'll be alright. I hope you're okay, too.
Maddie hit send and exhaled, determined to keep moving forward.

CHAPTER THIRTY-ONE

EMBRACING THE POSITIVITY

Maddie woke up to the sound of the text message. She glanced at her phone, and her face fell.

Lourdes: The post-op patients are lucky to have you. Take care of yourself!

Nothing in those two lines told Maddie that Lourdes cared more for her than a mere colleague. As she rolled out of bed and got ready for her day, she continued contemplating Lourdes' text. Why did Lourdes have to sound so cold? Perhaps she shouldn't have wasted her energy by sending Lourdes a text.

You're just disappointed. That's all. You feel let down that she's not falling all over you. But what can you expect? She broke up with you.

Maddie finished off her double shot of espresso and grabbed her keys. A morning jog was just what the doctor ordered. She only had an hour before she had to go to work, so Maddie settled on the hospital track and was grateful that she was the only one getting her run in. By the time she rounded the track three times, she had to get inside. She was undoubtedly a sweaty, energized mess. She ducked inside the bathroom to redo her hair and get ready for the day. Today was going to be the start of her healing journey. Maddie was determined to feel better, even if it was the last thing she did. She grabbed her phone and pulled up her Instagram. It'd been weeks since her latest post. It was time to get back on it. She typed out a message to her followers: *One of the hardest parts about maintaining a healthy lifestyle is finding balance. Remember to take time to actually enjoy your workout!* She snapped a sweaty selfie of her beaming in her scrubs. *Perfect.* She posted it and pocketed her phone, something new for her followers to read was always a great motivation.

She poured herself a cup of coffee and grabbed the last chocolate donut. She was already off to a great start. As she approached the elevator, her stomach tightened, and she clutched it, closing her eyes as the pain subsided. It was only the stress reminding her she still needed to take it easy. She popped the last bite of her donut in her mouth, hoping that getting some food in her stomach would make her feel better, and swallowed. Gradually, the pang in her stomach started to subside. The elevator doors opened, and Lourdes stood there.

The moment they met each other's gaze, Maddie felt her stomach twinge. "Uh, hey," she mumbled. They still worked in the same hospital. It was bound to happen.

"Hey, Maddie." Lourdes stepped off of the elevator, holding the door open for her.

"Have a great day at work."

"Um yeah, thanks." Maddie stepped on, and the doors closed, blocking them from one another, and Maddie clutched her stomach. *Don't let the sight of Lourdes stress you out.* She stayed in that position for a while, not remembering that she still hadn't pushed the button to her floor. Her head ached, and she frowned. Where did the headache come from? She gulped down another gulp of her coffee. If that continued, she'd have to reach for some aspirin.

When the doors opened, she spotted Jamie rushing in one direction as Sophie, another nurse, ran by in the other.

"Where's the fire?" Maddie asked, reaching for Sophie's arm.

Sophie glanced over her shoulder. Her face scrunched up. "A lot of emergencies through the night. One patient went into cardiac arrest. Another checked themselves out of the unit way too early." She shook her head, distressed, "I'm glad you're here. You'll be on your own today. Good luck." She rushed off as Maddie took another sip of her coffee and hurried to the nurses' station. Already, her head was spinning as she calculated her next steps, but she could do this. She took a deep, calming breath and reminded herself that as long as she put her mind to it, she would do well.

That theory was short-lived, though, when she rushed to the bed of Jack Porter, 59 years old, who had undergone emergency hernia surgery at three o'clock in the morning. He had chest pain and some heart arrhythmias after surgery and was at high risk for complications. The team was preparing to transfer him to the cardiac ward. This wasn't supposed to happen. He was supposed to be a quick recovery from hernia surgery, and now the goal was to ensure his heart returned to normal function. When she walked behind the curtain, Maddie was awash with a wave of sudden nostalgia. He was lying down, now hooked to an EKG and BiPAP. A woman, who looked to be his same age, was right next to his side. Maddie looked back at him and saw that his features reminded her of her father's. He had dark hair, a touch of gray, and a beard; even with the machines and the mask, she could almost see a smile.

"How are you doing?" Maddie asked, turning to the woman.

She gave a weak smile, "I've been better. I don't know what could have happened. Last night he was laughing, and within a few hours, he had such horrible pain and couldn't stop vomiting. Then I got a call he was having heart problems in recovery. Everything changed overnight."

"I understand how you're feeling," Maddie began. The woman looked up, her eyes glazed. Maddie went over to the machine and documented his vitals, "But I can see his numbers look good here, and he's improving. Heart problems may be a side effect of the anesthesia medications. He will be okay. You'll see. Besides, he's moving to the best department to handle his care. By these notes, we'll be able to move him as soon as a bed opens. We're looking at no more than an hour."

She nodded. "Thank you! Everyone has been so nice to me."

"We do our best around here, that's for sure. But I know it's still scary. My dad had a heart attack when I was in high school, and he's okay now. He's doing great, actually. But that fear stays with you. I want you to know that your husband is in the best possible place. Cardio is great, I worked there in outpatient for a bit, and the nurses there are going to do everything in their power to assure that your husband gets the best possible care," Maddie reassured her.

She sniffled, "I don't know what I'd do if something happened to him."

Maddie touched her shoulder and gave a slight squeeze. "You're not going to have to find out. I'll leave you for a bit, but let me know if you need anything. Got it?" One of the things that surprised her about post-op was that she had yet to be chastised for spending more time with patients and their loved ones. If anything, the other nurses on the floor encouraged it, especially during times like these when they were left trying to kill time before a transfer.

"Thank you...um..."

"My name is Maddie. Just give me a holler." Maddie left. This was the first time work made her smile since she transferred. She felt relief and pride knowing she had helped ease that woman's fears. For a moment, the pain in her stomach lessened. She reminded herself to drink some water, stay hydrated, and not get caught up in the chaos of the day. She was still a nurse. Even if the department differed, she could still help patients and their loved ones. Maybe Post-op wouldn't be so bad after all.

CHAPTER THIRTY-TWO

AGAINST ALL ODDS

Maddie's spirits continued to brighten as the days went on. The patients needed her. Some Covid restrictions still kept patients from having too many visitors except in dire circumstances. Most patients couldn't have any. She spent most of her time with those patients that seemed scared. Whenever they smiled, Maddie felt a swell of joy and hope. Maybe Post-op would actually appreciate her and her people skills. As the second week ended, she came into her element and, for the first time since the breakup, believed that maybe this was the best department for her. It was a rewarding feeling.

Maddie walked to Bed 12, where a little girl, Abby, seven years old, lay, looking sleepily around the room. Maddie approached the bed. "Hello, Abby. My name is Maddie."

The little girl looked up; her eyes were the deepest blue Maddie had ever seen. "Hello."

"Are you here alone?" Maddie asked, pulling up the chair next to the bed and taking a seat on the girl's right side.

"Mommy had to work. And daddy..." Abby's eyes dimmed.

"Mommy will be here when she's done."

Maddie nodded and looked down at the chart. Her left arm had a severe break that had to be repaired before she was left with worse issues as she grew older and her bones developed more. It wasn't typical for anyone to stay overnight for a procedure like that. However, the hospital had a policy that if the patient couldn't get proper care after the surgery, they would open a bed.

"How's your arm feeling?"

"Okay." She looked up, and her brows furrowed. "Will it always hurt?" she asked.

"Not in the slightest." Maddie closed the chart and leaned in to check the book on Abby's stomach. "*The Velveteen Rabbit*? That's one of my favorite stories."

Abby's smile deepened. "Daddy bought it for me right before...." Her words trailed off, and her eyes grew dim once more.

I'm hungry," she said, changing the subject.

"Alright. What would you like? You have to start with liquids. I can get you some juice or water Or perhaps a popsicle. You name it."

Maddie stood up as Abby lay there in thought.

Her eyes widened, "Popsicle!"

Maddie smiled. "I've gotcha. Give me just one minute."

Abby's eyes closed once more as Maddie left the room and went to the refrigerator at the nurse's station. Jamie looked up and nodded, "Just came out of Abby's room, I see."

"Yeah, the poor thing. She's here alone. I don't know how a family could leave their child right before surgery. It doesn't make any sense."

"Well, in these circumstances, I suspect it makes quite a lot of sense." Jamie looked back at the computer, but Maddie didn't even move a muscle, waiting for Jamie to continue. Jamie looked up and smiled. "Her mother is a single mother, attempting to get by. Abby has five other brothers and sisters. They're all older. Abby's father passed away a year ago. Abby's mom wasn't working at the time. Now, she has two jobs, and she's doing her best. Unfortunately, it's hard for her to manage when trying to maintain a household, put food on the table, etc."

"How do you know so much about the situation?" Maddie grabbed the popsicle from the refrigerator freezer and turned back to Jamie.

"Abby's my niece. My brother died in a motorcycle accident, which shocked everyone. Abby didn't have anyone else to watch her. The others aren't old enough to manage a rambunctious seven-year-old who needs to recover from a major surgery."

Jamie stood up from her computer. "Her mother will be here but not until after ten, and she has to stay in bed until then. Will you ensure they bring her what she can eat before eight?"

Maddie held the items in her hand, "You mean more than this popsicle?"

She smiled, "You betcha. I'll give the cafeteria a call as long as she does ok with liquids."

"Thank you!" Jamie called as Maddie headed back to Abby's room. Abby looked up and grinned.

"You're back?"

"I sure am! And if you do okay with liquids, you get to have real food for dinner! You name it, and I'll make sure it's ready for you." The smile on Abby's face was enough to light up the room. As Abby hungrily sucked on the red popsicles that Maddie provided her, Maddie left and went to the front desk. She dialed the cafeteria and gave them her order. "Chicken tenders, Mac and Cheese, French fries, and chocolate milk. Have it up here by 7:15. Thank you!"

Treva, another fellow nurse, approached the desk as Maddie hung up the call. "You're all smiley," Treva observed.

Maddie shrugged. "I guess it's just a good day. Mind if I take a break?"

"I'll be here - forever. Charting." Treva barely broke a smile before looking down at her computer. Maddie rolled her eyes. Nothing was going to hurt her good mood. A sharp pain returned to her gut when she got on the elevator. She held onto the side of the elevator and closed her eyes. Her stress was working its way out of her system. She had to give it time. Rome wasn't built in a day.

When she got to the break room, she went straight to her locker and grabbed some aspirin from her purse. She opened her bottle of water and downed the two pills. It wasn't coffee, but she would make do. Maddie fell against the locker and slowly massaged her temples until the pain subsided partially.

"Maddie?"

Maddie whirled around to find Eric. He ran over to her and threw his arms around her, knocking her back against the lockers. "Hey there!"

Maddie closed her eyes. The pounding in her skull was only a dull knocking at that point.

"I'm so glad to see you. How are things going? Tell me everything." Maddie barely had the door slammed shut on her locker before Eric pulled her over to one of the tables and sat them down. "How's Post-op? How are you? How's your dad? Well, you get the gist. How's life?"

Maddie smiled. "Things are good." *Despite the massive headache I just came down from.* "There's this sweet seven-year-old I'm managing today. She's all alone, and I can tell she needs someone to look out for her. And all the other patients have been amazing. I love my boss up there. Jamie and I are getting along great. And I'm slowly getting to know the other staff. There are a few obnoxious docs, but they're fine. She took a sip of her water. "All in all, though, things are pretty stellar."

"You're smiling, so that's a great sign." Eric reached out and squeezed her arm.

He continued, "Work has been going well, too. It's been busy, busier since you, well, you know."

Maddie sipped on her water, staring at the bottle. She'd be ecstatic if only the bottle would turn into a strong cup of coffee.

"Lourdes asked about you," Eric blurted.

Maddie frowned. "Oh yeah?" She took a long, drawn-out drink while staring at Eric. "What'd she say?"

Eric grinned. "That is proof you haven't forgotten her. You're brimming with hope, desire ... dare I say, love?"

Maddie's cheeks burned as she looked down at her bottle. "It was a simple question. When I hear that anyone is asking about me, I give the same response."

"Uh yeah, sure. But, anyway, Lourdes said that she hopes you are flourishing in Post-op and to tell you that she says hi."

Maddie's eyes widened.

"Well, I added that last part, but I'm sure she'd want me to tell you that," Eric admitted.

Maddie shook her head. "The hopeless romantic. But, if you get the chance, tell her I'm flourishing, so no worries there." She stood up from the table and tossed her water bottle into the trash can.

"It can't possibly be time for you to go back yet, can it?"

"I'm only on a break." She hesitated before smiling. "It was good to see you, Eric. Tell everyone I said hey." She winked and then hurried towards the door before she could change her mind on that last remark. If he wanted to share that with Lourdes, he could, and she wouldn't mind.

Maddie thought about it. She felt relieved that Lourdes even bothered to ask about her. Yet, she didn't want to get her hopes up. Maybe Eric was exaggerating. If she overthought the matter, she would send Lourdes another awkward text, which would get them nowhere.

Maddie stepped off the elevator and spotted Treva and Jamie at the nurses' station. The closer she got, she heard Treva's voice, "Maddie seems nice and all, but she really needs to up her game. I feel like I'm caring for triple the number of patients she does. I get she's new, but I'm tired of covering for her. She's slowing down the workflow. You know it as well as I do. If she doesn't change something soon, I will have to say something to Pauline. I'll have no choice."

Maddie's gut tightened as Treva's words rang in her ears. For the first time, she thought she was making a difference in a place where everyone understood her, but now Maddie was right back where she came from.

CHAPTER THIRTY-THREE

DISCOURAGED AND ANGERED

Maddie backed away from the nurses' station when she heard Treva talking about her. She felt hurt that Jamie didn't even stick up for her once. Maddie thought they were friends. It was disappointing to see how wrong she was. If she had been in the same situation as Jamie, she would have at least acknowledged that maybe everyone needed to evaluate their work ethic and patient relationships. Why was it that Maddie was the one that was in the wrong?

After overhearing the conversation, she tried to avoid Jamie and Treva. It would be awkward to run into them, and if Jamie caught her eavesdropping, Maddie would be mortified. To her relief, it was easy. Everyone was also avoiding her.

Two hours after she was supposed to be out of the hospital, she spotted the cafeteria worker bringing the food to Abby's room. Maddie greeted her at the door, "I'll take this for her."

"As you wish." The woman left the tray with Maddie, and Maddie entered Abby's room.

"Your dinner is here. Everything you asked for." She stopped when she saw Jamie sitting beside Abby.

Jamie frowned, "Your shift was over a couple of hours ago."

"Well, I had a few things I needed to get done."

189

Maddie pushed the tray closer to the bed. " I didn't know you were still here."

Jamie looked down at her niece, "I thought I would stick it out until my sister-in-law gets here." She then looked up. "But you probably should get out of here. I heard they're not happy now with anyone working OT."

Maddie shrugged, "I'll handle it. Have a good night." She turned and left Abby's room, a sharp pain caught in her stomach. She shook it off and made her way to the nurses' station. She was about to leave when she spotted Bill Bristow headed her way. Maddie groaned and looked around to see where she could dart or go unnoticed. It was too late as he stopped at the desk. Bill was the union rep for the hospital. It was never a good sign whenever he came out in the open, "Hello, Bill."

"Maddie." He stopped at the desk and looked down at the clipboard. "I'm just here to give you a friendly reminder. No OT is allowed, especially when you plan on working without pay. You have to stop this immediately, Maddie. And I know you have been warned about this before."

Maddie nodded, unable to muster up much strength to give her response.

"I need to know you truly understand the consequences that can come of this if you don't stop."

"I understand." Maddie dropped her gaze, and he nodded.

"I hope we don't have to see each other again. If I do, then you'll know...." His words trailed off as Maddie looked up and watched him leave. Just another negative mark on her record, and it broke her heart. She grabbed her water and hurried away from the desk, ready to go home even with her wounded dignity.

After clocking out and grabbing her things, she made her way to the elevator to get out of the hospital and to a safe place where she could cry. To her surprise, though, the tears didn't come. She sat in her car waiting for them, but she might have finally gotten to the point where she couldn't shed any more tears. Also, the anger inside her might have something to do with the tears staying away. She grabbed her phone and pulled up her father's number. She leaned back in her seat and waited for him to answer.

"Hello?"

"Hey, Dad. How are you doing?"

"Hey, Sweetheart. I'm doing well; no complaints here. How are you?"

Maddie sighed. "I wish I could say the same. The fact is, though, I'm just frustrated with work."

"Oh? I thought you said that the department was going well. You seemed positive about it. Something's changed?"

"It's just. I'm beginning to think I'm the only one that cares about patients. My boss reprimanded me for working overtime and not getting paid for it. But they don't allow paid overtime, so I don't know how exactly they expect me to get everything done, manage the care the patients deserve, and do it in a regular work shift. It annoys me."

"Honey, you sound stressed. I know You have been working late again. It hardly seems fair to you if you're not getting paid for it. Whatever happened to your puzzle? Did you listen to that meditation I sent you?" Maddie listened to what he said, but it wasn't fully sinking in. Granted, she was taking better care of herself than she was a month ago, but it was hard to resist the temptation to slip back into old patterns, especially when Maddie already felt like she was playing catch-up with her new department. She didn't mind going the extra mile for her patients.

"Okay, I haven't had time to work on my puzzle lately. I'll admit I've been pulling more than a couple of late nights. But it's fine. I'm fine. Everything's fine. Except it's not. But I'm fine," she insisted.

"Are you sure you're alright?"

"Yes, I'm fine." Maddie's stomach twinged again. It felt like her intestines were trying to eat each other. She made a mental note to run by Walgreens on her way home and buy more Tums. She held her stomach as if trying to tamp down the lies she spewed. "I'm just frustrated, but anyone that has to work for a living has to understand that. It's all good, though."

"I hope so."

"I promise you. I'm doing alright. I'll let you go. I love you."

"Love you, too, Sweetheart. Let me know if you need anything, okay?"

"I will," Maddie promised. She hung up the call, her hands clenching the steering wheel although she hadn't inched out of the parking lot. Maddie couldn't believe how alone she was when she thought she had finally turned a corner. She stared straight ahead, the hospital lights shining back at her. Why doesn't anyone care about her hard work, relieved that someone is finally picking up the slack for everyone? She shook her head. She got into nursing to be a beacon for everyone who needed help, but it wouldn't work if she were the only one who noted those struggling. And someone had to do something to make a change. Maddie didn't want to be the only one doing her part.

CHAPTER THIRTY-FOUR

HER WEAKENING

Maddie grabbed her keys and purse and headed for the car. She had plenty of time to get an extra long run in. After her double shot of espresso, Maddie was rearing to go. She had just reached the park when her phone started ringing. Eric's number came through her Bluetooth. She sighed. She had intended to ignore his calls. After the way her shift ended yesterday, she wanted to do what she could to avoid anyone, at least until she got to work.

"Hello?" She turned into the park and waited in the parking spot.

"Hey there? How's it going?"

"Since yesterday? I guess it's going alright. And you?"

"Great! So, my sister is in town. I thought you might want to come over for dinner or something when you have a free night. She'll be here a couple of weeks, and I think it'd do you good to hang with some friends. What do you say?"

"I don't know, Eric." Maddie got out of the car and started a slight jog as she slipped her earpiece into place. "I think I'd rather sit around and sulk."

"Come on, Maddie. That's no fun. I think you guys would get along splendidly. Wouldn't you want to meet my sister? After all, we've been friends for a while. I'd love for you to meet my family. You know, branch out a little bit.

"I've been out with you and James a few times." She continued to jog, this time picking up the pace. "It's just not a great time. Maybe sometime in the future."

He huffed. "I guess if I can't change your mind...."

"You really can't." Her breathing turned a little more ragged as she ran harder. "But it's not a no, just a not now sort of thing. Your sister's here for business all the time, right? I'm sure we'll catch up sometime soon. But I gotta go. I'm in the middle of a run. Talk soon, Eric." She disconnected the call and continued to run, the intensity burning in her legs and then her lungs. She wouldn't mind meeting his sister, but it wasn't the right time. As she ran, she squinted, drawing nearer to a man no more than a thousand feet from her. *I don't believe it.* The closer she got, the more she knew her eyes weren't deceiving her. She looked around, diverting her gaze from one side of the park to the other. Yet, she couldn't escape the awkward encounter, especially when his eyes closed on her.

"Maddie?"

Maddie came to a halt, and she smiled at him. "Mike! How are you doing?"

He pulled her into a hug, surprising her. "I was sad when I got the news," he said, slowly releasing from the grasp, "They said you wanted to transfer departments."

So that was the story they were going with. Maddie nodded, wanting to make it a little more bearable. "But I've missed seeing you! How are you? What's been going on? How have you been feeling?"

He stretched and grinned. "I've been staying healthy and fit, doing the exercises." His eyes dipped. "It hasn't been the same, though."

Those words tore at her, and she took in a breath. She couldn't cry, not when Mike was staring at her, expecting to see a woman who asked for this. "Honestly, I've missed you and all my other regular patients. I'm sorry I'm not there to greet you at your appointments."

He grinned. "As long as I know you're doing well."

"I'm doing alright." She glanced around, her eyes catching the distance. When she turned back to him, he had his arm around a boy who looked like his spitting image.

"This is my son, Myles."

"Myles, it is a pleasure. I've heard a lot of things about you." She shook his hand. ". Are you still playing baseball together?"

"We are." Mike beamed. "It was great to see you, Maddie."

"Likewise, Mike. You take care. Nice to meet you, Myles!" She waved to them both, then took back off on her jog.

As she left them, she felt the tears stinging the back of her eyes and forced herself to speed up into a sprint. She missed her patients. And she missed Lourdes. But neither would return to her if she didn't give it some time. When she returned to her car an hour later, Maddie was exhausted. She collapsed against the car and stood there, her legs wobbly and aching, her chest burning. Maddie clutched her stomach as the pain seeped through her body. She should have eaten the yogurt, along with the coffee. Maddie was hungry, no doubt. She'd have to grab a sandwich sometime soon. Her phone buzzed., It was a text from Eric with a photo that read, *My sister.* Maddie rolled her eyes and stuffed her phone back into her pocket. She couldn't handle the prospect of meeting someone new right now. *See? You do know your* limits, she consoled herself. Maddie opened the car door and reached into the console, retrieving some Ibuprofen and popping them into her mouth. She downed them with a large gulp of water and touched her forehead. She was soaked with sweat and needed to get to the hospital for her eight-hour shift. Maybe it wasn't wise to take such a long run on an empty stomach right before work. She'd also been inhaling aspirin. She collapsed into the driver's seat and lowered her head to the steering wheel, unable to stifle the sobs. She tried a breathing technique, but that just made her pay even more attention to the feeling that her throat was closing up into the size of a pinhole. Still, she had to be there for her patients if that was her only reason to persevere.

CHAPTER THIRTY-FIVE

OVERWORKED AND DROWNING

Maddie stifled a yawn as her alarm clock continued to ring. She groaned. *Why?* She finally had a day off, and she'd made sure to shut off her alarm the night before. Still, the alarm sounded. However, as the sound droned on, she realized it wasn't her alarm clock. She kept her eyes closed and reached for her phone. After a few seconds, her hand finally latched onto the phone and opened her eyes to answer the call.

"Hello?"

"Hello, Maddie? This is Pauline."

Maddie sat up in her bed, her supervisor's voice ringing in her ear.

"Hello, Pauline?" She glanced at her watch. Had she misread the schedule? Was she supposed to be at the hospital right now? It was just after nine o'clock, an hour after she'd usually be there. But she was confident that she had the day off. She'd been relieved that she had the day off. She'd planned her whole day the night before a healthy breakfast of avocado toast, followed by some quick morning yoga and a jog around her neighborhood, before finally dusting off her puzzle. Granted, she'd only had the edges finished, but at least her dad could finally stop badgering her to get a hobby.

"I'm sorry to bother you at home. I know you've worked seven days

TOO LITTLE TOO LATE?

straight, but would it be possible for you to come in today? I'll ensure you have tomorrow off if you can come in this morning and work until seven. I know it's short notice, but Jamie has food poisoning, and Sophie has a fever. It's all a mess. I'm really in a bind. I understand if you have plans, but I was hoping you could do me a favor, just this once," She rambled on so long, leaving little opportunity for Maddie to respond. As exhausted as she was, she couldn't turn down the invitation to work. Maddie was still trying to prove herself as an asset to the department. If she worked today, it would make her look dependable and seem invaluable.

After a beat, Maddie responded, "I'll do it. It's not a problem at all. And if you need me tomorrow, I'll be there, too,"

Pauline breathed a heavy sigh from the other end of the line. "That hopefully won't be necessary. I'm sorry I had to call you in on your day off. So, what time do you think you can get here?"

Maddie tossed back her covers and caught a glimpse of her clock. "I'll shoot for ten-fifteen. See you in a bit." She disconnected the call and didn't hesitate to hurry to the kitchen and put on her espresso machine. She hopped in the shower while it brewed. Maddie was showered and dressed in five minutes flat. Maddie poured herself two cups of coffee and raced out the door. She had plenty of time to get to the hospital when she quoted her boss. Once inside the hospital, Maddie hurried to the break room to clock in, then stepped into the bathroom to finally get a few minutes of deep breaths.

Maddie stared at her reflection in the restroom mirror. Her eyes were still red from crying all night. She was exhausted, and she couldn't fathom going on another minute. She raised her hand and filled it with two pills, placing them in her mouth, then downing it with her second cup of coffee. After all, it was the only thing that would help her to survive the day. She tossed the cup and leaned forward into the mirror.

"This is your eighth and final day, Maddie. You've got this. You are not going to fail now." It was an easy fix. She didn't have to be at the hospital this morning, but something in Pauline's voice tore at her, and she knew that if she helped her out, it would be a saving grace.

It took every ounce of her being to drive to the hospital just now. Maddie's hands shook as she covered her face, pulling her cheeks down to stare at her red eyes. No matter what, she would have to stand her ground if Pauline returned and said she needed to work again tomorrow. What Maddie needed was a good twenty-four hours in bed.

Maddie shook her head furiously. "Oh, brother." She reached for the knob on the sink, barely able to control it because her hands were shaking so badly. Once the water was falling, she loaded her palms and splashed some water onto her face. All she had to do was make it through the next nine hours. Then she'd get a twenty-four-hour break. She could do this.

As she left the bathroom, she spotted two nurses in scrubs walking past. They both glanced at her and nodded but kept on walking. Maddie's legs shook as she walked down the hall and to the elevator. As she waited for the elevator to come down to meet her, she leaned against the wall, her eyes zoned in on the numbers counting down. She started to feel light-headed and looked at the floor. The elevator dinged, and the doors opened. Luckily, she had the elevator to herself.

As the doors closed, she fell back against the wall. The dizziness continued, and she felt like the walls were slowly closing on her. Maddie's chest started to feel heavy, and her body went numb. *Is this how it feels to have a heart attack?* Maddie lowered herself to the elevator's corner, her knees to her chest, her heart racing. She rocked back and forth, desperate for her heart to stop racing.

"You've got this... you've got this..." she kept reciting, but the tears told her otherwise. The bell on the elevator dinged, and the doors opened. Maddie couldn't even look up as the pain in her body took over, and her eyes blurred. She looked down, her head nestled nicely against her lap. "You've got this...you've got this..."

"Maddie?" As she continued to rock, her head comfortably pressed between her legs, she felt arms around her. "Go get a wheelchair. Stat!"

"You've got this... you've got this...they need me. I have to get to work. You've got this."

"I have you, Maddie. You're going to be just fine."

Maddie swallowed, her eyes closing ever tighter. She had to get through this day. She was in a fog, and her body was full of tremors.

"You're safe. Just hang in there." The voice was soothing and controlling, but Maddie's tears were freely running down her cheeks. Her heart continued racing, and she felt the world caving around her.

"You've got this... you've got this... you've got this...I have to get to work. Pauline's expecting me. You've got this."

It felt like an eternity before the wheelchair appeared, and two people were lifting her into a seated position. Maddie dropped her head as someone took charge and helped her to another floor. It was all a blur, but before she could look up, she was being taken from the elevator and pushed through a set of double doors.

"We need help!" They called out, and then a crew of people came running toward them. Someone hauled Maddie onto a bed, her eyes finally attempting to open to stare at the ceiling.

"You've got this!" Maddie mumbled. "They need me. Pauline called me. I have to get to work. Where's Pauline? Someone needs to tell Pauline. You've got this."

Two nurses stood opposite her. One hooked her up to the EKG, and another worked on her blood pressure cuff and pulse machine. The beeping sound lingered in her mind as she felt her head swaying back and forth.

"Her BP has skyrocketed." The nurse helped her to open her mouth, and Maddie barely registered the dissolvable pill she slipped inside.

"We should call her family," a man spoke up.

"Someone needs to be here."

Tears stuck in the corner of Maddie's eyes as she held onto those words. What was happening? Was it a heart attack? She forced herself to push that thought to the side. Her dad would be devastated if that was what took her out of this world. As the staff ran around her, checking her vitals, the pain in Maddie's gut nearly jolted her out of bed. She grunted, but she wasn't able to move. The pain seared through her body, and darkness overcame her.

Maddie wasn't sure how long she had been out. But when she opened her eyes, a pain shot through her arm, and she looked down to see an IV stuck into her vein. When did that happen? She looked around. A nurse was documenting something in her chart. She looked up and gave a bright smile.

"There you are." The soothing woman's voice came to her, and Maddie blinked. Maddie looked around the room. She had wires coming out of her. A faint beep filled the room, deafening her ears. Maddie had no recollection of getting hooked up to the machines. She turned to the nurse. She vaguely remembered her. Susan, was it? Perhaps, Susie.

She opened her mouth, but words failed her.

"Don't try to talk. Have a drink of water." The woman thrust the cup in front of her and gently helped her to take a sip. Maddie swallowed and nodded, spotting her name tag as she did. Sue, close enough. She licked her dry lips and turned back to the machine. The numbers went up, then down, then back up again. Her blood pressure was a bit elevated.

"What?" she squeaked out.

The woman raised an eyebrow and once again tried to give Maddie water. Maddie pushed it away, swallowing hard, and took a deep breath.

"Why am I here?" Maddie whispered. "What happened? I have to get to work."

The woman tilted her head, "You don't remember?"

Maddie shook her head, frowning as she tried to focus on what brought her to that bed. The monitor beeped faster, and Maddie shot a look to her right.

"Just calm down," Sue replied.

"Everything is going to be alright."

"What?" Maddie pulled back as Sue moved in and hovered over her.

"You're restless, and your B/P is still high. I'll see if I can start you on pain medicine."

Maddie shifted in bed. She was in horrible pain. Her stomach clenched, and her heart started pounding. Maddie leaned back, and her eyes narrowed at the ceiling. Why wouldn't the pain go away? As her jaw tightened, she closed her eyes. Her head started spinning, and she couldn't hang on any longer. The darkness returned.

CHAPTER THIRTY-SIX

BREAKING POINT

Maddie woke with a start. She looked down at the IV and groaned. For a moment, Maddie thought it was all a dream. She frowned as she realized one crucial detail. She wasn't feeling any pain. They must've drugged her, and she wasn't sorry about that. She closed her eyes. She was so tired, though. The medication was doing its job, but why was she here? What brought her to need to be in the hospital bed, and how did she get there?

"You're awake!" She drew her eyes to the door as Sue came in, a smile on her face. "How are you feeling?" Maddie opened her mouth. Her throat was so dry. She swallowed and leaned back against her pillow as Sue rushed to her side. "Take this." She helped her suck on a straw, and Maddie sighed in relief as she sipped the cool water. It was like she hadn't had a drink in years.

"Thank you," Maddie whispered. "I'm feeling a tad better."

"That's what I like to hear." How was it that Sue was so cheery and happy? She wasn't in a rush to get out of there. She was handling Maddie's case with care. It was how Maddie recalled nursing should be without hospital politics.

"I'm going to step out and grab the doctor. He wanted to see you when you woke up."

Maddie nodded, closing her eyes. It wouldn't be long enough if she could sleep for a thousand years. "Maddie?"

She opened her eyes and saw a young man at her door. He couldn't be more than twenty-five. She gave him a once-over and glared. He smirked when she met his gaze.

"I'm Dr. Mallone. And I know what you're thinking, but I assure you I received my MD and everything." He winked, and Maddie dropped her gaze, feeling two feet tall. Why was she being sarcastic? She didn't have a thing to base her prejudice on other than he looked to be twelve. Okay, twenty-five, but still. He didn't seem like a seasoned professional. Yet, she wasn't there to judge. She was there to find out what had happened. And more importantly, who brought her to the ER to get help?

"So, that was quite a scary experience you faced earlier. I imagine you have questions, and I have questions."

He pulled up a rolling stool right up to her bedside. "Shall we get started?"

"I don't know," she barely squeaked out. "I'm not even sure how I got here, let alone why I'm here." She swallowed again and shot a look at the cup of water.

"Here. Allow me." He grabbed the cup and helped it up to her lips. She nodded as she took a quick sip.

"Thank you," she mumbled.

"So, I'm not sure if I'll be able to provide you with much insight." He'd have more luck talking to a wall. Or possibly the person that brought her to the ER, but for that to happen, they would both have to do some investigating.

"I see. Well, let's start with what you do remember. I mean, before waking up in the ER. Surely you've had some symptoms. When did they occur? What symptoms were you having? Maddie frowned. "What kind of symptoms? I mean, people have headaches and stomachaches all the time. It doesn't necessarily mean something's wrong with them." Maddie's heart picked up in speed, and she dropped her gaze. She knew what he was referring to, but if she confessed all, she was admitting that she had a problem. Still, it was nothing she couldn't work out herself. If she got home, she would be just fine.

"Dr. Mallone, I appreciate people's concern. I do. But if someone can get this IV out of me and let me go home, I will surely recuperate much better. I'm fine. I feel perfectly normal." Her head started spinning, and Maddie leaned back on her pillow and closed her eyes.

"Shall we continue?" he asked. Maddie groaned but nodded. "What you were most likely experiencing in the elevator was a standard panic attack. But I will run a couple of tests to rule out any other issues. This is a serious matter, Maddie. And my gut is telling me that you waited too long to be seen."

"Panic attacks? Elevator?"

His brows furrowed. "You really don't remember, do you? You must have lost time."

Maddie sighed. The only thing she remembered was waking up in the hospital room. She closed her eyes, dizziness creeping back into her brain.

"Dr. Mallone," she began. "Have things been stressful over the last month or so? Sure. Have I been handling it poorly? Undoubtedly."

She opened her eyes and shrugged. "But if I promise to take a couple of days off, don't you think I can get out of here?"

"Maddie, you do not quite understand the complexity of the issue. You're going to need off more than a couple of days. We have drawn your blood and are running more tests. The panic attack is merely the one conclusion I'm drawing here. I have diagnosed you with GERD. Gastro..."

She waved him away. "I'm a nurse. I know what it is."

She dropped her gaze to the blankets that covered her, "But I also know that doesn't usually require a hospital stay."

He raised his hand. "And a possible ulcer. Later today, they will come in and prepare you for an EGD." Maddie dropped her mouth, and he arched an eyebrow.

"We have to confirm or deny if it's bleeding. Again, this is a serious matter. And if you can't remember anything...." He stood up from his stool.

Maddie tossed her head back, "I've been under some stress." He slowly sat down on the stool. "That's been going on for almost two months. I've been supplementing the stress with coffee, soda, and a less than complimentary diet. But I've been trying to manage my stress better! I downloaded a meditation app!" He didn't need to know that Maddie never had time to open the app. She wasn't proud of how she'd been handling herself. She didn't even want to admit it, but if she was going to have any hope of getting out of the hospital anytime soon, she needed to start talking. Dr. Mallone continued to take notes, and Maddie felt this burden slowly lifting off of her.

"Maybe I needed to seek out help, but frankly, there haven't been enough hours in the day to have time to get that help."

He nodded and looked up, "So, you continued to do what was putting the stress on you. Day by day, week by week. And it led you to this hospital bed."

"You're the doctor," she muttered.

He smirked. "Well, it was only a matter of time before it would all catch up to you." He stood back up. "We'll get the EGD scheduled and possibly run some more blood work later. If you feel the pain return, call for the nurse, and she'll get you another round."

"As for this bed...." Her words trailed off.

"After the EGD, you'll be admitted and put in another room. You'll need to stay for at least another night of observation, no matter what the EGD points out. Staying overnight will give you time to really rest. Take it as your vacation."

"Some vacation." Maddie rolled her eyes.

He continued to smile. "You have a couple of guests that have been waiting until you were able to have visitors. I'll send one of them in now."

Maddie looked up. Guests? Who? She yawned as he left her room. She had to put on a smile and smile at whoever walked through the door. She could sleep once she had a few minutes alone. As she waited, she looked over at the monitor. Her BP was regulated now, perhaps because they gave her some medicine to lower it. Maddie released a shallow breath and nervously twisted her hands together. The last thing she remembered was stepping out of the restroom to rush off to her eighth day of work. *Work!* Surely the department knew what had transpired earlier and why she didn't show up to her shift.

Her thoughts were interrupted when her father rushed around the corner and into her room. "Maddie! I was so worried." He ran over to the bed, and Maddie couldn't control the tears as her father held her in her arms and consoled her. It was good to see her dad, but all she wanted to do was go home.

HER DAD CONTINUED TO STARE AT HER LIKE SHE WAS GOING to break at any minute. She cringed. "Don't look at me like I'm some porcelain doll."

He laughed. "So, in other words, don't look at you the way you looked at me when I was in the hospital."

Maddie scoffed. "That was different." He shook his head, and Maddie continued to wring her hands. He had been there only half an hour, but they hadn't said much to one another. Mostly he just watched her, observed her, and didn't bother making too many remarks. She was alright with that because she mostly feared that at any given moment, he would scold her, tell her she needed to take better care of herself and admonish her for letting it get to this point.

"Well, honey, as much as I wish I could stay here all day...." He got up from his chair, and Maddie followed him with her eyes. "There's someone else outside that is itching to see you." Maddie's eyes widened. Who could that be? *Lourdes?*

"He's been waiting just as long as I have."

"He?" Maddie asked, sudden disappointment hitting her straight to the gut.

"Eric. I'll send him right in."

Maddie smiled. Of course, Eric would want to come to see her. That was sweet of him to make an appearance. Her father gave her a quick hug and then was out the door to retrieve Eric from the waiting room. It would have been nice if Lourdes had decided to visit her, but she couldn't expect that to happen overnight. She and Lourdes were still in such a strange place. Lourdes probably thought she deserved this.

Eric rounded the corner, his face crumpling with worry. He sighed as he reached her. "Don't you ever freak me out like that again? You hear?" He wrapped his arms around her, and Maddie sighed with happiness that he was there.

"I have been pacing in the waiting room. I've nearly worn a hole in the carpeting. I get it. We still have COVID restrictions. You can only have one guest at a time, but I was about to break some knees if they didn't allow me in here."

Maddie laughed, then clutched her stomach as she shook her head. "Don't make me laugh."

"Do you want me to leave?" he teased.

"No!" She reached for his hand and pulled him closer to the bed, and he fell into the bedside chair. "I'm glad you're here. And I'm not surprised that the rumor mill went rampant, and you found out what happened."

Maddie shook her head. "What was it? Ten seconds flat?"

He quirked up his eyebrow. "Found out what happened? I was there when it happened, you goof. Of course, I knew you were here." He shook his head. "You had the whole department in a fury. Do you know that even Sierra blames herself? Don't get me started on Lourdes. She was screaming off orders like a drill sergeant.."

Maddie frowned. "Huh?"

They stared at one another, neither one's eyes diverting from the other until Eric frowned. "Don't you remember?"

"Frankly, I can't remember much of anything. I remember coming out of the restroom after taking three ibuprofen with my coffee. Then everything goes black."

He smacked his forehead. "Well, right there, explains it. Three ibuprofen with your coffee? Maddie, Maddie, Maddie." He shook his head. His nose scrunched up. "The elevator doors opened on our floor. I may never know why, seeing you no longer work in that department. You were huddled up in the corner of the elevator, just bawling. Lourdes was the first one to see you. She came running to your aid, barking orders, and wouldn't leave your side until she knew you were in good hands and she had a stream of waiting patients." He shook his head. "If that isn't love, I don't know what is."

For a moment, Maddie felt reassured. She knew that Lourdes loved her. Only Lourdes could make a breakup seem like kindness. But it felt nice to know that Lourdes was by her side. Still, she didn't want to get her hopes up. "She's compassionate and caring," Maddie argued. "I was probably just a patient in her eyes."

Eric huffed. "If that's the case, then why did she specifically grab me and ask me to relay the message on how you're doing? Maddie, you may think what you want. I'm telling you, seeing you struggle broke Lourdes' heart. She cares about you still. I think she's always going to care about you."

Maddie had a lump that wouldn't dissipate from her throat. She swallowed hard, but it remained. "Water."

He grabbed the cup and helped her to drink, but Maddie used it as her moment to think about his words. She wanted to believe them, but as her heart raced a little more, she wasn't sure if it was her illness or thoughts of Lourdes. Either way, Maddie wished she could talk to Lourdes right then. But Maddie's wishes weren't realistic. Lourdes was right to break things off. Maddie needed to learn how to take better care of herself, or her job and health would be at risk. Her shoddy attempts at self-care weren't enough. She had to make serious changes unless she wanted to wind up in another hospital bed. Lourdes saw the signs of Maddie's deterioration, even if Maddie was oblivious. It was funny, almost. Maddie had built up a following instructing others how to live their best lives, but she was the one who needed to make some lifestyle changes.

CHAPTER THIRTY-SEVEN

MUCH NEEDED VACATION

The past twenty-four hours were a flurry of activity, from the EGD to more blood tests, a nurse rushing in periodically to check on her vitals, and Dr. Mallone peeking in a couple of times to check on her. As it stood, there wasn't any news. While Maddie did have an ulcer, it wasn't bleeding. The only meds she needed were acid-relieving medications and a light regimen of antibiotics. Doctors were also adamant that Maddie had to fix her diet. Nutrition used to be so high on Maddie's list, so Maddie was confident that she could return to where she once was.

The next day after lunch, Dr. Mallone paid her another visit. Maddie was comforted by his confident smile. At least she was comfortable in her temporary surroundings.

"Hello, Dr. Mallone."

"And how's my patient?" He grabbed a stool and pulled it closer to her. "Are you feeling better today?"

She nodded. She had to admit that she could rest more here than she would be at home, even with the intermittent interruptions. Luckily they had medicines that were helping her to relax. At this point, she wasn't disappointed that she was missing work. They would survive until she could be back on her feet and ready to assist the patients. Her patients needed her to be rested and healthy anyway.

"Good to hear. So, I just wanted to warn you about something so you didn't feel like we were leaving you in the dark."

Maddie frowned. "Is something wrong? Did you find something on my tests? You can be straight with me. I'm a big girl."

He reached out and touched her arm. "Whoa, calm down. Nothing as drastic as that. It's just that the truth is the medication can only help you for so long. There's more than you'll need, but you also have to be open to it. We can't pressure you into anything, but I can make a strong suggestion." Maddie frowned. Whatever it was, it didn't sound great. He was preparing her for a grave situation. She could feel it. She looked down at her clenched hands. Maddie exhaled and nodded, prepared to hear whatever Dr. Mallone needed to tell her. "I have ordered a Psych evaluation for you for tomorrow."

"What?" Maddie squealed. "A psych evaluation? Dr. Mallone, I'm fine. Sure, I get anxious sometimes, but it's nothing I can't handle. I mean, yes, I've been more than a little stressed lately, but you said it yourself, I need some rest. I don't want to waste psych's time. I know we're slammed around here.."

"Now, Maddie. You're not being reasonable. The fact remains that you had a panic attack yesterday morning. It's not normal, and if you don't get down to the root cause, then all the medication in the world won't help you. It's a routine evaluation. It won't hurt. If anything, millions of people with anxiety have found that their lives have greatly improved once they introduced medication."

Maddie shook her head. She wasn't one of those patients. This all seemed inappropriate and unnecessary. "I appreciate your concern, but it's not needed."

He stood up. "With all due respect, you're being stubborn."

"Dr. Mallone, we need you in the ER. Five car pile up, and they're short on hands."

"I'm coming." He looked back at her. "Just consider it. Please. I understand you're concerned about how you'll be perceived. But I can promise you that none of that will matter if you find yourself back in the hospital. I have to go, but I'll wait for your answer."

He turned around and left the room. Maddie didn't want to be stubborn about the matter but was already getting medicine. Why couldn't that be the answer? She would seek out friends and her dad to get her help if she needed something else. That's what would be most beneficial to her.

There was a knock on her door. She looked up and saw Millicent, one of the morning nurses. "Good morning, my dear." Millicent was in her early sixties but still moving like she had forty years left. She had a bounce that reminded Maddie that age was merely a number. This morning she had flowers in her hand and placed them on the bedside table.

"For me?"

"Yep. Someone just dropped them off. There's even a card." She handed the card over to Maddie. "Do you need anything before I give you your space to enjoy the beautiful bouquet?"

"No. I'm good. Thank you!" Maddie waited until Millicent left the room, and she opened the envelope, revealing a card with flowers the same color as her bouquet.

The simple writing on the front read, *Thinking of you.* Inside, the inscription read: *Just wanted to drop you a line, Maddie, and tell you how much you have been in my thoughts over the past twenty-four hours. I hope that you get some much-needed rest. I care about you greatly and hate to see you in pain. With love, Lourdes.* Maddie read through the card three times, tears stinging the back of her eyes. If Lourdes cared enough to give her this beautiful bouquet and card, then maybe it was time for Maddie to follow through with her supposed lifestyle changes. She figured it wouldn't kill her to look into the meditation app. Maddie missed taking time to cook for herself. She used to make so many elaborate meals. Cooking used to be fun. For the past couple of months, she'd treated her body like an afterthought. It was time for her to take herself seriously.

Maddie flicked the tears from her eyes and hit the call button. It wasn't even a minute before Millicent rushed into the room. "You need something?"

"Will you please let Dr. Mallone know I'll consent to the psych evaluation?"

"Gladly, Maddie. Need anything else?"

"Maybe some more water."

"My pleasure." Millicent left, and Maddie read the card three times. It was just the right push she needed to ensure she would get better. For the past two months, almost everyone told her she needed to get better. But with Lourdes, it was different. She had never felt such genuine love before in her life, and she wanted to be worthy of that love. She wanted to be the best possible partner for Lourdes. But she also wanted to be the best nurse for her patients, to give them the care they deserved without whittling herself away into a husk of who she once was. She wanted to get better, not just because Lourdes loved her, but because she loved herself, too.

CHAPTER THIRTY-EIGHT

DOCTOR'S ORDERS

To say it was a relief to be home was an understatement. But two days later, when Maddie could rest in her own bed, she realized then how much she had taken for granted. Her dad had pleaded with her to allow him to stay at her place, especially when she was adamant that she was staying in her own bed. However, Maddie had to be forceful. She didn't need someone to take care of her. Maddie had gotten three peaceful nights of sleep and was thrilled to be in her own room. Despite her car being at the hospital, she allowed him to take her home, but he assured her he would get someone to help him drive her back to the apartment. She was satisfied when it meant being out of the hospital.

Cheddar meowed, and she scratched the back of his ears. He clearly didn't understand why she wasn't there to feed him. Her Dad periodically checked on him and filled his bowls, but Cheddar and Maddie were in a much better place.

"Maddie? Are you still there? You zoned out."

Maddie laughed and looked at her screen, "Sorry, Eric. It's been an exhausting day."

"I know, and I won't keep you much longer, but you were just about to tell me about the psych eval."

"Honestly, it wasn't as bad as I feared it would be. I'll admit that I felt much more at ease when it was done. I went into it, dreading it like I was about to get a tooth pulled. It was significantly less excruciating."

Eric laughed. "You still are full of drama, aren't you?" He winked, then pressed on.

"I just had some testing. I saw Peter Walters."

"Oh yeah? I've heard great things about him."

Eric grinned. "And I heard he's cute and single."

"Down, boy," Maddie teased. "You're cute, too, but you aren't single."

"Hey, a man can dream. I have never cautioned James about dreaming outside of our relationship. If anything, it keeps the love alive. Trust me." He clapped his hands together. "But now, what did Mcdreamy have to tell you?"

Maddie snickered. "He diagnosed me with Generalized Anxiety Disorder. He said it's not uncommon. Apparently, managing stress is key. He said I most likely had an acute anxiety episode, but it should all improve as I learn to manage my stress. He prescribed me a low dose of Ativan and said I only needed to take it if I feel another episode coming on. And a low dose of Zoloft for daily anxiety management. After the evaluation, I already felt much better."

"That sounds amazing, Maddie. I'm so happy that you took the steps. But what are the next steps to this healthier you?"

"Well, I have to do a follow-up with Dr. Mallone tomorrow after-noon. It's just to see how my first night back at the apartment treated me. And I have to pick up my prescription" She sighed and leaned back in bed.

"Uh oh. I know that sigh. What aren't you telling me?"

"Dr. Walters ordered me to stay off work for two weeks and no social media either! Two weeks, can you imagine?" She huffed and shook her head. She had already been off three days. That was torture enough. She wanted to be back to helping her patients out. What harm would that do if she had the assistance to improve?

"You do realize that staying off work for two weeks is only so your body can heal, right? You'll be back before you know it. It would be best if you had this time to rest. You might not think so, but your body knows so."

Maddie rolled her eyes. Deep down, she knew he was right, but it felt like a stab to her heart that she would have to steer clear of the patients she loved.

"I know, but it's still rough. Dr. Walters wants me to do outpatient therapy, as well. It's hard to imagine that working with patients has brought me anxiety."

"Well, it's not just working with patients. Maddie. You know, as well as I do, that your breakup was also a stressor."

"That was the reason we broke up. My stress was getting in the way of our relationship."

"True," he replied. "But that only added to the stress. You are such a kindhearted person that once the hospital started changing, you couldn't imagine letting the patients suffer. So you pushed yourself harder. You worked more. You dug so deep that it would cause strain on anyone in that position."

While he was right, Maddie's thoughts returned to Lourdes and the breakup. If she hadn't been so caught up in attempting to change the world, they might have still been a couple, and she might not have wound up in the hospital. She looked over at the flowers and smiled. She wanted to believe that as she evolved and grew, Lourdes would return to her side. "There you are again, in that zone." He laughed, tearing her eyes away from the flowers.

Maddie blushed and scanned the phone over to look at the flowers. "See those flowers?"

"They're gorgeous. Who are they from?"

Maddie turned the phone back towards her, "Lourdes."

His jaw dropped, and Maddie snickered. "Along with a card that said she was thinking of me and praying for me, and she hopes I feel better. ."

"Wow! That's certainly a step. I wonder why she reached out. Then again, she's probably just worried because she sees you as a patient. I'm sure that's it."

Maddie rolled her eyes, which elicited a laugh from Eric. "You know, joke all you want. I know it's a sweet gesture." She dropped her gaze back to the flowers. She wished she hadn't taken this long to see that she needed help.

"You guys belong together, Maddie. Just give it time. You'll be back in good graces before you know it. I would say this was just a start in the right direction." Maddie nodded. They could work their way back to each other, but he was right. They were slow in that process. "I best be going, but take care of yourself."

"I'll try. Talk later. Bye, Eric."

"Bye, Girlie."

She disconnected the call and smiled as she leaned back in her bed. Cheddar rested his chin on her leg. Maddie rubbed behind his ears, and he purred loudly. She was on the right track. That was the most important thing.

CHAPTER THIRTY-NINE

DECISIONS TO UNPACK

Maddie arrived at her appointment with Dr. Mallone thirty minutes early. If she was being honest, she was mostly hoping to catch a glimpse of Lourdes. Maddie could thank her for the flowers if they accidentally bumped into one another. She sent a short thank you text once she received them, but the only response she received was you're welcome. Even though it shouldn't have given her a lot to consider, her mind was racing with possibilities of what Lourdes truly meant by those words.

No matter how hard Maddie attempted to seek out Lourdes' meaning, she came up empty-handed. Instead, Maddie paced around the waiting room for thirty minutes. She kept checking her watch nervously. She didn't know why she was so frantic to get the appointment over. It was simply a checkup they could have managed over the phone. Yet, he was worried that, for some reason, she would be shoved back into a hospital bed, ready to submit to more tests. She rechecked her watch. Now, five minutes late. The lobby didn't seem very busy. She tapped her foot, growing impatient as the minutes ticked by.

"Maddie?" She jumped up, startled.

The receptionist tilted her head and gave Maddie a funny look. "Yes?"

"Dr. Mallone wanted me to tell you there's been an emergency that's kept him. If you don't mind waiting, he will be ready for you in another twenty minutes."

Maddie nodded her head. She had been there long enough. What difference would twenty minutes make? She sat down and waited. The longer she waited, the more nervous she became. She looked over to the hallway linking the waiting room to another department, and her heart skipped a beat. There stood Lourdes in her white lab coat and gorgeous smile. She was talking to another doctor, unaware that Maddie had her eyes off in her direction.

When Lourdes was through talking and turned her way, that's when their eyes connected. Lourdes nodded and started in her direction. Was she really coming to say hi? Maddie swallowed the lump that had formed.

"Maddie? Dr. Mallone is ready for you."

Maddie felt a wave of air rush through her body. The receptionist directed her to Dr. Mallone's office at the worst possible time. Lourdes stopped walking. Maddie could feel Lourdes' gaze on her back as she walked into the ward. Maddie wanted to scream; this wasn't how her romance novel was supposed to play out.

"Have a seat, and the doctor will be with you."

Maddie took a seat on the bed and waited, left to her own devices and nerves. Luckily, she was only there a few minutes before he popped into the room. "Good afternoon, Maddie. I'm sorry to have kept you waiting. How are you doing today?" Maddie nodded, but her heart was aching because her other half was wandering those same halls.

"This should be relatively painless."

He wasn't wrong. For ten minutes, they sat there and talked. Mostly about the weather and whether Maddie felt the psych evaluation was helpful. Maddie was quite honest with her thoughts on the matter. Dr. Mallone nodded and smiled as he listened.

"I'm glad I took the opportunity you gave me. I don't think we wasted a session," she admitted.

"I am happy to hear that. Keep up with your meds, and I am certain that in no time, you will be an even better version of yourself."

As Maddie left the room, she practically rushed around the corner, hoping that Lourdes would be waiting. She looked around and sighed. Lourdes had more important things to do than wait for her.

Before Maddie left the hospital, she went to human resources. She had to get the paperwork signed to start her FMLA leave. Her trip to HR ended up being far more discouraging than her visit with Dr. Mallone.

"I don't understand. What do you mean I have to attend a meeting?"

Clarissa, who covered the HR front office most days, didn't blink.

"It's protocol, Maddie. When someone has to take an FMLA leave for their mental health, the hospital wants to ensure that nothing like this will happen again. As your chart states, you are having trouble with anxiety and stress. These meetings are here as a mental health resource for our staff. Her phone rang, and she held up her hand. "Excuse me."

Maddie looked down at the paperwork in front of her. She was only on one signature and had a slew of others to read. Maddie skipped a few pages and continued to read. Much of it was legal jargon, which she didn't quite comprehend, but none sounded too bad. The only thing that made her nervous was the prospect of the meeting. It was bad enough that the whole hospital knew what had transpired in that elevator, but now she had to be humiliated again in front of the entire HR department. "Sorry about that. Now, where were we? Ah yes. The meetings. It's really an individual meeting, something you can set up on your own time. It just has to be completed before you return. There is one other option. But I'm not sure how you'd feel about it."

"Another option? What is it? Anything."

"Well, before attending a meeting, you can agree to switch career fields. Maybe nursing is too stressful for you after all. That's totally fine. There's no harm in that. If you choose to do so, you can change fields, and we'll call it an even switch. No worries at all."

She thrust a brochure in front of Maddie. "There are hundreds of options. You must scan the QR code in your spare time and choose the one that best suits you."

Maddie looked through the brochure and rolled her eyes. "I literally just came in here to sign the paperwork and leave. Is this necessary to make the decision now?"

"Of course not!" Clarissa opened the paperwork to the back page and pointed to the line. "Sign here, and you can choose your options later. I advise you to do it quickly so you don't get caught last minute."

"Understood." Maddie quickly signed. "Is that it?"

"One more thing. You have some mail." Clarissa reached under the counter and drew out a pile. She handed it over, and Maddie glanced at the top item. It was a card that read, "We'll miss you!"

"What's this?"

"You know how word gets around in CAPMED. Some of your co-workers wanted to express their wishes for improving your health." Her phone rang again. "I'll be looking forward to hearing from you. Take care." She grabbed the phone as Maddie ciphered through the cards. She felt like she wanted to cry. She dashed out of the hospital so no one would catch the tears in the corners of her eyes. It meant the world if people really wanted to wish her well.

There was a moment of hesitation where Maddie wanted to go to the Cardio floor and see Lourdes, but she dismissed that thought and left through the front doors.

Once outside, she scanned the QR code and pulled up the list of career choices. She skimmed down through them, mentally checking them off as not good enough. Then she stopped at one that caught her attention, *nursing informatics*. She read through the description and was mildly intrigued. For starters, she'd still be helping patients without being their direct caregiver. She considered that quietly. That might be something that would help her anxiety and relieve her daily stress.

She closed the browser window and hurried to her car. She could at least do some research. It would be a bonus if some of her classes transferred from the university. She felt rejuvenated for the first time since stepping into the HR office. She was ready for new possibilities.

CHAPTER FORTY

HER FATHER'S FLAME

Maddie didn't know why she was so nervous, but her palms hadn't stopped sweating since she left the apartment. She looked over to the small car parked behind her father's. Maddie wanted to meet Lydia and was relieved that her father had found a woman he enjoyed spending time with. However, she felt like a little girl again, ready to meet someone that could ultimately be her mommy. Maddie laughed at the possibility. She wasn't a child, and as long as her dad was happy, so was she.

The door flung open, and her dad pulled her into the house. "I'm so glad you could make it." He hugged her tightly, then kissed the top of her forehead. "Just seeing you now makes me confident that you will be alright.

Maddie nodded. "I'm going to be great, Dad." She squeezed him tighter, then spotted the woman standing behind him. She was around 5'7, with kind blue eyes and faint smile lines around her mouth. Her bleach-blonde hair was combed and coiffed. She wore a blue knee-length sundress and open-toed wedge heels. She smoothed her hands over the fabric of her dress, clearly nervous. Maddie pulled back and held out her hand. "And you must be Lydia."

The woman nodded, then stepped in closer. "I'm a hugger, do you mind?" Maddie shook her head. Lydia clutched Maddie to her, and Maddie's nostrils filled with the scent of a powdery, cloying perfume. "I've heard so much about you, Maddie. Your dad is very, very proud," Lydia gushed.

When Maddie pulled away and forced a smile onto her face, she swallowed, glancing between her father and the woman she was meeting for the first time. For some reason, she felt like she was about to burst into tears. "I've heard a lot about you, as well."

This was true, but her dad only started bringing Lydia up in conversation three weeks ago. How long had this relationship been going on? She was sure she would gather all the news throughout their meal. She took in a whiff.

"Dinner smells amazing."

"It's Lydia's signature dish," her father spoke, "Grilled Chicken and Rice. Along with steamed vegetables. I wanted to add Teriyaki sauce to the menu, but the warden refused." He winked at Lydia and reached for her hand.

Maddie couldn't believe how easy they were with one another. Yet, they were teasing one another like they were lifelong partners. It was refreshing.

Maddie glanced at Lydia. "And for that, I'm relieved. My dad needs someone to remind him to make healthy choices when I'm not around."

Her dad huffed, then chuckled. "Honey, go on in the dining room. We'll grab the food and meet you in a few minutes."

As Maddie went to the dining room, she stopped and looked at the same pictures they had on the walls from when she was younger and lived in the house. Most had stayed the same from when Maddie moved. She felt instantly at ease when she walked through the door, knowing she didn't have to question whether things would be different in her old home.

She sat down in the same seat that she always sat in. She could fully relax and look forward to a home-cooked meal that she didn't have to cook. It didn't take long for her dad and Lydia to have the food ready on the dining room table.

"Dig in. I hope you enjoy it," Lydia exclaimed. She was all smiles, almost giddy. It brought a smile to Maddie, as she looked just as happy to be there as her father looked to have her there.

After they each had their plates filled, Lydia didn't hesitate. "Do you mind if I give the blessing? It's been a long time since I've been around a table filled with food, and I always enjoyed these moments."

"Be our guest," Maddie's dad beamed with pride as Maddie lowered her head.

"Heavenly Father. We thank you for this meal this evening. Please look over my David and his daughter, Maddie. They will be great blessings in my life. Guide us in knowing what the future will bring us and how bright you can make it. In Jesus' name, we pray. Amen."

"Amen!" her dad declared. Maddie looked up and found him grinning from ear to ear. Maddie cleared her throat and looked down at the food. "It looks amazing, Lydia."

She took a bite and nodded with enthusiasm. "It tastes even better." She grabbed her napkin and dabbed her mouth.

"Thank you, Maddie," Lydia looked angelic as she grinned and continued to eat.

"So, do you come from a large family?" Maddie wondered.

"Ten brothers and sisters," she said.

"Growing up, we had two bathrooms. The girls and the boys." She laughed.

"When I went off to college, it was hard to believe I only had to share with my roommates."

"Wow! I can't imagine. It was hard enough with just my father and me." Maddie laughed, and her dad opened his mouth.

"Just kidding, Dad," She winked and took a sip of her water.

"But that's impressive."

"We managed. I wouldn't have had it any other way." Lydia's smile had never once left her face.

Lydia's seemingly endless optimism floored Maddie. She could only hope that she would one day be able to think about the future with the same level of excitement rather than the panic that usually settled in her gut when Maddie contemplated what she wanted to do next. "

So, tell me how you two met," Maddie was genuinely curious. Her dad wasn't suave.

Her father and Lydia gave each other a knowing glance, and then Lydia laughed slightly. "You tell it, David ."

Maddie smirked. The only time she'd ever heard anyone call him David was when he was stuck in line at the DMV. She didn't interrupt as her dad cleared his throat to continue their story.

"Frozen chicken," he began. Maddie tilted her head, and he laughed.

"You heard me right. We were both in the frozen chicken aisle at the grocery store. I was trying to decide between brands. Just as I reached for one, this hand came out behind me and snatched up the last bag." He laughed loudly.

"I was so astonished that I looked to see where the hand had come from. There she was, looking absolutely radiant in the middle of the grocery store, fluorescent lights and all Needless to say, we got to talking."

"I confessed that I didn't even want the bag. I noticed this handsome guy reaching for it and figured I would take the chance." Maddie's jaw dropped, and Lydia grinned.

"Next thing I knew, we had a dinner date. I was so nervous. I swore David was going to ditch me at the restaurant."

"I would have been a fool," he commented.

"That was the best chicken I ever bought." He winked, and Maddie thought she would melt in her seat. She couldn't remember seeing her father gushing like a lovestruck teenager, but it was sweet.

"That is so sweet," Maddie said.

"Do you have any children? Ever been married? Do you like kids?"

"Slow down, Maddie." Her dad laughed, shaking his head.

"Save the third degree for dessert." He winked at Maddie.

"Come on, Dad. You can't blame me for being curious. I've never seen him so excited about someone before," Maddie explained to Lydia.

Lydia reached out and took his hand. "I don't mind. I'm happy to share. I was married, briefly. We weren't right for one another and knew after about a year we needed to go our separate ways. We parted on okay terms, but it was meant to be. I never had children, but I have several nieces and nephews and love them each tremendously. So, yes, a big fan of kids. Both young and old." She looked over to Maddie's father and grinned.

"And I must confess I've never been this happy, either. Your father brings out the best in me."

Maddie felt an instant wave of relief wash over her. Those were the best words Lydia could have spoken. Truthfully, she was glad her dad had someone else looking out for him that wasn't her. While he would never tell her outright, Maddie figured that her dad had to be at least a little lonely. It was wonderful to see him smiling. Lydia seemed equally enamored. The last thing Maddie wanted was for her dad to be left pining for someone who didn't love him back. But watching Lydia and her dad interact throughout the night put any worries that Maddie had about Lydia and her intentions to rest. She wouldn't be calling her mom anytime soon, but she was genuinely excited for her dad.

TALKING TO LYDIA WAS LIKE TALKING TO A BEST FRIEND. SHE was thirty years older than Maddie, but Maddie didn't feel the sense that Lydia was there to be the motherly type. After all, Maddie had gone all these years with just her father. Lydia seemed to respect that. Honestly, it was refreshing to see that she cared for her dad and respected the existing relationship between Maddie and her father. She made a mental note to cross 'evil step-mom' off her list of worries.

"Can I get you both something to drink?" Her father stood up and grabbed the dishes.

Maddie arched her brow. "Dad, you're clearing the table? What have you done with my father? Let me do that." Maddie jumped up to reach for the plates, but he quickly pulled his arm back and shook his head.

"You two go ahead and get to know each other some more. I know you have more questions. I've got this." He offered Maddie a wink, which caused her to smile. Before shaking her head, she waited until he had left the dining room.

"The last time my father cleared the table, I was probably ten. You must be a good influence on him."

Lydia beamed. "I'm thinking it might be the other way around."

Lydia's eyes dimmed before she looked away at Maddie's contact. "I haven't been completely honest with you this evening, Maddie."

Maddie frowned. Here it was. The moment that Lydia dropped the ball. She didn't even want to swallow to break into the mood. She stared at Lydia, wide-eyed and nervous about what Lydia might share. Any harmful details involving her father would surely be the demise of Lydia and her father's relationship. Maddie would be sure of that. She took a deep breath and waited for Lydia to shatter her dad's hopes and dreams.

"It makes me nervous to talk about this."

"You can tell me anything," Maddie started. Still, she braced herself for whatever devastating news Lydia had to share.

"After my divorce, I dated only one other guy. I suppose it was a whirlwind romance. I was trying to get back on that horse, hopeful that anyone would be able to get my failed marriage out of my mind. I started a new job and went full force into it as if that job would be the only thing keeping me alive. It was there that I met Trevor. He was younger than me. But more importantly, he was my new boss. He promised me the world, and I was working hard, so I felt I deserved it. I didn't realize I was getting ahead solely because I was with Trevor."

Maddie's dad came in, and Lydia paused the story. He grabbed a few more dishes and then was gone. Maddie turned back to her, and she continued.

"As my stress levels rose, my relationship status with Trevor increased. Maybe God planned on me divorcing, only to get remarried a year later. I thought that Trevor and I were soulmates. But then, after a year, things started to falter. I was so stressed that my hair was falling out in the shower. Then, Trevor started to get abusive. He hit me to the point where I thought maybe I deserved it. The abuse made me question my life, but it made me believe that I had to keep working hard because I thought my job was the only thing that made me worthwhile. Clearly, I wasn't a good wife. Otherwise, Trevor wouldn't hit me, right? That's how messed up my thinking was. I justified his abuse by telling myself that I was the problem."

Again, Maddie's father returned to the room, and Maddie waited with her mouth agape, not wanting to disregard the story. He left as if he didn't see them, and Lydia released a breath.

"It took me an entire year and a hospital stay to realize I deserved better. I quit my job, and I went and stayed with one of my sisters and her family down south. I vowed that I wouldn't want to be in another relationship as long as I lived because the only happiness that mattered was my own. Fast forward two years, and I came back here, fully rested, ready for my life to continue. That's when I met your father. Now, I must admit; I'm telling you this because your dad told me about your incident in the hospital. I know that's a terrifying place to be when you feel like you can't trust your own mind or your own body. But I want to take this time to promise it will get better. It might not get better in a week or even a month, but it does. You have to trust that you deserve good things because you do. You deserve to be happy and healthy and have a job that doesn't make you want to panic every time you walk through the door. And I also know that making that change is really scary, too, so I'm here if you ever want to talk, okay? I'll have your dad text you my number, and you can call or text, whatever you're most comfortable with."

Maddie opened her mouth when she saw her dad pop back around the corner. "There, the dishes are in the dishwasher, and now we don't have to worry about them. How are my two favorite gals?" He walked over and placed a kiss on the top of Maddie's head before planting a sweet kiss on Lydia's lips.

"Will you excuse me?" Maddie got up and left the dining room, both pairs of eyes on her as she felt them when she rounded the corner. She entered the bathroom and closed the door, falling back against the door, Lydia's story still heavy on her heart. Maddie retrieved her phone from her pocket and pulled up the internet browser. Her search for careers was still readily available. She pulled up the description for Nursing Informatics and read the post over again. Maddie hit the speed dial to the hospital and waited for the prompts when she dialed in the HR voicemail.

"You've reached HR. Leave a message after the beep, and I'll return the call as soon as possible. Thank you, and have a great day."

"Hey, Clarissa. It's Maddie Anderson. Please call me back when you get this message. I have an inquiry to make about one of the other positions. I look forward to hearing back from you."

Maddie replaced her phone, then checked herself in the mirror. She wasn't crying. That was a good sign. She left the bathroom and returned to the dining room, where her dad sat alone.

She frowned. "Where's Lydia?"

He looked up. "She went outside to make a call. Her niece has a project due in school, and she thought you and I could use some alone time. Everything alright?"

Maddie nodded and moved into the seat next to him. "I really like her, Dad."

He grinned. "I was hoping you'd say that." He reached out and squeezed Maddie's hand.

"And before you ask, I knew about her situation with Trevor. We tell each other everything."

"So, she knows about my issues?"

"They're not issues. Lydia wanted to let you know that you're not alone. We all have problems to overcome. Some are bigger than others, but none of them are trivial. And she wants you to know she's here for you if you ever need someone to talk to."

After she got over the initial irritation that her dad had told Lydia about her problems, Maddie realized that it might not be so bad to have someone to talk to, especially someone who knew what she was going through. Lydia was right; these kinds of changes were scary. She squeezed her father's hand and leaned into him. "I love you, Dad."

"Love you, too, sweetheart." They embraced, and this was the first time Maddie felt that weight slowly lifting off her chest.

CHAPTER FORTY-ONE

NEW JOURNEY

As Maddie began her new career, pulling out of nursing and right into informatics, she realized it was an easier transition than expected. Informatics combined both healthcare and IT. Luckily, all of her classes had transferred. Nursing informatics still focuses on patient care. The only significant step she had to take to change careers was the paid training and a course the hospital offered. With the money she had in her savings, the lack of pay didn't even strain her. She also had her father's and Lydia's support, which made things all the easier.

It only took her two months to get everything finalized before she was prepared to start her course at the hospital. The three-month-long class covered the job and trained her to enter the field. Even better, they promised to offer all enrollees a position should they desire to extend their career with CAPMED. Another bonus of informatics was that Nursing Informatics specialists acted as the liaison between the IT specialists developing new healthcare software and the nurses on the floor, which meant that Maddie could still see her friends. For Maddie, she kept her options open to whatever her heart would choose. She wouldn't close any doors but felt hopeful about her new career.

Twenty people started the course aged anywhere from their late teens, right out of high school, up to Maddie's age. With one exception, a woman was returning to the workforce after having her three kids. Eva was fifty-four with blonde hair and green eyes. She was the most excited of Maddie's new classmates. Maddie smiled every time Eva asked a question. She felt inspired and moved by Eva's choice to change. If Eva could leap into a brand new career at 54, then Maddie could do so at 25. They became fast friends. Three weeks into the course, though, only five students remained. Maddie couldn't quite comprehend why so many people dropped out. She saw nursing informatics as a position to help people thrive. Yet, as the instructor stated, *It's just not for everyone.*

Eva remained, which was a relief to Maddie. She anticipated that both of them would be able to continue their Nursing Informatics career with CAPMED.

Their latest assignment was to analyze a real-life situation where they could evaluate the situation and decide the steps to take to process a patient's data. Maddie loved the course because it allowed them to throw themselves into real-life situations before starting the actual job. There were times when Maddie worried that she would fail the class altogether. But Maddie didn't let her stress get the best of her. Instead, she used some breathing exercises that her therapist taught her and started a 2-person study group with Eva. Soon, she was thriving in the class, which was fascinating in and of itself. "You can each email me the link to your online project, and I'll review it and have feedback for you next week. Have a great weekend!"

The five packed up their laptops and headed outside the room. Maddie waited for Eva to join her.

"How do you think you did?" Maddie asked.

Eva gave a weak smile, "Remember, it's been a long time since I was used to doing homework. And I'm still getting used to it." She laughed.

"But, all in all, I would say that I did the best I could. Isn't that what it's all about? You can only do your best, right?"

Maddie nodded, reveling in those words. Eva's positive outlook on life only gave Maddie room to think. They got on the elevator, and the doors closed behind them.

"How can you always be so positive?" Maddie asked. "You have a smile on your face 24/7. You never seem to let anything break your spirit."

Eva laughed, "Oh, Maddie. If my husband and kids heard you say that, they would certainly raise some eyebrows. We all have our moments. But then I take a step back and think and realize that my life could be so much worse. People struggle for a roof over their heads or food on their tables. People are struggling because their loved ones are sick, and they can't afford treatment. I decided I wanted to be in a position where I could eventually help them. I know I'm ancient, but I figured this would be the best way for me to help people in need. Plus, you never know until you try.

Suddenly the doors opened, and Maddie turned. Her jaw dropped. "Lourdes!"

Lourdes turned from the woman that stood beside her. Her smile faded almost immediately. But as they stood there, the smile started to return only slightly. "Maddie!"

Maddie swallowed the lump and then glanced at the woman beside Lourdes. The woman smiled, looked at Lourdes, and looked back at Maddie. Maddie's stomach dropped. The stranger standing awfully close to Lourdes also happened to be gorgeous. She was 5'10 with a blunt jet-black bob and large, green eyes. She had the same olive skin tone as Lourdes, with no blemishes in sight. She was dressed impeccably in a chic denim jumpsuit, a sharp contrast to Maddie's messy bun, day-old scrubs, and stress acne. "How've you been?" Maddie asked, stepping off the elevator and spotting Eva stepping next to her.

"Good. Great. No complaints." Lourdes glanced at her friend and then looked at Maddie. "This is Giselle. Giselle, this is Maddie."

"Nice to meet you," Maddie mumbled.

"Likewise," Giselle replied.

"I've heard so much about you."

With that, Lourdes nudged Giselle in the side and then turned to Maddie. "Um, so yeah, you're here, CAPMED."

She frowned. "Everything okay?"

"Everything is fine. Great." Maddie longed to ask why Lourdes had moved on so quickly. She looked at Eva. "This is Eva. A few weeks ago, we started a course in Nursing Informatics."

Lourdes' eyes widened. "That's great! I'm certain you're going to thrive in that."

Maddie's smile weakened. "Yeah. Well, it was good seeing you, Lourdes. Nice to meet you, Giselle, but we best get going. Tell everyone I said hi." She grabbed Eva's arm, and they hurried towards the front door.

"Friend of yours?" Eva asked.

Maddie didn't stop until they were outside. She turned to look back into the hospital but couldn't see either Lourdes or Giselle.

"Someone I used to know," Maddie muttered.

She sighed, "She looked happy, didn't she?"

Eva shrugged. "I mean, before seeing you, she looked pretty happy. I don't know her, so I can't really judge that."

Maddie huffed. "That's what I thought, though." She turned and started heading towards the parking lot, Eva close behind. "Lourdes and I used to be a thing until work stress got in our way. Well, it got in my way. We broke up a few months ago.."

Maddie stopped at her car and turned to Eva. "There hasn't been a day since I haven't thought of her or wondered what she was doing. I considered reaching out to her and telling her about my big change. But I always stopped myself. Lourdes wanted to move on, so I needed to respect that. And just like that, it looks like she has."

"Maddie, Dear. You can't tell that she's moved on. That could be a friend. Heck, you were with a friend." Eva laughed.

"Very possible it was something similar. Or a co-worker. You don't know."

Maddie tilted her head. "I've seen that look before. She's given me that look before. It's not a friend." She reached for her door. "I have to go. I'll see you next week!"

"Are you sure you want to be alone? We could go grab a drink or something."

Maddie shrugged. "That's really sweet of you, Eva, but I don't think I'd be the best company right now. I'll call you later." She got in her car and started it, a weight still holding her down.

As she got further away from the hospital, she cringed at her first meeting with Lourdes.

"Call Eric." She had worked so hard to make a difference, but seeing that Lourdes had moved on was enough to break her all over again. She reached up and flicked the tear away. Of course, this happened when she hoped she could fully get over Lourdes.

"Hey, girl."

"Can you talk?" Maddie sucked in a deep breath.

"For you? Always."

It finally happened. I ran into Lourdes at the hospital," Maddie started.

Eric sighed but said nothing.

Maddie continued, "I know that we said it was a possibility. After all, Lourdes still worked there, and the hospital was only so big, but I did not prepare myself for seeing her. What's even worse? I ran into her and her girlfriend."

"Girlfriend?"

They might have just started dating if Eric didn't know about it, but Maddie saw what she saw. "They were looking all chummy as I got off the elevator. It must be new if you sound so surprised."

"Well, Lourdes and I aren't best friends in any sense of the word, but we still work closely together. I would think I would have suspected if she had taken a lover. Are you sure?"

Maddie couldn't even giggle at Eric's use of the word lover, "I saw what I saw," Maddie huffed.

"I mean, it's been a long enough time. I don't know why I'm so surprised. Just because I haven't moved on doesn't mean Lourdes wouldn't. She deserves to be happy, and I am happy for her if she's happy."

"Whoa, slow down, Maddie. Let me do some investigating. I'm pretty good at that, you know." He snickered. "I'll see what I can find out. Don't go jumping to any conclusions. You're spiraling. I can feel the all-encompassing doom coming through the phone."

"Doom isn't exactly how I'd describe it. Heartbroken, maybe. It's the first time I'm seeing her in so long, and we loved each other." Maddie turned into the parking lot behind her building and sighed. "I guess I always envisioned we'd one day find our way back to each other, and since I got the help I needed and made the necessary change. I know I'm a better version of myself. I was looking forward to the day I could show up at her door and say,' This is the woman you fell in love with."

"And it could still happen."

While Maddie longed to believe that, her heart shattered from seeing the beautiful woman smiling before her and knowing she wasn't smiling because of her. Getting over a heartache like that would take longer than a few months, but Maddie had to trust that she would eventually get there.

CHAPTER FORTY-TWO

HEALING

No matter how hard I try, Maddie, I can't find any sign that Lourdes has a girlfriend. Eric had done his best, no doubt. She couldn't bicker with him over that, but as the days went on from that latest bump-in, Maddie knew that Giselle and Lourdes were bound to be the hottest item since Maddie and Lourdes broke up.

A month passed, and she threw herself into her coursework and did her best to just put Lourdes out of her mind. Thinking too long about their failed relationship was an obstacle she had to overcome. Otherwise, it would be the demise of her recovery.

Even though Maddie was busy with the course and studying when she wasn't at the hospital, she had to ensure she kept her eye on the real prize; staying healthy and leading a better life. She maintained her weekly therapy sessions and tossed herself into maintaining her health. Maddie resumed regular jogs. She only consumed the occasional burger. Her health had greatly improved over time.

Maddie took a long swig of water as she stepped out of her car and looked out over the park. She opened up her Instagram and smiled, taking a selfie at the start of the trail. *Hello, Friends. It's a gorgeous Saturday morning, and the birds are chirping! I'm about to head out to train for my next 5k for the American Heart Foundation this June. If you'd like to register to run or donate, the link is in my bio! Drop a comment below if you'll be there, and make sure to say hi if you see me! I love all of you, and I'll see you soon!* Maddie pressed "post," turned on her music, and started jogging. Tegan and Sara came on through her earbuds, and Maddie grinned. She didn't stop once throughout her run. She was happy to be back. The park was busy, but the kids and dogs didn't once interrupt her mood. Maddie closed her eyes and continued to jog, enjoying the fresh air and the soothing atmosphere. She could run like this for hours and never wanted to stop. Maddie no longer needed espresso shots to get her through a jog. She wasn't running to prove something to herself. She was running because it made her happy.

As Maddie rounded the trail, at least an hour of running already in, she spotted her. Lourdes was leaning up against a tree, her eyes closed. As Maddie drew nearer, she internally fought with two options, run right on by or stop and say hi. Lourdes was alone, and Maddie couldn't tear her eyes away. She still had the most beautiful and pristine complexion Maddie had ever seen. Maddie inhaled, and just like that, Lourdes opened her eyes. Their eyes met, and Lourdes offered a small wave. Was that Maddie's invention, or Lourdes wanting Maddie to wave and move on? Maddie's desire remained, and she slowed her jog.

"Hey!"

Lourdes gave a gracious grin as she nodded. "Hey!"

Maddie looked around, looking for Giselle, but Lourdes was alone. She saw the basket next to Lourdes and smiled. "Came out for a picnic, I presume?"

Lourdes shrugged. "Something like that. I saw this tree, and it seems like a great spot for a picnic. You know how that goes."

Maddie nodded. "I do." She glanced around, then turned to Lourdes. "I don't want to interrupt you and your alone time. Or, perhaps, you're waiting for someone. I..." She stepped back away from Lourdes. "I should leave you to it."

"Maddie, wait!"

Maddie paused. She would probably never want to leave if she stayed, but Lourdes deserved better than that. She deserved Giselle, who obviously made her very happy.

"I have more than enough. You could stay and join me."

Maddie turned around and looked down at the blanket and basket. "Are you sure? You're not waiting for anyone?"

Lourdes shook her head, "Unless you don't think your girlfriend would like you fraternizing with the enemy." Lourdes gave a nervous giggle.

Maddie frowned. "Girlfriend?"

"Yeah, that woman I saw you with last month. I figured that was a girlfriend."

Maddie's jaw dropped, and then she started laughing. She felt her chest caving in. Laughter bubbled up out of her mouth. She hadn't laughed this hard in a long time.

"You thought that was my girlfriend? Eva is old enough to be my mother." She continued to laugh, shaking her head.

"We're in class together. We're just friends, that's all."

She covered her face again, shaking her head. "I can't even imagine what you would have thought or why you expected she was, but believe me. She's not."

Lourdes beamed. "I guess I just assumed. And I know you like older women." She cupped her hand over her mouth.

"I shouldn't have gone there."

Maddie giggled.

"Well, older, maybe, but even Eva is out of the question. Besides, she's married with kids. She's just my friend." Maddie laughed, then rocked back on her heels. And yet, that wasn't the real issue there.

"I was more concerned that your girlfriend wouldn't want me sharing a picnic with you."

Lourdes snickered. "If I had a girlfriend, that'd be news to me."

Maddie arched an eyebrow. "Oh? You broke up?"

Lourdes frowned. "What are you talking about?"

"Giselle!"

Lourdes' eyes narrowed in, and then she started to laugh. Her eyes began watering, and she flicked the tears away. She hunched over, and Maddie watched her, but she couldn't stop joining the laughter. It felt good to laugh at the moment and not even know why they were laughing.

"Maddie, Giselle is my cousin. She came in from Texas, and I was giving her a tour of the hospital. You thought she was my...." She hunched over again and started laughing. "Wait until she hears that one."

Maddie fell back against the same tree Lourdes had once been leaning against. Could she have gotten it that wrong? When the laughter finally died, Lourdes shook her head and fell back against the tree.

"Maddie, we both got the wrong idea. Now that that's situated, will you please join me for a picnic?"

Maddie smiled and settled down onto the blanket next to Lourdes.

MADDIE AND LOURDES MADE THE SLOW WALK BACK TO THE parking lot. Maddie carried the blanket as Lourdes carried the basket.

"It sounds like you've made some great improvement Maddie. I'm so happy to hear."

"Honestly, when we broke up, it felt like the world was ending. But you were right. I needed to learn how to take care of myself. You didn't break up with me out of spite. You were trying to push me to actually take charge of my life. At first, I ignored you. I ignored everyone around me. I ignored literally every gut feeling that I had that something was wrong. I ignored myself so hard that I got an ulcer. The last thing I needed was to be in a relationship. So, thank you. Thank you for looking out for me when I couldn't look out for myself and pushing me in the right direction."

"I was happy to be that push," Lourdes commented. Things turned quiet, and Maddie felt the air brush against her skin. The morning turned out far better than she expected. As she sat with Lourdes, Maddie's anxieties slowly disappeared. They didn't dive into drama or the past. They just talked about life and what they had been up to since they last were together. They were both there just enjoying one another's company, and Maddie didn't want to waste a single minute. Lourdes released a breath beside her, and Maddie caught her, glancing at her from the corner of her eye. "May I be honest with you?"

"I wish that you would," Maddie softly answered.

"Well, the truth is, after we saw each other, I couldn't stop thinking about you. I was so happy to hear that you were doing well, but I was heartbroken to think that you had moved on and found someone that could make you happier than I could."

No one ever could. Maddie remained quiet and just processed the words as they came through. Maddie waited on Lourdes' to continue with bated breath.

"I wanted to be happy for you, but it hurt inside that you had moved on."

Maddie bit her lower lip, grateful to hear the exact words from Lourdes that she had also considered.

"I thought about reaching out to you but wasn't sure if you would even want to hear from me, so I just dropped it and told myself that you were happy, and that was all I needed to know. But I didn't like that we had completely fallen out of one another's lives."

"Neither did I," Maddie admitted. She stopped at her car and turned to Lourdes. "I wanted to reach out to you, as well. But I wasn't sure you wanted to hear from me."

Lourdes smirked. "It seems we both were mistaken." She took a deep breath, and her eyes darted to the ground. She looked nervous and unsure. "When I saw your Insta post, I decided to give fate a little push."

Maddie opened her mouth, snapped it shut, and allowed Lourdes to continue.

"If we couldn't connect long enough to have a picnic together, I would know it was time for me to move on. If I saw that you were happy with your girlfriend," She smirked and looked back up again, meeting Maddie's gaze. "Then that would be my sign to walk away and leave you to your happiness."

"So, you stalked me?" Maddie smirked, and Lourdes nodded.

"Sometimes you have to do what you have to do. I don't know what the future will hold. None of us do, but I know there's no hope for a future if we're not talking. And I wanted to see if there was any hope left. Are you mad?"

Maddie shook her head. "How could I be mad? I think today needed to happen. I also think we both needed a little push."

Lourdes sighed, a wave of relief washing over her face. "So, I'll see you around??"

Maddie nodded. If they could see where things could go, she was relieved beyond words that Lourdes had taken it upon herself. And part of her even questioned if putting it out to social media where she was, wasn't an open invitation to the woman that still had a piece of her heart. They'd already wasted so much time.

As Lourdes got in her car, Maddie pulled out her phone and found her post. She posted an update with a selfie grinning from ear to ear. *I can't express how much I needed this run and how much I'm now looking forward to what the future could hold. Love to all.* Before she got in her car, a notification sounded, and it was a like from Lourdes. Maddie grinned and slid into her driver's seat. The future was hers for the taking.

CHAPTER FORTY-THREE

BREATHING AGAIN

Maddie reached up way over her head, stretching to the ceiling and then leaning over and touching the floor. She exhaled as she made the movement and stayed in that position until she spotted Cheddar from the corner of her eye. She laughed and pulled Cheddar onto her lap.

"We've made great strides, haven't we?" She snuggled closer to him, pulled out her phone, and took a selfie. She went into her Instagram and added the caption: *just me and my stretching buddy. Have a great day, everyone!*

Her followers followed her on the journey from improving her health to her new career path. They had all been so supportive. It was only fitting that they would follow along as she started her new career. Maddie was in the middle of paid training in the medical records department. Both Eva and Maddie accepted that as their next step in nursing informatics.

Maddie's ulcer had healed entirely; it was the best time for her to take on the next challenge, and she was looking forward to it. A notification sounded, and she smiled when she spotted Lourdes' name. They were in a much better place. Maddie remained optimistic about where things could go.

Her phone rang, and she spotted an incoming FaceTime call from Eric.

She eagerly answered, "Hello, my friend."

"You're in a good mood today." Eric laughed, and she leaned back against the couch, scratching Cheddar's head and feeling at peace.

"And why not? Life is grand, isn't it?"

He smirked. "Did you and Lourdes finally reconcile in the bedroom?"

Maddie rolled her eyes. "Is it all about sex for you?" She laughed when she saw the appalled look on his face.

"I'm kidding. No. We're still taking things slow, but we're friends again, which is the most important thing. I can't express how grateful I am for that."

"You sound like a Hallmark card." Eric winked at her, then laughed. Maddie rolled her eyes as Cheddar jumped off her lap and went over to his bed.

"I'm glad that you're being so optimistic, though. I mean, I still think you two belong together. And it's great to know that you quit the stubborn act and are actually doing something about it."

Maddie crossed her legs and stretched out on the floor. They both knew that Lourdes had taken that first step. Semantics aside, Maddie was happy that someone other than her had taken the initiative. Someone knocked on her door, and Maddie jumped up from the floor.

"Just a sec, Eric. Someone's at the door."

Maddie padded to the front door barefoot and peeped through the peephole to find her father and Lydia.

"Do you know who it is?" Eric asked.

"You can never be too careful."

Maddie rolled her eyes. "It's my father and his girlfriend. I'll call you back."

"Talk soon!"

She disconnected the call. "This is a pleasant surprise." Maddie hugged her father, then leaned over and hugged Lydia. Over the past few months, her father's relationship continued to grow. Maddie had now come to view Lydia as a vital part of her life.

"Well, we just thought we'd pop in and see how you're doing!" Her father snaked his arm around Lydia's waist. Lydia hadn't once lost that sparkle in her eyes. Maddie glanced between her father and Lydia and then back again.

"Is that all?" Maddie inquired.

Lydia was the first to break her silence with a laugh. "I told you, David, that she wouldn't buy that. We're engaged!" She held out her hand and thrust her finger in front of Maddie.

Maddie grabbed hold of her hand and stared at the sparkling diamond. "Oh my goodness, I'm so happy for you both." She threw her arms around their shoulders, and they all embraced. Tears sprung to Maddie's eyes, but for once, they were happy tears.

———

LOURDES: GOOD LUCK TODAY. I KNOW YOU ARE GOING TO DO *great!*

The simple text from Lourdes left Maddie beaming as she entered the medical records department and looked around for a familiar face. Immediately, she spotted Eva, who hurried over to her.

"Oh my goodness, Maddie. I'm as nervous as a baby going in for their first shot."

"Don't be silly," Maddie replied. "Babies don't know they're getting a shot."

Eva smiled, and at that moment, she seemed to calm down. "I haven't had a medical job for ten years."

"You've got this, Eva. Besides, we're going to be doing it together. No need to worry. Got it?" Maddie exclaimed.

Eva nodded and sighed. "I don't know what I'd do if you weren't here with me."

All Maddie and Eva needed were those five minutes to relax. Eva wasn't the only one afraid. Maddie had taken on this challenge and was determined to do her best. A woman with dark hair and green eyes exited the back room and greeted them at the desk. "Hello, I'm Hadley. And you must be Eva and Maddie?"

"I'm Maddie, and this is Eva." Maddie pointed to her friend.

"We're both excited to be here."

Hadley smiled, "Let me show you both around." They took a tour that lasted just under an hour. What Maddie didn't anticipate was how big the hospital's medical records department was. It wasn't just on the tenth floor, but a whole basement of records housing all the archived files. Every time they entered a different room, they were in awe of how many files they would have to learn. Soon, both women were feeling o

Hadley introduced them to four other employees through the tour, each seeming busy but not filled with the nameless all-encompassing dread. The fact that no one seemed to be having a panic attack reassured Maddie. She could do this. Learning the ropes would take some time, but she would figure it out. Once they had wrapped back around the main floor, Hadley turned to them. "I do know it can be quite overwhelming but know that we do our best to keep our department adequately staffed. Eva, you can work with Beth. Maddie, follow me. I'm going to have you sit with Kristine."

Maddie looked over her shoulder as Eva looked like she had lost her best friend. She hoped Eva wouldn't let her insecurities get the best of her. Kristine got Maddie signed up on the computer system and then began going over how the system worked.

"Do you feel comfortable on the computer?"

"Absolutely!" Maddie was anxious to learn about doing an excellent job in medical records. When she met up with Eva, she felt like she was brimming with knowledge.

"I'm overwhelmed," Eva said, falling into the seat across from her. "Aren't you?"

"I am, but I think in the end, we'll figure it out. We both are smart. We both excelled in the course. So, I'm not going to let my anxiety get the best of me. I'm excited about what we'll learn. We can only go up from here."

"Ugh, Maddie. I wish I had the confidence you have."

Maddie was proud to hear the older woman state that. Maybe she had come along farther than she even knew herself. Her phone dinged, and she reached into her pocket and withdrew it to find the message.

Lourdes: How are things going? You can respond later, but would you be up for getting together later? We could go to the diner or something. Just let me know.

"Good news?" Eva asked.

"Huh?"

"You're grinning like a woman that has a secret. Or like..." Her eyes widened. "A woman in love."

Maddie blushed, looking away from Eva, confident she would see the truth written on her face. "It's not like that," she lied. "It's just a text. Nothing more. Nothing less." Her cheeks burned as she looked down at her phone, feeling Eva's eyes still lingering on her.

Maddie: I'm learning a ton. It's super informative. I get done here at five. I'll be free anytime after that.

Lourdes: I'll meet you at the diner at five-thirty.

"You may think I don't know what I'm talking about, but I have a teenage daughter, if you'll remember, and you have the same expression that she does."

Maddie laughed. "Is that so?" She slid her phone back into her pocket, appreciative of Eva's teasing. Maybe she looked like a teenage girl filled with love and hope. Maddie didn't want to ruin anything this time. She was ready to experience love once more.

CHAPTER FORTY-FOUR

RENEWED HOPE

When Maddie entered the diner, Lourdes already had the corner booth. She looked up, on instinct, as Maddie entered, and they greeted one another with a smile. Lourdes stood as Maddie reached the table.

"I'm glad you could come."

Lourdes didn't realize this, but Maddie had been waiting for this moment for months. Not only was she going to meet Lourdes, but she was also going to meet Lourdes as a happier and healthier version of herself, the version of herself that Lourdes knew she could be. "Thank you for inviting me."

Maddie and Lourdes sat down, and Maddie feared that the awkwardness would overwhelm her. What if they wouldn't be able to get past what they had gone through? They had a wonderful morning at the park, but that was an impromptu experience, where this felt more like a date. Maddie didn't want to pinch herself because if she did, she knew it would all be over. Yet, she was scared even to breathe. What if they couldn't fully overcome what caused them to break up? Already, she could feel her mind starting to spiral out of control. She walked herself through some deep breathing exercises that her therapist taught her.

Maddie and Lourdes ordered veggie burgers and fries, and Maddie felt herself relax. Once the waitress was gone, they fell into an easy conversation. It was as if no time had passed. There was no lingering awkwardness or feelings of regret. Instead, Lourdes was excited to hear about Maddie's new job.

Lourdes leaned forward, the booth squeaking under her, "How was your day?"

"I have some great co-workers," Maddie began, "Kristen is training me."

"Kristen Bridgeway?"

"You know her?" Maddie asked. Maddie was always stunned by the sheer amount of people who knew and loved Lourdes.

"She worked at the front desk in the ER when I started at the hospital. I'd heard she went to Medical records. She's a sweet girl."

"Yeah, I like her teaching style. And my boss, Hadley, I adore her. Oh, and my friend, Eva, is in the same department. So, I already know someone. But I think it's going to be a perfect fit. And once I'm done with training, I'll be put on the fast track to a nursing informatics specialist program. They are developing it for the hospital, and Eva and I are helping to develop it. I'm not sure that Eva is looking to go that far, so I could fly solo there. If I decide it's what I want to do. But the possibilities are truly endless."

"And you're literally glowing." Lourdes stared at her for so long that Maddie felt her cheeks burning again. She looked down at her glass of water, hoping Lourdes couldn't sense her embarrassment. She drank her water, trying to flush out her red cheeks.

"I gave up espresso -- no more double or triple-shots. I'll drink a cup of coffee every once and awhile. Other than that, I'm officially a tea girl. I feel better for it."

She took another sip of her water and then bit down on her lip. "But how have you been? How's work? The patients?"

"Work's been pretty good. I know some of the patients still miss you. If I'm being honest, I've missed you." Lourdes gave a slight smirk.

"But everyone is doing well. The department has hired a few part-time employees to take some of the stress off the rest of the staff. But, most importantly, I'm glad you're doing so well, Maddie. That really makes me happy."

"I..." Her words trailed off when the waitress returned and left them their food. She waited until they were alone again before continuing, "I know I have you to thank for much of this. You cared enough to show me that I needed to get help. For that, I'm indebted to you."

"Maddie, you don't need to thank me. I was happy to do it. Even if it meant taking the backseat for you to get what you deserved." Lourdes took a bite of her burger, and Maddie popped a french fry into her mouth. Even though so much time had gone between them, it was as if none of that empty time mattered.

They ate much of it in silence, yet when either of them talked, some genuine conversation kept the evening going.

"By the way," Maddie began. "Turns out you were right about memories. They tend to sneak up on you." Maddie sipped on her water, and Lourdes leaned in, her eyes wide. "I've started to remember a couple of things about my mom. She left when I was so young, but I recall good times, going to the store with her, singing songs in the car, and so forth. It helps me reflect on the fact that she wasn't always the leaving type."

"That's great, Maddie. I know sometimes memories don't always help in a good way. So, I'm happy to hear that you had some healthy memories coming to you."

Maddie smiled, and the table turned silent. Except for a few glances shared across the table, they remained present. They had been there for two hours, and Maddie appreciated every minute of their time in the diner.

"Maddie," Lourdes began. "There's been something eating at me, which I really want to discuss with you. I don't want you to think I'm drudging up the past or unsympathetic to everything you've been through. It's just something I've been thinking about a lot."

Maddie took a long sip of her water and slowly lowered her glass, unsure about the direction of the conversation. She nodded, waiting, anticipating every word Lourdes wanted to say.

"The patient that passed away all those years ago. The one that ultimately made me realize I needed to change my ways. There's more to that story. You see, she wasn't just a patient. We had started a romantic relationship. They always say you shouldn't get involved with your patients. Unfortunately, it hit me out of the blue, and there wasn't any turning back. The relationship nearly cost me my job. And when she passed away, it nearly cost me my life. I guess I thought I couldn't let things between us continue, especially while I knew you were in a tough spot. I didn't want to see you spiral into this abyss. So, I backed away. It wasn't just because you needed it. It was because I did, too. I needed space to process her death for real, no escape, no trips. At the same time, I feared I would lose you if you didn't get the help, and I didn't want to go through that again."

Maddie looked down at her empty glass of water and longed for another drink. She swallowed, hoping that would suffice.

She looked up and gave a heartfelt smile. "Do you wanna take a walk?"

Lourdes sighed and nodded. Maddie reached into her purse, grabbed some money, and tossed it to the table.

"You shouldn't do that," Lourdes argued. "I invited you."

"I want to," Maddie replied.

"Let's go." They left the diner, and Maddie laced her fingers through Lourdes' hand on their way out the door. They walked out into the crisp night air. Summer was just about to start. The sky was a luscious dusky blue. Maddie felt the weight of Lourdes' calloused palm against her own. She felt the tension release between her shoulder blades. Maddie was quiet, stunned at how someone else's presence could feel like relief embodied.

———

As THEY WALKED, THE SILENCE CALMED MADDIE'S ANXIOUS thoughts. They made it one block, then two. Lourdes never let go of her hand. "Do you know it's been three years since I've had a serious partner?"

"I didn't realize," Lourdes quietly stated. She swung their arms together in an easy rhythm. "I guess I didn't know when or how to let you know, but yeah, three years. I had a couple of little flings. But my last serious relationship ended in not a great place. We were tight, best friends. I was in college. She was working at a radio station. I thought we would get married. But I was young and naïve, and eventually, I realized that we wanted different things. But I thought we could work through our differences since we were in love. I threw my whole life into that relationship. I worked just as hard as I worked as a nurse. You could say I worked twice as hard to try and convince Raven to marry me."

"Wow, was it worth the effort?"

Maddie laughed. "Not even a little bit. While I was working hard to make our relationship work. She was working even harder to break things off. I just couldn't see it. I was blinded by what I thought was love. I nearly broke myself trying to be the perfect partner or at least the idea of what I thought Raven wanted. But, you see, I was Raven's first girlfriend. Ultimately she decided that it wasn't quite what she wanted. She wanted to be with a guy.

Meanwhile, I was dreaming up our wedding registry, but she had already decided that I wasn't the person she would marry. You can see how that would mess someone up. It made it really hard to get close to people. Even when I tried to move on, something stopped me from being able to be vulnerable. The minute I got close to someone, I remembered that pain. I threw myself into my job and told myself it wasn't worth the hurt."

"I'm sorry, Maddie. You don't deserve that."

"I didn't see it that way." Maddie stopped walking as they reached Millennium Park. The city was alive with the prospect of summer. The sunlight shimmered off of the metallic exterior of the Bean. Tourists snapped Selfies next to it, smiling at how the sculpture distorted their faces into cartoonish caricatures. Children played in the fountains, their bare feet slapping against the damp pavement. They splashed each other and screamed. Everyone in the park seemed giddy and full of life. Businessmen sat on the grass, loosening their ties and relishing the feeling of the earth beneath them. Families of tourists gawked at the collages of faces displayed on the massive LED screen behind the fountain, a rotating cast of Chicagoans.

Maddie and Lourdes found an open bench and sat down. She turned to Lourdes, who hung on Maddie's every word.

Maddie continued, "Every time I got close to someone, I heard Raven's voice in my head. Why wasn't I good enough? I was powerless to my tendency to self-sabotage. Whenever I would try to get close to some-one, I would do something to push them away. I didn't want to get hurt like Raven had hurt me. It all felt doomed from the start.."

"Maddie, your relationship wasn't your fault. Raven should have been honest with you and not had you jumping through hoops to be with her. She wasn't committed to you. That's on her, not you. As for pushing people away, it makes sense. Anyone would react the same way."

Maddie turned and looked off into the sunset. She brushed a loose strand of her hair behind her ear. Lourdes continued to hold her hand in the loving and caring way Maddie always longed for and desired.

"When you broke it off, I felt abandoned. But I see now that I need to work on myself for our relationship to thrive. So, I tried to start working on myself a bit, but then I was thrust into a new department out of nowhere, and suddenly I was right back where I started, working myself to the bone. So even though I thought I was getting better, I wasn't. I was stuffing my feelings down and telling myself that counted as progress. But then..."

She turned back to face Lourdes. "I learned that you were the one that helped me out of the elevator. You got me to the ER, which showed you would never abandon me. You were always there for me. I just didn't want to see it. I was too headstrong to see it. So now, I've been working on myself for real this time. Not for anyone, just for me. But I would like it if you were there to see me thrive, y'know? I feel like I owe it to you to let you see me when I'm healthy."

"Maddie," Lourdes reached up and touched the side of Maddie's face. Maddie closed her eyes. She had dreamt a million times of this very moment. Lourdes would look her in the eyes, say they had worked so hard to get to this moment. She waited for Lourdes to finally tell her that she wanted to pick up where they had left off.

Lourdes looked at her with nothing but love. "I never wanted to abandon you. It killed me that we couldn't be together.."

"I've missed you, Lourdes."

"And I've missed you."

Lourdes moved in closer to her, slinging her arm around the back of the bench and pulling Maddie close. "I want us to try again. We can be better than we ever were. But what do you want?"

Maddie grinned. She couldn't help but stare at Lourdes' luscious lips. She took a deep breath, "Well, my dad is getting married next weekend."

Lourdes' eyes widened.

Maddie shrugged, "It's a long story, but she's a great woman. Would you be my date?"

Grab the thrilling epilogue by scanning or clicking on the QR code below:
[or Type or Click here: https://BookHip.com/QGKVFMM]

Happy Reading,
Morgan
P.S: Thanks, www.kindlepreneur.com, for the QR code generator, and www.booklinker.com for the universal links.

At What Cost?

LIFE AND LOVE:
A Lesbian Medical
Romance Series

M.T. CASSEN

CHAPTER ONE

FOR THE CHILDREN

Anne

The world was lost in a soft silence when Anne Silva stepped outside the hospital hallway. She had spent all night restless and hopeful that today would bring smiles to the children's faces. Those fears could only linger as the rain pattered along her bedroom window. *What if the day got rained out?* She could already see the frowns forming on the children's faces when she broke the news. *We'll do it another day, I promise.* The cries would echo through the halls. They needed this. They needed a day away from the sterile antiseptic air of the hospital; they needed fresh air. Anne took in a whiff of the fresh air that she had long promised them and smiled. There was still a scent of rain but not a cloud in sight. All her fears washed away with the last puddle; today would be the day she only saw smiles. The workers from the local zoo were busy organizing the hospital courtyard as they had done for the past three years. Anne made it her duty to ensure that the kids stuck in the Pediatric ward could enjoy themselves but still access their medical care. It seemingly worked.

Anne glanced at her watch and grinned. She tossed her dark hair into a ponytail to get her bangs out of her green eyes. The courtyard would be flooded with children of all ages in just a few more minutes. Many of those children were stuck inside CAPMED for weeks due to their health issues —some with cancer and others with less severe cases of asthma. Anne carefully screened all participants to ensure they were medically fit to participate in the day's activities. Regardless of their health issues, everyone needed a break. It was the beginning of summer, and these kids deserved a chance to spend the day outside, like their peers who would be readying for summer vacation. Anne might not be able to give them a whole summer camp experience, but she could provide them with a day where they could just be ... kids. Anne turned and hurried to the elevator. And now, the best part was grabbing the children from their beds and pointing out the zookeepers and animals already filling the courtyard. There was a miniature pony, a face-painting station, and a small pen full of bunnies. Two baby goats munched on the overgrown grass. Today was just as exciting for Anne as for the young ones. She laughed as she stepped off the elevator.

Anne stepped into Willow Bixby's room. Willow, an inquisitive seven-year-old cancer patient, was already sitting in her bed. She had a round face framed by a blonde bob and large brown eyes. She looked like a cherub. "Is it time?" she exclaimed. Her enthusiasm was hard to contain.

Anne laughed. "You know it!" She wheeled the chair over to her and helped her to get seated. "Are you ready?"

"You betcha!" She clapped her hands together. "Mommy and Daddy are coming during lunch. I'm so excited!"

Anne laughed and leaned in, brushing her lips against the young girl's top of her head. "Same here."

The little girl giggled, and they exited the room. Already, the Pediatric staff had worked to gather the kids from their rooms, and Anne looked around at the organized chaos. "Cecilia," she called, waving her hand. Cecilia, a supervising nurse and one of Anne's old mentors, came over. She was tall and slender; she carried herself throughout the hospital with an undisputed air of grace that spoke to her experience. "Did you grab Maria?"

"No, she's the next on the list. I'll grab her and take Willow down to the courtyard for you. You're needed downstairs."

Anne frowned. "Downstairs?"

"HR." Cecilia shrugged. "But I'll take care of the rest."

"Alrighty then," Anne mumbled. She watched as the elevator was loaded with more patients and turned to head toward the stairs. What would they need her down in HR for? She shrugged it off and hurried down the stairs, as no one liked to keep that department waiting. As she drew closer, it hit her. They probably needed to verify the count of children so they got the payment correct. Clarissa looked up from the front desk the moment Anne entered. "Hey, Clarissa. I've been summoned." Anne laughed lightheartedly, but Clarissa didn't budge.

"They're expecting you. Go on in." She motioned to the boardroom, and Anne frowned. It seemed silly to make such a big entrance for a simple question they could have asked over the phone. But as she drew nearer, she thought even harder. And it was odd that they would need to have a count, as she was sure she had included that in her budget request. She shrugged and entered the room.

Robert Tucker sat at the head of the table. He was a burly man with ruddy cheeks, the CEO who kept everyone on the edge of their seats. He only made his presence known if there was a huge issue. Around the table sat Bill Bristow, the union rep, along with Henry Martin, her other mentor, who had a sort of Mister Rogers air about him. There were a few other faces that Anne could place, but she wasn't quite sure of their relation to the hospital. Callie North was also seated at the table, the nurses' representative. She was at least a friendly face. "Have a seat," Robert stated, motioning to an empty chair.

"Um, well, I don't know what this is about, but I have a courtyard of children waiting outside, and I'm supposed to make a speech welcoming the families. So, can we make this quick?"

"Please have a seat, Anne," Callie started. "That's what this meeting is about. It won't take long. Just have to get some things out of the way." Anne glanced at Callie, and she gave an encouraging smile and motioned to the seat beside her.

Anne slid into the seat and glanced over at Robert. "Alright, what's this about?"

"It's come to our attention that this event costs triple your proposed budget," Robert started.

Anne narrowed her eyes. In the last ten years she had been employed at

CAPMED, she had never been in such an awkward situation. In the previous five years in the Pediatric department, her career at CAPMED had soared, and things had never been better. Now, everyone stared at her as if they were ready for her to break right before them. She shifted in her seat, the awkwardness gripping her muscles.

"The staff was going through your portfolio, and while the depth of your organizational skills never ceases to amaze us, it seems that this year you had several unaccounted expenses." Anne frowned. She had gone through everything three times before submitting it. "Well, things come up," she hedged.

"The budget for snacks was double what it was last year." He pushed two papers out in front of Anne, and Anne picked up each one. She surveyed the one list, then the second, "The catering company raised their prices! Plus, this year, more than half the kids are gluten-free; that's going to be more expensive, but I didn't want anyone to feel left out." Anne looked over the list and nodded. "That's fair, but on page three, you'll see that the cost of the tents was double what it was last year as well."

"I had to find a new company! The other one went out of business because of COVID," Anne didn't want to sound like she was making excuses, but she couldn't shake the feeling that Robert was blaming her for circumstances beyond her control.

"I fixed it, though! Instead of renting folding chairs, I used the spare folding chairs in the storage room behind the cafeteria."

"And now there are no chairs for art therapy this morning," Robert finished.

"You see, Anne...." Robert pulled the lists back in front of him. "CAPMED, like all hospitals, is going through some tough times. Usually, mistakes like these would be permissible. However, the hospital board met last week to discuss the budget for the upcoming year, and we have to make some cuts. We need to cut some of the non-essential services, starting with family fun days." Anne sighed. "But Robert..." she began.

He arched an eyebrow. "There's no need for discussion. We went over the budget every way we could." A weight was heavy in Anne's gut, and she looked down at her hands. She could feel the children's disappointment when she announced today was the last Family Fun Day. "This will be the last one. Please inform the children and their families that our Halloween Haunt is canceled this Fall as well."

"You can't be serious." Anne glanced up and stared at him. "The children rely on these moments. You're letting the budget of all things snatch it away from them?" Robert didn't budge. Anne turned to Henry. He was always reasonable, but his gaze dropped to the table. She mentally groaned and turned back to Robert.

Robert shrugged. "The decision has been made. The hospital can't have any more events if we want to keep our doors open, especially the PEDS wing."

Anne cringed. "And there's no way that these cuts could be made in, say, the donor luncheons?" She crossed her arms in front of her.

"We are being reasonable here, Anne. I don't want your arguments, as they will only waste your breath." He grabbed his papers together and stood up from the table. "Now, if you'll excuse us, we have another meeting."

Anne stood up from her table, her head down as she exited the room. Clarissa's eyes were on her as she hurried from the HR office. This was ridiculous.

Willow grinned and waved at Anne when she arrived in the courtyard. "Nurse Anne! Come see the bunnies!" She called. She was holding hands with a taller blonde woman who was most likely Willow's mother.

Anne walked over to the wooden hutch containing a giant gray bunny.

"They're the cutest ever," Willow gasped.

"They are pretty cute," Anne agreed.

"Thank you so much for organizing this. I'm Ella, Willow's mom," She extended her hand, and Anne shook it.

"It's lovely to meet you."

"Seriously, I can't thank you enough. You have no idea how much it means to my husband and me to have a chance to be a normal family for a day." Ella gushed.

Anne's stomach sank. How was she supposed to explain to all these people that budgetary concerns were crushing their one chance at normalcy?

CHAPTER TWO

ROUGH MORNING

Anne

The radio played as Anne entered the kitchen; her cat, Whiskers, a gray-striped tabby, was not far behind. He meowed and nuzzled up against her, and she laughed and leaned down to ruffle the back of his neck. "Are you hungry, Whiskers? Is that what you're trying to tell me?" She ruffled the fur on his neck more, then walked over and grabbed a can of cat food from the cupboard. Whiskers proudly stood by his bowl when she walked over with the can and scraped it in. "Make it last. Mama's gotta work today." She smirked, then moved to the counter to pour herself a cup of coffee.

The clock on the wall read 7:05. She still had plenty of time to enjoy her morning before taking the ten-minute drive to the hospital. She leaned back against the counter and sipped on her coffee, glancing around where she had called home for fifteen years. What started as a dilapidated two-bedroom on the outskirts of Chicago quickly turned into her oasis. The first year was a lot of work. First, she ripped up the carpet to uncover the original hardwood floors. She replaced the grimy linoleum in the kitchen with chic laminate tiles she found online. She swapped out the Landlord special off-white paint for a soothing Robin's egg blue. On weekends, she scoured every corner of the Internet and every garage sale in the Chicagoland area for upcycled furniture. She found her round kitchen table in Bridgeport. The yellow velvet sofa was a cast-off of her sister, who couldn't risk a velvet couch with two young children. Her white iron bed frame was from an estate sale where she found her quilt. And while Whiskers didn't care about the decor, Anne adored the iron bird feeder shaped like a tiny cottage she stuck on the tree outside the kitchen window. It didn't take long for it to feel like that, a home. She took another sip and sighed. One more mortgage payment and the place would officially be hers, paid in full. Scrimping and saving down to the last dime hadn't been easy. She doubled her monthly payment so she could pay it off in half the time. But it had finally been worth it. She could imagine walking into the credit union and handing over the last installment. She planned on having two parties, at least. After all, her friends, co-workers, and sister would be happy to celebrate the joyous occasion with her. She finished the last of her coffee and placed the mug into the sink. Her life didn't have everything she desired, but had all the necessities. Now that Anne could pay off her house, perhaps she could find a woman to share it with.

Meow. Anne looked down and laughed at Whiskers as if he had read her mind. "Of course, she'll have to be a cat person." She knelt and scratched behind his errors. "Mama's off to work."

Anne never imagined she would be one of those parents who treated her pet as if they were human. But Whiskers was different. She met him a year ago on a date at a cat cafe with her ex-girlfriend. The girlfriend broke up with her a month later, but Whiskers was her friend for life.

Anne longed for a family one day. She knew that most therapists would tell her it stemmed from Anne's tumultuous childhood. Her father left them when she was still in elementary school. He said he fell out of love with her mother. Anne and her sister, Melanie, thought that was a lousy excuse. What about them? Did he not care what happened to his children? He was cheating with his secretary, a fact that only came out two weeks before the divorce was final. Anne and Melanie never did forgive him for deserting them. Where he wound up was simply a mystery.

Their mother, however, didn't let the divorce get her down. She worked as a government official in the Postal Service. Her friends at the post office rallied around her mother and family, ensuring they never had to do without. Unfortunately, as Anne was getting out of college, her mother was involved in an accident, killed by a drunk driver. The driver ended up in prison, but Anne vowed to preserve her mother's legacy of kindness, generosity, and being a great friend.

As for Melanie, Anne liked to believe she had gone down the same road. However, Melanie married a man named Josh, who was similar to their father. Yet, she didn't want to be the one who forced Melanie out of the marriage. Melanie would ultimately resent her, and her sister's relationship was the most important one she had, other than her relationship with her nieces. The four of them regularly got together for game nights and movies. She enjoyed getting to see her nieces grow up right before her eyes. That relationship was way too important to let it falter. Hopefully, one day, Melanie would realize the jerk Josh was, and Anne would be there to help Melanie and the girls get back on their feet.

Anne turned up the radio and began singing along to a Lady Gaga song. Traffic was light, which enabled her to go at her speed, and she started singing along. She was so close to paying off her house, which made her feel unusually buoyant. She was slowing down to ease onto the exit when she heard a loud crash, and her car jolted forward.

"Shit!" she groaned. Her car halted, the motor shutting off. She looked in the rearview mirror. She couldn't make out any features of the driver but saw a burgundy ribbon hanging down from the rearview mirror. The car stayed there, with no movement coming from the driver—a few cars whizzed by, but no one offered to stop. Anne reached for her phone and sighed. Not exactly how she wanted to start her morning, she grabbed the door handle, but before she could get out of the car, the driver backed up and sped around her, tearing off onto the exit and disappearing. "You've got to be kidding me!" Anne slammed her fists against the wheel and stared back at the now-empty spot.

Anne looked in her rearview mirror. There weren't any cars coming, and she opened the door and braced herself, walking around the car and looking at her bumper. The bumper was askew. There was a huge dent right where the two cars collided. Now, all responsibility was on her shoulders since the perpetrator had fled. She tilted her head from one side to the other. Maybe it wasn't that bad, and she could get by. If she planned on fixing it, she was looking at derailing paying off her house. She covered her face and shook her head as a truck whizzed by her, blowing on the horn.

She walked around and slipped back into the front seat. So much for the great big party she had planned. First, she didn't want to waste time getting it into the shop to be repaired. If only her car still drove. When it started, the radio resumed, and the engine roared to life. At least there was one plus. She drove off onto the exit, where the car disappeared, and looked around as the road drew to a T. She looked both ways, surveying each direction for a car that matched the red vehicle, but she rolled her eyes. She knew nothing about cars and couldn't differentiate one from the other. It was pointless.

She would call the shop later and see when she could get her car in and then worry about calling the insurance company. What was done was done. She had to get to work; she had never missed a shift. It'd been two months since hospital management shredded her budget, and the last thing she needed was another disciplinary meeting. Besides, there were times to shirk responsibility, and this wasn't one of them. She had to keep the pay coming, even more so now with an insurance estimate and repairs looming.

CHAPTER THREE

HIT AND RUN

Taylor

Taylor's grip tightened on her steering wheel, and she stared straight ahead. Her mind was fuzzy as she headed to the parking lot. She was too afraid to leave her car and see the damage she had done. A hit-and-run was far from her finest moment. But the car came out of nowhere. Then again, she was distracted, and her music was playing louder than a rock concert. It was the only way she could stay awake. She would have a long day ahead of her, and the neighbors had been in a screaming match all night.

Taylor slowly released a grip and opened her door. She stared at her front bumper and covered her face. The one good thing was that her car was still running. She groaned and got back in the car, slamming her door shut. A text dinged on her phone, and she grabbed it, spotting her brother's message.

GAVIN:

Hey, Sis. I just wanted to wish you a great first day on the job. You're going to rock it.

Gavin was just sixteen, a junior in high school, and her rock. Taylor believed that she should be the grown-up in the scenario. Their father was out of the picture when Gavin was only a baby, and their mother struggled with drugs and alcohol.

TAYLOR:

Hopefully, the day goes better than it started. Ugh.

GAVIN:

Who do I need to beat up?

TAYLOR:

You don't need to worry about anything. I got in a bit of a fender bender this morning.

GAVIN:

Oh no. Who's fault?

TAYLOR:

You're talking to her.

GAVIN:

Tay...please don't say...you can't afford that. You don't have insurance. How much damage?

TAYLOR:

I wouldn't know. I left the scene of the accident. I feel awful.

TAYLOR:

If I knew how to find them, I would gladly reach out and help them out. I'm a coward.

Taylor and Gavin had been in an accident before. One that left them in a homeless shelter as their mother tried to detox. The detox didn't work, and the accident left Taylor afraid of driving. Eventually, she overcame her fear enough to get her license, but panic lingered every time she merged onto the highway.

GAVIN:

Don't!! I'm guessing you bumped into an old dude with billions lying around.

GAVIN:

Let it go, Sis. You're better off.

Taylor laughed. It was easy to suggest letting it go, but was that even possible? She let go of a breath and tried to shake out her jitters. She couldn't lose this job before it even started. She was trying to save up for a nicer apartment for her and Gavin. It was nice that their aunt let them stay with her when Taylor was working her way through college, but her aunt's house was tiny. Taylor longed to move her family to a better neighborhood and life. Taylor got out of the car and looked over at the banged-up bumper. She did a number on it. She glanced down at her watch and heaved a sigh—only ten minutes to get the lay of the land of her new job. No pressure. Taylor started running toward the front of the building, leaving the accident behind her. She was about to reach the curb when she tripped. Taylor flew face-first toward the pavement. In the nick of time, she grabbed onto a pole to steady herself. She groaned, hopping from one foot to the other, a throbbing pain shooting up the heel of her foot and to her shin. If only no one saw her, she could shake it off and get inside.

"Are you alright?"

No such luck. Taylor grimaced and turned on her heel. Taylor's jaw dropped when she saw who was asking the question, a woman who looked to be in her mid to late thirties. Her complexion was flawless, her olive skin glowed, and her hazel eyes shone. Flecks of gold stared back at her from those captivating eyes. Her curly brunette hair was up in a messy ponytail, but she looked like she had just stepped out of a magazine.

The woman tilted her head. "Are you sure? I know curbs tend to jump out in the middle of nowhere."

Taylor was stunned. This woman was so gorgeous she couldn't think straight. Taylor cleared her throat and shifted her feet. "All better. It's just been a day, and that was the icing on the cake."

"Tell me about it. I'm having one of those days myself. I hope yours gets better. I hate to jet off, though. I'm running behind schedule. But, if you're sure you're alright..." Her words trailed off, and Taylor nodded, dazed. "Take care!" She waved and then rushed off, disappearing into the building.

Taylor snickered. Out of all the people she had to make a complete fool in front of, it was that dazzling woman. But it was nice to know there were still friendly people in the world. The woman didn't need to stop to make sure she was okay. She rolled her shoulders back and adjusted the burgundy ribbon she wore wrapped around her blonde hair. Who could blame her for trying to look nice on her first day?

Taylor slipped her purse back on her shoulder and picked up the pace to get into the hospital. She hadn't a clue where she was going and was already a few minutes behind. If only the day would improve.

CHAPTER FOUR

WE MEET AGAIN

Anne

"**Y**ou're scowling," Cecilia said, breaking into Anne's thoughts as she stared at the computer. She had tried to put the accident out of her mind when she entered the hospital. Yet suddenly, in the stillness of the Pediatric floor, the accident came rushing back to her. Who would just up and leave an accident like that? Someone with no conscience. As Cecilia raised an eyebrow, Anne released a groan and shook her head.

"Long morning."

Cecilia checked her watch. "It's just a minute past eight. I'd say the morning hasn't even begun."

Anne laughed. "You would think, but let me tell you about the start of my day. I'm on the highway, about to get off the exit, when *Bam.*" Cecilia jumped, and Anne leaned back in her chair. "I was rear-ended. As if that wasn't bad enough, the person left the scene so that I couldn't get their registration, license, nothing." She threw up her hands. "They left. Sped so fast that I couldn't even get the license plate number, as if my brain was even thinking that far ahead."

"Ugh," Cecilia grunted. "Could you make out the person? Male, female, make of the car, anything?"

"Red two-door. Does that help anything? If my head had been in the right place, maybe something would have stuck, but nope." Anne sighed. It didn't even help to talk about it. What would help is if she could go back to the highway and start over. She would have been more prepared. She would have snapped a picture.

"Sorry, Anne. That has to suck. People are downright rude." A light lit up at the nurses' station, and Cecilia backed up from her. "I have to grab the call. But chin up, stay positive. You always do."

"Thanks, Cecilia." Anne watched as she disappeared into a room and returned to her work. She was right. Things would improve as the day went on. It couldn't get much worse.

"Anne?" Anne looked up and saw Hailey, a fellow nurse, approach the nurses' station. She was younger than Anne and shorter. She had large brown eyes and blonde hair that she wore in a loose ponytail. Hailey clasped her hands together. She fidgeted from one foot to the other. She tossed a look over to the elevator and then back to Anne. "Do you have a few minutes?"

"Sure. What's up?" Anne leaned back in her chair, tearing her eyes away from the computer. Hailey appeared like she needed Anne's attention more than the computer did. Her eyes darted down to the floor, then back up. Anne nodded. "Are you nervous about training the new hire?"

Hailey sighed and even broke through a smile. "How'd you guess?"

"We all are there at some point in our careers. It's a tough job having to train someone. You want to ensure you don't forget anything, yet you also don't want to overwhelm them, especially on their first day. Just remember, everyone had to start new at some point. And it's a great pleasure that they think you're prepared enough to take on this challenge."

"Do you?" Hailey leaned against the counter. "Think I'm prepared, I mean."

"Absolutely! They asked me for a suggestion, and I instantly gave them your name. Hailey, you've got this."

"Do you have pointers?" she asked. "Advice on what to point out, what I can't forget, etcetera?"

"My advice would be to think about what you wish you would have known when you first started. Then make sure you do that. You'll want to give her a tour on her first day. That way, she does not feel like she's thrown to the wolves in a completely new place. Sometimes, it's the little things that make the biggest difference."

Hailey nodded, mentally taking notes of Anne's advice. "I don't know why I'm so nervous. I've been doing it long enough."

Anne smirked. "It's just one of those things. You have been doing it so long, but that's when you tend to forget. It's like a routine. When you do the same thing repeatedly, you can do it in your sleep. However, when you start talking about it, you can miss things." By the end of the talk, Hailey was back to her smiling and cheerful self. "But you're going to be fine. We all have faith in you."

Hailey smiled, her dimples returning. "Thank you, Anne. I needed to hear that."

"Anytime." Anne watched as the younger woman walked away.

She stared back at her computer and eased into the flow of the day. She had an initial consultation meeting with a new patient coming in for evaluation. That should take twenty minutes, then the rest of the morning, she would be free to work the patients through their usual routine. It shouldn't be too hectic, at least not until after lunch.

The elevator opened, and Anne glanced at the woman exiting onto their floor. Her jaw dropped as she stood up, trying to mask the obvious questions she wanted to delve into.

CHAPTER FIVE

GETTING THE TOUR

Taylor

Hailey was personable and left Taylor feeling comforted. The minute they left the desk, Hailey had Taylor on a full-fledged tour of the Pediatric floor. Taylor was in awe of how the floor catered to the pediatric patients. The walls were attractively decorated, from the bright and vibrant colors. Each hallway contained a new theme, along with the age groups that housed those rooms: oceans, jungles, cityscapes, and farm animals decorated each corresponding hallway. It was as if the hospital wanted to guarantee that the children wouldn't be bored if they were stuck inside all day. Taylor couldn't help but enjoy the view.

"Our motto is that if kids have to spend their nights here, we want to ensure they don't have to stare at drab surroundings."

"And I would say you do a fine job." Taylor traced the outline of a horse decal on the wall and glanced at Hailey. Hailey beamed, clutching her growing baby bump.

"I look like I'm about to pop, don't I?"

"What?" Taylor exclaimed. "Not at all. Quite the opposite. How far along are you?"

"Six months."

"Wow! You don't look old enough to have a child."

Hailey beamed, standing next to a room at the end of the hall. "That's a nice compliment. It's my first child. My husband and I were high school sweethearts and knew right after high school we'd get married. I worried that going to nursing school would be our demise. I heard horror stories about how being married and going to college full-time, only amounts to debt and arguments. Yet, it never happened to us." She giggled. "Mike is truly my best friend."

Taylor smiled. She would have given anything to have a relationship like that. But Taylor spent high school parenting her brother. She loved her brother dearly, but it was still a bummer that she spent high school playing Mom because her own mom couldn't step up to the plate.

"Do you have kids?"

Taylor shook her head. "My mother was a single mom who wasn't home often, so I helped raise my brother. It's not the same thing."

"Don't sell yourself short," Hailey argued. "I'd have to say that it's just as hard raising a sibling as raising your kid." Hailey touched her stomach. "I'm blessed to have this little bean right here. But it helps to have Mike in my corner. But I love kids. If you want to make it as a Pediatric nurse, you have to."

"You have a valid point there. I'm excited to start. I love kids, too. I think peds is a great fit for me."

"I imagine you're going to fit in great." Hailey grabbed Taylor's arm and gave it a slight squeeze. Taylor smiled, grateful to be part of a team of kind, dedicated people. Hailey walked over to the elevator and pushed the down button. They rode to the second floor. "This is medical records. We use electronic records most of the time, but we still have some paper records in case EMR goes down." Hailey explained when the doors opened. "It's all alphabetical, so quite easy to find what you're looking for. And if you need any help, you can be sure to ask any of us. We'll be glad to help you out. That's one thing about this department, everyone loves helping everyone else."

Taylor grinned -- another great sign. To her, it was as if they were looking at a family and not a workplace. She hoped she didn't relax too much; she had to remain on her A-game today. After Hailey finished her tour, they rode back up to the peds floor.

"We'll see if we can introduce you to some of the department staff. Dr. Newsome should be getting out of the room at any moment. They left the room and were headed down the hall, just as a door opened and an older woman exited the room. She glanced toward Hailey and nodded. "Speaking of…" They stopped next to the woman and Hailey made the introductions. "This is Dr. Newsome. She's been in the department for twenty years. The most senior physician the hospital has on staff."

Dr. Newsome was tall, with a neat silver bun secured on the top of her head. She rolled her eyes. "Hailey likes to make it sound like I'm ancient. I remember when the dinosaurs were roaming the halls."

That made the three of them laugh, and Taylor felt another wave of relief. In college, she heard stories about how you sometimes couldn't joke with the physicians because they always had to keep things serious. But with Dr. Newsome and Hailey, it felt like two friends hanging out.

The two of them continued their easy banter back and forth as Taylor watched them. "It was nice to meet you, Taylor."

"Likewise, I'm sure we'll be working more together in the coming days," Taylor remarked.

"I'll leave you two to finish up the tour." She waved and then turned a corner.

Taylor glanced at Hailey. "Are all the staff so easygoing?" she asked.

Hailey shrugged. "Mostly. Dr. Pohler can be a bit temperamental, but he is a great physician. You can get him to smile a few times, but mostly, good luck trying."

Taylor snickered. That might be a personal quest. She would have to consider it along the way. Anything was possible. Hailey and Taylor rounded the corner and Anne stood behind the nurse's station again. She was mortified when she realized that the one person who saw her outside, making a fool of herself, was the same person she would be working with. It almost felt like she was on a hidden TV show. What was more confusing was that the woman had this glow that left Taylor a tad speechless. She would have to figure out how to get over that quickly.

Taylor and Hailey made their way to the nurse's station, and Anne looked up. "So, how'd the tour go? Do you have the layout memorized?"

Taylor gave a soft laugh. "Hopefully. Guess I'll find out."

Anne nodded. "Good luck to you. Holler if you need anything." She hurried off. Taylor watched after her and didn't look away until Hailey cleared her throat. When she looked at Hailey, Hailey arched an eyebrow.

"What?" Taylor asked, sitting in the chair that Hailey had rolled over for her.

Hailey snickered. "You're not the first person to be enamored by Anne. She is one of the nicest and sweetest people to work in this department. And let's talk loyal. No one could even compare. The patients love her. The parents love her." She shrugged. "There's no one that doesn't."

"Enamored is such a strong word," Taylor mumbled.

Hailey laughed loudly, tossing her head back and her whole face lighting up. "I don't mean anything by it. She's wonderful. I can't find anyone with anything bad to say against her."

"Well, I know I'm new to the group, but you seem rather nice yourself."

Hailey blushed. "Flattery. It will get you everywhere. Now, this is the computer. You be nice to it, and it will be nice to you." She shrugged. "Sometimes."

Taylor laughed. Hailey was quirky. She liked that. She leaned in to study the computer as Hailey worked to guide her through the system. By the end of the computer tutorial, her head was spinning. She hoped to retain enough info to look like she wasn't a complete dunce. With notes going over everything, she was one step further in the learning and ready to make a difference like the rest of the staff.

CHAPTER SIX

GENUINE CHAT

Anne

Anne stepped into the cafeteria. She took in a whiff of the fish and scrunched up her nose. Today, she needed something less filling. She walked over to the sandwich bin, grabbed a chicken club, grabbed bottled water, and went to the cashier.

"Hey Kelly, how's it going?"

Kelly nodded. "It's been a busy morning. I'm looking forward to the lunch crowd dwindling. How are you?"

Anne wanted to lament about her car and how her day had started rough, but with any hope, it could only improve. However, there was a line behind her, and talking about her crummy day would only make her want to cry.

"The day is half over. So gotta love that."

Kelly smiled. "Yep. Enjoy the rest of it." She grabbed her sandwich and water and stepped away from the cashier. She was two seconds away from telling all about her morning. But she was relieved that she somehow let it go. There was no use complaining to anyone else. She glanced around the busy cafeteria until she spotted Taylor in the corner. She had her eyes pointed down at her cell phone and ate alone.

Anne glanced around again to see if anyone would go over and sit with her. When she was satisfied that Taylor was alone, she walked to the booth. "Hey."

Taylor looked up, her eyes wide. "Oh, hi, Anne." She shifted in her seat, quickly pocketing her cell phone.

"I don't want to interrupt. If you're busy, I can sit somewhere else. But truthfully, I tend to feel awkward eating by myself. So, if you wouldn't mind having company, you'll be helping me out."

Taylor quickly shook her head. "Not at all." Her cheeks grew a slight shade of red. "That's why I was staring at my phone. Somehow, I didn't feel so awkward being here alone." She smirked. "There you have it, my truth."

Anne sat down across from her. "Now we both don't have to feel so awkward." She looked at Taylor's sandwich and held up her own. "Welcome to the turkey club, club, I guess." She joked dryly.

Taylor sat up straighter, and her smile widened. Anne got to see her rosy complexion and bright eyes when she smiled. Her eyelashes were long and full. Her blue eyes shone as she stared back at Anne. She was a pretty woman. She was most likely in her early twenties, just straight out of college, but she held her head up in confidence, which is why it was odd to see her hiding behind her phone.

"How's your first day going?" Anne asked, opening up the plastic container that held her sandwich.

"Great! Everyone has been super nice to me, and I'm finding it easier than I could have hoped to acclimate myself to the area. I know it's only been five hours, but I feel like I will get a handle on my responsibilities."

"That's a positive note. Just remember that everyone has good and bad days. How you handle the bad days really makes a person."

They sat and talked for a bit, an easy chit-chat back and forth that surprised even Anne. When they first came into the department, most people were quieter and reserved, testing things out and ensuring they knew how the other co-worker would respond. But Taylor was laughing and joking around with her, almost easier than Anne could. They had good chemistry.

"What made you choose Pediatrics'?" Anne asked.

"I guess you could say Pediatrics chose me." Taylor popped the last bit of her sandwich into her mouth, and Anne stared at her, confused by how that one phrase sounded. She had said that multiple times, but no other person seemed to understand the same motivation. "I love kids. If ever I'm lucky enough to be a mother, I would want their nurse to be someone who cared for them as much as I cared for them. When contemplating what departments to do my residency, it was the only one that made sense."

"Inspiring," Anne mumbled. Taylor looked down, still blushing. "It takes a special person to see it through that way. It's rough to see kids suffering, and you will one day experience a loss you never thought you'd ever feel. And trust me, you never truly get over that loss."

Taylor stared at her, but Anne couldn't move her gaze away. Their eyes were locked, and Anne dared herself not to blink first. However, Anne failed and dropped her gaze to her water. She could feel the tension in the air between them. She was pretty sure if she touched Taylor, sparks would fly. And oh, how she longed to reach out and touch her. Taylor let out a breath and then started to laugh. That chortle brought Anne's eyes back up to Taylor's. Her jaw dropped slightly.

"I don't mean to laugh." Taylor covered her mouth. "I'm just reminding myself of how we first met this morning, with me practically diving face-first into the concrete."

Anne snickered. "You caught yourself. It was quite an impressive catch, indeed."

Taylor shook her head. "It was a rough morning. That was just the icing on the cake. I wouldn't have been surprised if I face-planted and broke my nose." She sighed. "But I am grateful I caught myself."

"Believe me, I know rough mornings," Anne groaned, suddenly thrust back into the accident that nearly left her late to work. Taylor stared at her, compelling Anne to share the story. She sipped on her water. "I was—." Her phone dinged a text message, breaking into her conversation. She glanced down at it and saw her sister's name, with a crying emoji as the text.

Anne groaned, then slipped her phone into her pocket. "I have to go." Without so much as an explanation or apology, Anne got up from the table.

She felt Taylor's eyes on her as she rushed away, dropping the trash into the nearest can and rounding the corner out of sight. She fished her phone out of her pocket and stared at the text again. If Melanie was upset, then she had reason to be. She called her and anxiously waited for her sister to answer.

"H...he...hello?" She sniffled, cutting deep into Anne's core.

"Mel, what's wrong? I got your text."

Immediately, the sniffling got louder, and Anne heard sobs. "I didn't mean to call you at work."

"Where are you? Are you in a safe place? Where's Lily and Rose?"

"Anne, will you stop?!" Melanie whined. "The kids are at the park with their friends, and I'm home alone. I didn't text you to get the third degree. I need someone to talk to and hoped you would listen."

Anne sighed. She would have to do her best. Josh wasn't the epitome of a great guy or even mediocre. In her eyes, he was the scum of the Earth, but Melanie loved him. She always defended him, and Anne sometimes needed to remind herself that she shouldn't be the motherly figure at that moment. She needed to be the friend.

"I'm sorry. I'm here to listen. What's going on?"

"Josh was out late last night. He said he had car trouble and needed to find a way home. It just doesn't add up. I smelled perfume on him. His car was fine this morning."

Anne sighed. If only Melanie would wise up and leave the loser. She released a breath, aching to spew all the hatred she could about her brother-in-law.

"Anne?" she inquired. "I know you want to tell me how much you despise him."

"I won't say those words," Anne replied. "But, Mel, you deserve better. That's not criticizing him. That's merely stating the truth. And I hope that you know you deserve better. He doesn't appreciate you."

"I love him." Then the whining resumed, and Anne could only stand there and listen, leaning against the wall, waiting for Melanie to stop crying over him.

"There's only so much love you can give someone that continues to treat you like that." She sobbed on the other end, but Anne left it at that. As much as she hated to hear that her sister and her husband were experiencing difficulties in their marriage, it reminded Anne that she wasn't the only one with problems. Melanie would cry for hours, possibly all day. Josh would apologize, and Mel would forgive him. It was the sad truth when it came to her sister's marriage. Anne could only hold onto hope that Melanie would eventually know that her happiness and the children's happiness were the most crucial things, and Josh wasn't the one to provide that happiness.

She returned to the floor and saw Taylor at the nurse's station. The conversation was still heavy on Anne's mind. If her sister didn't get out of the house quickly, who knew the damage Josh would cause? Not only to Melanie but to her nieces.

"Everything alright?" Taylor inquired.

"Yeah. Why?" Anne tried to play it off in the most lighthearted of ways.

"Well, you rushed off, and I thought we were bonding. Just wanted to make sure you were doing okay."

Anne sighed. "It's been a long day. I need to get back to work. And so do you."

CHAPTER SEVEN

FOR SHE'S A JOLLY GOOD LADY

Taylor

As the rest of the day went on, Taylor attempted to catch Anne's eye. See if there was some recognition of the moment they had spent together at lunch. It felt like they were talking, experiencing good chemistry with one another, even opening up in ways Taylor had never been able to do. Sure, she hadn't told Anne everything. There had to be more than just a few minutes between them before she was comfortable to dive in. Yet, things shifted the minute Anne ran away from the table. Was she paranoid?

With the day winding down, she saw Anne and prepared to catch up to her. She could be wrong, but she felt this pull toward Anne, and it seemed like Anne was even going to confess her darkest secret until something on her phone had her scurrying away. Although she wanted to catch up to her, Anne disappeared from the elevator.

Taylor frowned. Was Anne always this elusive? What happened to the friendly woman she met at lunch?

"Hey, Taylor. Heading out?" Hailey asked.

Taylor forced a smile and nodded. "Getting there." She hesitated. "So, Anne..." Her mind raced. Maybe it wasn't wise to bring up someone else's business. Hailey arched an eyebrow, waiting in angst as Taylor contemplated letting Hailey in. She shook her head. "Never mind."

"Are you sure?" Hailey tossed her bag over her shoulder. "If you are concerned, we can talk about it."

Taylor shook her head. "No, I'm good."

"Alrighty." Hailey reached into her bag. "I made a copy of your schedule for you. I nearly forgot it, so I'm glad we bumped into each other. First off, you did great today. I know the first day on any job can be a bit stressful, so good job."

"Thanks, Hailey." Taylor looked over her schedule, and her eyes widened. "Is this schedule for real? I have a ton of hours. If I weren't overwhelmed before, this would do me in."

Hailey laughed. "Trust me; there will come a time when you wish you had these hours." She shrugged. "I guess they just want to get your feet wet in all aspects. That way, you have the training. Just appreciate them for now because it won't last forever."

"If you say so," Taylor mumbled. She wasn't used to working full-time, and this gig had several double shifts. She had to remind herself that it was only getting her warmed up to learn all responsibilities. Hailey would know best.

"I have to run. I'll see you tomorrow." She tossed a wave over her shoulder and hurried to the elevator. Taylor looked back down at the schedule and groaned. This would leave virtually no time for activities outside of work. Sure, she had a couple of days off, but it was harder to maneuver around a work schedule so packed.

Taylor waited for the elevator to pick her up, then got on and took the slow ride down to the break room. She had gotten a locker and was able to house her personal belongings. It was bare when she got to the break room, or so she thought. She rounded the corner to the lockers and heard a muffled voice.

"Come to my place: you and the kids. You shouldn't be home with him. Who knows what he'll do?"

Taylor backed up, jamming her elbow against the metal door with a loud CLANG. She cringed, holding her breath. Anne peeked her head around the corner and stared at Taylor. "I'm sorry," Taylor whispered.

"It's fine," Anne mumbled. She pocketed her phone and then turned to a locker. Taylor stopped at her locker, the silence deafening at that moment. Taylor swallowed and glanced at Anne, who was fiddling with the combination. She groaned, moving the combination around several times. Taylor opened her mouth, ready to offer her assistance, when the locker fell open. "Finally," Anne grumbled. Taylor turned back to her locker and quickly grabbed her things from it. When she had her locker closed, she turned to Anne.

"Work tomorrow?" Taylor asked.

"Yep, bright and early. 6:00 A.M."

"I'll see you tomorrow, then." Anne turned and nodded, and then a smile slowly brushed her lips. "Have a good night!" Taylor quipped, then turned and hurried toward the door. If Anne wanted to be cold with her, that was her prerogative. After all, she did nothing wrong. At least nothing that she could recall. The phone call clearly soured Anne's mood. There was torment in Anne's voice.

Taylor entered her car and turned the key. Her car made a noise, then stopped. She groaned. Her car was pretty reliable in most situations. It was an older Toyota Camry, though. One that sometimes liked to be a tad picky. She tried the key again, pumping the accelerator and closing her eyes. All she needed was a little more gas. It started, and she released a sigh. She just needed to know how to work the vehicle.

When Taylor exited onto the highway, even though her radio was playing, she was more mindful of the traffic. It was when everyone got off work, and the highway was busier than in the morning. She tapped on her steering wheel and sang along to the song but focused on the traffic around her. She had to be careful because there wasn't any way she could handle getting into another accident. She was already letting the guilt settle in for the accident that morning. Someone out there was being forced to take care of damage they didn't cause. Why wouldn't she feel guilty?

Thirty minutes later, Taylor pulled into the driveway of her aunt's house. During the daytime, it wasn't anything to write home about. It needed a fresh coat of paint. The roof looked like it could cave in at any given moment. The street leading to the house was filled with potholes. The neighbors liked to get drunk, party, and have loud fights in the middle of the night. But since her aunt didn't force her to pay rent, it was the best she could find. However, she always dreamed of getting out of her house and into a better neighborhood, of course, taking Gavin with her. Maybe even find a place nearby that her aunt could afford if Taylor helped her out. They were all dreams but something to strive for.

Taylor approached the door and fumbled with her purse to find her keys. Before she could get her key out, the door swung open, and Gavin appeared in the foyer, wide-eyed, with a big smile. At seventeen, the baby fat had melted away from his face, revealing an angular jaw. He was starting to bulk up, too. He had biceps and a buzzcut. He played on the football team at his high school, a far cry from the kid who used to hide behind her whenever there were thunderstorms.

"Hey, Sis! It's about time you got home." He pulled her into the foyer, and Taylor smiled. Her aunt stood there with a homemade cake. She was still wearing her sea foam polyester work uniform from the restaurant. She was slim and in her late fifties, with smile lines bracketing her mouth and kind green eyes. She wore her hair in a loose ponytail. Her hands were red and raw from cleaning tables.

Gavin and Kristi both started singing For She's a Jolly Good Lady.

Taylor laughed when the song came to an end. "What's this for?" she asked. The lettering was sloppy, but the cake had writing sprawled across it, which read We're So Proud of You. She flicked a tear away, which had attempted to crawl down her cheek.

"Can't you read?" her aunt asked, laughing. "We're proud of you, and it's celebrating your first day on the job.

"And I'm starving," Gavin moaned. "So, let's have cake."

Taylor rolled her eyes. "After dinner." When he scowled, Taylor snickered. "I know. I'm so mean. Wash up. Aunt Kristi and I are going to make something delicious."

"I'm on it." He hurried out of the foyer, and Taylor reached for the cake.

"I hate that you feel the need to help," Kristi began. "You should be relaxing. After all, today was your big day. Besides, Gavin told me."

Taylor followed her aunt into the kitchen. "He told you what exactly?"

Taylor put the cake down on the counter and leaned back against it.

She would have hoped they could have had a few minutes of quiet, where Kristi didn't know that Taylor had fled from an accident.

"You know I don't approve of people that shirk their responsibilities." She held up a finger and wagged it in front of Taylor. Taylor felt like a little kid, ready for her scolding. She looked down at the floor as Kristi continued. "The truth is, I understand you felt it was your only option. But, honey, you have to remember that I'm here."

"I know, but you work two jobs to keep this house. The last thing you need is to help me out of a bind. Are you disappointed in me?"

Kristi opened the refrigerator and pulled out a casserole she had made special for the occasion. It was Taylor's favorite—sausage and hash browns, fit for dinner and breakfast. "I wouldn't say disappointed, exactly. You're a grown woman, worthy of making up her mind. Just think before you leap next time. I'm always on your side." She winked. "Set the table, and I'll warm this up."

In a way, it was a relief to have the truth out in the open. It could have been worse if she had waited to tell Kristi the truth or if Kristi had found out another way. So, ultimately, Gavin had done the right thing. Now, if only she could ease her guilty conscience.

TAYLOR STARED AT THE FIRE AS THE GLOW TOWERED OVER THE living room ceiling. Gavin was in bed, and at any minute, she'd have to be going, too. It was hard staying up, especially with a 7 A.M. call time. And seven o'clock was going to come soon. Besides, she had fourteen hours scheduled for the next day. She already felt the exhaustion.

"Want me to top off your water?" Aunt Kristi asked, startling Taylor from contemplating the fire.

"Just a bit." Taylor yawned. "I need to go to bed in a few minutes." She smirked when Kristi laughed. "What? You don't think so?"

"You're the one who lived off of coffee and energy drinks for the entirety of college." She winked, and Taylor snickered, sipping on her water.

"I'm different now that I have a job and real responsibilities. It's great to dream, but you sometimes have to be practical."

"Oh. So, this is practical, Taylor?" Aunt Kristi winked and sipped on her coffee. Taylor turned back to the fire. A lot had changed since she dreamt as a child. Back then, the world was hers to conquer.

"We haven't even talked about your day," Aunt Kristi began. "How was it? Outside of the accident, I mean."

Taylor snickered. "Yes, outside of that. But the day was good. You should have seen some of those kids that I worked with. And to see what they're going through; it just breaks your heart."

"And that's why you're meant for pediatrics, my dear."

"There isn't anywhere I'd rather be." Taylor sipped on her water.

"And your co-workers. I trust you're working with a great group?" Aunt Kristi arched an eyebrow, always the motherly figure. It gave Taylor great comfort to know that Aunt Kristi would always be there for support as she navigated her new job.

"Hailey is the one that trained me. She's six months pregnant and oh so tiny. She has a great heart. I lucked out when it came to working closely with her. I couldn't have asked for a better trainer to get me through my first day." Taylor dropped her gaze to the fire and thought back to the hours before when she started, not knowing where anything was, and left the day confident she could make this job work. "The physicians seem friendly enough. I heard there's a doctor that can be a bit temperamental, but I've seen plenty of guys like that."

"The neighbor in the back to mention one," Kristi teased.

Taylor laughed. "Mr. Landrin. Yep. He just might be one I was thinking of." Always yelling about the rickety fence that crossed their paths in the back. Even though it was on his property, he was insistent it was their nuisance. He and Aunt Kristi had yet to come to a resolution.

"There's always one grouch in the bunch," Aunt Kristi added. "Anyone interesting?"

Taylor's cheeks flushed, and she looked down at her glass of water. It was as if her Aunt had already read her mind. It was true; their bond was like no other, but she hadn't even breathed a word of Anne, and her Aunt was there to drag it out of her.

"Come on, Taylor. I see that sparkle in your eye, and your rosy cheeks don't exactly hide the truth." Aunt Kristi laughed. "What aren't you telling me?"

"Aunt Kristi, you're like a human lie detector." Her eyes lit up, but Taylor held up her hand. "Most of the time." Taylor laughed. "There isn't anything to tell. I mean, it's only been one day. The co-workers are nice, and we should leave it at that." She downed the rest of her water and stood up.

Aunt Kristi grimaced. "I am disappointed that you aren't going to tell me what you're hiding from me. But if that's the way you want it." She huffed and looked away.

Taylor sunk back down to her chair, and her Aunt grinned. Taylor shook her head. Her Aunt tended to get Taylor to talk, even if she didn't want to. But, in this case, Taylor wasn't eager to hide something. She was looking forward to getting something off her chest. It didn't sit well with her on how the workday ended, how she and Anne went from laughter to an icy silence.

"There is this one woman."

"I knew it," her Aunt said with a gleam. "Doctors and nurses always date each other. Am I right? Do tell."

Taylor laughed. "First of all, you can't know if it's something special after a few hours in the same space. Secondly, we ate lunch together, having a good time. Or so I thought. She then rushes off, like someone had lit a fire under her butt." Taylor shook her head. "I have no idea, but it was the strangest thing. Then she was almost cold when she saw me in the afternoon, and when I was grabbing my things from the break room, I saw her again. Nothing in that interaction said she even enjoyed getting to know me. So, whatever. Maybe that's why I'm single. I just don't get women." Taylor frowned. "I know that came out weird, but you know what I mean."

Aunt Kristi nodded. "Quite well. But you said it yourself; it's only been a day. Maybe she's shy and reserved."

"Not her," Taylor argued.

"It's hard to judge a person when you hardly know them. It's possible she just had a lot on her mind. Or some people are different. Your forever love doesn't need to be found on the first day, Taylor." Aunt Kristi stood up and walked over to her, taking the glass from her hand and kissing the top of her head. "Give it in time. Don't cut anyone out of the equation. You never know. Good night!"

"Night, Aunt Kristi." Those words played in Taylor's mind as she stared at the fireplace, then leaned back to watch the glow. It was true that Hailey said Anne was one of the sweetest people she knew. She didn't see Hailey as someone who would intentionally lie. Maybe Anne had a lot on her mind. Taylor got lost in the glow of the fire. She could stick around a few more minutes. Now, she hardly felt tired.

CHAPTER EIGHT

HOUSEHOLD VISITORS

Anne

The house was eerily quiet as Anne peeked into her spare room. Lily and Rose were asleep peacefully as if Melanie hadn't pulled them from the only home they knew. Anne was glad Melanie had agreed to come to the house, even though Anne spent the night with Melanie hashing over things.

He said it was a mistake. The affair is over. Anne rolled her eyes at that one. Josh had been caught. It didn't matter what he said. Anne wasn't about to believe him. She didn't understand why Melanie quickly let it go. She knew why, at least based on the one-word answer she usually got from her sister. *Love.* Was Melanie sure about that? Anne had been in love once, but it felt like forever ago. She couldn't imagine giving up herself and her beliefs for another person. But then again, abuse was a cycle.

True, he never hit Melanie. Or so she always tried to convince Anne. But there were other kinds of abuse; her sister and nieces needed and deserved better.

Anne rounded the corner, and Melanie sat at the table, a coffee cup in her hand. She looked up when Anne's slippers padded on the kitchen tile. Her brown eyes looked worried. Anne could tell Melanie hadn't been sleeping; bags were under her eyes. She looked exhausted. Melanie was always the girlie girl in the family. She loved makeup and clothes. Melanie wore no makeup tonight, and Anne could see her roots peeking out of her blonde hair. She looked like a shell of her former self.

"Just made a fresh pot. Help yourself."

"Don't mind if I do." Anne grabbed her mug and poured herself a cup. "Checked in on the kids, and they're sleeping like two snug bugs in a rug."

Melanie laughed. "It's been a long time since you said that."

Anne looked over at her sister, and she had the brightest smile. It felt like ages since she had seen that smile, and she had forgotten how much she missed it. "You know, sis, you and the kids can stay here as long as you want." She slid into the seat across from her and sipped her coffee. Melanie's face fell. She nodded but glanced down at her mug. "Okay, if staying here doesn't cut it, I can put you up in a hotel." After all, she wasn't going to get her house paid off this month anyway. What were a few hundred dollars spent at the hotel? If it meant her sister and nieces would be safe, she was all for it.

"Anne, I appreciate the offer. But I think we're going to head home tomorrow. If the kids were awake, we might even make it tonight." She smirked. "I was a little rash earlier."

Anne frowned, leaning back in her chair. "Did you hear from him? Is that why the sudden change of tune?"

"No!" Melanie argued. "He's my husband and the girl's father. What's running going to do? Absolutely nothing."

"Show me your phone." Anne held out her hand and waited. Melanie's jaw dropped. "If there's nothing on your phone from Josh, there's nothing to hide."

"With all due respect, Anne, I'm thirty-two and way too old to have my sister think she can control my life." She dropped her gaze, and Anne slammed her hand down on the table.

"Dammit, Mel. What did he say this time? How many tears do you have to cry before you realize that you're just being a doormat to your husband?" Anne didn't mean to sound so harsh, but watching her sister fall for Josh's same old tricks was frustrating.

"That's not fair." Melanie shook her head. "You're not married. You wouldn't understand."

Anne huffed and dropped her gaze to the table. She could stare at the wooden furniture for hours, and those words wouldn't hurt any less. But if that's what Melanie felt about it, then why sulk? She had made up her mind. *You know you don't feel that way. If she walks out that door and Josh takes his anger out on her, then you're going to be sorry you ever let her go.* "I may not be married, but I saw the pain in our mother's eyes, and I'm sure you did, too."

Melanie looked away from her. Her eyes darkening. Anne shook her head and stared at her coffee. If only her sister would understand that Josh was always going to be the man he was. He wouldn't change, and nothing could make that happen.

"I can't make you stay." The words came out, barely above a whisper. She bit down on her lip, fearing that tears would soon follow. Josh wasn't worth her tears, but her sister and nieces were. She reached for her coffee as Melanie looked at Anne.

"I know you don't get it. Hell, there are times when I don't, either. I don't want to rush back to him." She pushed the phone toward Anne. "3287."

"Huh?"

"My passcode. It's 3287." Anne reluctantly grabbed the phone and put in the code. Instantly, Josh's message came up.

JOSH:

> Baby, I'm sorry. We need to work through this.
> If you want me to see a counselor, I will.

"He's never offered to see a counselor before. That's a first step that could be our breakthrough." Anne slowly nodded, pushing the phone back toward her. "You don't believe him. Typical."

"Mel," Anne started. "I want to believe him. It would give me no greater pleasure than knowing he got some help and was the father your girls need and the husband you deserve. But I worry about you guys. You forget that I have seen horrible family situations at the hospital. Dads that abuse their kids and broken families. I don't want you in the midst of that."

"I get that, but I promise you, if we go back and things don't change, I will get us out of there. I'll be able to protect the girls. I know that I will."

If only Anne could believe that. But it was her sister's life, and arguing for her to stay could only drive a wedge between them. "Be careful."

Melanie smiled. "I always am." The smile never faded as she took another sip of her coffee. She licked her lips, then sighed. "So, what's going on with you? Anything new lately?"

Anne snickered, taking a drink of her coffee and nearly spitting it out. She didn't want to tell her sister about the accident when Mel had her own crisis brewing.

"My online shop is booming," Anne began. Anne knew she needed to drop the topic, and this was a nice detour. She made small, knitted items, from keychains to stuffed animals, and sold them online. It started as a hobby and slowly turned into another avenue of income, allowing her the opportunity to help with her mortgage and other finances. Anne never thought it would go anywhere, but she was pleasantly surprised by the reputation her online shop had earned. Getting noticed by reviews was sometimes a challenging goal to achieve. Now, she was finally starting to gain some recognition.

"That's great. What's popular these days?" Melanie asked, sipping on her coffee.

"Well, you know anything from *Mandalorian* is popular. People still request Baby Yoda." Anne was glad to have the reprieve from bringing up her biggest drama.

"That's great! I know the girls love the unicorns you made last year." Anne smiled. Lily was six. Rose was five. They were practically twins in Anne's eyes. Melanie and Josh wasted no time before they announced their second pregnancy. Back then, Josh was still a loser, but because he helped bring Lily and Rose into their lives, Anne pushed past his flaws. Now, it seemed there were too many to ignore. "Anything else going on?" Melanie asked.

There was no dodging that question. Anne had to tell the truth. "Your sister was in a little fender bender this morning."

"What?" Melanie stared. "Obviously, you're not hurt, right? But why didn't you tell me? Who's fault was it?"

"Well, I'm not hurt. It wasn't my fault." Anne sighed. "And the person fled the scene, so I'll have to pay for it out-of-pocket." Melanie reached out and touched Anne's hand, finding reason now to console Anne, but Anne didn't want the attention solely directed at her. Her sister was in a precarious situation and needed someone to always be on her side. "It's fine. It's just that when everything is going perfectly, and then it changes overnight, and you feel like everything you've worked toward is getting done for?"

Melanie's eyes widened. "I think you lost me."

"I guess I lost myself, too. I was about to make my last mortgage payment. I had parties planned, and I was super excited. Then this happened. Now, who knows how much this will cost me?"

"That totally sucks. Sorry, Anne."

Anne glanced at her coffee, then downed the last droplets. Perhaps it was her own naivety. She couldn't expect everything to go off without a hitch. Now was the time to survey the damage. No one else could help her out.

CHAPTER NINE

THE NEW TRAINER

Taylor

When the elevator doors opened, Taylor spotted Anne at the nurse's station. Taylor didn't know whether to approach her or avoid her. Unfortunately, the decision wasn't all hers. Anne looked up and offered a brief smile. Taylor sighed. Maybe she was in a bad mood the past couple of days. Yesterday, during her fourteen-hour shift, she had talked to Anne twice. Both times were because Anne needed a computer, and Taylor just happened to be sitting in front of the only free one. She wasn't gruff about it, but she felt none of the sparks during lunch two days ago.

"Good morning, Anne."

"Good morning. We are going to have a busy day today. Hailey called in sick; I'm guessing morning sickness. You're with me."

The air rushed out of Taylor's lungs. She had a strong urge to apologize to Anne. Maybe that would help. Yet, apologizing felt weird. Everyone had to learn sometimes. She feared that Anne and she wouldn't have the same working relationship she had with Hailey the two days before.

Anne continued, "We're down one nurse. It's going to get a tad hectic." Already, they had shared more conversation than they had in the last twenty-four hours; this was going to be awkward.

"Just put me where you need me." Taylor hoped she didn't seem anxious. Anne continued with a smile and nodded.

"Follow me. Our first patient is Willow. She's a frequent flyer around this ward. She has leukemia. She's been sick and moved to this department for follow-up. If things don't improve here, she will be transferred to a Cancer facility specializing in Children and cancer. The poor girl. She's been through a lot."

Taylor could hear the sadness in Anne's voice. She spoke from the heart, and Taylor could practically feel the pain oozing from Anne. Hailey had mentioned Anne had a big heart and was fabulous with the patients. Taylor experienced that from the first second Anne spoke, relieving Taylor's fears. Everyone could have a bad day, even two.

"Good morning, Willow. How are you feeling today?"

"Sick." She rubbed her stomach and frowned. "Can I get a Jell-O?"

"Absolutely. I'm going to get some vitals, and we'll grab that right away for you. Willow, this is Taylor. She's going to be assisting me today."

Willow gave a slight wave. "Hey, Willow. We're going to get you all better." Taylor grinned at the little girl, but from the corner of her eye, she saw Anne staring at her. Taylor shrugged it off. "What kind of Jell-O would you like when we're done?"

"Strawberry!" Her eyes lit up, and Anne hurried to the side of her, grabbing a thermometer as she passed the cart. Taylor stood there awkwardly. Hailey would tell her what to do, but Anne seemed focused on the patient. She understood, though, because it was just the two different work personalities. If she wanted to make it, she would have to be sure to understand the nuances of the hospital staff. After all, that, too, was part of a nurse's duty.

"Would you like me to grab the BP?" Taylor asked, reaching for the cuff.

"No, I got it. Just observe right now." Her tone cut through like a knife, and Taylor frowned, withdrawing her hand as if someone had just slapped her.

A lump slowly formed in her throat. Was Anne moody? For the rest of the visit with Willow, Taylor didn't even attempt to assist. Anne didn't seem like she needed or wanted the help. If that's how she felt, then Taylor would back off, but she made a mental note for future patients. Anne had excellent bedside manner, though. Anyone could see that. She knelt at her eye level and talked to her more than she even acknowledged Willow's parents. They were huddled on a couch, watching, observing. Taylor saw her mother's red, puffy eyes, and Taylor's heart went out to them. She bit down on her lip, hoping she wouldn't start crying. That was one thing Taylor hadn't considered: her inability to control her emotions. Yet, she needed to work through that because the patients weren't there to console her.

"We're all set in here. We'll grab you your Jell-O and be right back."

"Thank you, Anne." Willow's mother said. Anne turned to her and nodded, then turned back around and swiftly moved toward the door. Once they were both outside the door, Anne stopped and turned to Taylor.

"Are you nuts?"

Taylor cowered back, frowning. "Excuse me." Anne grabbed her arm and pulled her away from Willow's room, not stopping until they reached the nurse's station. "You can't seriously tell me that you thought it was a good idea to tell a little girl with cancer that she was going to get all better, right? Did your brain glitch? Because no one would think that was a good idea."

Taylor's eyes furrowed, and she thought back to the encounter with Willow. "Oh." She covered her mouth. "I wasn't thinking."

"That's painfully clear, but you need to start thinking because we have patients that die every year in this ward, who we would give our own breath to have saved. Many of those patients are Willow's age or even younger. Don't let that happen again." The last sentence stuck in Taylor.

"I'm sorry," Taylor mumbled. "It won't." She looked away, wary that a tear might fall. Anne was seething. Taylor didn't dare look in her direction. It'd only been two days, but Anne acted like she shouldn't mess up. Things were bound to happen, but maybe Taylor was destined to fail.

"Take this to Willow. She's waiting." Taylor turned back, and she had the Jell-O cup. There wasn't an ounce of a smile on Anne's face. Taylor grabbed it and dropped her head as if Anne scolded her as if she were a child. There had to be a way for her to show Anne she wasn't a complete failure.

She entered Willow's room, and Willow looked up, her eyes bright and expecting. "Here you go, Willow."

"Thank you!"

Taylor peeled back the top and handed over the Jell-O and spoon. She glanced over at her parents; her dad had snaked his arm around the mom's shoulder, protecting her. It was a noble sight, indeed.

"You let us know if you need anything. The doctor will check in on you in an hour or so."

"Thank you!" Her dad replied. Her mom appeared like she was ready to break. Taylor nodded and then left the room. When she returned to the nurse's station, Anne glanced up but immediately looked back down at the computer. "I can't imagine watching your child go through something like this."

"And for so long," Anne mumbled.

"Does Willow have any siblings?"

Anne sighed and looked away from the computer. Her eyes were still dark and hazy. Yet, there was still a vulnerability in them as Anne spoke. "Two brothers and a sister. The sister is older. The brothers are younger. They're staying with their grandparents while her parents can be here. The mom stepped away from her job. From what I understand, the dad's job is in peril. Their lives could be uprooted even more."

"So sad," Taylor whispered.

"Unfortunately, it's what we face around here. We need to get on to the next patient. Follow me." And again, they were off. Throughout the rest of the morning, when it came to Anne and the patients, she was phenomenal. Taylor watched her with curiosity. Hailey was right. As much as Anne loved her job and the patients she helped, the patients loved her just as much. Even the new patients seemed to have this connection with her and feel at ease.

While it was amazing to experience, Taylor couldn't help but notice that Anne was avoiding her. One screw-up, and it was like Taylor was dead to Anne. It was heart-wrenching because Taylor wanted to be there and learn from Anne.

The last patient of the morning was twelve-year-old Simon, and he needed labs drawn as he was getting ready to remove a benign tumor from his leg. Anne and Taylor entered the room, just like they had with so many patients earlier in the day. Only this time, something was different.

After Anne finished taking his vitals, she turned to Taylor. "Would you like to draw the labs?"

Taylor stared at her; her jaw dropped, beads of sweat popping up on her forehead. She glanced at Simon, who frowned and grabbed onto the bed, not looking interested in any mention of a blood draw. Then, he turned to his mom, who didn't notice Taylor's hesitation.

"Sure!" Taylor's voice cracked. The last time she had poked a patient was when she was doing her clinicals, and it wasn't a twelve-year-old boy. Instead, a fifty-eight-year-old woman didn't seem phased by getting her blood drawn. She had enough experience. During her clinicals, though, she had done several. She got some of the even tougher sticks, with which her teachers struggled. There was nothing to be concerned about except why Anne was suddenly putting her in this position. After barely two words to one another, when she wasn't introducing Taylor, this seemed like a sudden stretch.

She took a stride of confidence and walked over to the tubes Anne had already laid out before her. Feeling all eyes on her, she worked on getting everything set up. When it came to putting it in his arm, though, Taylor's mind blanked. She stared at the needle and then his arm. She had already disinfected the arm, but her mind was jumbled. Taylor released a breath and moved in. She felt again for the vein, swabbed the area with an alcohol pad one last time, and just went with it. There was no holding back, and it was a clean stick. One tube was taken, followed by another. She removed the tourniquet, pulled the needle out, and took a swab to his arm, but there wasn't a drop of blood.

"Let me know when you're done." He squeezed his eyes shut.

"I'm done." He opened his eyes and looked at his arm.

"I didn't even feel that."

Taylor breathed a sigh of relief. "I'm always happy to hear that." Taylor's words were cheery, but she was jumping for joy inside.

"We are all through here," Anne piped in. "The doctor has one more patient and will then be checking in to see if you have any questions on the forthcoming surgery. Let us know if you need anything."

They left the room, and Taylor finally released the pent-up sigh. "You did a good job in there."

Taylor stopped and turned to Anne. Those words filled her with more emotions than she had anticipated. "Excuse me." She turned and quickly moved to the restroom. When the door slammed behind her, she fell against the sink and tears flowed. After a morning where Anne didn't give her any acknowledgment other than to scold her, she needed that small compliment. She covered her face, shaking her head. But what if the blood draw had gone wrong? She would never hear the end of it and question her self-worth as a nurse.

She grabbed a paper towel and covered her face, trying to soak up all the tears. She needed more confirmation than she liked to admit. After a few minutes of standing there, gawking at her reflection in the mirror, her phone vibrated in her pocket. She reached for it and stared at the message.

AUNT KRISTI:

> Double shift at the restaurant today. I need to get the electricity paid for. Will you stop on the way home? Write a check, and I'll give you the cash to put back in your account.

Taylor groaned. It wasn't the first time Kristi expected to cover the household expenses, but her aunt eventually paid her back. Yet, there wasn't much in her bank account, so she hoped she had enough to cover.

Taylor heard a noise at the door, and she quickly pocketed her phone. Anne popped around the corner. "Sorry to interrupt, but," Her words trailed off. "Have you been crying?"

Taylor sighed. She didn't want anyone to think less of her, but she could already feel the condescending stares. "No, I'm good. Just caught in a coughing fit."

Anne shrugged. "You're wanted in HR. They said you have to take a test. I think it's just some basic stuff. But they said ASAP."

"Alright then! Thank you for the message. I'll head right there."

Anne left the bathroom and turned back to her reflection. She grabbed her phone again and pulled up her bank account. After making the payment, she looked at just having a couple of dollars left in her account. There weren't any other options.

TAYLOR:

Yep. I'm on it.

She had to do what she had to do, but she couldn't wait until her first paycheck. Two weeks wouldn't come quickly enough.

CHAPTER TEN

SEEING RED

Anne

The cafeteria was empty as Anne entered the room and looked around at their food options for the day. What she needed was a salad; what she wanted were a burger and fries. She groaned as the salad won. The week felt excruciating. She'd been busy at work. To top it off, she couldn't get anyone to fix her car. It wasn't due to a lack of trying. Every place she called was slammed with customers.

Anne headed toward an empty booth after she paid for her salad and water. The less she had to converse with anyone, the better. This week had put her in a foul mood. It wasn't like her, but it was hard to find a way out of it when every time she perked up, she encountered another blunder. For starters, it still bothered her that Melanie forgave Josh so easily and was willing to take the girls back to their house. Josh promised they could start couples counseling. But Anne had yet to see Josh follow through on a promise. Anne wanted her sister to understand that Josh would say what he could to get them back in his grasp. Anyone could see that except for the one person who needed to.

As she reached the booth, she spotted Taylor two tables away. That was another thing altogether. On the first day, they had a good chat at lunch. She was even mildly intrigued to learn more about the new resident. But then her life blew up. Now, she was stuck worrying about Melanie. She took her aggression out on the co-workers she knew the least, a.k.a Taylor. It'd been two days of being forced into working together. Hailey was still out sick, and there was concern over whether she could return.

Taylor did make some stupid judgment calls; telling Willow she would get all better was at the top of the list. But overall, Anne saw some potential in her. She was young, vibrant, and had the same drive Anne felt at that age. Anne could see that in her. She also noticed something else. Taylor had her emotions at the forefront at all times. She walked in on her crying and never once believed the story that she was in a coughing fit. Those were real emotions Anne saw in Taylor's eyes. She had been there before. At the start of her nursing residency, she wasn't nearly as poised as Taylor was.

"Mind if I sit here?"

Taylor looked up away from her phone. "Um yeah, sure, if you want." She wasn't the confident individual that Anne saw on the first day. Was that because of Anne's gruff tendencies? Taylor's mistakes made Anne frustrated, which she took out on Taylor. She knew this wasn't the best way to welcome a new hire, but she wanted to push Taylor to live up to her potential.

"Thank you!"

Taylor dropped her phone to the table, and Anne's eyes went to it. Taylor touched the phone, switching it to silent.

"You're not eating?" Anne asked. "You need to keep your strength up, especially for a fourteen-hour shift."

"I had a banana. I'm good."

Anne arched an eyebrow. She wanted to scowl and tell Taylor that just a banana wouldn't suffice, but she backed off and dug into her salad. Anne could feel Taylor watching her as she ate. "So," Anne began. "I owe you an apology."

Taylor scoffed. Anne fought the urge to reach across, grab hold of her, and tell her to stop being so nervous. She wasn't there to chastise her or fight her. She swallowed and took another bite of her salad.

"It's been a rough week. It started badly and only went downhill from there. So, if I offended you anyway, jumped on your case for Willow, or treated you poorly the last few days, know it wasn't personal. I shouldn't have been like that because it's no way to treat a new team member.

Taylor gawked at Anne. This time, Anne fidgeted from one side to the other. When the blonde's eyes were on her, she felt like Taylor could see right through her. The feeling was confusing, awkward, and even a bit exhilarating. While she was the senior nurse to Taylor, she was also intrigued by her. Anne had yet to decipher whether it was her looks or her personality, but with Taylor staring at her that way, she felt it was something she'd never experienced.

She laughed slightly. "Will you say something? Anything? Please."

Taylor dropped her gaze and slowly nodded. "Apology accepted. Although, I don't think it was warranted. You were right to talk to me about Willow. It was a blunder that I should have never made. And I totally get having a bad week. I've been there. So, consider it forgotten." Her smile widened, and Anne couldn't help but respond with the same. Already, Anne could tell that Taylor had a forgiving, loving spirit, which would make her perfect for pediatrics.

Anne dug into her salad again and then took a swig of water, finally relaxing. Taylor focused on Anne's salad again, almost as if she was salivating over it. When Anne caught her looking, Taylor put on a smile.

"Your salad looks delicious. I'll have to remember that for the next time."

"You still have thirty minutes in your lunch. I'm sure the banana won't hold you over."

"No, I'm stuffed. Really." Yet, Taylor's actions told otherwise. Was it a financial thing? Taylor had just been working there for four days. She wouldn't be getting paid for another week and a half. Anne didn't know her finances, but she knew her own. It was a rough road until she started making regular pay. Even then, she had moments where she still scrambled to make ends meet.

"Excuse me. I'll be right back." She got up from the table and went over to the salads. She grabbed one and then a water and went to pay for it. When she got back to the table, Taylor stared at her.

"What's this? I said I was stuffed."

Anne shrugged. "Just thought you could try it. That way, the next time, you'll know if it's something you want to buy. Just eat what you want." She sat down and went back to her salad."

"At least let me pay for it." Taylor was slow to reach into her purse, but Anne reached out and touched her hand. Taylor hesitated, and Anne smiled at her.

"Consider it the rest of my apology." She winked, then withdrew her hand.

"Thank you," Taylor mumbled. For someone who wasn't hungry, she started eating the salad with the enthusiasm of someone starving. Anne tried to tear her eyes away, but there was a piece of Taylor's story Anne didn't know. Maybe one day, she could understand Taylor a little more.

ANNE'S APOLOGY LESSENED THE TENSION BETWEEN THEM. THE rest of the work day flew by. Anne allowed Taylor to take on more responsibilities with the patients. Without Hailey, it made for some heavier workloads, but having Taylor there did help once Anne allowed Taylor to work solo for a bit. When the shift was over, Taylor finalized the documentation, and Anne watched over her shoulder to ensure Taylor didn't miss anything.

"Like that?" Taylor asked.

"Yep. Looks great. And our shift is over. It's been a long day. We can head on out." Since Hailey was out, Anne had to cover for her. She didn't mind the extra shifts, but it reminded her she wasn't as young as she once was. "You're doing great, Taylor. If I don't say that enough, just remember that."

Taylor grinned. "Thank you, and I appreciate your allowing me more freedom. And I must say, kudos to you for working with the patients. They absolutely adore you."

Anne snickered. "Thank you!" They stepped onto the elevator and rode it down. "I adore them all. I used to plan these excursions to the courtyard. The children would be able to experience the zoo. For the patients that have to stay here for days, weeks, months," Anne sighed. "They needed to have the same experiences that healthy kids get, you know?"

"That's awesome. I'm sure the kids love it. But you said, used to. You don't anymore?"

Anne nodded, leaning back against the wall of the elevator. "They did until budget cuts decimated the program." Anne rolled her eyes. "They've had to let some staffing go, so they bring on residents, who they can pay less." The doors opened, and Taylor frowned. "Not to say it isn't vital to have new nurses. It's the only way a hospital can grow."

Yet, that comment didn't sit well with Taylor, and Anne felt bad as they clocked out and grabbed their things from their lockers. It wasn't until they were out of the break room that Anne proceeded.

"I didn't say it to make you feel bad. It's not your fault. It's politics, and that sucks."

Taylor shrugged. "I understand. I can also see why it would be frustrating." They remained quiet as they left the hospital. Anne felt a pang of regret for even mentioning it. Just when they were back to being good, she had to screw things up and say the wrong thing. It had to be hurtful to hear.

"I really didn't mean anything by it. I was torn to pieces when they nixed the excursions, and I had to tell the kids that it would never happen again. They were understanding. It was me that went off the rails." Anne forced a smile as Taylor stopped in the parking lot.

"I'm sure it was hard to hear."

Anne sighed and looked down at the car they were standing by. "It is what it is," she muttered. Her eyes skimmed over the front of the car until it landed on the damage. She frowned. Then, she diverted her eyes to the rearview mirror, where a familiar ribbon hung. "Is this your car?"

Taylor nodded. "It's not much, I know. I aim to fix it or get a cheap used car within the year. Gotta have a paycheck for that, though." She laughed.

Anne didn't make a move to laugh. She kept staring. "Um, I gotta go." She backed up, her eyes burning into that fiery red color. She couldn't believe another rug had been pulled out from under her.

"Anne?"

Anne turned on her heel and ran away. Standing in front of her was the one person she wanted to see and ask how she could do it. Anne was at a loss for words. The anger was boiling inside, and she just needed to leave.

CHAPTER ELEVEN

SAYING GOODBYE

Taylor

What happened? What is it now? Those words floated through Taylor's mind as she tried to shake the image of Anne bolting out of her mind. They were good, then there was conflict, then they were good, and now it was like Taylor had burned Anne, and she wasn't even holding the flame. She had to figure out the root cause, or they would be stuck in awkward silence for another month.

The next day, she took a deep breath and entered the hospital. She had every intent of getting the hard stuff out of the way. When she saw Anne wasn't there, a flood of relief washed over her. They could worry about it later if she could ignore that interaction in the parking lot for a day. She would quickly, if not graciously, accept that. Hailey was back so today would be hopefully uneventful.

"How are you feeling?" Taylor asked.

"Better. This little one just wanted to make my life hell for a few days." She laughed. "I don't hold any grudge because, frankly, as the mother, I get to take revenge once he or she is born." She laughed, shrugging. "My doctor wants me to take it easy, but I'll be here while I'm feeling good. Did I miss anything?"

"Nope. Everything ran pretty smoothly. We missed you, though."

Hailey clutched her chest. "That's sweet. It's when you're gone that people really notice you." She wrapped her arm around Taylor. "I missed you guys and am super glad to be back. I hear you rocked the past few days."

Taylor frowned. "You did. From whom?"

"All of these love letters I received." She scattered them out on the desk. "When your main mentor isn't at the office, the other staff have to keep them in the loop. You got all enthusiastic praise. Kudos to you."

"Oh wow!" Taylor looked down at the papers, and she spotted Anne's immediately. She picked it up and read to herself. *I had the pleasure of working with Taylor over the last few days, and I'm pleasantly surprised. She's a brilliant nurse, and I only expect great things to come in her future.* " Interesting."

"And what about this one?" Hailey arched an eyebrow. "Taylor has great potential. She worked diligently and efficiently with our patients and always kept a smile on her face. She can work my rotation anytime. Signed Dr. Pohler."

Taylor's jaw dropped. "I didn't even notice that he noticed me." She was surprised to see the glowing review from Anne, but it made sense. Anne must have written it before the encounter in the parking lot. But Dr. Pohler, it seemed like everyone had taken notice, even when Taylor expected them to nod and shrug and barely know she was alive. "I'm sure it had something to do with my training."

Hailey shook her head. "I can't take any credit. After all, I trained you and then had to be off. I guess Anne would be the one who gets the credit. Either way, though. I'm proud of you."

"Thank you!" Taylor looked down at the raving reviews, and a knot dropped to the pit of her stomach. As nice as it was, she hoped she could speak with Anne and find out what exactly made her rush off.

"I have to drop these off to HR today. They'll go in your file for work; whenever they need to look at raises and promotions, they'll have all the necessary ammo they need." She put them into a neat pile and pushed them aside. "Today, I think it's safe to say you can work a little on your own. Willow is getting ready to be transported today." She grabbed a packet. "The info is right here. Whenever someone gets moved to a different facility, they will add a yellow sticker to her chart. It looks like, at 2:15, an ambulance is picking her up to transfer her to Tennessee."

"Does Anne know?" Taylor asked. "I know that she really cares about Willow. It would be nice if someone let her know. Seeing that she's off today and all."

"Good thinking. I can text her." She handed the chart over to Taylor. "Check on the family and see how she's doing. Ensure she doesn't need anything; if she does, get it for her. This transition will be rough for her, but we want to make her comfortable."

"I'm on it." Taylor grabbed the chart. She reached her room and took a deep breath before she dared enter. The moment reminded her of earlier in the week when she foolishly told Willow that she would be just fine. She deserved the scolding from Anne, but even that didn't deter a negative review. "Good morning! How are you all doing?"

Willow's mom looked at her, and her eyes were red. It was just Willow and her mom. Willow gave a weak smile. "Hi, Taylor." Her eyes widened as she sat up in her bed.

"Hello, munchkin." She brushed a strand of hair behind Willow's ear and then turned to her mom. "Do you have any questions?" Her mom glanced at Willow and then at Taylor, then back to Willow. "Do you want to talk outside?" Taylor asked. Her mom sighed and nodded. "How would you like a Strawberry Jell-O, milady?"

Willow eagerly nodded, and Taylor squeezed her hand. Taylor escorted her mom outside. With the door closed, her mother collapsed back against the wall. "I'm trying to be so strong for Willow, my other kids..." she hesitated. "And Paul."

"Your husband?" Taylor asked.

"He had to work this morning, or he would have been out of a job. We know traveling back and forth to Tennessee will be inevitable for him. I'll stay there all the time, but I worry that I'll break down in front of her, and I don't want to have that meltdown. But what if she isn't, okay?"

"Ella," Taylor started. "May I call you Ella?" She nodded, and Taylor continued. "I know it's difficult, but you have to have faith that Willow is going to be in the best place for her care. It's hard, I totally get that, but unfortunately, you have to be the strong one for Willow. She's going to look at you for your support." Ella sniffled and looked down at the floor. "I'm not saying that to upset you. But trust in the doctors, and we'll all be here rooting for her to get her health back."

"Thank you, Taylor." Ella leaned in and hugged her. When they parted, there were still a couple of tears in her eyes, but Leona smiled. "I better get back to her."

"I'll grab her Jell-O and be back in." Taylor squeezed Ella's hand, then turned to the nurse's station. As she grabbed the cup from the refrigerator, the phone started ringing. "CAPMED Pediatric Department. This is Taylor. How may I help you?" There was breathing on the line, and Taylor waited. "Hello?" The call went dead, and Taylor frowned. It had to be a wrong number; who else would prank call Pediatrics? Hailey rounded the corner before Taylor stepped away to go back to Willow's room. "Did you text Anne?"

"Yep. She said she'll be here to say goodbye." The phone rang again, and Hailey reached across the counter and grabbed it. "CAPMED Pediatrics' Department. This is Hailey. How may I help you?" Taylor turned and headed to see Willow. "Oh hey, Anne."

Taylor looked over her shoulder at the mention of Anne's name. It couldn't be. Anne wouldn't have blatantly hung up on her, would she? She shook that thought out of her mind and hurried back to Willow's room, telling herself it was a coincidence.

———

As Taylor got up from the table in the cafeteria, her phone started vibrating. Aunt Kristi flashed across the screen. Taylor gasped. The last thing she wanted was to see a call from her. She always texted. Aunt Kristi only called during emergencies.

"Hello?"

"How's work going? I'm not catching you at a bad time, am I? I would hope that if you couldn't answer the phone, you wouldn't."

"Um, is everything alright? I'm used to texts. Calls, not so much. So, I panicked." Taylor snickered, but only slightly, still fearing the worst.

"I'm sorry, dear. Everything is fine. I will be working late tonight and wasn't sure if I would catch you in the morning. I'm putting some money on the counter. Will you be a dear and pay the rent? You can bank what you need to cover the electricity bill you paid the other day. I just want to make sure they get our rent before we get a nasty letter from the landlords. If you don't mind, that'd be great. If I mail it in, I might not reach them on time, and I would much rather do it in person. Do you mind?"

"Not at all," Aunt Kristi." She tossed the banana peel. She was glad that her aunt mentioned the bill so she didn't have to bring it up. Now, she could replace the funds in her bank by the weekend, and it would be as if it never even happened. "I have to get back to work." She checked her watch. Just in time to see Willow onto the next chapter of her health journey. "Have a good night at work. Love you."

"Love you too, girlie."

Kristi hung up, and Taylor left the cafeteria and went to the elevator. As the doors were closing, she heard a woman. "Hold the door." Taylor reached out and kept the door from closing. She saw Anne hurrying to the elevator. When Anne spotted Taylor, she slowed her stride and looked up one way and down the other, hesitating before walking to the elevator. "Thank you," she mumbled.

She was dressed casually, wearing jeans and a T-shirt. The door closed, and the heavy silence continued. This was Taylor's chance, but she was hesitant to take the step. The fact that Anne barely looked at her told her everything she needed to know. The elevator ticked up the chains slowly, too slowly. Taylor felt anxious like the doors were closing on them, trapping them in this uncomfortable feeling. They had another floor to go, the last hint of a moment, before Taylor sighed.

"Did I do something to upset you?"

Anne laughed, then tossed a look to Taylor. Her lips curved upward in amusement. "I don't want to talk about it."

Taylor frowned. "Clearly, I did. I saw the review you gave. That wasn't made up. We were talking fine, and then, bam, nothing." The doors dinged and opened, and Taylor reached out to hold them open. "If I did something, I would much rather like to know what it is."

Anne stared straight ahead, Taylor watching her from the side. After what felt like an eternity, Anne crossed her arms. "Today, I'm saying goodbye to a little girl who means a lot to me. I don't know when I'll see her again. I would prefer not to have to deal with this, too. If that's too much to ask, then I'm sorry. But now is not the time." Anne hissed. Taylor dropped her arm and allowed Anne to exit first.

It was true that something was bothering Anne, but they weren't getting anywhere at that moment. As Anne stormed off to Willow's room, Taylor went to the desk to see where Hailey needed her. Those words weighed heavily on Taylor's mind. Whatever she did was something that Anne found unforgivable. What could have happened between the hospital and the parking lot was beyond her.

"Did I miss anything while I was on lunch?" Taylor had to force herself to stop thinking about Anne. Anne touched her hand when they were in the cafeteria the last time together. She felt a spark like there was this kinetic energy between them. It struck her so hard and now they were back to being enemies. How would she ever understand?

"We got a new patient straight from the ER. Matthew Sullivan. He goes by Sully. He's five and has flu-like symptoms. Will you start an IV on him? He's dehydrated, and I have three other crises I'm dealing with. His doc is Dr. Pohler, and since you guys are pals, now, I'm sure he'll be pleased."

Taylor groaned. "I feel you're teasing me." She tried to smile, but her heart was in the room with Willow and Anne. "I'll take care of it." Taylor glanced at her watch and grimaced. There was a strong likelihood that with this patient, she would miss the moment Willow left and never get a chance to say goodbye. "Hailey," she began. "Will you grab me before Willow gets transferred? I'd like to say my goodbyes. I know I don't know her as well as everyone else, but I feel we've formed a bond in this short time."

"Absolutely. You do the IV, and I'll make sure I get you before she leaves. He's in room 1140."

Taylor smiled, at least she would have her moment, however small. She went to the drug and supply closet, grabbed everything she needed to start his IV, and then pushed the cart toward the room. A guy was standing beside his bed. He didn't look much more than eighteen. Taylor smiled. "Mr. Sullivan?"

"Um yeah," the guy stepped back from the bed. "Well, I'm the younger Sullivan. My parents were working, and my brother didn't feel well. I hope I did the right thing. We couldn't reach them, and he needed emergency care. I hope I did the right thing."

"Trust me." Taylor touched his arm. "This is always the right thing." She thought back to her teen years when she had to care for Gavin. It wasn't an easy job, but at least Sully had a figure who could care for him. "And you are Sully, is that correct?"

"Hi!" He gave a small, meek greeting, before closing his eyes.

"He's always such an energetic kid." His brother replied. Taylor turned to his brother, and she saw the wariness in his eyes.

"What's your name?" Taylor asked.

"Trevor."

"Trevor, my name is Taylor, and together, we're going to help your brother so he doesn't feel so icky. Got that?" He nodded, his eyes filled with relief. "I'm going to get him hooked up to an IV."

"What's that for?" he asked.

"It's just so Sully gets hydrated. The worst thing that can happen is that he is dehydrated." Taylor knelt beside him as she remembered Anne doing with the other kids. "Would you like a Jell-O after this is done?"

He nodded, his eyes sparkling.

"Okay, give me a second, and we'll have you all hooked up in no time." She ruffled up his hair, and he already had pinker cheeks. "How'd you get the name, Sully?" Taylor asked as she prepped him.

"My brother," he whispered.

Taylor looked over and saw Trevor had tears in his eyes. "I'd say you have a pretty cool brother." She turned back to him, and he wore a small smile. Trevor watched her every move as Taylor felt his eyes on her. He was a brave young boy as she inserted the catheter and connected the tubing to the IV bag. When Taylor turned to Trevor, he had his hands clasped in prayer. Sully needed a brother like that. "Would you like a Jell-O?" Taylor asked.

"No, thank you!" He continued to pray.

The door flung open, and a woman rushed into the room. "My boys," she cried.

"Mom!" Trevor jumped up and they embraced. The room immediately felt lighter. Taylor left the room, feeling relieved to have experienced it. She also felt a bit sad to recognize the true love of a mother at that moment. Their mother was always too high to care.

She went to the nurse's station, grabbed a Jell-O and spoon, and headed back to see Sully when Willow's door opened. Hailey motioned for Taylor, and Taylor pocketed the Jell-O and hurried over to the room. She entered it, seeing Anne talking to Willow's parents. She hesitated, not wanting to interrupt, but Willow was lying on the bed, and her face lit up.

"Taylor!" she called. Anne turned and met Taylor's stare. Taylor snuck over to the bed and knelt beside her.

"You're going to get lots of medicine at the new hospital, and we look forward to the day you come back here and are big and strong. You got that?" In the back of her mind, she wondered if Anne was displeased, but she didn't promise Willow she would be back there. Besides, everyone needed to carry some faith.

Willow eagerly nodded. "Thank you, Taylor." She held out her arms, and Taylor hugged her. She felt her breath on Taylor's neck and didn't want to let go. Eventually, she had no choice and pulled back from the embrace. "Will you write to me?"

Taylor glanced over to Anne and her parents. How could she respond to that? Would her parents accept that? "We'll leave the address of where we're staying when we're in Tennessee. We'll make sure to get the letters to her."

"Then I absolutely will." She rubbed her thumb under Willow's chin. "Chin-up. We'll all be thinking of you."

"Thank you, Taylor." Taylor felt tears stinging the back of her eyes.

"I have to get going, but take care." She dropped her hand and turned on her heel, hurrying out the door before everyone saw her crying.

"Taylor?" Taylor turned around and Anne stood at the door. "I heard you were the one that said I should be notified about Willow's transport today. Thank you!"

"That's alright. You would have done it, as well."

Anne shrugged, then turned around and went back into the room, refusing to acknowledge their previous issues. Taylor reached her hand in her pocket and felt for the Jell-O, then hurried to Sully's room, where he was probably curious about what took her so long. Maybe she wouldn't know why Anne was so irritated with her. Perhaps Anne was just quirky. Either way, she had to accept it and see if there was any way they could work around the misunderstandings.

CHAPTER TWELVE

TRUTH REVEALED

Anne

Anne clocked out and headed to her locker. The day wasn't as bad as she thought. With Hailey there, she didn't have to bother being in close quarters with Taylor, and she could try to ignore the fact that Taylor hit her car, fled the scene, and subsequently delayed her mortgage. If it meant being the bigger person, then so be it. Bringing more drama into the hospital was not going to help anyone. Besides, she already knew that Taylor didn't live a life of luxury. She wished she knew why Taylor felt the need to rush off. Things would have been so much better if she had owned up to it and not rushed off like a child.

Anne's phone rang, and she grabbed it, spotting Melanie's number. "Hey, Mel. Perfect timing. I just got off work."

"I have a huge favor to ask." Anne waited, holding the phone to her ear to see if she heard anything that sounded like tears. To her relief, she didn't.

"Anything. What's going on?"

"Well, I feel like Josh, and I need a night alone. No kids. No distractions. Maybe that will show him we're where he wants to be."

Anne rolled her eyes. If it took that, it was clear he wasn't the right man. "Of course, I'll watch them. I'm off tomorrow, so bring them over at whatever time works for you."

"Thank you, Sis. I appreciate you."

"Not a problem. I love you. Talk tomorrow." She disconnected the call and slammed her locker shut. She left the break room and headed to the front door. She had just stepped outside when she spotted Taylor. She mentally groaned. She almost made it to her day off without an awkward interaction. Taylor gave a simple nod.

"Have a good weekend!" she called.

A crack of thunder sounded, and Anne looked up at the dark skies. She glanced at Taylor.

"You too!" Anne called, then sprinkles started, followed by a downpour. She ran to her car, wishing she had grabbed the umbrella from her locker. If she had only known, she reached her car and unlocked it with her fob, but not before her hair was drenched. "Good times," Anne mumbled. She looked out her window and saw Taylor running toward her car. "What now?" Anne mumbled. The rain started to dissipate as fast as it came. Sure, it would wait until she was already in the car. That was typical. Anne rolled her window down as Taylor approached her.

"I'm sorry to bother you." Taylor breathlessly leaned against the car. "My car won't start. You wouldn't be able to give me a jump, would you?" She clutched her hands together, a pitiful look clouding over her face. Anne looked up in the sky and saw several clouds had disappeared; they might have a few minutes before another blast of rain appeared.

"Where are you parked?" Anne mumbled.

Taylor motioned, and She took in a breath and exhaled. "Get in," Anne replied. If she was going to do the noble thing, she had to start it right. Taylor looked relieved as Anne unlocked the door for her to get in the passenger side. She backed out of the spot and drove to where Taylor had pointed. The car was eerily quiet, with only a few instances where Taylor would motion with her finger to show the direction to go. Before Anne reached the car, she frowned. "How'd you know where I was parked?"

Taylor dropped her gaze to her hands. "I watched you walk to your car."

So, she's a stalker; that's intriguing. Anne bit down on her tongue and closed in on Taylor's car. The spot across from her was open to allow easy access. She parked, and they both got out of the car. Anne spotted the mangled bumper, and her heart raced again. *Let it go. In the end, you'll feel better, and everyone can rest easy.*

"Do you have cables?" Anne asked.

"Um, I don't know. Possibly?" Taylor hurried to her trunk and dug through it as Anne tapped her foot, waiting for her to come out with her hand clutched around the jumper cables. She sighed. "I'm not finding anything."

"I think I have some." Anne went to her trunk and spotted her mangled-up bumper, just waiting for her to get it fixed. She shook her head. It was what it was. She reached for the cables and was about to close the trunk when she heard Taylor beside her.

"Shit!" Anne glanced at her; Taylor's eyes focused on the bumper. Her jaw dropped, and Anne waited for her to acknowledge it one step further. She looked up, her eyes darkening. "It was you."

Anne scowled, unable to handle the anguish running through her mind. "Yep, it was me, and it was you. You just left me there like nothing ever mattered. I don't get it. How could someone do that to someone else? Someone they don't even know? You didn't even check to see if I was okay, and you work in healthcare!"

Taylor's eyes dropped back down to the bumper. "So, you know it was me?" Taylor asked, her gaze dropping. When? How?"

"A couple of days ago. I saw the ribbon in your hair, and the dent in your bumper looks just like mine."

Taylor released a gasp. "When we were in the parking lot, you rushed off." She covered her face and shook her head. "I didn't mean to rush off like that. It was in the spur of the moment. I felt bad the minute I did it. I regretted it but never expected I'd find the person. I'm sorry, Anne. I'm so sorry."

"You're sorry? That's not doing a bit of good for me, now is it? I had my own problems. I needed that money, and now I'm stuck getting this fixed."

Taylor's brow furrowed. "We'll go to a shop right now." Taylor reached into her purse and withdrew her wallet. She opened it up, and

Anne stared at the wad of cash inside. "I'll use a credit card. If that will improve things between us, I'll do it."

"Are you kidding me? You have a wad of cash just sitting there, and you're trying to give me the guilt trip?"

"What?" Taylor balked. "You don't understand!"

"I think I understand quite clearly," Anne huffed. "It is what it is. A lot of good going to a shop will do. I've called around. I'm on a waiting list for every shop in town. Don't you think I tried? Do you think I like this mangled-up bumper? The answer is no, but there's not a damn thing I can do about it." Anne crossed her arms, the car suddenly a distant memory. "I'm outta here."

"You're just going to leave me?" Taylor argued. "Stranded?" Anne sighed and returned to her car, jumper cables still in hand. "I have an idea. I know someone, and I'm sure I can get you in, probably even tonight."

"Oh yeah, right." Anne snickered. "I've tried everyone. Are you not understanding?"

Taylor shook her head. "Please, jumpstart my car. I'll prove it to you."

Anne knew that Taylor was grasping at straws, but at the moment, she had to take advantage of it and hope that something good could come out of it, even if it ultimately bit her in the ass.

ANNE PACED BACK AND FORTH AS TAYLOR STOOD AT THE DESK, talking to the man who owned the shop: *Joe's Auto Body*. That was one place she hadn't tried. She couldn't even find a listing for him, but the parking lot seemed packed with cars. The shop was unlisted thanks to a recent name change. Anne just hoped that it wasn't another letdown. After several minutes, Taylor came back to her. Why Taylor asked her to wait by the door was beyond her, but if Taylor kept this promise and fixed her vehicle, she would be back on track to making her last house payment.

"I have good news, and I have bad news," she began.

"Let me guess, the bad news is there's a month turnaround, so it's back to the drawing board. At least you tried, right?" Anne held out her hand and tilted her head. "Give me the keys, and I'll just plan on one of the shops."

"Well, can't exactly do that. They're pulling your car in now. He said it could take twenty-four hours to fix, then another twenty-four hours for the paint to dry. But I have everything entered, and he knows I'm covering the costs."

Anne's jaw dropped. "I don't understand. His parking lot is packed. I checked the reviews, and they are nothing but high praise. And we're looking at the weekend."

Taylor shrugged. "He reworked his schedule."

Anne scrunched her nose, still confused but trying not to argue too much. She was one step closer to having her vehicle repaired, and unless Taylor let her down, she was getting it fully paid, like it should have been from the start. Seeing the money in Taylor's wallet did nothing but cinch the idea that Taylor had the means to get the job done and had only been playing the sympathy card.

"So, the bad news is I must get an Uber for the next few days. No biggie."

Taylor shook her head. "Not the bad news I was referring to. "Turns out my car is in dire need of a battery. He has to order one, and it won't be here until the morning."

"Oh," Anne muttered. "So, basically, we're both currently stranded."

"Appears that way." Taylor reached into her pocket and finally pulled out her phone. "I can call my aunt to pick me up. I can order you an Uber."

"Yeah, seeing you have all that money," Anne grumbled.

Taylor sighed. "Anne, it's not what you think."

Anne rolled her eyes, "I think you're a spoiled rich kid who's never had to take responsibility a day in her life, so you fled the scene of the accident. Who's Joe? Your Dad? Are you a body shop heiress?"

Taylor's mouth hung open, unable to reply.

Anne waved away Taylor's words. "I can get my own Uber."

Anne grabbed her phone and pulled up the app. Not exactly how she expected to spend her Friday night, as she fiddled with the app, Taylor called up her aunt. Anne didn't intend to listen to the conversation, but she was right there, and it was hard to ignore.

"Hey, Gavin. What are you doing answering Aunt Kristi's phone? Ugh. Are you serious? When do you expect her?" Anne looked up to

Taylor as Taylor turned her back away from her. "I need to be picked up. It's a long story. I forgot she works tonight. I'll see what I can do. I'll keep in touch. Bye." Taylor whirled around, and Anne quickly looked down so it wasn't obvious she had been listening to every word. "Well, it looks like I need to call one, too."

"Well, the closest ride is half an hour away. There's a Cubs game tonight." Anne slipped her phone back into her pocket. She shrugged. "My house is only about a mile up the road. I might head on out and take my chances before it rains."

"Alrighty then. I'll see if I can get that Uber. I don't mind waiting a bit." Taylor sat down in a chair, and Anne sighed.

"Or you could come with me. I have plenty of room. You can stay over in the spare bedroom and come get your car in the morning."

"Even after everything I put you through?" Taylor's eyes widened.

"Guess I'm just in a generous mood unless you'd rather stick it out here. It's your choice, but make it."

"A mile isn't so bad. I'm in." Taylor jumped up, and they left the auto body shop. They were quiet on the first part of the trip. The sky had darkened some, but that was due to the continuous impending rain. The walk was slow. Anne didn't mind.

As they rounded a curb, Anne spoke up. "So, plan on telling me how you got Joe to take in my car tonight?"

Taylor snickered. "Well, it's rather simple."

"Ex-boyfriend?" Anne interrupted. "I mean, he looks a bit older, but maybe you like the balding type.

She glanced over at Taylor, whose face was eerily pale. Taylor then burst into laughter. It was interesting to see her laughing when Anne ignored her in silence. It felt good to make her laugh.

"Not hardly," Taylor remarked. "He isn't quite my type. But he does have a crush on my aunt. She won't appreciate that I said she would go out with him, but I'm sure she'll understand it's for a good cause."

Anne snickered. "Interesting. I hope your aunt is the forgiving type."

"She can be," Taylor mumbled. Anne motioned toward a street, and they turned. At those words, a loud crack of thunder sounded. "Uh oh!" Taylor mumbled. They both looked into the sky just as big drops started to fall.

"We don't have too much further," Anne yelled. "Follow me." She ran as fast as her legs would carry her, with Taylor falling in closely behind. The rain continued to fall harder, and Anne felt the large pelts hitting the back of her neck as she focused ahead, not on what Taylor was doing. "My house is up here," Anne yelled. She ran up the walkway, thoroughly drenched, and fumbled with her key until the door was unlocked. She pushed through, and Taylor stumbled in after her.

"We are soaked!" Taylor said, coughing through the water that had covered her face.

Anne looked at her and then chuckled. "I should have grabbed an umbrella from the car."

"Now you think of that," Taylor said, laughing. Again, the radiant sound of her laughter echoed in Anne's ears, gently coming through the foyer and catching Anne off balance.

"If you follow me, I'll get you something to change into. Anything would beat these wet clothes." Anne hurried up the stairs, with Taylor padding behind her. She glanced over her shoulder and saw the awe on Taylor's face.

"You have a nice place," Taylor cooed.

"Thank you!" Anne mumbled. "Wait right here." She rushed into her room and dug around in her dresser until she had a t-shirt and lounge pants. She took it back out to Taylor and handed it over. "There's a bathroom down the hall. Feel free to change in there."

Taylor grabbed the items, and Anne waited until she disappeared into the bathroom. Anne returned to her room, pulled out her clothes, and quickly dressed in something more comfortable. By the time she was in the hallway, Taylor was still behind the closed door, so she went back downstairs to the living room. Anne worked on the fire, cooking up a lovely flame, when she heard shuffling coming down the stairs. She turned as Taylor entered the room. The t-shirt was extra-large compared to Taylor's thin frame. The lounge pants cupped her butt, hugging it and then slightly squeezing it. Anne's mouth hung agape as she gawked.

"Nice fire," Taylor replied, moving further into the living room. Anne turned away, glaring straight into the flames. It would be a long night.

CHAPTER THIRTEEN

WHISKERS IS MISSING

Taylor

T hings were awkward between them as they sat by the fire, Taylor staring aimlessly around the living room. "I'm sorry I couldn't muster up anything better than chicken. I'm sure you're more used to the glamorous meals."

"What? The chicken is great. You didn't even have to go to that bother. I certainly would have accepted a cold hot dog."

Anne snickered. "I'm sure." She rolled her eyes and dropped her gaze to her plate.

Taylor frowned; this was the second time Anne had insinuated that she was somehow too good for her, acting like she wasn't grateful for anything Anne had in the kitchen. It'd been a long day, and frankly, anything would have been acceptable. Anne acted like she was royalty or something. She looked down at her chicken and stabbed her fork into the meat before popping it into her mouth.

"It's quite delicious."

Anne stared at Taylor before shrugging and looking back down at her food. Again, awkwardness ensued. At least until another twenty minutes went by. Then Anne looked up and gawked, sending shivers down Taylor's spine. The way she stared at her, she wondered if she had horns growing from her head. Taylor nervously looked down. She didn't sense anything wrong. Outside of the elephant in the room, their cars were at the shop, and soon, she could hope the awkwardness was behind them.

"Why'd you do it?" Anne asked suddenly.

Taylor's jaw dropped, and then she snapped her mouth closed. She didn't have to inquire about what Anne was talking about. She knew.

"Why does anyone do something stupid? I was scared. I bolted." She shrugged. "It's like asking why bees sting. Or why does water flow down a waterfall? Hell, if I know."

"The latter two, you can search for the answer and most likely find one. But for why you ran from an accident, I guess you should search within your soul because I haven't a clue.

"Anne, I know you will probably never understand it, but you live in this fabulous place."

"A place I've worked hard to maintain," Anne quickly interrupted.

"I get that. Please let me finish." Anne didn't make another move to jump in as Taylor continued. "I have never had that luxury. I don't have the finer things. When I get a paycheck, I'll be living paycheck to paycheck. I don't have car insurance. Did I plan on bolting? No. Did I see any other way out? Not exactly."

"You are giving out this sob story, but I saw the wad of cash. Remember? That doesn't look like someone who has to fear living paycheck to paycheck."

Taylor shook her head. "And that's where you don't get it. As I've been trying to explain, that money isn't mine. My aunt needed me to pay the rent. I didn't get a chance to before my evening went to shit. She works two jobs to keep food on the table so my brother and I can stay with her. We aren't wealthy. I'm not the enemy."

Taylor's phone rang, and even though Anne stared at her, she reached for her phone and spotted Gavin's name.

"Hello?"

"Sis? Where are you? I've been worried sick. Sirens have been up and down this road, and I've tried calling you three times." She checked her phone and grimaced.

"Sorry. I didn't hear it. I meant to call you, but I'm staying at a co-worker's tonight."

"You are? Is everything alright?"

"It's a long story. I'll explain it tomorrow when I see you. You get some rest, and I'll call you in the morning. Love you."

"Love you, too."

Taylor hung up the call, and she looked back to meet Anne's gaze. "My brother. He heard sirens and was worried." Anne locked her gaze on Taylor's, making Taylor feel a few more nerves. She stood up from the couch and walked over to the shelves that housed Anne's DVD and Blu-Ray collection. "Wow, you sure have a ton of movies."

"Yeah, my sister will come over periodically, and we'll have movie nights. As you can see, there's a whole mess of Disney movies reserved for my nieces, and then when they fall asleep, we'll watch something else."

Taylor pulled out a movie and smiled as she looked over at Anne. *Labyrinth* is a great movie. It's easily my top choice. I blame David Bowie."

Anne slowly nodded. "Ugh, same! I used to love the soundtrack when I was a little kid." Taylor looked up, and their gaze met once more. She swallowed as that spark greeted her again, then returned to the movies. She replaced the movie, returned to the coffee table, and picked up her plate.

"It's getting late. I should help by washing the dishes. You get some sleep."

"You don't need to bother with that," Anne argued as Taylor reached for Anne's plate.

"It's the least I could do. You were nice enough to make us dinner. I know my way around a sink." She laughed, trying to make it lighthearted, but her chest caved in. She was exhausted, mentally more than physically. She went to the kitchen and started digging around the sink to find the stuff to wash the dishes, oblivious that Anne had made her way to the kitchen.

"I'm sorry," Anne replied. Taylor looked over her shoulder. "I apologize," Anne replied, moving closer to her. "I shouldn't have just assumed you were rich and trying to stiff me with the bill. After all, you put your card on file and made this all happen. I appreciate it."

Taylor shrugged. "You wouldn't have needed repairs if it wasn't for my carelessness. I was distracted, mainly because I was excited about my new job. And nervous. So, that's what happens when you're careless."

"Accidents happen," Anne commented.

Taylor arched an eyebrow. "Most people don't run. That's the cowardly thing to do."

"You were scared. Heck, I'm sure more people run than we even know."

"What are you doing?" Taylor whirled around and stood her stance, staring at Anne. "I'm trying to admit my fault in the whole thing, and you're trying to make me feel better. Why?"

Anne shrugged. "I was once young, too. We all make mistakes."

"Some with a higher price to pay," Taylor mumbled.

Anne reached for a towel and began drying the dishes that Taylor had already washed. They tag-teamed it until the dishes and kitchen were clean.

"But you're right. We should get to bed."

"Right. Should I make a bed on the couch?" Taylor knew this would be when things got more awkward. But Anne shook her head and motioned for Taylor to follow her. They went up the stairs, and she directed her to the spare bedroom.

"If you need me. You know where to find me." Anne started to disappear into her room.

"Anne? I am sorry, and I hope this will at least make things easier at work." Anne nodded. "We'll get there. Goodnight." She disappeared into her room, and Taylor considered those words. They were already one step closer.

TAYLOR SHIFTED IN BED, THEN FINALLY OPENED HER EYES. THE bedding was lush. The bed felt like a layer of clouds, but she couldn't even will herself to sleep. Sure, she could expect a hefty credit card bill, but at least she would have her dignity and smile, relieved that the truth was out there. How could they keep a working relationship going if there was the truth on Anne's side, with Taylor oblivious to their connection?

Taylor heard a noise, and she glanced over at the bedroom door. A light shone underneath the doorway. "Whiskers? Where are you?"

Taylor frowned, holding her breath and waiting.

"Whiskers! Come out, come out, wherever you are."

Taylor tossed the covers back, now intrigued. She moved to the door and flung it open, peeking her head into the hallway.

"Whiskers!" Anne came out of the bathroom, and her face flushed. "Sorry. Did I wake you?"

"That's alright. Do you have someone else living here who is named Whiskers?" Anne's cheeks reddened, and she shrugged.

"My cat. I haven't seen him all night." She frowned, opening another door, shaking her head, and closing it. "It's not like him. You didn't happen to see a little fur ball running around here, did you? He's knee-high and gray, with white feet."

"I didn't know you had a cat, so I'm sorry to say I haven't seen him. I can help you look, though?"

"You don't have to do that. I'm sure he's just hiding somewhere. You can go back to bed. I'll keep looking and eventually have to give up and hope he'll come out when he's good and ready. The storm earlier probably startled him." She shrugged. "It's no biggie."

Yet, her eyes looked panicked. Taylor could have returned to the room, shrugged it off, and shut her eyes, but she couldn't. Not when Anne seemed beside herself, her eyes filled with worry.

"Where's his favorite hiding spots?" Taylor asked.

"Under the bed, in closets, on the refrigerator." Taylor arched an eyebrow, and Anne laughed. "He doesn't hide well there but thinks he's invisible. But really..."

"It's fine. You take the downstairs, and I'll take the upstairs. We'll find Whiskers if it's the last thing we do." Anne gave a gracious smile and hurried down the stairs. "Oh, Whiskers! Where are you, Rascal?"

Taylor looked under the bed, and Whiskers wasn't hiding there. Before leaving the spare, she checked the closets and did not leave a single area untouched. Most likely touching the same place at least twice. Anne rounded the corner when she got downstairs, hope filling her eyes but quickly failing.

"I've looked everywhere. I even ran the can opener, which usually makes him sprint." Her eyebrows furrowed.

"He couldn't have gone anywhere, Anne. Does he go outside?"

"Never!" Anne shook her head. "He's always been an indoor cat." A loud crack of thunder sounded, and Anne's eyes went wide. "There was once, right after I rescued him. He got outside. He was gone for five hours, and I never thought I'd see him again."

"But you did. He knew where his home was. That's a promising thing, right?" Anne didn't even respond. She walked over to the window and stared aimlessly outside. "Maybe we should check outside, just in case."

Anne hurried to the front door and flung it open as Taylor went back through the kitchen. She had spotted a back patio. They would cover more area if they separated. When she was younger, Taylor once had a kitten, and she had gotten out. They weren't lucky enough to get her back, as a car came by and swerved, unable to miss her. That experience wrecked her long enough that she couldn't imagine what it would do to Anne, even if she was an adult and could handle disappointment.

"Whiskers!" she called out. "Where are you, kitty?"

Meow. She glanced around, fearful that maybe she had dreamt the sound of a cat. She held her breath and waited. *Meow.* That was definitely a cat. But where?

CHAPTER FOURTEEN

HEATED MOMENT ENTERTAINED

Anne

The rain was past them, but Anne still couldn't understand where Whiskers could be. He had never run off to the point where she couldn't find him. Other than those five hours a year ago. Even then, she didn't feel the dread and panic she felt now. Whiskers was a cat that liked to snuggle and held. He was way too skittish to be off by himself. Or so she thought.

"Whiskers?" she called. "Where are you?"

She shook her head. It was useless. Taylor was out helping her, but at what cost? They were both missing out on sleep, and she couldn't expect this to go on for the whole night. Anne entered the house with a feeling of defeat. Why should she be surprised? When it rains, it pours. She understood the cliche now.

"Anne?" Taylor called out.

"Yeah? No luck here." Anne headed to the kitchen, where Taylor's voice echoed. "We've looked everywhere, and you might as well..." Her words trailed off when she saw Whiskers nuzzling against Taylor's chest.

"I know there's a possibility I just brought a feral cat into your house." Taylor grinned. "I'm going out on a limb that this is—."

"Whiskers," Anne finished. She rushed over to Taylor and pulled the cat out of her arms. "Where have you been, my silly boy?"

"I found him under the porch. He probably got outside, and when the rain came, he looked for a place to stay dry."

Anne nuzzled her lips against his fur. "I've been a bit distracted lately. I probably didn't notice him run past me. I never realized how attached you can get to a pet until that pet is no longer here." Anne kissed the top of his head and then looked at Taylor. "Guess it's a good thing you were here."

"Nah, you would have found him soon enough. But, I'm glad I could get him back where he needed to be." On cue, Whiskers meowed, jumped out of Anne's arms, and hurried over to his food.

Anne laughed. "He's probably been out there all day. I'm sure he's starving. But I'll say it again. Thank you."

Taylor shrugged. "It's my pleasure. No need to say thanks." Taylor looked over to Whiskers as he ate, and a soft smile glistened on her lips. "He seems like a sweet cat. I can see why you'd grow so attached."

"I hope he feels the same way," Anne started with a smile. She heaved a sigh, and there was a long hesitation. Whiskers had been found, and they could go back to their rooms and try to get some sleep. However, she was on her second wind, and sleep wasn't on her agenda. "Would you like some coffee? The adrenaline kicked in, and I don't think I could sleep, even if I wanted to."

"Coffee sounds good," Taylor agreed. Whiskers meowed, and Anne looked down to where he stood at Taylor's feet.

"I think you just gained a friend for life." Taylor quirked up an eyebrow. "Whiskers, I mean. He's probably grateful for how you saved him."

A redness popped onto Taylor's cheeks, and Anne quickly looked away. She shouldn't notice her blushing, even though that was a sight she had already seen a couple of times. It punched her in the gut every time.

"I was glad to do it." Taylor picked Whiskers up in her arms and bounced him a few times as if he were a baby. Anne laughed under her breath.

"You make yourself at home in the living room. I'll make the coffee and be in shortly."

Ten minutes later, Anne had two mugs, a sugar container, and creamer lined up on a tray to present to her. When she reached the living room, she stopped short of entering. Taylor sat on the couch, Whiskers in her lap, slowly rubbing below her chin. On the other hand, she was holding one of Anne's knitted creations, and Anne couldn't tell if she was conversing with Whiskers or the doll Anne had knitted the night before. Either way, Anne didn't want to interrupt. She moved in further to hear her talking, and she smiled. The conversation, directed to Whiskers, was like someone talking to a new friend.

"You're such a good kitty, Whiskers. And so cute, too. If I had a cat, I'd want him to be just like you." Taylor nuzzled her lips into his neck, and Anne heard the loud purring from the other side of the room. "That's right, boy, such a sweetheart." She turned, her cheeks flushed. "And I'm embarrassed."

Anne laughed. "Don't be embarrassed. Whiskers is used to praise. We talk a lot. He's probably surprised to get such attention from a stranger, though. That'd be a new one. I didn't know if you wanted sugar or cream in your coffee."

"I usually take it black." She held up the doll. "Cute doll? Did you make this?"

"I dabble in knitting and crocheting," Anne replied.

She handed the mug over to Taylor. "Black coffee? You're hardcore," Anne said, impressed, changing the subject.

Taylor placed the doll back on the coffee table and grabbed the mug. "Well," Taylor began, then shook her head. "Never mind."

Anne arched an eyebrow. "You're leaving me just hanging here? Not cool," she teased, pouring some of the creamer into her mug and gently stirring it before taking a seat on the couch next to Taylor.

"Maybe for another time." Taylor gave a weak smile, then sipped on her coffee and nodded. "Simply the best. Thank you!" She scratched Whiskers until he jumped and scurried out of the living room. "Must've exceeded my welcome."

Anne laughed. "No, he's a pig and probably left to get more food. I doubt it had anything to do with you." Anne sipped on her coffee, and it was nice to sit in the living room, not have to reach for conversation, and even enjoy the solitude. If Anne listened hard enough, she could hear the gentle sprinkle of rain tapping against the window.

"Your crocheted doll looks a bit more than just dabbling. Then again, I don't have a creative bone in my body." Taylor laughed.

"Doubt that," Anne commented. "Everyone has some kind of creativity. It's just acting on it that requires strength. Knitting isn't so hard. I'm sure you could even learn if you had the patience."

"Patience...not always my cup of tea," Taylor smirked, sipping her coffee. She glanced around the living room, and Anne saw a hint of jealousy in her stare. "You have a beautiful home, Anne," Taylor began after several minutes of taking in that stillness.

"Thank you! It'd always been a dream of mine to own a home, not have to rent from someone or hold a thirty-year mortgage. It's been a long time coming, but I'm just getting to the point where this will soon be all mine."

"It's quite impressive. You're still so young."

"A few nights of only eating Ramen and drinking water never hurt anyway." Anne snickered, taking another sip of her coffee. And again, that silence hit her, but not in an overpowering way. She didn't need to stress over the conversation when there might not be some. She sipped on her coffee and watched Taylor doing the same. Yet, she noticed that Taylor's eyes dimmed slightly. "What about you?" Anne asked. "I imagine you have a nice place. You dress nice and all."

"Well, scrubs are all the rage," Taylor laughed loudly, her eyes lit up a smidge. "Let's just say I don't have a place like this."

"And we'll leave it for another time?" Anne inquired.

"Something like that. Can't show all my cards, right?" She quirked up her lips. Anne didn't pry, but it was clear that Taylor was reserved and wanted to keep up that wall. Anne couldn't object when they barely spoke twelve hours earlier. "This coffee was delicious. Glad you suggested it."

"I was going to make a cup for myself, so I figured you might as well join me."

Taylor nodded. "I appreciate it. I'll help you wash up, and I should be getting to bed."

"Yeah, me too. You don't need to help me. I'll just put it in the sink and take care of it in the morning. We both need to get some sleep."

Taylor's jaw dropped, and her mouth was agape. Her eyes were wide, inquisitive, her lips curved into a smile, and she laughed, then looked down. "You know what I mean. You in your bed. Me in mine."

Taylor vigorously nodded in response. "Of course. Nothing else crossed my mind."

Anne grimaced. It sure crossed her mind, and she didn't even know why. One minute, she was ready to have this woman's head on a platter for damaging her car; the next, she would smother her with compliments or kisses if she had her way.

She discarded the tray into the sink and met Taylor in the foyer. She reached for the railing at the exact moment as Taylor, their hands touching, and Anne quickly pulled back. A spark had hit her, and she had to step back and allow Taylor ample room to get upstairs.

"I apologize," Anne mumbled.

"No worries."

Taylor was cool and nonchalant, while Anne stood back red-faced and confused. They reached the top of the steps, and Taylor turned to Anne. "Thanks again for everything." Her words trailed off.

"Well, thank you for finding Whiskers." Anne reached for her door, glancing over her shoulder, and saw Taylor awkwardly gawking at her. There was this tension and pull between them, right? She wasn't feeling something one-sided, was she?"

"Anne," Taylor started. Anne whirled around, ready to give her full attention to that one mention of her name. Taylor shrugged. "Goodnight."

A breath escaped Anne. "Yeah, goodnight, Taylor." Anne reached for the door.

"Anne?" She turned around once more, baffled by the call of her name. "I can't go to sleep without doing something," Taylor whispered. She had already closed the gap, snaked her hand around Anne's neck, and pulled her to her. Her lips crashed against Anne's with a million watts of electricity crashing through her. Taylor's tongue dipped in and met Anne's, and Anne stood there, confused and anxious. Until she fully let that kiss embrace her, she grabbed Taylor's waist and pulled her closer. The kiss kept her thirsty for more. Her heart raced, and she envisioned pulling Taylor into her bedroom and allowing the heat to ignite up her room. After all, it'd been ages. Unfortunately, the kiss ended, and Taylor's eyes darted to hers. "I shouldn't have done that." Taylor gasped.

"Taylor," Anne argued. "I didn't exactly push you away."

Taylor shook her head. "I'm sorry. My emotions got the better of me. Goodnight." She turned on her heel, and the moment passed. Every part of Anne wanted to rush after her, but she stayed back and allowed Taylor to disappear into the spare room. They would talk in the morning and resolve so much. She wasn't sorry that Taylor had kissed her. The truth was, she wanted more.

ANNE STEPPED OUT OF HER BEDROOM. SHE DIDN'T GET MUCH sleep as she thought of Taylor just down the hall. So many times, she wanted to go to her and tell her she wasn't sorry the kiss had happened. Sure, it was unexpected, but was unexpected always a bad thing? She didn't think so. But the fact that Taylor seemed confused, she didn't make that move. If Taylor regretted making a move, then Taylor would need to communicate that.

Anne would support her. Taylor was young; who knows how long she'd been out? Anne looked to the spare room, and the door was open. Taylor was probably already up and ready for some breakfast. It did take Anne a little longer to get dressed, as she was fighting with thoughts traipsing through her mind. Anne went downstairs and first checked the living room. Taylor wasn't there.

"Taylor?" Anne rounded the kitchen corner, and still, she was nowhere. Maybe she was still upstairs, and Anne should have started there. She hurried back up the stairs and cautiously peeked her head in the door. "Taylor? Are you in here?" Silence. Anne frowned, stepping into the spare room. She looked around the room, the bed fully made, as immaculate as Anne had it before she had the visitor. Her eyes landed on the pillow, where a paper sat. Anne picked it up and started to read.

Anne –

Words can't express how sorry I am for so many things. You know what they are, but the truth is, the kiss has me a bit rattled. I feel like I startled or confused you. It's the last thing I want to do. I woke up early so it wouldn't be awkward. I will grab my car and hope that my embarrassment has dissipated Monday morning.

I'm sorry, Anne!
Please forgive me!
Taylor

Anne sunk into the bed. If she had known that Taylor would take it this hard, she would have forced her to have a conversation the night before. Anne reached for her phone and pulled up Taylor's number. At least she had the mind to get the number when they were working on the debacle with their cars.

"The number you have called has been disconnected. If you feel this has been an error, please hang up and try again."

Anne stared at her phone, Taylor's name staring back at her. She had entered the contact information. It couldn't be an error. Taylor was upset that she disconnected her number? She tried it again to ensure it wasn't a fluke but got the same recording.

"Ugh!" Anne groaned and stared down at the letter. Her only choice was to wait until Monday morning when they both worked, and she could square away the misunderstanding. Her doorbell sounded, and Anne jumped up from the bed. Or, she could do it right now, and Taylor was coming back to apologize for rushing off. She ran down the stairs and flung the door open. "Tay…" Her words stopped when she saw Melanie and her nieces. "Hey, you guys!" Anne put on a bright smile.

"Expecting someone else?" Melanie asked.

Anne shook her head but figured her face was bright red. "You are here earlier than I would have thought, though." She folded the note and stuffed it into her pocket. If Melanie had seen the letter, she would have had many questions that needed answering.

"What can I say? The kids wanted to get here."

Lily and Rose threw their arms around Anne's legs, and she held them. "And I'm glad to see you all. Put your bags in the living room. I have to wash up the bedding for tonight." She turned to Melanie, and Melanie arched an eyebrow. "What?"

Melanie shrugged. "You look weird."

"Gee, thanks a lot," Anne muttered. She grabbed her sister's arm and pulled her into the living room. She needed just a few minutes with her before she sent her back to her husband. But also, it wouldn't hurt to have a distraction.

CHAPTER FIFTEEN

AWKWARDNESS RETURNS

Taylor

When Taylor went in for the kiss, she had no intention of deepening it. Anne was right; she didn't exactly smack Taylor for kissing her. There was a moment when Taylor believed Anne was enjoying it just as much as she was. She grabbed onto her waist and pulled her to her in a moment of pure passion. She felt it down to her toes. When the sun rose, though, she had to leave. Taylor didn't want to face a morning where Anne would wake up with regret.

Taylor grabbed her phone and looked at it, grimacing. Anne had her phone number, and she'd be lying if she didn't say that she would have hoped Anne would have picked up the phone to call her. The fact that there wasn't one single call told Taylor everything she needed to know.

"Knock, knock." She looked up as Aunt Kristi entered the room. She smiled at Taylor, then grabbed the corner of Taylor's bed and made herself at home. Well, it was her home, but it wasn't often that she came into Taylor's room and just sat down to talk. Usually, they saved dinner time or the living room to hold conversations. With Aunt Kristi's busy schedule, they didn't allow much more time than that.

"What's up?" Taylor asked.

"I could ask you the same thing. It's the weekend. You're off, and I haven't seen you out of your room much more than an hour at a time. It's like you're hiding from me or something."

Taylor frowned. "Didn't mean to. I'm not hiding; I'm thinking. Besides, I know you're busy. Gavin's been out with friends. Guess I just needed to be somewhere I could think and not be in anyone's way."

"Honey, you're never in my way." Aunt Kristi caressed Taylor's cheek. "Do you have the money I gave you for the rent?" she asked, dropping her hand.

Taylor's mouth hung open, and she slapped her palm over it. "Oh my gosh, it completely slipped my mind." She never wanted to feel like she let her aunt down, but she could feel her aunt's disappointment at that moment. She got up from the bed and grabbed her purse. She opened her wallet and grabbed the cash. "I'm sorry, Aunt Kristi. I can get up early in the morning and drop it off."

She shook her head. "No worries. Barry called me last night and asked. I told him you have been super busy with a new job and forgot to deliver it, but that I would bring it over tonight before I go to work. He's understanding."

"I let you down, though. You asked me to do something simple, and I blanked."

"Taylor, don't be so hard on yourself. If you have other things going on, it's liable to happen. You have done plenty for this family, so don't stress." She hesitated, then smiled. "But, it's clear something is going on. We've always been able to talk, so I would feel better if you could tell me why this escaped your mind. Trouble at work?"

"Not exactly," Taylor mumbled. She looked down at her clenched hands, her heart racing as she relived the kiss again. She sighed. "Friday night, I was leaving work, and I had every intention of taking the money to Barry. Well, my car wouldn't start."

Aunt Kristi nodded. "Gavin mentioned that to me when I got home. So, you stayed at a co-worker's home. That seems reasonable enough. Did something happen?"

"Well, Gavin didn't know the whole story. And frankly, I'm still processing it myself." Taylor pulled her feet up under her butt and stared at her aunt. It turns out my co-worker is the one I had the accident with on Monday." Aunt Kristi's eyes widened. As surprising as that was, the details couldn't flow from Taylor fast enough. "She needed to get her car fixed. Frankly, I wanted to do anything I could to ensure she didn't have to wait another day. She tried everywhere. She did. Everywhere except Joe's Body Shop." Aunt Kristi arched an eyebrow. Taylor shrugged. "He was willing to do it and get me a new battery."

"I see." Aunt Kristi crossed her arms and stared back at Taylor. "He did this, no strings attached?"

"Well, not exactly." Taylor dropped her gaze. "I'm sure you can put it off as long as possible. Once the job is done, if you don't go out on a date, you don't. It's not like he can take back fixing the car."

"Wow!" Aunt Kristi shook her head. "We'll save that conversation for another time, seeing that I'm going to be late getting out of here." She rolled her eyes. "Continue."

"If it wasn't for Anne being one of the head nurses, I would have shrugged my shoulders and just said, oh well. There's nothing I can do. But I had to do something to salvage our relationship. The truth is, Anne, discovered that I was the one who hit her and ran from the accident. She didn't confront me with it, but things have been tense. Once I found out the truth, I had to do something to rectify our working relationship."

"Just your working relationship?"

"Yes, of course. Why do you ask?" Taylor sat up straighter.

Aunt Kristi shrugged. "You light up when you talk about her. I'm just wondering if maybe there's more to this than you're expressing." Taylor's cheeks burned, and she quickly looked away. If she mentioned the kiss, Aunt Kristi would surely see the truth. She swallowed the lump in her throat and shook her head.

"It's complicated."

"Affairs of the heart, usually are." Aunt Kristi reached out and grabbed Taylor's hand. She gave it a slight squeeze. "I'm proud of you for not shirking your responsibilities. I know it's not easy, as we are not rolling in dough right now, but you are doing the right thing." She stood up from her bed and grimaced. "And if I have to go out on a date with Joe to help my niece, then it's what I have to do." She gave Taylor a wink. "I'm heading off to work to drop off this money. Have a good night, love. I'll see you in the morning before you head off to work."

"Thanks, Aunt Kristi. I love you!" She blew Taylor a kiss and then disappeared from her room. Taylor grabbed her phone and stared at it. A simple message would suffice, but Anne wanted to ignore her. She tossed her phone to the side. The kiss meant nothing to Anne, and writing the letter was for the best.

———

TAYLOR PULLED INTO THE PARKING LOT AND PARKED AROUND her usual spot. She stared up at the front door of the hospital, a knot forming in her gut. If Anne had called, she would have been able to expect how the morning would go. However, with no call came no certainty. Other than that, she believed Anne would be back to ignoring her; that was a tough pill to swallow.

Taylor leaned back in her seat and groaned. She didn't want to have to face the hospital this morning. She wanted to call in sick, but how would that look? The staff would think she was an unreliable employee. Her shift was twelve hours, and she would have to smile and get through it. As difficult as that might seem. Taylor grabbed her water and took a swig.

"You can get through this, Taylor. You have no other choice."

With a deep sigh, Taylor exited the car and headed to the front door, extra careful not to trip on the curb, as she did a week earlier. The automatic door opened, and Taylor was about to enter the opening when she saw Anne. Anne stepped out of a shadow, and Taylor didn't know where her heart lay, but she knew there was a distinct moment when she wanted to bolt.

"Glad I didn't miss you. Can we talk?"

Taylor stepped back, let the automatic doors close, and then moved to the side. She looked around to see if they were alone, and it was just the two of them. There was nothing awkward about that. Or at least in a perfect world, there wouldn't be.

"I have to be in to work in fifteen minutes," Taylor commented.

"So do I." Anne moved past her and went over to the bench. Taylor followed her with her gaze, confused, as if they sat and talked for too long; they would both be late. But at least in good company.

Taylor sat down. Anne made no move to speak until she had. "I thought my letter explained why I left pretty well."

"Well, enough, I suppose." Anne tilted her head. "What I don't get is the need to rush off. I thought we'd want to talk about it. I guess I expected us to talk about it. But no, you rushed off like you were scared or something."

"Or something?" Taylor snickered. "I was scared. But that's beside the point. If you wanted to talk, you could have picked up the phone. You have my number. All you had to do was pick up the phone and say you wanted to talk. Perhaps then this morning wouldn't be so awkward."

Anne opened her mouth and shook her head. "First off, this morning is awkward because you ghosted me Saturday morning. Secondly, when I tried calling, I saw you disconnected your number. That's low. I can't exactly try to make amends when the other person is doing everything in their power to keep the other person at arm's length."

"What?" Taylor squealed, jumping up from the bench. "I never disconnected my phone." Taylor reached into her pocket and pulled it up. It still showed service, so she offered the front screen to Anne. "I wouldn't disconnected my phone just to avoid you. What kind of person do you think I am?" She frowned, then shook her head. "Don't answer that." Taylor had already fled a hit-and-run that made her look pretty flaky. "But I didn't disconnect the line. Heck, my phone is my life. I might do some shady-ass things, but that is not one of them." She shook her head.

Anne furrowed her brow, then pulled out her phone. Taylor watched as she fiddled with her phone, then held it up in front of her. "I dialed this number multiple times. Not once, not twice, but fifteen friggin' times. Each time, I got the same message."

Taylor rolled her eyes and fell to the bench. "Well, maybe you could put the right number in your phone next time. It's 5165, not 5156." She quirked up an eyebrow and stared at Anne. Anne looked at her phone and then sighed. Taylor watched as she typed something, then pocketed her phone. "So, you tried calling me fifteen times?"

"Give or take," Anne mumbled.

Taylor looked at her watch. "If we don't go now, we're both going to be late. Good chat." She turned and headed towards the hospital, not wanting to look behind her but hoping Anne had followed. When they reached the break room, she turned to see that Anne was on her heels, and

Taylor smiled. The fact that Anne did attempt to call her lifted her spirits, but that didn't change everything. She still didn't know how Anne felt about the kiss. They discarded their items in their lockers and clocked in, then walked side by side to the elevator. It wasn't awkward, other than the intense silence. When the elevator doors closed and Taylor pushed the button for their floor, Anne turned to her.

"There's still so much we have to resolve."

"Yeah, you're not wrong." Taylor fell back against the elevator wall, and Anne shook her head.

"You ran off without even discussing it. Just because you went in for the kiss doesn't mean I hated it. In fact," Anne took a step toward Taylor. "I would say that I enjoyed it. But clearly, I'm a terrible kisser because you bolted."

"Anne..." Taylor breathlessly gasped. Anne was inches from her, and Taylor's eyes dipped to her lips. If she took one step closer, there'd be no turning back.

The elevator dinged, and Anne stepped back. "Now's not the place or time, but you can't always bolt." She turned and exited the elevator, and Taylor stared after her.

"It's all I know." She released a breath and stepped off the elevator. Cecilia stood behind the desk, pacing back and forth.

She stopped, and her face was flushed. "I'm glad you guys are here. It's going to be a hectic day."

"What's going on?" Anne asked.

"Hailey is on bedrest for the remainder of her pregnancy."

"What?" Taylor asked. "She's got a few months to go."

"We'll make it work," Anne said, not missing a beat.

"I've been trying to get her shifts covered, but you know how that's going." Cecilia shrugged. "It'll be tough, but as you said, Anne, we'll make it work."

"We'll do what we have to do," Anne added.

Taylor leaned against the counter, the wariness already shaking her. But if the rest could handle it, so could she. She just had to be strong and hope that soon Anne and her could finish that conversation. For a minute, it felt like the heat was rising in the elevator. There was no way she misread that, even with the work day ahead.

CHAPTER SIXTEEN

OVER THE EDGE

Anne

Anne stifled a yawn as she stared at the computer. It'd been eight hours, and the shift seemed never-ending. With Cecilia off at meetings most of the day, it was just Taylor and her. She had to admit, she didn't know what she would have done if Taylor hadn't been there. Anne covered her mouth, another yawn escaping. Eight hours left, and she was already dead on her feet.

Anne was well aware that Taylor had it worse. Anne was used to the frenzy of a short-staffed shift. Taylor was only at the beginning of her second week. It would be a struggle for anyone who was in that position. She leaned forward, her eyes narrowing in on the computer screen. She sighed and fell back in the chair, rubbing her weary eyes. It was downtime for at least a few minutes. Taylor had finally been relieved for lunch. Anne could take a break when she returned. Perhaps. She didn't want to leave Taylor alone for an hour. Maybe she could eat at the desk. As she sat there, her mind drifted to Taylor. She was glad it was only a misunderstanding and Taylor didn't intentionally ghost her. She should have known it was a human error. But they still had so much to discuss, starting with that heated kiss — a kiss that Anne had yet to stop thinking about. If something so wild and passionate could abruptly send her in a tailspin, then maybe it was with exploring.

A light shone at the nurse's station, and Anne pushed herself up, grabbed her clipboard, and headed to the room. "You rang?" she asked, rounding the corner. The patient was Peter White, fifteen going on thirty. He had a wide grin.

"Catch." He tossed the football, and she caught it, clutching it to her stomach.

"Great reflexes," he said.

Anne laughed. "Well, I've come to realize this is going to be an everyday occurrence." She tossed the ball back into his grasp, and he shrugged.

"Gotta get my practice in here while I'm recuperating." He looked down at his leg and grimaced. "When did the doc say I can be released?"

Anne tilted her head. "Soon. Very soon. And next year, if you take it easy now, you'll be back on the field. Just give it time."

He rolled his eyes. "That's what all adults say."

Anne smirked. "Because we're all brilliant." She winked. "Not as brilliant as you, though."

He grinned. "I'm bored."

Anne scrunched up her nose. "I could see if the doctor wants me to order some labs for you. Let's see, how about four tubes?"

"Ha ha! You're so funny."

Anne laughed, straightening up his blanket at the foot of his bed. "I'm sure you didn't call me in here to play catch. However, I'm sure you're amazed by my athleticism."

"You never cease to amaze me." He laughed, a teasing grin playing on his lips. "But nah. May I have a milk?"

"Sure thing. Anything else while I'm out? A magazine, perhaps? Or maybe I can call your school and see if they can send you some homework."

He rolled his eyes. "It's still summer."

Anne snapped her fingers. "Oh, that's right. Well, maybe they'll put together a package for you to start early." She winked and could hear him laughing as she returned to the hall. She snickered and shook her head. Her favorite moments were working with the kids and enjoying the easy banter back and forth. She shared such great memories with all of them. When she got to the nurse's station, Cecilia was back there. She looked up and smiled. "You're back?"

"Yep. I thought you both could use a break. Where's Taylor?"

"I sent her to lunch. We had a lull and weren't sure when you would return to the hospital." Anne reached in and grabbed the milk. "A thirsty kid awaits." Anne held up the carton.

"You can pass that off to them and then go to lunch. I can man the fort until you're both back."

"Sounds good." Anne turned when Cecilia spoke.

"Oh, and I forgot. We got a letter from Willow. You can do the honors." Anne turned around, and Cecilia held up the letter, unopened.

"Thank you!" Anne slipped it into her pocket and hurried back to Peter's room. "Here you go, Bud."

"Thank you!" He had the TV on and was on to watching a football game, his spirits already looking to have improved.

"Let us know if you need anything else." He waved her away, barely acknowledging her, and Anne smirked. Just like that, she was forgotten. She turned on her heel and headed out of the room, pulling the letter from her pocket and ripping into it as she stepped onto the elevator.

Dear Hospital –

Hello everyone. I am at the new hospital. It's nice. I have already made a new friend. She stays in my room. We are going to be Besties. That's what my mom says. I am really happy, but I miss you. The doctors and nurses seem nice, but it might be a long time before they make me smile. I love you all. Miss you bunches. I can't wait to see you again.

With Love,
Willow

Anne held the letter to her chest as the doors opened, and she stepped off the elevator. It was good to hear from her, as not a day went by when she didn't think of her. Anne knew it'd only been five days, but that was five days too long. When she entered the cafeteria, she spotted Taylor sitting in the corner, phone in hand, with just a bottle of water in front of her. Anne grabbed two chicken club sandwiches and a water bottle, then paid for them.

Anne walked over to the table, and Taylor finally looked up. Her eyes widened. "You left the floor unoccupied?"

Anne shrugged nonchalantly. "The doctors are there." Taylor arched an eyebrow, and Anne laughed. "Cecilia came back and sent me to lunch. This seat taken?"

"Nope. All yours." Taylor pocketed her phone as Anne slid the second sandwich toward her. "What's this?"

"Accidentally bought two." Anne opened her sandwich, and Taylor shook her head, but that didn't stop her from opening it and mumbling thanks. "Guess who we got a letter from?" Anne handed it over to Taylor, and Taylor unfolded it. Her eyes widened when she skimmed it over.

Anne watched as Taylor read through the letter, her face brimming with a smile. When she looked up, there were even a few tears in her eyes. "She sounds good."

"Thought you'd want to see the letter." Taylor nodded and looked down at it, reading it over another time.

"Thank you!" She pushed the letter toward Anne. "And thanks for the sandwich."

"No problem. And since we didn't talk, I can tell you that I got my car back yesterday evening. Joe did a great job. I hope your aunt wasn't too upset with you that you offered her up for bait."

Taylor shrugged. "She understood, actually."

They settled into silence, and the moment wasn't right to bring up the forbidden kiss. But why call it illicit? There'd been a spark; maybe they needed to let it fly.

A WEEK WENT BY, AND ANNE DIDN'T PUSH THE SUBJECT. IT wasn't that she didn't want to. It was more that time had suddenly escaped them. Down a person, they were both working crazy schedules, many times on opposite rotations. Taylor's training transformed into a crash course, but even from the sidelines, Anne could tell she hadn't wavered. Her skills seemed to be at the level of expertise they needed, running on fumes. But since they were short-staffed, it was impossible to have it any other way. It didn't give them much more than a few minutes here and there to throw in a conversation, and when they talked, the kiss always seemed to be shelved. It was inevitable.

Now's not the time. We can naturally get to know one another; who knows where that will lead us.

The problem was, when there was little time for conversation, it didn't exactly form an everlasting bond between two people. As the start of another week arrived, however, they had a moment where they could chat at the beginning of Anne's shift.

As Anne stepped onto the curb to enter the hospital, she caught a side view of Taylor. Her eyes were down, looking at something on her phone.

"Hey you," Anne started. "Your shift was over thirty minutes ago, wasn't it? What are you doing still hanging around?"

Taylor looked up, and her eyes were frantic. She wouldn't have looked that high-strung, but she was three cups of coffee deep. Anne slid into the seat next to her and immediately focused on what was happening inside Taylor's mind.

"You look stressed," Anne began.

Taylor huffed and fell back against the bench. "I'm more than stressed. I'm exhausted. My legs feel like Jell-O, and I'm ready to fall into a corner with a pint of ice cream and a bottle of wine. That's a great combo, don't you think?"

Anne shrugged. "I don't know. For the right moment, it could be nice. Wanna talk about it?"

Taylor shook her head. "Not sure there's much to talk about. I just got my schedule. It's like a race to see what will fail first: my stamina or my body. These hours are ridiculous. When I started, Hailey said it was probably that they were getting my feet wet. We're going on three weeks, and the two-week schedule just came out. I don't know how much wetter my feet could be."

"May I?" Anne reached for Taylor's phone, and she willingly handed it over. Anne looked over her schedule. It was true. She had a lot of back-to-backs and several sixteen-hour shifts. At this rate, Taylor would be too tired to discuss the kiss. Maybe that wasn't such a bad thing. After all, the kiss would fade from both their minds at some point, and it'd be like it never even happened. *As if.* Anne swallowed and scrunched up her nose. "I'm sure it's an error. Don't get me wrong. They like to schedule the residents a bunch of hours to start for residents to understand the job's expectations."

Taylor arched an eyebrow. "Do you think they feel they still have to worry? I've been busting my ass, Anne." Her tone went up several notches, and she dropped her gaze. "Sorry."

Anne shrugged. "Quite alright, but I didn't get a chance to finish. They like to schedule the residents for many hours, but this is a tad overkill."

"A tad," Taylor snickered. "Do they want nurses or zombies?" Taylor took her phone and looked over her schedule. "Don't get me wrong. The pay will be phenomenal. It's not like I don't need it, but I also would like some sanity, and social life wouldn't hurt." Anne couldn't fault her there. Anyone would say the same. "It's not just me, Anne. I heard someone talking in the break room, and she said she was on her ninth night straight. Nine nights. That's unbelievable to me."

Anne furrowed her brows at that. Management was usually understanding. Situations happen, and mistakes can occur. The more Anne considered it, the more she was sure that this was a misunderstanding.

"You know, you could say something to scheduling about it. Maybe they have a new person working in the department. It wouldn't hurt to try, would it?"

Taylor gave a weak smile. "I suppose you're right."

"I'm sure of it." Anne stood up and checked her watch. "Let me know if you decide to bring it to their attention. I'll be happy to get Cecilia and Henry Martin on our side. They were both my mentors when I first started. Henry is in the HR department, so he's good to have in our pocket. You can just let me know." Anne backed away. "I better run, though, because I'm going to be late."

"Anne?" Taylor stood up, her eyes almost pleading as she stared at Anne.

"Yeah?"

"Well, we've both been busy. But I was hoping we could talk. You know it's been over a week since..." Her words trailed off. "You know."

And there it was. Anne nodded. "Sometime soon." She rechecked her watch. "But I have to go." She spun on her heel and hurried into the hospital, away from Taylor's wandering eyes. She groaned. If only they could have had another fifteen minutes, she would have stopped right there and let that conversation take place.

Anne dropped her purse off at her locker in a daze, clocked in, and exited the elevator. When the doors opened, Christal from the emergency room was at the desk, along with Cecilia. Christal left just as Anne reached the desk.

"Hello," Anne greeted Cecilia.

"Hey, so good news. I got the okay to hire a temp. She should be here next week to help you girls out."

"That's great!" Anne sighed. Maybe things would regulate, and Taylor could get a more reasonable schedule. She could hardly wait until Taylor got the news.

CHAPTER SEVENTEEN

KARAOKE NIGHT

Taylor

A s Taylor left the hospital, her entire body ached. As tired as she was, she did feel moments of a second and even third wind. Anne spoke with her three days earlier and clarified that Taylor could talk to HR. She still considered it, but for now, she had hours to work and just went with the flow.

She slid into the front seat and sat there momentarily, taking several minutes to do some deep breathing exercises before starting her car. The accident she had the previous month and the accident from her childhood taught her to be a wary driver. Getting behind the wheel wasn't a good idea if she was too exhausted.

Her phone rang, and she dug for it, spotting Gavin's name across the screen. "Hey, bro. I'm heading home. I thought I would swing through and grab some takeout. What can I get ya?"

"Actually," he hesitated. "First off, I know I usually have an eleven o'clock curfew, but there's a movie marathon playing at the Plex. All the guys are going. And a few chicks." He laughed, and Taylor rolled her eyes. "I was hoping that my sister would be a dear and say it was alright if I went out. Please. Aunt Kristi is working, and I thought the world's best sister would let me have some fun tonight.

"Flattery will get you everywhere." Taylor stifled a yawn. She was too tired even to argue. "What time will you be home?"

"Before I respond, remember it's summer. School will be starting soon, and I'm street-smart."

"What time?" Taylor asked, yawning once more.

"Two? Two-thirty tops."

Taylor laughed. She didn't have to be at work until six the following evening. She would be in bed, passed out when he got home, but he was right. He was usually smart when it came to not getting in trouble. Luckily, he didn't take after their mother that way.

"Okay, I will trust you."

"Thank you, sis. Love you!"

"Love you, too. Just be smart." She hung up the call and slipped her phone back into her purse. If she was going home alone, she might as well stop and grab something to eat. There was no point in making dirty dishes, and she could wake herself up a little more.

Fifteen minutes later, she turned into Bar None. It was twenty-five percent bar, seventy-five percent dive, but they had great burgers and fries. It wasn't too far from her aunt's house. She entered the restaurant and looked around. It was busy for a Thursday night, busy enough to stay out of the way and go unnoticed. The waitress came up and greeted her with a napkin and a smile.

"Welcome to Karaoke night. You going to get up on the mic?"

Taylor laughed. "Not hardly." She looked around. "I was wondering why it was crowded. A lot of singers, I suppose."

"Wannabe-singer," the waitress corrected. "My name is Vicky, and I'll be helping you tonight. What can I get fresh for you?"

"I'll take a bacon burger deluxe with curly fries and a beer."

"Coming up. If you change your mind, put your name in at the bar." She winked and then walked away.

Taylor shook her head. It was never going to happen. Five minutes later, Vicky had the beer back at her table. Taylor took a sip and sighed as a man and woman took the stage. They began singing *I Got You, Babe,* by Sonny and

Cher. Taylor watched them as everyone cheered them on. They weren't in tune, but they looked like they were having fun. Before the song ended, Vicky had the rest of her food. She was eating the fries, not recognizing the time, and enjoying as one after another, people piled onto the stage, sang, then left.

Taylor laughed, but the truth was some of the people could sing. It was the ones that made a joke out of it, which made everyone have a good time. "Get you something else to drink?" Vicky asked, popping around the corner, nearly startling the sandwich out of Taylor's hands.

"Sure, I'll take another beer."

Vicky left and was back within two minutes. Taylor took a swig and then finished off her sandwich. What had started as running in to grab a bite to eat had turned into enjoying the music and not wanting to leave. A song started playing, and she immediately recognized it. "Friends in Low Places" by Garth Brooks echoed through the restaurant.

She looked up, and her jaw dropped. Anne and three other women stood on the stage and started bellowing out the tune. She took a long swig of her beer and watched the foursome, with her eyes lingering on Anne for way longer than intended. Anne wore tight jeans that hugged the curve of her ass, and when Anne turned, Taylor got an indulgent view. She swallowed the lump growing in her throat and quickly broke it down with a gulp of beer. Was it hot in there?

Anne twirled around, looking fine, shaking her ass as the crowd went wild. Being older than Taylor, she had a way of moving that would cause every woman in her twenties to stop and stare. Taylor felt the heat radiating through the restaurant and feared she might pass out if it got hotter. Anne turned and looked straight at her, a knowing stare, a lingering glance, and Taylor gave a slight wave. Anne's smile brightened as the song came to an end. Taylor looked down at her basket of food. She could bolt or stick around. Before contemplating all options, she spotted the group headed her way.

"Hey, Taylor." Anne stopped, the other three stopping short, as well.

"Hey! You all sounded great up there." Taylor glanced between the four of them.

Anne turned to the other women. "Girls, this is Taylor. She works at CAPMED. Taylor, this is Melanie, my sister. Her best friend Josie and Josie's little sister Gwen."

"Do you have to call me the little sister?" Gwen mumbled.

"Well, you are," Josie pointed out, and the four of them laughed.

"It's nice to meet you all."

"Likewise," they spoke in unison. Melanie leaned forward and said something to Anne, and Anne nodded, then the other three skirted away from the table. Melanie and Anne looked alike. They had the same mannerisms, and right now, Melanie was making the same face Anne made when she looked over a file: she was sussing something, or someone, out.

"Was it something I said?" Taylor teased.

Anne laughed. "Nah, they're good. So, are you going to get up there and sing?"

Taylor snickered and shook her head. "I would need a few more of these." She tilted back her beer bottle.

"That can be arranged," Anne motioned for Vicky to come over to the table. "Two beers, please."

"Anne, I really shouldn't," Taylor argued. She knew her limit, and she had just about reached it. One more, and she for sure would max it. "I've had plenty, and I should be getting out of here. It's been a long day at the hospital. I'm beat."

"Just one more. You don't want me drinking alone, do you?" Anne winked and scooted into the booth across from Taylor. "Unless you were saving this spot for someone."

"Nope. Not at all." Taylor took a swig from the beer that Vicky dropped off at the table. "Do you come here often?" Taylor asked.

"Only when Melanie wants to get out of the house." She snickered, taking a sip of her beer. "Long story."

Taylor drank her beer, realizing that the heat had encased her as Anne sat only inches from her. Anne wore a white blouse that revealed her cleavage, and Taylor downed a quarter of the bottle.

"You girls were good up there," Taylor said, the music getting louder as another song started playing.

Anne laughed loudly. "Then you're hard up for talent if you thought that was good."

Taylor kept her eyes on the rim of her beer bottle but felt Anne's gaze on her. She looked up to see if she was right, and sure enough, there were those magnetic eyes. She grabbed her bottle and downed the rest.

"Want another?" Anne asked.

"I wouldn't dare," Taylor mumbled. Her head was hazy, and she could slowly feel the room spinning. She looked up, and Anne had a grin on her lips, obviously not knowing the position Taylor was in. "Anne," Taylor began.

Anne jumped up and grabbed Taylor's hand. "Come with me."

"What?" Taylor asked. Her feet flailed behind her as she stumbled after Anne and right up to the stage. "Anne," she hissed.

"Trust me," Anne said. "You're going to be great."

Taylor felt sick, the room still spinning. Anne said something to the bartender as Taylor stood there awkwardly. Then the song "Summer Nights" from *Grease* started playing. Anne began to sing, and the words blurred on the screen. When it came to Taylor's part, she didn't know where it came from, but she started belting out the tune, and the crowd roared to life. Taylor looked over at Anne, who moved in closer to her and snaked her arm around Taylor. They continued the song, not caring who watched them, but the crowd seemed pleased, and Taylor felt like she was on top of the world.

CHAPTER EIGHTEEN

TIMING AT ITS WORST

Anne

Taylor lit up on that stage. Anne wanted to see her let loose, but she didn't know she had a karaoke star on her hands. By the time the song played on, Taylor was flirting, hanging all over Anne, and acting like they had been doing this for years. Anne felt every word Taylor sang and couldn't tear her eyes away. Taylor was a beauty that only got more beautiful when she opened herself up.

They exited the stage, and Taylor laughed. "Anne, that was great." She fell against her, and Anne turned to steady her to her feet. Anne didn't expect that the last beer she got for Taylor seemed to be the one that took her over her limit. Now, Taylor was slurring her words, and that intoxicating beauty was coming from someone highly intoxicated.

"Taylor, you're drunk." Anne covered her face, feeling slight guilt over the matter.

"Nah, no, I'm not," Taylor argued. "I don't get drunk. I get even." She laughed louder than Anne had ever heard her laugh. Anne grimaced, wrapping her arm around Taylor's waist, then grabbed their purses and awkwardly stumbled toward the door. Once outside, the fresh air washed over her. Maybe that would help to sober Taylor up. "You're beautiful,"

Taylor moaned. "Do you know that? You're so beautiful." She caressed Anne's cheek, and Anne winced. She'd wanted to hear Taylor say those words but now wasn't the time.

"Come on! I'll get you home." She then frowned. *Home?* She didn't even know where Taylor's home was. She had no choice but to get her back to her house. Once they got to Anne's car, getting her into the passenger seat wasn't easy.

"Kiss me," Taylor breathlessly said. She snaked her hand around Anne's neck and pulled her to her, kissing her hard.

"Taylor," Anne argued. "Not now." Anne felt a gut punch. She wanted the kiss to deepen, not end, but how could she kiss her like that when Taylor was drunk and wouldn't even remember what happened the next day? "Not this way," Anne helped her into the seat, reaching across to buckle her up.

"Your lips are so soft. I could kiss you forever."

Anne jerked and stared at her. Taylor had a grin on her lips. "In the morning, you won't remember any of this." Taylor closed her eyes, and Anne shut the door behind her. She didn't want to believe that statement, but there was a strong likelihood it was true.

Anne looked around the small parking lot and saw Taylor's car. She would get her there the next day to pick up her car. At least Anne was there to see that Taylor got home safely. As Anne merged onto the highway, her phone rang, and she looked over to see that Taylor was sleeping, not even moving when the phone rang.

"Answer call. Hello?"

"Hey, sis. So, what's the story with Taylor?" Anne swerved at the mention of Taylor's name. She shot a look towards the passenger seat, but still, her eyes were tightly closed.

"There's no story. Taylor's just a co-worker. That's all."

"Hmmmm. Well, you lit up when you saw her."

"Shhhhh..." Anne sharply replied. "Can't talk now. But is everything alright with you? Is Josh home?"

"He stayed home with the girls while I was out, but then he went out with the guys once I got home." Anne rolled her eyes. She had heard that story way too many times. "I just wanted to check about Taylor. She's cute. If you like her, then go for it."

Taylor moaned in the seat next to her. "Gotta go!" Anne quickly disconnected the Bluetooth and looked where Taylor shifted in her seat. She held her breath, waiting, hopeful that Taylor would fall asleep. Taylor started snoring minutes later. Anne relaxed and drove the rest of the way home. Everything Melanie said, she had to push out of her mind. Sure, there might be something there. She sometimes felt it down in her bones when she looked at Taylor. The sparks always flew, but thinking of that now wasn't going to change the fact that there wasn't anything she could do about it. Taylor was in no position to respond reasonably.

ANNE SHIFTED IN THE CHAIR, ATTEMPTING TO FIND A comfortable position. She stretched, her neck cracking a few times. "Anne?"

Anne jerked and looked to the bed, where Taylor leaned on her elbows. Taylor looked around the bedroom and then back to Anne.

"You want coffee? You could use some coffee." Anne stood up, but even in the room's darkness, Anne saw Taylor's frown lines.

"What happened?" She groaned and touched her head, then looked up and met Anne's gaze. She released a growl. "Beer, that's what happened." She fell back into bed.

"Do you think you can make your way downstairs? I'll put on a pot of coffee."

"Yeah," she grumbled. Anne didn't wait for her to say anything else as she hurried from the room and straight downstairs to the kitchen. Taylor continued to flirt, and Anne continued to dodge her advances. Even when Taylor pulled her into the bed, it took all Anne's might to crawl off of the bed and keep her distance. If there was an award for perseverance, they both deserved it, but Anne was weakening, and with any more attempts, she might have caved.

Anne heard the shuffling on the steps, and she turned to see Taylor rounding the corner. Taylor dropped her gaze. Her cheeks were flushed. "Just in time. Your coffee is served." Anne poured two cups, and Taylor reached out for the table, steadying herself. Anne had been in that position one too many times. However, she was in her early thirties the last time it happened. "This should heal your headache in no time."

"I'm good," Taylor mumbled, falling into the chair and reaching for the mug. Anne scooted it closer to Taylor when it was clear that Taylor's depth perception was off. "Thank you." Taylor grabbed the mug and took a sip. She winced and then looked up, making eye contact with Anne. Anne gave her a consoling smile as she took a sip. "Usually, I never get too drunk to drive." Her eyes widened. "My car?"

"It's at Bar None, as it should be. Later this morning, I'll drive you there, and you can grab it. I didn't think you could drive home safely. I didn't want to overstep, but you were clearly under the influence." A vision of Taylor desperately placing the moves on Anne, only to get stopped in her tracks, attempted to wander into Anne's mind. Taylor's cheeks turned red, and she dropped her gaze.

"Do I even want to know?" she asked.

"Depends. What do you remember?"

"What did I do?" Taylor asked, still wide-eyed.

Anne smirked. "What do you remember?"

Taylor sighed. "The last thing I remember is singing with you."

Anne looked down and shrugged. "That's pretty much all that happened. However, it's a shame that you don't recall the crowd cheering you on."

"Are you sure they weren't boos?" Taylor asked.

Anne laughed. "You were a star up there." Taylor closed her eyes, opened them, and looked at her watch. "After you drink your coffee, you should lie down more. No need to rush off and get your car at this hour."

Anne took a sip. "Six o'clock. I feel like I've been asleep for forty-eight hours."

"Then I imagine the rest did you good since you've been working so many hours," Anne pointed out.

Taylor tilted her head. "Did you get any rest? I mean, you were sitting in the room. You didn't look all that comfortable."

Anne shrugged. "I can sleep anywhere. I'm fine. Just drink up."

Taylor took a sip, a little longer this time. When she dropped her mug, looking off into the distance. "I never do anything like that. After my..." Her words trailed off, and she clenched her hands together. Anne watched her, mild curiosity piquing her interest. "Water under the bridge. Just know that that's not like me."

"I wasn't judging," Anne remarked. "Besides, you might not remember that I practically forced that last drink upon you. Who knows what would have happened hadn't you taken that last beer on."

Taylor snickered. "Well, my limit is usually one. I recall drinking two myself, and it wasn't a hard sell to get me to go for the last one, that I remember."

"Yeah, I'm not much of a drinker either. I've seen what it can do to people. I don't much care for things that have that kind of effect on a person."

Taylor looked up from her drink. "I feel the same way," Taylor admitted. "My mom had a problem with alcohol and drugs when I was growing up. She changed in ways that hurt not only her but also her family. The fact is, when I was younger, I was in the car with her. She was under the influence, and we got into a nasty accident. One of the reasons I ran from our fender bender was that car wrecks triggered my anxiety. I had nightmares for years. I probably needed therapy, but the hardest thing is admitting you have a problem."

Anne slowly nodded. The heartfelt words that Taylor spoke left Anne hanging on her every word. She liked that Taylor felt comfortable enough to share such a personal story.

"I'm no therapist, but having someone to talk to is never bad. But I don't think your story requires therapy. It just requires understanding and knowledge that people are out there to listen. If you ever wanna talk, I'll listen."

Taylor smiled. "I don't have a lot of friends outside of a few here and there that I went to school with. So, I appreciate that."

"We all could use a few more friends. As you saw last night, my friends consist of my sister and hers." Anne laughed. "I hang out with a few from the hospital now and again, but everyone is so busy with life and their families. It's hard to find the time. But my sister, that's another story." Anne finished her coffee and stood up from the table. "Do you want a second cup?"

"No, I'm good. Thanks." Taylor moved the mug closer to Anne, and Anne turned to wash them in the sink.

"If you ever wanna talk, I'm here, too." Anne looked over her shoulder, and Taylor grinned. She reached up and massaged her temples. "Headache and all."

"I divulge info about my life, and you're bound to think my family is crazy. You might never want to hang out again." Anne smirked and turned, putting the mugs back in the cabinets. She hesitated and turned around, noticing that Taylor hadn't turned away. "My sister is in a rocky marriage. They have two loving daughters, and her spouse is cheating on her. He says it's over, but I see right through it. It's hard to know how to handle that. Being supportive is fine and all, but when he's mentally abusive. He drinks until he's passed out cold in the living room. There's something genuinely unsettling about him. It's hard to turn the other cheek."

"That's rough." Taylor scrunched up her nose. "I can't even begin to piece together what makes a happy relationship or how a marriage can survive in the long term. I haven't had a serious relationship, and who knows if I'll ever get married."

"You don't believe in marriage?" Anne asked. She knew that many younger lesbians were cynical about getting married, but most of her friends still thought that true love would conquer all. Anne wondered if Taylor was hesitant because of the patriarchal idea of marriage or if she didn't want to be bothered with the paperwork.

"I haven't met a marriage that's worked yet." Taylor shrugged.

Anne nodded, understanding. Yet, even though her dad up and left them for another woman, she still wanted to believe that, ultimately, when two people loved each other, a lasting marriage was inevitable.

"It's hard to argue when you have lived through marriages breaking up. I've been there and done that with my parents. My dad wasn't any better than my brother-in-law is to my sister. So, I get it. Yet, the hopeless romantic in me wants to believe." Anne shook her head. "Let me rephrase that the hopeless romantic in me has to believe that when two people are in love, they will move mountains to be with one another. I know when I find that love, I'll never want it to end."

Taylor's brow furrowed. "You seem so confident."

"When you're talking about love, how can you not?" Anne pushed into the chair. "If we get to bed now, we'll be able to get in a couple of hours. Now that I know you're okay, I'll lie in my bed."

"Sounds good to me." Taylor stood up. The color had returned to her cheeks, and she hesitated. "Thank you for making sure I got home safely."

"I'm glad I was there." Anne started to head out of the kitchen when her arm brushed across Taylor's. She looked up, and their eyes met. Anne smiled and went to look away, but the longing hadn't once wavered. *Dammit! She had almost escaped.*

"We never did talk about that kiss," Taylor began. "Perhaps the moment is gone, and we'll pretend it never happened. Or perhaps..." Before Taylor could finish that sentence, Anne moved in and claimed a kiss. Taylor had initiated so much between them; this was the least she could do. Standing in the kitchen, Anne reached for Taylor's shirt, aching to pull it over her chest, revealing her two breasts. Instead, she just held onto the shirt with one hand. With the other, she moved her hand up the back and rested it on her skin. Her tongue dipped in and claimed a moan from Taylor's mouth. This was where they had to end it. It was disappointing.

CHAPTER NINETEEN

GROWING CHEMISTRY

Taylor

Taylor stared at her phone as she stepped off the elevator. Wrapping up another day at the hospital, she was ready to go home, sleep, and be grateful she had the next day off. Taylor still hadn't said anything to the hospital about her schedule. While she was tired, no doubt, having the extra experience under her belt made her feel accomplished. Besides, did she want to complain less than a month into her career?

As Taylor stepped outside, the summer wind washing over her, she spotted Anne. There was a moment of hesitation where Taylor could have quickly walked past her and pretended she never saw her. But Taylor wanted to talk to her. It'd been two days since the encounter at Bar None and the even more awkward encounter the next morning. What she hadn't confessed to Anne was remembering more than she led on. There wasn't much Taylor had forgotten about that night at Bar None, whether it was the karaoke or her repeated attempts to seduce Anne. It turns out tipsy Taylor was also flirty Taylor. "What are you doing here? It's your day off."

Anne looked up and smiled. "I had to speak with HR about an issue with my bank. All taken care of." Anne started walking beside Taylor. A distinct heaviness was in the air as Taylor's mind returned to the morning at Anne's house-- a morning that felt like a lifetime ago. Still, she wanted more, and she could tell that Anne felt that way, too. "So," Anne continued. "Are you hungry?"

Taylor stopped in the parking lot and turned her head. "I could go for a bite."

"Meet me at the diner?"

Taylor nodded, and Anne hurried off to her car. Taylor looked down at her scrubs and groaned. It wasn't like it was an actual date, but she would have given anything to be out of her scrubs and dressed in regular clothes. There was no time to do anything about that, though. She pulled up the group text for Aunt Kristi and Gavin and shot them a message.

TAYLOR:

Grabbing a bite to eat with a friend. I'll be home late.

It wasn't entirely false. However, there wasn't a distinction between acquaintances and friendship. She and Anne were friends.

She pushed the thought from her mind and drove to the corner diner. Perhaps they would finally have a few minutes to talk. They had shared two passionate kisses and intimate moments that Taylor remembered vividly. They had to talk about it sometime. If Taylor didn't discuss it, she would surely lose her mind. How could they let something that palpable go undiscussed?

Anne pulled into the parking lot after Taylor got out of her car. Taylor waited for Anne to join her at the door before they entered. Since this wasn't a date, there wasn't any reason for awkwardness. Yet, her palms couldn't stop sweating.

They grabbed a corner booth, and Taylor didn't bother opening the menu. "You know what you want?" Anne asked.

"I usually get the fish basket."

Anne tilted her head. "A woman that knows what she wants is sexy. But if you're saying you have a usual, then you don't escape outside of that box, and you might be missing out on new adventures."

Taylor laughed. "Adventures in eating at the diner? I never considered that. So, what do you suggest?"

"Well, let's see." Anne skimmed through the menu, then returned to the first page and pointed. "Tenderloin basket. It's the best in the world, and ask for it with the gravy. I promise you; you won't be disappointed."

"You say it's the best in the world? How many places have you tried?"

"Twenty. No, wait a minute, I forgot Salt Lake City. So, twenty-one."

Taylor smirked. "You figured that out all in your head. I'm impressed." Anne continued to grin, and the waitress approached them.

"May I start you, ladies, off with something to drink? Or perhaps you're ready to order?"

"I think we're ready." Anne looked at Taylor and motioned for Taylor to take the reins.

"I'll take a water to drink, but I want the tenderloin basket with the gravy." The woman jotted down her notes and then turned to Anne.

"I'll take a fish basket. Water, as well." The woman took the order, then turned and left.

Taylor snickered. "After all that, you ordered what I was planning on?"

Anne shrugged. "I'm used to the tenderloin. It is the best, but I don't think I've tried the fish. I'm taking my advice and thinking outside the box." Taylor considered those words, then looked down at her hands, clenched on top of the table. There was something magnetic about Anne. If they had never worked through the accident, then she would have never been able to see the kind of person Anne was. She would have missed out on a great opportunity. But Anne was a personality that Taylor couldn't just turn away from.

The waitress brought them water, and they waited until the waitress had left before each took a sip. "Do you come to this diner often?"

"Quite often. It's just a hop, skip, and jump from the hospital. It makes for easy access." Anne took another sip, then looked up. "What about you?"

"Not that often. Aunt Kristi is a surprisingly good cook. I don't usually like to spend money if I can avoid it."

"That's smart," Anne replied. The table quieted, and Taylor questioned if that was because she brought up money. They hadn't talked about what it meant for Taylor to spend over a thousand dollars on her credit card. But Taylor didn't think it was necessary to point out those trivial matters when it was her fault, and rightfully so; she should be the one to have to pay for the damage. Besides, that got both cars fixed and could have been much worse. "Speaking of your aunt, though, did she have to go out on a date with that Joe guy."

Taylor guffawed. "Oh yeah, speaking of that..." Her words trailed off as the waitress brought their food. "Thank you!" Once the waitress was gone, she continued. "So, yeah. He called, and Aunt Kristi first attempted to ignore the calls. She's pretty busy, so she has a solid excuse, but he's called every day for the past two weeks."

Anne laughed. "Two weeks? She got him to wait that long?" She shook her head. "Is Joe that bad of a person?"

"I don't think it's that he's a bad person. My aunt has a type. She's been with the bad boys, and Joe rides a motorcycle. She gets the feeling that he's not the settling down type."

"So, your aunt wants to settle down and all?"

Taylor pondered over those words. Her aunt had a fiancée once, and everyone thought they would marry. It shocked everyone when they broke it off because they supposedly fell out of love—everyone except Kristi. "I'd say she's a lot like you," Taylor began. "You know, hopeless romantic and such."

"Far less cynical than you, I see." Anne smiled, then offered a wink when Taylor met her eye. She was cynical, but Anne had vibes that might turn her around.

"Maybe I'm not the cynic you think I am." Taylor tilted her head and grabbed her tenderloin. "This thing is huge."

Anne laughed. "Let's see if you can handle it."

Taylor choked on her bite as she comprehended the innuendo. She chewed so as not to swallow the sandwich in whole. "Delicious," she said as she swallowed.

Anne grinned with pleasure. "I knew you would like it." She took another bite of the fish. "And your recommendation is spot on."

They ate for a few minutes, letting the conversation drop off, but periodically, Taylor would look across the table, checking out what Anne was doing. In many cases, Anne had her eyes directed on Taylor until they both looked away.

"So, when do you work next Saturday?"

"Let me look." Taylor grabbed her phone and pulled up her schedule. "I work seven to seven. I have Sunday off, though, so the weekend won't be too bad. How about you?"

"I'm off, but I'm having a party. Some friends, co-workers, and my sister and nieces will be there. Nothing crazy. We'll have a bonfire, roast marshmallows, and do things like that."

"What's the occasion?" Taylor asked, grabbing two fries and putting them in her mouth.

"Last week, I made my last house payment. My house is free and clear. I vowed I would have a party to celebrate, and I'd love for you to come if you can make it."

"Sounds like fun. I could come after work." Anne nodded, and the conversation died again for a few minutes. "So, your sister...how's she doing? Have you talked to her?"

"Every day. Same ol' same ol'. She knows that she deserves better, but when your heart wants what it wants, it's hard to tell it differently. That's why I try to give her as many nights out as possible."

"Does her husband ever come around?"

Anne laughed. "He knows if he dared to come around, I'd kick him out. So, he stays away, and that's all the better." Anne dipped her fish in tartar sauce and held it there. "But, Taylor, I didn't just come to the hospital for HR. I had to talk to them, but I could have waited until the morning. I was hoping I'd catch up with you."

"You were?" Mildly intrigued, Taylor didn't move a muscle.

"I was. I didn't think I could let another day pass without talking to you about what's happening between us." Taylor clamped down on her lower lip, aching to pinch herself to ensure she wasn't dreaming. "When we kissed, it was highly likely I could just forget about it and move on. If we didn't discuss it, then it could be like it never even happened." She laughed. "And then, kiss number two occurred, and try as I might, I can't move on from it until I know what we're going to call this. I mean, maybe there's chemistry, but that's all. I'll nod and move on. But, if there's something more we should be exploring, then we owe it to ourselves to figure that out." Anne leaned back in her seat, putting the piece of fish in her mouth with a satisfied smile.

"I don't think we should ignore it." Anne grinned and leaned forward, and Taylor shrugged. "I mean, I've been thinking about it, too. And I think that there could be something there. I like being around you, and ever since we could move past the, you know." She looked down at her half-eaten basket. "It just isn't something I'm willing to look away from."

"I'm glad we agree." Anne clapped her hands together. "I was worried that maybe I was reading too much into it, but I'm relieved you feel the same way."

Anne and Taylor were on the same page. Now, all they had to do was figure out the next steps. They finished their food, and when it came time to pay, they reached for their wallet. It was Taylor who prompted a request. "How about this? We both pay for our own tonight. We can argue over the check when we go on an actual date. But surely, we can do nicer than this."

Anne nodded with enthusiasm. "That's a plan." They tossed money to cover their bills, left the diner, and walked to Taylor's car. When Taylor turned to face Anne, Anne was already inches away. Anne reached for her hand and pulled her to her. With no hesitation, she went in for a kiss.

CHAPTER TWENTY

IT'S MY PARTY

Anne

Anne glanced at her watch once more. She shot a look at the fence and sighed. Taylor said she would be there, yet she was already thirty minutes late. She tried to shrug it off. Taylor would be there. She promised. She took a sip from her water bottle and tossed it in the trash outside the circle of lawn chairs.

"Does anyone want anything to drink?" Anne asked, taking a stand.

"I'll take a beer."

"I'll take a water."

"I'll take a wine cooler."

She nodded and laughed, glancing around the fire pit where everyone had seemingly been enjoying themselves. "Anything else?"

"I'll take another burger. Well done." Her neighbor, Tyler, added. She rolled her eyes, ready to tell him he could grab that himself. But the truth was, she was just grateful that everyone had made it out to her party. She felt loved and couldn't have asked for a better turnout.

She had considered making it two parties, but the truth was that after giving it much thought, she realized just having a bigger party seemed to make more sense. Besides, she had help. Melanie had come over early with

Lily and Rose. They prepared the backyard. Then, her neighbors Mark and Aimee offered to come over. Aimee was a part-time DJ and said she would bring her music. Mark had a knack for grilling. Everything seemed to come together.

"As long as my memory doesn't fail me, your orders will be coming right up." Anne snickered.

"I'll help you," Cecilia commented, joining Anne in her journey to ensure she could fulfill everyone's wishes.

"Mark, will you put a couple of burgers on?" Anne asked, passing him to get to the coolers. "Well done for Tyler."

"Coming right up!" Mark turned from her, and Anne reached down to open the coolers.

"By the way, I heard from Hailey," Cecilia began. "I've been meaning to catch up with you. She's still on bed rest, but the doctors state she's improving. It doesn't look like she'll be coming back before her maternity leave is up, but I think we all figured that would be the case."

"Yeah. No surprise there." Anne frowned. "Was it two beers and a water?"

"No, your sister wanted a wine cooler," Cecilia commented.

"That's right. I'm glad you came along to help." Anne laughed, reaching into the cooler and pulling out a wine cooler." She looked over to where her nieces were playing games with Mark and Aimee's kids, and she reached in and grabbed four juice boxes.

"Let me help you here." Cecilia laughed. "I'm more than just the person that remembers the orders. I can deliver them, too."

Anne smiled. "Take this over to the circle, and I'll take the juice boxes to the kids and grab Tyler's burger."

"Teamwork makes the dream work." Cecilia winked and then hurried over to the circle. Anne sighed as she headed off to the table where the kids were.

"Who wants a drink?"

In unison, they all cried out. "Me!"

Anne gave them each a box and helped her nieces stick the straw through the hole. Mark and Aimee's kids, Ethan and Rory, were a bit older, at eight and seven, but she liked how they instantly took her nieces in and played games with them. That way, no one was feeling left out.

"Need anything else?" she asked. Anne ruffled Lilly and Rose's hair, and they looked up and grinned.

"We're good," Lily commented.

"Alright then. Holler if you need anything." Anne left the kids and went over to get Tyler's burger.

"Just in time," Mark commented, putting it on the bun and handing it over.

"Thank you, and you really should be taking a break. Have you eaten anything?" He shrugged, and Anne arched an eyebrow. "Precisely why I feared if you helped out, I would be taking advantage of you."

"You're not! I'm happy to be here." He smirked. "But I'll take a few minutes and make myself a burger. Does anyone need any hot dogs?"

"Nope. It looks like they have that covered over by the fire pit. Take this chance to rest. Promise me?"

He nodded. "Yes, Mother."

She playfully punched him, then turned to the fire pit. "Tyler? What do you want on this burger of yours?"

He laughed and stood up. "I was just coming to get it. I was only teasing. You didn't have to get it for me."

"Sure, you were." Anne laughed.

Tyler was only twenty-one. His parents had him at an older age, and when they hit retirement, they decided to move to Florida. Tyler inherited the house that was already fully paid off. Anne vowed that she would be sure to be there if he needed anything. Inviting him to the party was a no-brainer when he had no family in the area.

Anne's phone started ringing as Tyler grabbed the plate from her. She saw Taylor's name, and her face fell. Anne moved away from the crowd and answered the call. "Hello?"

"Hey, Anne. I just thought I'd check about tonight. I'm just now leaving the hospital, and I know it's late. So, if everyone is going to be leaving shortly, then I might as well not come. Right?"

Anne looked over to the fire pit, where Melanie and a few nurses were dancing to Aimee's playlist. "I don't think anyone is planning on leaving anytime soon. So, unless you don't want to come..." Anne held her breath. She didn't want to hear Taylor mumble that she would prefer to go home. She had been waiting all night to see her, a confusing situation.

"No, I'd like to come if the offer still stands." Taylor released a breath that washed through the phone. Anne smiled.

"Then it's settled. I'll see you soon." She disconnected the call and turned back to Melanie and her friends. Taylor was the only person missing from the group; she couldn't wait until Taylor arrived.

———————

ANNE CONTINUED TO WATCH FOR TAYLOR LIKE A HAWK. SHE tried not to be too engrossed in waiting for another person, so she brought her eyes numerous times back to the circle. She sipped on her water some and just waited.

"I want to believe Josh will change," Melanie said. "But seeing is believing, right?"

"You have to do what's right for you, Melanie. Josh will only change if he wants to. The sooner you remember that, the happier you will be." Tisha, a co-worker who happened to work in the psych department, said the exact things Anne had said numerous times to her sister. Yet, it was always easier to take news from someone else. And if Tisha could provide that to Melanie, then Anne wouldn't complain. She was surprised Melanie felt open enough to discuss her marriage, but it made sense, given Tisha's expertise.

Anne checked her watch for the millionth time that night. Taylor should be there at any moment. Or so she expected. She turned toward the gate, and that's when she saw her. Taylor gave a slight wave and smile.

"Where'd you get these chips, Anne?" Cecilia asked. "I've never had this flavor before. They were kimchi-flavored chips from a Korean market.

"Will you excuse me?" Anne jumped up and hurried toward Taylor, completely ignoring Cecilia's question. "Come here." Anne motioned for Taylor to follow her, and they went through the house's backdoor. "I didn't think you would ever get here." Anne turned to her and pulled her into her arms. She kissed her, the kiss taking Anne's breath away.

"That's some greeting," Taylor breathlessly exclaimed, breaking from the kiss.

"Too forward?" Anne teased.

"Not hardly. Too perfect," Taylor whispered. She moved in and pressed her lips against Anne's. They hungrily kissed, their tongues swerving through a fiery greeting. Anne had one thought: it wasn't going outside and rejoining the party. As far as she was concerned, she was ready for a party for two. Her tongue swooped in and claimed a moan from Taylor. She groaned and pulled back. Anne stared into Taylor's eyes, and a sparkle shone from her eyes. Taylor laughed and lowered her gaze.

"Anne?"

Anne whirled when she heard Melanie's voice. Melanie gave an awkward wave to Taylor, then turned to Anne. "Um, yeah?" Anne asked. Two seconds earlier, Melanie would have caught them entangled in one another's arms.

"It's getting late. I think I should be getting the girls home."

"Of course." Anne shot a look at Taylor, then quickly moved to follow Melanie into the backyard.

Melanie tilted her head. "Please tell me I interrupted something," Melanie hissed.

Anne felt her cheeks burning, and if it hadn't been dark outside, everyone would have noticed the embarrassment coursing through Anne's blood. "I plead the fifth," Anne whispered.

Melanie giggled and rolled her eyes. "Girls, we're going to have to leave."

"Do we have to?" Rose asked, clasping her hands together. "We're having so much fun."

Melanie shook her head and looked over to Anne. Anne shrugged. "Maybe you guys can come back sometime and play."

"Alright," Rose groaned, standing to her feet.

"Give me a hug." Anne opened her arms and hugged each of them; then they said their goodbyes to the neighbor kids. "Goodbye." She leaned in and kissed Melanie's cheek. "Call me if you need anything."

"I always do." Melanie grinned, and Anne walked them over to the fence and watched them leave. She waved when her nieces turned around and looked in her direction. They got in the car, and her sister drove away. Anne turned and spotted Taylor with the rest of the group. She was in a conversation with Tisha, Cecilia, and Kara from the hospital. Anne watched them until Cecilia and Tisha left the group and headed toward Anne.

"I have to be at a meeting out of town early in the morning. So, I should head out," Cecilia replied.

"And Cecilia is my ride," Tisha added.

"Thank you both for coming." Anne hugged them both.

"Congrats again on getting your mortgage paid off," Cecilia commented. "That's a huge accomplishment."

"You should be proud," Tisha added.

Anne couldn't control her grin. "Thank you! You guys drive safe, and I'll see you both later!" Anne waved, and they left through the gate. Kara started dancing with Tyler, leaving Taylor alone in the circle. She reached for a stick and then looked around, her eyes catching Anne's. She blushed.

"I'll confess. I've never made a S'mores before."

Anne's jaw dropped. "Is that so? Well then, I think you need a good teacher, and trust me, I have loads of experience." Taylor watched her as she showed her how to toast the marshmallows and then melt the chocolate over the fire. "Then you place them between the graham crackers and have a delicious masterpiece. Just don't burn yourself."

Taylor popped a piece into her mouth and sighed. Anne smiled and looked away so Taylor wouldn't see the heat radiating on her cheeks.

"You're right, Anne, this is amazing." Taylor's amazement had Anne raising her eyes to indulge in the satisfaction on Taylor's face. The intimate moment had passed, but it wouldn't for long. They could reconvene once everyone was gone. Anne was ready to get back to sharing some sweet moments.

CHAPTER TWENTY-ONE

SEXUAL TENSION RELEASED

Taylor

As the last guests left, Anne stayed outside to say goodbye to them, and Taylor kept to the kitchen. She had plenty of experience with cleaning since she spent her childhood cleaning up after her mother. Taylor heard Anne outside yelling goodbye to her neighbors. When Anne returned to the kitchen, Taylor washed the last dish and dried the counter from the water left behind.

Anne cleared her throat. "I didn't mean for you to get stuck cleaning up. You're a guest."

Taylor shrugged. "It was fun." She tossed the towel to the side and turned to Anne. "I know I got here late, but the whole night was a blast."

"Is that so?" Anne moved in closer to her. "What part was your favorite?"

Taylor scrunched up her nose in thought, then smirked. "Learning to make S'mores from a pro."

Anne leaned back against the table, and Taylor followed her eyes to meet Anne's. "Do I have experience camping? You could say that. My sister and I used to set up tents in the backyard. A million stars would be in the sky, and we would be crouched in a tent, reading to each other and making S'mores." She then shrugged. "But it wasn't just camping outdoors. I recall many adventures at campgrounds with my parents before my dad, you know." Anne sighed. "Camping was a favorite pastime of mine. What about you?"

"What? Camping? Didn't you see my mad fire skills out there?" Taylor giggled. "It's hard to go camping when you're living on the streets."

Anne frowned. "I'm sorry."

Taylor shook her head. "Don't say you're sorry. I'm a firm believer that your past helps dictate your future. Someone would take the rims off a tire a few times and use those for a fire pit. That would be when it was below zero." Anne's eyes widened, and Taylor laughed. "Don't look so serious. That was a long time ago. I've come a long way." She moved closer to where Anne stood and reached for Anne's hands. She intertwined her fingers with Anne's and ran her thumb slowly across her palm. "You know what?" Taylor whispered.

In her mind, a million thoughts raced. What funny or clever thing would she say, something riveting to mark the way to a compelling conversation?

"What?" Anne's breath released, and Taylor's mind went blank.

Taylor dropped her lips into a grin. "The house is so quiet and inviting. No one's here. It's just you and me."

Anne nodded. "And so, it is...just you and me."

"Wanna make out?" Taylor asked all inhibitions lost. She pulled Anne closer, and Anne's lips collided with hers. There was a moan, but Taylor couldn't catch if it were her or Anne. Anne slid her tongue between Taylor's lips, thrashing her wildly around Taylor's. After several minutes of heated kissing in the kitchen, Taylor pushed Anne back against the table. She reached her hand down, cupping Anne's ass in her palm, and held her, aching for so much more at that moment.

Anne seemed to read Taylor's mind, slipping her hand under Taylor's shirt and riding it up, revealing Taylor's breasts. Taylor broke from the kiss and stepped back, staring longingly into Anne's eyes. Anne grabbed Taylor's shirt and pulled it up and over her head, then tossed it to the side, with their eyes never wavering.

"May I?" Anne asked, reaching for the front clasp of Taylor's bra. If she didn't rip it off, Taylor would do the honors herself. She nodded, feeling the heat of Anne's gaze bore holes through her body. Anne flicked her wrist, and Taylor's bra opened. Taylor slipped out of her bra, and Anne moved in and captured Taylor's left breast into her mouth.

"Yes," Taylor cried. Her core throbbed as Anne sucked on her left nipple. If Anne didn't indulge quicker, she would come right there in the kitchen. Taylor arched her back and relished the feel of Anne's tongue flicking with pleasure against her nipple. She swiftly moved to her right breast, and again, a guttural groan shuddered through Taylor's body. "Ugh..." Taylor cried. Anne kissed her way around Taylor's areola, sending shivers through Taylor's spine. Taylor grabbed hold of Anne's hair and squeezed her fingers through her hair, enjoying the greed that Anne displayed between Taylor's two breasts.

Anne bit down slightly, just enough to cause Taylor to shudder, before releasing Taylor's left breast from her mouth. She looked up, and Taylor couldn't control the urge. She grabbed Anne's blouse and pulled it open, breaking a button or two in the process. Anne's mouth hung open, and Taylor laughed, slipping her tongue back in to capture another moan. Taylor was about to give her the ride of her life, and Anne seemed to be full throttle ahead.

TAYLOR SQUIRMED BENEATH ANNE AS SHE FLICKED HER tongue inside of her. "Oh, God," Taylor groaned, moving her body in time to Anne's thrusts. She closed her eyes and attempted to relax. It'd been a while since she had a workout in this capacity, and Anne knew how to make her body sing. Her stomach churned, and she thrust her hips harder. Anne greeted every move with pleasure. "Anne," Taylor whimpered, her mind going numb, her body slowly convulsing. She held onto the bed and cried as another orgasm raked over her.

Anne crashed against her, giggling as she hiked up Taylor's naked body. She looked down into Taylor's eyes and then kissed Taylor's lips. The alarm started going off, and Taylor groaned.

"Not now," she moaned between kisses.

Anne pushed herself up and longingly gazed directly into Taylor's soul. "Duty calls, and believe me, I don't want to leave." She rolled off of Taylor and stood to her feet. They were wrapped up in each other's arms for two days straight. Taylor hadn't even gone home to grab a change of clothes. Having Sunday off gave them plenty of time to explore each other in Anne's bedroom. She just hoped that when she got home, her aunt and brother didn't have too many questions to ask.

Taylor watched Anne's naked form as she stood next to the bed. Anne smirked and shook her finger. "What?" Taylor asked.

"You're oogling."

Taylor pouted her lips. "You don't like that?"

"On the contrary..." Anne moved in closer to her lips. "I love it, but it won't get me out of here any quicker. I can't be late for work."

Taylor snickered. "Well, you are taking a shower, right?"

Anne tossed a look over her shoulder. "I think I better. I can't be smelling like sex at work, can I?" She reached for Taylor's hand and pulled her up off the bed. Taylor laughed as they hurried into the bathroom, and Anne started to shower. Taylor cupped Anne's firm ass into her palm and kissed her neck as they waited for the shower to be warm, and then Anne pulled her into the shower after her.

Taylor closed the sliding door behind them and pressed Anne against the wall, the shower water cascading over them. They hungrily kissed one another, neither caring that the water could turn cold before anyone could shower. Taylor massaged Anne's breasts in her hands as the kiss lingered, tweaking the nipples as her thumbs approached them.

"Taylor," Anne gasped. "Work."

Taylor smirked, parting from the kiss. She grabbed the washcloth, lathered it up, and then fell to her knees to face Anne's femininity. Taylor ran the cloth up one leg and down the other, then moved her hand between Anne's thighs. As she caressed Anne's mound, Anne jerked. Slowly, Taylor moved in and out of her, washing her most sensitive spot.

Anne melted into Taylor's grasp, and once Anne was thoroughly cleaned, Anne did the same to Taylor. Taylor closed her eyes and enjoyed the intimacy that ignited in the bathroom. Taylor could get used to this.

She felt warm, hopeful, and renewed. Taylor always dreamed of a place like Anne now owned, free and clear. As the feeling hit her, it brought a smile to her lips, but maybe it wasn't a place like this that Taylor desired. Perhaps it was the security and love that went with it.

Getting out of the shower left her feeling a sense of dread. She longed to spend another night wrapped up in Anne's arms, but Anne had to work at seven, and Taylor had to work at five.

"I'll see you when I get in?" Taylor asked as they walked to Anne's car.

"I get off at four," Anne said, groaning. "What time do you get off? Maybe we can have a nightcap or something."

"I work twelve hours. I won't be off until tomorrow morning." Taylor dropped her gaze, missing her already.

"Meet me for breakfast tomorrow? Five thirty at the diner?" There was a continued twinkle in Anne's eyes, and Taylor could never turn away from that.

"I'll be there." Taylor moved in and planted a sweet kiss on Anne's lips. It was a kiss that would have to last them. She parted and waved to her, then hurried to her car. Once inside, she looked over as Anne backed out of the driveway and drove away from her. She grabbed her phone and looked down at it, noticing several missed calls and texts.

GAVIN:

> Sis, you better be having a good weekend because Aunt Kristi has lost her mind.

GAVIN:

> She said she doesn't care what anyone says. She's not going out with Joe on Saturday.

AUNT KRISTI:

> I must've been out of my mind for agreeing.

AUNT KRISTI:

> This guy has gone mad. He sent me flowers. Flowers. We haven't even gone out.

AUNT KRISTI:

> I'm not doing it.

Her phone flooded with messages once she typed in her passcode, including three missed calls from Gavin. She didn't want interruptions. With the heat that carried between them, could anyone blame her? She smirked and tossed her phone into the passenger seat. It was too early to deal with it now. She was confident she would have her aunt convinced when she had to go to work. After all, once she heard about Taylor's satisfying weekend, Aunt Kristi would be ready for anything.

CHAPTER TWENTY-TWO

HARD TO CONCENTRATE

Anne

Whenever Anne sat down or took two minutes to think, her mind immediately went to Taylor. Spending the weekend together was unexpected, but it was one of Anne's best weekends in a long time. She felt her cheeks warm as she thought of Taylor, the instant heat Taylor brought to her body, and the gentleness of Taylor's caresses. One could say simple pleasure, but to Anne, it was magical.

"Earth to Anne." Anne jerked to find Cecilia at the desk. She could feel the warmth of her cheeks and knew she had been daydreaming way too long.

"Hey, CC." Anne gave a bright smile, but her heart never ceased pounding.

"You were off in some fantasy world, I imagine. Anything you want to talk about?"

Anne blushed, quickly looking down at her computer. "I'm just daydreaming. You know, of what I will spend my money on now that I don't have the mortgage." It sounded logical. Anne nodded with relief.

She could pull that off with a snap of her fingers. Cecilia wouldn't think anything of it. Or would she?

"I don't know, looked more like a person in love sitting there." Cecilia snickered and sank into the seat next to her. Anne quickly looked down. *Love?* Now, that would be moving way too fast. This was nothing more than a fun, flirty fling. That's all. *Never mind that the thought of Taylor makes my heart clamor in my chest.* She quickly cleared her throat, removing the knot that lodged inside, choking her.

"I don't really have the time to meet someone right now. With my sister and..." She cut herself off. Cecilia had always been a great confidante, but even now, she didn't feel like divulging too much in that situation. "There's just no time. I'm daydreaming about finally going on vacation, that's all."

"You're still young, Anne. Just don't miss out on opportunities of finding love." Cecilia pulled up the computer, and Anne considered those words. Even if what she felt was the path where love was possible, she wasn't about to get into those murky waters. "We're admitting a three-year-old for some tests. ER just paged me." Cecilia changed the subject, which was a great relief to Anne.

"Oh no. Nothing serious, I hope." Anne went into nurse mode.

"She's experiencing stomach pains. We're putting her across the hall, making maneuvering easier for staff. They'll be doing a CT and X-ray scan of her abdomen this afternoon and plan on keeping her overnight for observation until Dr. Carr can see her tomorrow. Will you prep the room?"

"Absolutely!" Anne got up, grateful for the opportunity to concentrate on something else. Anne went to the room and was immediately hit by nostalgia. The room had been vacant since Willow transferred to her new hospital. Being back in the room, she gave it a once over. Willow was always there to bring a smile to her face, and aside from that letter they received, Anne hadn't gotten much info from Willow's family. She knew she was receiving treatment and responding well, but that was the extent of her knowledge. She just might've found the push to get her to write a letter to the seven-year-old.

Anne looked through cabinets, pulling out some extra bedding and prepping the room so they could bring her in and get her settled. She returned to the nurse's station and looked down at the information sent to them. She would need fluids and lab work done as well. Anne could take care of both things before she arrived on the floor. She had finished grabbing the tubes for blood work just as the elevator doors opened, and two orderlies wheeled her into the room.

"Savannah?" Anne asked, looking down at the three-year-old. She instantly looked scared, shooting a look at the woman beside her bed. The woman nodded, then reached over and squeezed the little girl's hand.

"My name is Vie," the woman said. "This is my daughter, Savannah, and she's freaking a little." She whispered the last words. The two men helped Savannah into the bed, and when they were out of the way, Anne moved in closer to her, kneeling to her level.

"I know you're frightened, but you can be sure I'm going to take great care of you. My name is Anne." She reached out and took hold of Savannah's hand, squeezing it slightly. A small smile appeared on her lips. "Now, let's do everything possible to make you feel better. Shall we?"

Next came the hard part: starting an IV on a three-year-old and drawing her labs, but her mom was there to assist. There was little apprehension from Savannah. When she finished the labs, the girl turned to her mom. "I'm hungry."

Anne looked over to Vie, and Anne gave a weak smile. "I'm sure you're hungry," Anne said, kneeling to the little girl again. "Unfortunately, we have to wait until the tests are done. Hopefully, it won't be long. Okay?"

"Okay."

"Good girl." Anne squeezed her hand, then turned and motioned to the door. "Vie, may I speak with you for a moment?"

She followed Anne out to the hallway, where Anne could speak to her more freely. "Is it bad?" she asked.

"No. Well, I'm not sure. We can't give her anything to eat in case she needs surgery. I know that sounds scary, but it might not be; this could be absolutely nothing. We have to go in prepared. We will get her something to eat as soon as we can."

"I understand."

Anne hesitated. "Are you alone? Will your husband or partner be joining us?"

"Probably not. We're separated, and he has other priorities." She shrugged. "It is what it is, but I appreciate you being so good to her. She's all I have."

Anne squeezed Vie's shoulder. "She's in good hands, and so are you." Anne smiled at her, then released her grip. "I'm going to go get her information loaded in and her bloodwork taken down to the labs. That way, we can figure this all out. If you need anything, you can just pull that lever by the bed."

"Thank you, Anne." She turned and disappeared into the room. Anne returned to the computer and entered the information, then started to take the blood to the basement, where the lab would work it. Cecilia came around the corner and waved Anne down.

"Two-year-old Jax fell off his bike and has a fractured ulna. He's headed up here and putting him in room 1012. Will you prep it?"

"Sure thing," Anne said.

Cecelia sighed, "Looks like the afternoon is turning into a crazy one."

Anne nodded and rushed off to the other room. It was hectic and possibly draining, but she enjoyed working with the toddlers the most. There were moments when she reached adulthood when she considered adopting a toddler. Then, the dreams drifted far from her. But now, she realized how maybe the dream hadn't entirely dissipated in her mind, especially if she had someone, such as Taylor, in her life.

Anne sighed, forcing the image from her mind. She took this too far and had too much going on to dwell on craziness. Even if the thought suddenly made her giddy.

CHAPTER TWENTY-THREE

MUCH NEEDED VISITOR

Taylor

Taylor felt the yawn coming on, and she patted her mouth. She leaned forward and stared at the computer, her eyes dipping to the time. "Ugh, two o'clock," she moaned. She still had three hours until Tessa would be there to relieve her, and she felt like her eyes were closing. She leaned back in the seat and stretched out, staring absently in front of her. "Wake up. Wake up. Wake up." She pushed herself up and began pacing. It was a slow night. She didn't mind it, but she was ready to fall once midnight hit. She continued to pace and checked her watch. Now, 2:02. She would never get to five o'clock with such moments.

She stopped pacing and leaned against the desk. To be where Anne was at that moment would indeed send exhilarating shocks through her body. She grinned, the image beckoning her to cave and settle into the erotic fantasy. The last thing she needed to do when, at any moment, an emergency could call on her, and she'd be left in a puddle of ecstasy.

Taylor moved around the ward, peering into rooms, many with parents asleep on the couch or chairs. After making her rounds, she returned to the desk twenty minutes later. She slumped in her chair and stared aimlessly at the computer. On the one hand, she was relieved tonight was slow. But she needed to stay awake. As she sat there, her eyes went to the room Willow once occupied. It now had a three-year-old. She didn't have to assist her much, but it did remind her of when Willow was there. She wondered what she was up to and if the hospital was treating her well. Taylor had promised to send a letter but hadn't had time. Taylor looked around the desk until she found a notebook. She sat there momentarily, thinking of everything she wanted to say, then began to write.

Twenty minutes into the letter, she heard the elevator spring to life. Taylor pushed the notepad away and glanced at her watch. It was just before three. Hearing the elevator at that time of night wasn't a thrilling moment. After all, it could only mean one thing: an emergency. The doors opened, and her jaw dropped.

"Anne? What are you doing here?"

Anne smirked, stepping off of the elevator. "I was in the neighborhood and thought maybe you could use some company."

Taylor snickered. "Neighborhood? At three o'clock? Are you trying to cruise the hospital?"

Anne moved in closer. "There's only one lady on my mind." She winked, swooped in, and kissed Taylor, taking her breath away. To say that those words caught her off guard was an understatement. She bit her lip, pulling back from the kiss. "Don't fret; chances of anyone catching us this time of night are slim to none."

Taylor blushed, looking down at her hands. Anne came to liven up her work schedule, and it surely would do that, but she was there to work. If they got caught, their jobs would be on the line. She looked up, scrunching up her nose in thought. "We're at work. It feels kind of dirty."

Anne smiled. "I'll admit, I never thought you'd shy away from PDA." She moved past Taylor and walked over to the nurse's station. "It makes me appreciate you all the more if I'm being honest. You're not the type that would go for a quickie in the supply closet—duly noted. I'm disappointed, but I can surely understand your concerns. I respect them." Taylor turned on her heel and stared at Anne. When she talked, it made her want to forget all her inhibitions, wrong or otherwise.

"What brought you here, Anne? Outside of being in the neighborhood, of course."

The smile never wavered from Anne's face. "Truthfully?"

"I'd appreciate the truth." Taylor stepped up to the counter, mere inches from Anne.

"I couldn't sleep. My mind kept returning to you, and I know how rough these mornings can be." She looked around and shrugged. "This is about as lively as it gets, I recall. So, I took a chance. I got dressed, jumped in my car, and here I am. The rest is history."

Taylor brushed her hand along Anne's cheek, and Anne's grin widened. Just one passionate kiss wouldn't hurt anyone. The kids were all nestled in their beds. The parents were out like a light, and she didn't have to do vitals for another hour. She moved in and pressed her lips to Anne's. Her tongue swiftly dove between Anne's lips, and her hand rested on Anne's heart. It thudded with every second that passed.

"I wanted you," Anne breathlessly spoke between kisses. "I couldn't resist rushing to the hospital."

If words caused a spark, Taylor was on fire. Her hand moved from Anne's heart and slipped beneath the buttons of her blouse, resting leisurely along Anne's breast.

"What if someone wakes up?" Taylor whispered.

"Easy enough." Anne winked and reached for Taylor's hand, pulling her after her. Taylor laughed until they entered the supply closet, and Anne pressed her against the door. Her lips eagerly sought her out.

"Anne!" Taylor gasped. "Now I won't know if someone needs me."

Anne turned and pointed to the wall, where the call lights for each room were conveniently displayed. Taylor laughed. She had forgotten that. In the heat of the moment, Taylor panicked. She swept her hand along Anne's neck and pulled her to her, melting into the kiss. Their tongues were back in a tangled mess, easily maneuvering one another. Anne slid her hands down Taylor's body, resting delicately on her pants. Taylor gasped as she gently pulled them down, taking her underwear along with them.

She didn't hesitate for a moment. She tossed her head back and groaned, Anne's warm breath resting on her inner thighs. *Do it already. She* wanted to cry. Her body tightened, clutched onto Anne's shoulders, and braced herself for the intimate connection. Her jaw dropped, and Anne's tongue eased into her.

"God," Taylor cried, bearing down and trying not to disrupt the smooth entrance. A beep sounded, and Taylor jerked from their intimate tryst. "Shit!" Taylor cried.

"It's okay," Anne said. She met Taylor's frantic stare. Taylor shook her head, yanking up her underwear and pants and glancing over at Anne, the moment quickly gone.

"It's not okay." She glanced up to where the light flashed on the screen and shook her head again. "I'm supposed to be readily available, and now...this." She rushed out of the supply closet, straightening her clothes as she hurried to Savannah's room. When she entered the room, she halted, hoping to calm her racing heart. Vie leaned over her daughter, and Savannah was wailing. "What's wrong?" Taylor asked, almost breathless from the moment that happened minutes ago across the hall.

Vie turned to her. "She woke up crying. She's so hot." Vie backed away from the bed as Taylor moved in. She felt her head and nearly pulled back from the heat. Taylor grabbed her stethoscope and leaned in to check her heart. Savannah wiggled underneath her, wailing and trying to reach for her mother's arms.

"I know, sweetheart," Taylor cooed. Her heart was racing, but most likely from the fever. She grabbed the thermometer and held it to her head. *One hundred and four.* Savannah's heart wasn't the only one racing. "We have to get the fever down. The doctor isn't in for a few more hours." She fought the urge to pace as Vie rushed back to the other side of Savannah's bed. *Think Taylor, think.* "I'll be right back." Taylor ran from the room where Anne was doing the pacing. She stopped when Taylor got to the hallway.

"I didn't want to come in and take over. Everything alright?"

Taylor shook her head. "Her fever is 104. She's boiling. I'll page Doctor Newsome. She's on a break, but it's an emergency."

"Shhhhh..." Anne reached out and touched Taylor's hand. "You've got this. She has a fever. What does she need?"

"She needs Tylenol, but if she has to have surgery..."

"Think about it, Taylor." Anne's voice was calm and soothing. "If she has a fever..." Her words trailed off.

"Combined with the abdominal pain, she could have appendicitis.

We'll have to operate." Anne nodded. Taylor sighed, relieved Anne was there for her.

"I paged Doctor Newsome," Anne said with a nod.

Just then, Doctor Newsome burst through the door, "Alright, what do we have here?"

"Three-year-old came in this afternoon with acute abdominal pain. We gave her abdominal X-rays, but now she has a fever," Taylor explained.

Doctor Newsome nodded and pressed a palm to Savannah's forehead, "She's burning up. Don't administer Tylenol orally; give her a suppository if needed." Doctor Newsome explained.

"Wait twenty minutes and see if the cold compress works," Anne added.

Doctor Newsome clapped her on the shoulder, "Good call, Anne."

"While Taylor worked around to get the cold compress and go back to Savannah's room, she left Anne behind.

"Just in case the doc decides surgery is necessary, we're going to try the cold compress." She pressed it against Savannah's forehead as Savannah quieted down some. "If after twenty minutes she still has a fever, we're going to give her the Tylenol. If it is appendicitis, we need to get her fever down. What's most important is relieving the fever; the sooner, the better."

Vie nodded, and her face wasn't nearly the frantic mess Taylor had initially found her. Savannah nodded back to sleep as Taylor stayed by Vie's side and waited twenty minutes together. When she returned to check on her, the fever had broken. Savannah was in a puddle of sweat and resting comfortably.

"She might not be out of the woods, but she's peaceful right now. Her fever broke. We'll recheck her in thirty minutes. I'll be right outside the door; don't hesitate to ring for me."

To her surprise, Vie leaned in and hugged her. "Thank you! I was so worried."

Taylor mustered up a smile. Vie wasn't the only one. "I'll be back soon." She left the room and looked around as Anne had vanished, or so she thought. Anne came out of another room, and their eyes met. "Everything alright with Samuel?"

She nodded. "He just wanted a glass of water. I got him taken care of. No worries. How are things?"

"The cold compress worked. I don't know what I would have done if you and Doctor Newsome weren't there."

Anne waved away Taylor's words. "You would have figured it out. This was your real first challenge, and many more will come. Believe me." Anne backed away from the desk. "I should probably head out and leave you to it."

Taylor widened her eyes. "Do you have to? I would prefer if you stayed." Anne stepped back in and nodded, leaving Taylor to sigh. It wasn't right to put all this work on one person, and it was true that before then, the morning had dragged on, but anything could happen. Emergencies happened constantly; it was far too much for one person to handle. Taylor needed to talk to HR before any other issues arose.

CHAPTER TWENTY-FOUR

WORLDS COLLIDING

Anne

"I appreciate you being here for me this morning." Anne walked Taylor out to her just after six thirty—an hour and a half after her scheduled shift was supposed to end.

"I'm telling you, I was glad to be here." Anne reached out and touched her arm. She saw the fear in Taylor's eyes. It was a new experience for her, and when Taylor asked, there was no way Anne would have been able to abandon her. "Luckily, Savannah seems to be doing much better. Dr. Newsome's scheduling her surgery for this afternoon."

Taylor rolled her eyes. "Not hardly. I would have been panicking in the corner if it was just me." Anne didn't believe so. Taylor didn't have the confidence in herself that Anne assumed she would have. But Anne knew that it just came with experience, and soon Taylor would be riding the waves of knowledge.

Taylor sighed. "We didn't even get that breakfast date."

"There will be other mornings. Trust me." Anne looked toward the hospital. She didn't want to say their goodbyes, but time was ticking, and she only had thirty minutes to get changed and get back to the Pediatrics floor. "I hate to bolt, but..."

"You have to get changed. I appreciate you, Anne. More than you'll know." Anne shook her head as Taylor leaned in and gave her a soft and gentle kiss. Passion was great, but the sweet and intimate moments really jolted Anne to life. "I hope we can see each other soon."

"I hope so, too." Anne stepped away from the car as Taylor got in and backed out of her spot. Anne waved, then walked back to the hospital and went to the break room, where she had an extra set of scrubs tucked away in her locker. As she dressed, she thought of Taylor. They had started going hot and heavy in the supply closet, only for things to get stopped so suddenly. It left her craving more, but the rest of the morning didn't seem right to try to start where they had left off.

When Cecilia arrived at five, she seemed confused about what Anne was doing there. Luckily, the ER paged her, sparing Anne. Yet, she knew the inevitable would occur, and to her unfortunate dismay, it happened sooner than she would have hoped.

When the elevator doors opened, Cecilia sat at the nurse's station and looked up. Anne did her best to play it off, moving to the computer and signing in with her credentials. She could look down all she wanted, but it didn't stop the eyes from boring holes into her. She turned, and just as she felt Cecilia's gaze.

"Do you need something?"

"Well, yeah. For starters, I'd like to know what brought you into the hospital early this morning. I checked the schedule and rechecked it, only to find that my eyes hadn't deceived me. You weren't scheduled until now. And there's the fact that you were in regular clothes, but now you're in scrubs, so clearly, you didn't misread your schedule. I feel that some explanation is warranted. Don't you?"

Not if I can help it. The truth is that I was in the neighborhood this morning. You know how it is when you're new, alone, and working the graveyard shift. I wanted to check on Taylor and see how she was doing."

"What time did you get here?" She arched an eyebrow, and Anne quickly looked away. "We have cameras, you know. It would be easy enough to find out."

"What does it matter?" Anne asked, sighing. "If it was midnight or five o'clock in the morning. Neither makes much difference."

"I want to know why you were roaming the streets to get here before I did. That's all." Cecilia threw up her hands.

"It was about three," Anne huffed. "My sister..." She hesitated. She was a horrible liar, and the truth would eventually come out. "I was just worried. Taylor is getting a lot of hours, and I wanted to ensure she was handling it. I couldn't sleep, so I came here. That's all there is to it. Besides, it's a good thing I was here because our newest resident needed assistance."

"Oh yeah? Why's that?"

Anne proceeded to tell her about Savannah as Cecilia nodded and listened. "Luckily, she's improved this morning, but Taylor is still fresh here. I just guided her along the way."

"Well, that's fine and all, but you can't work off the clock. Put in your hours, and I'll mark them for approval."

"Cecilia, that's not necessary. I was happy to be here."

"I'm not arguing this." Cecilia stood up from the desk. "I have to go to a meeting, but give me your hours, and you'll get paid for them."

Anne rolled her eyes but didn't comment on it. She didn't stop by with the intent of making a profit from it. Besides, the added attention she got from Taylor more than made up for lack of sleep and monetary value. But, if Cecilia insisted, there wasn't much sense in arguing. Anne turned back to her computer and pulled up the calendar when she spotted the notebook shoved into the back. Anne grabbed it and only saw Willow's name before tearing the page off and stuffing it in her pocket. She instantly recognized Taylor's writing and was intrigued to read the letter, but for now, she needed to get her day started, or at least the second part of it.

Dear Willow –

It's two o'clock in the morning. I'm at the hospital, staring at your room and thinking about you. I hope that you are getting the care that you deserve. I know we haven't known each other for long, but know that you are an extraordinary girl, and I wish only the best for you. If I ever have kids, I hope they're just as sweet as you are.

I trust that you're getting the best care in Tennessee. Are you getting plenty of Jell-O? Strawberry's your favorite, right? When you come back here, I will make sure you have a whole case of strawberry. Would you like that? I hope that you're able to make it back here soon. We all miss you. But we want you to get all better before you get back here. So, stay strong. Be well.

THAT'S WHERE THE LETTER HAD ENDED. WHETHER TAYLOR had wanted to add more and got interrupted, or if it was just her missing signature, the note just fell off, hanging out in the open for someone to complete it. Anne folded it and put it back into her pocket. The next time she saw Taylor, she would surely give it to her. It was hers to finish, but it reminded Anne of Taylor's sweetness. Anne wrote to Willow last night. Maybe they could send them off together. It almost made Anne smile when Taylor mentioned Willow. It wasn't out of the realm of possibilities that Taylor wanted kids. It was just one more thing that Anne liked about her.

The door to the break room opened, and in walked two women. Anne recognized them both. "Hey, Anne," Hannah spoke. She'd been working in the ER for just over two years. Anne didn't know her well, but she knew of her, and they were always cordial to one another.

"Hey, Hannah, Trista. How are you both?"

"No complaints," Hannah said.

"Well, I might have a few." Trista laughed and tilted her head back and forth. A pop sounded, and Anne smiled. Trista was a new one. Having been there only a few months, but also from the ER.

Trista and Hannah sat across Anne as Anne dug in her pocket and pulled out her phone. She went to her text messages and skimmed through them to find Taylor's name.

> ANNE:
>
> Thinking of you. I hope you're getting plenty of
> rest.

Before hitting send, her mind went to Trista and Hannah's conversation. "That's right, can you believe it? I mean, never in a million years did I think a newbie would have the nerve to call out HR." Anne glanced in their direction, trying not to eavesdrop but suddenly intrigued by the conversation.

Hannah's gaze met hers, and Hannah's cheeks reddened. "I didn't mean to gossip, Anne. I'm sure you know more about it than I do."

Anne furrowed her brow. "Know more about what?"

"Taylor. She's in your department, right?" Anne nodded. "Rumor has it, she went to HR this morning and complained about her schedule. I guess she made a pretty big stink about it."

Anne shook her head. "Don't believe everything you hear." Anne knew that she had walked Taylor out to her car. There wasn't any time to stop at HR. She knew that Taylor had considered it, but she never brought it up again. She told Taylor that she would help her make a move if Taylor decided to proceed. It was all just a misunderstanding. *Probably.*

"I don't know," Hannah replied. "Someone spoke with Clarissa from HR, and she said she could hear her talking behind closed doors."

"You know what they say about rumors," Anne offered. Yet, she grew more curious about whether they were simply rumors or something more. Anne looked down at the message, just hanging there for her to send. She deleted it and put her phone back into her pocket. If the rumors were true, she would have wished Taylor would have said something to her first. But what if Taylor was right and something shady was happening in scheduling? It wouldn't be the first time the hospital tried to cut corners and work on a staff shortage.

"Anne? Are you alright?"

Anne jerked her attention to Hannah, and she smiled. "Yeah, I'm good." She got up and waved. "See you, ladies, later." She hurried from the break room so they couldn't question the wheels running through her mind, but the gears hadn't stopped turning, and Anne didn't know if she should be angry with Taylor or HR.

CHAPTER TWENTY-FIVE

BURNING THREAT

Taylor

Taylor stepped into Savannah's room two days later. This time, Vie had a smile on her face and looked up, a rush of relief cascading over her features. "And how's the patient this morning?"

"Much improved," Vie said. "She's recovering like a champ." Vie ruffled her daughter's hair, and the color had returned to Savannah's cheeks.

"I'm so happy that you are both doing so well. Do you want anything, Savannah? An applesauce? Jell-O? Maybe some pudding?"

"I want it all." The little girl giggled. After her surgery to remove her appendix, her appetite improved significantly, which was a great sign.

"Coming right up." Taylor patted her knee and then left the room to retrieve the snacks. Hospital life had proven quickly to be Taylor's thing. She adored the kids and was falling into a groove. Yet, her exhaustion was overwhelming at times. She braced through a yawn and reached into the refrigerator. When she came up, she saw Cecilia approaching her.

"Hey, Taylor. You should head to lunch. You're wanted in Henry Martin's office when you're done."

Taylor frowned. "Henry Martin?" The name sounded vaguely familiar, but she couldn't quite place it or why the man would want to see her.

"He's on the Board of Directors. He handles hospital complaints." She shrugged. "I'm sure it's nothing to fret over. But he's expecting you at one."

Taylor frowned. "Alrighty then. Where can I find his office?"

"It's outside the cafeteria. You can't miss the nameplate. We'll cover for you." Taylor nodded and then went back to Savannah's room. It was daunting nonetheless. If only she could place this Henry's name. She was sure she had heard of him before.

"Here you go. Let the nurses know if you need anything else. I'm headed to lunch, and we'll be back later." Taylor smiled at Savannah and her mom, but the thought of meeting this Henry had her nerves running rampant.

As Taylor stepped off the elevator at the cafeteria, she glanced over to the wall of offices. Sure enough, there was Henry's name. She fought the urge to bust through his door and demand answers now. What good would that do her? *It might help ease my nerves.* Taylor grabbed her phone and pulled up Anne's name. It'd been two days of peace. She had texted Anne and even called her twice, but Anne seemed too busy to pick up the phone. Or she was avoiding her. That last thought had her laughing. What reason would she have to avoid her?

She stopped outside of the cafeteria and dialed the number. It went straight to voicemail. "Hey, Anne. I thought I'd try giving you another call. I hope you're doing well. I'm thinking of you and wish we could get together soon. Call me." She disconnected the call and looked over to Henry's office. *Henry Martin.* The thoughts trickled in, and she knew where she had heard his name. Anne mentioned it a couple of times when they had their conversations. He was a mentor to her when she first started alongside Cecilia. But Cecilia stuck around the department while Henry flourished and made a name for himself at the hospital.

Anne seemed to like him. If he was there to speak with her, there wasn't a reason to believe it was bad. Taylor stepped into the cafeteria and looked around. She loved many things about CAPMED so far, but the cafeteria food wasn't one of them. It was good enough, but her mind latched on the patients in the pediatric department and Anne. She never anticipated finding a girlfriend when she started her work there.

She felt her cheeks warm and never anticipated calling Anne her girlfriend. They'd only known each other for a month. But there she was, not imagining her life without having met Anne. A text sounded on the phone.

ANNE:

Been busy the past couple of days. More drama with Mel. Catch up later.

It wasn't the loving message she'd hoped for. Part of her expected Anne to ask her out on another date. Yet, it was a response. It had nothing to do with her and more to do with Melanie. She could relate to that, as she had her own family situations to deal with, so it was a text that she could understand.

TAYLOR:

I hope all is well with Mel and the girls. I look forward to catching up.

Taylor grabbed a salad and water and took it to her favorite booth. However, her stomach wasn't in the mood to eat. Her thoughts returned to Henry and why he wanted to meet. There were a million reasons, but none that she found to be all that thrilling. Taylor wasn't the type to get herself into trouble, and she feared that maybe a patient had complained. She had never had an experience with a patient or their parents that worried her. But when Cecelia brought up Henry, she put her guard up. An hour later, she only took two nibbles of her salad, and her water went untouched. "That was a waste of money," she mumbled. But there wasn't any way to force the food down. She went to Henry's office and tried desperately not to appear so shaken. She knocked, with a gruff voice coming from the other side.

"Come in!" She peered around the door cautiously.

"Hello, Mr. Martin. I'm Taylor, and I hear you wanted to see me. If now isn't a good time, I can come back." *Please don't make me come back. I'm scared to death and want some answers.*

"Now is about as good a time as any. Have a seat."

He was older than Taylor envisioned. He looked close to retirement age, with his gray hair pronounced and his wrinkles not hidden. Taylor grabbed the seat across from him. She turned at the closed door, wishing she had left it open. Now, she was stuck in this enclosure, expecting the worst.

"I called you into my office today to discuss the recent accusations you've made."

Taylor frowned. "Accusations? You mean the truth?"

He arched an eyebrow. "You're new, so I will pretend you didn't just say that. You see, Taylor, residents are a dime a dozen. There are a thousand more where you came from, and all of them would be eager to be in your position. We chose you because of your high marks and references, but I can assure you that no one would bat an eye to let you go, seeing that you're not happy."

Taylor's mouth went dry. She wished she had kept her water at hand.

"It's not that I'm not happy, Mr. Martin. And from what I can tell, I do a..." Her words stalled as she realized she was about to go off on this man who could literally hold her life in his hands. She released a breath. *Breathe in. Breathe out. Whatever you do, don't cry.* "I do a good job, Mr. Martin. I take pride in my work, and I want to be here. But hospital regulations are put forward for a reason. The hours that I'm working are unheard of. My schedule would cause anybody to break."

His face clouded. "Not anyone," he replied with a huff. "Maybe you're not as strong as you've perceived yourself on your application."

Taylor's jaw dropped. Tears threatened to fall. She worked long and hard to prove herself, only to have Henry Martin act like she didn't deserve to be there. And no one would speak to her that way and get away with it. Yet, she couldn't get the words out. She looked down at her clenched fists.

"If a resident can suck it up and stick it out, they will surely get better hours and higher seniority. If they can't, there's not much to do about it, at least on my end. If you want to get there, you must suffer the consequences. You don't get stronger by playing the victim." He looked down at his computer. "Now, I'm busy, and you should get back to work."

Taylor felt like Henry slapped her. She was in shock as she closed the door behind her and couldn't believe her day had resulted in a meeting like this. The anger welled up inside of her. Yet, she was frightened. How could she experience both emotions at once and not know which feeling would ultimately win?

CHAPTER TWENTY-SIX

EXPLOSIVE ARGUMENT

Anne

Anne tossed a crocheted turtle and started on her next one. A pile of animals rested on the couch beside her, and she sighed. What else to do on her day off? She had been crocheting starting at six and hadn't stopped to breathe. Even when she ate lunch, she continued to crochet. Was it because her online store was booming? Partly. But mostly because she was thinking about Taylor when she wasn't crocheting. And while she wanted to believe things were great with her, she knew that wasn't true. It was just after six, meaning she spent twelve hours crocheting. There was no doubt why she had a pile of creatures staring back at her. At least it would mean the paying customers wouldn't have to worry about waiting for their orders.

Crocheting was Anne's therapy, and it had helped today to keep her hands busy. She stifled a yawn and went back to crocheting a frog keychain. She was nearly finishing it thirty minutes later when a knock was on her door.

"Wait right here, little froggy." She said as she headed to the door and opened it. "Taylor!" she gasped. She was the last person she expected standing there. Her face fell. "What's wrong?" Tears cascaded down

Taylor's cheeks. As frustrated as she was about how things went down, she didn't want to see her upset. She reached for her hand, pulled her into the foyer, and closed the door behind them.

"Do you have a few minutes to talk?" Taylor asked between sobs. "I know you're busy with Melanie and all." She hesitated and looked past Anne. "Is she here?"

"Um, no." Anne stammered. She felt a pang of regret as she recognized how this would seem. She had sent the text on a whim, not even realizing what she was saying until it was too late. She needed space. She barely had time to think between work and Taylor's constant texts and calls. However, she also didn't want to seem like a cold-hearted bitch and not answer the phone when Taylor kept on it. "She's home now," she said, lying once more but feeling the angst coursing through her veins. "I have some time."

They walked into the living room, and Taylor glanced at the mountain of crocheted animals. Anne felt her cheeks burning, knowing that, again, the truth could come out that she had lied to Taylor. If things ever quieted down, Anne would have to straighten it out. For now, she couldn't backpedal.

"I've been working on these all week. Here, let me move it out of the way." She grabbed them in her arms, tossed them to the floor, and then turned to Taylor. "Sit down. Would you like something to drink?"

Taylor shook her head. "I'm good."

She obviously wasn't good, but Anne felt she was about to find out why. They sat on the couch, and there were several minutes of awkwardness. To go from the minutes they spent in the supply closet to suddenly not knowing what to say to one another, ate Anne up inside. She wanted to reach out and touch Taylor's hand, ask for her to look at her, plead with her to come clean. Only then could they make things right again.

"I don't know where to start," Taylor began.

Anne released a breath. "The beginning is always great." The space between them was too long, but Anne stayed in her corner of the couch while Taylor stayed in hers.

"Right..." Taylor released a breath. "The beginning. I spoke with HR about the scheduling."

"Yeah, I heard," Anne mumbled.

Taylor glanced up, meeting her gaze. "You did?" Anne nodded. "Now I'm thinking, as much as I'm glad I said something, maybe it was the worst decision I could have made."

Anne looked down at the couch; so many thoughts were playing in her mind, but she didn't know where to start. Taylor continued.

"I wanted to see if I was making a bigger deal out of it than I should. I thought if I said something, I could resolve many things, but now... I'm not so sure."

Anne looked up and shook her head. "Taylor, I told you to talk to me if you decided to go to HR. I said I would help you through it. Some strong personalities are in there; they don't take kindly to people trying to tell them what to do. I tried to warn you. You didn't even get me involved."

"I thought I could handle it alone," Taylor replied. She sobbed again, and a tear trickled down her cheeks. Her face was red and splotchy, and Anne felt bad for her, but she still couldn't reach out to touch her. "Today, I got called into Henry Martin's office."

Anne nodded. "Henry is a good man. That's not the worst thing that could happen."

Taylor's jaw dropped. "He practically threatened me. He said if I didn't want to work, he would find another resident from the thousands of applications they have. He was anything but pleasant to me."

Anne frowned. "I'm sure you just misunderstood. That doesn't sound like Henry."

"Misunderstood?" Taylor stood up from the couch. "He said residents are a dime a dozen, and there's a thousand more when I came from." The tears were thick in Taylor's eyes. The emotions were real. Anne could feel them, but the Henry she knew wouldn't be so cold and heartless. She couldn't believe that Henry would go down that road.

"You're emotional. Sometimes, our emotions cloud our conversations. Are you sure he said it like that? I mean, you could have easily misinterpreted things. I know that sometimes I take things the wrong way when I get overwhelmed."

"Are you taking his side? Do you not trust me? He said it that way, exactly. Clearly, you don't know your mentor like you think you do. He said I'm weak. Maybe that's how you feel about me, too."

Anne stood up and stared at Taylor. Her mind raced as she considered those words. "I know him very well, Taylor. And what you're saying doesn't sound like him. But then again, maybe he's different with new hires. I don't know. But I know you need to take a deep breath and stay calm. He's probably trying a new tough-love approach. I know he's had some problems with residents before. Maybe you just need to push your-self a little harder." Anne felt the fiery rage burning through her.

"Push harder? I push plenty hard. I'm a damn good worker, Anne. I never thought you'd take the hospital's side over mine."

"Taylor, I'm not," Anne argued.

"That's exactly what you're doing. Correct me if I'm wrong, but you said that the hospital stopped you from doing things for financial reasons. Don't you see how this could all be interconnected? I'm not crazy, Anne."

Anne stared at Taylor. She saw the tears flashing in Taylor's eyes, and there was a moment when she wanted to rush to Taylor and apologize, but she stayed her ground. Taylor shook her head and hurried past Anne. Anne stood there, stunned, and waited for the door to slam behind Taylor. Just as she expected, the sound came, and Taylor was gone. Anne sank into the sofa cushion and stared straight ahead. Henry wouldn't say things like that. He just wouldn't. She had to trust her gut, even though her heart just left the house.

CHAPTER TWENTY-SEVEN

RASH DECISIONS

Taylor

Taylor didn't know how she made it to work the next morning. She spent the entire night crying, wallowing in pity, shaken to the core by Anne's dismissal of how Henry treated Taylor. It was one thing for Anne not to take her calls or texts, but it was a different story when Anne acted like she was making it all up. Everything Taylor spoke when it came to Henry, Anne made an excuse for him.

She beat her hands against the steering wheel, tears stinging her eyes again. A notification sounded on her phone, and she quickly glanced at it. There was a moment when Taylor had hoped the notification would be from Anne, telling Taylor she was sorry she didn't believe her. Then again, she hoped it would come as a phone call. Instead, it was an ad for Viagra. She rolled her eyes and tossed the phone to the side.

She glanced down at her clock. It was just after eight o'clock. She still had an hour before she had to be at work. She was there so soon because she couldn't sleep. She didn't want to be in a place that could abuse their power and then laugh about it afterward. She groaned and stared straight ahead. If the money wasn't so good, she would have called in and quit in the middle of the night. She didn't need this stress, and she didn't need to work in a place that brought her only anger and dismay.

Another notification sounded, and she grabbed her phone again, instantly filling herself with regret. "Dammit," she groaned, tossing her phone to the side. Another ad, just for clothing, this time. But wishing and hoping it would be Anne was only killing her inside. Anne had made her choice when she stuck up for the hospital. She wanted someone who would stand by her side, not the big tycoons who could prey on the little people.

Taylor was used to mistreatment. However, this wasn't the same mistreatment she experienced growing up. Her mother had a sharp tongue that could reach out and strangle a person with just a few words. She saw the rude people around her, mainly because they were all in the same boat. Homelessness was brutal, and everyone had to find ways to survive; some struggled longer than others. Yet, those people always came around. There wasn't any redeeming grace from these superiors at the hospital. They had you locked in a place where you were desperate to be. After all, what good was an education without a career?

Taylor flicked away a tear; what she wouldn't give for her biggest problem to be the handful of assholes she encountered as a teen. At least then, she had the love and support of her younger brother. But she was there for Gavin, fighting for him, being the strong woman she needed to be. She resented Henry for saying she was weak because she was anything but. She'd be damned if she allowed Henry to see her cowering in a corner, doing nothing about it. She vowed to be strong and stick up for herself like she stuck up for Gavin. Taylor grabbed her phone again, this time not for notification but to check her schedule, which would surely be online now. As she stared at the schedule, the tears stalled on her cheeks. She couldn't even believe it. While she figured arguing with HR would give her a lessened schedule, she was looking at even more harsh hours. With a schedule like this, she would collapse by day ten.

She pulled up Gavin's name and busied herself, typing a message.

TAYLOR:

Hey, Gavin. Remember what we always say to abusive assholes?

She pocketed her phone and got out of the car. They might think that she's some weakling they can walk all over, but they had another thing coming. She had worked too hard in school to cry in the hallway. No man or woman was going to be the death of her career. She entered the HR office, where Clarissa looked up, her eyes wide at the sight of Taylor.

"Hey, Taylor."

"Clarissa." Taylor grabbed her badge from her purse and tossed it onto the desk. "You can tell anyone you want to know that yesterday was my last day. I quit." She spun on her heels and stormed towards the door.

"Taylor!" Clarissa called out. Taylor hesitated at the door and turned to face Clarissa. "You can't just quit like that. You have to give a formal resignation. That means it has to come in writing."

Taylor released a breath. "Alright. Do you have a piece of paper?"

Clarissa arched an eyebrow but handed her a sheet of paper as Taylor fished a pen from her person. She only added two words to the piece of paper. *I quit.* Then, Taylor signed the papers and pushed them toward her. "That should suffice, don't you think?" She waited for no response and stormed out of the office. It wasn't until she had exited the hall that she took a moment to breathe.

On the one hand, she felt crushed; on the other, relieved. Tears started to rush back to her when she stepped outside, taking in a whiff of the air. She would never see the kids again, and that feeling overwhelmed her, clenching at her chest.

A notification on her phone sounded, and she fumbled for it and read Gavin's reply: *We say, screw you.*

He was exactly right, and it was necessary as much as it hurt. If Taylor ever wanted to get her life back, she had to tell the administration what she thought of them, and that was the right step.

CHAPTER TWENTY-EIGHT

FAMILY EMERGENCY

Anne

Anne stared at the television; the reality dating show continued to play, but she rolled her eyes. "Love, it's such a waste of time." She turned off the show and leaned back against the couch. Her eyes drew to the cat she had crocheted, still sitting on the coffee table where she had left it. She had made it for Taylor, a replica of Whiskers. At this point, Taylor would probably never get it. She picked it up and stared at it as Whiskers hopped onto the couch and meowed.

Anne rubbed behind her ears and loudly purred, rubbing her head against Anne's hand. "She's not coming back. We both have to get used to that." Whiskers crawled into Anne's lap and lay there, getting all comfy and ignoring Anne's dire tone.

Anne tossed the cat she crocheted across the room and closed her eyes as I landed somewhere in the living room. She thought maybe Taylor was someone she could fall for. She was opening her heart to love with Taylor. The notion confused her but also excited her. But now, they weren't even on speaking terms, and there was little hope that would change.

Anne had no idea that Taylor could be so immature, though. That was a red flag. So, maybe it was a good thing that Taylor stormed out of the house and never returned. She at least got a chance to see the person that Taylor was. Taylor said that Henry called her weak, and by the looks of things, Taylor wasn't as strong as Taylor thought. She quit her job on a whim. And for what? To prove a point? Talk about immature. She couldn't just forget her responsibilities and leave without a word. Maybe that was what bothered Anne the most; Taylor never said goodbye.

"Stop thinking of her!" Anne fumed, jolting Whiskers out of her lap. "Sorry, buddy," she mumbled.

She fell back against the couch and stared at the ceiling. She watched TV so she wouldn't have to think about Taylor, but the TV only brought shows that made her think about her. It was a never-ending circle that continued to revolve. She jumped up from the couch and hurried upstairs. Perhaps sleep was the only thing that would soothe her. She changed into a t-shirt and lounge pants and fell into bed, her phone in her hand.

As she lay there, she pulled up pictures that she had taken of Taylor. She was so beautiful and independent. When Anne first got to know her, she believed that Taylor was this angel who could only breathe light into any situation. But now that this darkness had clouded around them, she knew it was only a mirage.

"Why didn't you say goodbye?" Anne whispered. It was true. That notion hurt her more than anything. She knew they had argued less than fifteen hours earlier, but the courtesy was to tell her. She wouldn't have bolted if the situation had been reversed. She tossed her phone down and leaned over to shut off her light. It was just after nine, but the sooner she got to sleep, the sooner she could stop thinking about Taylor.

How wrong she was. Her dreams immediately went to the woman she wanted to push out of her mind. Only it was her intimate fantasies that fell over her night.

Taylor's breath was like molten lava as they kissed, her tongue swooping against Anne's, wildly dancing, tasting like peach cobbler, only better. "I love you," Taylor whispered between kisses. Those words left Anne reeling with intensity. She couldn't stop the exact words from flowing out of her mouth. Why would she? She was in love with this woman, and their differences couldn't interfere with those three words.

Taylor straddled Anne, pressing her bare chest against Anne's. Anne just wanted to taste her nipples once more. As Taylor pushed herself up from Anne, Anne latched onto one nipple and then the next. She tasted so sweet. While she pampered each breast, she felt Taylor slipping her fingers down Anne's panties. Anne jerked, groaning, and Taylor moved her fingers in, pleasuring Anne with her touch.

"Yes, Taylor," Anne cried, breaking from Taylor's breasts to thrust her hips up and meet Taylor's fingers. She bit down on her tongue and anxiously rocked back and forth. "Don't stop. Just don't stop."

"Anne, the phone's ringing."

"What? Don't stop!" Anne's thrusts turned frantic as she begged each finger to slide into her.

"Anne! The phone!"

Anne jerked from her sleep. "Taylor?"

There was sobbing echoing on the other end. Anne quickly came out of her deep sleep. "Anne?"

"Mel? What's going on? Why are you crying?" Anne whipped her eyes and shook her head, clearing the image in her dreams.

"I was in a car accident. It's pretty bad. The car's totaled." She sniffled again. "CAPMED...please, can you?" The words came out broken, but Anne tossed the covers back and sprang out of bed.

"I'm on my way." Her head was fuzzy, but she had to get to her sister. She wasn't in her right mind. But something was wrong, and Anne needed to be by her side.

ANNE PACED BACK AND FORTH, WAITING FOR HER TURN AT THE ER. She checked her watch, then paced again. It'd been an hour since she had gotten the call from Melanie. So many thoughts were running through her mind about what had happened; if the girls were with her, how did it happen? Who's fault was it? She couldn't stop long enough even to think. Her head was a mess.

"Anne?" Anne rushed over to the desk, glad to finally get called. "You can go in now. E-7."

"Thank you!" Anne hurried through the double doors and went straight for the ER bed. She pulled back the current, and Melanie looked

407

up and started crying. "Mel." Anne rushed to her and held her in her arms.

"I just can't believe it. I wanted to think Josh would change, but it's impossible. He's a dirty rat, and I was the fool to always fall for it."

"Oh, Mel." Anne rubbed her hand along her hair. "What happened? Where are the girls? Whose fault was it?" Every question she had in the lobby came flooding back to her."

"It was awful." Melanie covered her face. The kids are with Josh's Mom and Dad. We were going to have a romantic night in. Or, so I thought. I went to the room to change into something sexy, and a text popped up on his phone. The man is clueless because he shouldn't have left his phone out, but he did. It was from a woman. I'm pretty sure it's the same one he'd been screwing. She talked about all these dirty things they would do together, and I confronted him."

"Oh, Mel. I'm sorry." Anne sat on the edge of the bed.

She shook her head. "Don't be sorry. I should have realized the guy I was married to. You tried to warn me, and I ignored you because I was in love. He confessed everything, though. He told me he felt he was in love with her and wanted to marry her one day." She started crying again. "I burst into tears and tore out of the house. I wasn't seeing where I was going. The tears blurred my vision, and I missed a red light. I tore through it, and a car hit me."

"Are you alright? I mean physically. You have some bruises, but is that all?"

"They ran some tests, and I'm waiting for the results, but I'm in some pain. Mostly, I feel stupid. How could I be so dumb?"

"It's okay, Mel. You're not stupid. You were in love," Anne did her best to soothe her sister. Even though Anne was far from Josh's biggest fan, Melanie didn't need to be chastised right now. Anne slowly realized that she couldn't make Melanie leave. Mel had to come to her conclusion by herself.

"I still am," Melanie admitted. Anne ran her hand down her sister's bed railing. "But I know that the girls and I deserve better."

Anne loved hearing those words coming from her. It was the first time Mel admitted that. "You do deserve better." Anne quickly added.

The curtain fell back, and Dr. Newsome appeared. "Anne? What are you doing here?"

"This is my sister." Anne then tilted her head. "What about you? A far cry from Pediatrics."

"Gotta go where the need arises, right?" She rolled her eyes. "I'll be here all week, but I hope to return to our home next week." She then turned to Melanie. "All tests returned and confirmed that it's just bruises and cuts. I do want to keep you overnight for observation, though. That way, if anything comes up within twenty-four hours, you'll be here but moved to an observation floor. I'll set that up and send the nurse back here to see you in a minute. How's the pain on a scale of one to ten?"

"About a seven," Melanie commented. Anne suspected the pain was mainly in Melanie's heart, but she didn't divulge that.

"We'll get you some pain meds to help manage the pain. See you in a bit." She left the room, and Anne turned to Melanie.

"It could have been a lot worse. Do you know how the person in the other car is doing?"

"They walked away from it, didn't even have to come to the hospital." Anne sighed with relief. The last thing they needed was any more heartache.

"I'm glad you're leaving him this time. No one deserves to be mistreated." Those words danced around Anne's mind. Taylor came to her mind. She forced her to exit her mind because thinking about her helped no one.

"I'm going to call the girls and see how they're doing." Melanie reached for her phone. "But I don't want them to know about the accident."

"I think that's smart. I'll give you some alone time." Anne slipped out of her room and fell back against the wall. She was relieved that Melanie only had some bruises and would completely heal. Even more so, she was glad Melanie would finally do herself a favor and escape the situation with Josh. She was on the road to a better life, and Anne would be by her side the whole way.

CHAPTER TWENTY-NINE

WORSE THAN SHE KNEW

Taylor

Taylor entered the house after a night at her friend Hannah's birthday celebration. She had considered not going, but staying at home and dwelling on her life wouldn't change the fact that she was out of a job. She didn't regret the decision because working at a place she didn't feel respected wasn't worth it.

"You're home early." Aunt Kristi looked up from the living room when Taylor entered the room.

"I only had one drink. I'm glad I went, but I kept thinking about work, or the lack thereof. I wasn't the best of company." She shrugged, then tilted her head. "You're all dolled up."

"Dolled up? This old thing." Aunt Kristi shrugged, but she looked great. She wore a tight-fitting black velvet dress, a flared skirt, and a sweetheart neckline. A bold red lip replaced her usual soft pink lip gloss. She wore her hair in an elegant twist.

Taylor squinted, "Hold up. Is that highlighter? Since when do you spring for a blush that isn't Mary Kay?"

"Since I felt like I needed a bit of a change. It's nothing. I'm just going out with a friend."

"You're wearing heels!"

"Well, my flats didn't go with this dress."

Taylor arched an eyebrow. "Aunt Kristi, be real with me. Is it a guy friend?"

Aunt Kristi rolled her eyes. "Well, you'll find out soon enough. It's Joe."

"Joe?" Taylor laughed. "I thought you had a date with him on Saturday. You're a night early."

"He has to work tomorrow at the shop. He called. I was going to blow him off, but I guess I realized I work so hard. Getting drinks with someone or dinner isn't the worst idea. I doubt it will be a late night. I have to work in the morning, and it's Joe." She shivered, but Taylor could only smile. She sure had a smile on her face for someone who appeared like she was dreading it. If things worked out, she could say she had a hand making it work.

"Well, I hope you both have fun," Taylor said, sinking into the couch.

Aunt Kristi frowned. "I feel bad leaving you here alone tonight. Gavin is out with friends, and after your week, I feel like you could use someone to hang with. I could call and cancel with him."

"Don't you dare!" Taylor shook her head. "I'll be fine." She'd be fine if she could get Anne out of her mind or CAPMED. Neither seemed likely, but she wouldn't want Aunt Kristi to stick around when Taylor felt this heaviness in her heart. She wouldn't feel right pulling Aunt Kristi down into her depression pit. "I'll be fine alone. It will give me time to think. At the party, it reminded me how tight the money would be. They were splurging at this party, which I think is great, but I need a job. The sooner, the better."

"We'll manage to get by. You honestly had to do what was right for you."

That's why Taylor appreciated her aunt and brother so much. They were there to be her support system. It wouldn't be easy, but they wouldn't abandon her, unlike some people. A chill fell over her just thinking about her fight with Anne. Or rather, the moment she rushed out on her. She didn't want to hear Anne making excuses for what CAPMED did. There was no excuse for their behavior.

A knock sounded on the door, and Kristi groaned. "That's him."

"Aunt Kristi, go out and have a good time. I understand you're wary of getting together, but Joe may surprise you. Just remember that he does have a good heart, and you don't get out nearly enough."

Aunt Kristi made a face. "But it's Joe."

Taylor laughed. "People have a way of surprising you. Don't sell him short. You never know."

"If you say so." She turned and headed toward the door, but she looked like someone being escorted to a funeral, not a first date. Taylor attempted to listen in on the conversation, but all she heard was some mumbles, and then Aunt Kristi appeared around the corner. Her eyes were wide, a bouquet in her hands. "Will you put these in water?"

"They're gorgeous," Taylor replied, rushing over to them. She peeked her head around the corner. "Hello, Joe."

"Taylor." He nodded, and her aunt made another face when she pulled back.

Taylor laughed. "You kids, have a great night." She patted her aunt on the shoulder, then added the flowers in the kitchen to a vase. She stared at them as they soaked in the water. She thought she had met someone that she would have showered with roses. Now she was home alone and didn't even know where Anne was.

Taylor returned to the living room and pulled her laptop closer. She could get through the night and find some jobs to apply to by the time her aunt or Gavin got home. However, it wasn't the job listings she found. Instead, Taylor ended up at Anne's online shop. She stared at the various creations, complete with a new listing. It was a replica of Whiskers. Taylor pulled it into her cart and stared at it for a moment. Anne would know that Taylor was still thinking about her if she purchased it, and she couldn't fathom answering. Taylor closed out of the shop, stopping herself just in time. Besides, she didn't have the money to spend on frivolous things. She could barely put food on the table.

Taylor then started to pull up Indeed for job listings when her eyes went to a previous site she had visited many times before. She nibbled on her lower lip and then went with it. Taylor searched Reddit: Nurses with toxic experiences at CAPMED. She held her breath. There was little chance it would find anything, but it popped up. Taylor stared at the list, then pulled the laptop to her lap and started to read through them. One after another, there were cases where nurses had issues while working at CAPMED.

I was so stressed that it took a toll on my body and health. The best thing I could have done was switch departments. I never looked back – Maddie.

All they care about is money; frankly, it's not a place where anyone should work. – anonymous

Taylor looked up after reading over thirty experiences that were much like hers. She wasn't crazy, but how could this information help her? Talking to someone who experienced the same could be helpful.

Someone should form a support group for those facing the same issues. I was a new resident, only a month in, and they treated me like garbage. My superior called me weak for complaining about my schedule when they scheduled me for back-to-back twelve-hour days. Quitting was the only thing that could help my sanity. I'm looking for another job, but I know I will get through this. – Taylor

Taylor stared at her message. Maybe she shouldn't sign her name, but the longer she considered it, the better she felt about that one decision. Taylor checked the box, stating they could email her if anyone wanted to chat and that the website helped her move to where she needed to be. She pulled up the job listings, a smile back on her lips.

CHAPTER THIRTY

FEELING THE PAIN

Anne

Anne woke up already exhausted. It'd been a rough couple of days. She stayed in the hospital with Melanie until she was released the next night, and they both went to pick up the girls. Melanie didn't tell Josh's parents about the mistress or their separation. The girls didn't even question when Anne returned them to her place. Melanie and Anne spent all night talking about Josh and how it wouldn't be easy on her or the kids. However, Anne knew that they would somehow make it work.

Anne told Melanie she and the girls could stay at her place for as long as Melanie needed. It beat the alternative, Melanie thinking they should go back and work through the problems because there was no going back.

But now Anne had to be to work early, and she was still tired from the previous days. She sat at the table, drank her coffee, and pulled up her schedule for the following week. Anne shook her head. She knew that things were going to be rough for everyone. After all, they were down a nurse, but Taylor was right; this was ridiculous, and something had to change, or she would be the next one to falter.

"Anne, are you sure that us being here isn't going to be a burden on you?"

Anne backed out of the schedule and looked to find Melanie in her kitchen. "Are you crazy? I'll be happy to have you guys here." She then got up from her place at the table. The truth was, with her work schedule, she wouldn't be there much, so someone should appreciate the house. "Want some coffee?"

"That'd be great!" Melanie slumped down in the kitchen chair as Anne turned to the coffee. "If things get hectic around here and you change your mind, we will find other arrangements. The truth is, I'm hoping Josh realizes the house was mine, to begin with, and gets out of there. But I can't go back until I know he's gone."

"Trust me. You guys aren't a burden being here, and you will remain here until you are ready to go back; that's an order." Melanie smiled.

"Have I ever told you how I'm glad you're my sister?"

"I trust we've both said that at some point." Anne turned back to the coffee and poured Melanie a cup. She took it to her, then clapped her hands together. "I'm going to be at work much of the day today. You can call me anytime you need me."

"We'll be fine," Melanie replied, sipping her coffee.

"Alright, then. I have to go finish getting ready." Anne patted Melanie's shoulder and then left the kitchen. When she got upstairs, she heard talking coming from the spare room. She peeked in the door and saw Lily and Rose sitting on the bed, speaking in hushed tones. Lily looked up and smiled.

"HI, Aunt Anne."

"Hey, sweeties. What are you both doing up here? There's cereal and French toast sticks. I'm sure your mommy will be happy to make you something."

"Just talking," Lily replied softly. "Is Mommy and Daddy getting a divorce?"

"What do you know about divorce?" Anne asked, taking a seat on the edge of the bed.

"My friend's parents are divorced. She moved."

Anne gave a weak smile. They were both too young to have to worry about such matters. "I don't know what will happen, but what I do know

415

is your mommy could use a hug. Do you want to go give her the biggest hugs you can?"

Lily and Rose nodded, jumped from the bed, and rushed out. She heard their feet on the steps and got up from the bed. She wished she could protect them from the world's sadness, but they would have to find out about it eventually.

Anne went into her room and looked around for her hair tie. She opened her dresser drawer and reached to the back, and her hand landed on some paper. Anne pulled them out and stared at Taylor and Anne's letters to Willow. In the hurriedness of the week, she had forgotten all about them, stuffed them in the back, and went about her day. But they needed to be mailed, and since Taylor wasn't there, Anne would take care of them. She stuffed them in her pocket and grabbed the hair tie by her bed. Anne pulled her hair into a ponytail and then left the room. She would be late if she didn't get out of there.

When Anne got down to the kitchen, Melanie had both girls seated, and she was speaking to them. She looked up and smiled at Anne. Anne grabbed her purse and keys and left the house without a word.

As she drew closer, she saw that it was cutting it close and that she'd make it on time, but for the first time, she didn't even care. She had something else she needed to do before clocking in for her shift. She didn't hesitate to go to Henry's office when she got to the hospital. What struck her, mostly, was the look he gave her when she busted through his door.

"I'm assuming this is about Taylor."

Anne frowned. "What? No. Not really? Why would I be here because of her?" If that wasn't an awkward statement, Anne didn't know what was. But there was no way Henry knew about their connection and that date. Hell, Anne wasn't even sure if she could call it that.

"Well, those in the same department usually become close. Just figured that you would have something to say." He shrugged. "So, how can I help you?"

"Well, this isn't about Taylor, but it could be." Anne pulled up her schedule in front of him. "Look at this, Henry. You can't tell me that this is normal scheduling."

He glanced, but only briefly, then shrugged. "Anne, I'm sure you know that hiring new staff is expensive. We don't have the budget for it.

And since Taylor quit so suddenly, that strains everyone else. It's the way it works. You can thank Taylor for that."

Anne sighed, pulling her phone back and tossing it in her purse. "Taylor quit, that's the truth, but these issues have been going on for a while. Don't deny it."

"Not you, too." He tossed his pen down and finally looked up. "We are doing the best we can, spreading out our little staff. People quit, and that puts more work on the ones left behind."

"Have you thought maybe there's a reason people quit?" Anne asked in a huff.

He rolled his eyes. "I have meetings all day, and I can't discuss this with you, but I'll see what can be done." He stood up, and Anne stared at him. He was different than she once remembered. He ignored her concerns, and now she had to figure out the next steps.

CHAPTER THIRTY-ONE

NEAR HER BREAKING POINT

Anne

Anne? What's the meaning of this? Lewis is allergic to Penicillin. You need to get your head in the game.

Anne felt tears stinging the back of her eyes as she drove to Melanie's place. It'd been two weeks since Melanie's car wreck, and the girls and Melanie moved back to their house. Josh was moving in with the mistress, and Anne was relieved he'd be out of their lives once and for all. Josh signed both the divorce papers and his custodial rights.

Currently, exhaustion was Anne's biggest problem. She was making stupid mistakes, and Cecilia repeatedly called her out on them. How did she get to this point? Anne sniffled, a tear rolling down her cheek. She often thought about messaging or calling Taylor, but she would only look foolish. Taylor was right; the hospital didn't care enough to monitor their employees' stress levels and hours. She couldn't believe she had to face the same issues before realizing the truth.

Anne turned into Melanie's driveway and sat there momentarily, not even having the strength to get out of the car. She stared at the garage and waited until she saw Melanie open the front door and step out onto the porch.

Anne gave a smile and waved, then stepped out of the car. Melanie tilted her head as Anne approached her. "Everything okay? You've been sitting out here for, like, fifteen minutes."

Anne laughed. "It wasn't that long." Melanie arched her eyebrow. Anne looked away from her. Maybe it was that long, and she had dozed off or something. "I'm well. Where are my nieces?"

"They went to Josh's brother's house."

"Is that a good idea?" Anne asked. "Josh doesn't want custody, so I don't see why his family should be a part of their care. Any judge might question things if you shirk your responsibility onto them."

Melanie groaned. "His family isn't like him. The girls love their uncle and grandparents. I can't see leaving them out of their picture. Besides, his family has been great and supportive. His mom even said that I should have divorced him long ago." She laughed. "For his family to say that we're talking a major revelation. And I thought it'd be best. They don't need to be here asking questions." Anne wasn't convinced but was too tired to argue her point. Josh's family were good people. Melanie was right; the girls deserved to spend time with their uncle, even if she and Josh were no longer together. Melanie led the way into the house, where boxes lined the foyer and living room. "Josh said he would pick up his crap. He hasn't. So, we'll load them up in the garage and wash our hands of them."

"Sounds good." Anne yawned and quickly covered her mouth.

Melanie sighed. "Are you sure you're okay? You look beat."

Anne smirked. "Well, you're not wrong. Work has been hectic. Ever since Taylor quit, things have been rough. But I'm hanging in there."

"Well, speaking of Taylor...have you spoken to her? You two could have something extraordinary, but it all disappeared."

"Yeah, well. We don't always get what we want. I'm not sure I'm ready to talk about her, but who knows what the future may bring." She moved to the first box. "But these boxes aren't going to move themselves. Let's go."

Melanie dropped it, and Anne was relieved. They started working on the boxes that Melanie had already packed. As they worked, they barely talked, which was alright with Anne as she focused on the task. Three hours in, Melanie crashed down to the couch. "Wanna stop for sandwiches? We're making good headway."

"Sounds good." Anne followed her to the kitchen, and Melanie pulled a pre-made tray from the refrigerator.

"What do you want to drink? Water? Milk? Juice box?" She laughed. "Or I've got something stronger." She wiggled her eyebrows.

Anne smiled. "I could go for some coffee." She turned her head and tried to mask a yawn.

"Coffee it is." Melanie grabbed a couple of pods to put in the Keurig and then turned to Anne. Anne saw that her eyebrows furrowed and her nose scrunched up in thought. She looked away, hopeful Melanie wouldn't bring up another heavy conversation. Being around her sister was good, but she wanted to keep the conversation light and fun. Getting rid of drama was always a plus. "I can see that you're more than just exhausted from extra hours, Anne." Anne lifted her gaze, concern etched on Melanie's face. "You look stressed, and being overworked is only a portion of that. Remember, I'm your sister. I know you well."

Anne rolled her eyes and dropped her gaze. Their relationship, especially the past six years, has been filled with her concern for her sister. Now that the tables were turned, she wasn't confident she liked that. She was the big sister and should be the one to have Melanie's back, not the other way around.

"I'm good. You shouldn't have to worry about me."

"Anne, I'm your sister. That's kind of my job. Besides, I owe you one for letting us stay with you when this all happened." Melanie winked, then turned around to grab Anne's cup of coffee. "Sugar?"

"Nah, I'm good." Anne took a sip, and then Melanie went back to her own. Anne nibbled on her sandwich and drank her coffee, taking in the extra energy boost she hoped the caffeine would provide. When Melanie sat down with her cup, Anne noticed that Melanie wouldn't give up on her quest to find more information. "It's just frustrating, you know? I put my heart on the line every day going into that hospital. I'm starting to feel like they don't care."

"Wow! That has to have taken a lot out of you to admit because I have seen the dedication you've given CAPMED."

Anne nodded. "That's why it's frustrating. The schedule is only half the battle. I've been working double shifts. It's exhausting, but I could handle it knowing that the hospital cared about its employees. All the nurses seem stressed and overworked. We're making mistakes." Anne sighed, sipping on her coffee. "I pride myself in not making mistakes, but they've almost become inevitable. You're bound to make mistakes when you live on caffeine and just a few hours of sleep. The management is mistreating its employees, and someone should take a stand."

"Oh, Hun," Melanie touched Anne's arm. "You deserve so much better than that."

Anne laughed, staring at her sister as Melanie flipped the script.

CHAPTER THIRTY-TWO

JOB INTERVIEW

Taylor

Maynard Pediatric's office was filled with seven kids aged two to ten. Unlike the dreary lobby of CAPMED, Maynard's lobby was decorated with bright green botanical wallpaper. Instead of fluorescent lights, large flower-shaped lamps lit the interior. The carpet felt soft under Taylor's feet. The mood of Maynard seemed significantly less frantic. The receptionist greeted her with a smile and told her to sit before taking a sip from a ceramic mug of tea. It was a far cry from the clipboards that constantly littered CAPMED's reception desk. Taylor watched as they played throughout the lobby, their parents watching them afar. A variety of toys covered the floor of the lobby. There was a train table in the corner and a pile of puzzles next to one of the chairs. They all seemed happy, albeit sick. Some were coughing to the point where they wore a mask. Others were most likely there just for their annual physicals.

"Taylor?"

Taylor jerked when she heard her name called. She'd been on four interviews thus far. But from the looks of the waiting room, Maynard Pediatrics could be a place Taylor could call home. Yet, she despised interviews, and as a resident nurse, she found that most offices were looking for someone more seasoned than she was. It was disheartening, but she could only hope she had finally found her home away from home.

"Hello, Taylor. My name is Jessie." Jessie held out her hand, and Taylor shook it with confidence.

"It's a pleasure to meet you." Taylor's voice didn't shake with nerves.

"Likewise. Take a seat. This interview will be short and painless."

Taylor hoped that Jessie was right. Some interviews lasted two hours, and she had to take a test before speaking with anyone. Others lasted fifteen minutes, and Taylor left, immediately feeling she had zero chance of getting a callback. So far, how she anticipated the interviews going, she was proven correct. She had gotten a call back from only one of them, but it was a polite no thank you.

"First, I want to give you a brief rundown of our office. We want to ensure that you'll not only be a fit for us, but we'll be a fit for you." So far, so good. Taylor liked the sound of that because every other place seemed all about what they had to offer and why she would want to be a part of their organization. She was left feeling like it was a big corporation, and she wanted a more cozy feel.

Jessie proceeded to go over the basics, from the number of providers to the specialties they serviced. She dove into the statistics and financial summaries, not holding back on anything.

"We have ten nurses currently and are looking to hire two more from our pool of applicants. The practice is growing, and the staff needs to grow with it." Taylor beamed. That was another great thing to hear. "Do you have any questions, currently?" Taylor quickly shook her head, feeling at ease at the start of the interview. "Why don't you start by telling me why you chose us."

"Well, I love kids. When I graduated college, I knew I wanted to work in Pediatrics. The resilience of children is amazing. They hold nothing back; they're relentlessly optimistic. They tell it like it is." Jessie continued to smile. "When I saw this job opening, I immediately applied, and when I got the call for an interview, I was overjoyed. I want to feel like I'm helping those who need it the most."

"That's great to hear." Jessie looked down at Taylor's resume. "I see that you worked in Pediatrics at CAPMED. If I'm being honest, many people tend to leave these doctor's offices to go to a big hospital. I find it

423

peculiar that you're choosing to do the opposite. May I ask why, and can we call your previous employer for a reference?"

Taylor felt like she had been kicked in the gut. It was the one thing she was sure had lost her job from the other perspective employers. She still honored herself by being honest, no matter the cost; this would be no different.

"Jessie, the truth is, CAPMED was a good place to work. However, I quickly found that I was overscheduled with hours, working eight, sometimes ten, days in a row. I voiced my concern. Then, suddenly, he was looked down upon as a troublemaker and even weak. I pride myself on being strong, but the stress and hours just got too much. I know what my body could handle, and it wasn't that. I don't like making problems, but I speak my mind. If that's a downfall of mine, then maybe one day I'll work on it, but I thought CAPMED took advantage of their employees, and I had to speak my truth."

Jessie listened quietly and nodded. When she spoke, she smiled slightly. "I started as an intern at CAPMED twenty years ago." Taylor's face fell, and she looked down. Another interview went down the drain, and it was a job she honestly thought she'd fit well in. "Back then, I thought I wanted to continue my career there. However, the daughter of the CEO came in and swooped in, taking the job out from under me. Even back then, I would say that they had some less-than-ethical business practices. I appreciate your honesty, Taylor. And I'm sorry that you were treated that way."

Taylor heaved a sigh, not able to hide the smile on her face. "Thank you!"

"I think I've gathered the information I need here. I'll confess we still have a couple of candidates left to interview." Taylor's face fell. "But don't let that discourage you. You'll be hearing either way by the end of the week." Jessie stood up. "Thank you for coming in!"

"Thank you for having me." Taylor shook her hand, but it wasn't as strong as when she first met her. It felt like the odds were stacked against her, but she had to have faith that she would be a good contender.

She left the doctor's office, wishing she had a clearer idea of whether they would hire her, but plenty of other jobs were out there. She would have to strike out and continue the search, even if it were a bitter pill to swallow.

Taylor pulled into the driveway. Exiting the car, she saw their neighbor, Mrs. Milligan, standing at her flowers, watering the rose bushes. "Hello, Mrs. Milligan," she called. The older woman scowled and kept on watering. No matter how often Taylor attempted to get friendly with the neighbors, they always gave her a cold shoulder. She checked the mailbox and found no one had picked up the mail, then hurried to the porch to the front door. When she got inside, she heard Aunt Kristi and Joe talking in the living room. In the past couple of weeks, they hadn't spent a lot of time away from one another. Taylor found it sweet, even though her aunt hated it when Taylor pointed it out. Joe was much sweeter than Taylor thought he would be and wasn't bad-looking either. He was 5'9, with some silver around the temples and a Mediterranean complexion. He was muscular from his years as a mechanic, with beefy shoulders and defined biceps that Taylor could see beneath his denim work shirts. He was also a bit romantic; he'd been leaving flowers on their porch daily for the past week.

"Hey, you two!" Taylor looked in the living room.

"Hey, Hun. How'd the interview go?" Aunt Kristi asked. She crossed her fingers. "It went well. But several other applicants are interviewing, and I don't want to get my hopes up." She looked down at the mail and skimmed through them. Her hand stopped on an envelope; Willow's name was scrawled in a seven-year-old's handwriting. She had thought about the letter she left behind at the hospital and considered writing to Willow again, but she was too depressed even to pick up a pen. "Here's the mail." She tossed the other envelopes onto the coffee table. "You kids have fun." She winked and hurried to her bedroom.

She ripped into the envelope and sat down on her bed.

Taylor –

Thank you so much for writing to me. It meant a lot. I'm doing great. My doctor said that I could be getting out of here soon. The medicine I'm on is improving my numbers, whatever that means. Mommy said it meant that I might no longer have cancer. I hope so. I miss you so much. You and Anne are my favorites in the whole wide world. The

Jell-O here isn't nearly as good as I got with you. Oh, and you're right, Taylor. I'm going to get all better. I know that I am. I can't wait to see you. I have to do tests, but Mommy will mail this to me.

Love,
Willow

Tears stung Taylor's eyes as she read the letter over again. She didn't understand. She hadn't mailed the letter, so how did Willow get it? There was a knock on her door, and she wiped her tears away.

"Come in!"

Gavin opened the door with a big grin. "Well, sis. How'd it go?" He plopped down onto her chair and wheeled himself over. "Are you crying? Why are you crying? Was it that bad? There will be more interviews; I know it."

Taylor shook her head. "I'm not crying because of that." She looked up, brushing a tear from her cheek. She held up the letter. "I got a letter from an old patient, and I guess it just brought back a lot of memories ."

He snatched the letter from her and read it. "Awwww, that's nice."

She nodded, then grabbed the letter and reread it. "The interview went well. Unfortunately, there are a million applicants, so the chances of getting it are slim, but I can't have everything."

He reached out and touched her arm. "I'm sorry, Sis. But you never know, right?"

Taylor shrugged. Her phone rang, and she grabbed it and stared at the number. "H...hello?"

"Hello, Taylor? It's Jessie from Maynard Pediatrics. I know I said you would hear from me by the end of the week, but I don't need to wait that long." Taylor's face fell. She could sense the rejection from a mile away.

"Well, I appreciate you calling me so soon." Taylor sighed, tossing a look at Gavin. He frowned, and Taylor turned back to the conversation. "If you know, you just know, and there are other jobs out there, so now I can focus my attention on those."

"Taylor, I don't think you understand. I'm calling you to offer you the job. If you accept it, you can come in tomorrow and fill out the paperwork with HR, and they'll go over benefits and pay."

"What?" She squealed.

Jessie laughed. "You stood out, Taylor. I think you want to be a part of the team almost as much as we want you to be a part of the team. If you come in tomorrow, you can have a tour and meet the staff. I know everyone would love to meet you."

"Yes, I'll absolutely be there. Thank you so much, Jessie, for giving me this opportunity."

"It's my pleasure. See you tomorrow."

"See you." Taylor disconnected the call, tears back in her eyes as she turned to Gavin. "I got the job. I got the job." She jumped up, the letter falling to the floor, and embraced her brother. Everything was going to be alright. She could feel it in her bones.

CHAPTER THIRTY-THREE

FINDING HER VOICE

Anne

Anne paced back and forth in the hallway. She had been off work for an hour and was still working up the courage to talk to Henry again after giving it much thought, talking with her sister at the beginning of the week. Anne gave the schedules a chance to change, and when they didn't, Anne knew she had to talk to Henry. Unfortunately, she hadn't worked up the courage to schedule a meeting. So, that left her outside, pacing. His current meeting would be done any minute.

Fifteen minutes later, the door opened, and she stopped walking to turn to see Henry and a young woman exiting his office. He shot Anne a look, and his eyes darkened before turning to the woman.

"It was a pleasure meeting you, Carrie. I'll be in touch." He shook her hand, and the woman left. He then turned and stared at Anne. "To what do I owe this honor?"

"We need to chat." She didn't give him a chance to turn away. Anne stormed into his office and waited for him to shut the door. She had taken her concerns to two other members of HR and was all told the same. Money is tight, but we're working to hire more. She called BS. At what costs would they finally hire some nurses? She was about to crumble and liked to believe she was one of the strong ones. When he closed the door, she looked up at him. "Please tell me that is one of the many nurses you're interviewing to work with us."

He snickered, slumping down into the seat across from her. "Carrie is nineteen. She doesn't have any nursing experience. She'll be doing her externship next year for medical records."

"At this rate, we could train nurses, which would be better than what we're experiencing now. Please give us an extern that you don't have to pay. I don't care, but I'm on the edge, Henry. You promised that you would look at doing some hiring, and I'm getting more hours now than I was when I first complained."

Henry sighed. "I am hearing your concern. We all are. Don't you think we talk? I know you have pleaded your case to everyone else, and frankly, you're wasting your breath, so why even try?" Anne opened her mouth, then shut it and took a deep breath. "Anne, you are a good nurse. I saw that from the very first time you entered this hospital. We would be lost without you. But, if you can't take the stress, your duties may be placed elsewhere. Other hospitals are hiring that might be more up your alley. Any one of us would be happy to give you a reference."

Anne huffed and stood up. She started pacing again as those words echoed in her mind. She hesitated and turned to him. "Henry, what happened to you?"

"Pardon me?"

Anne moved in closer to his desk. "You used to care. I don't know why I'm so surprised. You sat in the boardroom and allowed me to be humiliated that day and never once jumped to my defense. Yet, at the first mention that you threatened someone, I jumped to yours. Am I really that foolish?"

"Anne," he began.

"No, I'm seeing things clearer here. You have changed. Perhaps the power has gone to your head. It's sad. You were someone who could be the voice of those who needed you. I'm sorry you let some power go to your head. I don't want to give up on these children who still need a voice. I work my ass off, and now I'm just questioning if maybe that's another thing I'm being foolish about."

Anne turned and reached for his doorknob. "I haven't changed, Anne. I've always been this way. To get to the top, you have to be. You don't understand what it takes to run a hospital."

Anne looked over her shoulder. "With any luck, I never will because I couldn't do this. I couldn't watch the staff suffer for monetary gain. But you do you." She spun on her heel and left the office. She felt good about talking to him, even if it didn't get her anywhere.

Anne went home, the funk remaining with her, the conversation with Henry playing through her mind. She was hungry, but her stomach clenched whenever she tried to eat. Maybe the hospital had always been this way, and Anne refused to see it. She always thought CAPMED treated her well. She never wanted to abandon it. That was the point of going to school, right? Go to school, find a job that's not soul-sucking, and live your life. She covered her face, tears streaming down her cheeks as the realization hit her. Had her past screwed her up this badly?

Anne had put her loyalty in the wrong place. She should have trusted Taylor enough to know that she wouldn't make up false accusations. She had something wonderful going on with the younger woman, and she blew it to protect a place that didn't even care about her. Yet, the hospital management wouldn't protect them. That hurt more than anything. Taylor deserved Anne's support. Anne got up, dumped the soup down the sink, and shook her head. She wouldn't allow the management to have one more ounce of control over her. If they wanted to run the hospital on an overworked skeleton crew, they would have to do it without her because this was the last straw.

CHAPTER THIRTY-FOUR

DECISION MADE

Anne

Anne aimlessly walked down her stairs. She hadn't slept a wink the entire night, tossing, turning, praying, and looking for a sign. What should she do? She had always strived to be a supportive employee. She hated making waves and when she was getting into trouble. She was the first person to cower away from confrontation. Yet, in her heart, she felt the need to do something. She needed to take a stand and support her fellow nurses. Anne opened the refrigerator and stared at a fully stocked fridge. Yet, her stomach churned at just the thought of taking one bite. If only something could point her in the right direction, showing her the path. If only her mother were there. She felt a tear trickle down her cheek. She couldn't recall the last time she thought of how much she missed her mom. It never seemed to hit her. Sure, all women wanted the comfort of their mother's arms, but it'd been years since Anne felt she needed her mother's advice. She flicked the tear away and fell back against the counter. Decisions were tough, though, and how could she possibly know how to handle this based on intuition alone? A knock sounded on her back door, and Anne looked down at her messy robe. She groaned and headed to the door, peering through the curtains. "Tyler? What are you doing here?" She pulled her robe tighter around her.

"I'm sorry to bother you. You're always up so early and headed off to work, I just figured..." His words fell over her as he arched an eyebrow.

"I don't work until later. It's no bother. Wanna come in, have some coffee?" She stepped back to allow him to enter, but he stood there.

"Thanks for the invitation, Anne, but I can't stay. I got this in my mailbox a few days ago. Sorry I'm just now bringing it to you, but it's been a busy few days. Hopefully, it's nothing too important."

Anne grabbed the envelope and stared at it. Willow's name was neatly written in the corner. Her eyes widened. She had wondered if she had gotten the letters from her. Here was that answer. "Not a problem. I'm sure it's fine. Are you sure you can't stay for a coffee?"

He shook his head. "Thanks anyway. Take care." He waved and then hurried away. Anne sighed as she shut the door and stared at the envelope again. She ripped into it, anxious to read what Willow had to say.

Anne –

Thank you for the letter you wrote me. It made me smile. I'm not as sick anymore. The medicine has been working. I feel a lot better. Mommy and Daddy don't seem so sad now. Daddy visits when he can. I haven't seen my brothers and sisters at all since the move. Mommy will let me talk to them on the phone, and we'll FaceTime. I'm really good at it. Maybe they'll buy me a phone when I'm out of here.

Anne stopped reading the letter and sank into the chair, smiling as Willow's words seemed exuberant and hopeful. She talked about getting out of there, which was a great sign.

You always made me feel special. I don't have nurses here like that. They're nice but not as nice as you and Taylor. I miss you both so much. But the good news is that the doctors say I can leave here soon. And I would like to visit you when I do. Is that okay? I have to go. Mommy wants me to eat. The food isn't very good, but she says it will continue to make me stronger. I will talk to you later, Anne.

Love,
Willow

Tears stung the back of Anne's eyes as she tossed down the letter and stared ahead. Willow was on the path to getting better. She could jump for joy over that. She got up from the table and went to the refrigerator. The girl was also smart enough to heed her mother's advice. Food was fuel. She pulled out milk, a bowl, and cereal and poured herself a bowl.

Anne sat back down at the table and ate as she spotted Whiskers. She jumped onto the windowsill and peered outside, staring at the birds. She was observant, tilting her head to the side like a person. It cracked her up as Whiskers chittered at the birds, banging her paw against the glass. She grabbed the letter and reread it, her tears replaced by smiles.

ANNE:

I know what I have to do.

MELANIE:

I look forward to hearing all about it, and I support you in every way. Love you, Anne.

ANNE:

Love you!

She closed her eyes as she laid down the phone and took another bite of her cereal. Sometimes, she saw the decisions of her life branching out in front of her like tree limbs. From owning her home to having a loving family with her sister and nieces. Has her life been perfect? Not by any means, but what life was? But she was still growing. She wasn't stuck. She always had choices.

Her life was hectic right now, but she would be okay. She had the strength to weather the storms, just like Willow did as a seven-year-old.

Taylor came floating into her life when she least expected, and while their first days were bumpy, she quickly became someone that Anne could see weathering the storms with. Whether they could continue to grow together was yet to be seen. She needed to experience that to understand what she wanted in life fully. Anne knew now that she wanted a woman by her side. She blinked back tears and tried to shake those images away. To think that things would be over between them was heart-breaking, but just another hurdle.

Anne stood up and walked to the sink, dropping the dish down. Even if Taylor was gone forever, she had to take a stand. All nurses deserved that.

With a new bounce in her step, Anne hurried to the office and didn't stop until she was seated in front of her computer. She quickly typed out an email and read it three times before deciding that she spoke from the heart and only spoke the truth. She then went to the website for the time-keeper and pulled up her schedule, saving a copy and attaching it to the email. Anne stared at the email address to verify inaccuracies. The Board of Ethics needed the truth, and she'd be damned if she didn't provide them just that. She sent the email and ensured the copy was saved on her drive.

There wasn't any turning back now, and Anne was alright with that because if she had a second to change her mind, she would have chickened out.

Anne quickly got dressed and was anxious to get to the hospital. She had to take only one more stand, and this was by far the easiest of her decisions. When she reached Henry's office, his door was ajar. She heard talking as she crept forward, but nothing could stop her.

Henry looked up and met her gaze. She didn't blink or waver; she just stared at him. "I'll call you back." He laid down the phone and leaned back in his chair. "This is a nice surprise."

"Is it?" Anne crossed her arms.

He snickered. "If I'm being honest, I'm a bit surprised after our last encounter."

"Yep, and that's why I'm here." Anne laid down her resignation letter and pushed it towards him. "It should all be in order."

He grabbed the letter and looked it over, then shook his head. "You're making a mistake, Anne. Sure, things get tough, but they always improve. Give it a few more days or weeks. Ultimately, you'll see."

"You're not getting it. I quit. I have made up my mind. This morning,

I emailed the Board of Ethics explaining what shoddy management CAPMED has and how they should thoroughly review it. I imagine by next week, you'll all receive that call."

"You did what?" He slammed his fists down on the desk and stood up. "Anne, do you know the ramifications an email like that could have? You need to withdraw your complaint; say you were moody!"

"Or what, Henry? Are you threatening me as you did, Taylor?"

"Not this again," he groaned and sat in his seat.

"What? I shouldn't speak the truth?" Her voice got louder.

He looked up and met her gaze, his eyes darkening. "If you don't withdraw your complaint, I will ensure you're blacklisted in the city. No one would dare hire you." Anne stared back. "You think I'm kidding? Try me."

Anne shook her head. "You aren't the man I thought you were, Henry. But it doesn't matter. It's over and done, and I have made peace with it. Do what you think is best. It doesn't make me much difference because I'm quitting." She spun on her heel and stormed through his door, slamming the door behind him. Anne felt him staring at her but didn't make eye contact. She felt liberated as the tears started to fall once she got outside. Her past was behind her, and it was time to look toward the future.

CHAPTER THIRTY-FIVE

HEART'S CRY

Anne

Anne stared at the computer the same she had been doing the past week since leaving her job. "You did the right thing, Anne. You have to trust in that." There was little doubt that Anne could have continued the way she had, but it was still a scary place.

She scrolled the listings of another day until the list had reached its bottom. With all the places to work, she couldn't believe how difficult it had been to find a job she was interested in, or at least a bit intrigued. She turned from her computer and groaned. Another day, another dollar lost.

The fact that her house was paid off was the only reason she wasn't actively panicking. She had enough money saved up for her bills, such as her credit card and utilities, but eventually, that money would all run out, and that's when the panic started.

A text sounded on her phone, and she looked down to find a picture of Hailey holding her baby. Anne stared at it until tears sprung to her eyes. She was on the small side, as she was still born prematurely, but from the smile on Hailey's face, she was doing well—both of them.

ANNE:

OMG. Congrats to the parents. I want all the details.

She waited, staring at her phone for the text to pop through, when instead, her phone started ringing, and Hailey's name popped onto the screen. Hailey and Anne hadn't talked much since she was put on bed rest. A few times, she got the news of her health from Cecilia, but that was the extent.

"Hello?"

"Hey, Anne. Is this a bad time?" Hailey spoke so quietly, most likely not to interrupt a sleeping baby.

"No, it's a good time. How are you all doing? What's the baby's name? I'm sure you're both over the moon."

Hailey laughed on the other side of the line. "His name is Owen Michael. He was born yesterday. He's strong. Really strong. Just like his Daddy. He's definitely over the moon. We both are." She seemed happy, and that was important to Anne. "But I didn't call really to chat about Owen's birth. The truth is, I was calling to talk to you. I've been in contact with Cecilia. She's given me the details of the hospital. The good, bad, and ugly."

"Yeah, I'm sure she has," Anne mumbled. Anne had steered clear of two calls from Cecilia. She could imagine the disappointment from her mentor. But she wasn't the one who let anyone down. It was the hospital, which Anne had to tell herself. "Things haven't been great, Hailey. You've missed a ton."

"Yeah, it sounds like it." Then Hailey's voice turned small. "With everything that's going down, I don't think I will come back. I've done a lot of soul-searching and realized I want to be a stay-at-home mom. I didn't plan on saying that." She laughed. "Owen is the light of my life; if I can watch him grow up, I will do that."

"That's great, Hailey. You deserve it."

The phone went quiet, and Anne checked to see that she hadn't accidentally hung up on her. She opened her mouth when Hailey sighed. "So, how's Taylor? I know I didn't get to know her all that well, but I know that she didn't last long with scheduling. But she seemed like she could be the next Anne regarding nursing aspirations." Anne chuckled but didn't proceed in conversation. "I know the few times I did get a chance to talk to her, she seemed to have a draw towards you."

"What?"

"Yeah. I could tell that Taylor was quite intrigued by you. She would stare all awestruck. It reminded me of Mike when we first started dating. I guess there was a thought that maybe you two would develop into more than just a co-worker status."

Anne's brow furrowed. She leaned back in the chair, and her mind went to Taylor. "It's complicated. We had a falling out, so I haven't spoken with her."

"Well, that's too bad. You should act on it when someone looks at you as Taylor does. Trust me." Hailey giggled. Hailey was younger and didn't quite understand the reality of dating. She married her high school sweetheart. She didn't know what finding a spark with a near stranger was like. "If it was only that simple."

"Sometimes it can be. You should strive to be happy, Anne. How's the job search going?"

"It's not." Anne tossed a look to her computer and scowled at it. "But I imagine it will eventually work all out. You shouldn't worry about that. You have a baby to care for."

"You were a great mentor, Anne." The sincerity in her voice brought a tear to Anne's eyes. She quickly flicked it away. "You are going to do great things. That's inevitable."

"Thank you, Hailey." Anne sniffled.

"Well, I should let you go. Just know I'm here for you if you need to talk to anyone. Take care, Anne."

"You, too. Text me cute pictures of your baby, and I would love to see him soon."

"I will. Talk to you soon." Hailey disconnected the call first, and Anne slowly put her phone down. She glanced back at her computer, and Hailey's words came rushing back. She faced a huge regret, but Anne wasn't even sure where to find Taylor.

You have her number. You could give her a call.

She could, but it seemed way too impersonal if Taylor would even take her call. If she were going to get Taylor to forgive her, it would take a grand gesture, and that was not only for Taylor's sake but for hers.

CHAPTER THIRTY-SIX

HEART'S LONGING

Taylor

Another scream echoed through the living room as Aunt Kristi threw up her hands. "And I just bought your Boardwalk with a hotel. Hand it over." She wiggled her hand out over the table.

Marge groaned. "Has your aunt always been competitive? How did I never see this side of her?"

Taylor laughed, nodding. "I believe Aunt Kristi is changing." When Aunt Kristi met her gaze, Taylor gave her a wink.

"Not changing," Aunt Kristi argued. "Just going after what I want."

"Speaking of..." Violet asked. "How are things going with you and Joe?"

Taylor covered her mouth as Aunt Kristi's cheeks went red. Kristi and Taylor knew that would be the subject of conversation when they settled on game night. Typically, they got together monthly, playing games, eating snacks, and chatting about the opposite sex. But this had been the first girl's night since Joe and Aunt Kristi started dating. A loud noise sounded from Gavin's room, and Kristi jumped up. "I should go check on the boys."

"Sit down!" Marge argued. "It's just Gavin and the boys having fun on their video games." She laughed. "You are changing the subject, though. So do share all the juicy details." Four women sat around the table while Taylor hung back. She loved games, but for tonight, she was way too distracted to focus. "Earth to Taylor?" Taylor jerked from her thoughts, saw Missy had moved from the table, and joined her on the couch. "What's going on in that mind of yours?"

Taylor shrugged. "Not much," she lied. She tossed a look over to the table. "Don't you want to hear the juicy deets about Joe?"

Missy laughed. "I talk to your aunt at least twice a day. There's nothing she could say now that would be news to me. I thought I'd come over here instead. How's the new job going? Your aunt is so proud of you."

Taylor's cheeks were on fire, and she dropped her gaze. "The job is good." She shrugged. "You go in, work, get paid, then start over again." She had been actively working for two weeks now. And she couldn't lie that she couldn't recall ever being happier in the work aspect. She loved the patients, the co-workers, and, most importantly, the management. The pay was great, and she could see a lasting career working there.

Missy arched an eyebrow, to which Taylor gave a weak smile. "Are you coming back to the game?" Violet called out.

"Are you doing well?" Missy asked, ignoring Violet's call."

"Yeah, I'm doing okay." Taylor attempted to smile again. She looked away from the group. "I'm dying of thirst. Anyone else?" They each raised their glasses in response, and Taylor nodded. "Excuse me," she mumbled. Taylor hurried from the living room to the kitchen. She wanted to be okay or grateful for her job going well. But Taylor wasn't okay, not in any sense. Ever since Anne and her parted ways, she had this hole in her stomach, or maybe it was a little higher, such as her heart. It was hard to see if she'd ever have it filled again.

She reached into the refrigerator and poured herself another glass of lemonade. She was halfway through the glass when she spotted Aunt Kristi. She smiled.

"Did you change your mind?" She reached for a glass, but Aunt Kristi held up her hand.

"I didn't come for a drink." She walked over and wrapped her arm around Taylor's shoulders. "Are you doing alright?"

Taylor sighed. "Did Missy say something? I'm doing okay. Why can't that be good enough?" Aunt Kristi sighed, and Taylor dropped her gaze. "I'm sorry. I'm trying to feel satisfied with my job. I'm glad someone gave me the chance. I love my life and am happy to be living it. But..." Her words trailed off, and she looked away from Aunt Kristi's wandering eyes. She could feel tears stinging the backs of her eyes, and at any moment, she could have a downpour.

"It's rough losing the people you care so much about. When I lost my sister, I was heartbroken. She was on a downward spiral; no one knows that better than you and Gavin, but it didn't hurt any less."

Taylor frowned. She sometimes forgot that Aunt Kristi had lost her mom while everyone tried to get her better. "I'm sorry."

She smiled and shook her head. "You don't have anything to apologize for. Such is life, but I understand pain, and you were falling for Anne. I don't know Anne, but I certainly saw that in how you acted about her."

Taylor blushed and looked away. "She was the first person I could truly see a relationship with. I was getting to know her better, and so I guess that's why it's hard."

"You don't have to shut off your feelings." Aunt Kristi tilted her head. "And you don't have to lie about how you're doing. Not to Missy, not to me, not to anyone. We've all been there." She motioned with her head towards the living room. "Come in and play a game with us."

Taylor opened her mouth just as a text sounded on her phone. She looked down, staring at Anne's name.

ANNE:

Can we talk?

"Everything okay?" Aunt Kristi asked. "Your face just turned a sheet of white.

"Um, yeah." She held up the phone and showed her the message.

"Then, I'd say, you better get to talking." Aunt Kristi winked and leaned over, kissing Taylor's head. She left the kitchen, and Taylor returned to the text.

TAYLOR:

I'd like that. Do you wanna call me?

ANNE:

Actually, come outside. I think we should do it
in person.

Taylor frowned and left the kitchen, and went to the foyer. She opened the door, and Anne stood in front of the house. Taylor closed the door behind her just as thunder sounded. She looked up into the dark sky but then back to Anne.

"I don't understand. How'd you find out where I lived?"

"I have my ways," Anne smirked and moved closer to Taylor. Taylor didn't step in to close the gap. Anne snickered. "Joe. It took some begging, but I got him to give me the address."

"But why?" Taylor breathlessly asked.

Anne groaned and tossed back her head. "I'm not used to being vulnerable, especially around women I find intimidating, but I needed to see you. I needed to tell you how sorry I am for being a complete ass. I should have trusted in you. I should have been there to support you, but I was scared. I was scared to make a move. When I lost you, the world came out from underneath my feet. That's when I opened my eyes and saw what was happening."

"Anne," Taylor started.

Anne looked down at her phone and pulled something up before thrusting it in front of Taylor. Taylor grabbed it and read her message. It was powerful. It laid out everything Taylor had been feeling before leaving CAPMED. She looked up, and Anne had specks of tears in her eyes.

"I sent that to the Board of Ethics. Two days later, word spread and all the nurses at CAPMED revolted and went on strike. The Board came in and terminated the managers. They're starting from scratch. But it should have been started earlier. I should have listened to you." Anne took a breath. "Will you ever forgive me?"

"I already have," Taylor said, tears stinging her eyes and finally releasing. She stepped forward and reached for Anne's hand. "I already have." She whispered the words before she moved in and kissed Anne. The hunger had never died. The hole in Taylor's heart closed. Her tongue dipped into Anne's mouth as the thunder sounded again. The skies opened and engulfed them in rain. Neither one parted, letting the kiss overpower their emotions, and Taylor's love started growing.

CHAPTER THIRTY-SEVEN

WHAT FOREVER FEELS LIKE

Anne

Y our aunt is delightful," Anne said as Taylor and Anne walked hand-in-hand up to Anne's front door.

"She loved you," Taylor replied, laughing as Anne stopped to unlock the door. Anne looked over her shoulder and grinned. "What?"

"I'm just wondering if Aunt Kristi is the only one that loves me." She winked, and Taylor's cheeks turned red. Taylor reached up and brushed Anne's wet hair from her eyes. They had stepped into the house and got dried, mostly, as they played games with the four other women. It wasn't exactly a night that Anne expected to play out, but she found herself letting it feel like home.

"Let's just say that I could be getting there."

Anne smirked. "Let's just say you wouldn't be the only one." She opened the door and pulled Taylor in after her. She brushed her lips against Taylor's, and they kissed while standing in the middle of the foyer. "I've missed you," Anne whispered.

"I've missed you," Taylor whispered, followed by a moan as Anne cupped her hand around Taylor's ass. They parted from the embrace, and in the silence, Anne grabbed Taylor's hand and escorted her up the stairs.

She had plenty to talk to Taylor about, but she wanted Taylor back in her bed for the moment.

In the solitude of Anne's bedroom, they faced each other. They slowly began to undress, watching one another, surveying each other's bodies as each piece of clothing fell to the floor. Anne just wanted to enjoy the moment and not rush things. She wanted to savor every second. When they were both naked, Anne looked Taylor over, her eyes latching onto Taylor's breasts. She was always beautiful, but in this moment, they were astounding. Taylor's beauty had grown during their absence.

Anne moved in, brushing her hand against Taylor's cheek. Taylor closed her eyes in response, but only for a split second. She opened her eyes, and this sensual glimmer danced in her eyes. Anne moved in, kissing Taylor and letting the kiss linger with their bare chests pressed to one another's. Her tongue slid across Taylor's, and Taylor moaned before Taylor slipped her arm around Anne, drawing her in even closer.

Anne's heart raced in perpetual heat. She pressed Taylor down to the bed until Taylor was seated. Anne straddled Taylor's body with her legs wrapped around her waist. Taylor held her in those solid and unwavering arms. Taylor leaned back, pulling Anne after her, and then pushed her way up Anne's bed, with Anne following like a blanket. The kiss never broke until they reached the pillow. Anne broke from the kiss and sensually massaged her hands down Taylor's chest and to her stomach. She pressed firmly before moving her hands back to massage Taylor's breasts.

Taylor watched, a heat coming from those two sexy eyes, growling as Anne groped her breasts, acting like she needed to learn them all over again. Taylor's jaw dropped, and she shifted her body underneath Anne. Anne could feel her wetness already seeping, and Anne knew it wasn't just because of the ten minutes they were stuck out in the rain. With one hand still massaging Taylor's breast, she took her right hand and lowered it to Taylor's opening, slipping three fingers inside her.

"God, yes," Taylor moaned. Anne pumped her fingers, bringing a moan echoing into her room. She thought it was only Taylor's sighing until she recognized her cries. She had been anxiously picturing this moment for over two weeks, and it was finally there. Anne pressed in her fingers and held them, applying force and waiting for Taylor's cries to crash through her body. Taylor lifted herself up and then crashed down repeatedly until she seized on the bed. Her juices flowed from her, and Anne was ready to appreciate them. Anne shifted herself lower and went back to tasting Taylor. She lapped up every trace of what Taylor had to offer, then pressed her hands against the bed and hovered over Taylor's lips. "Damn," Taylor groaned, then laughed.

Anne slid her hand behind Taylor's head and pulled her closer until they kissed. How long had it been since she wanted to feel this very emotion? Way too long. She slipped her tongue in, grasping onto another groan. Their bodies intertwined as they held each other. It felt right.

TAYLOR TWEAKED ANNE'S NIPPLES, AND ANNE STRETCHED OUT her legs and just watched Taylor ravish her body. They had an equal share of exploring one another, getting reacquainted, and indulging in their tastes. This time was no exception. Taylor replaced her fingers with her mouth and sucked each nipple as Anne closed her eyes and grinned. Sleep was overrated, and if Taylor continued to get down and dirty with Anne, Anne would never leave her bed. Like she'd ever want to.

Taylor wandered up her body and kissed Anne, with Anne stretching her arms around Taylor, holding her down to her body. Taylor broke from the kiss and fell beside Anne, her body limp, her exhaustion evident.

"Never in a million years," Taylor whispered.

Anne snaked her arm around Taylor and pulled her closer. Taylor's head rested against Anne's shoulder. "I'm sure you're exhausted," Anne whispered. Anne, however, was on her third or fourth orgasm. She didn't want to go to sleep. She just wanted to spend the whole night talking and enjoying each other's curves.

"Exhausted, possibly." Taylor laughed. "Yet, I don't know if I could fall asleep. I'm exhilarated. I want more."

Anne smirked. They had the same beliefs. So, that was a great start to healing their relationship. "Let's talk and see what the next few hours can hold." She looked at her clock. It was only two. They still had plenty of romance and sexual tension between them. "So, tell me about your job."

Taylor giggled next to her. "It's honestly great, Anne. It's one of those things that I didn't want to get my hopes up and have everything let me down. I wanted to believe I would get the job offer, but so much was stacked against me. When I got the call the same day, I could hardly believe it. But it's where I want to be." From the corner of her eye, Anne saw Taylor shrug. "Well, besides here."

Anne laughed and turned her head, brushing a kiss against Taylor's nose.

"Where'd you learn about the job? It's been two weeks, and I don't feel I'm any closer to landing a job with which I can see a future."

"Well, it happened kind of unexpectedly. Did you know that Reddit has a slew of ex-nurses discussing their unfair working conditions at CAPMED? I met one ex-nurse online. She still works at CAPMED but found a position that worked best for her. She's working in Health Informatics. She said it's a world of difference. Then, another had just moved out of the area and told me how she left this position and knew they were hiring. It sounded perfect, so I applied, and the rest is history. Since you've quit, being a part of the group might be beneficial, too."

"I don't know, Taylor. I think I'm ready to wash my hands of anything CAPMED. Getting pulled back in by ex-employees might be my demise."

Taylor snickered. "Don't tell anyone, but I'm an ex-employee."

Anne rolled her eyes. "Present company excluded, of course." She reached out and pulled Taylor closer, her breath up against Taylor's lips. "You're the only one from CAPMED I still need to associate myself with." She kissed her.

"Great answer," Taylor grinned.

"Anything new and exciting, besides the new job, that I've missed from your life?" Anne asked.

Taylor scrunched up her nose. "Joe and my aunt are getting pretty close. I guess bringing them together wasn't such a bad idea. I could see them getting married someday."

"When I spoke with him this week, he seemed nice. I'm glad it seems to be working out between them." Anne caressed her hand against Taylor's arm, thinking of Taylor's last words. "What about you?"

Taylor's brows furrowed. "What about me?"

"Can you see yourself getting married someday?"

Taylor tilted her head; a thoughtful look appeared across her face. She then shrugged. "For the right woman, of course. You?"

Anne nodded. She had her house paid off and only a few bills trickling in. It wasn't wild to consider it. She felt she already found the right woman, though. It was only a matter of time. She cupped Taylor's chin and drew her to her for another kiss. Why delay the inevitable when it was obvious what her heart had already craved?

CHAPTER THIRTY-EIGHT

DREAMS FOR A FUTURE

Taylor

Anne stared at Taylor, and Taylor blushed. "You're staring again, Anne." She looked down at her eggs and dug in for another bite.

"I can't help it." Anne laughed. "I'm just so happy."

Taylor beamed. Hearing Anne express the same things Taylor felt made Taylor feel like she was on top of the world. She had never been happier and appreciated Anne making the grand gesture and finding her address to apologize. They both had a lot to apologize for, mainly being stubborn for allowing so much time to go by.

"I'm happy, too, Anne." Taylor cringed. She was so happy that she didn't want the morning to end it all, but she had to get to work as there was a busy day ahead of her. "I don't want to leave."

"Then don't." Anne shrugged. "It's as simple as that.

Taylor laughed. "Nothing is that simple. I've already called off for the morning. It's a busy afternoon and duty calls. Besides, I didn't exactly come prepared to stay all day. I have to get home and get a shower and dressed." Anne made a face. "Maybe tonight we can get together. We could go dancing or maybe hit up Karaoke."

Anne smiled. "I wouldn't object to Karaoke. After all, you were a little drunk the last time."

Taylor rolled her eyes. "A little? I was smashed." That got laughter from both of them. "Well, I know tonight there will be some Karaoke. So, meet me there at 6, and we can have dinner and sing to our heart's content."

"It's a date," Anne stood up. "I almost forgot." She hurried from the kitchen, leaving Taylor confused. Taylor waited and then saw Anne round the corner. She had something in her hand. "For you." She handed it over, and Taylor clutched her heart. "Do you like it?"

"I love it." It was one of the knitted replicas of Whiskers. She leaned in and kissed Anne. "Thank you! Just for this, I spring for dessert tonight."

Anne snickered. "I'd rather we made you dessert tonight." She winked.

Taylor couldn't have beamed any brighter. "I think that can be arranged."

Anne kissed Taylor, then pulled back. "I do like the sound of that." Her heart was already pounding. They got up from the table. Anne grabbed her hand and walked her out of the house to Taylor's car. They stopped short of the car, and Taylor turned to see Anne staring at the car. Taylor waved her hand in front of her.

"Where'd you go?" Taylor asked as Anne focused her eyes back on Taylor.

Anne gave a weak smile. "I was just thinking back to our first encounter, you know, on the highway."

Taylor covered her face in shame. She shook her head. "Not my finest hour."

Anne smiled. "But look, we came out stronger in the end. I feel bad that you paid for it, though."

Taylor's jaw dropped. "Why? I caused the accident and should have paid for it. I never should have run. My biggest mistake in all of this."

"Looking back, I can understand why you did." Anne stepped in closer, and they kissed. As rough as that day was, things were getting better. That was what mattered the most. "I'm just glad we found our way to each other."

"And we have CAPMED to thank for that." Taylor laughed.

Anne groaned. "At least one good thing came from it." The best thing came from it. That was the truth. Taylor reached for her door and opened it, then turned back to look at Anne. "Goodbye, Taylor." Even though they would still be seeing each other by the end of the day, Anne looked distressed when she said farewell. Taylor closed the door and turned back to her. "What are you doing?"

"I can't leave without saying something. Anne, you are the woman that makes me want to be a better person. Spending time away from you kills me. Spending time with you, I never feel more alive. I love you."

Anne grinned. "I'm glad to hear that because I love you, too."

Saying the words healed Taylor's hole in her heart, and they passionately kissed one another.

"Now, I really have to go." She stole one more peck, then turned and didn't look back. If she had, she would never be able to pull herself away, and there was still so much to do before she went to work.

When she got home, she was alone. Gavin had started back to school the previous week, and her aunt was still working. However, her evening job was having a lull, so her schedule wasn't nearly as hectic.

She took a shower and thought of Anne throughout it, imagining Anne was there pleasuring her while she got soaped up. It was disappointing that she was alone. But it also was a good thing since Taylor would most likely be late to work if she was there.

Taylor got dressed and was out the door with plenty of time to spare. She got to work and saw the parking lot was full, waiting for the providers and nursing staff to get off lunch. Taylor went through the back door and made her way to the nurse's station. She clocked in and started looking over the schedule for the day. She was only a few minutes in when she heard the commotion and saw the others returning from their lunch.

"Hey, Taylor." Susie plopped down on the stool next to her. "Have a nice morning off?"

"Yep, it was nice." She didn't elaborate. She didn't know any of her co-workers that way. "I hope I didn't leave you guys too empty-handed."

"Nah, it was easy this morning. This afternoon will be a bit of a challenge. But I trust we'll make it. You'll be with Dr. Radcliffe."

Taylor shifted the schedule to Dr. Radcliffe's name and stared at the first patient. She closed her eyes and reopened them, sure she was seeing things. She clicked on the name and read through the notes. *The mother called to establish a new patient. Remission from leukemia.* She covered her mouth.

"Taylor? Are you alright? Are you crying?" She reached for Taylor's shoulder.

"Happy tears," Taylor replied. "I know this patient." The light flashed that she was checked in. Taylor jumped up and grabbed her stethoscope. She hurried to the waiting room and scoured her eyes around the room where children were playing and enjoying themselves, and then she saw her. She was in the corner, playing with another girl. Taylor cleared her throat. "Willow?"

Willow turned and looked in her direction. She jumped up, glanced over to where her mother sat, and then ran towards Taylor. "Taylor!" She ran into Taylor's waiting arms, and Taylor just hugged her; it was full circle.

TAYLOR RUSHED INTO BAR NONE. SHE GLANCED AROUND until she spotted Anne sitting at a table on the other side. Ever since she saw Willow, there were so many times she thought about texting or calling Anne, telling her the great news. But then Taylor realized that she wanted Anne to experience the same shock she had felt. It made her heart sing when she recognized the name, and Willow ran into her arms. If Anne could experience that, too, she knew her lover would be equally happy. Anne got up from the table and greeted Taylor with a kiss. "I feel like it's busier tonight than it was even back then," Taylor started.

Anne laughed. "Probably just your nerves talking since you know you're about to upstage everyone with your singing talents."

Taylor groaned. "Don't remind me. I can't even get drunk because I work in the morning."

Anne smirked. "That's good because I don't think we need a repeat of last time." She winked. "But I figured you could use a beer after a long day."

"You were correct." Taylor took a sip of her beer. She fought the urge to tell Anne about Willow.

Taylor had everything planned and needed to trust herself not to blow the cover. She had a whole week to keep it under wraps, though. How would she ever be able to handle it?

"How was work?" Anne asked, sipping on her water.

"Great! How was your day? Or your afternoon since I know how your morning was."

Anne reached out with her leg and touched it with her foot. Taylor arched an eyebrow, and Anne laughed. "Just letting you know that I'm looking forward to dessert later."

"I'm sure you are." Taylor grinned, and Anne cleared her throat and dropped her foot.

"My afternoon was lonely. But, I took your advice and went on Reddit." Taylor looked up from her drink.

"Are you both ready to order?" Taylor and Anne turned to the waitress and took a moment to get their orders in. When the waitress had disappeared, Taylor turned back to her.

"Oh, yeah? And?"

"I was amazed, honestly. I recognized some of the names, but I had no idea everything they were experiencing at CAPMED. I spoke with a couple of women, and it seems they are great advocates for finding new jobs. One woman even said she could get me a job with her office. It'd be as a lead nurse, though."

"You would excel at that, Anne. Specialty? Or Family Medicine?"

"Family medicine, and I think maybe that's my next calling. I mean, Pediatrics was great and all, but I feel like seeing the kids suffer all day was grueling. You know what I mean?"

Taylor nodded. She understood, but with her job, she didn't fear facing death like she would at the hospital. "You have to go where you feel the calling."

"It'd be a big change," Anne admitted. "I guess that's a bit scary, but I owe it to myself to go in for an interview. Nothing bad would come out of it."

"I agree. You definitely should."

"Oh, and you know what else I was thinking about today that we haven't discussed since we got back together? Willow."

Taylor looked at her from across her water glass. She placed it down and swallowed the lump. Did Anne already suspect something? One mention of Willow's name and Taylor was already mush.

"I think of Willow often. A couple of weeks ago she sent me a letter. It was in response to the letter I had written to her. Confusingly, though, I had quit before I got the letter. I had left it at the nurse's station. So, I don't know how she got it." Anne looked down, and her face was red. "You?"

Anne shrugged. "I couldn't imagine not sending it. But what's confusing is I didn't know your address then, so I'm unsure how you got it. I had written a letter to her, too. I sent it out the same day. I also got a response. Maybe she sent it to the hospital, and someone was nice enough to mail it out."

Taylor nodded. That was a likely possibility. But she was focused on the fact that Anne had been thoughtful enough to send out her letter. She appreciated that beyond words.

Their food came, and they ate, mostly staying in an easy conversation, with only a few stale moments where they had silence, but even in those moments, staring across the table, it felt right. As they ended the meal, there was a lull onstage. Taylor looked up there, then back to Anne.

"Are you ready?" Taylor asked.

Anne crossed her arms. "I'm ready if you are."

Taylor got up and reached for her hand. "As long as we're up there together." They walked up to the stage, and Anne broke from the grasp. She went to the DJ and requested the song, with Taylor watching. Soon, "Unchained Melody" started playing, and Anne reached for her hand again. With the bar watching them, they began to sing together, and their eyes were focused on each other, not paying attention to the crowd. It was a semblance of their romance and everything they meant to each other.

After "Unchained Melody," they sang "I Got You Babe," followed by "Don't Go Breaking My Heart." Three songs in, and it seemed like the audience wanted more, but Taylor was exhausted and wanted to get home to be with Anne, alone.

"Are you ready to go home?" Taylor asked.

Anne smirked. "Home?"

"Well, your home. You know what I meant." Anne looped her arm in

Taylor's, and they got off the stage, despite some boos trying to keep them up there a little longer. They reached Anne's car, and Taylor stopped.

"Are you ready for some dessert?" Taylor asked.

"If that's you, then absolutely." Anne pulled Taylor to her, and she fell into her. Anne pressed against her car. A strong pull told Taylor to go home; she had to get up early for work. But on the other side, Taylor didn't want another night to go by where they didn't make love.

CHAPTER THIRTY-NINE

THROUGH A CHILD'S EYES

Anne

Taylor pulled into the park, and Anne turned to her. "So, is that the big surprise? A picnic in the park?"

Taylor looked around and then met Anne's gaze. "Did you bring a picnic because I did not?"

Anne tilted her head and then laughed and stared out the window. It'd been years since she had even considered hanging at the park, but from Taylor's wide grin, it was all Taylor wanted to do. She would have done anything to give Taylor everything she wanted.

"I'm excited."

"Are you?" Taylor reached out and touched Anne's hand. Anne looked down and stared at their hands clasped together. She looked up and moved in to kiss Taylor. "I love you so much, so if you want to spend the Saturday in the park, there's no other place I'd want to be."

"I love you, Anne." Taylor kissed her softly.

Yes, things had been going perfectly for them for the past week. They got out of the car, immediately joined hands, and started walking. The weather was gorgeous, the sun beating down on Anne's face. She took in a breath of fresh air.

"It's beautiful today," she replied with a gasp.

"Couldn't have planned for a better day. Then again, I had a stern talk with God." Anne laughed, and Taylor squeezed her hand. "Why do I think you're being serious?"

"Because I am. I didn't want anything to mess up this day." Anne nestled her head against Taylor's shoulder, and they continued to walk. Who knew how many days they would have with weather like this? There was no one she'd rather spend it with than Taylor. "Do you want to get some ice cream?" Taylor asked.

"I just want to wait here for another few hours, and then maybe." Anne laughed, kissing Taylor's cheek. However, Taylor didn't seem pleased by that answer.

"Are you sure? Because I want some ice cream."

Anne stopped walking and panned her eyes around the park, spotting the ice cream cart up ahead. She groaned. They had a late breakfast, and she wasn't all that hungry, but if Taylor wanted it, she would at least check it out. "Let's go."

They approached the cart, and Taylor looked around, hesitating. "Just a minute." She scanned the park and grimaced when she met Anne's stare; she shrugged. "I'm not really in the mood after all."

Anne frowned. "What's wrong?"

Taylor shook her head. "It's nothing."

"Aunt Anne." Taylor turned around, and Anne's two nieces, Melanie in tow, ran toward them. The nieces rushed into Anne's arms.

"What are you guys doing here?" Anne turned to Taylor. "Did you do this?"

Taylor shrugged. "I was afraid they weren't coming."

"We had a shoe crisis," Melanie said before she hugged Taylor. "Thank you for inviting us. Good to see you again." Melanie turned and hugged Anne. "Got the text and couldn't think of doing anything else this Saturday. The weather turned out perfect."

Anne laughed through tears. "Taylor's got an excellent track record with the man upstairs." She wiped her tears away. "But how? I didn't even know you had Mel's number."

Taylor shrugged. "I got it at the party. I guess I never deleted it."

Anne walked over and hugged Taylor. "This was the sweetest thing ever. I can never spend enough time with my sister and nieces. Thank you!"

Taylor nodded, but her gaze dropped. She eventually sighed. "There was more to the surprise, but I guess they couldn't make it."

"They?" Anne asked just as she heard her name.

Anne turned, her eyes narrowing on Willow as she ran toward them, arms open. Anne glanced at Taylor, who already had tears in her eyes. "Surprise."

Anne turned back to Willow, along with her brothers and sister. Willow led the pack, her parents and siblings not far behind. Willow threw herself in Anne's arms, and they embraced.

"I've missed you, Anne," Willow replied.

Anne started to cry, the tears landing on Willow's hair. "I've missed you, sweetheart." She pulled back and stared at her. "How are you doing? Are you healthy?"

She nodded. "In re...re..." she looked up to her parents. "What's that word again?"

"Remission?" Anne asked. Her parents nodded, and Anne pulled her back into her arms. It was the news she had been longing to hear. Holding the little girl in her arms, she couldn't control her emotions. And knowing that Taylor had done this for her made the moment all that more special.

ANNE WATCHED THE KIDS AS THEY RAN THROUGH THE PARK. She never thought she'd see Willow outside of a hospital bed. But watching her laugh and enjoying time with kids her age brought her back to the zoo Anne would incorporate into the Pediatrics Department. Just hearing the kids laughing and having a good time was a sign that showed her what she wanted. Anne wanted to experience all that. And she needed to work in a place that would allow her to enrich kids' lives.

"She looks so happy," Anne replied.

Taylor reached out and took her hand. Willow's parents entrusted her with Willow's care for the day.

"I can't believe you did this. How?"

"I'd say it was a miracle," Taylor started. "Monday, I went to work. I was already in a great mood; my first patient was Willow. I nearly fainted. I was giddy seeing her. She was so happy, in remission, and you couldn't tell anything was wrong. We talked after the appointment, and I wanted to surprise you. So, I decided that I would plan this out. I texted Melanie."

"I was immediately on board." Anne turned to Melanie, and she was grinning like a schoolgirl with a secret. "You guys are perfect together."

Anne rolled her eyes. "You're going to scare Taylor away."

Taylor laughed. "Never!" She leaned in, and they kissed. Anne's heart had started palpitating once more. "I'm in for the long haul. When I got there, I couldn't see Melanie and the girls, and Willow and her family weren't there; I got scared. I thought it all was going to backfire."

"A shoe was missing." Melanie laughed. "That's the only reason we were late.

"And gathering so many kids is hard, so that's why Willow's family was late," Taylor added. "So, all my insecurities about it were instantly vanished. Now look at that..." She motioned toward the laughing kids. "They're having a great time."

Anne turned back to watch them running after a football. It was true that they were enjoying themselves as only kids could do. Taylor reached out and grabbed Anne's hand, squeezing it slightly.

"It makes you think we could have that someday, right?"

Anne turned to Taylor, and Taylor was grinning from ear to ear. "And on that note..." Melanie got up and walked away, leaving Anne and Taylor alone on the bench.

"You haven't thought of it?" Anne asked. "Having a family someday?"

"I have," Anne began. "I just thought that maybe it wouldn't be something you'd want."

Taylor shook her head, then peered out at the six kids running around not more than twenty feet away from them. Melanie stood on the sidelines watching them while Taylor and Anne turned serious.

"I've always dreamed that one day I would start a family. Find a loving woman with whom to spend the rest of my life, then add a child or two. But, as I got older, I feared that maybe my dream wouldn't come true. Sitting here, watching the kids, reminding myself of all the joy I tried to bring them at the hospital, I feel like maybe I gave up on things too quickly. I want that." Anne motioned to the children. "Not only in my personal life but in my career."

"So, you're saying family medicine isn't your calling?" Taylor's smile grew as she looked at Anne.

"I'm saying that everyone has a purpose in life, and that just happens to be my purpose. And once you find it, you shouldn't let it go."

"I couldn't agree more." Taylor leaned in and kissed Anne. The kiss deepened, with Taylor's tongue slipping into Anne's mouth.

"Excuse me!"

Anne smiled as they parted from the kiss and turned to see Willow. She was glancing between each of them, her eyes wide.

"Are you guys getting married?" she asked.

Anne laughed, pulling her onto her lap and playfully tickling her. She continued to laugh until she couldn't breathe and then held up her hands to surrender. Anne looked over to Taylor, who hadn't wiped that grin off her face, and Anne smiled in wonderment. She couldn't help but feel like the whole world was opening up for Anne and Taylor and their future family.

Grab the thrilling epilogue by scanning or clicking on the QR
code below:
[or Type or Click here: https://BookHip.com/RDFQHFA]

Happy Reading,
Morgan
P.S: Thanks, www.kindlepreneur.com, for the QR code generator,
and www.booklinker.com for the universal links.

Passion without Tension?

Life & Love
Book Three

A LESBIAN MEDICAL ROMANCE NOVEL

M.T. CASSEN

CHAPTER ONE

PRODIGAL DAUGHTER RETURNS

Allie

"So, Doc? Am I dead yet?" Richard Roth winked, grinning as always. Allie rolled her eyes and looked down at his chart.

"First off, Richard, we've been through this at least a dozen times before. I'm no doctor. Secondly," she moved in closer to him, noting the numbers on the pulse oximeter clipped to his index finger. "Your oxygen level is stable today. Let me listen to your lungs. Take in some deep breaths."

He inhaled through his nose, drawing in oxygen from the nasal cannula tubing connecting to his oxygen tank. "Did you hear that Izzie is coming home today? She's helping out with the restaurant and will stick around here for a bit. I imagine that's also because her dear old dad is failing in the wind." He hesitated. "You haven't met her, have you?"

"Shhhh," she calmly whispered. "First, your heart and lungs; then, you can tell me about your daughter. Take in a big breath and hold it for me, please."

He took in a breath and held it briefly before releasing it. "Izzie is my heart," he replied. Allie grinned back at him.

"I'm sure she is, Richard. And that's a good thing." She leaned forward, arching her brow, "But if I don't get a good listen to your chest and lungs, then I'm not doing my job. So, just a little while longer, okay?"

He nodded and took a breath, holding it long enough until she asked him to release it and do it all over again. Allie turned from the couch and grabbed her notebook.

"Great job, Richard. And now, you were saying..." She looked up and met his gaze. His eyes lit up as he spoke about Izzie and her many accomplishments.

"I swear, whenever Izzie walks into a room, everyone is instantly drawn to her. She's coming back to help Cheryl with the restaurant. Unfortunately, it's not doing great, but Izzie will whip it into shape. She tends to intimidate people, but I think that's a great trait for any boss. You must know that you can't mess around, or people will walk all over you." Allie nodded, noting the pride in his voice.

In all honesty, she felt his pride every day she had the honor of working with him. The stories he would share about Izzie left Allie wishing she was more like that.

As a hospice nurse, Allie got attached to many of her patients over the past two years. That wasn't always a good thing. In hospice, the patients sometimes went as fast as they came. She'd been with Richard for a month now, longer than many of her patients. Richard had lung cancer, and even though he had tried all the treatments his oncologist recommended his most recent scans still showed disease progression, which is why they decided hospice was the best choice. Allie knew her job as Richard's hospice nurse was to help minimize the harsh symptoms of metastatic lung cancer, and make him as comfortable as possible. It amazed her that somehow he seemed to be dealing with the pain, difficulty breathing, and inevitability of death with a smile.

"I know you're proud of Izzie. That's admirable. May all kids see that kind of love and affection from their parents."

His cheeks were rosy, and he nodded. "I imagine you can relate."

Allie turned away from his gaze. Allie's family wasn't one to brag about her accomplishment. If anything, her family was greedy and selfish, expecting her to give up things she'd worked so hard for to fulfill their needs and desires.

So, no, she didn't have the luxury of a doting family. Yet, she always took it with a smile because it was what Allison Walsh did. She wanted to make people happy, both professionally and personally.

She cleared her throat and stood up from her chair. "On a scale of one to ten, how've you been feeling since yesterday?"

He shrugged. "No complaints. Maybe an eight. Been a tad tired." As if on cue, he yawned, shaking his head as if that could eliminate his drowsiness.

"It's been an exhausting time. Not just for me." Cheryl Roth's singing echoed from the kitchen. Allie turned back to him and smiled. She gave a slight nod of recognition. "I just worry about her and my Izzie."

"Well, Richard, we're not going to worry about that. For right now, you are here. Cheryl is here. There's still time to enjoy that.'

He gave a weak smile, then laid his head on the end of the couch. He closed his eyes and remained there.

Allie sat down and watched him as he slowly dozed off. Getting attached to the families was a difficult situation for her. When the patients passed away, it only made things that much harder.

Her phone dinged a text message, and she grabbed it to find the latest message from her mom. She rolled her eyes, ready to toss her phone and pretend as if she had never received the text.

MOM

When will you be off work? I need you to pick up a few things at the grocery store.

ALLIE

30 minutes or so, but Mom, I can't. I have to get an oil change. I'm already over my miles.

One of the many ways her family tried to hold tabs on her. She was twenty-five and sometimes felt like they were there to keep treating her like a little kid. She glanced down at her last text, and a knot formed in her stomach. Could she procrastinate changing her oil for another night?

Would that even make a difference?

Cheryl rounded the corner, holding some vegetables in her hand. "Did he fall asleep?" she asked.

Allie looked up and nodded. "We were done with his vitals anyway," she whispered. She reached over and ruffled her hand through their dog,

Harry's head. He hadn't left Richard's side. He rested his head on the man's legs.

"Izzie should be here any moment," Cheryl continued. "She's going to be hanging around this place for a while. He could use the rest. Once she's here, he won't want to miss out on a second."

Allie turned to look at the picture on the wall. Elizabeth Roth, from her picture, was a pretty woman. She smiled with her eyes. Her phone went off with another text message, but it was only her mom.

"A boyfriend?" Cheryl asked. "Or perhaps a girlfriend?" She winked when Allie looked up. Allie felt her cheeks breaking through with an embarrassing shade of red. She couldn't imagine telling her parents she had a girlfriend. In high school, she mentioned her attraction to women just once, and her mom immediately shut it down.

Her parents were always conservative, but even she was surprised at the level of hate her mom spewed.

"Neither. My mom." Allie had known she was a lesbian ever since she hit puberty. That didn't stop her from trying to appease her parents by finding a boy she could bring home. But it was hard to pretend you were something you were not. It felt wrong. She felt alone, scared, and insecure. She wanted to make her parents happy at the risk of her well-being.

MOM

> My car broke down, and I don't know when I'll be able to get to the store. Guess your father and I will have to starve until then.

And there it was. Allie sighed, relieved when Cheryl went back into the kitchen.

ALLIE

> Text me a list.

Her mom was smart, knowing what she needed to say to get under Allie's skin. But Allie allowed it. She longed for her parent's approval, no matter the cost. Sometimes, it cost plenty, thinking that she was unworthy of love. Only wanting to make her please them even more.

Allie pocketed her phone. The doorbell rang, and Allie turned to look in the direction.

"Mom? Dad? I'm finally here." Izzie rounded the corner to the living room. She dropped her purse to the floor, and Allie's jaw dropped. Izzie entered with that same commanding presence that Richard had spoken of her on so many occasions. It took Allie by surprise, nearly catching her breath.

She glanced over to the picture on the wall and then back to the person who had just entered the living room. The picture didn't nearly do her justice. But it was more than just her beauty on the outside. She was gorgeous, no doubt. She had dark blonde curls that seemed to bounce where there wasn't even a breeze. Breathtaking. She had a confident aura that went along with Richard's story. Cheryl ran into the room and embraced Izzie, giving Allie a few moments to take a deep breath and ignore her racing heart. When they parted, Izzie moved closer to Allie. Her piercing blue eyes bore two holes like lasers, and Allie forced a smile. Allie searched for words, melting under the scrutiny of Izzie's gaze. Richard was right. Izzie could be intimidating. Allie needed to speak before she passed out on the spot.

CHAPTER TWO

DOWN TO REALITY

Izzie

I zzie nodded and reached out, squeezing her mom's hand.

"I'm so glad I can be here, Mom." She pulled back and glanced at her dad, a pit forming in her stomach. He appeared so weak, almost lifeless. His breathing seemed even worse than the last time she was here. When she got the word that he was being moved to hospice, she knew where she wanted to be. The failing business was only an excuse to get her there. As a manager in Marketing, she figured she could help her family out more than she could help her own career.

"It's a pleasure," Allie replied. She was so quiet Izzie wondered if she'd spoken at all. She looked over and met Allie's gaze, with Izzie giving a slight nod before turning back to her dad.

"And how's he doing?" She moved in, ruffling her fingers through a piece of hair that fell over his forehead. She leaned in, planting a soft kiss on his forehead. The room remained still until Izzie turned to look at Allie, expecting an answer.

"Oh!" Allie nervously moved from one foot to the other, her eyes darkening -- this was the woman that her parents had fawned all over like she was the next Florence Nightingale? She seemed so apprehensive, unsure. Izzie cleared her throat, and Allie's eyes drew to hers. "Today is a good day. He seems comfortable. He's a strong man."

Izzie smiled. "That's my father. Always the strong one."

"Is that Izzie I hear?" She turned to him and knelt at his side. He held out his arms and pulled her into a firm hug. "I'm so glad you're home."

"Good to be here, Dad." She squeezed him tight, then pulled back and took in a whiff of her mother's famous Pot Roast. Her eyes widened. "Is that Mama's Pot Roast I smell."

Cheryl laughed. "Of course, we would have only the finest meal when our daughter comes home."

"I'm starving." Izzie headed toward the kitchen, then stopped and looked over her shoulder. "Not sure how this works, but do you stay for dinner?"

Allie looked up just as she flipped her purse over her shoulder. Her cheeks turned a rosy hue. Izzie focused on the color for a moment. It brightened her features and made her that much prettier.

"Yes, Allie. You should stay," her mother argued.

Allie kept fidgeting, and Izzie laughed. She couldn't remember the last time she met someone so quiet.

"I'd love to, and all," Allie started. "But I have some errands I need to run. So maybe another time."

Izzie nodded. "You're missing out. My Mama makes the best pot roast. She kissed her fingertips, then looked at her mom. "And I'm not just saying that." She shrugged. "Some other time, though. Nice meeting you."

"Likewise," Allie replied, this time with more of a zest in her step. Izzie disappeared into the kitchen and reached into the cupboard for the place settings. She hesitated as she stared at the kitchen table. She was guessing, unsure how frail her dad was or if he could make the trip into the kitchen. Just as the thought hit her, she felt a hand on her shoulder. She looked over her shoulder, and her dad grinned.

"It's great to have you home." He reached for the table to steady himself. Izzie helped him take a seat.

"We could have eaten in the living room, Dad. You shouldn't be pushing yourself, not on my account."

"She isn't wrong." Her mom's voice came from the entryway of the kitchen, and with her dad now seated, Izzie turned to see her.

She crossed her arms and raised her brow. "I told you we could do what we needed to stay at your level, Richard. You're now prancing out here, not even waiting for me to help you? That is why you have the wheelchair."

He shrugged. "You were saying goodbye to Allie. I didn't want to wait. Besides, I'm feeling much stronger now that Izzie is home. It's amazing how that happens." He winked at Izzie, but Izzie furrowed her brow. She didn't want her dad to jeopardize his health just because she was home. That wouldn't help anyone.

"Okay, we'll let it slide for tonight," Izzie started, placing the plates on the table. "But really, I wouldn't have minded the living room."

"Listen to your daughter," her mother scolded, moving to grab the food from the counter.

Izzie sighed. It was good to see that her dad was out there to join them, even if it was just for their first meal. As they sat down and started eating, they started talking about what was new in their lives, particularly the hospice nurse.

"Allie is such a sweet girl," her mother started. "It takes someone special who can handle the pressures and intensity of working with hospice patients. But more than that, it takes someone with a pure heart. And that's what Allie brings to the table."

"She seems quiet, more introverted than what I expected." Izzie took a bite of her potatoes.

Izzie shrugged. "I know I expected someone older. How much do you know about this girl that comes into your home?"

Cheryl laughed. "Our daughter, the cynic."

"Not cynical, just realistic." Izzie arched an eyebrow. "Someone needs to be." She tilted her head, almost in a scolding manner, but her mom continued to smile.

"We know as much as we need to know. Let me show you this." She reached into her pocket and withdrew her phone.

"Since when are phones allowed around the kitchen table?" Izzie laughed. "I remember you were both a stickler about that rule. What changed?"

"Nonsense!" Her mother grinned. "It was because the girls wouldn't stop calling you. If we had allowed you to have your phone, you would have never eaten a full meal."

She winked at Izzie, then held out her phone. Allie, her dad, her mom, and Harry posed for a selfie. They all looked so happy, crowded around the couch, beaming. Izzie nodded.

"One big happy family, it appears." She took a bite of her food and relaxed slightly. She was glad Allie was there, giving her father and mother reasons to smile. If Izzie couldn't be there, it was nice to see they had someone there to support them.

Her mother scoffed. "Is that jealousy, I hear? No need for that. Allie fits in the house. She came along when we needed it the most. Besides, I think that she needs us, too."

Izzie frowned, but her mother didn't proceed to explain. She looked down at her food and stared at the scraps left behind. "She seems nice enough. Just timid."

"Well, not all women are as confident as my Izzie." Her dad reached out and grabbed her hand. Izzie smiled and looked down at their hands clenched together. She dropped it. If they were happy with the nurse, she was just glad someone was there to help lift her parent's spirits. For that, she was infinitely grateful.

HER DAD CLOSED HIS EYES AS THEY HELPED HIM BACK TO THE couch. Izzie sighed. A trip to the kitchen for supper was enough to wear him out. She had to prepare herself that that was a possibility mentally. He said he felt good, though, which was soothing to hear.

She sat in the rocking chair, keeping her eyes on her dad. "So, we didn't spend much time discussing your life," her mother started.

"And for a good reason," Izzie teased, taking a swig of her water to buy her time. It always boiled down to the same question. Behind her mother's grin, she just waited for it. "Nothing new; that's about all you need to know." She smirked and took another drink.

"So, no new girlfriend?" her mother asked.

Izzie shook her head. And there it was. "I'm too busy with work to even mess with that." She stood up from the rocker. Even the thought of getting involved with someone else made her chest ache.

Relationships only brought trouble. Heartbreak made it hard to focus on the good that could come. Besides, it was nearly impossible to differentiate between the real and the fake in a woman. It was too discouraging to even try. "Speaking of work, I believe there's some accounting I need to look at as far as the restaurant is concerned?"

"Yeah, I emailed you the financial info earlier today." Cheryl grimaced. "It's not pretty. But with your dad getting sick,"

Izzie glanced over at him, mindful that discussing such matters in front of him could have an adverse reaction. "That's why I'm here. I'll take a look." She left the living room to grab her bags from the foyer, then passed back through the living room and turned to her mom. "You should probably get some rest, Mom." She looked at her dad, resting peacefully on the couch. "Does Dad just sleep here?"

Her mom nodded. "It's easiest on the couch. Besides, it seems the most comfortable. It's hard for him to breathe laying down. We put in for a hospital bed and should get approval within the week."

Izzie cringed. He didn't appear all that comfortable, but he rested easily and seemed to fall into a deep slumber. Her mother knew what was best. She had been by his side every day while Izzie tried to wrangle enough PTO to go home.

She smiled and turned to her mom. "I'm going to do some work and then go to bed. It's been a long day."

"Alright, honey. Don't work too late." Izzie nodded, bolted upstairs, and hurried down the long hall to her old bedroom. She dropped her bags and carried her laptop to the bed. She took a minute to glance around the room, which was full of memories. It was going to be a hectic time for her, with her duties at her full-time job not stopping and now her responsibilities of helping out the family restaurant, but she made a vow and was going to stick to it. Luckily, she had the option to work remotely and could do that at any time of the day.

She turned on her laptop, waited for it to load, and signed in to look at her emails. The first email that appeared made her want to gag. *We Value Our Employees.* The CEO liked to make it seem like they did anything to help the employees, but she was the first to laugh as one of the managers.

The fact that the pay was good. It was one of the few things keeping her from venturing into something new. However, she always wanted to question whether pay should be a deciding factor. She scrolled through the emails and pulled up the one from her mom. She looked at it, feeling a yawn coming on, and couldn't even stifle it.

She shook her head and refocused her eyes. Her dream was to ditch the corporate world and start her own company so she could work on her terms.

A text dinged on her phone, and she was grateful for the interruption. She snickered when she saw her mom's message.

> MOM
>
> Here's a cute pic from last night I forgot to show you.

Again, Allie, her parents, and Harry were in the picture. Allie and her parents were making a face, with Allie giving her dad bunny ears. Izzie laughed, shaking her head, then stared back at the woman in the center. When she saw pictures like this, it didn't appear like Allie was this timid wallflower. If anything, she glowed in every picture, and her parents looked excited to have her around.

When Izzie told her parents about providing a hospice nurse for her father, she didn't even blink at the money. She wanted to believe the nurse could offer more than just medical help. These smiles showed that Allie could do just that.

> IZZIE
>
> Dad's face is priceless. Thanks for sharing.

She stared back at Allie, then dropped her phone and looked at her laptop. Her work was going to take more time than the night would allow. She shut her laptop and pushed it off to the side. Izzie stood up and went to her nearest suitcase. Another text message chimed in.

> MOM
>
> It's late. Go to bed!

Izzie laughed.

IZZIE

Do you want to come tuck in your forty-year-old daughter, too? LOL. Night mom!

MOM

Goodnight, honey!

Izzie got changed for bed, put her laptop on the nightstand, and slipped under her covers. She looked back down at the picture that came through moments earlier and zoomed in on Allie. Her curves accentuated her body, drawing Izzie's attention to her plump breasts and trim waist. She traced her finger over Allie's features, then rolled her eyes and leaned back in bed. *Quit it -- the last thing you need is to crush on your dad's hospice nurse.*

The light was still on. Izzie groaned, tossing the covers back. She could manage a company and still go to bed without turning out the light. She laughed as she flipped the light off, then returned under her covers.

She sent her best friend, Mae, a quick text, along with the picture her mom had sent her.

IZZIE

Looks like my father is happy with one of the nurses on staff for his hospice care. Cute, right?

MAE

The picture or the girl?

Izzie laughed as a winky emoji popped up in the text. Mae was her best friend and knew her all too well. She shot back a tongue-out emoji, then typed in a text.

IZZIE

It's weird being back. My dad looks so frail, but seeing him smile in pictures like this warms my heart.

MAE

Must be rough, but I'm sure he's glad to have you there. You're a great daughter, Izzie.

Izzie smiled and sent a grinning emoji when another text came through.

> **MAE**
>
> Get some rest. I'm sure you're going to need plenty of it.

> **IZZIE**
>
> **Absolutely. Goodnight!**

She placed her phone next to her on the bed and closed her eyes, but the picture came back to her mind, and she grabbed her phone again to sneak a peek. She quickly swiped her finger across it to remove it from her main screen and dropped her phone to her bed.

I'm just happy and grateful that my parents are smiling during this trying time. She nodded, even though she knew Allie was cute. But she needed to focus on the present and her parents, not her dad's gorgeous nurse.

CHAPTER THREE

CHANGES TO COME

Allie

The sun was high in the sky as Allie stepped onto their porch at noon the next day. She removed her sunglasses and rang the bell. It wasn't long before Becky answered the door. She gave a smile and backed up for Allie to enter.

"How's the patient?" Allie asked.

"He's in excellent spirits. His daughter is here."

"Yeah, she came in last night before I left for the evening," Allie remembered seeing the gorgeous woman rush into the house as if she always belonged. There wasn't a hair out of place, and when she smiled. It seemed like she owned the room. Or maybe it was just Izzie's confidence shining through, which thoroughly impressed Allie. She only wished she could exude that same self-confidence. She glanced down at her hands, nervously clenched together. And now she'd be facing her again. If only she didn't stumble over her words.

"I must run to the hospital and catch up on a patient. Mr. Dennis was admitted last night."

Allie groaned. "I'm sorry to hear that. Hope it's nothing serious."

"Dehydrated." Becky made a face. "But I spoke with the on-staff nurse this morning, and she said that he's already greatly improved."

"Glad to hear." Becky followed Allie into the living room, where Richard sat in his wheelchair. Izzie was sprawled out on the floor, a pile of paperwork on her lap. Harry curled up at her feet and was sound asleep. Richard was the first to look up.

"And there she is." He had a bright grin on his face.

"Hello, Richard." Izzie looked up and gave a slight wave. "Izzie." When Allie said her name, the words came out so soft. Izzie didn't notice as she continued to talk to her father, discussing the papers she had tossed in the middle of them.

"I'm heading out," Becky replied. "If you need anything, you know how to reach me, but you're in very capable hands right now. See you tomorrow."

"See ya, Becky," Richard called out, remaining focused on his daughter's conversation.

"Nice to meet you, Izzie."

She grunted, and Becky snickered as she grabbed her purse and headed toward the foyer. Allie followed her to the front door.

"I've known her for a few hours, but she's a workaholic, that one," Becky replied, looking over her shoulder to Allie. "I know the type. My husband's the type." She laughed.

"The few minutes I got to speak with her last night, she seems nice, though," Allie replied.

Becky shrugged. "I wouldn't know. She didn't give me much of the time of day. Not that she needed to. I was here for her father, after all." Becky sighed. "Cheryl is at the restaurant, so you'll probably have to throw on something to eat. Unless Izzie decides to make that her gig, I'd say she's too invested in her work to add chef to her repertoire."

Allie gave a smile. "Thanks for the update. I'll catch up with you later." She stayed at the front door and waited until Becky got in her car and drove away. Becky was older than Allie, pushing fifty. She was also set in her ways, old-school, as some would say. But she was a great nurse. The younger generation looked up to her and wanted to follow in her footsteps.

When Becky glanced up at the door, Allie waved, then closed the door behind her and returned to the living room, where Richard and Izzie remained.

Izzie shook her head. "I don't know, Dad. It's just hard to understand some of these numbers. What was Mom thinking?" She tossed the papers down and groaned.

"Honey, I was the one that always did the books. When I got sick last year, your mom had to take over with almost zero notice. She's doing the best she can. She didn't sign up for this."

Izzie nodded. "And I get that, but she doesn't know how to make financial decisions. The restaurant has slowly started losing money this past year. Now," she hesitated before glancing up and shrugging. "I'm not sure how we can pull out of it. Mom is not the manager type."

"Excuse me," Allie whispered, trying to stay out of their way yet get started on his vitals. She felt like a fly on the wall, listening in on their conversation, but she had a job. Every shift started and ended with checking vital signs.

Izzie moved back, allowing Allie more space, and Allie gave her a gracious smile. Harry stood up and moved closer to Izzie, landing his head on her lap, and she ran her fingers through his fur. Allie caught herself watching the encounter, suddenly forgetting why she was there.

Richard cleared his throat, jerking Allie's attention back to him. He grinned, chuckling. Allie felt her cheeks burning as she reached out and touched his wrist. His pulse started palpating to her touch, and she tried to ignore the apparent looks he gave her. She checked his heart and lungs with her stethoscope, and his eyes remained focused on her.

"Let me grab your temp, and then you can get back to your meeting." He nodded, and she leaned across and grabbed the thermometer from the coffee table. Her stretch wasn't far enough. The thermometer fell to the floor. "I'm such a klutz today," she muttered.

Izzie grabbed it just as Allie's hand did the same. Their fingers embraced, and Allie quickly pulled back, taking in Izzie's gaze. Izzie smirked.

"Here ya go."

"Thank you," Allie mumbled, wishing the floor would open up and swallow her whole. Izzie seemed not to notice Allie's obvious sign of discomfort as Allie turned to Richard. He was staring at her with a massive, amused grin. Allie was uncomfortable, fumbling with his temperature. The strange look he gave her and his daughter being just a foot away made her hair stand up. "Temp is normal." She quickly moved away from her patient and sat on the overstuffed chair to document his vitals.

"I'm just afraid," Izzie began. "If the numbers look this bad now, who's to say what they'll look like in six months? As much as I hate to admit it, we might have to find someone to buy us out."

Richard groaned. "You're the expert. I feel bad having to let the staff go."

"Maybe the new buyer will keep on some of the staff. But ultimately, we can't fret over that. We have to do what's best for the company." She stood up from her position on the floor, with Harry looking up at her like *how dare you?*

"I think I'm going to head to the restaurant for lunch and see how things look from the outside."

Allie looked up, her cheeks warm at the thought of voicing her opinion. She was just a layperson who didn't know the corporate world. Her opinion most likely wasn't important. Yet, she was the average consumer, which might be more valuable than expected. "I don't mean to interrupt, but I have an observation."

"Any observation is helpful," Izzie began. "Speak up."

That gave Allie the extra push. "I was there last week, and the hostess was on their phone the entire time."

Izzie rolled her eyes and shook her head, glancing over at Richard. "Why is that not a surprise? Mom is just way too nice to be an effective manager. This restaurant has lost customers because of poor staffing. I'd imagine that many customers feel the same way Allie does. The staff needs to be more engaged with the customers instead of on their phones, doing who knows what."

Allie smiled, feeling proud that she had stepped up and offered her thoughts. Better yet, no one scoffed at her.

"I know you're right," Richard's voice was quiet.

Allie caught herself, giving another look to Izzie. Izzie was most likely one to get heads to turn. Aside from her physical appearance, her confidence was infectious. Though she was business-oriented, directed, and forceful in the career world, she was also a great listener. That was just as important as the physical aspects of a person, if not more.

"I'll start looking for a buyer." Izzie grabbed the papers and headed out of the living room and to the stairs. Allie could hear her feet as she ran up the stairs to the bedroom.

"My daughter has always turned heads with her beauty."

Allie turned and stared at Richard. He winked, and Allie looked down at the chart before her. "Beauty is only skin deep," Allie mumbled. She heard him give a slight chuckle. "Harry adores Izzie; that's clear."

"She's not the only one," he said, tossing his head back in laughter. Allie tilted her head, then turned away as the blush came on.

"I think I should get you something made for lunch. What sounds good?" She stood to her feet, hoping to steer the conversation away from Izzie. If she kept thinking about Izzie, she would never be able to concentrate.

CHAPTER FOUR

HELPING HAND

Izzie

The moment Izzie stepped into the house, the aroma of sizzling veggies and spices hit her. She took in a whiff and sighed. Something was cooking. Her stomach growled. She had been so busy at the restaurant that she didn't eat all day. One smell and her body quickly reminded her how ravenous she was. She released a yawn, adding exhaustion to the list.

She entered the living room to see her father resting in a hospital bed. He was sound asleep, and Harry settled at the foot of his bed. He looked at peace, but instantly, she was hit with a regular reminder. He wasn't doing well, and there was only a slim chance he'd come out of this. After all, once doctors transferred a patient to hospice, there was little hope for them. She quickly shook that thought out of her mind. If she dwelled on that, she would crumble in a corner somewhere.

She forced a smile and walked towards the aroma. Allie was busy at the counter, cutting veggies and tossing them into a pot. Izzie cleared her throat, and Allie turned to look at her, her face flushed. Allie touched her forehead with the back of her hand, her cheeks pinking slightly.

"I didn't hear you come in." She removed one earbud from her ear and slipped it into her pocket. "Jamming to Bach," she mumbled, returning to her veggies.

Izzie gave a slight laugh. "Oh, is that your cooking genre of choice?"

Allie shrugged, not bothering to turn in her direction. "It tends to relax me." She continued to toss veggies, and Izzie took in another whiff.

"I saw the hospital bed came," Izzie started.

"Yeah, earlier than we hoped. Unfortunately," Allie stopped, then looked over her shoulder. "And fortunately, a bed became available. I called in a few favors, and they delivered it a couple of hours ago."

"Nice," Izzie moved closer to the pot and peered over the stove. "Smells delicious, whatever it is."

Allie snickered, but her cheeks reddened when she met Izzie's eye. "When it's all said and done, it will be veggie lasagna."

"Enough for me, too?" Izzie inquired.

"Of course. I always make plenty." Allie's voice was soft, and her rosy cheeks continued to brighten her face. Izzie quickly looked away. Nothing good would come of having hots for a hospice nurse. Flirting was one thing. She flirted with an athlete's skill, but you could only take it so far. Izzie knew right when to pull back and when to move forward.

Izzie grabbed a carrot from the counter and chomped down on it. Allie's jaw dropped, and she laughed, returning to the pot. It appeared she was conjuring up a stew, but even though her parents started a restaurant, Izzie didn't have the kitchen skills required.

"Eating the ingredients, I see," Allie snickered, her face lighting up again.

Izzie shrugged. "I'm starving."

"Doesn't matter. I'm done. Now, we'll let that simmer for a while." Allie grabbed the remaining veggies and put them back in the refrigerator. She reached for a towel and wiped off the counter, with Izzie watching her from behind.

"Maybe my mom and dad should have hired you as the chef. The restaurant might be thriving by now." Allie laughed, tossing the towel to the side and turning. Izzie shrugged. "I mean, you know your way around a kitchen."

"Save your praise for after you've tried the meal." Her cheeks continued to hold a rosy color. "But I guess I have experience in this matter." She dropped her gaze. "So, how was the restaurant?" Allie quickly changed the subject, but Izzie didn't mind.

"For thirty years, my parents ran Stars and Stripes. If you haven't guessed, you could say it was my father's dream." Izzie scrunched up her nose. "My mom means well, but there's a difference between being nice and making an effective manager. None of us expected to have to switch roles. I don't know how long the restaurant can wait without looking for another buyer."

Allie slowly nodded as if she was taking in every word. "It's sad. The food is great, and no other restaurant can compete. It's a shame that there isn't some way to turn it around." Izzie glanced up, and there was this faraway expression in Allie's eyes.

"Not everything needs to change." Allie shrugged. "Such is life, I guess."

There was something genuine about Allie. She listened to Izzie when she spoke. That was a trait that Izzie hadn't seen in her past experiences. *But People can fake their interests. Just remember that.*

"I should get back to the lasagna." Allie turned from her and began shuffling around the kitchen.

"Would you like some help?" Izzie asked. She reached for the sauce just as Allie reached for it. Their fingers touched, and Allie quickly withdrew her hand.

Allie laughed, bringing a smile and laugh from Izzie. "Sorry. But yeah, that'd be great." Allie blushed again, and Izzie took a moment, stepping back and noticing the rapid color change.

She shook her head; thinking about it would only complicate things. Allie was her father's nurse, and that was all there was to it. "No worries." She handed the sauce jar to Allie, then reached into a cupboard and grabbed another apron. At that moment, to her surprise, she looked forward to cooking. People could look outside the box and find new activities to participate in; maybe this was what Izzie needed.

CHAPTER FIVE

ALL-AMERICAN FAMILY

Allie

L ater that evening, Allie unlocked the door to her apartment. It wasn't much: A one-bedroom, living room, and small kitchen nook, but it was home. In her eyes, it was much better than the house she grew up in, even if she only lived a couple of miles down the road. In a small town, you couldn't get too far from your parents, even when you moved away.

Cheryl arrived home just in time for dinner. They all sat around the table except for Richard. He seemed too fragile to get up from the hospital bed. When they finished, Izzie and Cheryl went to the living room and sat with Richard while Allie cleaned up in the kitchen.

During the meal, Izzie sat next to Allie, and it seemed like they were just two friends, hanging in her family's kitchen, with Cheryl only tossing in a word or two. They were total opposites, but the cliche rang true: opposites attract. The Roth family reminded Allie of a sitcom. They seemed to care about each other genuinely.

Allie couldn't even deny the jealousy she felt about that. She longed for something even remotely similar in her own life, but the prospects were bleak.

Allie slumped down on the couch and looked around the bare living room, a far cry from the laughter she left behind at the Roths. Allie's mind went back to Izzie, and she laughed. Izzie could make conversation with a brick wall. On the other hand, Allie only opened up when someone talked to her directly. Even then, she questioned whether it was her place to talk. It seemed impossible that Izzie would be attracted to someone like Allie.

Allie looked down at her phone as a text popped in.

> MARISSA
>
> Taking a break from studying. How ya doin' sis?

Marissa sent several heart emojis and exclamation points.

Allie smiled. Her younger sister was more like Izzie than Allie was. Marissa was optimistic, but she never let her optimism sacrifice her honesty. Allie was always impressed by that. When Marissa said she was going away to college, Allie wanted to be the one to talk some sense into her. How could Marissa move a thousand miles away when Allie needed her there? Allie couldn't manage her parents by herself. And, frankly, Allie was jealous that she hadn't decided to make the move. Yet, she was happy for her sister, even if she experienced occasional jealousy.

> ALLIE
>
> Studying? Last I checked, it was summer. I thought you were choosing to work this summer, and that's why you weren't coming home.

> MARISSA
>
> Ugh. Well, my advisor had a different idea. If I took Psych this summer, that would leave me the option of taking another course during the Fall semester. But I'm also working at the theatre for extra hours. College years are supposed to be stressful, right??

A few more emojis popped up at the end of the message, ending with the wary emoji and another three exclamation points.

Allie knew things couldn't be easy for Marissa, but she always thrived in chaos, so she was confident that Marissa only needed to vent for a bit.

ALLIE

Remember not to push yourself. No one will benefit if you end up in the hospital.

MARISSA

Are you kidding me? I'm as strong as an ox.

She added a bull emoji and then a muscle emoji, followed by a grin.

Marissa would be fine, but as the oldest sibling, it was Allie's job to worry about her. She stared at the messages, hesitating.

She needed someone to talk to. Marissa wasn't nearby, but she was the best option she had.

ALLIE

Remember back in high school when I had a crush on that girl?

MARISSA

That girl? Do you mean Susie Simcox? How could I forget??

Allie rolled her eyes. Marissa was only fourteen. It wasn't absurd to think that maybe Marissa didn't know what was happening. Even if it was all the house could speak of for twenty-four hours.

ALLIE

You remembered her name??

MARISSA

LOL. Of course. Mom was grossed out and pretended to be sick for a whole week over it. Dad was drunk and couldn't stop yelling over it. He said he wouldn't tolerate "unnatural" behavior under his roof. I thought for sure you weren't going to move out over it. If I had been in the same situation, I probably would have.

ALLIE

You were 14.

MARISSA

So, I would have made a backup plan.

Looking back, Allie wished she would have been more open to that, but instead, she blocked out her feelings and pretended nothing happened. It wasn't her finest moment, but there was no use hashing out the past.

MARISSA

What brings on this talk?

Marissa added the thinking emoji, and Allie sat there, unsure she wanted to continue the conversation. She took a deep breath and decided to go for it.

ALLIE

I met a woman, and I think she's great.

MARISSA

Really?? Is she drop-dead gorgeous and all that stuff?

ALLIE

Smh. It's more than the looks. She's confident. She knows what she wants. It's... hot.

MARISSA

Wow! Sounds intriguing. So, what are you going to do about it?

ALLIE

That's my issue. I don't know.

The fact that Izzie was older than Allie didn't stifle her attraction. She could get past the age difference. After all, it was only a number. But she had way more to consider.

ALLIE

I remember how our parents responded to it. I don't know that I can deal with that again.

MARISSA

You're older now, Allie. At some point, you have to choose your own path.

Allie scoffed. Sure, everyone wanted to march to the beat of their own drum. But letting people down wasn't something Allie could get past. If only she could throw up her hands and stop caring about what her family thought of her if only it were that easy.

> MARISSA
>
> How is Mom doing?

> ALLIE
>
> Still limping. She has some hip pain.

The car accident was six months ago, but her mom still had rehab she had to go through. She wasn't getting much better, and they had to discontinue the painkillers because they feared she'd be addicted.

> ALLIE
>
> The insurance threatened to cut off paying for rehab, stating that she should be better by now. How would they know? They're a bunch of idiots.

> MARISSA
>
> Yeah, she's getting screwed over.

A frowning emoji popped up on the text, and Allie nodded. That was the truth. Her phone rang, and she spotted her mom's number across the screen. She groaned and continued to let it ring, eventually going to voicemail.

> ALLIE
>
> Guess who's calling.

> MARISSA
>
> Mystery woman?

Allie laughed.

> ALLIE
>
> I wish!! Mom.

There was a moment of guilt that she didn't pick up the phone, but she waited for the voicemail. Instead, a text dinged on the phone.

MOM

You didn't answer my call. Surely, you can't
still be working.

Allie groaned. "No, just ignoring your call, Mom." She pulled up her mom's number, about to call her, when another message dinged.

MOM

I need some money. I have to buy some meds,
and the insurance isn't covering it. All I need
is $50.

Allie shook her head, her mind racing as she reread the message. "You've got to be kidding me," she mumbled.

ALLIE

Mom is asking for money.

MARISSA

I know how to stop that. Tell her you're
hooking up with a woman. She'll stop calling
you for days. LOL.

Allie sighed. If only she could find it laughable. Her sister was right, but Allie's stomach was in knots at the thought of telling the truth.

MARISSA

You know that it would work. She would, for
sure, leave you alone.

ALLIE

I know, but why is it so hard??

MARISSA

Sister dear, you have a pure heart.

If she could only have some fire to go along with that heart, then she wouldn't have people who should love her and accept her for who she is, taking advantage of her.

ALLIE

Sometimes too pure.

She again pulled up her mom's messages and stared at the last message.

ALLIE

I'll transfer it to your account.

She waited, hoping to get a message from her mom thanking her for once again caving in and sending the message. The text didn't come. Allie slipped her phone into her pocket and got up from the couch. At least one person would be accepting of Izzie if Allie pursued her. But it wasn't enough. She couldn't get attached to her. It would never work out. But even as doubt plagued her, she could feel her attraction to Izzie growing.

CHAPTER SIX

WORK OVERLOAD

Izzie

Izzie opened her laptop and logged into the system. Harry rested his head on her lap and whimpered when she moved unexpectedly.

"Sorry." She ran her fingers through his fur, covering the top of his head, and waited for her emails to pop up on her screen. She was on vacation, but work would be hell once she returned to the city. Currently, she could only stick around two weeks, and even that was pushing it. Izzie sighed and scrolled through her junk mail. She found an email from her boss and pulled that message up.

Hey Elizabeth –

I know you're on vacation. I hate to interrupt your time with family, but I need a second set of eyes on this document regarding the Morrison Tobacco case. We need to rerun the numbers. I can't seem to come up with the same results twice. Please take a look if you can. We're looking for a 2-3 day turn-around time, and I'm already getting this to you a day late, so the earlier, the better.

I know it's probably bothersome, seeing that you have this time off, but your opinion is the only one that matters to me. If anyone can figure this out, it's you. Please call me if you need me.

I look forward to hearing you soon.

Ryan

"Sure, Ryan. Anything for you." Izzie rolled her eyes. He was so manipulative it irritated her to no end. He laid it on so thick, most of the time. And Izzie allowed it because she valued the work she did there. She was a stickler about work ethic; if she could get the job done, she would.

She pulled up the document and looked it over. She already had a full schedule; between assisting the restaurant and trying to keep up with work, she had more than enough to keep her busy. This message from Ryan was only one more thing that would add to the pile. She minimized it and pulled her emails back up -- only two hundred left.

She skimmed through, dismissing the ones that didn't require any further reading. Eventually, she stumbled upon an email about an upcoming office party. It wasn't unusual for them to have a party to invite family members to see what was happening with the company.

Usually, spouses, kids, and other loved ones would take over a park in the city. They would have a potluck. It gave everyone a chance to get to know each other outside of work pressures. Izzie always tried to attend, even when she didn't have a plus one by her side. But the party was scheduled for the following month. She didn't know how long she would be sticking around, but expecting her to return to the city in a month was pushing it.

It shouldn't have been a big deal; it wasn't like the party was a mandatory affair. Yet, most of the staff frowned upon people who didn't make it a point to be there. Izzie had to admit that she was one of those employees. She moved on from the email and tried to push it out of her mind. If she was on vacation, she could do nothing about it. It didn't make sense to make a two-hour trip to a party.

She returned to the document her boss had sent her and pulled up the calculator. She started running the numbers as she saw them laid out. She documented the first total she got, then attempted to run them differently. The number came a few hundred higher. She returned to the previous calculation, worked the numbers, and came across the exact total from the first time. She frowned when she tried it a third time and got the same result.

"Who knows," she grumbled. She returned to the original email and sent her reply. She explained her results and assured her boss that she would look it over again but that the case was one that they couldn't dismiss. They needed to work with that company because they brought in a large percentage of their revenue. Ryan tended to catastrophize, and Izzie questioned if this was one of those times. As she finalized her email, a text message sounded on her phone. She reached across from Harry and grabbed her phone.

> BRANDY
>
> Just thinking about you. Wanna grab drinks?

Shortly after the message came through, a winky emoji followed it. Izzie sighed; this wasn't Brandy's first attempt to get through to Izzie. Right before Izzie left the city, Brandy had worked hard to get back in Izzie's good graces. Brandy was one of those exes who kept coming back. She wasn't any good for Izzie; she was only with her because Izzie was so successful. Izzie wanted to believe they could be together, but it always ended in heartbreak.

Izzie tossed her phone aside and ruffled her fingers back through Harry's head. "Don't worry, Harry. I know my worth and will not settle for anything less. Never again," she whispered, in case her mother could hear her.

Her mind went to Allie. Allie, on the other hand, seemed genuine. The fact that Allie chose an unselfish career was enough to show that she had a heart of gold. "Allie seems like a good person, boy. Doesn't she? And you like her, too, right?"

Izzie sighed and closed her laptop, setting it off to the side.

"Unfortunately, being a good person doesn't necessarily make you the right person. She's so young. What would others think?" She snickered.

She never cared what others thought. That's why she was in the position she was in. "I'm going home soon, so that should be reason enough."

Harry whimpered and looked up at her. She leaned in and kissed the top of his forehead. "You're a good listener, buddy." It just would never work out between them. Izzie had to set her priorities straight, which didn't involve starting a fling while on vacation. Besides, a girl like Allie could never be a fling. She was more confused than ever but had to push through.

CHAPTER SEVEN

HEALTHY INPUT

Allie

Allie taped another picture onto the cabinet and then looked down at the pictures still in her hands. She put a magnet on the refrigerator, then flipped through what was left, looking for the recipe for Vegan burgers she found online the night before.

As she fumbled through them, the papers went flying to the floor. "You klutz," Allie muttered, bending down to gather them.

"Mom? Are you home?" Izzie's voice echoed from the living room. "Where are you?" The words stopped, and Allie looked up to find Izzie in the kitchen.

"You're here?" Izzie bent down and helped Allie to gather the mess Allie had in the kitchen.

"Yep, my work never ends." She stood to her feet. "Thank you!" She grabbed the papers from Izzie's hands.

"I thought you at least had weekends off," Izzie commented, opening the refrigerator and snagging a jug of lemonade.

"Don't tell me my parents have you working so hard that you don't get a day off. I'll have to speak to them about that." Izzie poured a glass of lemonade. "Want some?"

"Nah, no, thank you!" Allie taped another picture to the cabinet. "It goes with the extra responsibilities. This gig isn't solely medical treatment, you know. I was hired to also assist with planning meals for the week. Which is what I'm doing." She held up the page in her hand.

Izzie snickered, taking a sip of her lemonade. "I knew it came with a hefty price tag. But I didn't know what it entailed. My dad is lucky to have you."

Allie was getting more comfortable with Izzie, but she still blushed. Izzie's demeanor didn't appear so cold around Allie. Allie placed the last page on the cupboard and peered at Izzie.

"I would say that I'm just as lucky."

"Gosh, could anyone be sweeter if they tried?" Izzie laughed light-heartedly. Now Allie was blushing. She shrugged and quickly looked away.

"Speaking of my parents, though, where are they?"

"Oh, right." Allie brought her eyes back to Izzie's. "Your mom and your dad took Harry out for a walk."

Izzie's mouth opened. "Is that even safe?" Her words came out like a slap to Allie's face. Allie gawked at her until Izzie sunk back to the counter. "I mean, I imagine that they received the all-clear."

"I wouldn't have allowed them to go if I didn't agree to it," Allie murmured.

"The walk and sun will do some good for him. If he stays cooped up in here for too long, he will go stir crazy."

Allie arched an eyebrow. "Imagine it was you in his shoes. Would you be able to do it?"

"There's no way." Izzie laughed. "And I get it. You're the boss regarding his care. And, as mentioned, he's lucky to have you." Allie smiled. Getting recognition from Izzie was nice. She wasn't used to that and would take the compliments as they came.

"So, what sort of meals do you think?"

Izzie looked around at the cupboards and refrigerator, surveying Allie's selections. She nodded. "I'm impressed. These aren't your typical burger and fries dishes like Stars and Stripes."

"Stars and Stripes are so much more than that," Allie pointed out. "There's a variety of options there, but maybe it wouldn't hurt to add a new style."

"Veggie burgers?" Izzie asked, still looking over the various suggestions.

"Just one option. Your father's health wouldn't allow all the greasy food, so I like to experiment and find new options for him so he does not have to eat the same old stuff. Your mother's garden allows for plenty of other food options. You have to work with what you have."

"That makes sense," Izzie quietly replied. "There's a vegan option at the restaurant, but it might not be something everyone would be interested in. So, maybe incorporating some new food choices on the menu would be helpful."

"And comfort food," Allie suggested. "People want to feel like they're getting a homecooked meal, even when they're at the restaurant."

"Such as..." Izzie turned around, and Allie's eyes dipped to Izzie's lip.

"Um, you have a," Allie pointed, but Izzie's eyes narrowed in.

"I have a what?"

"You have a mustache," Allie bit down on her lip so that she wouldn't laugh. Izzie attempted to lick it off and missed twice.

"Here!" Allie reached up and, with her thumb, wiped it away. Izzie's eyes locked on hers, and Allie felt a noticeable spark between them. She quickly pulled her hand back and smiled. "All gone."

She stepped back. "I don't like bacon, mac and cheese, for starters. Or you mentioned that your mom makes the best pot roast; maybe incorporate that into the menu. Change up the menu, and you could start to see a whole new wave of customers, along with your regulars."

"That's brilliant."

Allie smiled, sinking back even further away from Izzie. She wouldn't have called it brilliant, but Izzie was the professional, and getting affirmation from her was more than enough.

"I think this could work. We could broaden the menu, even keeping originals that are some of the biggest sellers but putting a fresh new spin on it. That would bring along a younger audience."

Her eyes lit up, and Allie stared at her, feeling the excitement that Izzie had in her tone.

"Allie," Izzie breathlessly replied. "We could do this. We could save the restaurant."

We? Allie couldn't dare look away. If Izzie were this excited, she would have to see it through. Allie didn't want them to lose Stars and Stripes. At that moment, she would have done anything to help make it a success.

CHAPTER EIGHT

OVERWHELMED BY EMOTIONS

Izzie

For the first time, Izzie felt hopeful about the restaurant. Maybe all they needed was a new menu for the new generation. She could only give it a shot. There wasn't much she had to lose. For the first time since she returned home, she felt hopeful and excited for the future.

"Are you sure you don't mind me using some of your ideas? What you have here is a great start." Izzie pointed to the various recipes. "Along with the mac and cheese, of course. That might be my favorite."

Allie smirked. "Mine too. But no, I don't mind. Heck, I didn't come up with these recipes. I liked how they looked and thought your parents would, too."

"We might come up with a different flair here or there, too. We can use this to start and grow the restaurant from there."

"I think that sounds perfect." Allie quipped. Izzie was attracted to Allie's agreeable nature, but she kept her distance; she wouldn't want to get any wrong ideas in the heat of the moment.

"It is perfect," Izzie replied. "My father will be so excited to see the restaurant doing so well and that we won't have to sell it. I was afraid of having to sell it before he passed away." The words hit her all at once, sending a sinking weight to the bottom of Izzie's stomach.

Dad might not be here next week, let alone next year. Tears sprung to the backs of her eyes as the thoughts rushed to her. She looked up and met Allie's gaze, and Allie started to reach out to touch her arm. "Excuse me." Izzie rushed through the back door and into the fresh air. She couldn't let Allie or her parents catch her breaking down. They would be back anytime, and she had pulled it together.

She sat down on the steps and breathed fresh air, relieved she had made her getaway.

"Can I sit down?" She looked up and saw Allie there, looking concerned. Izzie nodded, and Allie took a seat, not giving them much room. They sat shoulder to shoulder, letting the quiet settle between them. It was easy to be there.

"You know, Izzie, as a hospice nurse, I've had a lot of experience dealing with grief in families. I'm here to listen if you need it."

Izzie sighed and nodded. She wasn't great at discussing her problems. She preferred to stuff her feelings deep down and ignore them. However, she appreciated that Allie was there and ready to listen. They remained in silence. After several minutes, Izzie shook her head.

"I just don't know," she whispered. "I'm close with both my parents, but there's a special bond between me and my dad. Growing up, he was always in my corner, cheering me on every step of the way. If I wanted to do something that he thought was ridiculous, he never told me because he wanted me to find my footing along the way. Now, he wouldn't be supportive if something was dangerous, but he let me experiment and find my way." Izzie released a heavy sigh. "I just can't believe he'll be gone."

"Your father has lived a good life. What's even more important is the love he feels for you. He has always been proud of you." Izzie tilted her head, and Allie continued.

"He told me so. Before you came back, there weren't too many times he didn't talk about you, and his face lights up when your name crosses his lips."

"Really?" Izzie asked between breaths as the tears started to flow. Allie nodded, and their gaze was locked. The amount of care Allie had for her father was undeniable. They sat so closely together. She saw every detail of

Allie's face. Allie was beautiful, even more than Izzie had even noticed. As they sat there, she wanted to move in for a kiss. From the look on Allie's face, Allie wanted the same. The kitchen scene played out in Izzie's mind, where Allie reached up and wiped her mouth. Kissing Allie would feel right some other time. Getting caught up in the moment would diminish the connection, and she couldn't risk that. "Thank you, Allie." She jumped up and ran back up the stairs and into the house.

"There you are!" Her mother rounded the corner of the kitchen.

Izzie looked away and quickly wiped away her tears. "How was the walk?" she asked, forcing a smile.

"It was great!" her mother said. The back door opened, and Allie walked into the kitchen. "Allie, you did it again," Izzie's mother commented. "These recipes look great."

"They do, don't they?" Izzie said, breaking into the conversation.

Allie smiled, but it appeared weak. "As long as they taste just as good." She picked up her purse. "If you don't need me for anything, I have to be going. I have some errands to run."

Izzie watched as they said goodbye, and Allie only briefly tossed Izzie a look before muttering something incoherent and rushing out of the kitchen. The spark faded. The moment passed. But maybe something could ignite when the moment was right. Izzie just needed to give it more time.

CHAPTER NINE

AT THEIR BECK AND CALL

Allie

Allie moved the dust rag around absentmindedly as she considered the Roth house. She hadn't expected to get caught up with Izzie, but she felt a spark between them twice. It startled her, nearly taking her breath away, but it was there. Allie expected Izzie to pull away. After all, they both needed a reality check. Allie didn't deserve someone like Izzie. It was heart-wrenching to admit, but they'd gotten carried away.

Unlike most people, Izzie's beauty was all-encompassing, not just physical. Her beauty came from within. She had a pure heart. It made her human; she was more than just a commanding presence in a boardroom.

Allie tossed her rag to the side and sat down on the couch. Getting close to the families attached to your hospice patients is inevitable, but somehow, Allie knew this was different.

She didn't like Izzie because she was Richard's daughter. She liked Izzie, even though every fiber in her being begged her to stop. Falling for the patient's family member wasn't professional, but it sure didn't stop Allie. She grabbed her phone and opened up her gallery to a picture where Cheryl had sent her. Izzie sat next to Allie, and Izzie's dad was beside

Izzie's other side. Cheryl took the picture despite them telling her to get in it. It was a cute photo, but Allie zoomed in on Izzie. How could she not have caught feelings? She groaned, tossing her phone to the side.

She has never had these kinds of butterflies. The feeling was overwhelming and left Allie searching for an answer. She was entirely out of her wheelhouse. Allie didn't know relationships! She couldn't even trust her feelings. She grabbed her phone again and typed out a message.

ALLIE

Please tell me I'm a poor judge of character.

MARISSA

You're a poor judge of character.

ALLIE

Thank you!

MARISSA

But why am I supposed to tell you that? Wait. You're trying to talk yourself out of crushing on that woman! Aren't you?

ALLIE

Maybe. Okay, I admit she's charming.

MARISSA

Were your ex-boyfriends charming? Was Susie charming?

ALLIE

First off, nothing ever happened with Susie. Secondly, I thought so at first.

MARISSA

I thought your exes were all assholes.

Allie snickered.

ALLIE

Hey, I'm not arguing with you.

MARISSA

I think this will be good for you! You need a lover who's not some asshole, dude!

Allie sighed, slipping her phone into her pocket. Good for whom? If she acted on her feelings and everything went to shit, then who would be stuck paying the price? She would. She returned to work, determined to ignore her sister's teasing and forget about Izzie.

She could never be the one. It was wrong on so many levels. She busied herself with work, getting lost in cleaning her apartment, when her phone rang. She spotted her mom's number and considered not answering it before feeling overcome with guilt.

"Hello?"

"Where are you?"

Allie rolled her eyes and stopped in place. "I'm cleaning my apartment." She could have considered a thousand snide comments to make.

"Well, you were supposed to pick me up thirty minutes ago."

Allie frowned. "Pick you up from where? I don't have it on my schedule." Allie glanced at her phone, pulling up her calendar to prove that she wasn't losing her mind. But she'd written in bold: *Take Mom to the store.*

"Sorry, Mom," Allie grumbled. "I got busy with cleaning and completely lost track of time. Give me fifteen minutes, and I'll be there."

"You better be because the sale ends tonight." Her harsh tone echoed through the phone. Allie wanted to cry.

"I'm on my way," Allie mumbled. She disconnected the call, grabbed her purse, and hurried out of the apartment. Ten minutes later, Allie pulled up in front of the house, where her mom was waiting on the porch. She watched her as she limped slowly toward the car, anticipating her mom's complaints.

"I can't believe you forgot," her mother replied, climbing into the front seat. "Clearly, there are more important things on your mind than your mother nowadays."

Allie sighed. "That's not true. I'm sorry that the time got the better of me, but I had to clean my apartment."

The rest of the ride was silent. Her mom didn't respond to her excuse. Allie could hear her mom's foot slightly tapping impatiently. Allie didn't dare to look in her direction, which might have left them with another awkward conversation.

They reached the store. Even though her mom's walk was considerably slower than it once was, she was still two steps in front of Allie. Allie didn't mind. It gave her time to observe whoever else was stuck at the store on a Saturday night.

"I'm done," her mom said.

Allie glanced towards the cart. It wasn't even half full; she didn't have to do this tonight. Yet, she shrugged it off and followed her mom to the cashier. Allie helped pile the things on the conveyor belt and watched aimlessly as her mother dug through her wallet, looking for the amount the cashier had muttered.

"I'm short," she said, breaking into Allie's thoughts.

"How much?" Allie attempted to grumble while maintaining a calm expression. Nothing new, just a different night.

"Twenty-three dollars," her mom added.

"And seven cents," the cashier replied. The cashier tilted her head, giving Allie a discouraging look. Allie grimaced, not sure how this was her fault. Allie reached into her pocket and handed her mom some cash. She sifted through her pocket until she had it down to the last penny.

"Thank you!"

Allie looked to her mom, who never once even acknowledged the payment. Allie shrugged and started grabbing the bags from the counter. She left them on her wrists and maneuvered the cart back to the corral at the front of the store.

Her mom hesitated at the exit, and Allie stopped and tossed a look over her shoulder. "Are you ready? Or did you forget something?"

Her mom shook her head, and her facial expression clouded over. Allie turned to see what had caught her mom's attention. Two women stood laughing and holding hands as they headed toward the store entrance.

"Unbelievable," her mother mumbled. "I can't believe they feel they need to flaunt that sort of behavior. There are children here."

Allie frowned. The couple looked happy, as happy as Allie wished she could be. Her mother looked disgusted, squashing that dream before it could form.

CHAPTER TEN

STARS AND STRIPES

Izzie

L izzie was flooded with memories the moment she stepped into Stars and Stripes. The smells always hit her as she first stepped out of her car. Today, the restaurant was deserted. In the past couple of years, the restaurant's reputation has become downright dismal. Stars and Stripes transformed from a place of celebration to a place where people would serve their divorce papers with a side of fries.

Izzie pulled her phone out of her pocket and began taking pictures from one corner to the next. She hesitated and smiled as she snapped photos of the garden room, where she once celebrated her high school graduation. That night, the restaurant was packed. Every table was full of graduates brimming with hope for the future. She snapped a couple more photos and longed to restore the restaurant to its former glory.

A man entered the restaurant, and Izzie looked around. There wasn't a hostess in sight to greet him. He nodded in Izzie's direction. Izzie gave a bright smile and approached him. "Hello, just one of you?" she asked.

"There will be two." He gave a weak smile, and Izzie watched as his eyes clouded. Stress was radiating off of him like body heat. She grabbed two menus and motioned for him to follow her. She tossed a look over her shoulder. He followed her without making eye contact.

"Are you grabbing lunch with a friend today?" she asked, keeping her voice chipper.

"I wish," he mumbled. Izzie stopped at a table and placed the menus as the man slid into the booth. "Let's just say there's no such thing as a free lunch." He rolled his eyes.

"Lunch with the boss is never a good sign." His cheeks flushed. "But I'm a grown-ass man. If I get fired, so be it."

Izzie slowly nodded, then frowned. What kind of boss would bring his employee to a restaurant to reprimand him?

"Who knows? It might be something completely different."

He shook his head. "I know the signs," he grumbled. He grabbed the menu, stared at it, and tossed it aside. "Thirty years I gave that company. Thirty. And it's all going to end like this?" His words grew sharp.

Izzie didn't try to shy away from it. She understood. The corporate world was ruthless. Having someone think they were better than you was something she had to live with nearly every day.

"Toby..." Izzie turned and saw an older man standing behind her, staring at the table, glaring in their direction.

"Your server will be right with you," Izzie mumbled, spinning on her heel and hurrying to the kitchen. She burst through the doors, where Jess was gawking at her phone.

She looked up, eyes wide. "Izzie! I didn't know you were here." She slipped her phone back into her pocket.

Clearly. "Where's my Mom? Thought she was coming in today."

"She had to run out and get some groceries." Jess slowly nodded. "Who's the hostess today?"

"Kara," Jess replied, still leaning against the counter. "She's out taking a smoke break."

"Figures," Izzie mumbled. Jess arched an eyebrow but said nothing.

"Customers are waiting. Get to it," Izzie prompted.

"Of course." Jess left the kitchen, and Izzie glanced towards the back-door. She waited for five minutes before peeking outside, where she saw Kara making out with one of the other servers.

Kara was eighteen, while the guy she was kissing looked to be in his late twenties, possibly early thirties. Izzie burst out the back door, startling them both. She turned and then scoffed. Izzie narrowed her brows.

"Hey," Kara muttered before turning back to the guy.

Izzie cleared her throat. "Someone needs to be manning the hostess station at all times."

Kara chuckled and turned to face Izzie, her gaze dropping. "Oh. You're serious."

Izzie crossed her arms and was seconds away from tapping her phone. Didn't she pull off the attitude of how serious she was? "We have customers, and if no one is there to greet them, they don't feel welcomed. It's a known fact. Say goodbye and get back to work." She turned on her heel and stormed back into the kitchen.

Izzie waited in the kitchen until Kara finally entered the building. Kara shot her a look and started to walk past her.

"A little old for you, don't you think?"

Kara snickered and turned to face her.

"What are you, my mother?" The words came out sharper than Izzie expected, and Kara sighed. "I've gotten enough negativity from her. I'm fine, thanks."

"You're at a job," Izzie began. "That means you devote 100% of your time and energy to that job. You can do what you please when you leave, but for the next few hours of your shift, you don't step away from the hostess stand, got it?"

Kara rolled her eyes. "I work for the Roths. You're here on vacation for what, two weeks? What makes you think you can march in here and boss me around?" Kara spat.

Izzie stared at her, unsure of who would break first. Jess returned to the kitchen and took the order to the kitchen staff. Izzie backed up.

"I'm still a Roth. Be careful what you say. Get back to work," Izzie ordered.

A slight look of fear crossed Kara's stare before she shrugged and walked away. Izzie stared at the swinging door, the confrontation heavy in her mind. The staff didn't appreciate their job, and they certainly didn't fear they would lose it.

Izzie left the kitchen and glanced around the restaurant. So many good times filled the restaurant, but now it was a shell of the place it once was. The seafoam green paint was peeling; stuffing popped out of the booths, and the table tops were scratched. Izzie was excited at the thought of restoring Stars and Stripes. She appreciated the job she had worked so hard to secure, but her heart, in that moment, was with Stars and Stripes. Stars and Stripes meant so much to her family, the people who mattered to her most.

IZZIE SNAPPED A FEW MORE PICTURES, THEN HESITATED IN front of the restaurant. The restaurant was empty, except for the staff members and chefs who were cleaning.

Stars and Stripes had been begging for a makeover for nearly twenty years; the menu was equally antiquated. Izzie was determined to transform Stars and Stripes if it was the last thing she did.

The door to the kitchen opened, and she saw her mother. She gave Izzie a bright smile and waved for her to come over. Izzie pocketed her phone again and went to the kitchen.

"I heard you were here. Wanna help me grab some groceries from the car."

"Sure, Mom," now was the time to corner her mom about re-vamping Stars and Stripes. When they stepped outside, the warm air washed over Izzie.

"How long have you been here?" Her mom asked, opening the back of her SUV.

"Just under two hours." Izzie held onto the vehicle and took a deep breath. "I think we need to talk."

Her mom dropped the bag she had and turned to Izzie. She arched an eyebrow. "Sounds serious. Are you about to tell me about the birds and the bees again?" she joked, recalling the time twelve-year-old Izzie cornered her parents and gave them a sex talk.

Izzie laughed. "Well, it's serious, but it's an easy fix." She paused. "Did you know Kara has an older boyfriend?"

Her mom shrugged. "Yeah, but not really any of my business. She's not my child."

"I get that, but it's impacting her work performance. She was out back making out with the guy in this very spot a couple of hours earlier." Izzie rolled her eyes. "You can't be soft on these teens, or they'll run this restaurant into the ground." *As if they haven't already.*

"Nonsense." Her mom laughed. "We're not in that much trouble." She reached up and touched Izzie's arm. "Everything will all work out. You're here." She winked and turned back to the groceries.

For a few minutes, Izzie stood there, dumbfounded that her mom couldn't see the gravity of the situation. She grabbed a few bags and followed her mom back into the kitchen. When they finished, she turned to her.

"I know you don't want to believe that things are bad, but even if they weren't, you can always improve. Just don't let these employees take advantage of you."

"I hear ya." Her mom smiled, and Izzie wanted to believe she did.

"I'm going to head out of here. I'll see you later." She kissed her mom on the cheek and then left through the door and into the restaurant.

On the way to the front door, she grabbed a menu and spotted Kara staring at her from the other side of the restaurant. She ignored her and kept walking. For some things to change, she had to work at making it happen. She got in her car and headed towards the house.

Once she arrived, she parked in the driveway so she didn't block Allie from leaving. Walking to the front door, she remembered the intense attraction that seemed to have quickly developed between them. It wasn't just Allie's curves that intrigued Izzie; it was her sweetness and how close she had gotten to her parents. Izzie longed to get to know her better.

Izzie entered the house, and she heard. "Breathe, Richard. Just take an even breath. You're going to be okay."

Izzie rushed into the living room. "What happened?" she asked, her heart caving as she saw Allie leaning toward her father, her hand increasing the oxygen flow on his tank.

"One more even breath, don't force it." Allie's soothing tone echoed through the room. "You're going to be just fine, Richard." Izzie moved closer and saw her dad's face was as white as a sheet. The oxygen helped regulate his breathing.

"There, just like that," Allie said, keeping her tone even and focusing on Richard.

"Dad," Izzie whispered, reaching out to grab his hand. He gave a slight squeeze, and Izzie sighed. Allie continued to fix the oxygen machine and then turned to Izzie.

"There was just a brief stint where your father struggled to breathe, but we controlled it." She reached up and touched Izzie's arm gently.

"No worries." Her genuine smile left Izzie dumbstruck.

When she came home and saw her father struggling, her mind immediately went to the worst-case scenario, but Allie didn't even seem shaken.

"I just thought..." Izzie whispered. She looked over, and her father had his eyes closed. He looked more at peace, and that relaxed her. "There could be a time that I come here, and he's...."

"Shhhhh," Allie cooed. "You can't think like that. There are always good and bad days for everyone, especially my patients. But all is well. That's what you need to hold onto." She turned and went to a chart, then sat down and quickly took notes. Izzie studied her. It shocked her how much she liked Allie. But her father wasn't going to get better. He would only rapidly deteriorate, then where would that leave them? Allie would have no reason to come around, and Izzie would be back to her own life. A rock plummeted into her gut. Yet, the alternative seemed far worse.

CHAPTER ELEVEN

MENU ENHANCEMENT

Allie

Allie placed the dishes into the sink and reached for a towel. "Nonsense," Cheryl ordered. "You were our guest! The dishes can wait. Richard and I are going to go out for a breath of fresh air. I'd say we need it after today."

Allie nodded in agreement. It was scary watching Richard struggle to breathe, but his vitals were regulated. The oxygen was doing its job, so a little time outside would only help him.

"Do you need help before I go?" Allie asked. "I can help you with the wheelchair and oxygen tank." Cheryl quickly brushed away Allie's concerns, and Allie watched as she wheeled her husband and the tank with ease. Allie smiled and went to reach for the door, but Cheryl propped it open with her foot.

"Your mom's a strong one," Allie said, turning to Izzie.

Izzie snickered. "She's not the only one. I wish she'd be that strong when it came to handling her staff, but that's something entirely different." She frowned. "So, you're leaving?"

Allie shrugged. "No reason to stick around, is there?" She held onto that glimmer of hope that Izzie would give some sign that she just wanted her there, mirroring Allie's attraction.

"Well, I thought we could sit down and review the menu. We can talk about what we want to change. I have some ideas," Izzie shrugged. "You are the one that sort of put this idea in my head, so it wouldn't feel right if you weren't there every step of the way."

Allie blushed. That was almost the invitation Allie wanted. "If you can't stick around, though. I get it. It's not like your responsibilities continue after hours."

"No, I'm good with sticking around. I don't have any other plans."

Izzie's smile brightened. Her smile took Allie aback. Her cheeks were red, and her eyes were glowing. Once again, Allie felt a hint of a spark.

They entered the living room, where Izzie took over the couch and coffee table. She reached for the menu and held it up.

"This is the current menu, and these are all the new and improved menu ideas. Have a seat." Allie didn't hesitate to sit beside her and peer over her shoulder as Izzie glanced at the menu.

She groaned. "Some of these recipes are older than I am." She laughed and shrugged.

"Some will have to stay for sentimental reasons. But there are a lot of things we can improve. And items like this..." She pointed to the menu. "Americana Greens." She scoffed. "That's just a side salad. I checked our sales, and we've only sold one in the last year. Why go with something plain when you have all this variety."

Allie laughed. She bit down on her lip when Izzie tilted her head. "You say once in the last year? I would say it was me that bought it."

Izzie started laughing, shaking her head. "You're kidding."

"In my defense," Allie started. "I felt like I was coming down with a flu bug, and everything seemed to make me want to vomit, so I opted for something plain."

Izzie snickered. "Okay, I forgive you. But most people are most likely to indulge when they come to the restaurant. If they are in the mood for a salad, they'll grab the All-American Garden. You can use a ton of extra add-ons, like eggs, chicken, avocado," Izzie shrugged.

"The list is endless. No one," she paused, "typically, will go for something so simple."

"Unless they're sick," Allie pointed out.

Izzie tossed back and laughed. "Valid point. But I would suggest if you're sick, stay in bed."

Allie shrugged. Point taken, but there had to be a compromise between taking the salad away altogether and leaving it there for anyone who wanted something plain.

"How about a compromise?"

Izzie leaned back on the couch. "I'm listening."

"Keep the American Greens; now you can add any extras. If you want the American Greens, add in some chicken. Of course. Have them add as many proteins as they want: chicken taco meat. Whatever you want, we will do it, and all made to order."

"But, Allie," Izzie started. "So basically, you're talking about a small version of the All-American Garden." She laughed. "Why keep it? Instead, we can offer two sizes of the All-American. Win/win."

"Au contraire Allie flipped the paper around and grinned. "With the All-American Garden, you get various options in your dressings. There are over fifty varieties, isn't that correct?"

"You've done your research." Izzie gave a gracious smile, and Allie looked down at the recipe in her hand, feeling the warmth of her cheeks once again igniting.

"My point is, with the American Greens, we could give it a dressing that you can only get with this salad."

"Peach Mango? Do you really think someone would come to the restaurant wanting a Peach Mango Vinaigrette on the American Greens?"

"You really shouldn't knock it until you've tried it."

"And you have?" Izzie asked.

"One of my favorites." Allie waved the recipe in her hand. "And it's easy to make. I'll whip a batch, and you'll find it's one of the best."

"And if someone wants to add this dressing to another salad?" Izzie snickered. "What would be the response to that."

"It will cost extra because it is made for the American Greens." Allie shrugged. "I mean, we're not going to deprive them of it; they'll just have to spend a little more."

Allie's eyes widened. "You could bottle this up for resale at the counter. You have to admit, Izzie. It's not a horrible idea."

Izzie shook her head, an amused expression on her face. Allie moved a piece of hair behind her ear, looking down as her cheeks flushed again.

"What?"

"You're just full of surprises, aren't you?" Allie looked up and met Izzie's gaze, a smile deepening on Izzie's lips. That moment left Allie practically weak in the knees, and she felt like everything might work out.

"So, we agree that the loaded tacos are a bad idea." Izzie held up the recipes and tilted her head. Allie glanced between one recipe and the other, then nodded.

"I mean, I've never met a person that doesn't like a taco, but I don't think it's classy enough, do you? We want to keep Stars and Stripes with the same atmosphere, adding some unique dishes to spice the place back up."

Izzie turned the recipe around and glanced at it. She gave a slow nod but then hesitated. "Unless..." She continued to stare, and Allie could practically see the wheels turning in her head. They had been working on the menu for nearly two hours now. She was starting to intuit Izzie's likes and dislikes.

Amazingly, it felt like they were both on the same wavelength. They both added new ingredients and ideas to the recipes, leaving the other either eager for the suggestion or feeling less than stellar. But overall, they were on the same page every step of the way. "What if we do this? Give me your thoughts."

"I'm intrigued," Allie commented. Izzie's mother had already gone to bed, her dad was in his bed in the living room, and they had moved their operation to the kitchen table. It felt even more intimate, especially when Izzie moved her chair closer to Allie, only ten minutes in.

"Loaded Taco in a bowl." Allie arched an eyebrow. "Hear me out: same ingredients but layers in a bowl. You can choose your bowl, as well. From a flaky crust to a soft outer shell. On a diet, no worries, we'll pile it up in a regular bowl, and you get the same great taste without the breading."

Allie leaned back in her chair and considered it. Her eyes shifted away from Izzie's as she let the idea sift through her mind.

"You hate it." Izzie huffed and pushed the recipe away.

"No!" Allie reached out, and her hand brushed against Izzie's. Izzie quickly pulled back, and their eyes locked. As they sat there staring at one another, Allie wanted to lean in and go for a kiss. Fear and doubt kept her frozen in place. She shook her head.

"I don't hate the idea. In fact, I thought that Peach Mango Vinaigrette would go great with that. See, we're selling that already." She beamed, and Izzie chuckled.

"I think we have a winner." Izzie's words came out barely above a whisper.

"I'd say we do," Allie whispered back.

Izzie reached up and brushed a strand of hair that had fallen in front of Allie's eyes. She smiled and moved in. Allie braced herself, not wanting to faint. But just as Izzie was about to kiss her, Izzie's phone rang.

Allie fell back in her chair, defeated. Izzie grabbed her phone. "This is Izzie."

Allie looked down at the recipes sprawled out in front of them, hoping that her cheeks wouldn't betray her and show Izzie how much she longed for them to get back into the moment.

"I am telling you that we have to go in strong. If we don't, we can kiss this contract goodbye. I'm not about to sit back and watch that happen."

Allie looked up, enthralled by Izzie's take-charge attitude. She was confident and poised. It was thrilling to watch Izzie in her element. Seeing Izzie take charge only solidified her attraction; she had to make this happen.

CHAPTER TWELVE

PEACH MANGO VINAIGRETTE

Izzie

Izzie's dad was lying in the hospital bed, staring out the window, when Izzie walked into the living room. "Hey, Dad." He turned and smiled as she walked over and kissed him. "How's it going?" she whispered.

"Just thinking. Not much else I can do." He leaned back, with his head hitting the pillow.

When she left the house, he was still sleeping. She had noticed that his energy decreased as the days progressed. It gutted her. Anyone could see his time was running out. Izzie wanted to hold onto him for as long as possible.

"I'm good. Just a little tired, but nothing I can't overcome." The bright smile on his face was equally gutting. At least he remained so strong and optimistic. She could do the same. She winced; she always was the one who could control everything, but cancer was one thing she had no control over, and it killed her.

She squeezed his shoulder and stepped back. "The color is good in your cheeks, so just hang in there." He gave a wide smile. "Where's Allie?"

His smile deepened. "Every time we talk, you want to talk about

Allie." He winked at her, causing her to blush and look away. "You two seem to be getting along quite nicely."

Izzie rolled her eyes, even though there was an unmistakable grin that was hard to hide. "Don't be silly. She's helping with the restaurant."

"That's all?" Again, a wink.

That's all it should be. Izzie sighed. "And where is she?"

"In the kitchen."

"Thank you!" She gave him another kiss and then hurried to the kitchen. She hesitated before rounding the corner but then entered.

"Hey, Allie." she squeaked, her voice a full octave higher than usual.

"Hey. Just whipping up a salad for your dad."

"American Greens?" Izzie teased. Allie looked over her shoulder and grinned. They had a lovely time planning out the menu. They were in sync the entire time, which encouraged Izzie to go in for a kiss.

Unfortunately, her work had other ideas, and the mood had shifted considerably. She didn't know what the next few weeks would bring, but everyone deserved a little fun.

"Apparently, all this needs is...."

"Peach Mango Vinaigrette," Allie commented. "You wouldn't be disappointed, but do we have the ingredients? That's the question."

"My mom has a garden," Izzie pointed out, which caused Allie to laugh.

"Does your mom grow fruit?" She arched an eyebrow.

Izzie snickered. The chemistry between them was palpable, and no one could deny it.

"I never said I was the chef, but I imagine we'll find something around here. Doesn't hurt to look."

Five minutes later, Allie shook her head. "I can't believe you had everything needed for this dressing. Typically, I have to make it to the store at least twice because I forget something the first time around."

Izzie smirked. Allie didn't need to know that she had gone to three stores that morning to ensure she had everything they needed. She didn't think she would need everything today, but sometimes the universe had other plans.

Izzie grabbed two aprons from the cupboard, and they put them on.

She wasn't much of a chef, but she'd cook a five-course meal if it meant she could spend time with Allie.

"I'll let you lead," Izzie added. "After all, you've already made it before."

"Understandable. Besides, I tend to get relatively possessive in the kitchen."

"Just the kitchen?" Izzie asked. Allie's cheeks turned several shades of red, and Izzie clamped down on her tongue, immediately knowing how that sounded. "You're so sweet that I can't imagine you being possessive about anything."

Allie quickly looked away. "Guess when it's something that matters...." Her words trailed off, and Izzie relaxed, grateful that any tension diffused. Allie cleared her throat. "This should be fun."

She began whipping up the ingredients while Izzie stood back and watched. She wasn't wrong; she liked to take charge, but Izzie wouldn't deter her from that. Not when it felt like she was in her element.

"So, I've been thinking about other changes to the restaurant. Besides the menu, I mean."

"Oh yeah?" Allie asked. "Like what?"

"Well, I would like to give the place a new coat of paint. It needs it. Desperately, in fact."

"Yeah, that would be nice," Allie added.

"And I thought it'd be cool to hire a muralist to paint some scene on the walls." Izzie shrugged. "It's just a suggestion, but I see it in a bunch of restaurants around town."

"Can you afford that?" Allie looked over to Izzie, and Izzie considered the question. Not entirely, but if you wanted to make changes, you had to go big. Allie's sweet smile brightened her whole face.

"I always say that dreams are only worth achieving if you have to work hard on them." She shrugged. "Besides, I would love to give it the feel of an upscale restaurant with a small-town atmosphere."

"Then, I think you'll achieve it." She grinned again, and her beauty stunned Izzie

"Well, and I'd thought I'd had some plants. You know, cheer up the place." She continued, despite wanting to spend all day staring at Allie.

"Well, since we're discussing it," Allie softly commented. "I was thinking maybe LED lights strung all around the inside. If we do it right, they'll look like stars. It was just a thought, but what do you think?"

Izzie nodded. "I like the idea." She thought it was nice that Allie threw in some of her feedback. It made it feel like they were collaborating.

Allie grinned. "Looks like it's all figured out."

Izzie considered that. She didn't have everything figured out, but this was a start. "I want a picture of you."

Allie frowned. "You can't be serious. I'm a mess."

Izzie laughed. "You're beautiful."

That caused Allie's jaw to drop, and Izzie cringed. She hadn't planned on dropping that out there, and Allie's expression said everything. Izzie swallowed the lump that had quickly formed in her throat.

"Come on, Allie. I can't be the first person that's ever told you that." She snickered, brushing it off. "You look fine. Besides, I want to document the restoration of Stars and Stripes. Like it or not, you're a part of that."

"Fine." Harry wandered into the kitchen, and Allie knelt next to him, wrapping her arms around his neck. Izzie shook her head but smiled and snapped several pictures of them in their embrace.

"Now, may I get back to work?" She stood up and turned back to the counter.

"Of course. I'm going to grab a notebook so I don't forget any of these ideas."

"By the time you're back, I'll have a sample for you to try. Don't be long."

Izzie hurried out of the kitchen and up the stairs. She reached her room and pulled out her phone to stare at the pictures. She groaned and quickly typed out a message.

IZZIE

Too good to be true, right?

She sent the picture and began pacing, waiting for Mae's response, a response that was too unbearable to wait for. Just because someone seemed genuine didn't make them such.

MAE

I don't think she looks like your type.

522

Izzie frowned. Well, that was easy enough to push out of. She started to leave when another text message dinged.

> MAE
>
> Which is why I think you should consider it.
> What do you have to lose?

She ended it with a winky emoji, and Izzie sighed. She had everything to lose if it didn't work out between them, and with her returning to work, how could it?

She went back to the kitchen, and Allie turned around. She dropped her gaze to Izzie's hands. "Where's your notebook?"

Izzie looked down and shifted in place. "I knew there was a reason I went upstairs."

Allie laughed and shook her head. "Before you rush off again, have a taste." Allie dipped a spoon into a bowl and carefully stepped closer to Izzie. She held it to Izzie's lips, and Izzie locked gazes. Izzie tasted it from the spoon, tasting the bright citrus of the mango.

"What do you think?" Allie asked.

"The best dressing I've ever had." Like a schoolgirl, Allie clapped her hands together and turned back to the dressing.

"Exactly what I wanted to hear."

Izzie continued to watch her, mesmerized by her every move and wondering how long she could watch from afar before she gave in to her desires and went with it.

CHAPTER THIRTEEN

DINNER WITH PARENTS

Allie

Allie didn't know why she was driving to her parent's place. She usually only showed up when they wanted something, which was often. Maybe it was because the Roths showed her what it was like to be in a loving family, a stark contrast to her own.

She stared at the house, convincing herself to go home. Instead, she wandered up to the front door and knocked.

It was her dad, Nelson, who answered. "Allie? What are you doing here? Did we know you'd be here?"

"Do I need a reason to see my parents?" Allie tilted her head, anxiously awaiting his response.

He shrugged. "Not entirely, but we just ordered Chinese a couple of minutes ago."

"That's alright, Dad. I don't need anything." She shuffled from one foot to another."

"We could spare an eggroll." She looked past her dad to her mom, who hobbled into the foyer. Allie gave a weak smile.

"That would be great. Thanks." The smile faded when both her parents turned their back toward her and led the way into the dining room. Allie grabbed the nearest seat and waited for her parents to sit down.

Her dad held out the box for her, and she grabbed one. "Thank you!"

She took a bite and looked around the table. Awkwardness saturated the room. Allie anxiously nibbled on an egg roll.

"Want a beer?" her dad asked.

"No, thank you," Allie mumbled. She could have used water, though. But she said nothing.

"Before you stopped by," her father started, taking a sip of his beer. "I was talking to your mom about how damn frustrating it is. Insurance companies and all. They milk you for all you have, and when you're done paying their way, they milk you for more."

He shook his head. "Don't even get me started on having to cart your mom to her appointments."

"Nelson," Sandra began. "Maybe it would have been best for everyone if I just would have died. I wouldn't be this burden." Her mother's voice went up a few notches.

"Mom, don't say that," Allie scolded.

She sighed. "Well, your dad goes on and on about taking me to appointments like it's his job. Does he think I want to be this invalid?" She spoke to Allie like she was the only one in the room. Allie glanced between her parents, with her Dad slamming his hands against the table, shaking it.

"I'm just frustrated and tired," he cried. "The insurance company is all about corporate greed, aching to screw us over."

"Dad, that's not fair. I'm sure they aren't trying to screw anyone over. They have to make their money somehow."

He shook his head. "They have made their money and then some." He shot Allie a look. "And what about you?" Allie popped the last bite of her egg roll into her mouth and frowned.

"What about me?"

"Maybe I wouldn't feel the strain if you could help out a bit. It isn't just my responsibility. Your sister is off to school, so she can't help, but you're in town. You have no excuse."

Allie's mouth dropped. She stared at both her parents, but neither one made a move to suggest that he was only blowing smoke. She closed her mouth and looked down at the table, attempting to find the right words.

"Just a little more time goes a long way," he continued.

"When she has her appointments, I'm at work," she explained.

"There's always some excuse," he mumbled.

Allie sighed. "Maybe I can help by making calls to the insurance company or even giving you guys some money. It could be some help."

None of this was her fault, and if he needed to take it out on her, she would accept that. She already helped as much as she could; she hoped they would move on from the subject.

"Money won't give me back my time, will it? You should make a little more effort. Don't you have vacation time that you can take? We need all the help we can get."

"Dad, I couldn't possibly..." she began.

"So, there's something more important than your mom, I see."

"That's not fair." Allie stood up from the table. "I have a dying patient and can't just abandon him." She stared at her dad, unsure where the push-back came from, but in her head, she could picture Izzie and Izzie would never put up with getting bullied and guilted into doing something she knew wasn't right.

"Just sit down," her mother calmly stated. Allie glanced at her. The guilt returned, and she sat at the table.

"I'm sorry that I can't be more involved when taking Mom to appointments. If I were free, then I would do it." *And when I'm free, I do it.* "Calls and money are all I can do now until my schedule frees up."

He continued to drink his beer, and nothing was said on the subject.

"Always something more important," he grumbled. Allie frowned. *Is he right?* It felt like she was always at her parents' beck and call, but maybe not.

"So, Allie, what have you been up to lately?" Her mother asked. Whether it was to be nosey or change the subject, Allie didn't care.

"When I'm not working, of course, I've been helping a friend with some new recipes for a restaurant. She loves my cooking. It's been a great time." She looked down so her parents could see her red cheeks.

Her dad snickered, which caused Allie to look in his direction. "I remember when you made French toast and nearly burned the house down."

"Dad, I was four," Allie argued.

"Or when you burnt the chicken in your Home Ec class. Three kids went home sick, isn't that, right?"

Allie sighed. "It was only two, and there was no proof it was the chicken."

"You aren't going to poison the customers, right?" her dad continued. "Remind us never to darken the doorstep of that place."

"Ha ha, you both are hysterical. Do tell me more." She laughed, but their banter back and forth rang heavy in the room. Would it kill them to congratulate her? She didn't know why she was so surprised. When her boyfriend saw her cooking, he would always make excuses, saying that he needed to go home or that he would prefer they go out to eat. He wasn't any more supportive than her parents; it was no wonder she was drawn to Izzie.

At least with Izzie, she didn't have to worry about questioning herself. She could live in the moment. But at that moment, she wondered why she drove to her parent's place, expecting them to change when they never would.

Meet me at Stars and Stripes after closing. I have a surprise for you. You can come to the employee entrance. When the text came through, she was grateful to have an escape. She couldn't wait to get out of there, but driving to the restaurant, she grew apprehensive; what was this surprise? Why would Izzie even consider being with someone like her? Allie turned into the parking lot. It was empty. Allie drove down the small back alley. Izzie's car was the other one there.

She was nervous walking up to the door. She wouldn't be great company, not after the grueling encounter with her parents. Allie went to the door and tried the knob, but it was locked. She tapped on the door, then waited. It was pitch black, and every sound made her jump. Izzie had invited her here, so where was she?

She knocked again, this time a little louder. The door swung open, and Izzie stood there with a beautiful smile that made Allie blush.

"You look..." Allie started. She glanced over Izzie's outfit. Izzie wore a black dress with a white sash around her waist. The skirt appeared just above her knees. The sleeves hung off her shoulder. She looked classy, elegant, and beautiful.

"Or rather, I must look a mess." Allie looked down at her jeans and t-shirt. She had the same thing on that she wore to the Roth home to fulfill her nursing duties. "I didn't realize this was formal attire."

"Don't be silly." Izzie laughed. "You look exquisite."

"Sure, I do," Allie mumbled, entering the kitchen. If Izzie had warned her, she would have been able to adjust her outfit accordingly. But why? Why was Izzie all dressed up, and why did she summon Allie in the first place? There had to be a logical explanation.

"So, I imagine you're wondering why you're here."

Allie gave a weak smile. The thought had crossed her mind once or twice. "I'm intrigued." Even though she said one thing, her mind was a mess of nerves.

Izzie grabbed her hand and pulled her towards the door that led to the dining area. "Close your eyes," she whispered.

Allie giggled lightly. "Is that necessary?"

Izzie looked over her shoulder. "Trust me." Allie closed her eyes. The minute she did, her parent's words came rushing back. *You have no excuse why you don't help out more. Remember the time you burned the chicken?* She cringed. Her stomach clenched. "Are they closed?"

"Yes," Allie bit down on her lip. She needed to be in the zone to appreciate any surprise that Izzie had for her, but her mind was racing, lost in a different place. Izzie helped her through the door and then stopped.

"You can open them." Allie opened her eyes, and her mouth was agape. The lights were dimmed, and LED lights cascaded around the dining area.

"Wow!" Allie gasped.

"Is this what you had in mind?" Izzie asked. When Allie turned to her, she was glowing, with a smile on her face.

"I know you might have wanted to help, but I couldn't keep from doing it. I wanted you to be surprised."

"I am," Allie replied. Tears stung the back of her eyes, and she quickly looked around the restaurant. It was glowing almost as much as Izzie was staring back at her. A lump formed promptly in her throat, and she shook her head. She didn't deserve this. She didn't deserve any of it.

"I can't believe you did all this," she softly replied. "It's amazing."

Her cheeks warmed considerably. "And so are you." The words flooded out of her. Izzie looked around the room. Allie continued to feel that knot deep in her gut, letting her insecurities get the best of her.

CHAPTER FOURTEEN

SOMETHING'S OFF

Izzie

"So, since it's the garden room, I figured it could use some plants," Izzie looked over at Allie.

Allie nodded, but her eyes were blank, just as she had done every time Izzie pointed out something she was going to change or add to the restaurant. From the moment Allie arrived, she seemed unusually preoccupied.

Izzie couldn't tell if she was being paranoid or if Allie wasn't interested.

Allie glanced at Izzie as Izzie stared, then gave a more eager nod. "Sounds great!" She smiled briefly, then let the smile fade. Izzie quickly turned away as she frowned. It wasn't like Allie. She wanted to ask Allie if everything was alright, but she didn't want to make Allie uncomfortable.

The more she got to know Allie, the more appreciative she became.

Allie was nothing like her exes. Perhaps it was because Allie was younger, maintaining a sense of youthful optimism. Either way, Allie was someone Izzie wanted to get to know on a more intimate level. Izzie thought it was impossible to get to know Allie and not fall for her, but she maintained a realistic level of skepticism. Allie's job was to cultivate trust between herself, her patients, and their families. What if Allie only saw her as her patient's daughter?

"It all sounds great, Izzie." Allie turned to Izzie. "I can tell you're going to whip this place into shape."

Izzie smiled and reached for Allie's hand again. "Correction...we are."

Allie nodded slightly, then looked away. Izzie frowned. Something was on Allie's mind, and Izzie was determined to get her to open up.

"There's no way I would have been able to implement these changes without you."

Allie snickered. "I highly doubt that. I'm glad to help, but I'm sure you would have gotten there eventually."

Allie walked off, leaving Izzie to stand, gawking in her direction. Izzie left the Garden room and found Allie standing in the center of the restaurant. Izzie pointed to the wall where Allie faced. "That's where I want to put the mural. I think we can incorporate different aspects of the town."

Allie snickered, then looked over her shoulder. "But you're going back to the big city, right?" Izzie's face fell.

"I'm sorry," Allie began. "It's none of my business."

"That's not true, though, is it?" Izzie asked. Allie's brows furrowed. "We've gotten to know each other quite well. You have every right to know when I'm going back."

Allie shrugged nonchalantly. "You only have to tell me what you want to tell me." She turned away, and Izzie moved in closer to her. She had no definite date for her departure. It was inevitable, but the longer she stayed there, the harder it became to fathom.

"What are your hobbies, Allie?" Allie turned and tilted her head. "Likes, dislikes, annoyances," Izzie smiled. "Things like that. Surely, you have some. Everyone does."

Allie wrinkled her brow in concentration before answering, "Singing in the car and dancing. Mushrooms. Shady people."

Izzie laughed. "You like shady people?"

Allie laughed, her face softening for the first time that night. "Annoyances. I like to sing in the car and dance. I dislike Mushrooms, and shady people are annoying."

"I see," Izzie turned away from her and walked over to a stereo.

"What are you doing?" Allie asked.

Izzie smiled and turned on the radio until a slow ballad came on. She turned around and moved in closer to Allie. "It's not a car, but feel free to sing. I hate mushrooms, as well. And I don't see any shady people around."

"That only leaves one thing on the list," Allie replied, her words barely above a whisper.

"Dance with me, Allie." Izzie held out her hand, and Allie looked down at her fingers, then back up to meet Izzie's gaze. Allie reached for her hand, and Izzie pulled her closer. They slowly swayed back and forth to the music with their eyes locked. There was still some tension there, but Allie smiled sweetly, which was all Izzie wanted.

"I like to dance, but it doesn't mean I'm any good at it," Allie said. "Haven't had much reason for it lately."

"You are doing just fine," Izzie replied, gazing at Allie's lips. She quickly looked up. Allie nervously bit down on her lips, which made Izzie smile. "Allie," she began. "You're gay, right?

Have you ever had a girlfriend or anything?"

"As in what context?"

Izzie laughed, shaking her head. It was true; there were various contexts one could use. Had Allie ever been this close to a woman, dancing in her arms? Had Allie ever kissed a girl, let alone dated one? Allie had every right to question it, but as close as they were dancing, one question remained. Izzie was too shy to ask if Allie wanted her.

"It's your pick. I don't want to insinuate anything."

Izzie smirked, hoping the smile didn't spread too far across her lips.

"I haven't," Allie softly murmured, quickly diverting her gaze away from Izzie. Izzie considered drawing Allie in closer to her, but the timing seemed off.

"Have you ever wanted to?" Izzie arched an eyebrow when Allie looked back at her. Allie shrugged. Her lips curved upward.

"Maybe," Allie teased.

Izzie smirked before laughing. She held her arm out, releasing Allie from her grasp. Allie twirled around before being pulled back into Izzie's arms. Allie laughed as she fell into Izzie. Her mouth was agape as she stared into Izzie's eyes.

"Interesting," Izzie teased, stepping back as the song ended. She walked off to the stereo, glancing over her shoulder when she heard a huff. Allie's jaw dropped. "What?"

Allie shook her head. "Nothing, I suppose." She crossed her arms as if putting up an invisible fence between them. Izzie snickered and turned away from her.

"I'm glad someone thinks it's funny." Izzie turned and leaned against the table, catching Allie's stare. Disappointment radiated off of Allie in waves, pushing Izzie to take that step forward.

"I get the sense that something was on your mind from the moment you got here; wanna talk about it?"

Allie shook her head. "It's nothing." She looked down at the floor, and Izzie watched as she swirled her toe around, not wanting to look back up in Izzie's direction.

"Tell me, Allie," Izzie started. "Are there professional boundaries in your position? Such as you shouldn't get too close to so and so because you might get fired, or things like that."

"Like, would it be frowned upon that I was dancing with the daughter of one of my patients? Things like that?" Allie looked up, and Izzie nodded.

"I mean, you said it first."

Allie shrugged. "I suppose you could say there are rules in the handbook. You know, don't get too emotionally or physically invested in family members of your patients, but I feel like most companies would try to adhere to such a policy. I guess it's a don't ask, don't tell kind of scenario."

Izzie slowly nodded. "And who would tell?" Izzie asked. "Besides, I've always been a rulebreaker."

"I can see that," Allie replied.

Izzie snickered. "You must leave people guessing at some point in your life." She winked and twirled around in front of Allie. "So, this place will be amazing when it's all said and done. Don't you think?"

Allie followed Izzie's gaze around the restaurant, nodding. "I can't wait for the grand opening!"

Izzie turned back and saw Allie was still gawking around the dining room. Izzie's eyes latched on Allie's lips once more. In an ideal scenario, she would have leaned in and kissed Allie. She knew they both wanted it, but she still kept her distance. Allie met her gaze and stared. Izzie smiled.

"So, I guess we should get out of here," Izzie turned and led the way to the kitchen. She reached the door and held it open for Allie to enter, but Allie seemed hesitant to pass her. "Are you sure you don't want to talk?" Izzie asked.

"There is something," Allie started. Izzie waited, practically holding her breath. Then Allie shook her head. "It's all good." Allie stepped past her, now leading the way to the back door. Allie hesitated again, then whirled around. "I'm just going to say it. We're flirting, right? I'm not misreading the signals?"

Izzie's eyes widened. If Allie had to ask, then maybe she had been doing it wrong all along. "I think that's fairly obvious."

"Then why?" Allie asked. Izzie frowned. "Why haven't you kissed me?"

Izzie sighed, then took a step toward the door. She stopped when her hand touched the handle. "Allie, when we kiss, I want it to be perfect. And the moment needs to be right." She shrugged, opening the door. "Trust me. We'll get there." She stepped outside and held the door open for Allie. Allie quietly walked by her. She was silent.

But Izzie knew she had to take things slow; Allie wasn't like her previous partners. She wanted to make this worthwhile.

CHAPTER FIFTEEN

MISSING IZZIE

Allie

A llie took in a whiff of fresh air as she rolled Richard onto the back porch. "It's a beautiful day out here," Allie replied. "I thought you would like the fresh air."

"Perfect," he replied. His voice was a bit breathless today. Allie noted his vital signs. His breathing was labored. She didn't like to see that, but his BP was great, and his pulse seemed strong. Fresh air could just be what she ordered.

"There's my sweetheart!" he commented when Cheryl walked out onto the porch with a pitcher of lemonade and three glasses.

"Did you miss me?" Cheryl asked with a grin, leaning in to kiss his forehead. Harry ran off the porch and bounced into the yard, chasing after a squirrel before rolling around and playing with his tail. Allie laughed and then turned back to Izzie's parents.

"Always, love. Always." He grinned.

Allie sank into a chair. Their love was the kind that most people would strive to achieve. Allie had never experienced such love when it came to her parents, but it was sweet to see that Izzie grew up surrounded by love.

"Thank you," Allie grabbed a glass from Cheryl and slowly sipped on it. As she watched them, she wondered what Izzie was up to. She had only been gone twenty-four hours. Allie hadn't expected to miss her already. She took another sip and then looked off into the sunset.

"I wonder what Izzie is up to," Cheryl commented.

Allie glanced in her direction, and Cheryl gave a light wink as if to say she had read her mind. "Probably working her butt off, so she can get back here as soon as possible." Cheryl took a sip, then licked her lips. "She's always been a hard worker."

"That's the truth." Richard laughed. "With that level of confidence, I don't think anyone was surprised when Izzie took on the corporate world. It was only fitting she would find her niche out there, where this small town couldn't help her to soar." As he spoke, his face lit up in talking about his daughter. It never ceased to amaze Allie how much love she could find in his words. She took a sip when she felt her cheeks burning as she just thought about Izzie.

"She's a captivating presence," Allie whispered. As they stared at her, her cheeks warmed again. *Had she said that out loud?*

"But no matter where she is, she likes to lift others, too. She's support-ive, maybe a bit of a dreamer, believing that anything is possible in the world," Cheryl noted. Allie smiled. In the past couple of weeks, Allie had received Izzie's unlimited support first-hand.

"She's a little guarded, though," Richard added.

Allie turned to him. She opened her mouth to respond but then snapped it shut. Her throat went dry, and she took a quick sip, finishing off her lemonade.

"I think she finds it difficult to trust people. She's been through a lot of heartbreak." Cheryl spoke quietly, looking off into the distance.

Allie could see that and even understand it. "But, somehow, she still sees the good in people and their strengths. I'd say it's what led her to her marketing job.

Allie considered the last statement from Cheryl. If that was the case, what did Izzie see in her? What were Allie's strengths? Why was Izzie paying so much attention to her? True, they'd been flirting. But Allie couldn't shake the feeling that Izzie saw something in her she couldn't see in herself. She looked down at her empty glass.

"Would you like some more, dear?" Cheryl asked.

"Maybe just a smidge." Cheryl poured a little more into her glass, and Allie graciously took a drink.

"You have done some great work here, Allie," Cheryl replied. "We wanted the best for Richard's care and certainly got the best."

Allie blushed. "Thank you! I'm glad that you think so." She took a drink and felt unexpectedly proud of herself. Izzie wasn't the only one who liked to light people up. The Roths were a family that Allie could be inclined to accept into her life forever.

She glanced over at Richard; he was staring out into the yard, watching Harry, perhaps not even paying attention to what Cheryl had just said. He seemed so at peace outside.

"Let's get a picture." Allie finished the last of her second glass and put the glass down.

"Something to commemorate this beautiful weather."

"Selfie time," Cheryl said, laughing.

"Nope, just the three of you. I'll sit this one out." Cheryl tilted her head but didn't push to change it.

"Harry, come here, boy!" Cheryl called. He ran up to the porch and instantly put his head on Richard's laughed. Cheryl wrapped her arm around Richard, and they posed for the picture, with Allie snapping a few extra shots.

"Perfect!" Allie pocketed her phone. "Are you both done with the lemonade? I'll bring the pitcher inside and get the dishes washed from dinner."

"Dear, you don't have to bother with that. Just enjoy the outside. I can get that after you've gone." Allie shook her head. She needed to get away for a moment before thoughts about the future consumed her.

"I got it." She grabbed the tray with their glasses and the pitcher and carried it into the house, taking a deep breath as the solitude sucked her in. Allie placed the tray on the counter, then pulled up the last picture she had snapped. Cheryl had snuck in a kiss on Richard's cheek, and Richard was grinning like a schoolboy with a crush. She sent the picture to Izzie, along with the caption: *Just here missing you.*

IZZIE

> They are lucky to have you. And they're not the only ones.

A winking emoji popped up after the message. Allie smiled and started to pocket her phone again when another message popped up.

IZZIE

> I love the pic, but someone's missing. Fix it for me?

Allie smirked and then puckered up her lips into a pose. She snapped a flirtatious selfie, followed by one where she was smiling. Once she approved of both pictures, she sent them to Izzie.

IZZIE

> That's what I like to see. And I must add you're looking gorgeous and much happier than the last time we saw each other. That makes me happy.

ALLIE

> Thank you, and yeah, I'm feeling better. Hopefully, that can continue once you're back here.

Allie sighed, her heart swelling as their flirtations lit up the screen.

CHAPTER SIXTEEN

FALLING

Izzie

The restaurant had dim lighting. Soft music filled the air as Izzie took a bite of her escargot and then leaned back in her seat. "Maybe I should add this to my menu back home." She laughed, and Mae arched an eyebrow. "What?"

"You just called it home? Again, this is the third time tonight."

Izzie rolled her eyes. "It's simply a word, nothing more." She shrugged. "Nothing less."

Mae scrunched up her nose. "I'm not so sure. Before returning to Sunnydale, you wouldn't even fathom that being your home. The big city is you. Or at least it used to be. But I'm sensing a change."

Izzie looked around the elegant restaurant. She was only teasing; the patrons of Stars and Stripes would think escargot looked like a science project. However, she noticed that some of the recipes Allie had come up with were merely simpler versions of what the restaurant had to offer. It brought small-town living into a new realm. Allie was full of surprises. She let a smile linger.

"And you're smiling again," Mae commented. "Let me guess, you're thinking about her."

Izzie looked up, a laugh caught in her throat. "You're delusional. You need to cool it with the romance novels." Izzie took a sip of her wine.

"It's not a bad thing, Izzie. You seem more relaxed going back to Sunnydale. I get it. Everyone needs a break from the city sometimes. But you're glowing. I can tell it's been good for you to be with the people closest to you. You deserve a little hometown fling."

Izzie blushed. "Well, you're wrong. Allie and I haven't even kissed." She popped a bite into her mouth, and Mae snickered, taking a bite of her salad.

Izzie looked off toward the distance, and Allie popped back into her mind. Allie was never far from her thoughts these days. She dropped her gaze to her salad and took a bite.

"You know what would make this salad even better?" Izzie stated. Mae shrugged. "Peach Mango dressing." Mae arched an eyebrow. Izzie snickered. "Allie has this recipe that would make any salad better. Trust me."

Mae snickered. "But you don't think about Allie." She shook her head and continued to eat.

"I'm making a point. Allie is helping me with recipes for the restaurant, and the moment I took a bite of that dressing, I knew we had to add it. With her help, Stars and Stripes is going to be back on the map in no time."

Mae slowly nodded. "Sounds like Allie is pretty much perfect." Izzie stared at her. "I mean as a co-restauranter." Mae winked and then took another bite of her salad.

Izzie blushed. If only she could get over herself.

Allie was perfect, and not just for the restaurant. But she was holding back; that was clear from their last encounter. There was a disconnect between them that was more than just Izzie's trust issues.

"I thought that was you over here." Izzie looked up and saw Cassandra, one of her longtime clients.

Izzie smiled. "How are you?"

"It's been a few months, Cass. Long time no see. I'm good. And you?"

Cassandra looked over her shoulder to a table, and Izzie followed her gaze. A woman sat with her back to them, then Cassandra rolled her eyes. "Pretty good. On a blind date from hell." She winked at Izzie. "But gotta be friendly, right?"

Izzie nodded. "But if you're not feeling it, you might want to be honest. No point in wasting either of your time."

"When you're right, you're right," Cassandra replied. "But hey, I didn't mean to interrupt." She glanced between Izzie and Mae, then back to Izzie. "Maybe you should give me a call sometime."

"Is there an issue with the campaign? We could tweak it to your liking. Call the office anytime. I have some family stuff I'm dealing with. I won't always be around, but my assistant here would be happy to take any messages."

Cassandra smirked. "I wasn't talking business." She winked. "Give me a call." She turned on her heel and walked back to her table.

"That was weird," Izzie mumbled.

"Weird?" Mae laughed. "Um, that woman was drop-dead gorgeous, and you practically ignored her." Mae tilted her head. "And don't say things like, she's not your type, because she is exactly the type you'd use to go for."

Izzie opened her mouth to argue when her phone buzzed. She glanced down at it and saw a picture of her parents and Harry, along with a small message from Allie. She smiled, immediately turning her attention to her phone. Two images popped up of Allie, and Izzie grinned.

"Um, do I need to leave you alone with your phone? I feel like I'm interrupting." Mae laughed.

Izzie looked up. "It's nothing. Allie just sent me a picture of my parents. That's all." She shot back a message and grinned. "Nothing more than that."

Mae shook her head. "I'm your assistant, yes, but I'm also your best friend. Your trust issues are holding you back from telling Allie about your feelings. Don't even try to lie to me. I've seen it before."

"It's not that," Izzie argued. "There's more to it, anyway. The distance, for one."

"And you can work remotely, right?" Mae argued. "There comes a point where you can't look at all the reasons something won't work but think about how you'll make it work."

Mae tossed a look over her shoulder, then turned back and grinned. "You saw Cassandra as a client!"

"She is nothing more than a client." Izzie took a sip of her wine.

"Okay, but before the two of you would have hooked up in the bath-room. That says something. You have feelings for Allie; trust them."

Izzie considered that, then snickered. "You missed your calling, Mae. You should have been a therapist."

Mae shrugged. "I'm stating the obvious. You'll thank me later, and I want an invite to the wedding." She took a bite of her salad.

Izzie blushed. Everything that Mae said made sense. She looked at the last text, grabbed her phone again, and typed a message.

IZZIE

How about a picnic once I'm back in town?

She put down the phone, not waiting for the response. It was time to do something to progress things, even if it was scary. Sometimes, the best things were.

CHAPTER SEVENTEEN

PICNIC UNDER THE STARS

Allie

I *know it's your day off, but I want to see you.* Allie couldn't hide her smile when she saw Izzie's text. Luckily, she was home alone. Allie knew Izzie was back in town and considered making an excuse to go to the Roths, but she couldn't think of a reason.

She stood before her closet for what felt like an eternity, considering the perfect outfit before landing on a sheer, champagne-colored tank top and a pair of high-waisted jeans. It accentuated her curves in a way that she hoped Izzie would appreciate.

She knocked on the front door just before eight o'clock. Cheryl answered the door. Allie opened her mouth, too stunned to say anything.

"Allie, come in!" Cheryl grabbed her hand and pulled her into the foyer. "Izzie is waiting for you. She's getting impatient."

"Mom!" Izzie scolded. Allie looked past Cheryl to the stairs, where Izzie approached the main floor. Izzie's checks were red, which Allie found endearing. Allie bit down on her lip so she wouldn't burst out laughing.

"What's wrong with saying that?" she asked, shrugging. "You two have fun." She winked, then turned from the two of them. Allie hovered in the foyer, hoping to catch a better glance of Izzie.

Izzie wore a short-sleeved dark linen blouse that showed off her muscular biceps. The top three buttons open. She wore dark-wash jeans. A silver chain glinted around her neck. She wore her hair in a low ponytail. Allie tried not to stare at the opening in her blouse and failed.

Izzie snickered. "I'd say my parents are more excited than even I am." She shrugged. "Then again, I'm pretty excited."

"Excited? For what?"

Izzie reached out and grabbed Allie's hand. "You're about to find out." She escorted Allie from the foyer and to the kitchen. Allie took a moment to glance in the living room, where Richard lay in his bed. Cheryl sat up against his side, not moving her eyes away.

"How's he doing?" Allie asked.

"Good moments and bad, but I'd say you know that better than any of us." Izzie glanced over her shoulder, and Allie gave a weak nod. To her dismay, she did.

Izzie opened the door and held it open for Allie to go outside. Allie grinned as Izzie held her hand, guiding her down the porch steps.

"You planned this?" They stopped walking. Izzie had spread a picnic blanket across the lawn. She'd also set up a wicker basket, an entire cheese plate, and what looked like a bottle of wine.

"Were you expecting more?" Izzie asked, a playful grin on her lips.

"This is perfect." Allie sat down on the blanket and kicked out of her sandals. She was glad she had bothered to give herself a pedicure.

Izzie kicked out of her shoes and joined her.

She grabbed the basket. "So, you've got your standard charcuterie spread: smoked gouda, brie, some grapes, crackers. But I also have chocolates, angel food cake, strawberries," she wiggled her eyebrows. "Pick your poison."

"It all sounds so delicious," Allie said, clapping her hands together. "You choose where we start."

Allie looked up into the sky as the sun was nearly out of sight. She grinned, making her gaze around the backyard. How could Allie not fall for Izzie when she planned all of this?

"It's so beautiful out here," Allie added.

"And romantic," Izzie whispered. Allie turned to make her gaze. Izzie grinned and held up a single strawberry. She held it out to Allie's lips, and

Allie maintained eye contact as she took a bite, chocolate dripping off the strawberry onto her lower lip. She licked it off. She noticed that Izzie's gaze lingered on her lips. Izzie popped the remaining part in her mouth and grinned.

"Delicious."

Allie blushed. Her skin was on fire as Izzie stared at her. She sighed and slipped one leg over the other, hoping that Izzie couldn't sense how shy Allie felt at that moment. "No one's ever done anything like this for me."

Izzie shook her head. "That's a shame because you deserve only the best." Izzie reached into the basket and withdrew bottled water. She handed it over, then quirked up her lips. "There's wine, too, if you prefer something stronger."

"Water is perfect." Allie took a swig and then nodded. Izzie's eyes never once wavered from Allie as she drank. When Allie glanced in her direction, Izzie shook her head and reached back into her basket to grab a container with two slivers of cake already divided. "What?" Allie inquired.

"Nothing." Izzie plopped a piece onto Allie's plate, then grabbed her own. Periodically, she would look up, and Allie caught her staring, but only because Allie also had her gaze fixed on Izzie.

"I just never," Izzie began. She snickered. "I never thought, or expected, or even dreamed I would find something or someone that would want to keep me coming back here. Other than my family, of course. But now," Her words trailed off.

Allie blushed, looking down at her piece of cake. She grabbed it and took a bite, hoping it would give her ample time to consider Izzie's words. Allie worried she would let Izzie down. She licked her lips, hoping to grab all the crumbs before letting those words fully sink in.

"You know, Allie. My family is important to me."

Allie slowly nodded. It's not that her family wasn't important to her; she was sick of failing to live up to their expectations. But Izzie didn't stop there.

"There's something special about you. Watching you with my family only reaffirmed that. It takes a special sort of person to work in hospice."

Allie grinned. "Well, I must admit that your attachment to family is one quality I admire. I've worked with a lot of families, but your family is pretty special."

Allie looked up at the house, and a pit formed in her stomach. She would fight for her family if they showed her a tenth of the kindness the Roths lavished on her daily.

"You have a good heart. That's hard to find in a person. It doesn't hurt that you're gorgeous."

Allie turned her head. "You know how to make me blush."

Izzie snickered. "Listen, all I'm saying is it hasn't gone unnoticed." Izzie winked. "You are sweet and caring. I feel like I can trust you with all my heart."

"Izzie," Allie softly replied. "You take my breath away the moment you walk into a room. Your confidence is sexy."

Izzie popped a piece of chocolate into her mouth, and Allie drew her eyes to her lips; what she wouldn't give to lean in and kiss her at that moment. She sighed and looked up.

"And it doesn't hurt that you're gorgeous."

Izzie grinned. "So, we're equally attracted to one another. Is that what you're saying?"

Allie sighed. She reached into the basket, leaning in closer to Izzie, feeling the magnetic pull of their attraction. Allie grabbed a piece of chocolate and unwrapped it before pulling back from Izzie. She placed it in her mouth, letting the chocolate melt on her tongue.

"I think attraction can only take things so far, though," Allie replied. "That's why it's your mannerisms, love for your family, and confidence that leaves me breathless every day."

"Damn, keep talking like that and..."

"And what?" Allie whispered.

Izzie stroked her hand against Allie's cheek before drawing her in and kissing her. The evening sky had grown darker, and the stars had begun to appear. As they kissed, Allie scooted in closer to Izzie. It didn't feel like their first time; if anything, it felt like they had been together for years. Izzie's lips were soft. Allie tasted something earthy, chapstick, maybe? Allie pulled back, licking her lips and focusing on Izzie's.

"I won't rush you," Izzie whispered. "I know this is your first," Before finishing the sentence, Allie snaked her hand around Izzie's neck and pulled her in closer. They kissed while Allie took the lead, dragging her tongue along Izzie's. Izzie groaned.

Allie pushed Izzie back down to the blanket, letting the kiss deepen and straddling Izzie, feeling the heat radiating off her jeans. She slipped a hand under Izzie's blouse, cupping her breast, giving it an exploratory squeeze. Izzie smiled as they kissed, threading her fingers through Allie's hair. The warmth she felt against her sent shivers down Allie's spine, and she wouldn't ever pull back.

CHAPTER EIGHTEEN

CONFLICTING FEELINGS

Izzie

Izzie stared at the laptop, contemplating hurling it across the room before realizing she would have to pay to replace it and still work for another eight hours.

She had made the trip back to the city earlier in the week, hoping that that would keep her from returning any earlier than necessary. However, now, her boss was barking orders, changing up the project, and acting like Izzie was doing everything wrong. When was he going to realize that she was the one who was supposedly in charge of the project?

Instead, she felt like a simpleton who didn't know how to do her job. He was making her look bad, especially in front of the clients. She slammed her laptop closed and pushed it to the side. She wasn't sure how long she could last in a career that wasted her potential.

I hope your father is doing better. That was how he ended the latest email, but it wasn't sincere. He didn't want Izzie to up and quit on the spot. That fake sincerity could only go so far before Izzie bowed out and pursued something else.

Come on, Izzie, you know that's not likely. You like your job and the clients you work with, and the pay is good enough to stick around. It didn't hurt that she could also work remotely, but if she had to return to the city every week, what good did all the perks do? Her job brought her crashing back down onto the Earth.

Last night was one of the best nights Izzie had had in a long time; it was fleeting.

Izzie sighed and left her room. She went downstairs and spotted her dad in the living room. The baseball game was on. He was sitting in his chair watching while remaining unimpressed.

Izzie went to the basement, where her mom was folding laundry. She looked up and greeted her with a smile.

"Hey, dear. How's it going?"

Izzie shrugged. "Been better."

She frowned. "That's not what I like to hear." Her mom tossed a pile of clothes into the washer and then turned to look at Izzie. "Thought last night went well. You seemed happy. I know I was in bed when you got inside, but you got back pretty late."

Izzie smiled. "Last night was fun. Great. But I just got some work emails I'd prefer to ignore."

"Work isn't so great, right?" Her mother shot her a sympathetic look, and Izzie tried to force through a smile. "Work can be like that, unfortunately."

"My boss just has unreasonable expectations. He gave me this time to come home. It was all worked out, but then he flies off the handle expecting me to be right there at his beck and call."

Izzie shrugged.

"Not always possible." She clapped her hands together. "Again, I don't want to think about it. I don't want to sell the restaurant. So, I'm taking that off the table. What if we have a grand re-opening to showcase the new menu?." She could feel the excitement welling up inside. "I think some of these ideas will turn the place around."

Her mom continued to frown. "You work too hard. Is this reasonable when you won't be able to stick around forever? And where does Allie fit in the mix? I think you guys could be cute together, but in the long term, what are you thinking? Going back to the city could put a damper on all of that."

A rock plummeted into Izzie's gut. Izzie prided herself in her rationality, but now her mother had the questions flying, and Izzie had no answers for her. She grimaced. "And just like that, I'm stuck thinking about the inevitable." She turned on her heel to leave.

"I don't mean to be a downer, Izzie. I want everything to work out for you. You know that. I am one of your biggest cheerleaders."

Izzie hesitated. "I know, Mom. Sometimes, I don't want to be the rational thinker." With that, she headed back upstairs. She fell back against the wall at the top of the stairs. The pain kept gnawing away at her gut. She reached into her pocket for her phone and pulled up Allie's name.

IZZIE

Can't wait to see you. ;)

Logically, she knew she shouldn't text Allie when so much was up in the air. Yet, she longed to talk to Allie again. She had to see her to remind herself how the previous night felt. She returned to her room, and the text popped on her phone.

ALLIE

Looking forward to it, as well. Last night was amazing. I can only imagine if my parents knew.

It ended with a laughing emoji, and Izzie read over that message a few more times. Was Allie closeted? Did her parents not know she was gay? That text message worried Izzie. Allie was everything that Izzie wanted in a woman, but if she was hiding her sexuality from her parents, maybe they shouldn't be together. She tried to push that thought out of her mind. Izzie was reading too much into it. Or so she hoped.

CHAPTER NINETEEN

I NEED YOU

Allie

Allie caught herself looking for Izzie. She took Richard's vitals and prepared lunch for him because Cheryl was off to the restaurant to accept a shipment. However, it was Izzie that Allie longed to see. She didn't want her emotions to get in her work, but getting closer to Izzie seemed like a welcome distraction.

They said Izzie was working in her room, but with the text earlier in the day, Allie assumed that meant Izzie would be waiting for her. To Allie's dismay, Izzie didn't seem interested in Allie's arrival.

Once Allie had prepared the tuna salad, she decided it was her time to find Izzie. If Izzie were too busy to come to her, she would go to Izzie. She approached her room with caution. She had never been to Izzie's room but longed for a midday rendezvous. She knocked lightly on the door. When she didn't hear a response, she opened the door slightly.

"Izzie?"

"I'm on a conference call," Izzie hissed.

"Sorry!" Allie quickly closed the door, then hurried down the stairs and to the kitchen. She didn't breathe until she was far from the bedroom. The look on Izzie's face spoke volumes: she thought Allie was a nuisance.

Allie forced a smile, even more, confused than before. She put a sandwich on a tray, with some water and ice chips, and carried them into the living room for Richard.

"Are you ready to eat?" she asked.

He nodded weakly but still smiled. Harry lay at the foot of the bed, sound asleep, as Allie placed the items on Richard's cart and wheeled the tray over him so he had easy access.

"Need anything else?" she asked.

"I could use some company," he said. She smiled. "Grab your food and come sit with me."

Allie left the living room, grabbed her food, and then returned to sit on the chair closest to him, which Cheryl usually occupied. "How are you feeling, Richard?"

"Today? Pretty good. Today is a good day." He kept smiling as he took small bites of his sandwich.

"Those are the best days," Allie replied. She looked down at her food, trying not to think about her awkward interaction with Izzie.

"You like my Izzie, don't you?" She looked up when Richard asked the question. "I see the way you two look at each other. Cheryl and I still look at each other like that."

Allie blushed. "I can assure you, no matter how hard anyone tries, they could never have the kind of relationship you and your wife have. People can only strive to have that one day."

He chuckled. "Izzie is a Roth. She gets her fight and fire from her parents." He winked. "So, it could happen." He took another bite and then started to choke. Allie jumped up and hovered over him.

"Are you okay, Richard?" He nodded, continuing to cough, but the spell slowly died.

"I want my daughter to be happy. You make her happy." His words were soft, barely above a whisper. "I'm not very hungry."

"At least take a few ice chips." Allie leaned in, helping him to take the chips. He fell back, looking even weaker than he had moments ago. Allie returned the tray to give him more room, then sank into the chair. His breathing was light as he closed his eyes. Allie stared at him, tears stinging the backs of her eyes. Richard was a fighter, but at some point, his fight would end. She quickly brushed a tear from her eye and jumped up. She hurried from the living room and stood at the sink, staring at her dirty dish. Allie closed her eyes. *Lord, watch over this family as Richard's health fails; help them to see that you'll take them to a better place.*

"Allie?"

Allie turned to find Izzie. She arched an eyebrow but didn't comment on the tear streaming down Allie's cheek. "I made tuna. Do you want some?" She went to the counter, but Izzie quickly shook her head.

"I have to go. I don't think I'll be back before you leave. Just wanted to let you know." She then turned and left the kitchen.

Allie frowned, then ran from the kitchen to meet her in the foyer. "Out? Is everything alright?"

Izzie spun on her heel and nodded. "Why wouldn't it be?"

Allie shrugged. "You tell me. You texted me that you couldn't wait to see me, then practically ignored me while I was here."

Izzie sighed, then moved in closer. "I wasn't ignoring you. I was busy working." She leaned in and softly kissed Allie. "But now I have to go out. I'll see you around."

Allie nodded and watched as Izzie left the house. She heard the padding of feet behind her and turned to see Harry. He walked over to the door and whimpered, then lay down in front of it.

"I know the feeling, boy." Allie turned away and went back to the kitchen. But why Izzie was suddenly so cold was beyond her.

IZZIE WAS RIGHT. ALLIE DIDN'T SEE HER THE REST OF THE DAY. Allie pulled into her parking lot of the apartment building, wishing against everything that Izzie would have gotten back to the house and they could have talked. She would have even settled for a text message, where Izzie apologized for being distant. Sure, they kissed, but the kiss wasn't nearly the exciting experience she anticipated.

Allie walked up the stairs to her apartment, and that's when she saw her. "Izzie?"

Izzie turned and stared at her. "I was beginning to think I was at the wrong place."

"I didn't even know you had my address." Allie moved in closer to her.

"You're taking care of my father. I needed to do a thorough background check." She shrugged. "I wouldn't have stalked you or anything, but I needed to see you."

"I'm glad you're here. I think we need to talk." Allie opened the door and held it open for Izzie to enter. When she closed the door, Izzie turned around to face her. There was still this desire in her stare. She felt it tingle down to her toes. She opened her mouth, but Izzie held up her hand.

"I need to start, or I don't know if I'll ever be able to get it out. So, please, let me go first." Allie nodded. "You said something in a text earlier about your parents. So, they don't know you're gay, right?"

Allie sighed. She had practically forgotten she had put that on the text. She wasn't even sure why she had. "I spent my whole life trying to be with the person they wanted me to be, trying to avoid my attraction to women. They would disapprove. So I keep it to myself. What they don't know won't hurt them." Allie shrugged. "It's no big deal."

"No big deal. So, you're fine with lying to your parents about who you're with. Man, woman, whatever, you throw up your hands and say no big deal? So, us being together, to you, was no big deal?"

"That's not what I'm saying. It was a big deal to me, but my parents didn't need to know who I was with every second of every day. They wouldn't understand, and if it's easier to keep it to myself, that's what works for me. I went in for the moment, doing what felt right. I'm of age and clearly shouldn't have to beg for my parent's approval. Just because they feel one thing doesn't mean the rest of the world does. I'm happy."

Allie moved in closer to Izzie. "For me, that's what matters." Izzie just continued to stare. "I'll tell them, especially as we are getting closer. Soon. Very soon."

Izzie nodded, then finally smirked. "Your happiness, you're right; that's what should matter. That's all that should matter. But I don't want to cause more issues with your parents."

"It's not like that. You never could. I've just never had reason to mention." One day, Allie would have to tell Izzie everything, but if this was why Izzie felt so distant earlier, then Allie didn't want to make that moment right now. "You were so cold earlier."

Izzie shook her head. "I was stressed for a lot of reasons. Mostly work, though. I might have to go back to the city."

"For how long?" Allie wondered out loud.

Izzie shrugged. "Two days? A week? I don't know. And I don't want to go. Yet, work might depend on it. And dammit, I didn't want there to be another reason that would keep me here."

"So, in other words, I'm wreaking havoc on your life?"

Izzie groaned. "Yes, but in the best way." She wrapped her arm around Allie and pulled it toward her. They kissed; this time, the hunger in the kiss was undeniable. Their tongues fought magnetically with one another, standing in Allie's small living room.

"I want to be with you in every sense of the word," Allie whispered.

"Are you sure?" Izzie pulled from the kiss, staring into Allie's eyes. Allie nodded, reaching for Izzie's hand and pulling her to her bedroom.

"I need you to stay." Once they were in the room, Izzie pushed Allie down to the bed so she was sitting on the side. She grabbed Allie's shirt and pulled it up and over her head. Allie's breathing turned ragged as Izzie reached behind her to unhook Allie's bra.

"You're so gorgeous," Izzie murmured. She leaned in and hungrily kissed Allie before dropping her lips to Allie's breasts, trailing her tongue along the underside of each breast before suckling each nipple. Allie arched her back and growled, letting Izzie enjoy the taste. She was ready to let loose and allow Izzie to have her from start to finish. All of her doubts fell away. She trusted Izzie. She was ready to see where they could go.

CHAPTER TWENTY

THE LONG GOODBYE

Izzie

Izzie grabbed hold of the bed, swooping her legs over Allie's shoulders as Allie trailed her tongue along Izzie's swollen clit.

"Oh, God!" Izzie cried. She bared down, her body shaking uncontrollably. "Damn," she gasped. "Are you sure you've never done this before?"

Allie laughed, greedily sucking at her clit. She lifted her head and trailed kisses slowly up Izzie's body. She went in for a kiss, then breathlessly kept her lips hovered over Izzie. "I've had a lot of time to fantasize."

She kissed Izzie, slipping her tongue into Izzie's mouth as Izzie wrapped her arm around Allie's body. At first, it seemed Allie expected Izzie to top, but slowly, Allie took charge. Where the shift happened, Izzie didn't know. She also didn't mind. She was incredibly turned on. When the kiss died, Allie fell beside her, and Izzie pulled her closer, their soft breathing entering the dark bedroom.

Izzie closed her eyes and let the breathing ring in her ears. When she showed up at Allie's apartment, she doubted they would end up in bed together. However, when she saw Allie, those words came rushing out of her mouth. How could she walk away from this when Allie was everything she needed?

"So, what'd you think?" Allie whispered beside her.

Izzie grinned. "About what?"

"Be honest. Am I good in bed?" Allie asked.

Izzie turned to Allie, drawing her closer.

"Always, Babe. In my eyes, you could do no wrong." Izzie cradled her, kissing her harder and holding her tightly, wishing they could stay in bed forever. They closed their eyes, and it wasn't long before Allie's breathing turned even softer. Izzie opened her eyes, watching her sleep. It was magical to be there together at that moment. She closed her eyes again, expecting to drift off to sleep, when she heard ringing.

It wasn't her ringtone, but Allie never even budged from the place. Izzie held her breath, hoping the ringing didn't wake Allie. It ended abruptly, but a few minutes later, a text message sounded on the phone. *What if it's an emergency?* Izzie thought, reaching down into the pockets of Allie's scrubs. She dug into her pockets and finally withdrew the phone.

> MOM
>
> Why aren't you answering the phone?
>
> MOM
>
> Don't forget your cousin's wedding is coming next month. I need your help to find the perfect present.
>
> MOM
>
> Hello?

"What are you doing?" Izzie nearly dropped the phone when she heard Allie's voice. Izzie turned, and Allie's eyes widened.

"I thought it could be an emergency." Izzie handed over the phone. "I'm sorry."

Allie checked the messages, then shrugged. "No worries. It's not like I have some deep, dark secret." Allie put her phone on the nightstand, then turned back to Izzie. "When do you think you'll have to head out of town?"

She barely blinked when it came to the missed text messages. But Izzie finally comprehended the level of Allie's parents' disapproval. Yet, being in Allie's arms, it seemed so right.

"Um, possibly tomorrow. I will call my boss in the morning to see if I can work some things out."

"Well, then, we shouldn't waste another minute." Allie leaned in and kissed Izzie. But Izzie was now more curious about Allie's parents than ever before. As Allie dipped her tongue in, releasing a moan, Izzie slipped her fingers behind her head and held her in place. If Allie had something she wanted to tell her, then she would. For now, Izzie wanted to appreciate the resolution of months of sexual tension.

She moved in, wrapping her legs around Allie and pressing her down in bed. They were already both wet. As they kissed, she reached down and pressed two fingers inside Allie. Allie jerked, and she saw a small smile dancing on Allie's lips. Izzie moved her fingers in deeper. Allie groaned in pleasure, tossing her head back. Izzie grinned, satisfied by that reaction.

She pumped her fingers in, causing Allie to shift beneath her. Izzie closed her eyes and focused on the motion until the wetness intensified. "Yesssss..." Allie cried.

"Don't you dare." Izzie laughed, moving in to replace her fingers with her tongue. She held onto Allie as Allie crashed against the bed, an orgasm washing in waves across her body. She came in a gush, leaving Izzie hungry for the taste of her, relishing in the salt on her skin.

The cell phone was out of her mind, and she moved back up Allie's body, kissing her, just glad they were experiencing intimacy together. But it would be that much more complicated if she had to leave.

IZZIE SIGHED INTO THE PHONE. "RYAN, I ALREADY CAME BACK last week. You promised I could take off as much time as needed. I'm working my ass off to ensure everything's finished on time. None of this requires me to be in person."

"Cassandra says otherwise. Your family is important. I get it, but I'm only asking for a few days. Surely your family will be fine without you. You said there's a nurse, right?"

His tone was so calm. Cassandra only wanted her there to entertain her delusional fantasy that Izzie was interested in her. Since Allie came along, Izzie had no interest, and if Cassandra didn't see that, then Izzie didn't want to spell it out for her.

"What time's the meeting tomorrow?"

"Noon," he replied. "I would like you here by ten so we can go over the meeting agenda."

Izzie shook her head. "Three days tops. That's all I can give you. If something happens to my dad while I'm gone, I'll never forgive myself. So, I'm coming back on Saturday; if that's not enough, then I don't know what to tell you. Understood?"

"We'll make it work. I'll see you in the morning." He disconnected the call before they said their goodbyes.

Now there was only one thing left to do. Izzie left her room and went down the stairs, where she heard her mom talking with Allie and her dad in the living room. She peered into the room; the TV was blaring, and Allie was engrossed in conversation with her mom.

"Allie?" Allie looked up and smiled, but Izzie never once broke into a grin; this wasn't a conversation she wanted to have. "I need to talk to you for a minute. I thought we could go over the menu one more time."

"Sure!" Allie got up and followed Izzie into the kitchen. "What's this about, Izzie? The menu is all worked out." Izzie grabbed Allie's hand and pulled her out of the backdoor. The further they got away from the house to talk, the better chances her parents wouldn't hear her.

"And now you're scaring me," Allie said.

They stopped walking about the middle of the backyard, where they had had their picnic a few days prior. "I just got off the phone with my boss. I have to go back to the city in the morning. There's a meeting that I can't get out of. I guess the contract relies on me being there."

She looked away from Allie's gaze as it dropped to the ground. "Dammit, I don't want to go."

"We knew it could happen. We took the chance to get closer, always knowing that one day you'd have to leave." Allie threw up her arms. "It is what it is."

Izzie reached out and grabbed her arm. "This isn't forever. I told you that I'll be back. We're looking at three days at most. I'll come back as soon as I can ensure that contract is safe."

"But for how long?" Allie shook her head. You come back another week and then go for another two? Come on, Izzie. It's not practical." Izzie pulled her back to her, causing Allie to crash into her, and their lips connected. Izzie wrapped her arm around her and held her to her.

"I'll make him see that this is it."

"Again, for how long?" Allie whispered.

Those words rang through Izzie's ears. Allie had a point: for how long? At some point, Izzie would have to go back forever, but she didn't want to dwell on that.

"I can only think about today." Izzie quietly replied. She slipped her fingers through Allie's hair, pulling her back to her. They kissed again, with Allie finally relaxing in her arms. Was it careless? Izzie didn't even mind at that moment.

"Follow me," Izzie replied.

They returned to the house, and Izzie held up her hand for Allie to remain there. She peeked into the living room to find her mom and dad watching a sitcom from the eighties. She returned to Allie and grabbed her hand, pulling her through the back hallway and up the stairs to her bedroom.

"Izzie," Allie hissed. "I'm on the clock."

"Consider this helping out the daughter." Izzie winked and crashed her lips against Allie's. Allie laughed but didn't hesitate. Izzie grabbed Allie's shirt and pulled it up and off of her, only breaking from the kiss to remove her shirt.

"Your mom and dad will hear us," Allie argued.

"They're busy. I want to be with you tonight if I'm leaving tomorrow. So kiss me already."

Allie moved in for a kiss as Izzie removed her bra. While they kissed, she kneaded Allie's breasts in her palms. Allie melted at her touch. She pushed Allie down to the bed, cutting off the kiss. As Allie watched her, Izzie got undressed, quickly tossing her clothes to the side.

Allie shimmied out of her pants and spread her legs out, her nakedness on display. Izzie crawled on top of her, and they passionately made out. Allie threaded her fingers through Izzie's hair, giggling as she drew her closer. Izzie pulled the covers back, and they slipped underneath, getting lost under the covers. Izzie ground onto Allie, letting the molten core of her center guide her as she slipped her index and middle finger into Allie's damp entrance.

"Do you need me?" Allie panted, slipping her tongue between Izzie's lips.

"Always, babe." Izzie hungrily kissed Allie, and they let the bed swallow them whole. If her parents asked, she would say they were saying goodbye, but she knew they'd understand.

CHAPTER TWENTY-ONE

HARDER THAN EXPECTED

Allie

IZZIE

I miss you!

Allie felt herself tearing up. It'd been only three days and felt like a lifetime, unable to see Izzie, talk to her, touch her, or even flirt in the kitchen. She swallowed the lump in her throat.

ALLIE

I miss you, too. When are you

"Someone has a secret."

Allie dropped her phone mid-text, looking up to see Cheryl at the kitchen entrance. Allie's jaw dropped, and she quickly shook her head, grabbing her phone. "No secret." She pocketed it before she could even finalize her text. She'd have to get back to it, hopefully sooner than later. Nothing like leaving a woman hanging. "Thought I'd whip you guys up a salad?" Allie gave a smile and rushed to the cabinets.

Cheryl laughed. "You don't have to hide from it. I'm no prude. I see how you look at Izzie. We're both glad that Izzie and you have connected in the way you have."

Allie froze. *Connected? What did Izzie tell her parents, or what was Cheryl implying?* "You can never have too many friends," Allie replied, her words nearly in a mumble, which caused Cheryl to laugh out loud.

"So, that's what you're calling it these days? A friendship?" Allie looked over her shoulder, and Cheryl grinned. "I can't recall Izzie looking at any of her *friends* like she looks at you. And vice versa."

Allie winced. Why did Cheryl insist on finding ways to embarrass her? She stammered, shrugging, then frowned. "So, you think Izzie could see it as more than a friendship?"

She latched down on her tongue as the question came out. She could only hope that Izzie felt the same way for Allie as Allie felt for her. She dropped her gaze to her feet, wrangling her growing affection.

"The salad can wait, my dear," Cheryl began. "Have a seat."

Allie hesitated. "Richard will probably be getting hungry."

"He's still sleeping like a baby and will probably be long after you've made anything. Take a seat."

Allie nodded and took a seat across from Cheryl. She placed her hands on the table, then her lap, then back on the table, until she eventually sat on them, hoping she wouldn't get fidgety.

"We've always known Izzie was into women. We never judged or questioned her beliefs because we always believed that Izzie would know what she wanted out of life. Unfortunately, we've seen Izzie's heart break too many times through the years. When a parent has to witness their children in pain, it's one of the most devastating feelings they experience."

Allie dropped her gaze. If only her parents felt the same. She longed for that kind of emotional love connection with the two people who should have unconditional love and concern for her.

"When someone comes into their life and gives them a reason to smile, there's no greater joy. And I can see that smile on Izzie's face. Sweetie, you made that happen."

Allie's cheeks reddened. "Things just aren't so cut and dry." Allie's words were barely above a whisper. Izzie is eventually going to go back to the city full-time. My job and life are here. I can't see how a long-distance relationship will overcome the hurdles." Allie sighed; even if she wanted to jump all in, it felt impossible.

"Do you even know when she's coming back? What if I get invested, and she bails?"

Cheryl's eyebrows furrowed. "No one knows what the future will hold. Did I think that one day I would have to watch my husband's health fade, and so quickly, too? No, not at all. But here I am." Allie dropped her gaze. "I'm not trying to be depressing, but the point is that everything happens for a reason, and sometimes you might not understand the reason. I just think that this could all work out in your favor. You shouldn't give up hope." Cheryl touched Allie's hand, giving it a slight squeeze. She then stood up and turned from her, hesitating but only slightly.

"Salad sounds nice, my dear. Holler if you need anything." Allie pulled her phone from her pocket and stared at the half-written text while leaving the kitchen. She deleted the message, then began a new one.

ALLIE

Any idea how long you'll be in the city?

IZZIE

Is this your way of saying you're missing me, too? ;)

Allie smirked.

ALLIE

Maybe.

IZZIE

She's beautiful and cryptic. A deadly combo. Lol. Let's just say I'm hoping to be home before your bed gets cold.

Allie blushed. Whenever things seemed too good to be true, something went awry.

ALLIE

I'll hold you to it.

She hit send before she could rethink her text. Izzie had her mind in a twist and wanted to go full force, no matter how difficult.

CHAPTER TWENTY-TWO

TEMPTATION BREWING

Izzie

"Dinner with a client at six, followed immediately at eight for drinks." Izzie nodded and entered the information on the calendar on her phone. "Any other questions?"

"Just one," Izzie began. "I need to be getting back home. I've already been here a week, four days longer than intended. So, I would appreciate a definitive answer on when I can leave." She sighed. "It's stressful being away from my parents."

Ryan grimaced. "I understand, but it's stressful when you're not here. You keep talking about home, but from what I've gathered, *this* is your home."

"You know what I mean," Izzie grumbled. "When your family is struggling, you gravitate toward that place, and I've been working my ass off from my office/bedroom and doing a great job, or so I thought. So, I don't see why you needed me to be here."

She looked down at her phone.

"Dinner and drinks with the clients seem like a lame excuse."

She could feel her frustration with every breath, but nothing would change until Ryan understood how strongly she felt about it. And the truth remained that she needed to be there for her parents. Plus, she missed Allie. Maybe even a little too much.

"If tonight goes well, then maybe a few days." He shrugged. "But it all depends on how tonight goes."

"Sounds a bit like blackmail to me." Izzie tilted her head. He looked up from his computer and smirked. Izzie shook her head. "Well, I should get home and prepare for tonight. After all, if I want tonight to go well, I have no other choice."

She rolled her eyes and turned on her heel. "See ya tonight," she muttered, then closed the door behind her, letting it slam a little too loudly.

Izzie didn't live far from the office, but the drive was monotonous, thanks to the endless barrage of speeding cars. And she used to think this was the only place where she could thrive.

Izzie pulled into her driveway and stared at the house, which seemed to radiate a newfound hostility. Suddenly, everything felt like the world was in a gray hue. She cleared her throat and got out of the car. A text message dinged on her phone when she got into the house. She withdrew it from her purse and smiled, Allie's message popping up on the screen.

ALLIE

Just thinking of you. I hope the city is treating you well.

IZZIE

I've had a crazy day, but this message made me smile. I should be home in a few days, though. That's encouraging.

ALLIE

I look forward to it. My sheets have gotten a tad cold. :(

Izzie laughed. For a moment, Izzie was comforted by the thrill of mutual flirtation.

IZZIE

Well, we'll have to fix that soon. ;)

She groaned as she headed to her bedroom. The last thing she wanted was to get dressed up for dinner and drinks with a client who wouldn't blink twice to disappoint her. She rummaged through her closet, pulling out one dress after another, finally settling on a blue suit she'd worn a thousand times before. Usually, she didn't even second guess having dinner and drinks with the clients; but if cocktails with sales execs prevented her from getting home to her parents, she'd scowl every time.

She got dressed and stared at her reflection. "Good enough," she mumbled. She left her bathroom and grabbed her bag as another message dinged on her cell. Hope arose as she glanced at the message; her face fell.

RYAN

Not going to make it tonight. Marisa has a stomach bug. I can't leave the wifey home to deal with that alone. When you have kids, you'll understand.

"Unbelievable," she mumbled. Whether it was the truth or an excuse Ryan used to get out of the client dinner, she'd probably never know. Izzie's mood only worsened.

IZZIE

Hope she feels better.

Izzie tossed her phone back in her bag and shrugged it off. A sense of impending doom followed her to the restaurant. Maybe Izzie could only stay for drinks? It wasn't like that was deciding whether a client signed on. She would tell them it'd been a long day, and she'd have an early morning. It was no big deal. Who could fault her for that?

She went into the restaurant. The hostess looked up and smiled. "How many today?"

"Um, two, I believe. I'm here for a Jackson Myers."

"The Myers party is here already. I'll show you to your table." Izzie couldn't even thank her as she trailed behind the hostess to a table far in the back. As she drew closer, her eyes narrowed on the woman sitting at the table. She looked up and greeted Izzie with a table.

Izzie frowned, stopping short of the table. "I don't understand. I'm here to meet with Jackson Myers of Myers and Sons Industries. That, well, it's not Jackson. And they're not a son."

The hostess looked from Izzie to the woman standing at the table, almost as if she anxiously awaited that moment. "It's alright, Susan. She's at the right table. I'll take it from here."

Susan shrugged and turned, walking away. Izzie crossed her arms and stared at Brandy. "Mind telling me what is going on here? There's no deal on the table, is there?"

Brandy tilted her head. "That's not true. Have a seat, and I'll explain everything." Izzie shot a look toward the seat across from Brandy. "Please. If I explain and you want to leave after that, then I won't argue."

Izzie cautiously moved towards the table; this was precisely the sort of shady scheme Brandy loved to orchestrate. While Izzie could hardly believe they dated now, there was a time when she pictured spending her life with Brandy.

She took the seat and stared at Brandy. "I don't want any games, Brandy. I want the truth. You have five minutes."

Brandy arched an eyebrow, then nodded. "I'll be honest that I was hoping that once we saw each other, no time would have passed, and you would understand that I'm not trying to deceive you, but that's not happening."

Izzie glanced at her watch. "Four minutes and counting."

Brandy opened her mouth, then her brows furrowed. "Okay, so here it goes. There is a deal out there, and that deal is with Myers and Sons, as we told your office."

Izzie tilted her head, unsure if she could even believe that much. "I'm the new account manager of Myers and Sons; they're looking to go through a merger. I thought that maybe your company could assist us through the merger. We need advertising and financial advising, which are your specialties. At least in my opinion."

"So, you want me to believe this isn't in some attempt to get me to fall back in your clutches?"

"Why would you say that?" she asked, frowning.

Izzie laughed. "You have been trying to flirt your way back into my life."

"And failed miserably," Brandy huffed. "But the bottom line is perhaps I thought this would be a way to get to you. I thought I could convince you it was the best route for your office."

She turned to the empty seat next to Izzie. "Where's Ryan?" she asked.

"His daughter is sick," Izzie muttered.

"Well, don't forget I thought he was coming, too. So, this wasn't a ploy to get you alone. I am here for all business. Give me a chance, and you'll see."

"Hi, my name is Henry. I'll be your server tonight. What can I start you off with to drink?"

Izzie sighed, glancing between the two of them. She wanted to bolt, but Ryan would find just one more reason to make Izzie stay longer if she didn't at least put in a valiant effort. "I'll take a water."

"Your finest red wine," Brandy stated.

Izzie snickered. "All on Ryan's dime, right?" The waiter walked away, and Brandy smirked.

Izzie regarded Brandy with a healthy level of suspicion.

Dinner dragged on. Despite her best efforts, she laughed at some of Brandy's lame jokes. But it felt like Brandy did have a grasp on what she wanted out of Izzie when it came to business, and Izzie was impressed.

"I hope you can see the vision and want to be a part of it."

"I'll consider your viewpoints and pass them along to Ryan. After all, it's his call."

"But you'll be the one that gives him the recommendation one way or another, right?" Brandy arched an eyebrow.

"Since Ryan isn't here, I'll guide his decision." Izzie shrugged. "I suppose you could say I'm leaning towards signing the deal." Brandy's lips grew into a huge grin. "It is a good deal, but this is business only. You need to understand that."

"I do." She eagerly nodded, then clapped her hands together. "No one would be disappointed if this business arrangement takes place."

"Alright then." Izzie dug in her purse and pulled out the business card.

"We still have drinks," Brandy argued.

Izzie shook her head. "You've already downed two and a half glasses of wine."

"I'm not drunk," she argued.

Izzie smirked. "No, you're right. You don't look drunk. It's been a long day, and I have an early morning."

"You could allow me to buy you one drink, just as a thank you for giving an affirmative recommendation to Ryan."

Izzie shook her head. "Not necessary." Brandy's eyes zoned in on hers, and she remembered Brandy's endless stream of texts asking if they could grab drinks. She looked around and met Henry's gaze, motioning for him to come over and get her tab.

"It could be a celebratory drink," Brandy replied.

"We'll celebrate when Ryan signs the paperwork. We can make him pay."

"You're all set?" Henry asked.

"Yes, thank you." Izzie handed over the bill and card. When she turned back to Brandy, she looked disappointed. Izzie sighed and looked down at her hands, nervously waiting for Henry to return her receipt copy.

"I feel like we had a good time tonight," Brandy began.

"For a business dinner, it was alright," Izzie replied, shrugging.

She glanced around and was relieved to see Henry return to their table. "Thank you." She quickly grabbed the receipt, added the tip, and signed it before looking back at Brandy.

Brandy dropped her gaze. There was a smidge of regret. She shouldn't have allowed the dinner to happen when she knew Brandy had other intentions. She just wanted to believe that there could be something else to it.

"We're over, Brandy. The sooner you can acccpt that, the better off things you'll be. You want us to work in a business arrangement, but I don't even see how that's possible when there are feelings on your part."

"Both of our parts," Brandy argued.

"We have a history together, and nothing can change that." Izzie shrugged. "I'm sorry." She got up from the table, turned, and quickly walked through the restaurant. She took a breath of fresh air once she got outside.

"Izzie!" Brandy called, following after her. Izzie stopped at her car and turned around.

She opened her mouth as Brandy moved in and kissed her. There was a moment of hesitation, maybe due to nostalgia or stupidity, but Izzie allowed the kiss to linger either way. However, once Brandy's tongue swooped in to touch hers, Izzie pushed her back.

"That will never happen again."

Brandy stared at her. "You can't tell me that you felt nothing at that moment. There's a spark between us. If you're going to lie and say that I misread the signs, then maybe I don't know you anymore."

Izzie laughed. "Maybe that's your problem, Brandy. You never really did know me; that's where our relationship problems started." She touched her door handle. "I won't base my judgment on what happened here, but I can't do this anymore. I left us behind a while ago. If you have a problem with that, I don't know what to tell you, but I know I have to do what's best for me." She shrugged. "And that isn't us."

She opened the door and slid into the driver's seat, with Brandy still staring at her from outside her driver's side window.

Izzie put the car in reverse and pulled away from her, desperate to get even a block away from the nightmare that had just occurred. She was mentally kicking herself for allowing the kiss to linger a second longer than needed. She played the memory back in her mind, shaking her head as she pulled into her driveway.

She dug around for her phone until she found it and pulled up Ryan's number.

IZZIE

I'm sorry, I can't do this anymore. I'm heading out of town tomorrow.

She exited her car and hurried to her front door, feeling relief finally flooding through her. Once inside, she heard the text message response.

RYAN

Can we discuss this?

IZZIE

Ryan, I've made up my mind. I need to be there. If you can't accept that I'll be working remotely for the foreseeable future, then maybe you'll decide that you have to let me go. If that's your decision, I'll accept it.

Ryan didn't respond. She stared at her phone, waiting for Ryan's decision, ultimately accepting whatever he said. She swallowed when the response popped up on her phone.

RYAN

You've given me some things to consider. We can discuss it in the morning.

Izzie tossed her phone aside and let the night play out with a nice long shower. If Ryan wanted to fire her, she couldn't object. It wasn't even something that would push her to change her mind. She had every clue she needed to know where her heart wanted to be, which wasn't in the city.

CHAPTER TWENTY-THREE

WELCOME HOME

Allie

"H e's getting weaker," Cheryl noted as Allie entered the kitchen. "He still has good days," Allie began. "This is probably just an off day. They're bound to happen with every hospice patient." She kept her tone pleasant despite fearing that the end was near.

"He misses, Izzie."

Allie dropped her gaze. They weren't the only ones that missed Izzie. It felt like she had been gone an eternity rather than a week. "I have an idea. Let's get a picture and send it to her. I'm sure she misses you both, as well."

"Good idea." Cheryl smiled, jumping from the kitchen table to follow Allie into the living room. Richard's eyes zoned in on the television, but only a commercial was playing. Allie cleared her throat, and he looked at her, offering a weak smile.

"We thought Izzie would like a picture to brighten her day. Cheryl, you stand next to Richard's bed," she instructed. Harry perked up, staring straight ahead. Allie smiled and held her phone up. "Smile."

She snapped a few pictures, then looked down at her phone. "Let's get another selfie with the four of us. I know that'll make Izzie smile." Cheryl was grinning, and so Allie moved in closer to the bed. At this point, she'd do anything for the Roths. She held out her arm, and they all grinned at the phone. Even Harry looked like he had an extra big smile on his face. She snapped a couple of selfies and stepped away from the bed to text her.

She added all the pictures to the message and typed out her text.

> ALLIE
>
> Just some pictures to say don't forget about us. :)

"And sent." Allie stared down at the pictures again, scrolling through them. It made her smile. She just hoped that Izzie wouldn't think she was trying to pressure her to return when Izzie's job needed her in the city.

"So, what do you want to eat?" Allie slipped her phone into her pocket and turned to Richard. He shrugged. "You have to eat and keep up your strength, Richard."

"Allie's right, Dad. You better eat."

Allie turned towards the sound of Izzie's voice. Izzie wore a big smile. "Izzie!" Cheryl ran to her daughter, and they embraced. "This is a nice surprise. You didn't let anyone know you were coming home today."

Izzie shrugged as they parted. "It was a last-minute decision." She shot a look toward Allie.

Allie hung back, unsure if she should run to her or play it cool. Izzie tossed her a genuine smile. "Hey, Allie."

"Hey!" Allie quipped.

"Would you like some help with lunch?" Izzie asked as she moved in closer to Richard.

"Welcome home, sweetheart," he said. Izzie kissed him on the forehead and squeezed his hand. It was a sweet yet heartbreaking reunion. Richard looked like the world had gotten brighter, but he was too weak to celebrate.

Izzie looked over her shoulder and met Allie's gaze. "So, what'd we settle on for lunch?"

Allie shrugged. "Still up in the air." She looked over to Richard. "Did you decide?"

He grinned. "I'll eat, but you both decide. Don't make a fuss."

"Do you need my help?" Cheryl asked.

"No, we're fine, Mom." Izzie led the way to the kitchen, with Allie following after her. Once in the kitchen, Izzie turned and pulled Allie toward her, kissing her with the long-awaited passion that made Allie's toes curl.

She gasped. "Your mom could walk in," she breathlessly replied.

Izzie gave a cheeky grin and shrugged. "Let's give her a show. I'm sure she wouldn't mind." She pulled Allie back to her and left Allie wanting more. She nearly forgot how intense their chemistry was. When Izzie pulled back away from it, she smiled.

"It feels good, right?"

Allie nodded, and her heart continued to race. Allie leaned back against the counter and stared. "So, last minute, huh? Was this meant to be a surprise?"

Izzie quirked up her lips. "Well, there's more to it than that. I'll tell you all about it eventually. What are you doing tonight? It occured to me I've never taken you out on an official date."

"I don't know," Allie began. "I mean, the picnic here was pretty special."

Izzie smirked. "Well yeah, but I can do better than that. We could go to a nice restaurant, movie, or whatever you like. I want to get out and do something, and tonight seems like just as good a night as any. So, what do you say?"

Allie swallowed the lump that had quickly formed in her throat. She wanted to say yes, but more pressing worries had invaded her mind. If they went out on a date, they could run into her parents, and she would face scrutiny. She hated how her parents dominated her life by shoving her into the closet.

"You have to think about it for that long?" Izzie laughed lightly, but her face had clouded over.

Allie quickly shook her head. "No, dinner would be nice. You choose the place."

Izzie leaned in and brushed a kiss across her lips. "I won't disappoint. We have a lot to talk about." She parted, giving a soft wink.

"Now, let's figure out lunch." She turned and went to the cupboards as Allie watched her. She wanted to be as carefree as Izzie, ready to pursue and conquer the world. But if she wanted to be out and proud, she would have to figure that out on her own.

ALLIE GLANCED AROUND THE RESTAURANT IN AWE. SHE HAD never been to a French restaurant before, even if this one was just a few blocks from her apartment. There was no way she could afford it, and it's not like Allie was going to scrape by her rent for some coq au vin.

"Are you sure you want to eat here?" Allie asked. "I feel a bit underdressed. You don't need to break the bank."

Izzie snickered. "I want to do extravagant things for you. Besides, I made the reservation, and we're already seated. It would be inconsiderate to get up and leave." She gave Allie a wink. "Just enjoy it."

Allie nodded but still glanced around the restaurant as if she had never seen chandeliers. The truth was, she had only seen the glass ones in movies. She didn't know how to respond to this level of luxury. She felt this overwhelming sense of insecurity as she looked at the various clientele that graced the restaurant. Maybe she was a tad underdressed. She looked at her blue floral print sundress. Izzie complimented her numerous times before they even made it to the restaurant. Why was she so nervous all of a sudden?

"You look gorgeous," Izzie softly replied, as if she could read Allie's mind. Allie looked up, and Izzie couldn't have smiled any brighter. "Never more beautiful."

She gave her another generous wink, making Allie blush. Allie looked down at her menu, mentally reminding herself not to look at the side where the prices were displayed. Izzie was treating her, and as hard as it was to accept that, she had to let it go.

"Hello, my name is Tiana, and I'll be taking your order today. Can I get you both started with something to drink?"

Allie looked over to Izzie as Izzie opened her mouth. "We'll take a bottle of your finest red wine."

Tiana nodded and turned from them. Allie smirked. "I know what you're trying to do."

Izzie tilted her head. "Give you everything your heart desires? You caught me." Izzie picked up a glass of water they had already placed on their table and took a sip. "I'm shameless that way."

"I was thinking more along the lines of getting me drunk." Allie quirked up her lips in a flirtatious grin.

That brought a laugh from Izzie. She shook her head. "Darling, neither of us needs liquid courage at this point."

Allie's cheeks burned, and she situated herself in her seat. Izzie had a point there. She quickly looked down at the menu, and by the time the waitress returned with their wine, she was ready to order. Izzie motioned to her for her to go first.

"I'll take the Sole Meunière and French Onion Soup on the side."

"And for you?" Tiana asked as she turned to Izzie. Izzie's eyes had narrowed in on Allie inquisitively before she cleared her throat and looked down at the menu. Allie placed her order, ending with a side of Escargot. Allie shivered at the mere thought of eating snails. When Tiana left, Izzie glanced back at Allie.

"I'm impressed," she said.

"By?" Allie inquired.

"Well, I didn't know you spoke French." Izzie laughed

She shook her head. "You never cease to amaze me." She swirled her glass of wine in front of Allie.

"Well, I took four years of French in high school. Also, I know what Escargot is and can't imagine anyone choosing to eat that."

Izzie laughed. "You'd be surprised how good they taste. Don't knock it until you try it."

"I'll take your word for it." Allie picked up her glass and swirled it around as Izzie had done moments ago.

"I propose a toast," Izzie replied before Allie could take her drink. Allie raised her glass. "I hope we always find beauty, love new people, and never shy away from uncertainty." Izzie arched an eyebrow, and that was Allie's cue.

"To letting your heart take the lead." Allie smiled.

"Always, babe." Izzie winked, and then they both took a drink. Allie heaved a sigh, placing the glass down on the table. "I can tell something is on your mind."

"I'm curious. You showed up out of nowhere this morning. How did you even get here?"

Izzie looked down at her glass of wine. "It all started last night." Allie listened as Izzie told her the story of Brandy and how the evening unfolded. She didn't interrupt. She focused on her wine and absorbed the information.

"Things with Brandy ended long ago, but I suppose she's been itching for us to get back together." Izzie released a groan. "Frankly, I'll confess that last night only cemented the idea that I'm done with her."

"So, you didn't feel anything, even when she kissed you?" Allie was hesitant, but she had to ask.

Izzie stared at Allie, unmoving. Tiana arrived with their plates. The question hung in the air between them. "Thank you," Izzie replied, still looking at Allie. Tiana left, and Izzie began. "So, you know how sometimes, you see someone from your past, and it's like your past comes flooding back?"

Allie slowly nodded.

"I guess that when Brandy and I talked, I thought we could focus on the good times. Then when she kissed me...."

"It meant nothing to me. It was then that I realized I needed to get out of there. My boss, Ryan, only cares about what he wants, not what is better for his employees. I've been over it for a while now." Izzie dropped her gaze to the plate of the Escargot perched beside her salad. "It could have cost me my job, though."

"What?"

Izzie laughed and looked back up, shrugging. "If it happens, it happens." She picked up Escargot with her fork and put it on Allie's plate.

Allie shook her head. "I wouldn't want to eat your food. Thanks anyway!" She pushed it back to Izzie's plate. Izzie snickered.

Izzie sliced off a sliver of it and held it up to Allie's lips. "Just one bite."

Allie decided to be brave despite her snail-based reservations. She opened her mouth and took a bite. On the first bite, she wasn't sold, but then, slowly, she could appreciate the taste.

"Good, right?" Izzie asked.

"I'll be honest. It's not bad." Allie wiped her mouth off and grinned. "I would order it again."

"See, you never know until you taste that first bite." She winked, and Allie coughed, not wanting to laugh. They were talking about more than just the first taste of Escargot, and she was happy that she could finally accept that.

CHAPTER TWENTY-FOUR

SOMETHING GOOD

Izzie

Izzie sat back in her chair and tilted her head. "So? What do you think?"

"You're showing all sorts of new things, aren't you?" Allie laughed, and Izzie watched as she licked her lips and nodded approvingly. "You are right, though. The Dreamsicle is among my top three favorite ice cream flavors."

Izzie clapped with glee. "I didn't think you would be disappointed. I can't believe you've never tried it before." Izzie dug into her cup of ice cream. She pointed to the cup that sat in front of Allie. Vanilla and chocolate are so plain for someone like you."

Allie laughed and shrugged. "I know what I like! What can I say?"

Izzie took a bite of her ice cream and swirled her spoon into the cup. "You surprise me every day." Allie's cheeks turned a deep red.

"Tonight was nice," Allie began. "I'm glad you're back here, even if you might lose your job. I hope your boss realizes it would be a terrible decision to fire you."

Izzie quirked her lips into a smile. "Well, like I said, whatever happens,

happens. Tonight made my week." Izzie finished her cup of ice cream and looked at Allie's. "But, I hope that it's not over."

"What'd you have in mind?" Allie asked, a teasing grin gracing those beautiful lips of hers.

"Well, why don't we get out of here, and you can find out."

Izzie reached out and grabbed Allie's empty cup, then grabbed her hand. They got up from the table and walked hand-in-hand past the trash can. Izzie tossed their empty cups into the trash. Allie's grasp felt so small in her hand but warm.

They walked to Izzie's car, and Izzie opened the door for Allie. Before Allie could get into the car, Izzie pulled her toward her and kissed her. Izzie's tongue slipped into Allie's lips, and Allie fell against her. Izzie snaked her arm around Allie, holding her tight.

"Some people just don't know how to get a room. The last thing I want to see is two lesbians sticking their tongues down each other's throats." A man huffed as he walked by them. Izzie pulled from the kiss and turned to him.

"The last thing I want to hear is some old dude being a prude while I'm out with my girlfriend! Get a life!" Izzie called.

"Izzie, quit it," Allie muttered, yanking back on Izzie's shoulder. Izzie turned to Allie, and Allie dropped her gaze.

"This is exactly why I moved away," Izzie huffed.

"I'm not going to have some ancient asshole spewing homophobia at us when we're literally existing. Screw him. I bet he's fucking miserable."

Allie sighed but dropped her gaze to the ground. Her brows furrowed, and Izzie sensed Allie's discomfort.

"Allie," Izzie started.

"Let's just get out of here," Allie muttered. She slid into the car and pulled the door behind her.

Izzie fell back, waiting cautiously before hurrying to the car's other side and entering the driver's seat. The ride to Allie's apartment was tense. When Izzie looked over to say something, Allie quickly looked out the window. Izzie decided to let it go. She didn't want to fight or let that old dirtbag take up any more of her energy.

At the apartment, Allie was the first one to speak. "We can say our goodbyes out here," she mumbled. She met Izzie's gaze. "Goodbye. I had a good time."

Izzie rolled her eyes and looked away, "You had a good time until I told off that octagenarian homophobe."

Allie shook her head. "It had nothing to do with that. I understand why you would say something. People should mind their own business, but..." She glanced away, staring out the passenger window. "I'm just not sure what to think." She turned back to Izzie.

"Maybe I'm not cut out for this." She gave a nonchalant shrug. "Goodnight."

She opened the door, but Izzie was two steps ahead. She quickly opened the door and hurried after Allie, not letting her reach her door before she grabbed her arm to stop her. Allie turned around, and a few tears stuck to her cheeks. "You're better off with someone else, Izzie. Trust me."

"There is no one else, Allie." Izzie stepped in, closing the gap. "You need time? I'll give you time, but don't shut me out."

Allie opened her mouth, but Izzie had already moved in and kissed her, not letting Allie utter whatever words were hanging in the back of her throat. "We could have something good here, Allie." Izzie rested her forehead against Allie's.

"Don't run away from it just because you're scared." She slid her fingers through Allie's, then turned and walked away.

"Don't go!" Allie called.

Izzie turned around and breathlessly stared at Allie. Allie reached for Izzie's hand and pulled her down the hallway toward her room. She fumbled with the key, then finally got the apartment opened. Izzie fell into the door after Allie, and they embraced, the hunger once against returning.

Izzie grabbed Allie's zipper and helped her out of her dress, slowly falling to the floor of Allie's living room. Allie pulled Izzie after her toward the bedroom. Their lips crashed back together, their tongues wildly colliding with one another's. "I don't want to be scared," Allie whispered. While they kissed, she undid her bra and let it fall to the floor. She fell back onto the bed and stared at Izzie. Her nipples were pert.

Izzie slipped out of her dress, letting it fall in a pile at her feet, then kicked out her panties and pulled off her bra. "With me, you'll never have to." She knelt in front of Allie and grabbed onto Allie's panties. Their eyes connected, and she slipped the panties off and down Allie's legs. She moved her fingers between Allie's legs and slipped them inside, watching Allie close her eyes and rest in a satisfied grin. She needed Allie to trust her.

"What do you think?" Allie asked, holding up the plate in front of her. She shifted her body from the right to the left, and Izzie dropped her gaze to her hips. She smirked, then looked up and met Allie's grin. "I mean, about the pattern."

"I know, and that's quite disappointing." Izzie winked and moved in to grab the plate from Allie.

"If you go with the one with the stars, that's pretty self-explanatory." She kissed Allie. It was right out in the open, and Allie didn't once attempt to pull back. It'd been three days since they had that awkward encounter in the parking lot. Izzie appreciated that Allie seemed to be quite content making out in public.

They had decided to go to the department store and pick out some items to refresh the Stars and Stripes look. Izzie loved having Allie by her side. She couldn't imagine doing the task without her vision and input, even if it took Allie a couple of minutes to speak up.

"How many do you think you'll need?" Allie placed the plate back in its spot and turned to look at Izzie.

"Well, I'm expecting a large turnout for our grand opening, so at least a thousand to start with. If it comes down to it, we can always use the current dinnerware for a backup plan." Izzie looked around the dinnerware section as Allie hurried over to the glasses.

"Look at these," she excitedly exclaimed. "These glasses match the plates, and they have the stars etched into the glass."

"And look at these." Izzie grabbed another glass. There are hearts. We could buy some that we use for special occasions."

Allie tilted her head. "That would be adorable." She then frowned. "Is there going to be enough money for this, though? With your job and all...." Her words fell off.

"You know the saying; it takes money to make money." Izzie shrugged. "Besides, with Ryan, no news is good news. As I said before, I refuse to worry about it. We'll figure it out. I say we'll take five hundred of these glasses."

Allie wrote down the information and then moved on to the cloth napkins. Izzie watched her for a moment, relishing in how much she cared about this woman, nearly taken back by surprise by that overwhelming feeling.

Allie turned around on her heel and held up a pattern. "What do you think?" she asked.

Izzie smiled. "What do you think?"

Allie's jaw dropped, and she looked up, her cheeks turning a soft pink. "I asked you first." She looked back down at the napkin and nodded enthusiastically. "I think it would like with the place setting." She looked up as Izzie moved in closer to her. "But my opinion doesn't matter nearly as much as yours does."

Izzie laughed and grabbed the napkin from her. She surveyed it, closing one eye, then shifting her gaze before nodding. "I think it's quite nice."

She tossed it to the side. "But, I think you're more exciting to stare at." She winked and brushed her hand along Allie's cheekbone before pressing her lips against Allie's.

Allie gasped, opening her mouth slightly. "In the middle of a depart-ment store? So scandalous." Allie giggled, then stepped away from her, keeping distance between them. "How many should I put down?"

"I'd say a thousand."

Allie opened her mouth and looked over her shoulder. "People can get messy."

"They come in a pack of twenty-five. So, we're getting twenty-five thousand napkins?" She arched an eyebrow, then laughed.

Izzie scrunched up her nose. "Too many?"

Allie shrugged. "Well, you did say people can get messy, so maybe it's necessary. Before we place our order, we can reevaluate."

"Whatever you say, darling." Izzie moved in and brushed a kiss across Allie's nose. Allie grinned, and their eyes met. There was a second where Izzie wanted to swoop in and pull Allie into her arms. Feeling this way about a woman made Izzie feel like she was floating. She opened her mouth, aching to express how much the moment meant to her.

"Allie? Is that you?"

Izzie turned to face that man who had invaded their intimate moment. His eyes dropped over Izzie, and then he gazed at Allie. Allie quickly stepped back from her.

"Sean! Long, um, time no see." Allie dropped her gaze to the department store floor as Izzie stepped back to give them more space. Allie's cheeks were a fiery red, and Izzie quickly looked away, suppressing her urge to stare.

"Yeah, it's certainly been a long time. It looks like you've got a lot going on." He laughed loudly, then shook his head. Izzie drew in her gaze and glared in his direction.

He snickered. "Allie! I never would have thought I'd see the day." He shrugged. "I guess that explains a lot."

"What?" Allie began.

He arched an eyebrow. "Things between us always seemed off." He snickered again. "I guess I didn't have the parts you were looking for."

"Now listen here," Izzie started. "I don't know who you are or what your deal is, but you can't go around talking like that about anyone, especially Allie."

Allie's cheeks deepened as she quickly looked away from Izzie. Izzie turned away. She had probably said too much already, but it pained her to see Allie frozen in her spot, looking terrified.

"Do your parents know, Allie?" Izzie glanced in his direction, and he had nudged his head in Izzie's direction.

"Sean," Allie began.

He shook his head. "See ya around," he muttered. He moved past Izzie, mumbling something under his breath. It was so low that Izzie couldn't make the words out, but it wasn't anything that she figured would be a compliment.

"Sean!" Allie hollered. "Sean, wait." She hurried after him, leaving Izzie behind. Izzie reached for the napkin she had tossed to the side earlier and fluffed it back into place. She glanced in the direction of Allie, who walked back over to her, her gaze downward.

"Are you alright?" Izzie asked. The mood shifted; any levity she'd felt with Allie was gone.

Allie shrugged, then looked down at her notepad. "Do you mind if we finish this up some other time? I'm not feeling well."

"Not at all." Izzie barely got the words out before Allie turned and led the way to the front of the store. Izzie hung back, her heart breaking from the sadness clouded over Allie's face.

All Izzie wanted to do was pull Allie in her arms and tell her everything would be okay.

CHAPTER TWENTY-FIVE

NEAR BREAKING POINT

Allie

Allie stared out the window for the first half of the ride back to her apartment, unable to face Izzie's disappointed face. She knew that Izzie was most likely seething in the driver's seat. She sighed and looked over her shoulder. Izzie stared straight ahead, a frown on her face. Allie wrung her hands together. The tension in the car was palpable.

"Do you wanna tell me what that was all about?" Allie looked up and met Izzie's stare before Izzie turned back. Allie opened her mouth, then swallowed and turned away. "I've been debating whether I should say anything; maybe it would be best to let you deal with this how you want to. But I care about you, Allie. I don't want you hurting, and it's clear that Sean or whoever ruined your day. If you want to talk about it, I'm here." She shrugged. "And if you don't..." She released a breath and shifted her gaze back to Allie's. "I'm still here."

Izzie closed her mouth, her thoughts rushing back to hearing how Allie's parents would disapprove of their relationship, but was that all this was about? She bit her lip to tamp down her questions.

Allie sighed next to her, and Izzie waited. "Sean is an ex of mine," Allie began. "It was years ago, but I guess those wounds are still so deep. It wasn't like we were destined to be together or anything." She stared back out the window. "Maybe my parents hoped it was more than what it was. But we could never be together."

"I see," Izzie softly replied. "So, your parents would approve of him, but not me?" Izzie cast a look out of the corner of her eye. "Sean was surprised to see you being affectionate with a woman, so let me go out on a limb here. Your parents aren't the only ones that wouldn't approve, right? Are you not out to anyone?"

Allie shook her head. "No one knows you're a lesbian? Not a single person? You've never told anyone?" Izzie didn't want to believe it. How could their relationship exist in the real world if no one knew about it?

Allie sighed. "My sister, I suppose. I thought I was bi for a while. It's no secret that you were my first. I've been pretty clear about that, but I've been in relationships with guys." She huffed.

"They put me down, and I couldn't get my parents to see this. So hiding my true self was the only thing I could do."

"That's bullshit." Izzie shook her head, and Allie's jaw dropped. "I'm sorry, Allie, but it is. You have to stand up for what you believe in. You are an adult, and you ran after your ex, begging him not to tell your parents like you got caught sneaking out after curfew."

Allie sighed, her mouth closing. "Am I wrong?"

"You don't get it," Allie mumbled. She turned to look out the window. "You've grown up in this perfect little house with this perfect family. You couldn't possibly understand what I've had to go through."

"You're making excuses, Allie."

Allie looked down, her arms crossed. "Again, you don't get it."

"I get that what you might think looks like this perfect life on the outside doesn't mean that I have everything my heart desires. If it did, I would have been married long ago. You aren't the only one, Allie, who has faced relationship challenges. We all have a different story. That's all."

Izzie pulled into a parking spot, and Allie glanced at the door handle, wondering how quickly she could grab the handle and launch out of the car. She was liable to burst into tears if she didn't leave soon. Instead, she stayed, turning to see Izzie's eyes focused on her.

"You have to decide what's important in life, not your parents," Izzie shook her head. "You should have gotten past that stage of your life long ago."

Allie turned away and reached for the handle. At the same time, Izzie did, too.

"You don't have to," Allie argued.

Izzie sighed and walked Allie to her apartment. A heavy silence hung between them. When Allie reached the door, Izzie grabbed her hand, her fingers tracing over Allie's.

"Don't let one person ruin your life. Got that?"

Allie looked up and gave a slow nod before Izzie leaned in and offered a soft kiss. It was short, and she turned and walked away, leaving Allie gawking. Allie grabbed the keys to her apartment and unlocked the door. When the door closed behind her, she grabbed her phone and texted Sean.

ALLIE

I'm begging you. Don't tell my parents.

Allie stared at the text. With just one click, she could have the message out there. She closed her eyes and deleted the message, slipping her phone back into her pocket. If they knew, she could finally break free from her parent's expectations, even if it would wreck her relationship with her family.

CHAPTER TWENTY-SIX

MOVING FORWARD

Izzie

I zzie stared at her phone; she hadn't heard a word from Allie in two days. A slew of other nurses showed up to care for her father, and Izzie would be lying if she didn't question if that was on purpose.

Izzie looked back at her phone, closing her eyes and willing it to start ringing. She'd even accept a text message, something short and sweet, to tell Izzie that she wasn't upset with her. They had left things up in the air at Allie's apartment, and Izzie didn't want things to stay too distant between them. She pulled up Allie's number and went to call her when her phone rang. Her face fell when she saw Ryan's name flashing across the screen --this could only mean one thing. Either he was calling to fire her, or he wanted to talk about business. But if he wanted to talk about business with her, he could email her. Something wasn't right.

If he fires you, you're certainly better off. Besides, you'll have too much to do. You're still fixing up the restaurant. Remember that everything happens for a reason.

"Hello?"

"Didn't think I'd catch you; the phone rang longer than expected." He sounded formal and did not indicate whether this phone call was good or bad.

"I was in the other room," she lied. "May I help you?" If he wanted to talk business, then she could do the same. Two could play it cool. The number one rule of business was never to let someone see you sweat.

"Well, I wanted to give you an update on things. We signed the papers with Myers and Sons Industries this morning."

Izzie's mouth dropped open. "And?"

"Well, I thought you'd want to be kept in the loop since you'll be the leading person on this account."

"So, I'm hearing that you have decided that I'm more valuable as a remote employee than as a non-existent employee. Is that what you're saying?"

"Come on, Iz. You knew that I'd never do without you. We're a team, and there's no way the company would survive without you."

Izzie rolled her eyes. "I don't know if I believe that," Izzie started. "Besides, I don't think I can work on the Myers and Sons account."

"Elizabeth, you have to be joking. Why? It has to be one of the biggest accounts that have ever come across our desk. Any employee would be ecstatic to have it."

Izzie sighed. "Then give it to someone else. I don't want the account." There wasn't any reason to believe Brandy was the one who greenlit the deal. But if Brandy wanted to get them in this situation, she wouldn't play along with it. She didn't want Brandy to lord anything over her.

"You don't understand," Ryan huffed. "Without you, there isn't a deal. They have seven days to back out, contingent on you signing the paperwork. I was going to email them to you after we get off this call."

"But why?" Izzie asked.

"They want the best, I assume. We all know you're the best."

It wasn't likely. "I don't know," Izzie mumbled.

"Do you want more money?" Ryan asked. "You say the word, and I'll get you more money."

"What? It has nothing to do with the money, Ryan." A knock on the door jarred Izzie away from the conversation. Her mom peeked in the room, and Izzie motioned to her cell phone.

"Allie is here. I wanted to let you know," her mom whispered.

Izzie nodded and then turned back to her conversation. "I have to go. Send over the contract, but I'm not committing to sign it."

"Izzie," Ryan began. Izzie disconnected the call and pocketed her phone.

She had been wondering what she would say to Allie; now that the moment was there, she needed to figure it out quickly.

Izzie hurried downstairs, and she could hear Allie's voice coming from the living room. "You look good, Richard," she replied. "And I've been getting some great feedback from the other nurses. I'm relieved to see your pain is improved today."

"We've been missing you, though." His tone was still weak. Izzie entered the room as Allie looked up and met her gaze.

"I've missed you, too." She gave a weak smile to Izzie before turning back to look at Izzie's dad. "All of you. It was nice having a couple of days off, but it's good to be back."

"I have to run to the restaurant," Cheryl called from the corner of the living room. "Does any of you need anything before I head out?"

"I'm good, Cheryl. Thanks." Allie sat down on the rocker and jotted down some things in his chart.

"I'm good, Mom," Izzie muttered. Izzie stayed back and waited for her moment to enter and bring in a conversation with Allie.

"How have you been feeling, Richard, since your last observation yesterday?" Allie asked.

"Can't complain. I have my two favorite women here that are happy and healthy. What guy could complain about that?"

"I'd have to say you have much to be thankful for." Allie looked over to Izzie without smiling. "But I was more thinking about your pain. On a scale from one to ten, where is your pain today?"

"Four," he said with confidence.

"That's better than yesterday." Allie took some more notes, then put the chart to the side. "So, do you want something to eat or drink?"

"I'll take some water," he replied. Allie turned and again met Izzie's gaze before hurrying past her to the kitchen. Izzie hesitated but then turned and followed her to the kitchen.

Allie turned from the sink and halted when Izzie entered the kitchen. "Allie, I'm sorry."

Allie looked away from her and shrugged. "Sorry for what?" she asked.

Izzie stepped in closer to her. "I'm sorry if you thought I was frustrated with you. I wasn't frustrated with you; I was frustrated with the situation. We didn't exactly end the night on a great note." Allie looked up. Izzie wondered if Allie would fully open up, and when Allie nodded without saying anything. "So, I'm sorry."

"I'm sorry, too." Allie held up the water. "I should get this to your dad." Before she could pass Izzie, Izzie reached out and grabbed her wrist.

"But are we going to be okay?" Izzie asked.

Allie slowly nodded. "Everything's fine." Izzie released her wrist, and Allie fled from the kitchen. The warm fuzzy feeling she usually felt with Allie was gone. The room was cold.

She stepped out of the kitchen and heard Allie's gentle voice wafting in from the living room. She could turn her feelings off, but Izzie didn't want to. She still cared greatly about Allie and longed for Allie to voice what she felt. Izzie left the living room and went back up the stairs to her room. She grabbed her laptop and pulled up Ryan's email. If she signed the contract, she said she had no qualms with how the company worked. She would surely be saying she was ready to quit if she didn't. Izzie needed to make the difficult decision sooner rather than later.

IZZIE'S PHONE DINGED WITH A TEXT MESSAGE. SHE HAD BEEN staring at her email off and on for hours but hadn't come any closer to deciding whether she would sign the contract. It was never about the money, but maybe something else could persuade her if she was that deadset against working with Brandy.

She grabbed her phone, and the message from Mae popped up.

MAE

Can you talk?

IZZIE

Sure. What's up?

Immediately her phone started ringing. "Yeah?" she answered.

"So, have you decided whether to sign the contract?"

Izzie snickered. "So, did Ryan put you up to this? Is that what this is about?"

"What? No. Never." Izzie had been friends with Mae long enough to know when she wasn't being truthful. She didn't reply, and Mae cleared her throat. "Are you still there?"

"I'm here, but I find it interesting that the day Ryan reaches out to me, you also reach out to me. No, I haven't signed the contract, and I'm honestly going back and forth. I'm weighing my options. I don't think it would be healthy for me to work with Brandy."

"Well, Izzie, you must do what you feel most inclined to do, but can I give you my two cents?"

Izzie laughed. "Have I ever stopped you before?"

"Well, true. The fact that Brandy snuck into a business dinner and tried to kiss you isn't great. It's pretty bad. I totally get it, and if you sign this contract, you'll need to set some pretty hardcore boundaries. Starting with making sure she knows where you stand. But, I think you need to ask yourself if Brandy tempted you or if you don't think you can trust yourself to work closely together."

Izzie sighed. "I guess the way I look at it is there was a moment where Brandy and I were laughing and carrying on like things used to be, but it wasn't in a sensual or intimate sort of way. We just clicked in a friendly manner. Part of me wishes we could be friends. We could work together and not have to dance around each other, wondering if something sexual would happen. And then she kissed me out of nowhere."

"When she kissed you, did you realize you still had feelings for her?" Mae asked.

Izzie shook her head, then snickered. "Honestly, it wasn't until she kissed me that I realized nothing like that could ever happen again. I'm over her; a thousand percent. I know that that's true. There's only one woman that I want to get close to."

"You see? Then what do you have to worry about?"

Izzie considered the question. She didn't have to worry about herself. It was Brandy that she had to worry about. Yet, if she could trust herself, then there was nothing Brandy could do to affect her.

"I need to go. I'll call you later." Before Mae could say goodbye, Izzie hung up the call, pushed her computer to the side, and rushed from her bedroom. She hurried downstairs, where her dad was watching television. "Allie?" Izzie entered the kitchen, but there was no one. She went to the living room, but her dad was alone. "Where's Allie?"

He turned from the television. "She had to leave. Her mom called and needed help with her meds or something."

Izzie frowned. "She just left you? You might have needed something."

He laughed. "She knew you were here. Her mom needed something. Don't try and tell me you wouldn't help your parents if they asked."

"I suppose," Izzie mumbled. "Do you need anything?"

He shook his head. "Physically, I'm good. But I could use a chat with my girl." He patted the side of his bed, and Izzie smiled and moved to take a seat. "So, what's going on between you two?"

"Us two? Like Allie and myself?"

He nodded. "Yep, those would be the two I'm referring to." He gave her a wink, and Izzie glanced toward the television.

"Not much to say," she softly replied. "I'd rather discuss the restaurant."

"Allie is helping you with that, right?" He gave another wink, and Izzie snickered. Before that moment, Allie had been helping in most aspects of Izzie's life.

"Anyway, I'm getting ready to order some new place settings and napkins. The grand re-opening is going to be great. I'm getting excited about it."

"That's great, honey." He leaned back in his bed and turned back to her. "It's good to have you home. Have I told you that lately?"

"Every chance you get. And I'm glad to be here." Izzie reached out and took his hand, squeezing it tightly. As he held her hand, he closed his eyes. Izzie looked away as tears stung the backs of her eyes. There would come a day when he wouldn't be there for her to talk with and hold hands. She couldn't fathom that day approaching.

"I'm not afraid to die," he said. Izzie turned back to him, and he watched her like he could read her mind. "People say you find the stages of grief, but I have to say I've never felt this fear of dying. I'm afraid my family won't be able to cope when I'm gone."

"Dad, you don't have to be afraid of that," Izzie whispered. "Dying is a part of life. We'll miss you, of course, but that shouldn't be something you have to think about."

"Life is too short," he whispered. "You never know when you'll take your last breath. So, that's what reminds us not to waste one minute. There's more to life than work. You have to find happiness and hold onto it. Just remember that." He smiled, then closed his eyes as their fingers remained intertwined. Izzie brought his fingers to her lips and kissed them before releasing them down to his side. She turned the television off and left the living room to return to her bedroom.

Her dad was right, there was more to life than work, but she couldn't leave jobs unfinished. She grabbed her laptop and pulled up Ryan's email.

Ryan –

I will sign this on one condition. I can terminate it anytime if I feel things aren't working out. There is no exception; I get the final say at every turn. They can take it or leave it, but that is my stipulation. Let me know, and if they agree, I will send it back to you.

Elizabeth

There, that was what she could live with. Hopefully, they would be willing to compromise.

CHAPTER TWENTY-SEVEN

A HARD ROAD

Allie

Allie glanced up the stairs, a weight in her chest. It wasn't the first text she had received from Sean since bumping into him at the department store. She'd been able to ignore him. One more text wouldn't hurt.

A week had passed, and Izzie and she hadn't said more than a few words to one another. She had hoped by now things would have blown over and she would have been at peace with where their relationship was going. Yet, every time she considered calling Izzie, a text appeared, or her parents needed something.

Izzie seemed distant, and while Allie understood Izzie's frustrations, she had her own to overcome.

She entered the living room, where Cheryl and Richard were watching television. She didn't want to interrupt them; frankly, it was Izzie she needed to talk to. She grabbed a folder from the table and headed out of the living room. When she got upstairs, Izzie's door was ajar.

"It's open," Izzie called after Allie had knocked. Allie pushed the door open but was careful not to step over the invisible line that led straight into Izzie's bedroom. She couldn't cross that boundary, even if she wanted to. Izzie looked up from her computer, then quickly stood to her feet. "Hey, I was going to come down a bit later and see if any of your Cranberry pie was left. That stuff is some of your best work." Izzie licked her lips, still smiling.

"Thank you." Allie blushed, glancing down at the folder in her hand. "I know you like it, so I added it to the menu." Allie held it up. "And speaking of, the full menu has been finalized."

"Great! I look forward to checking out the final product." Izzie moved in and grabbed the folder from her. "Come sit. Do you need a break or anything?" Izzie motioned into the room and tilted her head.

Allie quickly shook her head. "That's alright. I'm fine."

Izzie mumbled something but didn't speak up so Allie could hear. She looked down at the folder and leafed through each page, nodding as she skimmed through each one. Allie stayed in place, nervously waiting for Izzie to comment one way or the other.

"This looks great," Izzie commented after several minutes of looking over the dishes Allie had added to the menu. She looked up and grinned. "And the advertising that the restaurant is getting is causing quite the buzz for this reopening. I really can't thank you enough for all you've done."

"I haven't done much." Allie looked down at the floor. "I just hope that it's enough." She shrugged and stepped back from the bedroom. She would have given anything for Izzie to close the distance between them. Instead, they stayed firmly planted in their respective spots.

"It's going to be great," Izzie commented.

Allie nodded, her eyes grazing over Izzie's lips and then her cheekbones. She had contemplated a moment where they would fall into each other's arms. Perhaps Izzie would push her into bed, and they would make mad, passionate love to one another again. But, for them to be together, Allie had to come out of the closet.

"I returned to the store and ordered the place settings and napkins. They'll all be ready to deliver in a few weeks."

A pit formed in her gut-- she should have been there, but then

599

bumping into Sean terrified her. What kind of life would it be if she constantly ran from her fears?

"It's all going to go great," Allie replied. "Well, I should let you get back to work."

"Right! I'll see ya around." Izzie closed the door, and Allie turned and stepped toward the stairs as another text came to her phone. She sighed and grabbed her phone.

SEAN

What's your plan? If you ignore me, it's just not going to go away. If you have nothing to hide from, why not shout it from the rooftops? LOL. Never mind, I know the answer to that.

Allie rolled her eyes, but he kept texting.

SEAN

What's being a lesbian like?

A winking emoji ended the message.

ALLIE

Shut up, Sean!

The moment she sent the text, she felt regret. Why did she let Sean get under her skin? She didn't feel guilty for being gay. Then why did she even care what Sean had to say? He was back to controlling her, infuriating her beyond words. She thought about so many responses that she could get that closure she needed, yet none of the words flowed. She stomped downstairs in disgust. She'd get there, but it wasn't the right time.

CHAPTER TWENTY-EIGHT

A FRESH PERSPECTIVE

Izzie

Izzie looked over the menu again. It was clear how much hard work Allie had put into it, and she would be lying if she said that it didn't endear her to Allie again. If only that were all she needed. She needed Allie to be truthful and not give her reason to doubt the woman she came to know.

She pulled up the picture of Allie on her phone, the very first one she had ever taken of her. Harry made a whimpering sound, and she looked at him and ruffled her fingers through his scruff.

"I know, boy. I feel the same way."

Maybe Allie's perfect smile was only a facade, and Allie wasn't the perfect being Izzie once saw her as. She closed her eyes and shook her head. It wasn't true. Allie was genuine and kind-hearted. She was someone Izzie could envision the rest of her life with. Just because people had hurdles they needed to overcome didn't mean this wasn't a relationship worth fighting for.

She stared back at the picture of her, and immediately Izzie smiled. Allie was the woman that she believed she was, past and all. No one was perfect. Allie needed Izzie's empathy right now more than ever. Izzie's parents had accepted her without so much as a blink. She couldn't imagine being trapped in the closet in her mid-twenties.

They needed to have difficult and deep conversations. Izzie knew Allie was worth fighting for; she could feel it in her bones.

Izzie pulled up Mae's number and dialed it. "Hey, you've reached Mae. I'm not able to talk right now. Leave your number, and we'll chat later."

"Hey, it's Izzie. Call me back when you can."

She disconnected the call and looked over at her computer. Instead of thinking about Allie, she needed to concentrate on work. She pulled up her email and skimmed through it, landing on an email from Ryan. It was the first time she had heard from him all week. She did work on the side, trying to stay ahead of the flow of clients without overextending herself in case Ryan fired her. The fact that he hadn't said anything when she was clocking in led her to believe he wasn't entirely through with her. But now, an email could be her make or break.

"Here goes nothing," she muttered.

Elizabeth –

I spoke with them, and it's official. They readjusted the contract with your demands. You get the final say on every-thing; if you want to discontinue the contract at any point, it's your prerogative. Please sign the papers ASAP so we can get this deal going.

Ryan

Izzie was surprised, but a deal was a deal. She pulled up the contract and read through it once more. To finalize it, she documented her name with its electronic signature and then gave the contact a once-over before sending it back to Ryan. Now she needed to get to work, and if that meant maintaining communication with Brandy, she would figure it out.

Her phone rang. Mae's number flashed on the screen. "Hello?"

"Sorry, I missed your call. What's up?"

"Well, for starters, I just signed the Myers and Sons contract, so that's official." Izzie continued to rub the top of Harry's head.

"Whoa, I didn't actually think you would sign." Mae laughed lightly. "But, guess it gives us more work, so yay." Izzie could hear the slight sarcasm, and that caused her to snicker. "But, I already sense there is something more."

"I need some advice. One woman to another."

"Always. What's up?" Mae asked.

"It's Allie. I'm starting to fear that maybe she's hiding some things from me. Well, maybe a few things, but she's not out of the closet to her family or anyone that truly matters in her life."

Mae exhaled. "Honestly, that's a hard thing to do. If she's never had a relationship with a woman, it's no wonder. People have to do it at their own pace." Mae took a breath. "How'd your parents react when you came out?"

"They were surprised," Izzie admitted. "But, ultimately, they embraced me. They said they wanted me to be who I wanted to be and would support me in any way they could. They love me unconditionally, no matter who I happen to love."

"Well, not everyone has the same loving family. You are lucky in that respect. So, if Allie is having a hard time saying the words or speaking her truth, it could be because she never found the support that you have."

Izzie slowly nodded. That was true, but if Allie couldn't open up to her about that, how would Izzie ever be able to commit to her emotionally?

"When I first told my mom I liked a woman," Mae laughed. "It wasn't a pleasant experience. There was a moment when I thought she might never accept it. She would try to set me up with her friend's sons or friends of friends, and so on. It was like she wanted to change me, and it was frustrating. My dad seemed more understanding, but then again, it's not like he's ever truly given me the time of day, so he probably just shrugged it off."

Mae came from a single-mom home. Her dad took off when she was eight. He was still in the picture, but barely, and both Mae and her mother seemed fine with it. Mae knew from a young age she was bi-sexual. But her current girlfriend appeared to be the love of her life. Izzie was envious. "I can empathize with how Allie feels. I found Cass, and I can't imagine being happy with anyone else. Eventually, Allie will get there, but it could take some time."

Izzie thought about that for a moment before commenting. "So, what do you think I should do? I want Allie to feel like she can open up to me, not hide how she really feels."

"Then I think you need to talk to her about that. It takes some people longer to warm up and see that even though they don't have support from their family, it doesn't mean they don't have support elsewhere. You could be her support system. But I wouldn't give up on it until you have given it a shot."

Izzie just wanted Allie to stand up for herself, but maybe she was putting too much pressure on Allie. She needed to listen to Mae. She needed to give it time.

CHAPTER TWENTY-NINE

CONFESSION

Allie

"Talk to your mother," her father warned. "She's going to wind up dead, and it will be your fault." As the words sunk in, Allie cowered back on her couch. She could already feel the pressure building inside of her. Why did her father have to add so much more?

"Dad?" she argued. "Hello? Hello?"

"Allie, is that you?" Her mother's voice came onto the phone.

"Mom?" Allie sat up straighter on the couch. Her father told her the bare minimum, just that her mom refused to go to the hospital because of the exorbitant bill insurance wouldn't cover. "What's wrong, Mom?"

"My stomach has been causing me issues. I'm sure it's nothing, no need to fret." Allie was surprised by her nonchalant attitude.

"You probably should go get it checked out. It's the weekend. If you wait until Monday, it could be a lot worse. Do you need a ride or something?"

"I don't need to go. I don't want to go. I have enough bills to deal with from the accident. Who knows what the insurance company will do to screw me over this time."

"But, Mom," Allie began. "If you're in that much pain, you really need to get checked out."

"I'm fine," she repeated. "I have to go. I have a roast in the oven."

"Alright, goodbye." Allie disconnected the call, then pulled up her dad's number.

> ALLIE
>
> I'll try again a bit later. She's adamant about not going, but I'll see what I can do.

Before she got off her phone, a text message popped up. She stared at Sean's name. *Dammit, leave me alone, Sean.*

> SEAN
>
> Hi, Allie.

He ended it with a Devil emoji. Even a simple text like that was enough to send Allie spiraling. There was more to the greeting than saying, "*Hey, how are you doing?*

> ALLIE
>
> Why can't you leave me alone? You are a self-righteous jerk. And all you deserve in life is to be miserable. I hope you find someone that is just as miserable as you.

She sent the text and tossed her phone to the side; her body shook as anger raked through her body. Why did she always let Sean get to her? She stared blankly at the phone, instantly wishing she could take back the text. It was one thing to let things slide off her shoulders, but she was allowing herself to stoop to his level, and she was better than that. Or, at least, she wanted to believe she was better than that.

SEAN

> Don't ever talk to me like that again. If you do, you can be sure I'll tell the whole world that you're a lesbian. And if I ever see you with another woman, I'll be sure to snap pictures, too. And If I ever find out the name of the woman you were with last time, I'll make sure she pays the price of all your sins. Don't mess with me. You won't like what you find—got that?

Allie stared at the text message. How she could have been with a man like that was beyond her. But he said some things that struck her. If he ever found out Izzie's name, he could ruin her. She did not doubt that. The grand reopening was only a few weeks away, and she didn't want to give any ammo to Sean. It would be worth it if she did nothing but try to protect Izzie.

Allie was supposed to be at the restaurant that evening, but now, she couldn't dare take any chance with Sean on her heels.

A knock sounded on her door. Allie pocketed her phone and went to the front door. She peered through the peephole and saw Izzie. Allie hesitated at the door. Now was her chance to protect Izzie and her family. The Roths didn't need that sort of stress in their lives.

"Izzie," she greeted.

"Hey, Allie, do you have a moment to talk?" Allie leaned against the door jam. "Please, it won't take long."

"I don't know that we have anything to talk about. We've been drifting apart, haven't talked. I'm not sure there's much we can say to each other," Allie choked out.

If only she could pull Izzie into the apartment. Take her into her arms and tell her everything she was currently facing; all of it would work out.

"You really believe that?" Izzie asked. Allie slowly nodded. "Say the word then. If you can look me in the eye and tell me you want me to leave because we have nothing to say to one another, I will walk away and never turn back. Just say those exact words, Allie."

Allie hesitated. She moved from one foot to another, stricken with nerves, unsure how to escape her awkward situation. Izzie shook her head.

"If you can't speak, I don't know what to expect. Goodbye." She spun on her heel.

"Izzie, wait!" Allie called out. Izzie turned and stared back at her. "Don't go."

Izzie didn't hesitate to move back to her. "Just talk to me, Allie."

Allie opened the door and invited Izzie into the apartment. It wasn't going to be an easy talk. But they needed to clear things up.

ALLIE HESITATED BEFORE SHE STARTED THE STORY, BUT THERE was no stopping once she did. "My parents are old-fashioned," she concluded. "If they knew about my lifestyle, they would surely disown me. No one would describe my family as 'loving,' but they are my only family."

Izzie listened intently as Allie tried to be completely upfront about everything, leaving out the most dysfunctional news, such as the badgering texts from Sean.

"You must learn to live your own life, Allie. It's going to be hard, but you'll feel so much better when you're living life on your terms."

"And I get that." Allie sighed. Not too many people would understand the hesitancy she faced. She didn't want to disappoint anyone; it had to be in her own time. Plus, with her mom's health, it wasn't the most opportune time to make such a huge announcement. Allie opened her mouth to continue when her phone rang. Her dad's number flashed on the screen. "I have to get this." She answered the call, looking away from Izzie. "Hey, Dad. What's up?"

"It's your mother. She said she was in extreme pain, doubled over, then nearly passed out before she agreed to let me call for help. The Ambulance is taking her to the hospital."

"Okay, I'm on my way." Before her dad hung up, she dropped the call and got up from the couch. "I have to go."

Izzie frowned. "What's wrong?" Allie looked around for her purse, her hands shaking as she grabbed it from the rack by the door. Izzie reached out and touched her hand. "Just calm down; what's wrong?" she asked, her soothing tone taking over the apartment.

"My mom is being taken to the hospital. Her health hasn't been great, but that's a story for another day. I have to go."

"You can't drive, Allie. I'll take you."

Allie quickly shook her head. How could she get out of that one? If she went there with Izzie in tow, her parents would immediately suspect something. She did not want to face that while her mother was ill.

"That wouldn't work. I mean, after all, I just said..." Allie flung her purse over her shoulder. "I can't even imagine the look on my parent's faces if I show up with a woman."

"Allie, calm down." Izzie reached out and touched her arm. "It's not like I would go in there and be like, 'Greetings, in-laws! I'm your daughter's girlfriend.' I wouldn't do that. I can be just a friend or rather a daughter of your patient. You could have been at work, and I just offered you a ride. We can think of an excuse later."

Allie tilted her head. "Allie, you're shaking, and I can't allow you to go alone. It wouldn't be in your best interest."

As much as Allie wanted to be strong and stand her ground, she knew Izzie was right. "Alright, you're just a friend."

Izzie nodded and stood back, and Allie led the way out of her apartment. Even that one phrase caused Allie's chest to ache. She wanted to be strong and tell her parents everything. But again, the timing was off; this was the best option for now, at least until her mother's health improved.

CHAPTER THIRTY

ONE NIGHT OF HEAT

Izzie

Izzie watched Allie as she walked back and forth in the waiting room. Allie stopped and turned to her. "How long has it been?"

"Two minutes since the last time you asked me. Will you please stop pacing? I'm sure they'll let you in to see your Mom any minute." It'd been two hours since they had arrived at the hospital. Izzie couldn't imagine how she would cope with the waiting game if it were one of her parents stuck in an ER bed. Still, eventually, they would come out and allow her time to visit with her Mom, and then, hopefully, she would have a better understanding of everything that was happening.

Allie began pacing again, causing Izzie to laugh softly. Izzie grabbed a magazine and flipped it open, skimming the articles but staring at the pictures.

"Allie?"

Izzie looked up as Allie stopped pacing. "Yes?"

"You may both go in; the doctor is in with your mothe, and your father is with her."

"Thank you!" Izzie stood up, but Allie whirled on her heel and stared at her. "I think I should go in alone."

"Of course!" Izzie smiled and sank back into the seat as the nurse pulled Allie away. Izzie went back to reading her magazine, but she couldn't concentrate. She tossed the magazine to the side and stood up, pacing back and forth as Allie had done moments ago. As she did, a call came through on her phone. Her Mom's number showed up on the screen.

"Hello?" She sank back into the chair.

"Have you heard anything?" she asked.

Izzie had sent out a text when she first arrived at the hospital, so her parents wouldn't wonder where she was. "Allie just went back to see her Mom. The doctor was going to let her know what was happening. I'm sitting out here in the lobby waiting. Hopefully, I'll know something shortly."

"Keep us both posted. We're thinking of her."

"Thank you, Mom. Love you."

"Love you, too, honey. Give Allie a kiss for us." Izzie smiled. She had to appreciate the love and affection her parents gave her; she never had to question if that love would ever fade. She hoped Allie would know love wasn't conditional someday soon.

Izzie disconnected the call and leaned back in her seat, her eyes directed toward the Emergency entrance where Allie had disappeared moments earlier. Ten minutes passed, and the doors swung open. Allie walked over to Izzie.

"How's she doing?" Izzie asked as she stood up.

"The doctor said that the blood work and CT scan of her abdomen didn't find the reason for her pain. The doctor thinks her symptoms are likely due to adhesions from her previous accident and subsequent surgeries, but they'd have to do an exploratory surgery to know for sure. Unfortunately, her insurance won't pay for the surgery unless there is an emergent medical complication from the adhesions, like if the scar tissue was to cut off blood flow to part of her intestines. And right now she is in pain but there's nothing to warrant emergency surgery. So, she's cleared to go home."

"That's good to hear she can go home," Izzie smiled and looked past her to a man that exited through the same double doors Allie had left moments ago. He headed straight towards them. He was a middle-aged man, a little gray at his temples.

"Allie," he began. Allie turned around her mouth agape. He looked over to Izzie, who awkwardly shifted from one foot to another.

"Um, Dad, this is Izzie. She's, um," Her cheeks were red.

"My father is one of Allie's patients. She was at our house when you called, so I drove her here." She offered him a hand. "Nice to meet you."

"Yeah, you too. Thanks for getting her here." He shook her hand but didn't offer much more than that. He then turned back to Allie. "Your mother and I are in a pinch. She needs this medicine, but I'm broke. Can you fork over some money to help us out?"

"Um, sure, Dad." Allie dug into her pocket and pulled out a wad of cash. She didn't even count it as she handed it over.

"Thanks." He then turned and hurried away from them, not offering much more than a wave of the hand.

Allie looked at Izzie, her cheeks flushed. "Thanks for that," she mumbled.

Izzie shrugged. Seeing Allie's father made it almost understandable why Allie hid her truth and feelings. If Allie wanted to introduce her as a friend, she would be a friend.

They exited the hospital, both of them remaining. When they reached the car, she turned to Allie. She opened her mouth, but she was at a loss for words.

"I'll get you home." She went around the car and got in, with Allie trailing behind. As she drove home, she fought for words, finally settling on the only thing she knew best. "I got a text that the order was shipped to the restaurant. We're one step closer to getting the restaurant back open for business. Everything is on schedule."

"That's great." Allie continued to look out the window, her words barely audible.

Izzie slowly nodded, sighing as she turned into the parking lot of the apartment building. "Oh! I gave the chefs your menu, and they're excited, but I think they have some questions. Do you think that maybe you could come into the restaurant sometime this week for a meeting? It shouldn't take long. I think it would help them feel a bit better about the opening. After all, I hired a few new employees. I don't want them to feel like we're setting them up to fail."

Allie turned to her; her eyes narrowed in. "Actually, I was going to talk to you about that." Izzie parked and then waited, turning her head slightly to the right. "Um, so the thing is," Her words trailed off as Izzie kept her focus on her. "You see, it's like this..." Again, a pause.

"What's going on?" Izzie wondered aloud.

Allie reached for the door, then smiled. "I'll be there. Just name the time," Allie mumbled.

Izzie frowned, struck by the look in Allie's eyes. "Allie?"

Allie quickly shook her head. "Just forgot what I was going to say. Thanks for the ride. I'll see you tomorrow when I come to the house."

Izzie nodded. "Yep, I'll be there." She still sensed this tension between them, and she couldn't shake it. She stayed motionless, but her brain worked a mile a minute.

"By the way," Izzie started, keeping Allie in the car. "I spoke with my boss. I signed the contract." Allie tilted her head. "You know, the one with Brandy."

At first, Allie frowned but then quickly nodded. "Anyway, laid out the deal that if Brandy does anything to hinder our working relationship, I can pull out of the contract. No questions asked."

"That's good," Allie replied, her frown slightly returning. "I hope you two can work things out." She gave a weak smile. "Goodbye." Allie opened the door, and Izzie watched her head up to her apartment building. Confusion remained etched on Allie's face as she walked away from Izzie.

Izzie could only imagine the stress Allie felt. When her father got sick, Izzie thought the stress would destroy her. She grabbed her phone and pulled up her Mom's number. Her Mom answered on the first ring.

"So, what do you know?" Her Mom sounded concerned.

"She's going to be alright. She had a bad accident a while back and has some residual scarring, but it's not too bad."

"Oh, thank heavens. Happy to hear." Izzie started to put her vehicle in reverse until she saw Allie running toward her. She halted the car and stared.

"Um, Mom. I'll have to call you back." She disconnected the call and opened the door as Allie ran to the driver's side. "What's going on?"

"I want you to stay." Allie panted, leaning against the car. "We'll figure out everything later, but for now...I need you."

Izzie stepped out of the car, her purse still inside as she leaned toward Allie. She pressed her lips against hers and didn't pull back because that was all she needed to hear. *Stay!*

IZZIE'S LIPS TRAILED DOWN ALLIE'S STOMACH AS ALLIE mumbled incoherent thoughts. Izzie smiled because her mumbles were in sync with Izzie's. Izzie had waited days for them to reconnect. She wouldn't have been able to turn down the invitation, even if she wanted to. She slipped her tongue into Allie's navel, and Allie released an exuberant sigh. Izzie grabbed Allie's hips and helped her thrust them toward her.

"Izzie," Allie gasped. Izzie grabbed Allie's thighs and pulled them back, opening Allie up to her. With Allie's legs pulled apart, Izzie moved in, anxious to taste her again. Allie released a groan, which brought Izzie in even deeper. *Yes, Allie, I'm yours.*

"Wait," Allie groaned, mid-thrust in action. Izzie pulled back, her heart racing, but her mind just as fast. Allie shuddered, releasing a breath. Izzie swallowed, holding onto Allie's eyes.

"You're killing me." Izzie released a soft chuckle but swallowed again; her body was electric.

Allie closed her eyes and gave a firm nod. "Proceed." Her legs started shaking as Izzie held firmly onto them.

"Are you sure?" Izzie groaned. She needed Allie to be sure. There was a reason Allie had stopped. If she weren't ready to get back to it, they would slow down.

"I think," Allie whispered. Her eyes opened and clouded over. "I don't know." A tear pressed at the corner of her eye, and Izzie leaned forward.

"I...I don't know when I'll be ready to come out."

"Hey," Izzie whispered, pressing her thumb along the corner of Allie's eye. "I'm not going anywhere. Today was a long day. If you don't want to have sex tonight, I'll understand."

Allie pressed her sweat-soaked body against her, and Izzie gave her an encouraging smile. "No pressure, Allie."

She meant those words, as much as waiting frustrated her. Mae's words came into her mind. She needed to allow Allie to make the move.

"Promise," Allie whispered.

"Cross my heart." Izzie started to pull back, but Allie grabbed her wrist and pulled Izzie on top of her. She kissed her hard, forcing her tongue in between Izzie's lips. Allie snaked her hand around Izzie's neck, slipping her fingers up and into her hair, taking immediate control of the situation. Izzie hungrily returned the kiss, not pulling back as Allie did the tantalizing dance with her tongue.

While they kissed, Allie pressed her hand between Izzie's thighs and weaved her way up to her opening. Izzie moaned, then shifted her head to the side, breaking from the kiss.

"If we do that, there will be no stopping." She laughed, pressing her hand against Allie's chest to free herself.

Allie smirked. "Fuck it," she moaned.

Izzie's eyes widened as Allie firmly yanked on Izzie's hand to pull her closer to her. Allie passionately kissed her again, thrusting her tongue between Izzie's lips. Izzie didn't know what had gotten into Allie, but she liked it. She grabbed Allie's shoulders and fell next to her, with Allie shifting her weight and moving on top of Izzie. Allie intensely broke from the kiss and slid down Izzie's body until she was in between Izzie's legs.

"Allie..." Izzie moaned. She spread her legs further apart and anxiously waited for Allie to move in and invade her entrance. Izzie thrust up to meet Allie's tongue, and Allie excitedly crashed in and out of her opening. Allie pressed her hand against Izzie's stomach, holding Izzie into place. Waves crashed over Izzie's body, sending rippling shivers up and down her spine. An orgasm sunk its teeth into Izzie. "Yes," Izzie cried. "Harder. Oh fuck yes. Allie. Damn!" Izzie cried out, the bed shaking as Allie did every-thing to keep the satisfying feeling thundering into Izzie. "Ahhhhh...God, yes!" Izzie reached back and held onto the headboard, the ripples slowly dying to mini tremors. She gasped, her fingers slowly slipping from the headboard as Allie slithered back up her body.

Allie had a generous grin on her lips. "Well, what do you think?" Allie asked.

"Babe, you're a bombshell." Izzie trailed her fingers around the back of Allie's neck and pulled her to her. They kissed in a passionate embrace. Tonight Izzie's mind was free from doubts; there was only Allie.

CHAPTER THIRTY-ONE

ONE NIGHT OF REGRET

Allie

Allie looked over where Izzie slept soundly. A smile was on Izzie's face, which caused Allie to grin even wider. She didn't plan on having Izzie back in her bed. The truth was, she had decided that ending it would be better. With Sean lurking around the corner out for revenge, it might be the most logical option. But Izzie about everything that happened with her mom. She even was starting to understand why Allie was having trouble coming out. It felt right. Besides, hearing Izzie state that she gave the stipulations to Brandy, Allie knew she could trust her. Running back to the car only took her thirty seconds to decide.

As they made love repeatedly through the night, Allie knew there was only one thing she could do afterward: try to make amends with Sean. She felt confident that Izzie would give her the time and space she needed to tell her parents. So it was only fitting that Allie attempted to get Sean off her case. He had no right to terrorize her. As long as he would back off and not ruin Izzie in the process, her and Izzie's relationship could continue to grow.

Allie leaned in, gave Izzie a soft peck on her cheeks, then tossed the covers back and slipped out of bed. Allie looked over her shoulder to ensure Izzie was still sleeping, then grabbed a t-shirt and slipped it on before leaving the bedroom and heading to the living room. Her phone lay in the middle of the floor, discarded the moment they started ripping each other's clothes off.

She unlocked her phone and pulled up her text messages, her face falling the minute she saw her messages. The first picture in a line of messages from Sean was a picture of Izzie smiling. It was her bio from the website for the marketing firm where she worked.

SEAN

It wasn't too hard to figure out who you were fucking. I'm surprised by how easy it was. LOL.

SEAN

Now that I have a name to the face, it makes it much easier to crush her.

SEAN

Oh, look! A grand reopening of Stars and Stripes, hosted by none other than Elizabeth Roth.

SEAN

Special guest, my very own Allison Walsh. What a coincidence. Is that when you guys got all hot and bothered?

SEAN

What was it like, Allie? Don't spare any of the details.

SEAN

You're all quiet now. Are you guys doing it nonstop? I wonder what your Mom and Dad would think if they knew their princess was sleeping with a woman. Come on, Allie, what do you think they would say?

SEAN

You're going to wish you never saw me that day. Hahahaha!!

Allie fell to the couch, her eyes clouding over with tears. She covered her mouth and stared at the last message. Why was he doing this? Was it to make a point? Was it to embarrass her?

ALLIE

Again, why are you doing this? Who I'm with is none of your damn business? Ruining her life is ridiculous. Just tell me why you're doing this.

Allie stared at the screen, anxiously waiting for his response. She glanced at her watch. It was just after three. Chances are, she wouldn't even hear from him until later in the morning. She closed her eyes and fell back on the couch. If he kept threatening her, then she would have no other choice.

A text dinged through, and she quickly looked down at the message.

SEAN

Because I can.

ALLIE

You would humiliate two people just because you can? I don't get it.

SEAN

How humiliating do you think this is for me? Hell, I had sex with a lesbo; talk about humiliating!!

ALLIE

So, you're ruining us because your manhood took a hit. Grow up. I knew you had issues, but even this seems a new low for you. She's done nothing to you. We haven't spoken in what, three years? I'm asking you nicely just to let it go. What my parents think is none of your concern.

SEAN

No, but it would be pretty damn funny to be the one to break it to them. LOL. That might even make it a little less humiliating for me.

ALLIE

Go to hell!

"Allie? There you are, babe. I was looking all over for you."

Allie turned to see Izzie. Izzie wore a robe that opened up in the front and sauntered to Allie. Allie lowered her gaze as the previous text returned to her mind.

"We need to talk," Allie whispered. She sniffled, the words choking her a bit.

"Of course." Izzie sat down and reached for Allie's hand, but Allie pulled back and even moved a few inches from her, unable to turn to look in her direction. "Wait, are you okay?" Izzie mumbled.

Allie looked up; a tear trailed down her cheek. Izzie looked away, not even willing to brush it away. She felt paralyzed by pain.

"I'm sorry," Allie whispered. "I think we rushed back into things."

"You think?" Izzie asked. "But why? I told you I would give you time. I'm trying to be understanding and let you figure this out at your own pace."

"I know," Allie argued. "But the timing is all off." She dropped her gaze. "For everything. It just isn't going to happen right now. I'm sorry," she held her breath, worried she would start crying.

Izzie stood up from the couch. "So, what are you saying? We're just going to stop sleeping together, stop being together?"

"No," Allie started. "I mean, yes. I mean, I don't know. But I think we need some time apart, and I think I should bow out of the restaurant reopening."

Izzie arched an eyebrow. "We were doing that together. Or so I thought."

Izzie shook her head. "I don't know what's happening here, but something seems strange. What am I missing?"

"Nothing," Allie lied. "Just please understand that I'm not taking this lightly. I have just made up my mind, and I'm standing my ground. I need time to think. I need some space. Please, Izzie."

Izzie threw up her arms. "Alright then. You'll get your time away from all of this." Izzie turned on her heel, grabbed her clothes, and then hurried out of the living room. Allie fell back down to the couch, tears stinging the backs of her eyes. She quickly flipped the tears away and went back to her phone.

She deleted the message that she hadn't sent. Being snarky wouldn't help her case; nothing would.

ALLIE

It's over with Izzie, so you might as well call off the dogs. You won. Happy now?

She didn't get a reply as she waited for Izzie to finish getting dressed. Her eyes were downward when Izzie stormed past the living room. Allie jumped up and hurried to the door. "Izzie!" she called out. "I'm sorry!"

Izzie huffed. "Yeah, you and me both." Then opened the door and let it slam behind her as Allie leaned back against the wall, the tears unable to stop. Her heart was out that door, and she didn't know how to get over that.

CHAPTER THIRTY-TWO

TIME TO DECOMPRESS

Izzie

I zzie looked like a zombie as she walked down the stairs and peeked her head around the corner. Her father was still asleep. She had gotten home late and didn't want to wake anyone. She snuck up to her bedroom, stifling her sobs, unable to face her parents.

It was early morning. The sun peeked through the windows, but the ache in Izzie's chest remained. She didn't understand how things could go so poorly. She thought she and Allie were finally back on the right track until Allie got cold feet.

She smelled coffee in the kitchen. Her mom sat at the kitchen table, paper in one hand, coffee mug in another. Izzie wanted to tease her that no one read the regular newspaper anymore, but she wasn't in the mood to even joke around. Izzie cleared her throat, to which her mother looked up and smiled.

"I stayed up until midnight until it was clear you weren't coming home." She gave Izzie a lighthearted wink. "I was surprised seeing that when we talked, it sounded like you were just leaving her apartment. Things must've gone well after you hung up." Again, a wink.

Izzie gave a weak smile. "I need coffee," she mumbled, ignoring the

622

insinuation her mother had left her. Her mother turned to her, and Izzie could feel her eyes on her back, but Izzie didn't dare turn to look. She poured her cup, then took a sip.

"So, it didn't go well?" she asked.

Izzie sighed and turned around to face her. "I'll be honest that I don't know how to respond to that. Things were going well, or so I thought." She smirked and took another sip, not wanting to go into that sort of conversation with her mother. "I never realized how difficult it would be to get into a relationship with someone who isn't out of the closet yet."

"Oh," her mother looked down and took a drink. "I see."

"When I came out to you and Dad," she began.

"We weren't immediately understanding, Izzie, if you should recall."

Izzie frowned. She couldn't remember her parents being anything but supportive. Both her parents seemed willing to understand what she wanted out of life. They were willing to take her in with open arms. At least, that was how she remembered it.

"Your father and I know that you should be able to choose your own path. It's not necessarily the path we would have laid out for you, but as the days went on, we both realized how happy you were, and that was the important part." She shrugged. "But you have to understand that not everyone has the same home life that you do."

"That's what Mae said," Izzie mumbled. Izzie took another drink. "The thing is, I could totally understand that. As frustrated as I am that she won't just say, this is me, and take it or leave it, I get that everyone has to do it in their own time. I can accept that and even told her I could accept that. But then, things went downhill. And fast. It was like someone had flipped a switch, and all of a sudden, Allie didn't want any part of this."

Izzie dropped her gaze, the ache quickly returning. "She's not even coming to the re-opening."

"Seriously? You both have put in so much effort. She should be there."

"You're telling me," Izzie grumbled. "I don't know." Izzie took a seat across from her mom. "Maybe it's because she's scared that someone will find out, and she can't face that. Or maybe…"

"Maybe she fears that you're disappointed in her, and it would be easier to end things." Her mother shrugged. Izzie opened her mouth, but her mother continued. "Izzie, you can be very strong-minded and opinionated. Sometimes you can even come across as intimidating."

"In my career but not personally," Izzie argued. Her mother tilted her head, and Izzie frowned. "I don't mean to be."

"You have a good heart, Izzie. And so does Allie, You're a lot alike in that respect, but maybe you freaked Allie out a bit. Maybe she didn't want to disappoint you, so she ended things before they began." Izzie looked down at her coffee cup.

"Did you discuss it with her, or just leave it at that?"

"I tried," Izzie began. "She seemed pretty confident that this was what she wanted. She kept saying; I just need time. I just need time." Izzie shook her head. "So, it was left at that. I said I would give her space from all of this and stormed out."

"Don't count her out," her mother began. "Give her space. She's never dated a woman before, right?" Izzie slowly nodded as her mother reached out and took her hand, patting it softly.

"I'd imagine it's pretty scary for her. Wouldn't you think?" She smiled when Izzie met her stare. She stood up from the table, not waiting for Izzie's response. "What do you want for breakfast?"

Izzie smiled and shrugged. "Whatever you want to make." She grabbed her phone and looked down at Allie's contact. Just a few clicks of the button, and she could send her a text and tell her she understood, and Allie could take all the time in the world, but that would be a lie. She didn't understand, and despite getting a talking-to from her mom, she only saw how Allie changed, not how she needed to change.

It's my fault for falling for someone so young. Izzie wanted a strong woman who knew what she wanted. Allie was strong, but she was also young and inexperienced.

IZZIE

I think I'm going to come to town for a few days. I really could use a change of scenery.

MAE

Uh oh. What happened?

624

IZZIE

Believe me, you'll hear all about it soon
enough. Do you think Cass could set me up
with a lady friend? ;)

MAE

???

IZZIE

Come on, double date. I'm not picky. LOL.

MAE

Girl, you're a mess. Just get your ass here so I
can hear all about it.

IZZIE

Can't be soon enough.

Izzie downed the rest of her coffee. "I think I'm going to head into town a few days. Maybe that will help me to shed some light on all of this. Besides, with this new contract, I could use some face time with the CEO."

Her mother turned around. "Are you sure you're not just running away because you're hurt? If you run, nothing will get resolved."

"Mom, I love you, but I'm not running." Izzie kissed her cheek. "If Allie wants space, you can't get much further than the city. Besides, it won't be easy seeing her coming in every day to take care of Dad. But if anything happens, I'm only a couple of hours away. It's really for the best."

"If you think so." Her mom scrunched up her nose, and Izzie nodded. She did believe so because risking the chance of running into Allie would only complicate things. If Allie wanted space, Izzie would give her space. At least, that's what she would tell herself.

THE CLUB WAS LOUD FOR A TUESDAY NIGHT. IZZIE GRABBED the seat across from Mae and looked down at the menu. Mae grabbed the menu out from under her nose and arched an eyebrow. "You aren't here to eat and have a drink, are you?"

Izzie laughed. "Of course. Isn't that why a person goes into a club?" She grabbed the menu back. She smirked when Mae rolled her eyes and glanced back at the menu. "I'm in the mood for some chicken wings."

"Sounds delightful," Mae mumbled. "I'm in the mood to get the juicy details on why you decided to come to town."

"I'll spill the tea," Izzie replied as she looked up. "After we have something to eat."

The waitress walked over and put down two napkins. "I'm Greta. Can I get you started on something to drink?"

"A beer, whatever's on tap," Izzie replied.

Mae nodded. "Same." The waitress turned away, and Izzie glanced out to the dance floor. A group had already formed with a blonde woman dancing in the center. Izzie nodded toward the floor, and Mae glanced over her shoulder. "What?"

"The blonde center stage. Wonder what her story is."

Mae rolled her eyes. "I'm not buying that for a sec. So, did Allie break your heart or something?"

Izzie huffed. "Allie? Allie, who?" Mae stared at Izzie, and Izzie quickly glanced away. "Just because I was falling for the woman and she decided to rip my heart out and stomp on it doesn't mean that broke my heart. I'm stronger than that. And I'll tell you this..." She stopped when Greta put the two bottles down on the table.

"Ready to order?"

Izzie motioned for Mae to proceed as she took a quick swig of her beer. When it was her turn, Izzie opened up the menu. "Chicken wings basket with fried pickles and another beer."

She tipped her head. "I'm thirsty tonight." Greta giggled, then turned on her heel and walked away. Izzie smirked. "Greta looks more my age. Maybe I'll slip her my number and see if she's into women." Izzie winked, and Mae cocked an eyebrow.

"You'll tell me what?" Mae asked as Izzie took another drink.

"Huh?" Izzie inquired.

"You were saying before Greta brought us our drinks that you would tell me something."

Izzie frowned, then nodded. "Oh, right. Just something about Allie's age. Not worth mentioning." She took another swig, then glanced back to the dance floor. That same blonde was out there dancing, but the longer she stared, the more she felt like she was cheating. She looked away, and her eyes clouded over.

Mae's brows furrowed. "You're worrying me, Izzie. I don't think I've ever seen you like this before."

Izzie laughed. She had never been like this before because she had never been with anyone that had pulled her in, in the way Allie had. "I think Allie's scared. She said she needed a break from all of this." Izzie motioned with her hands, then shrugged. "Whatever that means."

"Did you ask her?" Mae asked.

Izzie's jaw dropped. "You and my mother are cut from the same cloth. I am giving her the space that she needs and clearly wants. And if she needs space, then fine; that means I'm free to do what I want. Right?"

"No one could stop you but yourself." Mae shrugged. "If you feel that you're ready to find someone else, perhaps someone more mature and older than Allie, then I think you should. You asked me and Cass to set you up with someone while you're here." Her eyes brightened. "I think she did. I just wanted to chat with you and make sure you want to do this before I set anything up." Izzie watched as Mae fumbled with her phone. She held it out in front of Izzie. A woman with fiery red hair stared back into the camera. "Beautiful, right?"

Izzie glanced at it, then looked up at Mae, gauging if Mae was teasing. Yet, there was no sign of it. She was pretty enough. Some people would define her as gorgeous. Although, Izzie couldn't see it because she was still fixated on Allie.

Still, this could be the break she needed. She trusted Mae and Cass; she decided to go with the flow. She nodded.

"Set it up!" She finished her beer just as Greta returned to the table with another beer and their baskets of food. Mae typed something into her phone, then pulled her basket closer to her.

"I texted Cass." Mae took a bite of her burger. "Her name is Mercury."

"Like, retrograde?" Izzie mumbled. "Age?"

"Forty-two. Looks good for her age, don't you think?" Mae looked up from her fries as Izzie took a bite of one of her wings.

"I suppose." Izzie shrugged. "If just looking at the blonde on the dance floor was cheating, then Izzie already felt like she crossed a line. She took a sip of her beer, but her stomach churned, and she put it down. "How does Cass know her?" Izzie inquired.

"They work together. And you won't have to worry about her being in the closet. She's been out since her early teens. So, it should be a great match. I'm honestly not sure why we never considered it before. She could be your perfect partner. "

"So, you're all of a sudden super excited and ready to get me hooked up with someone else?" Izzie popped a pickle into her mouth and slowly nibbled it.

Mae shrugged. "What can I say? I want you just as happy as I'm with Cass. Is that a crime?"

Izzie frowned, staring down at her food. It was a shame to consider since she thought she was already that happy. How could she suddenly jump into something else when her heart was crushed back home? She wasn't thrilled at the prospect of a first date, but maybe this would help her move forward. What was the harm in exploring something new?

CHAPTER THIRTY-THREE

HEARTBROKEN AND TIRED

Allie

I'*m not feeling well; I need someone to pick up my shifts for the next few days.* It was an excuse, but Allie had to do what felt right. If she went to the Roth home, she would surely see Izzie, and her heart wasn't ready to face her. The Roths could survive without her for a few days.

She turned into her parent's driveway and hesitated before getting out of the car. She settled for the pain of keeping secrets instead of being honest with her parents. *In due time, Allie. In due time.* For the moment, she would have to hope she wasn't too late with Izzie when she finally told the truth.

With her mother still in pain, she had to visit her. The insurance company was still refusing to cover the surgery until it was absolutely medically necessary. She knocked on the door and waited for the door to open. Her father flung the door open as the ringing phone started. She entered, with him answering the call.

"I know. I'll be out in the door in five. Maybe sooner. Yep, see you soon." He nodded a greeting. "Just in time. Your mother's been complaining. She needs her meds."

Allie frowned. "Where are you going?" she asked as he grabbed his wallet and keys from the table.

"Poker night with the boys. That's why you're here, right? You said you would stay with her while I was out."

Allie mentally groaned. She didn't expect to stay. She had hoped that she could drop the medicine and get home. Not that she had any place to be.

"You're staying, right?" He motioned to her.

Allie shrugged. "I suppose I am now."

"Great! I'll be home late, so stick around until midnight or so."

Allie nodded and tossed her purse to the side. If she had to stay, she might as well make the best of it. Her dad left without saying goodbye to her mother. Or maybe he did that before Allie arrived. Either way, there wasn't this tender goodbye that Allie would associate with a loving marriage.

"Allie?" Instantly, her mother called out for her. Allie grabbed her pills and went to the kitchen for a glass of water, then carried it down the hall to her parent's bedroom.

"Thought I heard you here," her mother commented.

Allie held up the pill bottle and water like a prize and walked over to where her mother lay, looking helpless. Allie read the bottle, popped off the lid, and slipped a pill into her palm. She handed the two items to her mother. She took them, choking out as she swallowed them down. Allie leaned in and patted her back; it was her job as a nurse and dutiful daughter.

"Are you okay?" Allie asked, taking the water from her hand, and she nodded.

"I do hope this medicine kicks in. My body is a mess."

"I got a call from the doctor, and he said they found a pinched nerve. Along with the scarring in my stomach." She shook her head. "I feel that I'm never going to be back to myself before the accident." Her mother huffed, releasing a cough. "And I'm exhausted."

Allie knew the feeling. She turned to leave when her mother made a soft noise. Allie looked over her shoulder, and her mother winced. "Do you need anything? Perhaps a pillow to prop you up?"

Her mother scrunched up her nose. "Some ice chips would be nice.

And I'm sure the house looks atrocious. Could you dust and sweep while you're here?" Her mother shifted in bed. "That way, I don't have to fret over what needs to be done while I'm stuck in bed."

"Of course," Allie mumbled. She left the room and went straight to the kitchen. She pushed the button for crushed ice and watched as the glass filled up, then grabbed a spoon and hurried back to her mother. Her mother was sitting up in the bed, still shifting uncomfortably. "What do you need?" Allie asked, leaning into her mother.

"Two more pillows would be good."

Allie left her with the glass of ice and hurried to her old bedroom, where she grabbed the pillows off her bed and returned to the master bedroom. Allie helped to place the pillows behind her back, and her mother settled into them.

"Is that better?" Allie asked.

"I guess," her mother muttered. Allie started to leave to get the housework started. "Guess who we ran into the hospital when we were leaving," she began.

Allie shrugged. "I have no idea. Who?"

"Sean." She kept her eyes closed, and Allie gawked at her, the name setting in. "You remember Sean, right?"

"Um yeah, of course," Allie mumbled. "What was he doing at the hospital?"

"I don't know; visiting a friend or something. I haven't seen him since you broke up with him. That was ages ago. I wonder what made you break up with that sweet guy. He's still single, he says. Maybe you two could reconnect?"

Allie sighed, stepping back closer to the door. Her mom's eyes opened, and she looked like she had aged twenty more years. "Do you still have his number?"

"Wouldn't know," Allie replied quietly. "It's been eons since we've chatted. I really should get to the housework." She turned and hurried out of the room, practically falling against the wall once she was out of sight. It seemed too predictable like maybe Sean had set up the meeting. Was he following them? She quickly shook the thought from her mind. He was a creep.

Allie got to work, dusting off the living room and finding that the dust wasn't even noticeable and certainly didn't require a once over, but she continued to do it so her mother wouldn't harp at her. Halfway through the dusting, she heard movement from the bedroom.

"Allie? You still here?"

Allie heaved a sigh and hurried towards the bedroom. The two extra pillows lay halfway across the floor. Allie walked over to them and picked them up, confused about how they would have made their way across the room. Her mother gave her a feeble smile.

"Sorry about that."

Allie tried to hide the eye roll as she headed back to her mother's side of the bed and helped to prop the pillows up behind her. "No worries." Allie turned and left the room, grateful she didn't get stopped again. However, that was short-lived, as her mother quickly took advantage of Allie's presence. Whether it was to get her mother a glass of water or fluff up her pillows for the third time, Allie was pulled in several different directions, leaving her ready to collapse at the end.

She fell back against the wall, just outside her parent's room, her head throbbing and her legs aching with exhaustion. "Allie?"

"Yes, Mom?" Allie rounded the corner, dragging as she moved closer to the bed.

"Will you open the window a tad? It's all stuffy in here." Allie obliged, opening the window but immediately getting halted. "Not that much," she scolded. Allie lowered it slightly. "Better."

"Good," Allie grumbled, moving past the bed.

"Allie?"

Allie hesitated, heaving a sigh as her mother's words came out. Allie turned to stare at her. "Yes?"

"You really should think about Sean. He's a good man, and you need someone. You'll be an old maid if you don't settle down soon. Your father and I got married when we were twenty."

And look how you turned out. Allie seethed the words that ached to come out. Instead, she forced a smile and nodded. "I'm happy, Mom. I don't need a man." She turned and stomped out of the room. She went to her old bedroom and collapsed on the bed, tears staining her cheeks almost immediately. She reached for her phone, and the first picture she pulled up was a picture of Izzie.

She would give anything to be in her arms right now. She shook her head, forcing the image out of her mind. If things weren't so screwed up, then maybe it would be a possibility, but with Sean somewhere in the background and her parent's cruelty, she had to let something go.

ALLIE

Love you, sis! I'm glad you got away. :(

She tossed her phone to the side and let the tears freely fall down her cheeks. Maybe she was only good at allowing people to use her; the thought made Allie's chest ache.

"Allie?" Her mom called out again, but Allie couldn't bring herself to go. She had to let the tears out so her mother didn't see her weakness.

CHAPTER THIRTY-FOUR

TRYING TO FORGET

Izzie

"Izzie, this is Mercury. Mercury, this is Izzie." Mae made the introductions, beaming.

Izzie put on her best smile and shook Mercury's hand. "Hi, Mercury. It's a pleasure."

"The pleasure is all mine. I've heard so much about you." Mercury offered Izzie a wink and shifted in her place in the club. "But your pictures don't do you justice, I must confess." Mercury gave Izzie a once over. There was one time when Izzie would have flirted back but now wasn't the time. Izzie gave a sweet smile, then turned to Cass and gave her a nod.

"Izzie, good to see you again," Cass offered.

Likewise, Cass, it's been too long." Izzie took her seat, with Mercury sliding in next to her, a bit too close for Izzie's comfort.

"Ordered the drinks, babe," Mae replied.

"You always know what I like." Cass leaned in. They made out, and Izzie felt herself staring. She quickly looked away, catching Mercury glancing in her direction.

"Isn't it beautiful when two people are in love?"

Izzie nodded and then looked away from Mercury's wandering eye.

She stared out at the dance floor, and her brows furrowed as she zoned in on the crowd already forming on the floor. The blonde she had seen the previous night was back on the floor, and Izzie smirked.

"Your beers," the waitress commented, approaching their table, breaking Izzie from the stare.

"Thank you," she mumbled, grabbing one of the bottles and taking in a gulp.

"Are you ready to order?" the waitress asked.

The table each nodded as they placed their orders, and the waitress was gone. Izzie took another sip, sighing as the liquid went down her throat.

"I hear your father is ill," Mercury started. "I know the pain that cancer can cause a family. I hope his prognosis is okay?"

Izzie met her curious glance as she slowly shook her head. "He's on hospice." She dropped her gaze, fearing that she would burst into tears, then quickly grabbed another drink.

"I'm sorry. I'll be praying for y'all." Mercury's words seemed genuine, catching Izzie off guard.

"Thank you," she muttered before quickly taking another sip. She glanced across the table at Mae, who was lost in conversation with Cass. Izzie shifted in her seat.

"There's a band playing tonight," Mercury continued. "I hear they're fire, like my hair." She laughed loudly, which brought Izzie's attention back to her. She had a loud and boisterous voice. She didn't care if she turned heads; that was an excellent quality when the mood called for it. Izzie dropped her gaze and sipped on her beer. "I love this club," Mercury continued. "Do you come here often?"

"Um, yeah," Izzie stammered. "When I'm in town, anyway. It has a nice atmosphere."

"Izzie owns a restaurant," Mae supplied, "Stars and Stripes. It's super cute."

"Is that so? That's cool. Maybe I can come to visit." Mercury reached out under the table and stroked her hand along Izzie's leg, landing on her knee. Izzie wondered if she was always this forward or if Izzie just caught her on a strange night.

"It's my parents' restaurant," Izzie softly replied. "Just trying to help renovate it. It's taken some work, but we're almost there." She downed the rest of her beer in one gulp, with Mercury's hand still holding onto her knee.

When the waitress brought them their food, Izzie couldn't have been happier. She was uncomfortable sitting at the table, unsure how Mercury would take the flirtation to another level. She sipped on her second beer and let the conversation carry around her, only adding a few *yeahs and uh-huh* to the mix.

"I love to dance," Mercury stated after Izzie was down to just a few fries in her basket. "What about you?"

"Not really," Izzie muttered.

"Izzie," Mae laughed. "You know that isn't true. You love to get out there on the dance floor."

Izzie glared in Mae's direction, and Mae's smile faded. "Um, Mercury, want to go to the restroom with me?" Cass asked, already getting up from the table.

"Sure!" Mercury got up, and they left the table, leaving Izzie to stare at Mae.

"What?" Mae asked.

"What? Why are you acting this way? Stop trying to push it. If we don't vibe, we don't vibe." Izzie shook her head. "I don't understand it."

"You don't understand it? Well, I don't understand you. You are moping around here, and I'm trying to help. If things aren't going to work with you and Allie, then why not try something new?" Mae shrugged. "Could do you some good."

"Would you like another beer?" The waitress reached their table, glancing between Mae and Izzie.

"No thanks," Mae started.

"I'll take one," Izzie quickly replied, downing the rest of her beer. The waitress left as Cass and Mercury came back to the table. Izzie shrugged and stood up. She held out her hand to Mercury. "Let's dance."

They rushed onto the dancefloor as a fast song played. She danced with strangers all the time; nothing was notable about it. The song ended, and a slow song came onto the loudspeaker. Izzie hesitated as Mercury continued to smile. Izzie held up her hand and went to the table. She grabbed her beer and took a couple of swigs before walking back to the dance floor. Mercury pulled her closer. What could one slow dance do? Nothing, as long as they both knew the boundaries.

The room spun along as Mercury twirled her, then pulled her to her. Izzie fell into her, laughing. She relaxed in Mercury's arms. Her fourth beer heaved in her stomach, but she wouldn't let the alcohol get to her. She swallowed the lump in her throat as they swayed to the side.

"Tonight exceeded all of my expectations," Mercury said. "I hope you feel the same."

Izzie laughed, her head warm as she pressed the back of her hand to her forehead, then slowly nodded. "I didn't realize I needed this night. To get out there and have some fun."

"Sometimes it's good to take chances," Mercury wrapped her arms around Izzie, and Izzie wondered if she should bolt. Again, she swallowed.

"Mercury," Izzie quietly started. "Ya see, there's this...." Mercury raised her finger to Izzie's lip.

"You don't have to say a word. I can feel the chemistry between us. Can you feel it?"

Izzie couldn't tell if it was chemistry or her mind playing tricks on her. She liked to believe it was the latter. "Mercury," Izzie whispered.

"Don't fight it," Mercury stated. She moved in and softly pressed her lips against Izzie's. Izzie gasped, opening her mouth slightly.

"Mercury!" Izzie pressed her hand to Mercury's chest, pressing her back. "I can't." She turned on her heel and hurried to the table where Cass and Mae stood.

"I have to get out of here," she grumbled.

"I'll drive you." Mae jumped up and hurried after Izzie. Izzie didn't stop until she got outside and could get some air. Izzie lowered her head to stare at the ground.

She shook her head; she couldn't do this. It was too soon. She wanted to kick herself for even allowing it for a second to continue. "Are you okay?" Mae asked, wrapping her arm around Izzie's shoulders.

Izzie shook her head. "I'm not okay. I drank way too much. It's not what I want. I thought I was over Allie, but I'm not." She felt a tear stinging the back of her eyes and turned away from Mae. "Just get me home." Izzie led the way to Mae's car, her head spinning. She focused on a spot on the ground, hoping that that would cause the spinning world to end.

The drive back to her house was a quiet one. Izzie stared at her phone, contemplating texting Allie. But she closed her eyes and leaned back in the car, the spinning returning.

In the driveway, Izzie reached for the door. "I'm sorry," Mae said quietly.

Izzie turned to Mae. "You don't have to be sorry. I didn't know I wasn't ready. Hey, you were trying to help."

Mae reached for the door. "I'll make sure you get in and get a shower. It's the least I could do."

Izzie didn't object. They walked up to the door and got inside. When the door was closed, Mae grimaced. "What?"

"I have to be honest with you. I wanted to see if you were truly over Allie, so I got this plan in my head. Get a beautiful woman and put her right in your path."

Izzie arched an eyebrow. "So, you made up this date? So, who's Mercury?"

"She's an actress," Mae replied. "And she's married...to a man."

"Wait, what?!" Izzie turned away from her.

"Are you mad?"

Izzie laughed, then shook her head. "I mean, that's pretty fucked up, but I'm also a little relieved?" Izzie turned around to Mae. "I mean, she was laying it on thick. I was surprised you thought we would get along." Izzie threw up her hands. "Now it makes sense she was acting. She sounded scripted now that you mention it." She moved in and kissed Mae on the forehead. "You were only trying to help, but next time... don't." She gave her a wink and then turned away. "I'm going to go take a shower.

Feel free to let yourself out." She went into the bedroom, grabbed her pajamas, and went to the bathroom.

She heard her phone ringing in the other room. "Mae, will you grab that for me?" she hollered. "Tell whoever it is, I'll call them back in a bit."

She turned on the shower and leaned against the sink, shaking her head at Mae's scheme.

"Izzie?" There was a tap on the bathroom door.

"Yeah?" Izzie opened the bathroom, and Mae held out the phone. "It was Allie. The minute I answered, she hung up." Mae scrunched up her face. "Maybe you should call her back."

Izzie stared at the phone, then shook her head. "It probably was a mistake. I'll wait until she calls again."

Mae arched an eyebrow. "Are you sure?"

"Yep, positive. Thanks." She backed into the bathroom, closed the door, and stared at the recent calls, hoping Allie would call her back.

CHAPTER THIRTY-FIVE

LEARNING AND GROWING

Allie

Whardhen another woman answered the phone, Allie felt broken. Here Allie was upset about how things were going between them, and Izzie was off having fun with another woman. It put things into perspective. If that were how Izzie wanted to respond to her request for space, she would accept it and move on.

Allie pulled her car into the driveway. She wanted to check on her mom again. When she left, her mom was sound asleep. But if she was in as much pain as she claimed, someone needed to pay close attention to her.

She knocked on the door and waited for someone to answer. After another knock, she heard movement. Her mom opened the door and leaned against it, even giving a light smile.

"You look better today," Allie said, entering the house and looking around. "Where's dad?"

"He went out with a friend. I'm feeling a bit better today. The pinched nerve isn't hindering my movement as much, and the pain med is actually doing something. I thought I would walk around and try to get some energy. I can't stand for too long, but I don't want my muscles to weaken."

Allie furrowed her brows, turning away so her mom couldn't see. Her mom never mentioned exercise before this.

"I'm glad to hear it. Do you want me to stick around? Do you want company?" It was one way to take her mind off of Izzie. Since she hadn't been working with Richard, she had to find something to keep herself occupied. Her mother was one option.

"Nah, you've done enough. You can head out and do something at home."

Allie tilted her head in shock. "Alrighty then." She turned to head to the door.

"There is one thing," her mother began. Allie hesitated. She should have known she wasn't entirely out of the woods yet. She hadn't stepped back in her car, so there was plenty of time for her mom to change her mind. Allie turned, waiting. "With your father going out last night and again today, I'm not sure I'll be able to cover rent. The doc is looking at a medicine that could help the scarring in my gut to heal. And there it was," she explained.

Allie slowly nodded. "Oh, and if you could stop off at the grocery store and bring me back a few things. I think I have my list some-where." Her mother turned and walked towards the kitchen. Allie watched her walk, surprised by how quickly the pinched nerve had healed itself.

She dropped her gaze, infuriated that her mother would find so many ways to use and abuse her. When she returned, she had a list in her hand. "Mom, I can't," Allie began.

Her mom's eyes widened. "Huh?"

"I can't help you out today. I already helped pay for your meds. I have to work later today." She was suddenly filled with lies, surprised by how easily the lies could come out.

"You're going to abandon us?" her mom asked.

Allie huffed. "Mom, how much does Dad spend on beer a month or going out? Way more than he needs to. If you guys need the money, he should stay in once or twice."

"You know he would never do that," her mother argued.

Allie nodded. "Right, and sadly, that's not my problem. I'm sorry, but have Dad grab the groceries on his way home." Allie turned and walked out of the house, a sense of relief washing over her. Finally, she had taken the stand, and it was about time.

On the ride home, Allie felt her heart aching. She had sought out her parent's approval for so long. But for what? They were the problem, and it was time that she finally started acknowledging that. Unfortunately, it was too late for her to make amends with Izzie, but it was never too late to start standing up for herself.

Allie turned into the parking lot of her apartment building when her phone started ringing. She saw Marisa's number on the caller ID. "Hey, Sis."

"Hey. Sorry, I missed your text last night. I was at a party and didn't get home until late. I should have left sooner, but that's college, you know?" Marissa laughed, and Allie forced a smile. "Is everything okay? Are Mom and Dad giving you hell again?

Allie sighed. "Everything is starting to be okay. I finally realized that our parents don't need to run my life. I'm a grown woman. It's freeing. I can live my life how I want."

"Wow! That's awesome, Allie. It's about time."

Allie grinned, letting disappointment sink into the back of her mind that she didn't allow herself to feel this way from the beginning. She could have saved herself from a lot of heartache. "How is school going?" Allie asked.

"Great! Looking forward to the day I'll be finished, but I imagine you felt like that when you were this close."

"Oh, I remember those days." Allie laughed. "You're getting there, and I'm so proud of you."

They talked for a few more minutes until Marissa had to get off and go to study. "I love you, Allie."

"Love you, too, Sis. Talk later." She disconnected the call and turned to her text messages, pulling up Sean's name.

ALLIE

Who I like should be no one's business but my
own. I hope you understand that because I
have every right to be happy, just as you do.
I'm sorry I let my temper get the best of me,
but I won't allow you or anyone else to stand
in the way of my happiness. I wish you only
the best.

Allie hit sent and smiled back at the message. It was time to do what she wanted, even if it would surprise everyone. Her happiness was the most important thing. Satisfied with her realization, Allie got out of the car and went to her apartment. That was one thing no one should take from another person, their happiness.

A WEEK PASSED, AND IZZIE STILL HADN'T RETURNED TO TOWN. Allie wondered if she ever would. After a few days off, Allie was forced to get back to work. She couldn't desert Richard, even if the thought of seeing Izzie made her nervous. As it appeared, though, she didn't have to worry about that. Izzie was having the time of her life in the city, romancing every lesbian in sight. Allie wasn't going to let that interfere with her life.

"How are you feeling right now, Richard? On a scale of one to ten." She poised her pen and sunk back into the rocking chair. He gave a generous nod and then continued to think.

"Seven, I suppose. Always have bad days that interfere with the good." Allie nodded. She could say much of the same. "But, I'm living to see another day." He coughed, leaning forward as Allie jumped up to pat him on the back. He sputtered out another cough, covering his mouth with the offered towel. "I wish my Izzie girl would get home," he replied.

Allie gave a weak smile, then returned to her place on the rocker. "The grand opening is next week. She'll have to be home soon, right?"

He quirked up an eyebrow, then grinned. "You are right. Cheryl is doing her best to keep busy at the restaurant, helping the staff get organized. I know she wishes she could be spending her time at home with me.

Although, I wouldn't mind if she got away to do something for herself. What I would like is if Izzie could come back home and take her mom to get a manicure or something like that. Women like that, don't they?"

Allie snickered. "Most women do. Who wouldn't like to be pampered? Maybe they can do that after the grand opening. It might be a good idea for them to decompress."

"That is true, but I know both Cheryl and Izzie like to sit around and worry about me. Even though Izzie isn't here, she's called."

"And hasn't mentioned anything about what she's doing or," *Who she's doing it with?* Allie clamped down on her tongue. "I imagine she misses you both greatly."

Richard sighed. "I'm sure she does, but she's vague and doesn't like to make promises. I get it. She doesn't want to disappoint me. I just want her home."

"Have you told her that?" Allie inquired. He quickly shook his head. "Don't want her to feel obligated." His eyes widened. "Maybe you could call her for us."

Allie opened her mouth when she heard the front door opening and then Cheryl's voice. "Things are coming along quite nicely at the restaurant, Richard. You would be impressed."

He turned, dropping the subject. "That's great. I look forward to seeing the smiles on everyone's faces. Allie hoped he would be feeling up to making it to the restaurant for those smiles.

"Will you be working that day?" Cheryl asked, turning to Allie. "I mean, I hope you're going to be there, but I'm sure you will be busy helping out. After all, you'll be a guest of honor."

Allie opened her mouth, not wanting to have this conversation. "I, I'm really not sure. Haven't given it much thought." Allie hadn't thought about much else other than the opening. She still hadn't decided if she was going in the first place.

"I'm going to throw on some veggie burgers," Cheryl began, changing the subject. "Are you sticking around for dinner?"

"Actually, I have to do some running around for my mom." Allie stood up. "But today was a good day, Richard. I'm glad to see you're doing so well."

He gave Allie a wink. "I'll see you tomorrow, Allie."

Allie gave a wave, then turned away and reached for her purse. "Bye, Cheryl! Richard," she called, then hurried towards the door, wanting to get far enough away that neither one could talk anymore about Izzie. She got out the front door and dug her phone out of her pocket. Immediately it came to Izzie's contact info. She'd considered calling Izzie dozens of times throughout the past few weeks. She quickly slid the contact info off the screen and walked to the car. Until she could talk to her in person, it was best not to do anything.

CHAPTER THIRTY-SIX

AWKWARD MEETING

Izzie

Izzie stared at her phone. Allie's picture stared straight back at her. She ran her hand over her face and closed her eyes. She didn't know why she couldn't get her out of her mind, but there was still this magnetic pull to her. So many times, she had considered calling her, asking her why she hadn't called her back. Now two days after being home, she still hadn't had the opportunity to see her, and it was slowly killing her inside. She knew what she wanted. She wanted Allie.

Izzie pushed her phone away and leaned back in her bed, but clearly, Allie had chosen the opposite. She hadn't so much as glanced in Izzie's direction. And it seemed that she knew the exact moments Izzie would be out of the house so they wouldn't have to bump into each other. And if that's how Allie felt, then Izzie didn't want to be the one to change her mind.

Izzie stood up from her bed and left her room. She headed down the stairs, grabbing her purse from the railing. "Mom, I'm heading to the restaurant. I..." Her words fell off when it was Allie in the kitchen. "Oh," Izzie gave a slight smile. "Where's Mom?"

"She took your dad out for some fresh air. I showed her how to hook his oxygen tank to the chair so she doesn't have to try to carry it and push him." Allie shifted her gaze, and the tension grew in the living room. Izzie looked over her shoulder and back to the stairs. Allie knew she was there and opted to stay in the kitchen alone.

"I see," Izzie mumbled. She shifted from one foot to another.

"So, you're back," Allie softly stated. Izzie turned to meet her gaze. "I mean, obviously." She cleared her throat and moved to the sink, where a pile of dishes remained. Without turning to look in Izzie's direction, she began running the water.

"Sooooo," Izzie began. She sighed. "Good to see you, Allie." She turned away and left the kitchen. She had reached the foyer when she heard the shuffling of feet.

"When should I tell your parents you'll be home?" Allie asked.

Izzie snickered and hesitated at the door, then turned to Allie. "I'm a grown woman. I don't have a curfew, Allie." Allie looked down, and Izzie instantly regretted it. That was snarky, and no matter how Izzie felt, Allie didn't deserve a comment like that. "Just tell them I have some errands and won't be late."

"Alright then." Allie turned on her heel, and Izzie stayed in that position for a moment. How could they have been driven so far away? Izzie reached for the door, but that magnetic pull kept her grounded. She turned and returned to the kitchen, where Allie stared at the kitchen linoleum. She quickly looked up when Izzie coughed.

"I didn't mean to be snarky," Izzie replied.

Allie shrugged. "No worries. It's not my problem. It is what it is." She went back to the dishes.

"How'd we get here?" Izzie calmly asked.

Allie paused at the sink before looking over her shoulder. Her gaze was emotionless. "We're just two different people." Allie shrugged. "Can't change one person. It's hard enough to get past your demons and work on yourself. The fact that we didn't work isn't a failure on either of our parts. Things happen."

Izzie leaned back against the wall. Staring at Allie, it was like she was seeing someone for the first time. "So, just like that, it's not worth it? That's what you're saying?" Allie opened her mouth, then snapped it shut.

"I see," Izzie whispered. "Well, maybe we are way too different."

The back door opened through the kitchen, and her mother's voice came through. "It was such a great walk. It's beautiful outside." Her cheery tones left a sour feeling in Izzie's stomach.

Izzie swallowed and turned to her mom. "Look who emerged from her cave," Cheryl joked.

She glanced over to Allie and back to Izzie. The tension in the kitchen was palpable.

"Dear, help me to the living room, will you?" Her father asked, breaking the awkwardness.

"Um, I'm running to the restaurant. I'll be home later," Izzie started to turn.

"Allie, you should go," Izzie's mother chimed in. "I mean, you collaborated on the re-opening, right?"

Izzie turned to Allie, and Allie's eyes widened. "No, it's for the best I go alone," Izzie argued. "I have a ton to get done, and I couldn't interfere with Allie's work here. I'll see you all later." Izzie darted from the kitchen and didn't stop until she was outside. She fell back against the front door.

In one instance, it was good to see this side of Allie, the immature side, unwilling to change. In another, it was hard to face that she could have been wrong about her. She pushed away from the door and headed to her car. At least she found out before they had gotten too far into the relationship.

CHAPTER THIRTY-SEVEN

HER WORLD NEVER STOPS TURNING

Allie

Allie leaned back on the couch. Her latest encounter with Izzie hadn't gone how she expected. If anything, she had high hopes they would see each other, put their differences aside, and leap into each other's arms. Yet, they were now not even speaking, and Allie wasn't sure where it all went wrong. Allie did suspect that it was somehow all her fault.

If she called now, she would be groveling. She needed to give Izzie some time to cool off before she reached out. She got up from the couch and went down the hall to her bedroom. A bedroom that never felt so cold. She pulled back her covers just as a knock came from the front door. Allie glanced at her watch. It was nearly midnight. Who could that be?

The knock sounded again as Allie headed down the hallway. "Coming!" Allie called out. She peered through the peephole to see Izzie standing at her door. "Izzie?" Allie opened the door. Izzie looked up, and her eyes had a tinge of red. Had she been crying?

"May I come in?" Izzie asked. Allie nodded and stepped back for Izzie to enter. Before the door was closed, Izzie started. "Don't talk until I've gotten this out there. I have some things to say." Allie nodded. Izzie began pacing. "I just don't get it. One minute we're hot, and the next, it's like you can't even look at me. I have been driving around for two hours, wondering what I should do about it. It ultimately led me to your door because the truth is, until I can get out what I have to say, I won't be able to sleep." Izzie took a deep breath, and Allie nervously bit on her lower lip.

"Allie, I get that you're scared. You're not out of the closet, you're afraid your parents will disown you, and you're willing to give up on your happiness if that means you can keep everything under control. But there comes a time when you have to realize that people are going to think what they want to think. It doesn't make them right. You have a right to like whomever you like, and if someone wants to belittle you for that, that's their problem. Not yours." Allie opened her mouth, but Izzie held up her finger to halt her. "Just because you aren't willing to come out of the closet doesn't mean we have to walk on eggshells around each other. You should have been at the restaurant. We had so many plans, or have you forgotten that?" Izzie hesitated, waiting.

"I haven't," Allie whispered.

"Then why the hell have things been so tense between us? I told you I would give you time."

"And then you abandoned me," Allie argued.

"You're being a bit overdramatic. Abandoned you? I wouldn't take it that far." Izzie crossed her arms in front of her. "You called me, and I thought you were saying that you were ready to move us forward, but you never called back. I waited for your call."

"I'm sure you did," Allie huffed, turning her gaze away.

"What does that mean? How would you know? You never called me back. Or, maybe you didn't mean to call."

"I meant to call," Allie's voice went up a couple of notches. "But I didn't expect to find that you were with another woman that night. Imagine my surprise when I get a woman on your phone. It was like a smack to my face. Or perhaps that's what you wanted. Here I'll show Allie. She's going to be sorry. Was that your plan?"

Izzie frowned. "What are you talking about?" She shook her head. "My friends took me out because they knew I was having a rough time. I went back to my house." Izzie arched an eyebrow. "And Mae answered my phone. You remember Mae. She's my best friend and my assistant?"

Izzie stared at Allie, waiting for Allie's reply.

Allie thought back to that moment. Had she been wrong this whole time?

"She answered, and I thought..."

Izzie shook her head. "You thought wrong. How could we ever have a relationship when there's no trust between us?"

Allie tilted her head. "That's not fair. We weren't exactly in a good spot. A woman answers, what am I supposed to think?"

"You're supposed to trust me," Izzie quietly answered. "You're supposed to know me enough to know that I wouldn't be out inviting women back to my home when the only woman I wanted to spend my time with was you."

"Izzie," Allie began. "I'm sorry, I...."

Izzie held up her hand. "I don't need you to explain. We had too many obstacles in our way." She scrunched up her nose and shrugged. "We have too many obstacles in our way. I'm just sorry for my part. I clearly didn't do enough to show you could count on me." Izzie moved past Allie as Allie reached out to touch her arm. Izzie shifted slightly, releasing Allie's grasp. "Maybe in another lifetime, things would have been different. Goodbye." Izzie hurried away from Allie, and Allie could only stand there and watch.

Allie had ruined everything. Now, her world was crumbling down at her feet as Izzie walked away. If only Allie could convince Izzie, she'd changed.

CHAPTER THIRTY-EIGHT

GRAND RE-OPENING

Izzie

Izzie saw the line for the grand re-opening the minute she turned the corner; a knot welled up in her stomach. She hadn't wanted to do this alone. And even though dozens of people waited to get inside, she never felt more alone. She would have given anything to have Allie by her side. She turned into the parking lot and spotted her parent's van in the first parking spot. At least they were there in her corner, but it didn't feel the same.

She entered the back entrance, and her mom was the first one she greeted. "Honey, did you see that line?" she asked, her eyes welling up with tears. "Your father and I are so proud." She pulled Izzie into a hug.

"Thanks, Mom. It's really exciting."

Her mom pulled back and frowned. "Yet, you look like you're ready to cry, and those don't seem like happy tears. What's going on?" Before Izzie could respond, her mother continued. "Allie, right?"

Izzie gave a slight nod. Everything was so messed up. They hadn't spoken in the past few days since she stopped at the apartment. She thought talking in person would help, but it only seemed to create more misunderstanding.

"Do you think she's going to come?" she asked.

"I doubt it," Izzie mumbled.

"Izzie, I can't find the ingredients to make the dressing." Shelbie from the front of the kitchen called out, her voice filled with panic.

"There's no time to dwell on everything. I have a restaurant to re-open." She pushed past her mother and went to Shelbie. She was determined to ensure that the restaurant's re-opening went smoothly. A lot was riding on tonight. After all, it had to be successful if there was any hope of turning a profit.

And for an hour straight, she was busy taking care of the mini-fires, including finding all the ingredients to make Allie's special salad dressing.

"Where do you want these?" Izzie turned as Kris, another employee, entered the kitchen. She held three platters of star-shaped cookies decorated with red, white, and blue icing. It was just like she and Allie pictured.

"Where'd you get these?" Izzie asked.

Kris shrugged. "Some woman. She said she just wanted to drop them - -."

Before Kris got out all the words, Izzie hurried out of the restaurant. "Hey, darling. I'm impressed. Look at this crowd."

"Thanks, Dad, but" She glanced around, not seeing Allie anywhere in the dining area. Then again, it was jam-packed; every seat was occupied. "Have you seen Allie?"

He frowned and shook his head. "Maybe she..." Again, Izzie didn't wait for him to finish talking. She ran through the dining area and out the front door. She looked up and down the street, but still no Allie.

She frowned, feeling dejected, and went back into the restaurant. Perhaps it wasn't even Allie. After all, star-shaped cookies seemed like the most obvious choice. But it felt like something Allie would do.

She approached her dad's table, and he raised an eyebrow. "I'm glad you could make it, Dad."

He nodded. "Me, too. You didn't find her?"

Izzie shrugged. "Maybe someone else dropped them off. I'm not going to worry about it. Besides, I have customers to greet." She patted her dad's shoulder and then went back to the kitchen. She clapped her hands together to get the employees' attention. They all stopped what they were working on and turned to face her.

"I'm going to greet everyone and give some thanks, and then the customers will be ready to eat. So, you better be all prepared. Thank you for everyone's hard work. You all are great." She looked over to her mom, who placed the cookie platter on a table. She turned and met Izzie's gaze. Izzie approached her. "Do you know anything about the cookies?" Izzie asked. "Like, where they came from?"

Her mom shrugged. "It was a sweet gesture, wherever they came from. Don't you think?"

"Yeah, but..." She stared at them, overwhelmed with emotions. If it was Allie, why did she duck out of there so fast that Izzie wasn't even able to say thank you? She shook her head. Again, dwelling on it would only wreak more havoc.

"I better greet everyone." She grabbed her mom's hand, and they left the kitchen. It felt like even more people had gathered while she was in the kitchen. If they got any more people hanging around, they would have to worry about the fire code.

Her mother sat next to her father, and Izzie approached the microphone. She tapped on the microphone, drawing a hush from the crowd, and all eyes turned to her. Izzie gave her best smile.

"Hello, everyone. I want to greet you all and thank you for coming to the grand re-opening of Stars and Stripes. Let's just say it's the same place you know and love, updated for the twenty-first century." A round of applause sounded, and that caused Izzie to grin even brighter. "This opening never would have happened without the help of some very important people."

Izzie swallowed and turned to the table where her parents proudly sat. "Of course, I can't go without thanking my parents, Cheryl and Richard. My father opened this place when I was just four years old. He deserves a round of applause."

Everyone cheered, and Izzie felt choked up, glad her father was there to experience the moment. He waved proudly from their table, and Izzie scanned her eyes around the crowd. She stared out to the back, where Allie stood, still clapping, eyes zoned in on her parents' table. Allie turned, and their gazes locked. Allie stopped clapping as Izzie turned back to the mic, her throat dry.

"I also need to thank my friend, Allie. She helped me along the way with some of the new menu items. I'm sure you will all fall in love. I couldn't have done it without her." Again, clapping, this time with Izzie leading the applause.

Allie smiled, waving to people before glancing back in Izzie's direction. She gave a slight nod as Izzie turned back to the crowd. "I won't keep you all, but you'll all see some comment cards at your table. If you could leave the comments, the good, bad, and ugly, in that box," she pointed, "I would appreciate it. Also, follow us on social media. Leave reviews wherever you prefer, and tell your friends to do the same. Enjoy!"

She quickly left the stage and hurried to where Allie was so she wouldn't take off. Allie was pacing by the door when Izzie reached her. Allie wore a pale pink dress. It accentuated her curves, and Izzie caught herself staring.

"Hey," Izzie said.

Allie stopped pacing and smiled. "Hey."

"Thank you for the cookies."

Allie nodded. "It only felt right. We had all these plans, and I like to keep promises when I make them." Izzie took in those words. Despite everything going sour between them, it was good to know that Izzie could still count on her. "I couldn't miss tonight."

"I'm glad you're here," Izzie replied, her words barely above a whisper. Now it was just figuring out how she could keep her there without losing everything.

CHAPTER THIRTY-NINE

I LOVE YOU

Allie

At first, Allie agonized about whether or not she should even show up to Stars and Stripes. She decided to bring the cookies as a nice gesture. She and Izzie could remain civil for one night. It was bad enough that Allie needed to continue her role as Richard's nurse. They needed to figure out how to get along.

"I need to talk to you," Allie started. "But not here." She turned and led the way to Izzie's parents. Izzie wasn't far behind, which was a relief because Allie felt courageous and needed to use that momentum. Otherwise, she was liable to chicken out and go home.

Richard and Cheryl grinned when she approached. "Allie, I was hoping you would make it," Cheryl exclaimed.

"We all were," Richard said, hugging Allie. Richard looked over to Izzie, and they seemed to communicate silently. Richard knew how important it was that they were all together to celebrate their hard work.

Allie turned to Izzie. Izzie quirked up an eyebrow and waited. "Izzie?" Allie sighed. "I've been a fool. I pushed you away because I was too scared of my feelings. That is the truth, and I know I probably don't deserve you."

Izzie's jaw dropped, then a smile slowly crept on her lips. "But I'm telling you anyway. I'm not going to run anymore. I'm going to do what I want to do. To hell with everyone else. You are what matters to me," Allie declared.

"Are you serious?" Izzie asked quietly.

Allie nodded. "I care about you so much, Izzie. So tonight, in front of your parents and this restaurant full of strangers," Allie laughed. "I want to ask you if you want to make our relationship work. I'm not scared anymore." Allie cast a glance to the side and saw Sean peering at them. He had a smirk on his face and a phone facing them. He was filming the whole thing.

Allie pulled Izzie towards her and planted a heated kiss on her lips. The crowd around them cheered, including Richard and Cheryl from where they sat at the table. Allie smiled as she pulled back, turning to find Sean staring at them in disgust. She snickered and turned to Izzie, the only person in that room that mattered.

"I just hope that you feel the same way."

"Are you kidding me?" Izzie moved in closer. "This is everything I've ever wanted to hear." She wrapped her arms around Allie, and they kissed again, only this time Izzie took the lead, slipping her tongue into Allie's mouth.

Allie parted and turned to find that Sean was no longer standing there gawking. Izzie turned to her parents and the rest of the customers surrounding them.

"What's everyone staring at? Haven't you ever seen PDA?" She laughed. "Eat, drink, enjoy!"

"Can we get away and take a walk or something?" Allie asked, leaning into Izzie's ear.

Izzie grabbed her hand and escorted her to the front of the restaurant and out the door. They continued to hold hands as they slowly walked down the sidewalk in front of the restaurant.

"I'm sorry, Izzie," Allie began. "I'm sorry I've been so guarded. I'm sorry that I believed you were off sleeping with some other woman."

Izzie stopped walking and turned to Allie. "I think I can understand the last part. I mean, you wouldn't know. We weren't on the best terms, and I used to be a bit of a player. So, I forgive you, and I get it."

Allie smiled. "My family just can't understand how two people could love each other if they're not cis, straight people."

Izzie grinned. "Did you say love?" Izzie continued to smirk, and Allie laughed.

"I'm so in love with you, Izzie. It scared the crap out of me, but I can't run from that anymore. I longed to be happy, but when I could picture what my parents would think of me, it shut me down. Then when I saw Sean...."

She sighed. "He was here tonight, snapping pictures and videos of us, and I don't even care. He can think or say or do whatever he wants. It's not going to define me. We dated for years. My parents pushed me to marry him out of college, but I felt it wasn't right. How could I marry someone that I had no feelings for? He wasn't a good man back then, and today, he's even worse."

Izzie squeezed Allie's hand, comforting her. Allie looked up and met Izzie's tender gaze.

"He threatened to take our relationship to my parents, and that got to me way more than it should have. I should have ignored him, but I allowed it to break me. For that, I'm sorry."

"Babe, I get it." Izzie caressed Allie's cheek, and Allie closed her eyes. It felt amazing to have Izzie's hand back on her skin. "I don't trust easily. As I fell in love with you, it scared me. You seemed so perfect, and I thought I was broken or something. I didn't know if I could trust you because those I trust tend to let me down. Part of me wasn't sure if I wanted to trust you. Ultimately, I had to open my heart because not loving you was just too hard."

"So, you do love me?" Allie whispered.

Izzie grinned even wider. "Always, babe." She wrapped her arms around Allie, and they kissed in front of the restaurant. It was the happiest day of her life, and nobody would take that away from her.

CHAPTER FORTY

COMFORTING ARMS

Izzie

Allie's hand was warm as she escorted her back into the restaurant and over to her parent's table. As they passed tables, customers reached out to stop them. "This food is delicious, Izzie," One commented.

"We have Allie to thank for that." Izzie squeezed Allie's hand, and Allie beamed next to her, even offering *thanks* periodically.

"I knew they'd love you," Izzie whispered. "Almost as much as I do." She gave Allie a wink, and Allie's cheeks turned a soft peach. She leaned in and kissed Izzie in the middle of the crowd of customers. Izzie could get used to her fearless side. Who knew what the future could hold?

"I love you," Izzie whispered.

"I love you," Allie volleyed back.

They reached Izzie's parents, who were beaming with happiness. It was a mix of the success of the grand re-opening and that Allie and Izzie were finally together.

"I'm glad to see you out, Richard," Allie commented, brushing her hand on his shoulder. "How are you feeling?" Izzie watched the caring attention that Allie gave her father. Who wouldn't fall in love with a woman like that?

"I'm doing pretty good," he said. "I couldn't miss Izzie's big reveal." He paused to catch his breath. He inhaled deeply, breathing in the oxygen coming from his nasal cannula. "We're both so proud of her, and it's clear how much the customers love the new look." He paused a little longer this time. "The décor is magical. I can't imagine how much the sales will improve. We have both of you to thank for that."

"And I know from personal experience how much Izzie worked to make this happen. You both should be proud." Allie leaned in and kissed Izzie's cheek. Izzie grinned, with her mom clapping her hands together.

"I'm just so happy to see the two of you looking so in love. It makes a momma's heart swell with pride."

Allie smirked, and Izzie kept her eyes on her. "I say we should commemorate this moment with a picture," Izzie suggested.

"Yes!" Allie eagerly responded. "We could put it on the social media pages for the restaurant. What better advertisement?"

Izzie quirked up an eyebrow. "Are you certain?" she asked. "I mean, then your parents might see it...."

Allie shrugged. "Kind of the point. That way, it's out there, and I don't have to run from it. I want the whole world to know that I'm your girlfriend, and nothing makes us happier than being in love. Let's do this."

"Well, when you put it that way." Izzie winked and then wrapped her arm around Allie. She held up her phone, and the four of them grinned, with no one smiling as hard as Allie was. She wasn't running, and Izzie was ecstatic. Izzie uploaded it to the page and captioned it: *Elizabeth Roth, her girlfriend, Allison Walsh, and her parents have a grand opening for Stars and Stripes.* "What do you think?" Before hitting send, she held up her phone for Allie and her parents to see.

"Perfect!" Allie commented.

Izzie hit send, then glanced at Allie. "What are you doing?"

"Texting my mom with the link. I might as well get that part over with. It's not like she can say anything to change my mind. I'm officially out and proud. I've never felt better," Allie said.

"I love you so much!" Izzie replied.

Allie looked up and met Izzie's gaze. "That's good because you're stuck with me." Allie squeezed Izzie's hand, then lifted her hand to her lips. She kissed her knuckles, and Izzie's heart melted.

"So, can I see the text?" Izzie asked.

Allie leaned into Izzie and showed it to her. *I want you to meet my girl-friend Izzie and her family. Check out this link. I've been working with the Roth family, and they're amazing. But Izzie is everything.*

Izzie smirked. "When you go all out, you really go all out."

Allie laughed. "The truth is, I'm just tired of worrying about what they think. If they can't support me, they don't get to have me in their life. It's that simple." A text message popped onto the screen within minutes.

That's a disgrace. You can't be serious. Tell me you're only kidding.

Izzie gave Allie a side glance, and Allie shrugged, pocketing her phone.

"Let them stew," she quickly replied. "They can spew hate all they want. I'm still happy. I'm still gay."

Izzie loved seeing Allie be so confident about coming out, but she had to wonder if Allie's mom's disapproval still hurt. They were family, after all. And if Allie did want to cut them out of her life, it would be a significant change.

"Izzie? Some customers would like to greet you." Tami, one of the servers, popped up around the corner.

Izzie reached down and grabbed Allie's hand. She kept her by her side the whole night as they greeted customers and were both complimented on the revamped menu and interior It was wonderful to watch people enjoy a place her father worked so hard to build.

After greeting numerous guests, her mother motioned them both to return to the table. "Your father is getting tired. I'm going to take him home."

"Alright. So happy you could come, Dad." She hugged him and kissed his cheek.

"I'm so happy I could see this restaurant thriving once more." He had tears in the corner of her eyes, and as she stared at her dad, Allie squeezed her hand. Izzie put on a smile and nodded. Izzie returned home to revitalize Stars and Stripes before Richard was too sick to see it through. She'd achieved her goal with the help of Allie's love and support. Now that Allie was back by her side, Izzie knew anything was possible. She was ready to help him live his best life with what little time he had.

"Did you tell your parents you wouldn't be home tonight?" Allie asked as they entered her apartment.

Izzie laughed. "I doubt my parents thought I'd be home." She heaved a sigh. "It's funny, you know? Tonight was exhausting, but I've never been on such an emotional high before. It's like I could never sleep, and that would be alright."

Allie wrapped her arms around Izzie's neck. "Babe, I feel the same way." She kissed Izzie sweetly, pecking her lightly on her lips. "I'm so in love with you, Elizabeth Roth. I doubt you have any idea how much."

"I have a pretty good idea," Izzie replied with a wink before pulling her closer and holding Allie's body to her as they kissed heatedly. Izzie's phone went off, and Allie pushed her back.

"Is that a notification from Stars and Stripes?" Allie asked.

Izzie laughed. "Um, we were kind of in a moment, weren't we?"

"And the moment can continue, but I want to see the reviews. Don't you?"

Izzie snickered. The reviews were the last thing she cared about, especially during a passionate kiss with her girlfriend. But she would check the reviews to appease Allie, and then they could return to where they left off. Izzie glanced at her phone, and several notifications flooded the screen.

"I'm a little nervous," Izzie admitted.

"Why? You heard the praise from everyone. Everyone loved it. The reviews are just the icing on the cake." She peered over Izzie's shoulder while Izzie pulled up the site. She clicked on the reviews, and they started from the top as five-star reviews continued to display one after another. *Delicious. I can't wait to go back. This is what our town needs. We loved it, and the ambiance was terrific. The food was the best I've ever tasted. Looking forward to making this our family tradition.* "See?" Allie wrapped her arms around Izzie. I told you everyone would love it. You did this, babe. Kudos."

Allie continued to slide through the reviews until a message popped up on the screen.

Lesbians? Disgusting – Anonymous One Star.

"What?" Allie grabbed the phone from Izzie and stared at it.

"There's always someone," Izzie argued. "It's not a big deal."

"But it is," Allie replied. She turned and stared at Izzie. "I saw Sean at the restaurant. He was snapping pictures of us, and then he was gone. I thought he got the message when I didn't turn away from you. It sounds just like Sean."

"And it doesn't matter," Izzie replied. She grabbed her phone back.

"But that's not all," Allie muttered. "Remember when I slept over after the hospital?"

Izzie nodded. "It's pretty hard to forget. My heart shattered in the morning. I thought that we were in a good place. I had hoped that all would work out, but then..." She shook her head. "That doesn't matter. I don't want to think about that. We're finally in a better place. We love each other, and Sean can kiss my ass. I got the woman."

"I need to be honest here, though," Allie commented. "Things went wrong because of Sean. He continued to text me, practically warning me that he would do something like this. Following us seeing him in the store, he didn't stop badgering and bullying. He threatened that something like this would happen. He discovered who you were. It was all because he was humiliated. He's deranged and thinks he's somehow less of a man because his ex is gay now. I called things off between us because I was afraid he would sabotage the re-opening if I didn't."

"Wow! That makes sense. I was wondering what had happened. It was like a switch flipped. We were great one minute, and then everything fell apart overnight."

"It broke me," Allie continued. "But, if Sean can make good on his promise to ruin you, then I can't be the cause." Allie turned from her. Izzie saw the pain on her face, and it broke Izzie, but her words didn't worry her.

"Allie!" Izzie reached out and touched her arm, stalling her. "I'm glad you were honest about it and told me. That morning hurt me. Well, I'm sure you realize that because I left town." Izzie smirked. "But it all makes sense, but Sean can do nothing to you or me. As for the restaurant, it will thrive despite what Sean is trying to pull. It's words; they're not stopping anyone. Look at this."

She clicked on the replies, and over a hundred were listed under his review, defending Izzie and Allie. "The customers that matter are making their voices heard. So, what one idiot thinks doesn't make a difference, does it?" Izzie tossed her phone to the side, and it landed on the couch. "I throw my hands up. If someone wants to throw shade at us, that's up to them, but that means they are the problem. Not us. Got that?" Allie nodded.

"I'm just sorry you had to deal with that jerk because he isn't worth your time or energy." Izzie pulled Allie closer to her. "I love you, and no one will say something is wrong about that, especially Sean. He's probably just jealous that he doesn't have love. Screw him."

Allie grinned. "Screw him." Allie wrapped her arms around Izzie and swooped in for another kiss. The passion instantly ignited, and Izzie guided Allie back to the bedroom while they both frantically tore at one another's clothes. "I love you," Allie groaned, arching her back as Izzie moved her lips down to her neck. Allie fell to the bed and reached for Izzie's breasts, bringing one into her mouth and starting to suck as Izzie broke from her neck. She grinned, tossing her head back and allowing Allie to devour each breast.

Allie pulled back and moved to Izzie's lips, and they entangled their bodies. Izzie pressed Allie down to the bed and straddled her body, the kiss deepening. The naysayers could complain as much as they wanted, but Izzie had Allie.

CHAPTER FORTY-ONE

(ALMOST) ONE BIG HAPPY FAMILY

Allie

Allie looked over to Richard as he lay resting in his bed. It'd been three days since the grand re-opening, and his color seemed paler. She surveyed him, taking her notes as she watched him trying to rest, but his breathing was jagged. His oxygen requirement has increased. Violent coughing spells kept him exhausted and also prevented him from sleeping. She shook her head and looked down at her notes, a tear sprung to the corner of her eyes. Initially, he perked up when Izzie got home, but now it looked like he had aged twenty years. She carefully flicked her tear away so it wouldn't drop on her notes.

Cheryl peeked her head out into the living room. "I just grabbed some veggies; wanna help me in the kitchen?"

"Sure!" Allie looked away so that Cheryl wouldn't note the tinge of sadness on her face.

"His breathing is getting worse, and he's getting weaker," Cheryl replied.

Allie glanced in her direction. "Maybe he'll perk up tomorrow. I mean, that's the story with cancer. Some days are just always going to be better." Allie gave a generous smile. "I'm sure he still has plenty of good days."

She bit her tongue. Why did she say that? She had always vowed that she would never give families false hope. But Richard and Cheryl were different. They weren't just any family. They were now part of her family, or as close as she could get, without marrying Izzie. Now they were closer to her than her own. She needed to try and cheer up Cheryl.

"He's getting weaker," Cheryl whispered. "You know it, and I know it." She dropped her gaze as they entered the kitchen. "I just don't want him to wind up in some facility or hospital at the end of his life. Promise me that that won't happen."

Allie opened her mouth, and Cheryl gave her a pleading look. Allie closed her mouth and nodded. "I'm going to do what I can to ensure that he gets to continue peacefully rest at home," she said gently.

Cheryl sighed and nodded. "Now, let's make something for us to eat."

Allie and Cheryl worked on chopping up the veggies and putting together dinner while talking like mother and daughter. It was nice, with no mention of cancer and Richard's failing health. When they had the stew on a boil, Cheryl turned to Allie.

"Izzie should be finished with work shortly. Want to go see if she's almost ready to eat?"

Allie smirked. She turned and started to leave when Izzie rounded the corner. "I'm famished," she said. "Hello, beautiful." Izzie leaned in and kissed Allie. "How are you doing?"

"Better now," Allie whispered.

Izzie wrapped her arm around Allie's waist. "Dinner smells amazing." Izzie took a whiff. "Mom, can I steal Allie away for a moment?"

"Of course. You both enjoy yourselves." Cheryl turned to stir the stew as Izzie grabbed Allie's hand and pulled her through the kitchen and out the back door. She sighed as the door was closed.

"I needed some alone time," she replied. She wrapped her arms around Allie and pulled her into a kiss.

"I needed this, too," Allie quietly added, breaking from the kiss and beaming. "How was work today?"

"Ugh, work." Izzie laughed. "Not hardly worth mentioning. How have you been?"

"Well, good moments and bad."

"Start with the good." Izzie offered a wink. Allie scrunched up her nose, then smiled. "I'm in love with the most beautiful woman in the world."

"Not even," Izzie smirked. "You're the most beautiful." She grabbed Allie's hand and pulled her closer to her. Allie nestled her head against Izzie's as they stood on the patio and enjoyed the solitude. "And the bad?" Izzie asked.

"Sean strikes again." She dug her phone out of her pocket and showed it to Izzie. "Despite all the support, Sean is determined to ruin you. Or us," Allie mumbled.

Izzie snickered as she read the latest comment, this time signing off with his name. *Now the whole world will know what a freak Allison Walsh is. And her "partner" will look just as disgusting. Yuck – Sean*

"You do realize that your ex is starting to look like a psycho," Izzie replied. She then released a laugh. "It's not even working. People are still supporting us. You don't need him to be okay with what you're doing. We're not doing anything illegal."

Allie nodded. Her old self was working its way back in, trying to tear her down, and the worst part was that she was starting to let it. Izzie slid her hand around Allie's neck and lifted her chin to look into Izzie's eyes.

"You are a better person than Sean ever will be. Remember that, Babe."

Allie smiled and nodded. Izzie caressed her lips, and they stood on the patio kissing, Allie's body growing limp next to Izzie's. "I love you so much, Izzie."

"I love you, too." They kissed once more as the back door swung open.

"Dinner is ready," Cheryl called.

Hand-in-hand, they walked back into the house, where Cheryl had started to set their places. "Is Dad awake?" Izzie asked.

"Yeah, but he's too weak to come out to the kitchen," Cheryl frowned. "He said that for us to enjoy, and then he'll eat."

"Nonsense," Izzie replied. "We have that card table in the basement. I'll grab it." Allie helped Cheryl take the plates and utensils into the living room, where Richard looked up.

"What's this?" he asked.

"We're having dinner in the living room for a change. It will be a nice change of scenery, and we can all eat together."

"You don't have to do that on account of me," he argued. "It's so much hassle."

"Nonsense!" Izzie replied again, entering the living room with a table in hand. "Allie, wanna help me grab three chairs?"

"Absolutely!" Allie hurried behind her, and they went down to the basement to get the chairs for the three of them to use while he sat up in his bed. "This was a great suggestion. Your father shouldn't be left out."

Allie nodded enthusiastically. "Smart idea."

Izzie shrugged. "There's no guarantee how much longer we'll have together. I want to cherish the time we do have." Allie nodded, the mood growing solemn as they went upstairs with the chairs to meet her parents. Once they got to the living room, they set everything up on the tables. Cheryl went in to grab the food. Izzie tossed a look over to Allie. "Have you heard from your parents?" she asked.

Allie shook her head. They hadn't said a word to her over the past three days. She had considered reaching out to them but decided it wasn't healthy for her. If she had to grovel, then their love wasn't worth it.

"I spoke to my sister, and she's happy I'm finally out. I guess that's all that matters. Besides, I have your family to live vicariously through."

Izzie smiled. "Always, Babe." She leaned in, and they kissed. Yet there was this burning pain in her chest. Allie pushed the pain aside and told herself she was better without them.

CHAPTER FORTY-TWO

LOVE IS WORTH IT

Izzie

Izzie's heart raced as she stared at the house before her. *What's the worst they could do?* Slam the door in her face, that's what. For thirty minutes, she had been driving around in circles, giving her a pep talk, convincing her to stop the car and knock on that door. For thirty minutes, she came up with the same decision. If they slammed the door in her face, at least she took the chance. But now, staring up at the house, she was a jumble of nerves.

It was true that Izzie was used to commanding boardrooms, so trying to talk sense into two people she didn't even know, should have been easy enough. But if she ruined her one opportunity, she could destroy Allie's chance of making amends. For that, she'd never forgive herself. Izzie tapped the steering wheel and tilted her head. *I'll also never forgive myself if I don't take the chance.*

"Imagine it's the boardroom and jump straight into the deep end. You'll never float if you don't try."

Izzie released a breath and got out of the car. Every step had to start somewhere. She knocked on the door, the knock sounding loud and forceful.

No one came to the door. Izzie knocked again. Still...no one. *Great! They're not even here anyway.* She looked down at the doormat before glancing straight ahead. Just once more, she knocked on the front door. After another moment of hesitation, she turned away.

Just as she did, though, she spotted someone peeking out behind a curtain. She dropped her gaze and shook her head. Maybe the Walshs weren't someone she could reason with. Not even worth her time.

She started down the sidewalk and paused. Allie was worth her time, though. She turned back on her heel and stomped toward the door. She knocked again. "Mr. and Mrs. Walsh, I know someone is in there. Will you please answer the door so that we can talk? Ignoring this isn't going to help anyone. Allie deserves this much."

She brought down her hand as the door slowly opened. A woman stood at the door but barely opened the door wide enough for Izzie to see inside the house.

"Mrs. Walsh?" Izzie asked.

The woman nodded. It was a start.

"My name is Elizabeth Roth. Everyone calls me Izzie. I know you know who I am, but I'm asking you to please hear me out. I love your daughter, Allie, and it would mean the world to her and me if we could somehow make peace."

"I don't see how talking is going to change anything. Allie's been lying to us, and she knows how we feel."

Izzie nodded. "And how you feel is why she's been lying to you." Izzie looked around, surveying the area to see if anyone was eavesdropping on their conversation. When she looked back at Allie's mother, her eyes were dimmer. "If I could just have ten minutes of your time. If you want me to leave after that, then I'll go. But I think we would both be more comfortable if we did this inside your house."

Her mother gave a slight nod, then opened the door so Izzie could enter the foyer. She led the way into the living room, where she sat on the couch, and Izzie sank into a chair. Izzie was sure the ten minutes wouldn't last long, so she continued.

"Is your husband home?" Izzie asked.

"No. You wouldn't be sitting here if he was." Her tone was harsh, and

Izzie felt it from across the room. She swallowed the lump that had worked itself into her throat.

"First off, how is your health?" Izzie began again.

"I'm fine. It's not really a concern right now. Your time is ticking." Allie's mother looked down at her watch and then back up to Izzie.

"Right," Izzie mumbled. "Anyway, I know that hearing the news the way you did was overwhelming and confusing, but from what Allie has told me, she's always had feelings for women." Allie's mom shuddered, and Izzie continued.

"It's never easy coming out to your parents, especially when you know they're so against it. Allie's brave in that respect. But, you see, you don't have to understand or even like it, but all I'm asking is that you try to look from Allie's perspective. You can't choose the ones you love."

"I don't agree with that," her mother huffed. "Allie had other options. She used to date a nice young man. He would be perfect for her."

"Is this Sean?" Izzie asked. Her mother arched an eyebrow. "Sean has been threatening your daughter, badgering her, practically stalking her. I don't see how this would be a man you would want your daughter to be with." Her mother's jaw dropped.

"I don't know Sean personally; we haven't been introduced. However, he bumped into us once and, from that moment on, has been threatening that he would come to you first. From what I can gather, he's been harassing her via text." Allie's mother dropped her gaze.

"Your daughter deserves better than that. And I want to believe that you know she does."

"Well, I..." Allie's mom stammered. She then shrugged and didn't proceed.

"Mrs. Walsh, I came here because your opinion of Allie has always meant so much to her. I think she cares about what you think a little too much. She doesn't know I'm here, but I wouldn't be the woman Allie fell in love with if I wasn't willing to give this a shot. I'm asking you if you could at least think about it and try to accept it, not for my sake, but for your daughter's," Izzie pleaded.

The door opened, and then her father appeared. Izzie recognized him from the hospital trip. She stood up as he entered the living room. "What are you doing in my house?" he asked.

"I let her in." Izzie glanced over to Allie's mother. "She just wanted a few minutes, but her time is up."

Izzie's face fell. She nodded. "Yeah, I was just leaving." Izzie walked past both of them, then looked over her shoulder. "Just please think about what I said."

No one said a word as Izzie left the house and returned to her car. She sat there for a moment; her heart pounded in her chest. She had never encountered two people that were so hard to read, but from the looks of things, she hadn't even made a dent in getting through to Allie's mother. Plus, she hadn't been able to speak two words to her father. It was a wasted trip, but at least she could say she tried.

CHAPTER FORTY-THREE

ROAD TO FORGIVENESS

Allie

I *can't wait to see you. Wear something sexy. ;)* Allie read the text for the hundredth time. "If you insist, Izzie." She stood in front of her bedroom mirror, wearing a sheer blue dress with a negligee hidden underneath. As soon as Izzie lowered the dress, she would get an exquisite view. She giggled and twirled around in front of the mirror. She went to the store earlier in the day to find something nice. They rarely got a chance to go out on the town together. They could have dinner, go dancing, or even walk in the park; anything sounded thrilling with Izzie by her side.

She reached for her necklace and held it up to her collarbone. It was the perfect addition. A text dinged on her phone, and she grabbed it from her dresser and read the message.

IZZIE

Waiting for you can be torturous. I'm just sitting here, all alone.

Izzie had snapped a provocative selfie of herself, puckering up her lips and staring back at her camera phone. Allie grinned. How could she have gotten so lucky?

ALLIE

I'll be there in five minutes. Don't miss me too much.

Using the same pose, Allie snapped a quick selfie before sending the message to her and a winking emoji. She grabbed her purse and hurried out of her bedroom. Allie threw the front door open and fell back when she saw her parents at her door.

"Mom? Dad? What are you doing here?"

It wasn't exactly the greeting she had intended if she was to see them again, but there it was out there. She stepped back, and her mom balked at Allie's outfit.

"Are you going out?" she asked.

"Um yeah." Allie shifted her gaze from her parent's sight. "I'm going on a date with Izzie. And if there isn't anything constructive you're here to discuss, I will be late. She's waiting for me."

"That Elizabeth. She seems like a persistent one," her mother replied.

Allie frowned. "Excuse me?"

Her mom arched an eyebrow. "She didn't tell you that she paid us a visit?"

Allie slowly shook her head. "Well, perhaps she wanted to keep it secret until she found out how it turned out."

Allie's brows furrowed. "I'm sorry, but I'm confused. Did she come to your house? I never asked her to do that, and I assure you I'll be talking with her. She should have left you alone, especially knowing how you both obviously feel."

"Now, calm down," her dad said, speaking for the first time since Allie opened the door. "May we come in for a bit and sit down? We have a few things to square away."

"As I mentioned," Allie began. "I have somewhere to be, and I shouldn't keep her waiting, but if you want, we can talk some other time."

"Allie, please," her mother pleaded. "This will only take a second."

Her mom's eyes were dark, and from her tone, Allie saw that putting them off would only cause more strain in their relationship. She nodded and led the way to the living room. They all sat down, with Allie fidgeting in her seat. She grabbed her phone from her purse and quickly sent out her text.

ALLIE

Slight delay. I'll be there ASAP.

She looked up and gave a nod, and her mother began. "She stopped by yesterday. I was the only one home, and she said she wanted ten minutes. I invited her in, expecting it to be a slow ten minutes, but then she talked." Her mom glanced at her dad and then back to Allie. "I realized then that there's one thing for certain, and Izzie loves you. And when it comes to a relationship, that's the only thing that matters. I wasn't expecting to come to that conclusion, but as I said, she's persistent."

"What are you saying?" Allie asked, her words barely audible.

"Your mother is trying to say that we might not understand it. We might not even condone it. But, your mother has discussed it with me, and we both feel it's only right that we try to accept it."

"Seriously?" Allie stood up from the couch, sharing from one to the other.

Both of them started to nod. "You are a grown woman, Allie. And you should make your own decisions. Given time, maybe we'll be able to understand it. For now, we have to say we're just willing to give it a chance."

Allie ran to them, throwing her arms around both of them. Hearing that her parents were willing to try and accept her was a start to mending their relationship. This was the first time they had listened to her as an adult.

"You'll really like her. I know you will." She pulled back, feeling the urge of tears touching the backs of her eyes. Neither one made a reply, but Allie knew it wouldn't happen overnight, but if they were willing to try, she was ready to understand that it could take them some time. And she would accept that.

"We love you, Allie. I know sometimes we take that love for granted." Her mother commented, and Allie had to flick away a tear. They stood up and moved closer to the front door.

"And I love you both," Allie replied. No one forced her to say it. She loved her parents because, for once, they were willing to try.

675

"When you both are available," her dad began, "let us know, and we'll get together."

"I'll discuss it with her tonight," Allie replied. "Thank you for coming over here."

She stood at the door and watched them walk down the stairs, her head reeling from the past conversation. She wanted to be optimistic about it, but there was a nagging thought that maybe they were trying to trick her.

Doubts are crowding their way through. Just enjoy the possibilities.

She left her apartment and locked the door behind her. They wouldn't have made a special trip to her place to trick her. Allie was sure of that.

Allie arrived at the restaurant in five minutes and found Izzie in the back corner, reading through the menu. As Allie got closer, Izzie smiled. "I was starting to get worried," she said.

"Sorry, but I had an interruption. You stopped by my parents?" Allie asked.

Izzie's mouth hung down. She snapped her mouth close and shrugged.

"I'm sorry. I was going to tell you tonight when we were out. I went there yesterday. I wanted to try and reason with them."

"First off, how did you know where they lived?"

Izzie smirked. "I told you that I had to do a pretty hefty background check when we hired you s the lead nurse, including finding your parents' address. I assure you that I never looked into them until yesterday. I just really needed to talk to them. But, sadly, I doubt it did much good. Your dad kicked me out the moment he got home."

"Well, it did much more than you may think." Izzie tilted her head. "They stopped by my apartment and said they would try to accept it. They want us all to get together soon. So, I would say that your visit might have helped them to turn a corner."

"Are you serious?" Izzie clapped her hands together.

Allie grinned. "I love you so much, Izzie. You have no idea what this means to me that you did this." Allie reached out and touched Izzie's hand. If it all worked out, Allie might even discover a new side to her parents, and she was excited for what was to come.

CHAPTER FORTY-FOUR

CHANGE IS A GREAT THING

Izzie

"A re you sure you feel strong enough?" Izzie asked, helping her dad onto the back porch. He gave a soft chuckle, as she was so used to hearing from him.

"Izzie, girl, as long as you're by my side, I'll always be strong." His words weren't nearly as loud as she would have liked, but Izzie needed this time alone with her father. The time she could never take for granted. She helped him into one of the chairs on the back porch and then laid a blanket across his lap. Harry sighed as he lay down at her father's feet.

"Mom is at the restaurant, so it's just the two of us." Izzie propped herself into the chair next to him and reached out to touch his hand. "Are you comfortable?"

He nodded. "This is perfect. Just me and my Izzie." He gave her a wink, and Izzie felt her cheeks burning. She ran her finger along his palm and looked out over the landscape. "It's a beautiful night," he said as if reading her mind.

"That it is. The weatherman said to enjoy it because there won't be too many clear nights; we're in for a steady run of rain." Izzie smiled. "Not that it's unnecessary, but I like these nights where you can just enjoy the stars outside." She looked up and gave a generous nod. "And it's a beautiful night to watch the stars."

"There's one even brighter than the rest." She turned to see her dad had his eyes zoned in on her. She smirked and shook her head. He always knew what to say to get her to smile. Ever since she was a little girl, she was the epitome of Daddy's Little Girl. As she got older and moved away, their relationship remained idyllic. "I mean it. You pulled the restaurant opening together as if your life depended on it."

"Well, part of me feels like it did. I wanted to make you proud, Dad."

He grinned. "Darling, you always make me proud." Izzie ran her hand over his, and he continued to smile. "When I'm gone," he began.

"Dad, tonight we're not supposed to be talking about that. No tears, no pain. Just enjoying the night. That is all." She looked away from him, a tug quickly pulling at her heart.

"But, this has to be said. No one knows how much time one will have, and I need you to know my wishes before it's too," His words fell off, and Izzie turned to look in his direction.

"I know your wishes, Dad," she whispered. "Without you even having to say them." He arched an eyebrow. "You want me to run the restaurant."

He chuckled. "Would that be a bad thing?"

Izzie shrugged. It's not like she hadn't considered it, but just thinking about it made her nervous. If she took that plunge, she knew where her life would be. She wanted to be there, with Allie, without worrying about her nine-to-five job. "It'd be a big change."

"And my daughter has never cowered away from change." He gave her a wink and squeezed her hand. "Think about it; I mean, your life is here, right? You're happy. I've never seen you happier. Then again, I would say that's because of the younger woman in your life."

"Dad!" Izzie playfully slapped his hand, then laughed. "Well, I'm not the only one that went for a younger woman." She winked, and he gave a breathless laugh to chime in with her. "She is pretty great, though, isn't she?"

"I couldn't have picked a better woman for you." He gave another wink, and Izzie leaned in and gave him a soft peck on his cheek. "I'm just glad that you both figured out how much you needed one another."

"You and me both," Izzie agreed. Izzie reached down and ruffled her fingers through Harry's fur, then looked at him. He leaned back in the chair and closed his eyes, a slight smile on his lips. Izzie turned away, gazing into the moon as it appeared in the sky. *Protect my father, Lord. I don't want him to feel any pain at the end of his life.* A brush of air washed over her as her hair flew in the wind. She grinned and nodded, feeling her prayers answered.

"I've lived a good life," her father wheezed. Izzie turned to him, and his eyes opened again. He gave a slight nod. "And I can rest well knowing that my daughter is going to live her best life."

"I love you, Daddy," she whispered.

"Haven't heard those words in a while. You used to call me that when you would climb into my lap, and I would read you a bedtime story."

"Or twelve," Izzie joked.

He laughed. "You did love your stories."

"You read them the best. Mom didn't do voices." Izzie replied.

"Will you help me inside?" he asked. "I'm getting a bit tired."

"Of course." Izzie got up and offered her arm, then helped him out of his chair and back into the house. The walk was slow, but she didn't want it to end. She helped him into his bed, and he looked up and met her stare.

"I'm glad you came home."

"Nothing could have kept me away." She leaned in and hugged him.

"Goodnight!"

"Goodnight, My Izzie."

As Izzie walked away, a weight sat on her, and she looked over her shoulder to watch her dad settle into bed. "You know, with the restaurant, I'll have to quit my job and come home."

He nodded. "That was kind of the point." He gave another weak wink before closing his eyes. Izzie stared at him, and she felt another gust of air pass over her, only this time, there wasn't anything that should have caused that. She turned away, a tear trickling down her cheek.

Izzie got upstairs and grabbed her laptop. She sat on the edge of her bed and typed in Ryan's name. With just a few sentences, she could submit her resignation. She bit her lower lip.

"What you doing?"

Izzie jumped and turned to Allie, who was buried under her covers.

Allie grinned like a schoolgirl and shimmied out of the bed. She was already dressed in a sexy negligee, leaving little to the imagination.

"What am I doing? What are you doing?" Izzie laughed, unable to look anywhere but Allie's perky breasts that were inching closer to her. She quickly flipped away a tear on her cheek and turned back to Allie. "Hiding in my room? You naughty girl."

"I can be really naughty when I want to be." Allie grabbed the laptop away from her and put it on the floor, then moved back in closer to Izzie.

"Work can wait. Now's the time to play." Allie nibbled on Izzie's ear, and Izzie arched her back. Allie pulled back and tilted her head. "Is that a teardrop, I see?"

Izzie quickly shook her head. "I'm excited to see you, that's all."

Allie pulled back and looked Izzie over before shaking her head. "Your eyes are red."

"I must look awful." Izzie looked away. She bit back the tears, but Allie brushed her hand lovingly along Izzie's cheek. "I had an emotional talk with my father. I guess it's finally hitting me that there won't be too many more conversations like that."

"I'm sorry, Izzie. Do you want to talk about it?"

Allie wrapped her arm around Izzie and locked eyes with her. Izzie smiled and shook her head. "You look gorgeous. I don't want to kill the mood. All is well." She leaned in and kissed Allie's nose before shifting her lips to Allie's. Allie didn't let the kiss linger as she slowly pushed Izzie back.

"And I've already brought the mood down, didn't I?"

"No," Allie argued. "But you don't have to always be strong for me. I can be your rock, too, you know."

Izzie grinned and nodded. She wrapped her arm around Allie and pulled her back in the bed, resting her head against Allie's. At that moment, it just felt good to have Allie in her arms.

"What would you say if I told you I'm thinking of quitting my job, moving here full-time, and making the restaurant my top priority? Well, next to you, of course." She kissed Allie on the forehead as Allie turned to her and gawked.

"Are you serious?"

Izzie nodded. "I can't be worrying about work when I have more important things on my mind."

Allie laughed, fell into Izzie's arms, and gave her a kiss filled with hunger.

"I take you like the idea?" Izzie inquired teasingly.

"I love the idea!" Izzie held Allie, and Izzie silently contemplated everything she would say to Ryan. It wouldn't happen overnight, as she had some loose ends to tie up, but she knew in her heart she was making the right decision.

Grab the thrilling epilogue by scanning or clicking on the QR code below:
[or Type or Click here: https://BookHip.com/WVQXLBN]

Happy Reading,
Morgan
P.S: Thanks, www.kindlepreneur.com, for the QR code generator, and www.booklinker.com for the universal links.

MT CASSEN BOOKS

Available In Paperback, Ebook, And Audio Formats. Click Image:
https://mybook.to/MELODYINHERHEART

Available In Paperback, Ebook, And Audio Formats. Click Image:
https://mybook.to/FIGHTINGHERTOUCH

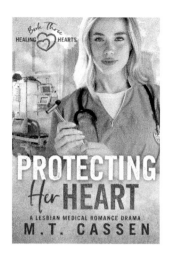

Available In Paperback, Ebook, And Audio Formats. Click Image:
https://mybook.to/PROTECTINGHERHEART

ABOUT THE AUTHOR

Morgan Cassen

WITH ROXIE

Morgan Cassen writes Lesbian Romance. Her mission is to make the world safer for sapphic stories to be told. Yes, she knows that there are millions of romance writers and billions of romance novels. So, why would she even think of adding to the pile? Well, Morgan has seen enough to know that the truly interesting stories are not what happen between human beings. That gig can seem pretty tame. At least compared to its older, tempestuous sister. Let's bring out Ms. Inner Conflict, the queen of all drama in the human world -- the ruler of the emotional map. Yes, the conflict between everything you've worked for and everything you want. You never imagined that all your hard work would put you so far away from everything you wanted. Also, how about the conflict between the past and the future? Being true to the past would require you to keep the future so far away in the future. But, how long can you postpone the future? What if your whole framing of the past can't stand the scrutiny of thoughtful analysis today even as you resolutely push the future away?

Huh, what do you do with that kind of conflict? The conflict between human beings can look so tame compared to the real thing: conflict between you and you. You are the hero and villain at the same time, but the problem is that the villain thinks she is the hero, while the hero is all caught up in doubt. Which you will you choose? No, nobody else will make that choice for you. You get to make that choice, and your comforting, trusty friend--procrastination--can't seem to do the trick this time. The time has come for you to choose. See, inner conflict is where it's at. Inner conflict is what Morgan writes about in her books. Please join her as she writes the stories of breakup and love that tug at heartstrings.

Morgan is indebted to Sarah Wu (copyeditor) and Dr. Peter Palmieri and Nurse Karen Stockdale (medical advisors) for their extraordinary work and diligence. This book is so much better because of their efforts.

Stalk the author using the link below:

www.mtcassen.com

ABOUT PETER PALMIERI
(MEDICAL ADVISOR)

Peter Palmieri, M.D., M.B.A. is a licensed physician with over 20 years of practice experience in Chicago, Dallas, Houston, and the Rio Grande Valley in Texas. He received his B.A. from the University of California San Diego, with a double major in Animal Physiology and Psychology. He earned his medical degree from Loyola University Stritch School of Medicine and a Healthcare M.B.A. from The George Washington University. He is a regular  contributor of original articles to a variety of health and wellness blogs.

ABOUT KAREN STOCKDALE
(MEDICAL ADVISOR)

Karen Stockdale, MBA, BSN, RN is an experienced nurse in the fields of cardiology and medical/surgical nursing. She has also worked as a nurse manager, hospital quality and safety administrator, and quality consultant. She obtained her ASN-RN in 2003 and her BSN in 2012 from Southwest Baptist University. Karen completed an MBA in Healthcare Management in 2017.
She currently writes for several healthcare and tech blogs and whitepapers, as well as developing continuing education courses for nurses.

Karen's websites are:
https://www.linkedin.com/in/karen-stockdale-5aab2584/
and
http://writemedical.net/

ABOUT OLIVIA HALVORSON
(MEDICAL ADVISOR)

Olivia Halvorson, MSN, FNP-BC, BSN, RN is a board-certified nurse practitioner with over 10 years of medical experience. She has worked in the fields of emergency medicine, urgent care, oncology, hematology, and home health. Olivia obtained her BSN in 2015 from the University of Connecticut and her MSN in 2018 from King University. She currently works in research, as well as writes healthcare blogs, and edits fiction and non-fiction books.

Peter and Karen were advisors for "Too Little, Too Late?" and "At What Cost?"

Olivia was the advisor for "Passion Without Tension?"

ABOUT ROSIE ACCOLA
(COPYEDITOR)

Rosie Accola is a queer poet, editor, and zine-maker who lives in Michigan. Their writing explores how reality t.v. functions as autofiction and the intersection between pop culture and poetics. They graduated with their MFA in Creative Writing from Naropa University in 2022. In 2019, they published their first full-length poetry collection, "Referential Body," with Ghost City Press. You can find them on Substack, where they publish the RoZone, a monthly newsletter about the craft of writing and arts and crafts.

Printed in Great Britain
by Amazon